George Mifflin Dallas, Alexander James Dallas

Life and Writings of Alexander James Dallas

George Mifflin Dallas, Alexander James Dallas

Life and Writings of Alexander James Dallas

ISBN/EAN: 9783744660099

Printed in Europe, USA, Canada, Australia, Japan

Cover: Foto ©Raphael Reischuk / pixelio.de

More available books at **www.hansebooks.com**

LIFE AND WRITINGS

OF

ALEXANDER JAMES DALLAS.

BY HIS SON,

GEORGE MIFFLIN DALLAS.

PHILADELPHIA:

J. B. LIPPINCOTT & CO.

1871.

I THINK it right, in giving this volume to the world, to say that it was fully prepared for the press by my father in 1862,—two years before his decease,—and that its publication has been delayed by circumstances over which I had no control.

JULIA DALLAS.

PHILADELPHIA, 15 February, 1871.

PREFACE.

A DELAY of forty-five years in issuing this publication can be ascribed with justice only to the exigencies of professional, and the duties of public life.

Nor do I regret the delay. Numerous changes in the plan first formed have been calmly considered and adopted. Immense piles of correspondence were subjected to repeated winnowing. The desire to simplify and compress as much as a distinct development of character could authorize, increased with the lapse of time.

Some of the letters to and from Mr. Dallas are incorporated in the text, furnishing, as they do, the best possible insights into particular periods of his life, and connected, as they are, with events of the day. Those of Mr. Madison and Mr. Duponceau are set apart as entitled to separate preservation, because they were revised and returned to me by their respective writers with that view.

So also, as illustrating argumentative and oratorical powers, extracts are made from certain speeches, more or less ample, as perspicuity or the importance of the subject seemed to require; but no formal collection of innumerable and brilliant displays at the bar is attempted. Such a collection, while it could have but little general interest, would necessarily lead into a labyrinth of detail.

In the effort to avoid, as far as possible, the seductions to frequent eulogy, I tremble under the apprehension lest there may have been too stern an adherence to cold facts and incontestable records. My personal feelings, however, could not be allowed to intrude themselves on the reader; and I have never doubted that plain, unexaggerated truth, as respects my father's life, character, and services, would constitute the noblest monument to his memory.

G. M. D.

PHILADELPHIA, 10 July, 1862.

CONTENTS.

(vii)

LIFE AND WRITINGS

ALEXANDER JAMES DALLAS.

THE subject of this sketch was born in the Island of Jamaica, on the 21st of June, 1759. His father, Robert Charles Dallas, had emigrated from Scotland, and, after a career of much reputation and success as a physician, returned from the West Indies, for the double purpose of benefiting his own health and of educating his children, first to Edinburgh and subsequently to London.

The family name would appear to have originated on the verge of the Scottish Highlands, to have gradually extended through various shires, and, from remote times, to have stood in high credit. Its derivative meaning is *Dal* and *uisg*, "the house in the dale." In a rich and beautiful quarto volume, "The Book of the Thanes of Cawdor," printed in 1859 by the present earl, it often recurs, as early as the fourteenth century, associated with important transactions, and undergoing the transitions of "*Dolace, Dolles, Dales,* and *Dalace,*" springing from variety of pronunciation.

While a pupil of the celebrated Elphinston, whose academy was at Kensington, in the immediate vicinity of London, Alexander became distinguished for his proficiency,—so much so as to attract the kind attention of two illustrious visitors of his teacher, Dr. Benjamin Franklin and Dr. Samuel Johnson, the former often inviting him to his house, and the latter sending him, as a testimony of approbation, a copy of his "Rambler."

His progress and prospects were interrupted and clouded by the death of his father, whose estates in Jamaica, greatly reduced in productive value by their owner's absence, passed finally into the hands of testamentary trustees, and were, as usual, neglected.

His mother, a lady of Irish descent, and originally called "Camac," married Captain Sutherland, of the British navy, after a short widowhood; and, aware of the nature and probable treatment of their distant property, encouraged her sons to look to other sources for support and independence. Of these there were three besides the subject of this memoir: two older, Robert and Stuart, and one younger, Charles. There were also two daughters, Charlotte and Elizabeth.

Alexander, in his fifteenth year, was without the hope or the means of completing the course of study he had advantageously begun. Hurried by parental solicitude to seek active occupation, he at first enrolled his name at the Temple as a candidate for professional life, but was soon induced to take what was considered a safer and shorter path and to engage as clerk and accountant in arranging the business of a merchant of the name of Gray, who had married the sister of his mother, and whose concerns were alike extensive and embarrassed. It was during this trying period of early, unlooked-for, and incessant drudgery that he contracted the powers and habits of industry for which he was ever afterwards remarkable, and that he exhibited, even while excessive toil and confinement undermined his strength, his well-known unsubdued buoyancy of spirit and great versatility of talent.

At the expiration of about two years, Mr. Gray suddenly left his pursuits and his country, and Mr. Dallas rejoined his parent and sisters, then residing in Devonshire. Once more relieved from compulsory labor, he renewed, with unabated ardor, his application to ancient and modern literature, and hastened, with the aid of a private instructor, to acquire that portion of scholarship and learning seen judiciously displayed in his speeches, writings, conversation, and amusements. Here, too, borne away by the fashion of the place and of the day, he combined the soldier with the poet, procuring a commission for the one, and for the other successfully appealing to the tastes of his friends and the public. And here he formed that attachment to Arabella Maria, daughter of Major George Smith, of the British army, to which he has ascribed, in his will, all the happiness and prosperity he subsequently enjoyed. Their union was solemnized at Alphington church, in Devonshire, on the 4th of September, 1780, himself being then but just turned of one-and-twenty, and his bride scarcely sixteen years of age.

Mrs. Sutherland having recently gone to Jamaica, the youthful couple proceeded to London, in order to follow her, in the fleet then preparing to sail; and, after residing some months with their elder sister, Charlotte, shortly before married to Captain George Anson Byron, of the navy, they finally quitted England. On landing in the West Indies, they were welcomed by all the members of their family, among whom was Major Smith, whose constant absence from home on military duty had prevented his seeing his daughter since her infancy, but who, with many friends, greeted them with the utmost affection and cordiality. Inducements were offered to Mr. Dallas to make his stay permanent. Governor Dalling appointed him a Master in Chancery. Lucrative business was promised, and promotion in fortune and honors confidently predicted. He soon perceived, however, that the climate disagreed with his wife; that the patrimonial estate had been fatally involved by mismanagement; that the most painful and irreconcilable of all controversies, domestic ones, had arisen among those whom he loved best, and that the place of his nativity was the least auspicious to his happiness or his ambition.

While meditating a return to England, and half tempted by the frank offer of a curacy in Ireland, to devote himself to the church, a casual incident sufficed to kindle his enthusiasm, to confirm his enterprise, and to fix his future destinies. At the country residence of Major Smith, he met Mr. Lewis Hallam, who had lived for several years in the united colonies prior to their revolution, whose literary tastes and talents were congenial with his own, who had personally witnessed the causes and progress of the great struggle then terminating, and who delineated in terms of animated eulogy the social condition, free principles, and high hopes of the American people. His resolution was formed, and remained inflexible. Collecting as rapidly as possible what of his father's special bequest to him could be rescued from the general wreck— a sum not exceeding three thousand dollars—and with but two letters of introduction and of credit to Mr. William

Bingham and Mr. Robt. Morris, he embarked for the
States on the 10th of April, and on the 7th of June, 1783,
after a voyage of much peril and extreme tediousness,
reached New York. He immediately proceeded to Philadelphia, and, on the tenth day after landing, took the
prescribed oath of allegiance to the Commonwealth of
Pennsylvania.

At this epoch the war for independence had closed.
A cessation of hostilities had been proclaimed on the 19th
of April, although the definitive treaty of peace between
his Britannic Majesty and the United States of America
was not signed till the 3d of September, 1783, and Sir
Guy Carleton lingered in garrison with his troops at New
York, which he did not finally evacuate before the 25th
of November following.

At the age of four-and-twenty, with a wife whom he
tenderly loved, with scanty provision for an uncertain
future, but with dauntless moral energies and large intellectual resources, Mr. Dallas found himself the citizen of
a new world, in the midst of strangers, and without any
definite pursuit. He had placed an ocean between him
and all his past associations. The refuge of kindred, the
encouragement of friends, the sustaining and soothing
consciousness of being known and appreciated, the thousand aids and alleviations which, in places of birth and
continued residence, give certainty as well as sweetness
to exertion, he had voluntarily and sternly abandoned.
A vigorous hope never deserted him. Prepared for every
sort of mental activity, he felt assured of attaining at last,
however slowly, the success rarely denied to willing perseverance.

His personal exterior and accomplishments were fitted
to attract and conciliate. To a figure at once tall and
erect was united a deportment alike frank and graceful.
His complexion was florid, his nose aquiline, his eyes
large and blue, his forehead high and open, and his mouth
formed with uncommon distinctness and delicacy. Vivacity, candor, and cordiality were blended in the general
expression of his countenance. These traits, embellished
by the freshness of youth, and a ready colloquial talent,
could not but constitute an ample passport in ordinary
intercourse.

On entering the city of Philadelphia, as utterly friendless as unknown, a happy chance led him for lodgings to a boarding-house in Front Street, above Arch, the principal rooms of which were occupied as offices by Mr. Jonathan Burrall, commissioner for settling the accounts of the Commissary and Quartermaster's Departments of the revolutionary army. An acquaintance with this gentleman was immediately formed, which rapidly ripened into mutual esteem, and ultimately into a friendship that no circumstances afterwards, in the slightest degree, interrupted or impaired. It is due to the basis and ardor of this attachment, prolonged and uniform for thirty-three years, to add that its parties were, from first to last, with equal sincerity and almost equal warmth, of opposite sentiments in politics.

At the outset of his American life, Mr. Dallas encountered an obstacle as wholly unexpected as it was serious. He left Jamaica under the impression that he could, with little delay, on his arrival here, act upon his long-cherished preference for the legal profession, and find in the profits of an attorney an adequate security against want. For this purpose he had sedulously prepared himself. The rules of the courts, however (modified, as peace approached, under the dread of interfering immigration), exacted, as a qualification for admission to practice, a residence in the State of two years, and he was thrown, at the most critical moment, upon expedients and projects to which he had not before thought of appealing. He bore the disappointment patiently, improved the interval by closely studying the statutes of provincial, congressional, and State legislation, and cheerfully gave himself to any honest exercise of his faculties for compensation.

Mr. Burrall, in the course of an intimacy of a few weeks, perceived in his fellow-lodger the rare sagacity and accuracy in explaining and adjusting matters of account which he had acquired in the service of his uncle, Mr. Gray. He was invited, at a moderate salary, to a desk in the commissioner's office, and, speedily confirming the trust reposed in his skill and industry, soon enlarged his reputation, and with it his employments and means. Before the year was out, his confidence in his prospects was such as to justify his forming his own establishment in a neighboring house, which he rented from Mr. James C. Fisher.

Early, too, in the spring of 1784, he enlisted with zeal and ingenuity in a project with which Mr. Lewis Hallam returned from Jamaica,—the introduction of the regular drama into Philadelphia. Theatres were, as yet, little known and much reprobated in the United States. Public opinion and prohibition had been strongly and steadily opposed to them. The private performances at Boston in 1750, the fitful efforts of a strolling company of players at Providence and at New York in 1758 and 1762, and the languid pretensions of Mr. Hallam himself as a manager, before the war, had only confirmed the general dislike. Economical habits and strict principles recoiled from an amusement which, in its then rude and imperfect condition, could manifest none of its ameliorating and instructive tendencies, and seemed chiefly dangerous to simplicity of manners and purity of life. During the contest with the mother-country, men had neither leisure nor wish for diversion of any kind, and perhaps the known fact that dramatic representations were a favorite pastime among the officers of the invading army deepened still more the prejudices of those whose sufferings and wrongs appeared to be mocked by such ill-timed frivolities. In Pennsylvania, they were explicitly proscribed under the statutory classification of "vice and immorality;" and were, besides, the objects of a condemnation even more impressive and uncompromising than that of law, from a religious society whose numbers, virtues, and wealth exercised an almost irresistible influence. Nevertheless, the memorial of Mr. Hallam to the local legislature was drawn by Mr. Dallas, soliciting the exemption of his plan from the operation of the act of Assembly; and, during the pendency of that application, instantly, loudly, and ably opposed, though ultimately granted, Mr. Dallas devised a mode of, in some measure, disarming the repugnance and inoculating the taste of the community. The dexterity of the contrivance and of its execution was repaid by complete triumph. Obtaining the written opinion of Mr. Jared Ingersoll on the lawfulness of the proceeding, Mr. Hallam opened his "*Lectures upon Heads and other subjects,*" in the course of which, himself the only actor, he personated many characters, and adroitly, by recitation or mimicry, refined the feelings or provoked the merriment of his audience. His "*Long-room*" was always thronged. The utmost industry of Mr. Dallas and his best talent at various composition were taxed to mould and diversify the "lectures." Their effect more than met the expectations of the author or the performer; to the one the profits were ample, to the other they brought an enlargement of reputation as a writer, and finally the success of a good cause in the reconciliation of popular sentiment to a regular theatre.

A fondness for dramatic exhibitions in their higher grades, is inseparable from cultivated intellect. To see brought as near to present reality as possible the incidents of history, the moral combinations of fiction, the delineations of peculiarities, whether national or individual, the tendencies of uncontrolled passions, the alleviating sallies of wit, and the native glories of virtue, is a diversion the zest of which augments with every increase of reading, reflection, or experience. Perverted and debased as it sometimes is, like every other human art or faculty, it can never fail to be alike instructive and ennobling in its true condition. It was thus that Mr. Dallas appreciated the stage, and ardently sought its establishment. His memory was laden with the pages of Shakspeare, of whom he was an enthusiastic admirer, and familiar with the choice productions of the later English dramatists. He witnessed several performances of David Garrick, at Drury Lane, during the closing years of that great reformer of the art. And having essentially contributed to the popularity and success of the theatre in Philadelphia, he regarded it as, in a measure, his own creation, with a partiality which the toils of law-practice, the solicitudes of politics, or the cares of state, could never damp or repress. An autograph fragment found among his manuscripts indicates his having prepared the plot of a sentimental comedy, seemingly to conciliate public sympathy towards a certain class of American loyalists, and its beauty, purity, and point, short as it is, make us regret that he should have left his design unfinished. At times, and for special occasions, he wrote unacknowledged addresses, prologues, and epilogues, for the benefit of those whom he esteemed as actors or cherished as friends. He habitually, during a series of years, repaired from the court-room, as soon as its business was adjourned in the evening, to the theatre, where he remained for about half an hour, in the farthest corner of a distant box, giving himself wholly to the relaxation, and enjoying his favorite department of criticism.

Mr. Dallas displayed, while young, and never ceased to possess one rare faculty, often remarked by those who knew him intimately, and which eminently conduced to his own happiness and to the happiness of all around him. Most persons of vigorous and disciplined understandings are competent to severe and protracted exertion. Intense thought and study seem in some the natural course of existence. Others achieve wonders by temporary seclusion and labor. It falls to the lot of very few, however, to be able to reconcile the most effective throes of mind with the readiest social intercourse; to exert the power of compressing instantly the intellect to its utmost force, and of as instantly unbending into ease and vivacity. The effects of abstraction are seldom dispelled by mere volition; they cling to the animal spirits, shade the countenance, benumb the organs of speech, and are slow in yielding to external exigencies. Hence they whose stations or pursuits exact profound meditation gradually cease to be what are termed men of the world, and, at home or abroad, are incapable of that prompt and light communion so fertile of domestic endearment and so graceful in general society. It was otherwise with him of whom we are treating. He would retire to his office, grapple at once with the most abstruse question of law, arrange an entangled mass of facts, or resume a current of original composition, without any apparent effort: when, too, thus involved, he was regardless of interruption, and at the call of affection or of frolic would break off with joyous abruptness, and betray not the slightest symptom of preoccupation. How constantly did these transitions surprise and delight his friends! Most frequently they were manifested when his children, heedless of his labors, invoked his enlivening presence, always finding him in their fireside sports of "*Musical pantomime*," "*How do you like it*," "*So does the mufti*," and others, their gayest companion. During his most arduous professional toils, which day after day attested at the bar the devotion of his zeal and the elaborateness of his preparation, he would mingle, with unclouded freshness, in scenes of conviviality and amusement. A single instance may adequately illustrate this trait of character. Late in the evening he was busily engaged in methodizing notes for his argument in the morning before Judge Washington in the celebrated " Olmstead case," while his family circle in the adjoining parlor were equally intent on framing a set of original " conversation cards." The youthful party undertook to write on one side of each blank card an emphatic or leading word, and on the other side an appropriate couplet. A burst of boisterous mirth drew him from his office, and being immediately apprised of the nature of the pastime, and called upon to assist, he remained for about fifteen minutes absent from his papers, and endorsed several of the cards with lines of poetry.

MISS LIVINGSTONE.

O'er lifeless marble let Pygmalion moan,
We hail the graces of a Living-stone.

FRIENDSHIP.

The delusions of life will teach you ere long
To compound for no good, if you suffer no wrong ;
For friendship romantic in search while you go,
Every man is my friend, sir, who is not my foe.

HOME.

That home is home I can't agree ;
For let me with my Mary roam
Through ev'ry land, o'er ev'ry sea,
I still will find myself at home.
The spot of birth, the seat of fame,
The cottage thatch, or palace dome,
May mark an era, give a name,
But Mary's bosom is my home.

The term of probation having expired, Mr. Dallas was admitted as attorney and counsellor in the Supreme Court of Pennsylvania, on the 13th of July, 1785. At that period, the law was "*rudis indigestaque moles;*" but happily its administration and practice were in the hands of men fitted by strength of mind, integrity of principle, and untiring energies to settle the foundations of a system in harmony with the real wants of the people and their new political institutions. If some errors were committed which subsequently demanded bold remedies, it is never-

theless scarcely possible to exaggerate the services rendered to the Commonwealth of which they were citizens
by the McKeans, the Wilsons, the Bradfords, the Inger-
solls, the Rawles, the Lewises, and the Tilghmans of that
day. The individual fame of lawyers is not often wide,
and seldom outlives, except in the ranks of the profession, the generation to which they belong; but the
good they do as a body constituted of bench and bar,
when learned, patriotic, and indefatigable, remains, perhaps forever, operative and imperishable. In a young
and free country, where impulse and consistency are to
be given to the maxims of liberty and the rules of right;
where constitutional injunctions are to be rigidly enforced,
and property to be acquired, transmitted, and protected,
conformably to fresh modifications of legislation and untried structures of jurisdiction; no class of intellectual
laborers produces results equally permanent and extensive. Becoming the agents of every other class in succession,—to advise, vindicate, or redress,—the general
tendency of their united influence is to impart confidence
to truth, boldness to freedom, and stability to order. The
epoch of '76, especially as delineated by the doctrines
of the Declaration of Independence, required social as
the necessary adjunct of political change. It was obvious
that the pyramid, alleged to be an appropriate emblem
of monarchy, could not be converted into the republican
cube without resettling the base and altering the bearings
of all the parts. No two citizens could thereafter have
precisely their former relations to each other, without
imperfection in the substituted code. Rank, privilege,
primogeniture, entail, freehold, coercive church, tithes,
and the countless other minute props of aristocratic organization were destined to be practically met and demol-
ished wherever found lurking. The spirit, as well as the
letter, of recognized truths was to be carried out in all
the channels of men's business; and the great idea
equality, at all times, with all persons, and under all circumstances, to receive its just application. For the execution of these high objects, our lawyers offered, besides
their abilities and virtues, the guarantees of mutual watch-
fulness and public discussion. Very few years elapsed
before Mr. Dallas ranged himself among the foremost to
whom we have referred; and his professional exertions

were often made on occasions of extreme public and political interest.

His spare time was employed in superintending several literary periodicals, among which *The Columbian Magazine* attracted most regard. This miscellany appears to have been assigned by its proprietors to his management in 1787, after having been under the direction of the justly-celebrated Francis Hopkinson, whose merit as a writer was established by a number of effective satires, in prose and in poetry, as well as by essays of a severer cast. The circumstance of his superseding this veteran author, at so early a period, as editor of the publication, is strong proof of the respect which he had already inspired for his attainments and qualities,—a respect in which his predecessor, the Admiralty Judge of Pennsylvania, very frankly united.

To the labors of law and of literature Mr. Dallas soon added the distracting ones of politics. To a generous and enlightened mind no field of public action could be more attractive than that presented by the United States. A people accustomed to the enjoyment and exercise of liberty in their social relations had begun the experiment of self-government, whose foundations were laid in an independence proclaimed upon the broadest principles and consummated with unrivalled wisdom and acknowledged valor. Their country was extensive, their products and resources were abundant and various; their habits of life were unenfeebled by luxury and wealth : as detached communities, each of their Commonwealths was a scene of progressive activity, intelligence, and happiness; while as a confederacy their combined power had been proved adequate at least to the purpose of common defence. Still, however, nothing political was settled save great maxims. Amid the absorbing dangers of a first war, the Union, by which alone it could be waged, was imperfectly organized ; the separate sovereignties, actuated by a wholesome jealousy of central power, had been too sparing in the faculties they conferred upon their common agent, the General Congress; and the return of peace, bringing into view other objects besides those of battle, soon disclosed the expediency of replacing the existing Articles of Confederation by some scheme of government less slow, complicated, and uncertain. The local constitutions of the

States, hastily arranged at the epoch of '76, were also unsatisfactory, and even that matured by the sage Franklin was destined to early abandonment. The sources, distribution, and restriction of authority became subjects of universal interest and discussion. With no ambitious chief to propitiate, with no conterminous jealousy to dread, and as yet with no faction to inflame or obscure, the minds of men were everywhere exploring the forms and arrangements best adapted to pure and permanent republicanism. Differences of opinion naturally prevailed, which grew wider and more distinct as the period for movement ripened. Correspondence, conversation, the public journals, the halls of legislation, and voluntary associations, all contributed to swell and elucidate the theme on whose solution so much in future of freedom, peace, prosperity, and glory depended. It seems to have been a special allotment of Providence that America should teem, at her great crisis, with master-spirits, whose philosophical temperament and discriminating sagacity were only surpassed by the singleness and expansion of their patriotism. Debate, though protracted and adorned by the development of countless theories, was enriched by the fruits of profound study and sobered by the lessons of experience. Human society cannot hope to witness a region more congenial, a time more propitious, or a race more fitted for the trial of a democracy as simple and as thorough as physical causes will permit. The call for a convention to deliberate on trade and commerce, made by Virginia in January, 1786, and the meeting of such a body at Annapolis in September following, were only prefatory to that extraordinary assemblage which opened its sessions at Philadelphia on the first Monday of May, 1787, and concluded them by submitting to the confederated republics, for adoption or rejection by their respective peoples, the existing Constitution of the United States; and this bright national creation, at every step of whose formation and in every subsequent scene of whose amendment prior to final confirmation floods of light were shed on the nature of American institutions, led directly to similar organic improvements in several of the narrower but perhaps more vital spheres of State polity, and earliest in that of Pennsylvania.

The politics of Mr. Dallas were formed in the progress

of these events, and were exclusively of American growth. In England, whether from youth, distaste, or other cause, he had been led no farther than may be implied in a profound veneration for Franklin and a warm admiration of the parliamentary eloquence of Charles James Fox. He had never ranged as Whig or Tory, and it would be a mistake to suppose that, like several of the prominent men with whom he subsequently associated and sympathized, he had fled to the New World as a retreat from the factious furies of the Old. His choice of a home was voluntarily made, almost as soon as he attained manhood. For the pursuit of happiness, independence, and honor, he selected the American soil; allured, no doubt, by the bright future then opening upon it, but impelled by no past persecution or prejudice. His indefatigable studies preparatory to professional practice imbued his mind with the spirit and character of our legislation, customs, opinions, and manners; his convictions and his feelings harmonized with the most liberal doctrines; and he attached himself to the first germ of the Democratic Party of the United States.

The origin of the two permanent American parties is distinct as matter of history, and honorable in all its incidents. It preceded national organization. The principles destined to agitate the government by their collision were enunciated before that government existed. Power was yet unknown; no court to propitiate, no club to terrify, no treasure to covet, ambition was without an object, avarice without temptation, and servility without an idol. The substitution of republicanism for monarchy had been · almost an act of unanimity, and the subsequent ripening of the Federal Constitution was an intellectual process, during which the wise and the virtuous differed as to the means of attaining the same end, without for one instant subjecting themselves to the ordinary and odious imputations of intrigue, faction, interest, or fear. Mind was at work, not on what already *was*, with countless complicated and contradictory influences, but on what was *to be;* and, in advance of every selfish motive, and of every bias inimical to pure and honest patriotism, leading statesmen promulgated with rare ability their respective schemes of polity, developing in their differences the struggle which must unavoidably precede the creation of the new system, as well as forever accompany its administration. The obvious integrity and transcendent talent with which opposing views were sustained inspired universal forbearance, and the very compromises made in order to achieve some definite result attest the existence of principles in themselves irreconcilable. It may be said, indeed, that what was thus early yielded has only tended to give to both the parties greater identity of character and more precision of purpose, and that each, in a natural course of action, avails itself of every opportunity to reclaim in practise the concessions it originally made to theory.

The new government of the Union went into operation on the 4th of March, 1789; the new form for the Commonwealth of Pennsylvania in December, 1790. Mr. Dallas acquired and exercised all the rights of American citizenship six or seven years before either of these events, and largely participated in the public discussions and agitations by which they were preceded. His ability in transactions of business, his strength and eloquence as a lawyer, —displayed in all the courts, federal or State,—and the power of his pen, rapidly made him conspicuous. On the 1st of May, 1790, he issued from the press the first volume of a series of reports of cases argued and decided in the courts of Pennsylvania before and since the Revolution, which he afterwards extended to four volumes. This publication was most cordially welcomed by the bench and the bar. Dedicated, in terms of warm but just acknowledgment, to Chief Justice McKean, that eminent and remarkable man transmitted a copy of the work to Lord Mansfield, who, in reply, spoke of the compilation and of the judicial learning it embodied in language of high and polished praise. General Thomas Mifflin, elected the first governor under the new Constitution of Pennsylvania of 1790, on being apprised that he was the author of certain attractive essays then publishing, sent his friend Mr. Edward Fox to invite a visit and acquaintance, and immediately offered him the post of Secretary of the Commonwealth. The commission, which bears date early in 1791, was unsought and wholly unexpected; but it was accepted in a spirit of friendship as frank and lasting as its presentation was generous and graceful. Reappointed in 1793 and in 1796, at the subsequent re-elections of Governor Mifflin, he remained the principal adviser and aid of that popular and patriotic chief magistrate during all the three official terms to which the constitution—and that alone—restricted his eligibility.

In this manner, at the age of thirty-one, Mr. Dallas began a career of public life which he can scarcely be said to have intermitted until very shortly before his death. At that time such a career was peculiarly genial to his varied acquirements, conciliatory manners, and cultivated tastes. Philadelphia was far the most imposing and promising city of the continent. It was the capital of two freshly-formed governments; the abode of much, if not all, of the best literary and philosophical intelligence in the country,—of Franklin, Rush, Rittenhouse, Logan, Hopkinson; the most active mart of commerce, and the point of social comfort and repose sought by strangers and travellers. Though ardent and firm in preferring the most popular principles in politics, he indulged no proscriptive sentiment: fond of society, and gifted with uncommon powers of making it agreeable, he pursued genius, learning, wit, merit, and accomplishment, of whatever party and wherever he could find them, and threw the doors of his domestic hospitality wide open for their indiscriminate reception. In this essentially, and not in the mere office he held, however important as an accessary that certainly was, consisted the real publicity of his life. His profession, to which he always clung as to a sheet-anchor, uninterrupted by the routine of administrative duties, expanded in its range and increased in its emolument, and thus sustained the expensive buoyancy of his spirits and rewarded an unflagging industry.

The nine years of Governor Mifflin were marked by a wise course of local policy and by incidents of national moment. While the General Assembly showed every disposition to advance the prosperity of the State, and energetically led the way to important improvements in its laws, trade, intercourse, and institutions, there were referred to, and dependent upon, the talent, vigor, and management of the executive many subjects at once novel and embarrassing in character. Of the five hundred and seventy-four acts of Assembly passed during this period, a number were necessary to adapt the operations of the government to the provisions of the new constitutions; the great body of them related to the ordinary objects of legislation; but many indicated enlarged and sound views of the true policy and interests of the Commonwealth, and still remain in operation to attest the wisdom of their authors. As illustrative of the last description, we would briefly refer to the acts providing for the construction of the Lancaster turnpike and other roads; for opening and improving navigable waters; for building the permanent bridge over the Schuylkill and various other bridges; for incorporating associations for literary, charitable, and religious purposes; for regulating the descent of intestate estates; for abolishing the punishment of death in many cases and graduating the crime of murder; for facilitating the barring of entails; for regulating writs of partition, and for regulating county rates and levies. The governor, a man of revolutionary patriotism and service,—the first aid-de-camp of Washington in 1775,—who had long acted as a member of the old Congress and for a period as its president, reposed unlimited confidence in his secretary; and they two, harmonious always in sentiments and views, fulfilled at every juncture their high trust with uniform and signal success.

/The position occupied by Mr. Dallas in the arena of politics, when invited by Governor Mifflin into his councils, was a conspicuous one. Notwithstanding his professional and literary exertions, he had for several years devoted much time to associations and arrangements of a party character, that were gradually assuming shape and taking deeper root. The leading men in the various sections of Pennsylvania were personally known to him; and with those whose public sentiments he shared, such as Gallatin, Findley, Smilie, Addison, he maintained an active correspondence. In the city he was the efficient and stirring spirit of a republican phalanx distinguished by learning, purity of life, and patriotism. His consultations with these gave authenticity and weight to what the promptness of his writing disseminated through the interior; and the influence he acquired, which his adversaries endeavored to make odious by exaggerating, was the legitimate consequence of an enlightened and persevering zeal in spreading and consolidating the foundations of a party which, though then in a minority, was destined soon to take and long to hold the direction of affairs.] It would greatly embellish this biography were

its author able to sketch the lives and characters of those
in unison with whom Mr. Dallas thus acted. More, aye,
much more of gratitude and fame is due to them than has
yet been awarded. Contemporaneous malice and heredi-
tary prejudice have labored, and yet labor hard to mis-
represent their principles and underrate their work; but
an unassailable monument to Dr. James Hutchinson,
Thomas Mifflin, Jonathan Sergeant, George Bryan, David
Rittenhouse, Peter S. Duponceau, Dr. Samuel Jackson,
Thomas McKean, Edward Fox, John Barclay, Thomas
Leiper, J. Swanwick, and others of their associates may
be found in the simple fact that the doctrines for which
they struggled and were denounced are now inseparable
from the being and exercise of government in America.
They were the doctrines adjudged to have their truest
representative in Mr. Jefferson. That morbid bigotry of
opinion is surely deserving of nothing but reproof, which
can rake among the ashes of extinguished contests in the
hope of rekindling detraction against men whose wisdom
and sincerity are affirmed by sixty years of positive
history."

It was much less easy at that inexperienced epoch than
it now is to perceive and to preserve the true relations
between the States, and between them and the general
government, with the boundaries of their respective
spheres. Yet it is curious and gratifying to record some
instances of original and clear sagacity on this critical
subject which lapse of time has at least not improved.
The very first year of its operation had hardly closed
when, on a point in respect to which much sensitiveness
has always existed and must long continue, the executive
of Pennsylvania officially proclaimed, and enforced with
irresistible power of argument, a construction of the Constitution of the United States, of great importance to its
duration. It arose out of a criminal prosecution instituted in Washington County, where an indictment was
found by a grand jury, at a court of oyer and terminer,
against several persons for forcibly carrying off a free
negro with intent to sell him as a slave in another State,
in violation of a highly penal act of Assembly. Governor
Mifflin received authentic information that these offenders had taken refuge in Virginia, and he immediately
applied to the chief magistrate of that State for their

3

delivery up as fugitives from justice. His application was refused. It was repeated, with more emphasis and formality. A correspondence ensued which displayed considerable ability on the part of the authorities of Pennsylvania, and proved them to be signally "regulated by a due regard to the dignity and rights of the Commonwealth," as well as by "a sincere respect for the sentiments of a sister State," and a disciplined anxiety "to avoid all invidious and unprofitable altercation." The controversy was prolonged for several months. In addressing the legislative body on the 25th of January, 1792, the message made the following lucid exposition of the stand which had been taken:

"This representation from the State of Virginia appears, in some respects, to be founded upon misinformation as to the facts, and, in others, upon a misconception as to the law. In the case of the demand for delivering up the persons who had forcibly carried off a free negro, it is indeed avowed that the fact was committed; but the authority of this State to render it criminal, the circumstances which constitute a flight in the offenders, and the operative sanction given to the demand by the present Constitution of the Union, are still doubted and denied. I trust, however, that it will not be thought necessary at this day to assert the sovereignty of the State within her own territory upon matters of internal policy. She had the unalienated power to legislate upon the subject which has produced the controversy: her law defined and declared the offence; and it is the duty of her officers, if they cannot prevent, to punish every violation. The offence, it is true, can only be committed or punished within the jurisdiction of the government by whose authority the law was enacted; but when committed, whether by citizens or strangers, the federal obligation of the States expressly provides against that impunity which flight into another country might otherwise afford. The documents that have been transmitted by the executive of Virginia, proving that the citizens of that State made an irruption into Pennsylvania, with the immediate purpose of carrying off the negro in question, the moment that the act was committed, those persons became offenders in the contemplation of law; and the moment that they retired from the jurisdiction of this State, they became fugitives from justice within the meaning of the Constitution of the United States. Nor can it be of any importance to the inquiry whether the circumstances stated respecting the original condition of the negro are true or not, since the laws of Pennsylvania, though they will not permit violence or injustice, supply an adequate remedy for every wrong. If the negro was not lawfully emancipated, he would have been restored to his master upon a peaceable application to a competent tribunal; but if by the benevolent operation of an act of the General Assembly (which has long been esteemed an honor and an ornament to our code) he has obtained his freedom, it is surely incumbent on the power that bestowed the blessing to protect him in the enjoyment of it. Thus the claim to the services of the negro, if just, did not require force to maintain it; and if unjust, force can never alter its nature, or expiate the injury which, in effect, it perpetrates.

"But, independent of these considerations, it will be remembered that in the case of the negro who was deprived of his liberty, as well as the case of the Indians who lost their lives on Beaver Creek, the grand inquest of the proper county have brought the several accusations against the persons that were named in the respective requisitions presented to the executive of Virginia. The investigation of the facts, therefore, rests with another tribunal, and ought not to be unnecessarily discussed in an extra-judicial manner; but if the facts stated in those several presentments amount to crimes, or, in other words, if our laws have any force even within the boundaries of the Commonwealth; and if strangers, who having wilfully committed an offence against the municipal law of Pennsylvania retire to a neighboring State, may be denominated fugitives from justice, then every member of the section of the Federal Constitution which authorizes the demand as a preliminary to the trial of the offenders is amply satisfied on the present occasion; and neither policy, justice, nor candor will admit a construction of that constitution which, at the time of the ratification, shall place the citizens of the Union in a state of nature, and declare the antecedent period to be now free from every federal compact or obligation."

The grounds on which the executive of Virginia declined complying with the requisition as originally made, were, *first*, that the offence described in the indictment was not a felony or other crime within the meaning of the constitution; *second*, that, as a trespass, the violence complained of was equally cognizable in Virginia as in Pennsylvania, and, therefore, no removal of the accused was necessary or proper; *third*, that it did not appear that the accused had *fled* from justice; *fourth*, that there was no legal evidence of their having been *found* in Virginia; and, *fifth*, if all the prior objections failed, there remained the insurmountable one that Congress had not prescribed the *manner* in which the constitutional injunction should be fulfilled, or, in other words, through whose agency and by what sort of authorization the delivery and removal were to be made. We must not say that the first four excuses for inaction were uncandid and frivolous, for they had weight with some strong and independent minds; but it was the fifth only which appears to have suspended the interposition of President Washington, to whom Governor Mifflin submitted what in his judgment constituted a dangerous disregard of one of the most delicate and salutary guarantees of the national compact. Out of this case, and in consequence of the resolute attitude assumed in vindicating the rights of the State, sprung the act of Congress of the 12th of February, 1793, which has since furnished the rule of action on all such cases. Fugitives from justice, and persons escaping from the service or labor to which they have been held, are equally embraced by that act. It is impossible to repress a regret that, on a point like the extradition of persons, whether culprits or slaves, which has become one of such extreme tenderness, the authors of the constitution were not more precise, or that the legislature, when the embarrassment first came under notice, had not devised a single plan of proceeding less liable to disturb the natural sympathies of men, and more effective to secure the covenanted rights. Some subjects do not seem to admit of their being disposed of in a manner unusually summary; they, in fact, are facilitated and fortified by the ordinary dilatory process; and, among a people so sensitive on matters of personal freedom and safety as are the American people, they can only be successfully regulated under the sanction of high and paramount authority.

Many provisions in the constitution contemplate and require legislative enactment before they could be carried into execution; but to rank among these the two clauses of the second section of the fourth article is a mistaken refinement, and might subject them to an ordeal not originally intended,—namely, the uncertain inclination of a congressional majority. They enunciate distinctly enough the purposes of the convention and of the people, —criminals to be surrendered on executive demand and slaves to be surrendered on claim of the owner; and both purposes, thus sanctioned, are easily attainable with known forms, and upon established principles of social action, without the slightest additional direction. They were not to be rendered nugatory by the neglect of Congress, nor could it be designed to leave them liable to be frustrated by complicated or cumbersome devices. It is strange to find their dependence upon mere legislation first asserted from the State of Virginia, a State that would now be reluctant to acknowledge that a repeal of the act of February, 1793, could take from them all practical efficiency.

The solicitudes and labors of Mr. Dallas's office were greatly enhanced by disturbances which had been gradually fomenting in the western parts of Pennsylvania, and which, ultimately assuming an insurrectionary character, made the interposition of military force necessary to the maintenance of order and the enforcement of law.

At the first Congress under the new constitution it became evident that, to supply the public wants, an increase of national revenue must be provided. After the assumption of the revolutionary debts of the several States, estimated as an aggregate of twenty-one millions of dollars, the Secretary of the Treasury, Mr. Alexander Hamilton, recommended an excise upon domestic distilled spirits and stills as the best means of paying the augmented annual interest. A clamor immediately arose. The very name of excise was odious and inflammatory. The citizens assembled in many places, listened approvingly to angry harangues, adopted resolutions denouncing the project, and forwarded their remonstrances to the legislature of the Union. This quick outcry seemed partially successful, and the bill failed on its first trial. Yet, notwithstanding a vigorous and excited opposition, both in and out of Congress, the scheme became a law on the 3d of March, 1791; and resistance to its execution, at once, and in Pennsylvania particularly, proclaimed itself loudly and boldly. The population of four large western counties of this State—Washington, Fayette, Alleghany, and Westmoreland—among whom the distilleries were numerous and profitable, exhibited great exasperation. Meetings gathered at Redstone and Pittsburg in July and September; and in the early part of the latter month one of the collectors of the excise and persons entrusted with the service of judicial process connected with the matter were assaulted, tarred and feathered, and otherwise cruelly treated. Similar and worse outrages continued to be perpetrated during the whole recess of Congress, which again convened, agreeably to a special law, on the 24th of October, 1791. A reduction of the unpopular duties, by an act passed in May following, accompanied by modifications of a conciliatory character as to the manner of assessing them, produced no other effect upon the discontented than a belief that their proceedings had intimidated the government and that farther displays of violence would soon extort an absolute repeal. Combinations of disguised and armed men made their appearance throughout the extensive districts already mentioned, overawing and silencing the friends of order, and visiting with fire and sword the revenue officers who failed, on being summoned, to surrender their papers and resign their commissions.

There were, indeed, many distinguished men who, though hostile to the excise, were yet more hostile to forcible and lawless attempts to obstruct its collection. These, particularly William Findley, David Reddick, Albert Gallatin, Hugh Brackenridge, and Alexander Addison, while unable to arrest the torrent raging round them, exposed their persons to danger and their characters to suspicion by efforts to assuage its fury and to direct its course into safe and constitutional channels. As is usual, the spirit of party recklessly confounded them with the general body of disorganizers; and as they ranked high for ability and usefulness among the minority, composed of Democratic Republicans, unsparing obloquy was for a time heaped upon their names.

Before President Washington would consent to regard the outrages of conspirators and rioters in the light of insurrection or treason, demanding the interposition of military force, he required to be satisfied that they were formidable enough, not merely to impede the execution of an obnoxious law, but to defy the power of the judiciary and to endanger the peace of the country. Governor Mifflin and Mr. Dallas were extremely reluctant, and so expressed themselves in conference with the President and his advisers, to believe the civil authorities of Pennsylvania incapable of maintaining the ascendency of the laws. On this, and on this alone, turned a difference of opinion which prevailed as to the most expedient course of action for suppressing the disorders. In the estimation of the executive of the State, the incompetency of the judiciary department of the government to vindicate the violated laws had not been made sufficiently apparent; and the military power of the government ought not to be employed, until its judicial authority, after a fair experiment, had proved incompetent to enforce obedience or to punish violations of the law. There was, up to a certain period of time, just foundation for this view of the subject. If judicial inefficiency existed, it was not discernible by or in the courts of Pennsylvania; that it might be seen and felt by the federal judges, in their steps to pursue and punish offenders, was other matter, out of the cognizance of the State functionaries. No one could doubt that the mass of the people of Pennsylvania, and all her magistracy, were conscious both of the right to disapprove the policy of the excise and of the criminality of resisting its collection. As in various other places, in the county of Chester the riotous abuse of an exciseman acting under that law had been prosecuted, a verdict of conviction obtained, and an exemplary punishment inflicted; and on that occasion the foreman of the grand jury by whom the indictment was found, addressing himself to the attorney-general, declared that *he* was " as much or more opposed to the excise law than the rioters, but would not suffer violations of the law to go unpunished." Nor was it a violent presumption to suppose that, bad as matters really were in our trans-alleghany section, their enormity was somewhat highly colored by those who either could not tranquilly bear to see a favorite system thwarted, or eagerly imputed every crime committed as a necessary consequence of political doctrines opposed to their own.

When President Washington, therefore, invited Governor Mifflin to say whether he deemed the circumstances to be such as would warrant his calling out a portion of the militia of his State, a correspondence sprung up between the two executives, which was conducted with striking ability on both sides, and was considered of great interest and moment. (*Appendix, No.* 1.) It treated elaborately, and with exclusive relation to the suggested movement, of the responsibilities of the highest officers of the Union and the Commonwealth, of the boundaries which both separate and connect their respective spheres of public duty, and of the incompetency of the judiciary to fulfil its purposes,—an incompetency affirmed by the one to be manifest and denied by the other to be sufficiently shown. The act of Congress of the 2d of May, 1792, providing for " calling forth the militia to execute the laws of the Union, suppress insurrections, and repel invasions," furnished a plain and practical rule of proceeding to the President; but the governor had no such chart by which to steer, and if he invoked the physical power of his State without legislative sanction, and upon the inherent vigor of his office only, he would naturally first desire to see that the emergency was such and so recognized as to justify him under any result. Both these patriots were, however, relieved from all the embarrassment that might have followed upon a contrariety of impressions by a notification addressed, under the date of the 5th of August, 1794, to the President, by James Wilson, an associate justice of the supreme court of the United States, and of the circuit embracing Pennsylvania, certifying, as prescribed by the second section of the act of 1792, that there existed in the counties of Washington and Alleghany combinations too powerful to be suppressed by the ordinary course of judicial proceedings. The proclamation of the President was at once issued; requisitions for quotas of militia were addressed to the four States of New Jersey, Pennsylvania, Maryland, and Virginia; and before the close of September an overwhelming army of fifteen thousand men were put in motion to concentrate in the region of disaffection. No portion of this force was more prompt or more faithful than that from Pennsylvania,—attesting the sincerity of Governor Mifflin when, at the conclusion of the leading letter in the series referred to, he said: "It is proper, under the impression of my federal obligations, to add a full and unequivocal assurance that whatever requisition you may make, whatever duty you may impose, in pursuance of your constitutional and legal powers, will on my part be promptly undertaken and faithfully discharged."

Mr. Dallas accompanied Governor Mifflin on this expedition as his aid-de-camp; and perhaps it would now be impossible to portray its characteristic features with as much distinctness and authenticity as they appear in some

letters written by him to Mrs. Dallas, which lie before me. As illustrating, too, his own views of the insurgents and of the measures in progress to disperse and punish them, and as unfolding his character generally, they are the best materials for biography, and could not, without injustice, be withheld from the reader.

1.

"READING, 23 Sept. 1794.

"After a jaunt of great fatigue and filled with fifty eccentric incidents, we reached Pottsgrove at half-past 11 o'clock last night. This day we dined at Reading; and the governor delivered his address in a Presbyterian church to a very numerous audience. At least two-thirds of them were Germans, and did not understand a word of what he spoke. The effect, however, has been very great, although this county is greatly disinclined to the present exertions."

2.

"WRIGHT'S FERRY, 28 Sept. '94.

"I must reserve a general detail of our journey till I have reached Carlisle. It has been successful as to its principal object, but certainly not a pleasant one. There is an inconceivable degree of confusion in every department, and you know the necessary consequence—my being harassed with everybody's business. Colonel Gurney's regiment leaves Lancaster to-morrow. McPherson's Blues left it yesterday. The military rage is completely inflamed, and the whole country seems in motion."

3.

"YORK-TOWN, 29 Sept. '94.

"We have travelled through a delightful country for two days past. The roads are bad, but our journeys are short, from the capital of one county to the capital of another. The governor acquits himself with great address, and has everywhere been received with the highest respect and applause. He certainly surpasses every expectation that I had formed of his management in conciliating the troops. The want of supplies has given ample occasion for that kind of exertion."

4.

"CARLISLE, 4 Oct. '94.

"The soldier's life has fairly commenced. The change which the dress has made in the appearance of all our acquaintance is trifling compared with the change which their duties seem to have made in their dispositions and manner. Thus we prove ourselves the creatures of habit. My habit has hitherto been a love of my family and of business; it has afforded me so much satisfaction that I never shall be tempted to change it. Every call to the camp-scene I resist as a snare; and, unless when forced by business, I pass my time at my quarters in Carlisle.

"The President arrived here to-day. He was introduced with considerable state, and expressed great satisfaction at the appearance of the troops. He and Mr. Hamilton, the governor and myself, dined with a number of others at Mr. Montgomery's. The President's toast was, 'A happy issue to the business before us;' and his sentiments respecting it are so elevated, so firm, and yet so prudent and humane, that I am charmed with his determination to join us. Two men have been killed,—one by the Jersey line, and one by the Pennsylvania line. I believe that both either provoked or deserved their fate; but the events are calculated to excite alarm, particularly when exaggerated, as they have been, by the enemies to the measures of government. The President, in a candid and manly manner, regretted that the deaths had happened, and observed that men who are engaged in the duty of supporting the law should be the last to violate it. This declaration was, fortunately for me, made in the presence of several who thought me lukewarm for inculcating a similar doctrine a day or two before the President's arrival. I enjoyed the triumph.

"When shall we return? I have asked myself, I have asked everybody around me, the question; but every attempt at an answer, applied to the whole army, is in vain. In the case of the President, however, we may calculate his return to be on the first of November, because at that time Congress will meet. In the case of the governor (if questions of rank do not shorten the period), we may calculate his return in the course of November, because at the beginning of next month the legislature will meet. In my case, unless particular business of a public nature detaches me sooner, you may calculate as in the case of the governor. But in the case of the army at large, I can furnish no rule of calculation. The western counties are overrun with banditti. If they are uncontrolled during the winter, they will acquire strength; and it will be difficult, by a similar exertion of the militia, to overawe them hereafter. Hence I conclude that at least a part of the troops will be stationed in that quarter for several months; and, in order to evince the determination as well as the power of the government to support itself, I think it probable that the whole will be marched to Pittsburg. An opinion partially prevails that an abject submission is contemplated by the western insurgents; and a meeting is appointed, we are told, to take the critical state of their affairs into consideration, with a view of coming to that result. I wish the case may be so; but, after what has happened of violence and deception,

I confess that I am at a loss to fix any criterion by which the sincerity of such overtures could be ascertained. The terror, excited by the approach of the army and the deaths of the two men who have been killed, is universal and excessive; but, as there is no reason to suppose that one convert has been made, remove the cause of that terror and you revive the spirit of opposition. In this very town we daily pass and repass the most violent abettors of the insurgents; nay, the most active partisans in raising the whiskey pole in the high street parade, without insult, through the camp. The pole has been taken down; but it is obvious that the disposition which set it up has not been subdued."

5.

"CARLISLE, 6 Oct. '94.

"The President gave a dinner to-day to the governors of Pennsylvania and New Jersey, and their families. He seemed in excellent humor, free and full of conversation. I believe Wayne's success, the appearance of the camp, and a greater facility in settling the questions of rank among the leading officers than was expected, have raised his spirits. Lee will probably command; but the governor says he will serve in the humblest capacity rather than not serve at all. This is not the case with General Irvine; nor, it is hinted, will it be the case with the principal officers of the Jersey line, who claim a superior rank in the army to that occupied by the proposed commander during the war. There are about four thousand men encamped here. They are in high spirits and eager for the fray; but for my own part, if I dared to indulge a pacific wish in so warlike a scene, it would be for the restoration of order without the further display of the power of the government, or the indulgence of a vindictive spirit. A meeting was to be held by the insurgents on the second instant, which may lead to that event."

6.

"CARLISLE, 9 Oct. '94.

"The great secret of arrangement is at last divulged. Governor Lee first in command, Governor Mifflin second, and Governor Howell third. Mifflin commands the Pennsylvania and Jersey lines, till the two columns unite at Bedford. General Hand is appointed adjutant-general for the whole army. The march is to be commenced on Friday, the tenth, and the President expects that we shall reach Bedford on the sixteenth.

"I mentioned to you that a meeting would be held by the insurgents on the second instant. The result has been a declaration of submission, and the appointment of Mr. Findlay and Mr. Reddick as commissioners to entreat that the army may not enter their country. The general opinion spurns at this puny expedient, suggested by mere panic; but I cannot help regarding it as a favorable symptom of a short campaign,—at least of a bloodless one. The commissioners are expected this day, and it is not improbable that they will arrive in time to meet the President before his departure for Fort Cumberland. The best consequence that I expect from the visit is the President's explanation of the evidence of submission that will be satisfactory to him; and I think that a general declaration of obedience to the excise system, and an immediate surrender of their leaders, will be among the essential conditions.

"The accounts continue to be various from various quarters with respect to the probability of an opposition. One fact, however, seems well authenticated. Bradford, having himself subscribed the terms of pardon originally proposed, recommends submission to his followers on this avowed footing, that they may take time for better preparation to effect their object; and one Hamilton (a man who has hitherto acted under Bradford's auspices) has bound five hundred insurgents, in the neighborhood of Washington, by a solemn oath to support each other or die in the attempt, if the army should offer to seize or injure any of them. Notwithstanding this, and a thousand other reports of a disposition for resistance, I believe the troops will march in perfect safety to Pittsburg and back again. Some accidents may happen in parties sent out to apprehend particular characters, but I am confident there will be no general encounter of hostile bodies."

7.

"CARLISLE, 18 Oct. '94.

"Never was there so narrow an escape! As I was passing down the main street towards the Jersey camp, in company with Mr. Hoge, of the State Senate, and Mr. Brown, a ball passed within three inches of my back, and shattered a stone in the wall of a stable about five yards on my left. B. had stopped at the door of the post-office, ten yards behind, and Hoge had advanced about two yards before me. We started at the report of the gun. For a moment I suspected design, and looked anxiously around to discover the person who had fired. It proved to be a gunsmith, trying a rifle for an officer of one of the corps, and in his great wisdom he had placed his mark in a direction that crossed the principal road within point-blank shot. The accident has cost me some reflection, and I may be the safer for it in future.

"Though a very small part of the Pennsylvania quota had reached the rendezvous on the arrival of the President, the state of preparation obviously exceeded his expectations. He spoke publicly in terms of encomium; and Mr. Hamilton did not hesitate to tell me that the exertions of the governor had been successful beyond the most sanguine hopes of the friends of the

government. Notwithstanding, indeed, the flashes of the other
States, particularly of New Jersey, the Pennsylvania militia
have been the most numerous and the most expeditious in assembling; and, I will add, they are as well arrayed and as well
disciplined as any body of troops that were ever collected on a
similar occasion. The only counties that have failed materially
in turning out their quotas are Northampton and Bucks. The
deficiency, however, is amply supplied by volunteers from counties not included in the requisition and from counties that have
furnished more than their quotas. All the Pennsylvania militia
have reached the rendezvous. The Maryland and Virginia
militia, who are to rendezvous at Fort Cumberland, about twenty-
five miles from Bedford, had not reached that station a few days
ago, but were marching rapidly towards it. Some troops of
horse and a volunteer corps of infantry, under General Freling-
huysen, are still expected at Carlisle from New Jersey. It
appears to me, however, that every corps which arrives after this
time will be too late to participate in the business of the campaign. But it is certain that a sufficient force for the purposes
of government has already proceeded towards Bedford, there to
unite with the column of Virginia and Maryland troops. On
Friday, Saturday, and Sunday about seven thousand five hundred men took up the line of march. Friday was the first day
that my lame leg suffered me to limp abroad, and I went to view
the departure of the army. The sight was inconceivably awful
and interesting. The cause of the expedition, the characters
engaged in it, and the doubts that hang upon the catastrophe
were calculated to produce the most affecting sensations; and
when I saw the President lift his hat to the troops as they passed
along, I thought I caught a glimpse of the revolutionary scene.

"When I speak of doubts that hang on the catastrophe of this
expedition, I do not mean to excite the least doubt of the success
of the government, but how long it will take to restore order;
whether any resistance will be made, and to what extent; how
many accidents may occur; who will be treated as delinquents;
and, to sum up all, what atonement will expiate the offences of
the western counties and appease the resentments of the army,
are questions painful to conceive and difficult to decide. Messrs.
Findlay and Reddick have repeatedly conferred with the President. They report, in the warmest language the manly, candid,
and firm though moderate complexion of his conduct and dis-
course, and express the greatest solicitude that he should accompany the army. This, however, he stated to be impracticable;
but assured them that he would take every precaution to preserve
discipline, and to insure safety to those who had acceded to the
propositions for submission, as well as to the uniform friends of
government. It is evident, notwithstanding this assurance, that

they are dejected and fearful. They were anxious to ascertain the evidence of submission that would be satisfactory. From the nature of the inquiry, he could not give an explicit answer; but he stated a variety of facts that had recently occurred, and observed that to any man of common sense and reflection the principal means of evincing a restoration to order must readily occur. They have promised to do everything that men can do; but they have not authority, and they do not seem to possess confidence to pledge themselves for a general acquiescence in the excise laws; nay, at the very moment of their negotiation, they acknowledged that General Neville could not return to his desolated farm with safety. Findlay asked my opinion; I gave it as I believe I have already given it to you, that a surrender of the leaders, an entry of the stills, and a renewal of the oath of allegiance to the United States were indispensable before any specific overtures from the insurgents could be attended to. Both the commissioners, with apparent sincerity, have declared that they are not acquainted with any man who can be denominated a leader that has not saved himself under the propositions for an amnesty. David Bradford wrote a letter by them to the governor, in which he not only pleads his submission in time, but alleges that he has acted with a view to befriend the government from the commencement of his diabolical career. This state of things, however, only serves to perplex and irritate the troops. It strengthens the necessity of their march, and I have no doubt that the commander-in-chief will be prepared on the spot to designate the objects of seizure and punishment. It is in cases of detachments sent to apprehend such characters that I principally fear the effusion of blood. A desperate man will be disposed to fortify his house or barn and muster all his friends to defend it. Before that effect is produced, however, I expect that another will be generated by the approach of the army. The friends to government, who have hitherto been awed into silence and inactivity, will unfurl their standard. The disaffected or the lukewarm, who have not mingled in the riots, will endeavor by striking actions to secure themselves from suspicion and danger. All who have made themselves obnoxious to punishment will either attempt to excite the populace to resistance or fly from the country. In this fermented state of things the insurrection may work itself pure without any aid from our military chemists, but the process will be dreadful. The arm of government, uplifted against the insurgents, may be interposed to prevent the waste of property and the destruction of life among them. A war conducted as such a war would be, under the influence of personal enmities, cannot be contemplated without horror."

8.

" BEDFORD, 19 October, 1794.

" The uninterrupted march of six days has precluded me from all opportunity of writing to you. If that pleasure could be supplied by any other, the sublime scenes which have been exhibited from the summits of the loftiest mountains that I have ever viewed would go far to compensate me. Two days after we left Carlisle the army encamped at a small village called Strasburg, at the foot of the North Mountain, which rises in a bold and awful manner to an amazing perpendicular height. At first the mountain seemed inaccessible; but, winding through a narrow gap, we formed an excellent road, which left nothing for complaint but what could not be remedied,—the steepness of the ascent. The journey was overpaid by the prospects. Before us lay a valley of immeasurable depth and extent. Behind us, the horizon, at the distance of many leagues, was bounded by the eastern ranges of the mountains in the neighborhood of Carlisle. Every object was upon a large and striking scale. The change of the scene had a wonderful effect upon our feelings and vision. I saw nothing that could excite the common sensations of pleasure,—no rich vales, no cultivated farms, no populous settlements. One vast pile of mountain upon mountain, or one continued range of wilderness and forest, alternately fixed the attention. But my mind was overcome by awe. I felt at one time an inclination to weep; at another, I stopped my horse to indulge in a fit of laughter. When I gazed across the valley, I experienced an insurmountable solicitude, something like what occurs when a man cannot comprehend a subject that is proposed to him; and when I advanced to catch a glance of the precipices that bounded the road upon either side, I felt terrors and propensities that I can only compare to the terrors of guilt and the propensities of madness. I wish to give you an idea of the scene from its effects; but the hand which created can alone describe it. Nature and Nature's God were everywhere visible to the eye and sensible to the heart. You know that our sight is the most deceitful of our senses; in truth, it communicates nothing to us exactly in the light in which it is received. The army, while we continued in the low-lands, appeared astonishingly numerous; the men that composed it appeared, from their port and equipments, gigantic; and every horse moved with the solemnity and stature of an elephant. The moment these objects came in contact with the mountains and the forests, they diminished in the apparent size and number. On the top of the Tuscarora, our army appeared like a race of dwarfs, and our cavalry like a race of mules.

" Judge Peters afforded us considerable mirth on the road. He strings puns as well and as closely as your old friend Ad-

miral La Forey. I observed to him, after having slept together
at a petty tavern, near the crossings of the Juniata, in a room
which had little covering above and was open to the cold wind
on every side, that I had no idea of the existence of so rude, so
uncultivated, so barren, so uninhabitable a country within the
boundaries of Pennsylvania. 'I differ from you,' cried he; 'I
think it the most hospitable country that I ever travelled through,
for all the inhabitants *keep open house !*'

"You would suppose that on the mountain's top the goddess
of Health had raised her temple. The air, too, appeared fresh
and clear; but, throughout the country, intermitting, remitting,
and ague fevers have made dreadful havoc; and even on the
summit of the Tuscarora a numerous family presented themselves
as objects of charity, depressed with poverty and emaciated by
disease. Taking into view all that has passed before us, one
would imagine that the army is the only healthy body of men
in the State. The sickly region seemed to commence before
we reached the Susquehanna; and we are told that it will terminate when we have scaled the Alleghany. Besides the permanent inhabitants who are afflicted, the road is crowded with
itinerants, who are flying from the feverish swamps of Maryland
and Delaware to Westmoreland or Kentucky. A small, ill-con-
trived wagon, drawn by a single, old, and meagre horse, was met
yesterday ascending a hill, after having disgorged ten passengers,
who were of ages from eighty years to three months. Every
one of them was worn down with fever and ague. I expressed
to the grandfather of the brood my surprise at their undertaking
a journey in such circumstances. 'Providence is very kind,' says
the old man (and he shook with age and ague as he spoke),
'Providence is very kind; he does not suffer the fever to attack
us all on the same day; and so we take it by turns to drive the
wagon and to nurse the sick.' 'But what can tempt you to
transplant yourself at your time of life into so rough and remote
a country?' 'Fifty years, man and boy,' he replied, 'I have
been afflicted with this cruel fever; it has become constitutional
with me. I do not expect to get rid of it by the journey; and
old age is a disease which may be increased but cannot be cured
by a change of residence. As I have suffered, however, I know
the extent of the calamity. It has soured every morsel I have
eaten and embittered every drop that I have drank. My labor
produced no profit, and my family no delight. When, therefore,
I beheld my sons and their children exposed to the same blight,
I resolved to lead them forth and to make a last effort to preserve
the life which I had given them. We are poor, the road is
rough, and our asylum is remote; but the very hope of acquiring
health supports and exhilarates us in every step we take.' The
wagon had by this time reached the top of the hill; the wretched

family again entered it; and you will join me in wishing them success in their search for health.

"If I were less interested in our correspondence, I had the means of gratifying an indolent, or an indifferent, disposition presented to me yesterday. A coarse-looking fellow, with a red woollen cap on his head and a shaggy beard on his chin, was writing, in an affected posture, while a dozen soldiers sat round him, with countenances expressive of great attention, admiration, and pleasure. I wondered what could be the nature of the business. The amanuensis soon satisfied me. Having finished a sentence, he began to read his composition to his audience in the following words: ' My dear wife, we have had a long and troublesome march. It made me very unhappy to go so far from you ; but, my dear wife, my country called me. When we have thrashed the whiskey-boys, I shall return with rapture to your arms. Till then, don't make yourself uneasy on my account. My dear wife, I hope the children are well, as I am at this writing, etc.' The person for whom the letter was written could hardly restrain his ecstasy while it was half spelled and half read, ' à la mode de Darby.' At the close of the reading the group united in one burst of applause, and each man begged that a copy of the letter might be made for him. One, however, asked if it could not be so altered as to serve for a sweetheart as well as a wife; and another wished the part about children to be left out, if it would not hurt the composition, as he had not been married long enough to do more than lay the foundation for being called a father. The cost of each letter was two-pence ; and you now perceive how easily and how cheaply I might keep up our correspondence in this mechanical mode.

"The President is expected here to-day. The right column, said to be six thousand strong, under General Morgan's command, have marched from Fort Cumberland, by the way of Braddock's road, into the revolted counties. We expect our column will be put in motion on Wednesday next. Before then I will write to you by an express."

O.

" BEDFORD, 23 October, 1794.

" Every idea of resistance has vanished, and the entrance of the army into the western counties can only be with a view to manifest the power of the government. That will be accomplished by the march through the country, and we now understand that it will only take six or seven days to carry us to the ultimate point of our route. It is said that Parkynson's Ferry will be the place of general rendezvous. From that to Fort Pitt is a distance of about twenty-five miles.

" If ever I leave my home again for a soldier's life,—but I will

4

make no protestations. I have, indeed, no reason to complain, comparatively with others, of my accommodations and treatment. Our stores have lasted admirably, and cannot fail for the period which I have mentioned. I have never slept in a tent, but must do it to-night. With respect to the rest, I shared at first in the odium of certain imprudences, but my sequestration from head-quarters restored me to full credit. The incessant scene of business in which I have been engaged has afforded the opportunity to acquire the friendship of some, to command the approbation of all, and to remove the prejudices of many members of the army.

"The army took up their line of march yesterday. The rear is at this moment leaving the town. I viewed the parade of their departure from a lofty hill. It was grand. The infantry, about six thousand; the cavalry, about two thousand; and the baggage wagons, about seven hundred. The expense and waste of such an army are inconceivable; but I think the government will be amply compensated by the effect which the prompt appearance of such a force upon such an occasion must produce throughout the continent and throughout Europe.

"Judge Peters and Mr. Rawle accompany us in our march. The President took his leave of the troops in a manly, judicious, and affectionate letter, in which he recognizes, in strong terms of praise and gratitude, their patriotic exertions, and warns them against any excesses that can sully the reputation which they have already acquired. He adds a declaration (a very necessary and a very beneficial one) that it is intended to employ the military in strict subordination to the civil authority. Upon that principle our campaign has already opened. The judge and attorney have been incessantly engaged in issuing warrants to apprehend the principal rioters in this county, and the process is regularly executed by the marshal, under an escort of cavalry. In this way Filson, Lucas, Husband, and Wisecarver, four notorious rioters, have been seized, and are on their way to Philadelphia jail, with a guard of twelve troopers. We shall collect the group of leading insurgents in other counties by similar exertions, if they stand their ground. But we receive daily accounts of numbers that are endeavoring to save themselves by flight. Boats loaded with fugitives are constantly passing down the Ohio. Bradford hugs himself in an imaginary indemnity, and * * * * * * * seems to think that he has persuaded government into the belief of his having acted under a mask with a view to facilitate the restoration of order. These men have been delinquent, and merit the punishment that awaits them. But there are others who, without having participated in the violences of the opposition to the law, are inconceivably obnoxious as the original propagators of the doctrines which have eventually produced these violences. The names of Findley, Smilie, and Gallatin are at the head of this catalogue. I never undertake to defend any man's conduct at this season and upon this subject, but I am persuaded that these gentlemen are safe in point of law."

10.

"PREATOR'S, at the top of the Alleghany Mountain, 26 October, 1794.

"The march from Bedford has been inexpressibly tedious, but I think a day more unfortunate could not happen than yesterday. We had a march of ten miles to encounter, in order to gain the summit of the celebrated Alleghany Mountain. The preceding evening was cloudy, and during the night the whole country was deluged with rain. When the signal for taking the line of march was given, a heavy fog covered the face of the earth, which occasionally assumed the appearance and effect of a cold, penetrating sleet. At the place from which I am now writing, the army divided,—the Jersey line pursuing the route to a solitary tavern, called Black's, and the Pennsylvania line proceeding to a small Dutch village, called Berlin. The roads, upon every rational calculation, seemed impassable, but the troops reached their stations about dusk. The baggage wagons, however, were all detained till midnight, and many of them were overset, broken, etc. The Pennsylvanians in general were accommodated in the village churches, houses, and barns, but the Jersey troops could not find the least covering to shelter themselves from the most inclement night that I ever witnessed. The order was issued for renewing the march this morning, but the officers declared that the situation of the men rendered it impracticable. The frequent recurrence of such scenes will at least try the zeal and patriotism of the troops. The strongest constitutions and the firmest patience will hardly bear them out. The language of discontent has already been heard. There is no enemy to encounter, no object evident to common optics to be attained by transporting such a force, at such a time, into such a country. Why, then, proceed? Or, if you will proceed, why expose the men to weather and to want in a way which many say was never known during the Revolutionary war, and which I say no European general would attempt in conducting a disciplined army into the field? Such are the present ideas upon the subject. I shall be happy if they continue so temperate throughout the march; but I am already prepared to join a soldier who, in a tent adjoining mine, kept me awake all night with singing, 'A soldier's life's a lazy life, a drunken life, a slavish life, a blackguard life.'

"The song was sung the only night that I slept in a tent, which was the one preceding the storm that I have described.

Not pleased with the experiment, and warned by the clouds that hung upon the mountain, Mr. Brown and myself hastened a few miles ahead of the army to shelter ourselves under the roof of a wretched tavern. In this asylum we have escaped being drenched and frozen, and therefore it would be ungrateful to note the smaller inconveniences which we encountered. Under any other circumstances, however, I should have found even those insupportable. Little to eat, only whiskey to drink, bad cooks, noisy companions, a wet room, and stinking beds are not pleasant subjects to brood upon; and yet, as long as the weather continues as it is, I shall cheerfully accept them in lieu of colds, fevers, agues, pleurisies, etc., and the catalogue of calamities to which the army is constantly exposed. I am not in pursuit of military fame, and the value which you place on my life increases the natural anxiety to preserve it.

"I wrote thus far without knowing how I should send my letter. An express has just stopped at the door of the tavern, and tells me he goes with letters from the camp (about five miles off) to the President. The tempestuous weather continues; and I think it probable that the object of the present express is to procure authority for altering our route. At all events, I shall leave the army, on my return to Philadelphia, on the fifth or sixth of November. Notwithstanding the storm, there seems to be a disposition to order the troops to march at nine o'clock to-morrow morning. If so, I must go."

11.

"CAMP, at Bonnet's, near Cherry Mill,
31 October, 1794.

"I have at length the pleasure, by way of paradox, to decline any further correspondence with you. I shall certainly leave the army on or before the fifth of November. That I should be tired of the jaunt is not extraordinary, for I never promised myself much gratification in commencing or pursuing it; but the same solicitude for its termination prevails among the most frolicsome and the most patriotic heroes of the army. The effect is easily traced to its cause. With many the expedition was undertaken during the effervescence of a transient resentment, produced by the popular clamor against the insurgents. With some it was entered into as a frolic. Most people thought it would not carry us beyond Carlisle; no one imagined it would transport us across mountains and precipices into this rude and almost unexplored region. Every calculation being erroneous, no wonder the calculators are dissatisfied. The disappointment, however, might have been subjected to the rules of a philosophic acquiescence, if any object could be discovered for the perseverance of those who have led us sometimes into the clouds, and sometimes into the depths of the earth ; but fifteen thousand men have been marched three hundred miles without a symptom of opposition, and they are, at this moment, in the heart of the enemy's country, with plenty around them of everything but avowed enemies. The fact is so farcical that it would excite laughter, did we not reflect upon the public expense and the waste of private happiness which it has produced. I do not mean to say that the expedition was impolitic or improper ; but that it has been protracted in a manner that appears to me wantonly extravagant."

12.

" BEDFORD, 8 November, 1794.

"As it is possible that the post may pass us on the road, I have taken the chance to apprise you of our arrival at Bedford on our way home. Mr. Ingersoll and myself were equally eager in prosecuting our journey ; and I think I shall have the pleasure of seeing you on Thursday or Friday next. The first will be our object ; but if we attain the other, it will bring us within my old precept: attempt the impossible and you will achieve the extremely difficult.

" We left the army as soon as its ultimate point of march was fixed. The main body of our column will remain on the east bank, at Budd's Ferry, and the main body of Governor Lee's column will remain on the west bank of the Youghiogeny, till the line of march for returning to their respective homes shall be taken up. This will be in the course of a week. The light troops of both columns will form a junction, and be employed in sending out detachments to scour the country, seize whiskey-boys, etc. during the residue of the campaign. It is probable, because indeed it appears necessary, that a competent force will be left in the refractory counties to keep them in awe during the winter ; but this measure must originate in Congress, as the existence of the present army expires, agreeably to the limitation of the act which authorized its being raised, in thirty days after the meeting of that body. It does not appear to me that any trust can be put in the principles or remorse of the rioters ; there is nothing but fear and coercion that will insure their submission. Many of them have fled, it is said, into the woods ; of those that remain, several have been hardy enough to threaten a renewal of their violences as soon as the army is removed ; and the smiling countenances which others assume are not sufficient to conceal the hypocrisy at their hearts."

These letters, without entering into minute details, enable the reader to form a fair judgment respecting the

military expedition to suppress the outbreak commonly
called the Whiskey Insurrection. While the Union was
yet in its infancy and unconscious of its herculean energies, it was the part of wisdom to permit its safety to be
placed as little as possible at hazard. No one can question the prudent and humane policy which actuated the
President in determining to relieve the nation at once
from every possible danger by a demonstration of irresistible strength. At this day, however, we should look
with a smile, or with alarm, upon an executive requisition
for an army of fifteen thousand men, to quell an agitation so local and limited as the one that has been depicted.
Our present confidence is the offspring of experience,—
springing from an ascertained certainty that the form of
the government is deeply rooted in the affections and
veneration of the people. We rely upon their nearly
unanimous attachment to the constitution, that on all
occasions of civil discord thins the ranks of disaffection
more surely than artillery. No troops additional to those
already in garrison were deemed necessary, in 1831, to
maintain the laws of the Union, vehemently disclaimed
and subverted as they seemed to be by a State at once
united and inflamed. A single regiment, legally put in
motion, would, in any part of our country, be more than
sufficient to disperse and destroy an ephemeral rebellion
against a mere act of Congress. It is, indeed, not extravagant to say that such a single regiment, especially if
employed as aids and agents of judicial authority, might
more rapidly, quite as effectually, and at comparatively
no cost, have overcome and banished every symptom of
the insurrection to encounter which fifteen thousand
militia concentrated in the western settlements of Pennsylvania. That we are able to entertain this supposition
upon a full after-knowledge of the facts, and at the expiration of sixty-eight years, implies no censure of the measures actually pursued by those on whom the occasion
broke with the force of novelty, at a critical juncture of
political experiment, and under exaggerations which could
neither be detected nor fail to stir a panic. No general
proposition is more true than the one stated by Chief
Justice Marshall in his Life of Washington, that "when
the mind, inflamed by supposititious dangers, gives a full
loose to the imagination, and fastens upon some object

with which to disturb itself, the belief that the danger exists seems to become a matter of faith, with which reason combats in vain."

All insurrectionary symptoms having been dispelled, Mr. Dallas was furnished an opportunity by the legislature, at its next session, to place upon record a clear and unanswerable exposition of the patriotic conduct of the government of Pennsylvania. He seized with avidity the occasion of a mere letter of inquiry addressed to him by a committee, and framed his answer in the shape of an elaborate report.* Nothing could be more authentic in its details of facts, nothing more cogent in reasoning, and nothing more conclusive as vindication. In thus silencing forever the calumnious assaults too readily indulged in against Governor Mifflin and his associates, he exhibited a power only surpassed by a similar effort twenty years afterwards, in his justly-celebrated pamphlet delineating "the Causes and Character of the War" of 1812.

This disproportionately huge military movement against the western malcontents had an unforeseen tendency to augment the bitterness of political strife. Although the jealous friends of liberty could rejoice in the bloodless restoration of order, they perceived, for the first time, with amazement and alarm, the immense power placed by the federal constitution practically in the hands of the leading advisers of the executive. Such a power was unsafe while lodged with men, some of whom were believed to incline towards a rule of force, rather than one of opinion; of rank and wealth, rather than of simplicity and equality. Candid observers remarked how eagerly were filled from adjoining States the files of an army destined to avenge and enforce a favorite measure of a favorite secretary in those districts of Pennsylvania supposed and represented to be peculiarly averse to his policy. The patriarchal presence of Washington seemed the only guarantee against the excesses of a vindictive and licentious soldiery. It was the fashion of the day also to retail the exaggerated accounts given by English newspapers of every revolutionary excess in France; to invoke a rigorous support of government by all the delineated terrors of Parisian clubs and mobs; to stigmatize every association formed

---

* See Wharton's State Trials of the United States, page 161.

for political vigilance, information, and criticism as Jacobinical; and to ascribe the insurrection, not to the unnecessary, abrupt, and unexpected harshness of the law
it resisted, nor to the criminal passions of individuals, but
to the decried and destructive principle of democracy.
Unfortunately, this restive impatience of obstacle received
countenance from the highest quarters, and came to be
considered as essential among the supporters of the administration. Under ordinary circumstances it might
have passed by without much result, as an expedient
substitution, on a party emergency, of cant and clamor
for argument; but at a moment of martial demonstration,
while swords and bayonets were being handled by the
partisans of power, it assumed the character of a menace,
and instantly awakened to fresh and fiercer activity the
very spirit it was designed to paralyze.

The strength of the opposition had been gradually
growing. Denunciation is at once the very feeblest and
the most exasperating weapon with which differences of
opinion can be combated. The Democrats, among whom
no one was more conspicuous than Mr. Dallas, stood their
ground. The effort to crush them with the odium of
having caused or stimulated the insurrection, and of being
disciples of Robespierre and Marat, was defeated and
rebuked by a vote in the popular branch of Congress;
and very soon, a measure of executive policy absorbing
public attention, their ability and energy were concentrated against it from all parts of the country, in a manner
equally signal and impressive.

At this distant day it is difficult to realize the excitement which sprung up on the occasion of "JAY'S TREATY,"
sent by the President for consideration to the Senate of
the United States, on the 8th of June, 1795. The negotiator had been withdrawn the year before from his office
of chief justice of the supreme court, and commissioned
as minister plenipotentiary to Great Britain, at a moment
when projects of a retaliatory nature against that nation
were actually pending in the House of Representatives.
His appointment naturally arrested those projects, although his known political predilections precluded the
hope that the sentiment or purpose in which they were
founded would receive his attention. He was welcomed
at the court of London with open arms; and, giving to the

objects of his mission and his instructions both assiduity and ability, a treaty of amity, commerce, and navigation, of unusual length and complexity, was signed by Lord Grenville and himself on the 19th of November, 1794. A feverish and impatient solicitude prevailed among the agricultural and commercial classes of America while the negotiation was in progress; and as the result did not reach our government before the seventh of March, and was not submitted to the specially-called Senate for more than three months afterwards, ample time was afforded to allow that feeling to become intense and universal. It was our "*coup d'essai*," since the era of independence, at diplomatic arrangement with England, and there were various topics of which both our interest and our honor exacted a definite and just settlement. The vehemence with which the friends and journals of the administration had, during all the operations for extinguishing the whiskey insurrection, fulminated against everything *French*, inspired a general distrust that shameful and injurious concessions were being made to a partiality for everything *British;* and the secrecy of senatorial consultations, protracted for weeks, though ultimately broken through, did but sharpen to the utmost the public curiosity and apprehension. When it was found that even the Senate could assent only to a qualified or conditional ratification, and that the Republican minority of that body had deemed the treaty extremely defective and objectionable, suspense gave place to widespread popular agitation. In the course of July, and in rapid succession, meetings were held in all the principal cities, apparently with the expectation of inducing General Washington to withhold his final approval. In BOSTON, the instrument was declared to "*be highly injurious to the commercial interests of the United States, derogatory to their national honor and independence, and dangerous to the peace and happiness of their citizens.*" In PORTSMOUTH, New Hampshire, the citizens desired "*to express their most hearty disapprobation thereof,*" because it *rigorously enforced debts due to British subjects,* but forgot the claims of our own citizens; because it involved "*a direct invasion of the rights of individual States;*" because "*its regulations of trade, commerce, and navigation must prove destructive to those American interests;*" because "*the list of articles contraband of war was extended, to the injury of France, Hol-*

land, and Sweden," and because it was *"not conducive to the interest, honor, and lasting peace of our country."* In NEW YORK it was pronounced, with a long detail of reasons, *"injurious to the agriculture, manufactures, and commerce of the United States, derogatory from their national honor, and dangerous to their welfare, peace, and prosperity."* In CHARLESTON, after a selection from *"many well-founded objections,"* it was apprehended *"that great evils would result to these States from this treaty."* In BALTIMORE *"a disapprobation of said treaty"* was briefly expressed. In TRENTON it was condemned as *"degrading to the national honor, dangerous to the public interest, and destructive of the commercial and agricultural views of the United States."* In PHILADELPHIA, then our commercial and political, our national and State metropolis, repugnance was stronger, keener, and more emphatic than elsewhere. Mr. Dallas took a leading and effective part against it, as well in writing as in public speaking. With zeal and labor he analyzed and explained the whole subject,—the omissions, ambiguities, latent dangers, and obvious errors of the treaty were vividly depicted, and the practical operation of many portions shown almost conclusively to jeopard the material interests of the American people, or to impair their character by striking covertly at their best revolutionary friend and ally. Embodying his views, at once methodically and eloquently, in a paper of some length, under the title of *"* FEATURES OF JAY'S TREATY*"* (*Appendix No.* 2), they were actively disseminated, in pamphlet form and through a daily journal. While, according to the invariable practice of the writer in his deliberated productions, the language and tone towards the persons implicated in manufacturing the treaty was respectful and measured, the argument for its condemnation was pressed with a perspicuity and force wholly unanswerable. The effect was immediate and powerful. A numerous assemblage of *"* citizens of Philadelphia, the Northern Liberties, and the District of Southwark,*"* held in Independence Square on the 25th of July, 1795, adopted a memorial addressed to the President, and confided it for transmission to a committee composed of the following gentlemen, most of whom were then and for many years subsequently eminently distinguished, viz.: Alexander J. Dallas, Thomas McKean, John Swanwick, Charles Pettit, John Hunn, Moses Levy, Abraham Coats,

William Coats, Stephen Girard, John Barker, William Shippen, Jr., Frederick A. Muhlenberg, Blair McClenahan, and Thomas Lee Shippen. As this memorial was penned by Mr. Dallas, and contained a comprehensive epitome of the grounds upon which he and his Republican associates were strenuously opposing the consummation of a measure of executive policy, it may be appropriately inserted here at length :

" To George Washington, President of the United States.

" The Memorial of the citizens of Philadelphia, the Northern Liberties, and the District of Southwark, in the State of Pennsylvania, respectfully sheweth :

" That your memorialists, sincerely and affectionately attached to you, from a sense of the important services which you have rendered to the United States, and a conviction of the purity of the motives that will forever regulate your public administration, do, on an occasion in which they feel themselves deeply interested, address you as a friend and patriot,—as a friend who will never take offence at what is well intended, and as a patriot who will never reject what may be converted to the good of your country.

" That your memorialists entertain a proper respect for your constitutional authority ; and whatever may be the issue of the present momentous question, they will faithfully acquiesce in the regular exercise of the delegated powers of the government ; but they trust that, in the formation of a compact which is to operate upon them and their posterity, in their most important internal as well as external relations, which, in effect, admits another government to control the legislative functions of the Union ; and which, if found, upon experience, to be detrimental, can only be repealed by soliciting the assent, or provoking the hostilities, of a foreign power, you will not deem it improper or officious in them thus anxiously, but respectfully, to present a solemn testimonial of their public opinion, feelings, and interest.

" That, under these preliminary acknowledgments of the duty and of the design of your memorialists, the following objections to the ratification of the treaty lately concluded between Lord Grenville and Mr. Jay, are submitted, with implicit confidence, to your consideration :

" The treaty is objected to,

" 1. Because it does not provide for a fair and effectual settlement of the differences that previously subsisted between the United States and Great Britain, inasmuch as it postpones the surrender, and affords no compensation for the detention, of the western posts ; inasmuch as it cedes without any equivalent an indefinite extent of territory to the settlers under British titles, within the precincts and jurisdiction of those posts; inasmuch as it waves a just claim for the value of the negroes who were carried off at the close of the war, in violation of positive compact; and inasmuch as it refers all hope of indemnity, for the recent spoliations committed on the commerce of the United States, to an equivocal, expensive, tedious, and uncertain process.

"2. Because by the treaty the federal government accedes to restraints upon the American commerce and navigation, internal as well as external, that embrace no principle of real reciprocity, and are inconsistent with the rights and destructive to the interests of an independent nation, inasmuch as it unreasonably fetters the intercourse with the West Indies, with India, and with the American lakes, by means of navigable rivers belonging to the British; inasmuch as, in many instances, it circumscribes the navigation of the United States to a particular voyage; and inasmuch as some of our staple commodities (exempted by the treaties with France, Holland, Prussia, and Sweden) it makes liable to confiscation as contraband; and others (exempted by the law of nations) it makes liable to seizure, upon payment of an arbitrary price, as articles useful to the enemies of Great Britain.

"3. Because the treaty is destructive to the domestic independence and prosperity of the United States, inasmuch as it admits aliens, professing a foreign allegiance, to the permanent and transmissible rights of property peculiarly belonging to a citizen, and inasmuch as it enables Great Britain to draw an invidious and dangerous line of circumvallation round the territory of the Union by her fleets on the Atlantic, and by her settlements from Nova Scotia to the mouth of the Mississippi.

"4. Because the treaty surrenders certain inherent powers of an independent government, which are essential in the circumstances of the United States, to their safety and defence, and which might, on great emergencies, be successfully employed to enforce the neglected claims of justice, without making the last dreadful appeal to arms, inasmuch as the right of sequestration, the right of regulating commerce, in favor of a friendly and against a rival power, and the right of suspending a commercial intercourse with an inimical nation are voluntarily abandoned.

"5. Because the treaty is an infraction of the rights of friendship, gratitude, and alliance which the republic of France may justly claim from the United States, and deprives the United States of the most powerful means to secure the good will and good offices of other nations, inasmuch as it alters, during a war, the relative situation of different nations, advantageously to Great Britain and prejudicially to the French republic; inasmuch as it is in manifest collision with several articles of the American treaty with France; and inasmuch as it grants to Great Britain certain high, dangerous, and exclusive privileges.

"And your memorialists, having thus, upon general ground, concisely but explicitly, avowed their wishes and opinions; and, forbearing a minute specification of the many other objections that occur, conclude with an assurance that by refusing to ratify the projected treaty you will, according to their best information and judgment, at once evince an exalted attachment to the principles of the Constitution of the United States, and an undiminished zeal to advance the prosperity and happiness of your constituents."

Few things are more difficult to determine than the positive merit of treaties; and certainly no one can feel the slightest disposition to underrate Mr. Jay's. Agreeably to his own representation, the compact, imperfect and unsatisfactory as it might be, was the most favorable one for his country which the British ministry would consent to make. Undoubtedly learned, patriotic, laborious, and faithful, he was, nevertheless, not suited to cope, on such questions of trade and international policy as it involved, with the practiced officials of London. A remarkable proof of this was furnished by the twelfth article, the extraordinary character of which could scarcely be palliated by the subsequently ascertained fact that Mr. Jay was, unhappily, wholly ignorant of the commercial importance then assuming by the great southern staple. He was hurried, too, in his work, by the consciousness that it was wanted for cabinet purposes at home. Nor can it be said that, tested by experiment and time, the treaty either fulfilled the promises of those who applauded, or verified the forebodings of those who condemned its terms. It constituted, however, one of the early battle-grounds of political party. The principles upon which it was assailed, and the men who assailed it, were of the Democratic opposition; and those principles and those men, invigorated by every exercise, and steadily advancing, as they were, to the direction of national affairs, are entitled to be understood. It is especially wished that Mr. Dallas may be understood; and that his just fame, in connection with this particular subject, may not be impaired by rash expressions even from pens of imposing authority.* The "FEATURES OF JAY'S TREATY" and the

---

* "With this course of *passionate declamation* were connected the most strenuous and unremitting exertions to give increased energy to *the love*

memorial cited exhibit the platform on which he took his stand, and to which he rallied "*an immense party in America.*" They cannot be read with care and candor, without communicating the impression that their author had perfect mastery of his subject, and handled it with consummate ability.

It is possible that the rapid spread and harmonious activity of the Republican party, as attested in the agitations against the treaty, can be, in some measure, ascribed to proceedings which were soon made the objects of special and unmeasured animadversion by those in power. Since that period, similar proceedings have become so universal, and are now esteemed such legitimate modes of inculcating and uniting opinions, that modern politicians can scarcely understand, much less approve, the grave censure with which they were at first received. I allude to the voluntary associations or societies formed to diffuse favored doctrines of government, to secure co-operation against the progress of errors, and to be ever on the watch to detect covert encroachments upon public liberty or right. These agencies of popular sentiment were extremely odious to all official functionaries and dependents: and, perhaps, a prophetic instinct as to their ultimate tendencies exaggerated their capacity for mischief and colored their dangers too highly. No doubt they were liable to abuse, and might be perverted into instruments of disorder; but in this they shared with the constituted authorities themselves the essential fallibility of every human arrangement.

We must not forget, however, that the tales wafted over the Atlantic from London and Paris were ill calculated to recommend these political unions to American adoption. British ministers, judges, and parliamentary committees could find no language sufficiently strong to

---

which was openly avowed for *France*, and to *the detestation not less openly avowed for England*.

"But an *immense party in America*, not in *the habit of considering national compacts, without examining the circumstances* under which that with Britain had been formed, or *weighing the reasons* which induced it; *without understanding the instrument*, and in many places *without reading it*, rushed impetuously to its condemnation, and seemed to expect that public opinion would be *surprised by the suddenness* or *stormed by the fury* of the assault; and that the Executive would be compelled to *yield to its violence.*"—*Marshall's Life of Washington.*

convey their abhorrence of "*The London Corresponding Society*," "*The Society for Constitutional Information*," and "*The Society of the Friends of the People;*" whose conspicuous members, the Hardys, the Muirs, the Palmers, the Gerralds, the Margarots, the Sinclairs, the Skirvings, and the Horne Tookes, were undergoing prosecution and transportation. At the same time, the excesses into which ran the saturnalia of the French factions, inflamed and misled by Marat, Danton, Robespierre, Collot D'Herbois, and Billaud Varennes, threw discredit as well upon mere forms of organization as upon the bold bad men who made them means of insurrection and terror.

.Contented with the liberties, constitutions, and laws of the country, no Republicans of the United States could entertain a desire beyond that of seeing them confided to those by whom they would be administered in the preferred spirit of democratic strictness, simplicity, and economy. Instead of wishing, they deprecated, change; for the change they most feared was that retrograde one into which the supposed monarchical theories and habits of certain eminent statesmen might gradually glide. What, therefore, in Europe was represented as subversive could here be in reality only progressive and conservative. The great jeopardy of the newly-established freedom is to be found, as very recent, like former events, on the eastern continent, have shown, in the reactionary inclinations for the abolished system. It is unnecessary, and would be painful, to speculate upon the consequences that might have ensued, had any of the precautionary and honorable steps been omitted which peacefully and persuasively paved the way for the election of Mr. Jefferson in 1801.

At least, such were the views that swayed the enlightened and patriotic citizens by whom the principles, articles, and regulations of "*The Democratic Society of Pennsylvania*" were adopted and publicly proclaimed on the 4th of July, 1793. Among these gentlemen, Mr. Dallas was undoubtedly foremost. His associates were eminent for their attainments, their public spirit, and their irreproachable standing. The astronomer, David Rittenhouse, was *President;* and Mr. Dallas headed the committee, on whose abilities and labors devolved the task of achieving the objects of the association. The constitution, first circular, and other explanatory papers, were drafted by him; and he energetically opened and perseveringly maintained a correspondence coextensive with the Union and everywhere salutary and effective.

As the establishment of this the leading society has, as I have said, been authoritatively censured, it may not be amiss to seek a just appreciation of its impulse and designs in the original documents that frankly and distinctly developed them.

The following is extracted from the statement preliminary to the principles, articles, and regulations:

"At this propitious period, when the nature of Freedom and Equality is practically displayed, and when their value (best understood by those who have paid the price of acquiring them) is universally acknowledged, the patriotic mind will naturally be solicitous, by every proper precaution, to preserve and perpetuate the blessings which Providence hath bestowed upon our country; for, in reviewing the history of nations, we find occasion to lament that *the vigilance of the people has been too easily absorbed in victory,* and that *the prize which has been achieved by the wisdom and valor of one generation, has often been lost by the ignorance and supineness of another.*"

The following are enumerated as "the fundamental principles of the association:"

I.

"That the people have the inherent and exclusive right and power of making and altering forms of government; and that for regulating and protecting our social interests a REPUBLICAN GOVERNMENT is the most natural and beneficial form which the wisdom of man has devised.

II.

"That the republican Constitutions of the United States and of the State of Pennsylvania, being framed and established by the people, it is our duty as good citizens to support them. And in order effectually to do so, it is likewise the duty of every freeman to regard with attention and to discuss without fear the conduct of the public servants in every department of government.

III.

"That in considering the administration of public affairs, men and measures should be estimated according to their intrinsic merits; and, therefore, regardless of party spirit or political connection, it is the duty of every citizen, by making the general welfare the rule of his conduct, to aid and approve those measures which have an influence in promoting the prosperity of the Commonwealth.

IV.

"That in the choice of persons to fill the offices of government, it is essential to the existence of a free republic that every citizen should act according to his own judgment, and therefore any attempt to corrupt or delude the people in exercising the rights of suffrage, either by promising the favor of one candidate, or traducing the character of another, is an offence equally injurious to moral rectitude and civil liberty.

V.

"That *the people of Pennsylvania* form but one indivisible community, whose political rights and interests, whose national honor and prosperity, must, in degree and duration, be forever the same; and, therefore, it is the duty of every freeman, and shall be the endeavor of the Democratic Society, to remove the prejudices, to conciliate the affections, to enlighten the understanding, and to promote the happiness of all our fellow-citizens."

The Circular.

"FELLOW-CITIZEN,—We have the pleasure to communicate to you a copy of the constitution of 'The Democratic Society,' in hopes that after a candid consideration of its principles and objects, you may be induced to promote its adoption in the county of which you are an inhabitant.

"Every mind capable of reflection must perceive that the present crisis in the politics of nations is peculiarly interesting to America. The European confederacy, transcendent in power and unparalleled in iniquity, menaces the very existence of freedom. Already its baneful operation may be traced in the tyrannical destruction of the constitution, and the rapacious partition of the territory of Poland; and should the glorious efforts of France be eventually defeated, we have reason to presume that, for the consummation of monarchical ambition and the security of its establishments, this country, the only remaining depository of liberty, will not long be permitted to enjoy in peace the honors of an independent and the happiness of a republican government.

"Nor are the dangers from foreign sources the only causes at this time of apprehension and solicitude. The seeds of luxury appear to have taken root in our domestic soil; and the jealous eye of patriotism already regards the spirit of freedom and equality as eclipsed by the pride of wealth and the arrogance of power.

"This general view of our situation has led to the institution of 'The Democratic Society.' A constant circulation of useful information, and a liberal communication of republican sentiments, were thought to be the best antidotes to any political poison with which the vital principles of civil liberty might be attacked. For, by such means, a fraternal confidence will be established among the citizens, every symptom of innovation will be studiously marked, and a standard will be created to which, in danger and distress, the friends of liberty may successfully resort.

"To obtain these objects, then, and to cultivate on all occasions the love of peace, order, and harmony, an attachment to the constitutions and a respect to the laws of our country, will be the aim of 'The Democratic Society.' Party and personal considerations are excluded from a system of this nature; for, in the language of the articles under which we are united, men and measures will only be estimated according to their intrinsic merits and their influence in promoting the prosperity of the State.

"From you, fellow-citizen, we hope to derive essential aid in extending the society and maintaining its genuine principles. We request, therefore, an early attention to the subject, and solicit a constant correspondence."

The current occupations of a practising lawyer are scarcely to be esteemed worthy, under any circumstances or for any object, of patient analysis or consideration. They are toils applied to the shifting and fading vicissitudes of life and the emergencies of business, very limited in their influence, really interesting to those only who are parties to them, and passing so rapidly and numerously as to fix no attention. On the surface of this general stream, however, there may sometimes be discerned, by careful discrimination, buoys or beacons which mark the anchorage of some great principle or some historical incident. The professional position of Mr. Dallas attracted to him, during a series of years, beside the ordinary causes of litigation, a number, both civil and criminal, having their origin in public measures and feeling, and connected more or less intimately with the constitution and government of the country. Some of these last demand notice. As he never became a member of the legislature, either State or federal, and very seldom partook in popular meetings, these controversies of mind and opinion may furnish important though certainly not the only means of accurately appreciating the originality, powers, resources, and integrity of his intellect. Perhaps we shall find, on recurring to the most conspicuous among them, that, notwithstanding the continued torrent of detraction he breasted while living, but could not silence when in his grave, his devotion to equal rights and well-ordered liberty shone forth in the construction of every law; that his sympathies were invariably enlisted and fearlessly expressed against oppression or usurpation; that having carefully watched the progress of the convention of 1787, he profoundly reverenced as he thoroughly comprehended the Union it prescribed, and that he brought to the aid of what may be called his uniform forensic democracy, extensive learning, quick ingenuity, vigorous reasoning, and a rhetoric which, disdaining to be figurative, was alike polished and perspicuous.

I. It was by a simple but sound reference to the true characteristics of the constitution that, on the trial of *Robert Worrall*, in 1798, for an attempt to bribe a commissioner of the revenue, he led or confirmed Judge Chase in the authoritative and important declaration that the United States, *as a federal government*, have no common law, and that consequently no indictment can be maintained in their courts for offences merely at the common law. His course of argument was briefly as follows:

"All the judicial authority of the federal courts must be derived either from the Constitution of the United States or from the acts of Congress made in pursuance of it. To maintain the jurisdiction of the court it was therefore necessary to show that an offer to bribe a commissioner of the revenue is a violation of some constitutional or legislative provision. The constitution contains express provisions in certain cases, designated by definitions of the crimes, by a reference to the characters of the parties offending, or by the exclusive jurisdiction of the place where the offences were perpetrated; but the crime of attempting to bribe, the character of a federal officer, and the place wherein the present offence was committed, do not form any part of the constitutional express provisions for the exercise of judicial authority in the courts of the Union. The judicial power, however, extends not only to all cases in law and equity arising under *the constitution*, but likewise to all such as shall arise under *the laws of the United States;* and besides the authority specially vested in Congress to pass laws for *enumerated purposes*, there is a general authority given to make all laws which shall be necessary and proper for carrying into execution all the powers vested by the constitution in the government of the United States or in any department or office thereof. Whenever Congress think a provision necessary to effectuate a constitutional power of the government, they may establish that provision by law; and whenever it is so established a violation of its sanctions will come within the jurisdiction of this court, which, by the eleventh section of the judicial act, has 'exclusive cognizance of all crimes and offences cognizable under the authority of the United States.' But in the case of the commissioner of the revenue the act constituting the office does not create or declare the offence; it is not recognized in the act under which proposals for building the lighthouse were invited, and there is no other act that has the slightest relation to the subject.

"Can the offence, then, be said to arise under the constitution or the laws of the United States? and if not, what is there to render it cognizable under the authority of the United States? A case arising under a law must mean a case depending on the exposition of a law, in respect to something which the law prohibits or enjoins. There is no characteristic of that kind in the present instance. But it may be suggested that, the office being established by a law of the United States, it is an incident naturally attached to the authority of the United States to guard the officer against the approaches of corruption in the execution of his public trust. It is true that the person who accepts an office may be supposed to enter into a compact to be answerable to the government which he serves for any violation of his duty, and having taken the oath of office, he would unquestionably be liable, in such case, to a prosecution for perjury in the federal courts. But because one man, by his own act, renders himself amenable to a particular jurisdiction, shall another man, who has not incurred a similar obligation, be implicated? If, in other words, it is sufficient to vest a jurisdiction in this court that a federal officer is concerned; if it is a sufficient proof of a case arising under a law of the United States to affect other persons that such officer is bound by law to discharge the duty with fidelity, a source of jurisdiction is opened which must inevitably overflow and destroy all the barriers between the judicial authorities of the State and the general government. Anything which can prevent a federal officer from the punctual as well as from an impartial performance of his duty—an assault and battery or the recovery of a debt, as well as the offer of a bribe—may be made the foundation of the jurisdiction of this court; and, considering the constant disposition of power to extend the sphere of its influence, fictions will be resorted to when real cases cease to occur. A mere fiction that the defendant is in the custody of the marshal has rendered the jurisdiction of the king's bench universal in all personal actions. Another fiction, which states the plaintiff to be a debtor of the crown, gives cognizance of all kinds of personal suits to the exchequer; and the mere profession of

an attorney attaches the privilege of suing and being sued in his
own court. If, therefore, the disposition to amplify the jurisdiction of the circuit court exists, precedents of the means to do so
are not wanting, and it may hereafter be sufficient to suggest
that the party is a federal officer in order to enable this court
to try every species of crime and to sustain every description of
action.

"But another ground may, perhaps, be taken to vindicate the
present claim of jurisdiction: it may be urged that, though the
offence is not specified in the constitution nor defined in any act
of Congress, yet that it is an offence at common law, and that
the common law is the law of the United States in cases that
arise under their authority. The nature of our federal compact
will not, however, tolerate this doctrine. The twelfth article of
the amendments stipulates that the powers not delegated to the
United States by the constitution, nor prohibited by it to the
States, are reserved to the States respectively or to the people.
In relation to crimes and misdemeanors, the objects of the delegated power of the United States are enumerated and fixed.
Congress may provide for the punishment of counterfeiting the
securities and current coin of the United States, and may define
and punish piracies and felonies committed on the high seas, and
offences against the law of nations: and so likewise Congress
may make all laws which shall be necessary and proper for carrying into execution the powers of the general government. But
here is no reference to a common law authority,—every power is
matter of definite and positive grant, and the very powers that
are granted cannot take effect until they are exercised through
the medium of a law. Congress had undoubtedly a power to
make a law which would render it criminal to offer a bribe to
the commissioner of the revenue; but, not having made the law,
the crime is not recognized by the federal code, constitutional or
legal, and consequently is not a subject on which the judicial
authority of the Union can operate."

It is impossible not to observe with what cogency and
clearness this short argument of the professional advocate
sustains the cardinal principle of constitutional construction on which the political party of his preference had
taken its stand. No latitude, and hardly liberality, of
interpretation. "*The constitution is a federal compact:*"
"*every power is matter of definite and positive grant:*" "*the
objects of the delegated power of the United States are enumerated and fixed:*" and though Congress may make all laws
necessary and proper for carrying into execution the
powers of the general government, and so might, by adop-

tion, bit by bit, legislate the common law into the federal code, yet, until that be done, it could not be appealed to in maintenance of the jurisdiction of the federal courts. That this reasoning met persevering opposition which has now become nearly obsolete; that its truth and weight have long since given it an impregnable lodgment in the American mind, under the force of amplifications in every sphere of discussion, are unquestionable facts: yet it should be recollected that at the date of Worrall's trial it was comparatively fresh, the distinctive feature of a political organization in a minority, and in direct conflict with the theories and inculcations of those who made and administered the laws.

II. The impeachment of *William Blount*, a senator of the United States from Tennessee, resolved upon by the House of Representatives in the summer of 1797, gave rise to proceedings of equal novelty and interest. The crimes and misdemeanors imputed to the accused were substantially a conspiracy to wrest Louisiana and Florida from Spain, then at war with England, in violation of our treaty obligations; and acts of bribery or intimidation connected with our Indian agents, in order to excite the Cherokees and Creeks to hostilities against the neighboring subjects of the Spanish crown.

The members of the House of Representatives charged with the management of this impeachment were distinguished for parliamentary and professional ability. Among them the three most prominent were Samuel Sitgreaves, of Pennsylvania, Robert Goodloe Harper, of Maryland, and James A. Bayard, of Delaware. The first-named gentleman is believed to have drafted the articles. The counsel of William Blount were Mr. Dallas and Mr. Jared Ingersoll, of the bar of Philadelphia. Necessarily, the sphere of action was the most august of American judicatures, the Senate of the United States. On the 24th of December, 1798. that tribunal, through the lips of its presiding officer, Thomas Jefferson, the Vice-President, permitted a plea to be filed on behalf of the defendant: and the matter alleged in that plea proved fatal to the prosecution.

The substantial averments of the plea were, *first*, that William Blount was not *then* a senator (he had been expelled the body by resolution on the 8th of July, 1797);

and *second*, that although he was a senator at the periods
referred to in the articles of impeachment, he was *not a
civil officer of the United States;* that he was not charged
with any crime or misdemeanor, or any malconduct, or
any abuse of public trust, *in the execution of any civil office;*
and that by the constitution, no persons but the President,
Vice-President, and *civil officers of the United States* are
liable to impeachment.

Let it not be supposed that any one could be insensible
to the fruitful ingenuity and close logic with which the
managers encountered this plea, nor unmindful of the
impressive and copious learning of Mr. Ingersoll; but
our specially assigned purpose, the illustration of the
course of Mr. Dallas, forbids expansive deviation. In
repelling the arguments with which the plea was assailed
by Mr. Bayard, he took three general positions under
which to arrange his remarks, and maintained them with
a power altogether conclusive. Again he was obliged to
resist, at the outset, an impetuous effort to establish the
English common law as the source whence to deduce, in
the administration of *federal* jurisprudence, the rule of
right.

"As the honorable manager had contended that the constitutional grant of a power to institute and to try *impeachments*
extends, *ex vi termini*, to every description of offender, and to
every degree of offence, a just respect for the high authority
which he represents, as well as for the talents he has displayed,
compels the defendant's counsel to follow him into the wide field
of controversy that he has unexpectedly chosen. A claim of jurisdiction so unlimited, embracing every object of the penal code,
annihilating all discriminations between civil and military cases,
and overthrowing the boundaries of federal and State authority,
ought surely to have been supported by an express and unequivocal delegation: but, behold, it rests entirely on an arbitrary implication from the use of *a single word;* and while the stream
is thus copious, thus inundating, the source is enveloped (like
the sources of the Nile) in mystery and doubt. The constitution
declares that '*the House of Representatives shall have the sole
power of impeachment*,' and that '*the Senate shall have the sole
power to try all impeachments:*' hence it has been urged that
as there is no description of the offenders or the offences in the
constitution itself, where the power is vested, every offender and
every offence, impeachable according to the common law of England, must be deemed impeachable here; and it is alleged, that

the common-law power of impeachment extends to every crime
or misdemeanor that can be committed by any subject, in or out
of office.   Such a doctrine is contrary to the principles of our
federal compact; is contrary to the general policy of the law of
impeachments; and is contrary to a fair construction of the very
terms of the constitution."

And Mr. Dallas proceeded under these three subdi-
visions into extended argument.

That it was *contrary to the principles of the federal compact*,
he deduced from the design with which the government
of the United States was established.

"Although it is in some of its features federal, in others it is
consolidated; in some of its operations it affects the people as
individuals; in others, it applies to them in the aggregate as
States: yet, in every view, all the powers and attributes of the
national government are matter of express and positive grant
and transfer: whatever is not expressly granted and transferred
must be deemed to remain with the people, or with the respective
States; and as the motive for establishing the federal constitution
arose from the want of a competent national authority in cases
in which it was essential for the people inhabiting the different
States to act as a nation, so far the people gave power to the
federal government: but the delegation of that power is evidently
limited by the reason which produced it.   Thus, in the creation
of a national judiciary, we find that in criminal as well as in
civil cases, no authority is vested in the courts but upon the
appropriate subjects of national jurisprudence.   Crimes and misdemeanors, which have no connection with national objects, are
left to be prosecuted and punished under the laws of the State
in which they are committed.   And yet it is asserted that for
any crime or misdemeanor which could only be thus the object
of State jurisdiction, which could not be tried upon an indictment
in any federal court, a State officer or a private citizen may be
impeached before the Senate of the United States!   The mere
investment of a power to impeach and to try impeachments is
considered as an instrument destined to carry the government
beyond its natural sphere, and to give to the censorship of the
Senate a scope and efficacy of which the general judicial authority
of the Union does not partake."

The manager having referred to the English common
law for an exposition of the import and operation of the
power of impeachment, Mr. Dallas contended that

"The United States, as a federal government, had no common
law in relation to crimes and punishments.   The crimes punish-

able under the authority of the United States can only be such as the constitution defines or acts of Congress shall create, in order to effectuate the general powers of the government. How did the government of the United States acquire a common-law jurisdiction in the case of crimes, and by what standard is the jurisdiction to be regulated? When the colonies of America were first settled, each colony brought with it as much of the common law as was applicable to its circumstances and it chose to adopt; but no colony adopted all the common law of England, and there was a great diversity, owing to local and other circumstances, in the objects and extent of the common law which the different colonies adopted. The common law is, therefore, the law of each State so far as each State has chosen to adopt it; but the United States did not bring the common law with them. There are no express words of adoption in the constitution; and if a common law is to be assumed by implication, is it to be the common law of the individual States, and of which State?· or is it to be the common law of England, and at what period? Are we to take it from the dark and barbarous pages of the common law, with all the feudal rigor and appendages? or is it to be taken as it has been ameliorated by the refinements of modern legislation? Would it not be absurd to refer us to the ancient common law of England? And, if we are referred to its improved state, do we not rather adopt the statutes than the common law of that country? And is the common law to fluctuate forever here as it may fluctuate there?"

Continuing his line of argument, Mr. Dallas urged that the doctrine of the managers was also inconsistent with the general policy of impeachments, and with a fair construction of the terms of the constitution.

" To suppose that these terms include a jurisdiction over all persons, for all offences, is to annihilate the trial by jury where a punishment more severe than death, to an honorable mind, may be inflicted; it is to overthrow all the barriers of criminal jurisprudence; for every petty rogue may be tried by impeachment before this high court for every offence within the indefinite classification of a misdemeanor."

The chief point of his subsequent reasoning went to prove that a senator was not embraced by the constitutional phrase " *civil officer;*" that the verbal criticism which drew a distinction between civil officers *of* and civil officers *under* the United States was unfounded; and that no man is an officer of the United States, in the sense of those clauses of the constitution which vest the power of impeachment, unless he has been appointed and commissioned by the President.

"The President and Vice-President have their commissions from the constitution itself; and the Speaker of the House of Representatives is emphatically an officer of the House—not of the United States. As the President does not commission himself and the Vice-President, and as it was intended to affect them by the impeachment power, therefore they are expressly named. The President does not commission senators and representatives, but it was not intended to affect them by the impeachment power; therefore they are not named."

Legislation is *a trust*, not *an office.* This distinction is not a novelty; it is drawn in the articles of confederation, in the federal constitution, in many of the State constitutions, and in acts of Congress. But, independent of all precedent and authority, this distinction is founded upon the very nature of a free government.

"The legislature is, in theory, the people; they do not themselves assemble, but they depute a few to act for them; and the laws which are thus made are the expressions of the will of the people. Over their representatives the people have a complete control, and if one set transgress they can appoint another set, who can rescind and annul all previous bad laws. But the power of the people is only to make the laws; they have nothing to do with *executing* them; they have nothing to do with *expounding* them; and hence arises the diversity in the modes of remedying any grievance which they may suffer from the conduct of their representatives or agents. If a legislator acts wrong, he may be expelled before the term for which he was chosen has expired; he may be rejected at the next periodical election; and the laws which he has sanctioned may be repealed by a new representation. But if an executive or judicial magistrate acts wrong, the people have no immediate power to correct,—prosecution and impeachment are the only remedies for the evil. Then it is manifest that, by the power of impeachment, the people did not mean to guard against themselves, but against their agents; they did not mean to exclude themselves from the right of reappointing or pardoning, but to restrain the executive magistrate from doing either with respect to officers whose offices were held independent of popular choice. The subject is made more plain by two considerations: *first*, that, although either house may expel a member, they cannot (on the principles of the constitution, without any express prohibition) expel him twice for the same cause; *second*, that the President is not empowered to pardon in cases of impeachment. In the case of expulsion, the member is sent to the people ; but if they choose to return him again he has a perfect right to his seat. In the case of an impeachment, the delinquent officer is dismissed ; on the general power of the executive, he might be reappointed ; but, to guard against the abuse of that power, the constitution superadds a sentence of perpetual disqualification."

There can be no certainty in ascribing to any given causes or reasons the conclusion reached by the Senate on this memorable occasion. The course, however, of the debate in that body after the professional discussion had closed, would seem to indicate that, in the convictions of the majority, a senator was not an officer of the United States, in the constitutional sense, liable to impeachment, and that, at all events, after having been expelled, no such proceeding could be entertained against him for crimes and misdemeanors alleged to have been committed while he was a senator. The court deliberated during a period of five days. Two affirmative propositions, in the form of a resolution, were submitted on the first day for adoption, in substance that a senator was a civil officer of the United States, and that the articles imputed offences to William Blount committed while a senator. On the fourth day of discussion, these propositions were *negatived* by a majority of fourteen to eleven, and on the sixth day, all parties being convened for the purpose, MR. JEFFERSON pronounced judgment as follows :

" Gentlemen, managers of the House of Representatives, and gentlemen, counsel for William Blount, the court, after having given the most mature and serious consideration to the question, and to the full and able arguments urged on both sides, has come to the decision which I am now about to deliver. The court is of opinion that the matter alleged in the plea of the defendant is sufficient in law to show that this court ought not to hold jurisdiction of the said impeachment, and that the said impeachment is dismissed."

This was the first case of impeachment under the existing government, and there have been but three since, namely, those of John Pickering, Samuel Chase, and James H. Peck, all judges of the United States. The lapse of more than half a century without a single additional attempt to apply the power of impeachment to *a*

legislator, countenances the impression that the reasoning
of Mr. Dallas has been accepted as in harmony with the
principles of our polity and conclusive on the true reading
of the constitution. Such a result must be esteemed fortunate. Had the opposite view prevailed,—had the mys-
teries and incongruities of English common law received
recognition as an exhaustless fountain of federal authority,
and every delegate or agent of the people been held amenable to this process of official disqualification, the mischiefs,
especially at times of high political excitement, must have
been endless and intolerable. It is practical wisdom to
remove, in advance, from the reach of contending parties
the means of mutual injury. A magnanimous adversary
in a mere trial of strength puts aside the dangerous weapon
to whose use he might be tempted by the sudden heats of
rivalry. Mr. Dallas pressed with admirable spirit the
great inconveniences incident to the construction he resisted, by destroying the independence of both branches
of the legislature, by arming a majority with instruments
of vengeance, and by rendering senators the judges in
their own cause.

III. A trial which, at about the same period of time,
awakened much local interest, and produced a strong and
wide effect upon public opinion and sentiment, took place
in the superior criminal court, held at the State House, in
Philadelphia, upon the indictment of *William Duane*, then
editor of a political newspaper called *The Aurora*, and
several others, charging them jointly with an ordinary
riot.

It will be recollected that the act of Congress, passed
on the 6th of July, 1798, known as the Alien Law, vested
in the President of the United States an immense discretion over persons resident here but born abroad, and not
yet actually naturalized,—giving him the power to apprehend, restrain, secure, and remove them, and to establish
any regulations he deemed necessary respecting their treatment. This was one of those *ultra* and utterly inexcusable
devices by which inflamed factions sometimes fancy they
can intimidate or coerce their opponents, but which really
betray their own unworthiness and prepare their own
downfall. It aroused the utmost jealousy and resentment,
kindled a generous sympathy for those who were considered unconstitutionally oppressed by vindictive rulers, and

was greeted everywhere, except in the presence of official authority, with clamorous condemnation.

The defendants in the prosecution were conspicuous and resolute in denunciations of this law. To a great extent its enactment may be ascribed to the exasperating stream of bold and energetic attack upon the federal administration which flowed, without ebb, through the columns of *The Aurora;* and the editor of that print, with his known associates, were watched, with a corresponding zeal, as likely to commit themselves, under a galling sense of wrong, by some breach of the public peace. They had determined to obtain, if possible, such a pressure upon Congress by means of popular petition, as would lead to a repeal of the act; and in pursuance of this plan they caused a placard to be posted on the exterior wall of the church at which, on a particular Sabbath, the numerous congregation to which they belonged, assembled. This placard was the following short invitation : " *Natives of Ireland who worship at this church are requested to remain in the yard after divine service, until they have affixed their signatures to a memorial for the repeal of the Alien Bill.*" That a matter in itself so simple and harmless, so entirely within the sphere of constitutional right and order, even supposing the locality and the day unreflectingly chosen, should meet resistance and occasion violence, is a strong proof of the diseased and sensitive state of the public passions. Some took fire at the proceeding as *Jacobinical,* some termed it a profanation of the consecrated edifice, others a desecration of the neighboring graves, and many an insult upon the pious attendants at the altar ! The impulse to all this indignant invective, however, was obviously the party spirit then hotly raging. It is difficult to repress a smile at the extravagance of the honest chief magistrate of the city of Philadelphia, who, officially reporting the outrage for prosecution, described it as an act "*done with intent to subvert the government of the United States !*" The utmost extent to which the evidence carried the disorder of the scene was, that *one* of the implicated, while being pushed from the churchyard, exhibited, without using, a pistol he had in his pocket to protect himself against a totally different and unconnected assault !

Mr. Dallas addressed the jury :

"These gentlemen who have been, with sonorous emphasis, charged with a design to subvert the government, were relieved, by the very evidence adduced to criminate them, from every imputation or even suspicion of having been guilty of the commonest casual affray. But you have heard them called *Jacobins!* And has it already been settled that an exercise of the invaluable right to petition for a redress of grievances is *Jacobinism?* Are forms of proceeding, expressly recognized and warranted by the constitution, thus early after its adoption, converted by the judgment of reckless faction into criminal acts? Is it possible to treat the defendants as lawless outcasts of society because they received, from those who were willing to give them, signatures to a memorial whose contents do honor to its author? And is it possible that for this they are additionally asserted to have forfeited all privilege of counsel on their trial, with open threats that he who undertakes to represent and defend them shall himself be denounced and victimized?

"There can be no doubt that this is *a party case,*—a party question altogether. Look abroad, is not party marshalled, nay armed, for violence? Has not party entered into the recesses of private intercourse, poisoned its roots, and destroyed the possibility of its existence among those who differ on political principles? Is not the population of the whole country almost equally divided by the spirit of party? Where is the hope of safety, where the expectation of retaining even the soothing civilities of society, if these furious passions are to be introduced upon all, the slightest, occasions before a court of justice? I appeal to you, gentlemen of the jury, is this picture overdrawn? is it not strictly true?

"And what object had these defendants in view? Was it a legal and meritorious one, or a lawless and culpable one? I cannot conceive it possible that, in a city so populous and enlightened as this,—a seat of government, where the written constitution is in the hands of every man, and the exposition of its principles undergoing constant emanation from the chambers of Congress, —that to solicit signatures to a memorial for the redress of grievances, in its tone and character so dignified and decent, should be esteemed criminal. If it be a crime, who is he, on one side or the other, that is guiltless? Is a proceeding which all citizens are bound to encourage and promote,—a proceeding dear to every one who values the liberties and constitution of our country,— a proceeding positively recognized by the constitution itself, and which all men and all parties should support at every hazard; is such a proceeding to be stigmatized as riotous?

"I will not consume your time by reading this memorial; its perfect propriety is universally conceded: wherever read, by whomsoever spoken of, whether by the friends or by the enemies of the act of Congress, none have denied that it was honorable to its writer, respectful in its language, and a fair exposition of the sufferings inflicted by the law upon those against whom it was enacted. It is neither my intention nor my purpose to discuss that law itself, or to arraign any measure of the honorable body which passed it; I may be allowed, however, merely to remark that it was adopted when a special policy seemed inflexibly to trample down every obstacle in its path: and this I will say, without fear of contradiction, that if its passage was within the constitutional competency of Congress, equally indisputable is the right of the people to complain of its operation as a grievance and petition for its repeal. Ah! but these petitioners are aliens! Be it so. But citizens, in all quarters of the country, and many of the national representatives in both houses of Congress, remonstrated against the law as of doubtful constitutionality and of exceeding severity; why, then, should the memorialists, the very sufferers themselves, be condemned as criminal, for adopting and imitating, with unexceptionable words, the example thus set them? Let it not be pretended that by petitioning for a repeal, they meant violently to resist the law; to overturn the constitution and the government: such an idea is too preposterous to be entertained for a moment by this court or jury. Disobedience to the statute was not contemplated; and as long as the judiciary sanctioned it, they, in common with all good citizens, were bound to submit to it. But this orderly acquiescence did not, and cannot, preclude them from seeking its repeal in the strictly constitutional mode to which they resorted. Or, gentlemen, are we to be told, that aliens resident in this country have no rights, no claims to freedom or to justice? Is it true that men are invited, by the most flattering views of our independence, liberty, and social security, sustained by an admirable constitution and by equal laws, to come and enjoy with us these American blessings; and that when they do come, with all the ties of family affection around them, bringing their industry and talents and gratitude to their new asylum and their permanent home, they are destined to suffer the bitterest disappointment, to find these beckoning promises illusory, and to feel their hopes crushed? They fly from tyranny, they quit oppression, exaction, and persecution, allured by the glorious prospect and the loud promise of liberty and protection here; but they are suddenly told—'You are subject to the mandates of an individual; you may be forced to leave your home and occupation at his bidding; your treatment is what his will may prescribe.' Far be it from me to say that their treatment will be tyranny; but it depends upon the character of one man, as fallible as all other men; and I solemnly ask whether in the shelter and safeguard of the judicial tribunals, in the confrontment of accuser and accused, in the ordeal of a jury, and in the publicity of trial, aliens are not substantially outlawed by this legislative ordinance?

The individual on whose discretion they are dependent may himself be wise, virtuous, honorable, and just ; but, of necessity, he acts upon information derived through others who may possess none of these qualities."

The indictment had been framed with several counts, in the expectation that a conviction might be obtained on some one of the phases of offence imputed. It was ardently and eloquently pressed by Mr. Joseph Hopkinson, author of "Hail Columbia," and subsequently eminent as a member of Congress and as judge of the federal district court. But it signally failed; the jury, after a brief consultation, pronouncing a verdict of not guilty as to each and every shade of the accusation.

Some of the remarks we have cited as made by Mr. Dallas on this trial, so temporary in its interest and importance, more than half a century ago, are not inapplicable to the leading doctrine zealously inculcated by a party organization which the circling course of events indicated within a few years back, as on the eve of assuming the management of public affairs. If there be in reality a trait peculiarly characteristic of American polity, it is the very great facility with which foreigners, discontented with their homes from whatever cause, political oppression, classified social inferiority, ecclesiastical intolerance, unappreciated talents, or adversity, have been admitted into the equalizing sanctuary of our citizenship. The Republicans who, at the instant of its passage, condemned the Alien Act and perseveringly prolonged an opposition to it as unconstitutional, unjust, and irrational, until repeal was accomplished and its victims or their families were indemnified, never could, and their disciples probably never will, predicate patriotism or fitness for public service from nativity alone. Their sense of the history, spirit, and institutions of each State and of the Union rejected, as inconsistent and derogatory, every sort of exclusiveness not essential to the maintenance of order, liberty, and law. Such exclusiveness had prevailed for ages, and had been plausibly cherished and fortified, in Europe, when they cut the ties that bound them to that continent; but it was never American. They welcomed the immigrant as a fellow-being. They frankly accepted his regenerating oath of allegiance and abjuration. They felt no fear that the blessings of a country so free as theirs could be voluntarily assailed by those in full enjoyment of them. They advanced no discriminating claim to special gratitude, because by what they did they acquired as much as they gave,—a worker in the common hive, a defender of the common safety, a contributor to the common treasury. Making their system of government an object of affection, as the offspring of all, and of pride, as the protector of all, instead of a standing usurpation and a perpetual menace, they believed that, whatever might be the conflict of opinions and the change of administrations, sedition and treason had become almost impossible crimes, certainly crimes little to be dreaded. It might be that, as a security to the immigrant himself against sudden misdirection, or even to the State, a probationary period had best be defined; but, in general theory, all men of mature years, sound in mind and in morals, were competent to assume the responsibilities and exercise the rights of citizens; and, indeed, the locality of the cradle in which they were first unconsciously rocked had as little to do with the political philosophy of the question as the texture of their first wrappers, the properties of the air they first inhaled, or the wholesomeness of the nutriment of which they first partook. The title to accredited manhood is that of actual possession, requiring no backward tracing, and is independent of birth here, there, or elsewhere. It is not amiss to remember that in a frame of government, adopted in 1776 under the direct auspices of Franklin and in the fresh and full vigor of revolutionary reconstruction, the forty-second section expressly provided that every foreigner, having taken the oath of allegiance, " shall, after *one year's* residence, be deemed a free denizen, and entitled to all the rights of a natural-born subject of the State, except that he shall not be capable of being elected *a representative* until after *two years'* residence."

They who esteemed native birth an essential civil qualification quit the hard rules of logic, and rested upon the persuasive suggestions of sentiment. They asked the Democrats of '98, and they appealed to the immigrants themselves, whether it was possible wholly to release the mind from its youthful convictions, to extinguish in the heart the fond attachment for early scenes and associates, and inflexibly, for the sake of the new, to sacrifice all

6

remembrance of the old country? If upright nature could give but one reply, then was there not a practical, though it might seem to be an illogical, necessity for guarding our institutions against the operation of these latent influences on human conduct? Did they not at least exact such a term of precautionary novitiate as would hold out a promise that purely American ideas and affections would spring up and effectually acquire ascendency? Unfortunately, this view of the subject, in reality a narrow and delusive one, catches promptly the unreflecting ear; and it was, moreover, strengthened by the frequency with which the foreign born of our population, French, Irish, Scotch, English, or German, formed, sometimes for purposes of benevolence, sometimes for military tuition and parade, sometimes for conviviality, and sometimes for political conference, associations, contradistinguished from American fellowship, and of a tone and a ceremonial exclusively transatlantic. These associations were construed as living and ostensible proofs of a wish and a determination on the part of immigrants themselves to keep up the distinction between the native and adopted citizens, to avoid sinking into a homogeneous mass, and to transplant hither antipathies, tastes, practices, and prejudices, which had not found a natural growth on our soil. The question could not easily be answered, why are we to overlook the locality of birth and to ignore it as unimportant, while they, in whose favor we should do so, insist thus upon retaining it as a link of concert, a shibboleth, and a pride?

A great organic principle, once and with unanimous sanction deposited as the corner-stone of a free and just and beneficent structure of government, cannot be trimmed and fashioned anew to suit every light and transient jealousy. It is there for universal and perpetual use,—not to be shaken by partial evils or casual incongruities, but to outlive the errors and excitements of centuries and of generations. If there be in the Constitution of the United States an unwise or even hazardous contempt as to the personal genealogies of those for whose protection, prosperity, and happiness it was formed,—if, among the vast discoveries of modern genius, it has suddenly been found that "there is much virtue in blood" and more in nativity,—if that which the noblest assemblage of sages

ever convened embalmed in their work as an essential
feature of American republicanism—the baptismal efficacy of naturalization—be wrong and suicidal, the people
may ultimately resort at least to the power of amendment.
It would be discreet, however, to avoid defacing one of
the fundamental originalities of our sense and system of
human liberty, until its dangerous tendencies were established by something more palpably true than sentimental
casuistry, something less flimsy and fugitive than party
strife. In the constitutional enumeration of the powers
of Congress, the fourth is "to establish a uniform rule of
naturalization,"—a phrase whose import requires no comment; and, in the entire instrument, eligibility to office,
as a civil right, is restricted to the natural-born citizens,
or to citizens at the time of its adoption, only in the cases
of President and Vice-President. Every other legislative,
executive, or judicial functionary, superior or subordinate,
may be *law-born* instead of *natural-born*. When the expediency of extending or contracting the period of *residence*
as a qualification in members of the Senate or of the
House of Representatives was discussed in the convention
of 1787, the truly American doctrine, in utter scorn and
hostility of the admitted European one, broke forth. MR.
MADISON "thought *any restriction* unnecessary and improper. Improper, *because it will* give a *tincture of illiberality
to the constitution.*" DR. FRANKLIN was not against a reasonable time, but should be *very sorry to see anything like illiberality* inserted." "We found in the course of the Revolution that *many strangers served us faithfully*, and that *many
natives took part against their country.*" "When foreigners,
after looking about for some other country in which they
can obtain more happiness, give preference to ours, *it is a
proof of attachment which ought to excite our confidence and
affection.*" MR. EDMUND RANDOLPH "reminded the convention of *the language held by our patriots during the Revolution* and *the principles laid down in all our American constitutions*. Many foreigners may have fixed their fortunes
among us under *the faith* of these invitations." MR. JAMES
WILSON "rose, with feelings which were perhaps peculiar,
mentioning the circumstance of *his not being a native*, and
the possibility, if the ideas of some gentlemen should be
pursued, of his *being incapacitated from holding a place under
the very constitution which he had shared in the trust of making !*

He remarked *the illiberal complexion* which the motion *would give to the system*, and the effect a good system would have in inviting meritorious foreigners among us, and the discouragement and mortification they must feel from *the degrading discrimination proposed.*" No one can doubt that Americans should govern America,—Americans *law-born* or naturalized as well as *natural born.* There is but one real calamity to dread, and that is that Americans may undertake to govern America upon principles wholly un-American, not reconcilable to the genius of the Revolution nor to the import of the constitution.

Perhaps no more appropriate occasion than the present will occur, in the progress of this sketch, for referring to an incident by which the composure and candor with which Mr. Dallas regarded this matter of foreign birth may be appreciated. He was, like Alexander Hamilton, born on an island in the West Indies; but he came to the United States as early as 1783, was a citizen at the time of the adoption of the federal constitution, and was therefore eligible to the office of President. In 1816, when his energy and ability in retrieving the almost hopeless bankruptcy of our national finances had inspired an ardent admiration, several of the representatives in Congress from Kentucky requested permission to put his name forward as their candidate for the chief magistracy. He declined, without hesitating, and on two grounds: one, as the fast friend of James Monroe, and the other, because, although undoubtedly embraced by what may be called the temporary reservation of the fourth clause in section 1, article 3, he deemed it most suitable and respectful that, as regards that eminent station, the policy designed as the permanent one should at once be frankly adopted and pursued. While he could eloquently insist upon the legitimate and lineal fruits of naturalization in its countless but inferior bearings, he thought it by no means unbecoming or harsh, and clearly involving no breach of plighted faith, though it might not be strictly logical, that the American people should prefer depositing their executive power in native hands.

IV. The impeachment of *Alexander Addison*, president judge of the court of common pleas for the circuit composed of the counties of Westmoreland, Fayette, Washington, and Alleghany, before the Senate of Pennsylvania, furnished another occasion for the striking professional displays to which we are cursorily adverting.

Mr. Dallas was of counsel to aid the managers appointed by the House of Representatives. Although the proceeding hinged upon incidents in themselves of slight dignity and importance, the legislative body could not well abstain from its institution. The freedom with which Judge Addison, exercising his functions before juries, habitually indulged in allusions to topics of a political bearing, had given much offence, and provoked one of his associate colleagues on the bench, Judge Lucas, to counteracting efforts. The president of the court bore with restless impatience what he regarded as a sort of mutiny among his subordinates or staff. Possessed of fine abilities, and admirably qualified as a lawyer, he was nevertheless prone to unnecessary assumptions of power, was fond of irrelevant dissertation in his official addresses, and probably believed that the rapid and ominous advance of the democratic element in the social state excused, if it did not imperiously exact, a check from all persons in authority. Judge Lucas, a plain, uneducated man, of sterling integrity of purpose, inexperienced in the forms of legal tribunals, but keenly alive to every encroachment. no matter how plausible, upon popular rights, was at first overawed; and when he at last undertook to dissent, found himself incapable of a successful stand against contemptuous arrogance, loud menace, or dexterous management. He was publicly, from the seat of justice, sneered at as one whose opinion was not worth hearing; silenced, on attempting to speak to a jury; and finally, when prepared with written remarks, he was ordered to abstain from reading them under an intimated penalty of imprisonment. Many citizens, who witnessed the circumstances which thus reduced one of their magistrates to the unmerited condition of a cypher or pageant, addressed themselves, for inquiry and vindication, to the legislature. The personal treatment of Judge Lucas, though it effectually disabled and depreciated him as a public officer, was frivolous and unaccompanied by actual violence; yet it was apparent that the engrossing pretensions of Judge Addison involved principles of considerable nicety and importance; that he obstinately and perseveringly pushed those pretensions; and that, if the established system of associates, in judicature, was to be maintained, their independence must be vindicated by the only competent authority.

It has been said that in America, the judiciary, of all the departments of government, is the most open to attack and the least capable of resistance. The remark may be just; but it would be uncandid to omit adding that this exposure and this weakness were, at the time of which we are writing, greatly aggravated by the rash manner in which judicial functionaries had frequently drawn into doubt their impartiality or purity of motive. In this respect time has ripened a change in the highest degree honorable to the spirit of our institutions and the wholesomeness of public opinion. Judges are now, as well in State as in federal spheres of action, not merely learned and laborious, but inaccessible to corruption of any sort, and as little liable as human agents can be to the suspicion of bias. Certainly, on questions connected with the constitutions, or involving principles of construction, decisions must be expected to conform to that school of politics to which the judge belongs and from which he was intentionally selected; but in the ordinary administration of justice, touching the enforcement of contracts, the prevention or redress of wrongs, and the execution of the criminal code, we are free to doubt, even in presence of the illustrations of France and England, whether the rule of right has, in any country or at any time, been fulfilled by legal tribunals, more wisely and virtuously than it now is throughout our republics.

The speech, in maintenance of the impeachment, was remarkable for its clear development of constitutional law, its compact and forcible reasoning, and its singular aptness of illustration. Nearly two days were occupied in its delivery. Let it be observed that although the amendments adopted in convention, in 1838, were interesting and important, especially in the tenure of the judicial office, the remarks of Mr. Dallas are as just commentaries upon the present as upon the former constitution of Pennsylvania. We will refer to such portions only of this deservedly celebrated address as include matter of general and permanent interest and as seem to us particularly replete with the manner of thought and diction which characterized its author.

The prosecution was supported under *three* points of

view: 1, that it is the right and the duty of an *associate* judge to address a grand jury, as well as a petit jury, upon subjects judicially before the court; 2, that by depriving Mr. Lucas of his right, and preventing his performance of this duty, Judge Addison has been guilty of an illegal, unjust, and unconstitutional misdemeanor in office; and 3, that for an offence of this description, an impeachment is the appropriate remedy.

After reading the entire section of the constitution respecting the judicial power, Mr. Dallas said:

"I lay it down as a general result to be deduced from this article, that the president and associate judges of the courts of common pleas, in their powers and duties as judges are placed on a strict footing of equality, and have equal coextensive authority. This equality arises, indeed, not only from the constitution of the office, but from the very nature of the judicial character.

"Here then is no distinction made in the constitution between the powers of the president and associate; and if the constitution recognizes no distinction, the legislature can make no distinction; and certainly no act of the judges themselves can possibly overleap the constitution and the law, to create a distinction by bartering or surrendering rights, which they possess for the public benefit. We must not be misled by words or names. A *president* does not mean a person who is to direct, influence, control, and command the court; but in this, as in all public bodies, from necessity, there must be an organ to declare its sense. Thus, in the supreme court there is a chief justice, in the senate a speaker, and on the grand jury there is a foreman; they all mean the same thing, and nothing more.

"Nor are we to be misled on account of a distinction made in the act of Assembly for organizing our courts, by which a professional character is required to be placed as president of a court of common pleas. The president does not by this distinction acquire any additional power, nor is he raised to any greater degree of eminence. You find nothing in the constitution that prescribes that the president shall be a legal character, though the act of Assembly enjoins it; and, although it might be a question, whether the legislature had the power under the constitution to place this restraint on the appointments of the executive, it has nothing to do with the present discussion. In point of convenience, however, the introduction of a law character on the bench might be well,—he may unquestionably be useful; but he cannot be supposed entitled on this account to abridge the rights, or to prevent a performance of the duties of his associates, as declared in the constitution.

"This constitutional inquiry is necessary, because, I think, after establishing that the constitution gives equal power and equal rights, and imposes equal duties on the president and associate judges, we shall require something more than an outdoor agreement of the judges to destroy this constitutional equality, not only as to the parties to the agreement, but as to their successors forever.

"The first idea of the judicial character which presents itself is that a judge only exists in the exercise of his own judgment. A judge cannot act by deputy, for he cannot delegate the powers of his judgment to another; he cannot, for the purposes of judgment, receive information through the eyes, ears, or understanding of another. The very nature of the judicial character, I repeat, requires that he should see, hear, and understand for himself. He violates the trust if he substitutes the judgment of another for his own, or even if, by his silence, he permits a jury to infer that he is satisfied with the opinion of another, at whose opinion he revolts; nay, he is more bound to give his opinion and to assign the reasons for it if he is dissatisfied, or even doubts, than when he concurs in the sentiments of a colleague. What sort of a judge would he be that should suffer it to be understood that he agreed in a charge from which in fact he dissented? No man will assert that such conduct would furnish the mind with an idea of the judicial character. Different circumstances, says the defendant, will strike the minds of different persons in a different manner. True, it is so in the moral and in the physical world, and emphatically it is true in the science of the law, which is a department of the moral world. There is scarcely a topic of legal investigation which does not produce contrariety of sentiment and sometimes of decision. It is not a difference among lawyers merely; but you scarcely find an argument at any bar that does not occasion a diversity of opinion on the bench. But this very view of the subject leads to the conclusion that every one ought to assign his reasons, whether he agrees or dissents; and we ought not to say to an associate judge that you may think, but you shall not utter your thoughts; you may form an opinion, but you shall not deliver it; you may sit as a judge, but you shall never display your own judgment, unless it coincides with the judgment of the majority of the bench. Alas! would this be consistent with the judicial character? Further, we know from our own times, as well as from the history of ancient days, that a majority of the judges in courts of law have been capable of delivering illegal, unconstitutional, and even criminal opinions. On such occasions were the minority bound to silence? Whatever may have been the rule of the day, in the case of the ship-money and the case of the seven bishops, mankind have since consecrated to everlasting fame the names of those who honorably

spurned the slavish doctrine. Let the doctrine prevail, and I
see not why a puppet or a China mandarin would not form as
good an associate for the honorable president as a Coke or a
Mansfield,—a judge who may agree in silence, but cannot dissent
in speech; who may ruminate, but dare not divulge his sentiments; who shall be considered in law a party to the judgment
of the court, and yet cannot in fact declare that he thinks the
opinion of the court either erroneous or criminal. The powers
created by the constitution, the rights inherent in the judicial
character, point at equality and independence among the judges.
In every court, whether superior or inferior, the maxim prevails,
'*Inter pares non est potestas.*'

"From every source of judicial authority, from the constitution, from the acts of Assembly, from the maxims of the common
law, and from daily practice and experience, the same undevi-
ating result is deduced. A brother justice cannot be bound even
to his good behavior for using such expressions in court as
would authorize the commitment of a private person. But let
me appeal, likewise, to any member of the Senate at all acquainted
with proceedings of courts, whether his sense of decorum would
not be wounded if, seeing a division of three to two judges upon
a case before them, he should hear the majority declare that the
minority might think, but should not speak? And what would
be his indignation if this threat was added, 'If you of the minority
are not silent, we of the majority will send you to jail!' But is
this the extent to which the mischief leads? May not the
majority of every public body act upon the same principle with
equal right? and shall we not in the end encourage a usurpation
by which all the independence of individuals, of minorities in
public assemblies, and even of the departments of the government,
may be undermined and destroyed? Carry it one step further,
and if the judges divide two against two, mere manual strength
or brutal force must decide the judicial conflict."

The following passage cannot fail to be specially impressive. Uttered in the presence of a numerous audience, the description of the partisan habits of judges
has the weight of contemporaneous testimony, and exposes
one of the greatest evils of those days. Such bold and
eloquent condemnation could not come from the lips of
an eminent public man before a court of impeachment
without the warrant of notorious and incontestable facts:

"Inquiring more particularly, however, whether there is any
difference in the authority of the several judges constituting the
same court to address grand juries (their other official powers

being clearly equal), we are to look for the origin of charges
to the English courts. I have not the books here to refer to ;
but, if my recollection be correct, the practice originated with
the justices in Eyre and Assize, who, in the course of their judicial circuits and visitations, collected a number of persons competent to inquire into the state of the country, for the purpose of
discovering the offences that had been committed and bringing
the offenders to trial and punishment. The selected inquest
usually assembled at the chambers of the judges, where the
principal judge delivered to them an abstract of the crimes and
offences of which they were to inquire, comprising nothing more
than a short definition of the several offences and the punishment
annexed to the perpetration of them. The length of the charge
naturally increased with the increase of offences and the extension of the penal code to new objects ; but still it long preserved
its original character of a mere abstract of crimes and punishments, and consequently no opportunity could occur on this part
of a judge's duty for a diversity of sentiment. *From the useful
simplicity of this practice, however, it has been the passion of
modern judges greatly to depart, but in no country has the departure been more bold or pernicious than in our own. Even
in the judicial history of England, where the spirit of party
has sometimes raged with the most dreadful consequences, you
will find it difficult to trace any instance to countenance the
political declamations, the party invectives, which have of late
become a sort of prelude to the commencement of every session
of our courts of justice.* The moment the original ground was
left, from that moment a new series of consequences ensued. We
entered our courts, not as to a scene of administrative law, but
to a scene of political speculation, in which no precise object was
presented to the mind ; but, instead of a definition of crimes and
punishments, the attention was engaged by theoretical declamations or the feelings were exasperated by the forensic denunciations, and every mind drew different conclusions from the display,
having different prejudices and opinions to indulge.

"In every instance of a charge to a grand jury relative to their
duties, it is admitted that there is a concurrent right in the associate judge to address them, but it is said by a witness, 'that as
to all *extra matter*, it was left exclusively to the president, under
a chamber agreement of three of the associate judges and the
president, to say and do as he pleased.' '*Extra matter!*' But
though the definition has not been given by the defendant, or
his witness, there are materials before us from which to form
a tolerable idea of the meaning of those who used the term.
It is then, I presume, matter delivered to a jury, with which
they have nothing to do. It is matter to dissuade them from
the impartial discharge of their duty, on the score of party

animosity. It is matter to excite in their breasts a spirit of persecution against their neighbors who differ with them in political
or religious opinions. It is '*extra matter*' to inculcate doctrines
to the people, from the bench, in favor of the party to which
the presiding judge has attached himself. We will put a case
(authorized by the testimony) of a political discussion in which
is brought into view that farrago of absurdity, falsehood, and
wickedness that glares in the pages of Barreul and Robertson;
or which is portrayed in the ' Bloody Buoy' with all the filth of
Porcupine; and we will suppose the presiding judge to declare
that the evil spirit which appears in those works to have destroyed Europe, has extended its baneful influence to this country, and already corrupted and diseased the very heart of the
body politic; if, in proof of such assertions, he would refer to
the legislative proceedings of our sister States, Virginia and
Kentucky, and point emphatically to the result of our own
elections; and if he should lead to the conclusion that every
man participating in those reprobated acts was an enemy to religion, good order, and civil government; an object fit for general
execration, and meriting to be banished from the social world;
I ask, whether any judge sitting on the bench, hearing this
wild, irrational, unfounded, and dangerous invective, ought to
be expected to pass it over in silence; and by that very silence
to expose himself to the suspicion of approving and assenting?
Grant this, and the effect would be dreadful! A president of a
court of common pleas having the exclusive right to detail all
'*extra matter*' according to the dictates of his own taste and
passions, would soon pass from general declamation to personal
denunciation; consigning his fellow-citizens, one after another,
to popular hatred and fury, as the partisans of a faction, Jacobins,
and Illuminati; or as members of the Middle Creek Secret Association, till all security of the laws in relation to persons, reputation, and fortunes would be annihilated. If, at least, this
extensive mischief was not produced, it would be owing more
to the mild temperament, the happy manners of our citizens,
than to the conciliatory disposition of the judge.

"Let us again put a case, hypothetically. Suppose the president and three associate judges, being of the same political party,
make an agreement that the president shall deliver all '*extra
matter*' to a grand jury; and, in pursuance of this agreement, he
eulogizes one party at the expense of the other; shall a judge
belonging to that other party be doomed to sit in silent anguish,
while he, his friends, and copatriots are vilified and traduced
without just cause? Must he listen patiently to the commenda-
tion of measures which he condemns, and to the arraignment of
motives which he approves? In short, must he exhibit, from
time to time, the culprit, and not the judge, upon the bench;

while the political charges of the president, acting uniformly and constantly on the public mind, like drops of water continually falling on the same spot, work a deep impression? or like the influence of a stone upon the smooth surface of a lake, extending circle beyond circle from the jury and auditors to their families, their neighbors, and their distant acquaintances, until the whole community is affected by the political tendencies of the judicial politician?

"It is said by Lord Bacon, 'that the best law is that which leaves the least liberty to the judge; and he is the best judge who takes the least liberty to himself.' True, in the present instance, the law left no liberty to the judge to address grand juries on points foreign to the ends of their institution; but it is equally true that the judge assumed more power than was ever contemplated to be given to a court, much less to an individual magistrate."

On this particular topic, we will restrict ourselves to a single other extract. It is not alone condemnatory of "judicial politicians;" it manifestly, though covertly, exults in the success of the very cause which the defendant had desecrated the bench by repeatedly assailing; and, avoiding a revulsion of feeling which might be provoked by too much triumph, it brings, with equal brevity and skill, the whole weight of that cause to bear upon the minds of the senators whom he addressed.

"We will not go into a detailed examination of Mr. Addison's charges to grand juries; but it is evident that in the best of them he largely indulged himself in speculative points. In those instances, however, let us be satisfied in reflecting that if he did no good, he did no harm; except, indeed, by a waste of that public time, of which he was so parsimonious, when a brother judge wished to share a part. Yet, if the system of Mr. Addison's charges was to elevate one set of citizens and to depress another, fair play required that both sides of the question should be heard; and in relation to the '*extra matter*,' or political portions of his judicial lectures, it was unjust and dishonorable to deny to Mr. Lucas, for himself and his friends, the opportunity of vindication and reply. If Mr. Addison enjoyed a superior degree of learning, and a more extensive sphere of influence, his delinquency was proportionably greater in the abuse of his official trust, to disseminate party politics, and to excite domestic animosity. Nay, the topics of the president's charges were often treason against the vital principle of our government. A representative republic must languish and expire if the source of its life and duration, the right of election, shall be poisoned, or cut off, or brought into contempt. When, therefore, the presiding judge inveighed against the issue of the general elections, as symptoms of popular corruption, he attempted in effect to undermine the confidence and attachment of the citizens in the republican institutions which they had established; and as far as in him lay sought to subvert what he had sworn to support. When such an attempt is made by an allusion to the influence of the Illuminati, Jacobins, Democrats, and secret societies upon our elections, he ought to be corrected, and the manner in which Judge Lucas attempted to correct him was certainly not too severe for the occasion. We have heretofore heard the tocsin of alarm sounded; tales of plots and conspiracies have been anxiously fabricated and circulated by '*the friends of order and good government;*' and our women and children have been terrified with the impending horrors of taylors, tubs, clues! Nay, the very letters of the alphabet have been marshalled against the peace of the community; and X, Y, and Z were, for awhile, the symbols of corruption and outrage, of foreign hostility, and of domestic discord. But these bubbles have vanished into air, 'thin air;' the mask has been torn from the face of the impostor, and the triumphs of the republicans have produced nothing which patriotism or humanity can deprecate or deplore. But if the State of Pennsylvania deserved to be denounced by Mr. Addison for the result of the elections of 1799, which only gave a majority of five thousand votes in opposition to his wishes, what must be the depravity and degradation to which her citizens have since sunk, when we find that the majority in 1802 has swelled to the unprecedented amount of thirty thousand!"

One of the difficulties in this impeachment, and practically that which required much dexterity to surmount, lay in the really light and colloquial circumstances which constituted the overt acts of wrong. To give gravity to these incidents, to magnify their import, and so to prevent their being dismissed as trivialities, called for more than ordinary effort and tact. How Mr. Dallas managed this portion of his task will be seen more distinctly than it has yet been seen in the fragment we next introduce. The picture with which the orator closes is masterly in its coloring and in its minute details. It is impossible not to see, as if actually occurring, the humiliation and expulsion of the associate, the chuckling audience, and the contemptuous and victorious president; we sympathize with the wounded, and we follow his dejected figure as he steps down from the bench and slowly retreats to the door; and then, as he disappears, we are roused to the consciousness that, in a sneer, a taunt, and a smile, the temple and the votaries of justice have been degraded by lawless arrogance and outrage.

"I have reached that stage of the discussion which calls for some caution to prevent a departure from the moderation that I have prescribed to myself. We have seen a judge degraded and a court violently dissolved ; but it remained, to stimulate an honest indignation, that a magistrate's functions, duties, and rights should be superseded and annihilated, under the terrors of a threat, delivered in open court, by his brethren of the bench! The lumber of our professional libraries contains, we know, much absurdity ; but this affords no ground for reflection on the law itself, which is a system of refined common sense, adapted to the various conditions, situations, and pursuits of mankind. Thus the difference of time and place makes often, in law and reason, an essential difference in the delinquency and punishment of an offensive act. The giving the lie in a street, or a tavern, is a breach of good manners, and generally terminates in a personal rencontre, yet it is not an offence in the law ; but if the same indecorous expression be pronounced within the precincts of a court of justice, its consequences are highly penal. A blow given in the highway is a mere misdemeanor ; but if given in Westminster Hall it has been regarded as a species of treason. Let us apply the principle of this determination to the present case. If a private citizen, in a private room, were to threaten a judge for any part of his conduct in court, such a threat, all will agree, would be greatly reprehensible ; and yet how venial it is compared with the fact that one judge has threatened another judge sitting on the same bench, in open court, for an attempt to exercise what is now an acknowledged right! State the defence of Mr. Addison as involving a proposition, that two judges of the court may lawfully commit the third judge to prison for attempting to express an opinion on any subject before the court, and what mind can yield its assent? Then, where is the distinction between the actual commitment which removes the judge from the bench, and the menace of the commitment which awes him into silence while he remains there ? Hardly would it appear a greater outrage to me if, instead of sending the judge to jail, or threatening to send him thither, the president had boldly struck him from his seat.

"It is true, sir, that the terms of the threat uttered by Mr. Addison were not expressly that he would send Mr. Lucas to jail ; but this was its natural and necessary import. The witnesses use different words, but they concur in substance that Mr. Addison ordered Judge Lucas to be silent, and declared that if he did not desist from the attempt to speak the court would find means to make him. What are the coercive instruments of a court in any instance of contempt of its authority? Fine and imprisonment. It would be a pitiful subterfuge to say that the president intended merely to direct the grand jury to withdraw, for he might, with equal effect, have done so in the morning; and certainly, if nothing more was intended, he might then have given the direction at once without the addition of the threat. The pride, if not the candor, of the defendant will prevent his resorting to so palpable an evasion. Nor will it answer his purpose to allege that he meant to coerce Mr. Lucas by the imposition of a fine only; that would be as unlawful as a commitment to prison, and the means would not be suited to the end, since a fine might operate as a punishment for speaking, but could not operate as a gag to make him hold his tongue. The commitment to jail, therefore, was the threat. Such was the interpretation of the words in the mind of Judge Lucas, and the effect upon his conduct was in perfect correspondence with it. He sunk, mortified, dejected, and confused upon his seat; he paused for a moment's reflection and self-collection; he trembled at the disgraceful and injurious conflict which must inevitably ensue if he longer asserted his rights; he saw his character and usefulness as a judge completely destroyed. With shame and affliction he retired from the court, and the bench and the bar, the jury and the audience, united in a laugh of triumph, a sarcastic smile, in which (says Mr. Gazzan) I was sorry to observe the president take a conspicuous part!"

Judge Addison replied in person, with much ability and force. He was answered briefly by Mr. Joseph B. McKean in support of the impeachment. The trial began on the 17th of January, and consumed an entire week. On the 26th of January, the question was taken in the Senate on the articles jointly in the following form: "Is Alexander Addison guilty or not guilty of the charges contained in the articles of accusation and impeachment exhibited against him by the House of Representatives?" Twenty members replied "Guilty," and four "Not guilty."

Mr. Dallas had, with a just forbearance, argued that the terms of the constitutional provision prescribing that "the judgment shall not extend further than removal from office and disqualification to hold any office of honor, trust, or profit under this Commonwealth," amounted to a limitation, and not to a grant of power; that the Senate,

therefore, possessed a discretion to apportion the punishment to the degree of the offence, and might modify their
sentence, on conviction, either to a simple removal or to
a removal and a disqualification to hold any judicial office.
This view was embraced by Mr. Addison, and by him re-
called to the mind of the Senate, in a letter addressed to
that body immediately after they had voted; and accordingly, on the succeeding day, was formally pronounced by
the Speaker a judgment of removal and also a disqualification " to hold and exercise the office of judge in any court
of law within the Commonwealth of Pennsylvania."

V. Perhaps a still greater detail of the professional
exertions of Mr. Dallas might enable some readers of this
sketch to form a fuller and more accurate conception of
his legal attainments, and of his ability and attractiveness
as a forensic speaker. The occasions were numberless,
and their features infinitely various. But as this is not
the aspect of his character which interests the present
age or posterity, further elaboration upon it would probably be unwelcome. Let us restrict ourselves, therefore,
to one or two additional cases; and first, that of the impeachment of *Edward Shippen, Chief Justice, Jasper Yeates
and Thomas Smith, Assistant Justices of the Supreme Court
of Pennsylvania;* which, after the loss of three years in
preliminary movements before the House of Representatives, reached the stage of trial in the Senate, sitting at
Lancaster, on the 7th of January, 1805.

The public functionaries formally arraigned by the
popular branch of the government for misdemeanor in
office were universally known in the State, were advanced
in years, were of acknowledged learning, and of unques-
tioned purity of life. They were charged with a single
" *arbitrary and unconstitutional* " act, to wit, sentencing
Thomas Passmore to imprisonment for thirty days and a
fine of fifty dollars for a " *supposed contempt* " in libellously
posting at a frequented coffee-house, in the city of Philadelphia, one of several defendants, against whom he had
previously instituted an action within their judicial cognizance. The article of impeachment briefly set forth the
facts on which it was founded, but abstained from any
imputation whatever, direct or inferential, of corruption,
venality, cruelty, or malice. It is quite clear that the
irritated complainant must have failed in his appeal to

the legislature for redress or revenge, had he not fortunately, and perhaps even to himself unexpectedly, fallen upon a condition of speculative and party politics in that body auspicious to his aim. The occurrence for which he claimed the infliction of punishment might possibly be regarded as an error of judgment: that alone, however, could not sanction a proceeding by impeachment: but it presented nevertheless a distinct occasion for parading certain theories or prejudices warmly urged and rapidly advancing to the controlling influence they subsequently exercised.

Many of the most active and prominent politicians of Pennsylvania conceived that the revolutionary principles which achieved a separation from the British crown were yet imperfectly carried out. They wished for more thorough and practical changes in every department of public agency. The constitutions of 1776 and 1790 were half-way measures, halting under the interpretations given them by courts and counsel. The broad substratum of the jurisprudence of the Commonwealth was still in fact, to their disquiet and disgust, *the common law of England.* Their independence was incomplete or illusory. They ascribed to judges and lawyers a spiritless inability to quit the routine of precedents set in Westminster Hall, and push the new and elevating doctrines to their logical results. Judges and lawyers, therefore, had become targets at which to aim: compulsory suits were if possible to be superseded by arbitration: and the citation of British adjudications, made subsequent to the 4th of July, 1776, was to be peremptorily forbidden.

The trial opened with due solemnity by a speech from Mr. Nathaniel B. Boileau, the principal manager on the part of the House of Representatives, a gentleman of French descent, of considerable adroitness and talent, who was rising fast on the political horizon, and afterwards became secretary of the Commonwealth under Governor Snyder. The prosecution had the aid of Mr. Cæsar A. Rodney, an eminent member of the Delaware bar, at that time the Attorney-General of the United States, by selection of President Jefferson. Mr. Dallas and Mr. Jared Ingersoll were enlisted by the accused to conduct the defence. Twenty days, as well afternoon as morning, were consumed in the examination of witnesses and the

7

arguments on both sides. On the 28th of January, 1805,
the Speaker of the Senate announced from the chair to
the chief justice and his associates that they were
acquitted: the vote previously taken on the question,
"Are the judges guilty or not guilty as charged in the
impeachment?" having stood 13 for guilty and 11 for not
guilty, and the constitution requiring for conviction the
concurrence of two-thirds.

The junior counsel for the venerable accused made on
this occasion what cannot but be considered, notwithstanding the imperfection of the stenographic report
which has brought it down to us, one of his most powerful addresses. During four entire days he pressed with
unfaltering vigor upon the tribunal, a majority of whose
members he knew to be unfavorable, a copiousness of
learning, an aptness of illustration, and a directness of
reasoning, altogether overwhelming. Even his legislative
adversary, Mr. Boileau, in replying, exclaimed, "When I
behold the mass of books under which the floor of the
house groans, I am reminded of the giants of old, piling
mountains upon mountains in order to reach the skies
and hurl Jupiter from his throne."

The line of argument boldly and justly confronted the
political prepossessions which have been adverted to.

1. A contempt of court is technically an offence,—not
against personal feeling, but against the administration
of justice, and exacts summary process.

2. This summary process is derived from the common
law,—every country has its common law.

3. The common law of England was brought over with
them by the original settlers of Pennsylvania, as far as
it was applicable to their new situation, and is our birthright and inheritance. It is declared to be a part of our
law by legislative acts and judicial decisions.

"I repeat, that in Pennsylvania, we should have no security
for our persons, our property, our reputation, and the regular
proceedings of courts of justice, without the common law. The
constitution of Pennsylvania, sir, would be a dead letter without the expository power of the common law. That constitution says that 'every man for injury done him in his property,
person or reputation shall have remedy by due course of law:'
and I aver with confidence that this provision can never be of
any avail without the auxiliary of the common law. All wants

are to be supplied, all grievances redressed, but *how?* Unless it be left to the common law to expound, it is utterly unintelligible and impracticable. Suppose a man attempts to put you out of your estate 'by due course of law,' *how* is he to attempt it?—by the common law. *How* are you to defend your estate?—by the common law. *How* are you to get satisfaction for an assault and battery?—by the common law. Suppose a man libels my reputation, the dearest thing in life: nay, the man who does it does something worse than take from me my life: *how* am I to seek for redress?—by the common law. There is no act of Assembly for it: the common law alone entitles me to redress."

4. How are we to acquire a knowledge of this common law?—by the books, or, as Mr. Jefferson called them, "*usual monuments*," wherein it is registered.

5. These books view the act of Passmore, although committed out of court, as a contempt at common law, punishable by attachment, fine, and imprisonment.

6. Neither of the constitutions of 1776 or 1790 contains anything in letter or spirit incompatible with or annulling this current of legislation and judicial decision. "Trial by jury *as heretofore*," and "No man can be deprived of his liberty or property without the judgment of his peers OR the law of the land," are fundamental maxims, in no degree violated by the summary treatment of contempts.

These propositions were severally elucidated with great research, and enforced by all the power of argumentative ability and eloquence. They rescued the clients of Mr. Dallas from a painful and perilous predicament; and it may confidently be said that they established, in relation to the source, composition, and character of the law of Pennsylvania, a conviction never since shaken.

The impeachment, however, though formally a failure, in reality attained the objects of those by whom it had been planned. It was a means of ventilating and inculcating certain extreme doctrines. In truth, there was very little sympathy for Thomas Passmore, though much was loudly professed; and as to the fate of the judges, indifference prevailed. The rising malcontents had their field-day, exhibited an imposing ascendency in both legislative chambers, and, through the speeches of Messrs. Rodney and Boileau, spread an *ad captandum* gloss over their peculiar views. The trial had scarcely closed, when they felt themselves strong enough to summon a caucus, to scheme an attack upon "the stern Trojan," Thomas McKean, the actual chief magistrate, to systematize serious changes in the existing constitution, to clamor against the sophistries and pretensions of lawyers, and to nominate as their candidate for the office of governor, to be supported at the election in October following, Mr. Simon Snyder, then Speaker of the House of Representatives.

To counteract so bold and threatening a movement, it was thought necessary to arouse and organize for combined action all the citizens of Pennsylvania, without regard to their established party lines, who deprecated *ultra* and illiberal measures. Hence sprung *our* "TERTIUM QUIDS," or, for brevity's sake, the Quids,—a phalanx, self-named Constitutional Republicans, composed equally of Democrats and Federalists, united for a short campaign only and for a single object of common interest.

As soon as the association was formed in Philadelphia, about the beginning of March, 1805, resolutions preparing the way for an explanation of their motives and purposes were adopted, and a numerous committee of correspondence appointed, whose names conciliated respect and confidence. They were "Alexander James Dallas, William Jones, George Logan, Richard Bache, Sr., Peter Muhlenberg, Samuel Miles, Samuel Wetherill, Sr., Jonathan Bayard Smith, Peter S. Duponceau, Guy Bryan, Chandler Price, Edward Heston, James Gamble, and Manuel Eyre, Sr." These gentlemen were instructed, "in order to ascertain fairly the deliberate and authoritative sense of the majority of the people of Pennsylvania, to prepare and publish a memorial and remonstrance to the legislature against the existing project of calling a State convention, and to express only such sentiments and language in that memorial, directed to that single object, as may be honorably subscribed by every citizen of the State, who is opposed to the project, whatever may be his party attachments, prejudices, or principles."

Mr. Dallas, as chairman of this committee, discharged its duties with indefatigable perseverance, transmitting a memorial to the legislature without loss of time, addressing, in the early part of June, his fellow-citizens at great length in a paper esteemed to be one of the happiest and most forcible productions of his pen (*Appendix No.* 3), and maintaining with every town and county of the State an unremitting and vigorous correspondence during the whole of that summer. He was earnestly seconded by popular meetings in all directions, and his labors were amply rewarded by the abandonment of the project of a convention and by the re-election of McKean.

The circumstances just recited seemed so linked with the impeachment of the judges that it has been thought best to overlook the irregularity of their being told slightly in advance of the narrative.

Mr. Dallas had accepted from Mr. Jefferson the appointment of District Attorney of the United States on the 10th of March, 1801. He was then secretary of the Commonwealth, recommissioned as such by Governor McKean in 1799. On his withdrawal from the secretaryship, delayed only by an embarrassment as to his successor, two mutually kind and respectful notes were interchanged, which, as attesting what he depicts to be "an interesting act of his life," are entitled to a place here.

To his Excellency, Thomas McKean, Governor of Pennsylvania.

April 24, 1801.

"MY DEAR SIR,—The business of the attorney of the Eastern District has so increased that I was ashamed to trouble Mr. Ingersoll with it, and consequently I heard with pleasure that you had fixed upon a successor to me in the office of secretary of the Commonwealth. Mr. Trimble will probably be here on Tuesday, and I mean to enter on the duties of my new appointment next Monday or Tuesday. Be so good, therefore, as to consider this letter a resignation of the commission which I have had the honor to hold under your administration. The records and accounts of the executive department are left with Mr. Trimble in complete order.

"There are many considerations that render this an interesting act of my life. The flattering manner in which the office of secretary was originally conferred on me by Governor Mifflin, the cordiality with which you continued me in the station, the consciousness of having endeavored, for a period of eleven years, faithfully to discharge an important public trust, and the reflection that the fury of party, while it assailed me in every other quarter, has never found or fabricated a pretext to arraign my official conduct,—are sources of pride and pleasure that will enliven the success, or alleviate the disappointment, of every future scene.

"Though our official separation is at this time unavoidable, be assured, sir, that I never can feel indifferent to your honor and your happiness. As a professional man, as a public man, and as a private man, my respect and attachment have been uniform, disinterested, and unequivocal; and I claim from you, as the best proof of a reciprocal sentiment, frequent opportunities to evince the sincerity of these declarations.

"I am, dear sir, your faithful friend and servant,

"A. J. DALLAS."

REPLY.

Alexander James Dallas, Esq.

"PHILADELPHIA, April 26, 1801.

"MY DEAR SIR,—I received your favor of to-day, expressing your resignation of the office of secretary of the State of Pennsylvania.

"When I reflect on your assiduous, able, and faithful discharge of that arduous trust for the last eleven years,—years teeming with difficulties, tumults, and anxieties that have rarely been exceeded in this or any other country; that you have passed over ground before untrodden, and have finished your career with honor to yourself and reputation to the governors with whom you have acted: when I reflect on your disinterested attachment to my person and your avowed regard for my public and private character: when I consider the loss Pennsylvania will sustain by your relinquishment of this office, and am perfectly sensible that I cannot supply the post with an equal, it cannot be concealed that I part with you not only with reluctance but the greatest regret.

"Your affectionate expressions of friendship and that your assistance on occasion will not be wanting, notwithstanding our official separation for the present, the advancement of your happiness which I profess to have at heart, and a sincere wish for the advancement of justice and to promote the ease and honor of Mr. Jefferson's administration, impress it as a duty upon me to acquiesce in the loss of such a coadjutor. From my soul I wish you comfort and prosperity in your new station, and every other to which your merit may raise you.

"Accept the friendship and a tender of the best services of, dear sir, your most obliged and obedient humble servant,

"THOS. McKEAN."

VI. The only other illustration of professional ability and skill which it is deemed necessary not wholly to overlook, occurred several years after Mr. Dallas had assumed the office of District Attorney of the United States, and but five years before his entry into the Treasury Department at Washington at the invitation of President Madison. This controversy was very ancient and complicated, had assumed many shapes successively, and in the end found its way into the circuit court of the United States on the trial of a criminal indictment. It ranged, unsettled, from the revolutionary epoch of 1778 to the constitutional one of 1809, and finally, by furnishing occasion to sweep through its channel of progress, elicited a discussion of extreme interest on conflicting principles of fundamental politics.

During the war certain prisoners, captured by the British, were placed on board of a sloop called the Active, and were ordered to be transported from Jamaica to New York. Among these was Gideon Olmstead. On the voyage, the prisoners rose, and, headed by Olmstead, took command of the vessel, confined the officers, crew, and passengers in her cabin, and steering for a friendly port, had nearly reached one, when a Pennsylvania brig, Captain Houston, overhauled them, seized the sloop as prize, took her to Philadelphia, and there libelled her in *admiralty under a statute of the Commonwealth.* Olmstead and his companions filed their claims for both vessel and cargo, resisting the pretension that they had not completely subdued the enemy when Houston came up. The jury who tried the cause found a general and unexplained verdict, giving to Olmstead and his associates only one-fourth, and the remaining three-fourths to their opponents. On appeal to the *court of appeals established by Congress*, this sentence was *reversed*, the entire prize decreed to Olmstead and his associates, and the court of admiralty directed to effect sale and to pay the proceeds accordingly.

The competency of the superior jurisdiction thus exercised, that is to say, in setting aside the verdict of a jury and in prescribing a wholly different judgment and distribution, was disputed by the court below. The judge of that tribunal, instead of conforming to the mandate from above, disregarded it, received himself the proceeds of the marshal's sale, and paid over to the treasurer of Pennsylvania, Mr. David Rittenhouse, so much thereof as had been originally awarded to the Commonwealth by the jury, taking a bond of indemnity in which the obligor was described as treasurer, and as accepting the fund for the use of the State. This fund was in fact in the form of loan office certificates, which, upon the death of Mr. Rittenhouse, came into the possession of his representatives Mrs. Sergeant and Mrs. Waters, and were libelled for execution by Olmstead under the decree of the higher court. This libel, too, was determined in his favor, in January, 1803. It was shortly after this that the legislature of Pennsylvania took part in the controversy; but it was not until the 27th of February, 1809, that Governor Snyder, watching the course of judicial action, deemed it his duty to maintain the rights and honor of the State by executing the enactment and calling out a portion of the militia to protect Mrs. Sergeant and Mrs. Waters from any process in the hands of any officer under the direction of any court of the United States.

Amid very great local excitement, the marshal, with his writ of attachment in his hand, and anxious peacefully to execute it according to the principle of forbearance advised by Mr. Dallas, was nevertheless forcibly obstructed and repelled by a numerous military guard, which surrounded the residence of the ladies, under the command of General Michael Bright. With some firmness, much composure, and great address, he penetrated to the interior of the house and effected the arrest.

An indictment, founded on a penal act of Congress, against *Michael Bright* and eight others being presented and returned by the grand jury, came up for trial in the circuit court of the United States on the 28th April, 1809, before judges *Bushrod Washington* and *Richard Peters*.

Occasional collisions, in federative systems of government, between the local and the general authorities are shown by all history to be unavoidable. The lines which divide the spheres of action are on the borders so narrow, and, under the fading influences of time become so indistinct, that they are constantly in danger of being practically overstepped. Such, too, is the infirmity of human intellect and virtue, that an aggression, once committed, never lacks defenders or apologists; and an error which quiet good sense might at the outset have rectified, rapidly swells into a noisy and impracticable shibboleth of party. The stand taken by the legislature of Pennsylvania against the rights of Olmstead, and the course of judicial appeal, was untenable; and yet it was perseveringly bolstered by legal provisions and executive conduct for many years, until it finally took an alarming and critical aspect. In opening the evidence, Mr Dallas said:

"When the grand jury found this indictment *a true bill*, what was the spectacle exhibited in the streets of Philadelphia, what were the consequences that menaced the peace of the city, and what were the feelings that agitated every patriotic heart? An armed force, raised under the orders of the governor of the State to resist and defeat the judicial authority of the Union; a marshal officially compelled to summon a part of his fellow-citizens to oppose with force another part; and the authority of the United States in action, leading to the result of arraying the whole power of the confederation, if necessary, in arms, against the whole power of one of its members! Not only the inhabitants of Philadelphia, but every citizen of every State,—nay, every friend of republican liberty throughout the world must be appalled in contemplating so momentous a crisis. It was not simply a question of property, a question of jurisdiction, or a question of State sovereignty that was involved; but the great questions which are so interesting to mankind seemed to be at issue,—whether a free government, established and administered by the people themselves, can possess sufficient energy for its own preservation; whether the republican representative system is constructed of materials fitted for stability and duration, and whether liberty, driven from the regions of Europe, Asia, and Africa, shall find a dwelling-place on the face of the terra-queous globe."

The solemnity of this exordium was neither exaggerated nor misplaced. Let us remember that, though the Constitution of the Union had been in operation but twenty years, the tendency to disregard its provisions was already thrice and seriously manifested in Pennsylvania. In 1794, an insurrection to resist an excise on whiskey stills; in 1799, another to resist a mistakenly-called window-tax; and now a threatened rebellion to secure for State pretensions a supremacy expressly conferred upon the national jurisdiction. This last was far the most formidable and dangerous; it rested vaguely upon the popular and undiscriminating doctrine of State rights; the sovereignty of the Commonwealth seemed enlisted; the executive and both branches of the legislature gave it countenance; it preceded by a quarter of a century the discontents of South Carolina, and yet bore all the worst features of nullification.

The eloquent and patriotic counsel who, as we are aware, had profoundly explored the origin and structure of the American Union, and reverenced it as the wisest of human works, could not resist this suitable opportunity to press its excellence upon a public tribunal. During the subsequent fifty years we have rejoiced in many able commentaries and vindications; but the lucid, just, comprehensive and powerful exposition given by Mr. Dallas, in advance of all these, merits special preservation. Nothing can do equal justice to the purity of his love of country, the soundness of his judgment, and the clear richness of his elocution; and nothing at the present epoch of strife is worthier of analysis and study. We may venture on extracts of unusual length.

"In the management of the prosecution I shall not step aside to arraign the policy of the State of Pennsylvania, nor to derogate from the character of her magistrates. To assert the authority and jurisdiction of the United States it may be necessary to question the constitutionality of the course that has been pursued in Pennsylvania and to demonstrate the errors that have been committed by her public functionaries; but it can never be necessary to ascribe an improper motive to human actions when the fallibility of human judgment will fairly account for whatever is or seems to be wrong; and it is in the capacity of a private citizen, not in the office of a public prosecutor, that I permit myself to deplore and to deprecate the policy of the State government. Even under the opinion that Pennsylvania has erred, I shall speak of her with reverence and attachment. My remarks will be confined to the evidence, the law, and the principles of the case. And I confidently hope that the event of the discussion, so far from disgracing Pennsylvania, will be the instrument of her vindication, restoring her to the high and merited rank which she has hitherto enjoyed among the sister States.

"The offence charged against the defendants is of a nature as serious as any that can be charged against the citizens of a free government. I do not except treason as it operates against the government, nor murder as it respects an individual. In its first aspect, indeed, it differs from those crimes; but it gradually assumes the front of treason, and murder naturally follows in its train. Even, however, this tendency to accumulate guilt is not the great evil and danger of the offence to which I now advert. *The open, bold, and ostensible movements of treason—for instance, the levying of war to subvert the government, or to sever the territory of the Union by the range of the Alleghany or the western waters—will always present an object which the vigi-*

*lance of our administration may readily detect and the power of
the nation will certainly defeat ;* but if a resistance to the regular
operation of the laws, administered through the medium of the
courts of justice, shall pass with impunity till the offence becomes
habitual among the people, the disease will not be perceived till
it is incurable ; the foundations of the government will be undermined before the approach of danger is suspected, and the fabric
of civil liberty which the valor and wisdom of your patriots have
raised will, in a sudden and tremendous fall, overwhelm you with
destruction and dismay. Remember, then, I pray you, that the
existence of the government depends essentially upon the existence of all its departments, and that treason in arms against the
executive and legislative departments cannot be more certainly
fatal to the vital principle of the government than habitual opposition or popular contempt manifested toward the judicial authority. This is, in some degree, the case in every form of government,
but in monarchical governments the ready assistance of military
force may always be obtained to execute the judgments of the
law. It is under a free government, constituted by the people,
and forever dependent upon their good will, under which the
civil authority is declared to be supreme, while military force is
designated as an object for jealousy and control, that the dominion
of the laws must in a peculiar manner be held sacred, for otherwise (as it has been already said) the government itself must
cease to exist. When the decrees of justice can no longer be
enforced by the marshal and the writ, you must resort to the
soldier and the bayonet ; and, whatever you may choose to call
your government, depend upon it you will no longer continue
to be a free people. *A resort to arms in obstructing the operation of the laws must inevitably lead to a resort to arms in
maintaining them. Nor can it make any difference in principle
whether the execution of an act of Congress or the judgment of
a court be resisted, whether the resistance is attempted by an
individual or by a multitude, in the rage of wanton violence or
under color of spurious authority.*

"But opinions have been scattered abroad in pamphlets, in
newspapers, and in declamatory harangues, which are, I confess,
well calculated to pervert the public mind, and to excite the
public feelings on the peculiar subject of the present prosecution.
It is weakly, if not wickedly, said that an opposition to the judicial process of our courts is not an opposition to the laws; and
*that persons who act under the authority of the State in making
such opposition are guilty of no offence.* Against a doctrine so
radically vicious it is a duty most solemnly to protest: nor can
I safely approach the immediate ground of the prosecution without first endeavoring to rescue your judgment from its baneful
influence. I claim, therefore, the attention of the jury for a

short, but, I hope, *a satisfactory development of the principles
of our social compact in its federal as well as in its State characteristics.*

"There is no truth more certain, none to which I more sincerely subscribe, than that *the sovereignty of the nation resides
essentially and everlastingly in the people. From this sovereignty emanates the powers of government, whether they are
vested in the federal or in the State system; and whether in
either system, they are assigned to the legislative, the executive,
or the judicial department.* The institution of government is
thus an exercise of the sovereignty of the people, in their own
way, and for their own good. The people acting as the creator,
assign to the subject of their creation, the form, attributes, and
operation necessary to its use. *In dividing the powers of
government into federal and State, the sovereignty of the people
is displayed, not surrendered:* and in dividing the government
into departments, the separation is made for the preservation of
each in its legitimate sphere, and not with a view to render any
one department superior to the others. *Hence, while the sovereignty resides inherently and inalienably in the people, it is a
perversion of language to denominate the State, as a body politic or government, sovereign and independent.* If, indeed, the
word 'State' is used as a collective for the people of the State
(in which sense, and in a sense descriptive of territorial jurisdiction, it is sometimes used), there is no objection to the phrase:
but a State, meaning the government of the State, is never itself
sovereign, though it may discharge those functions of sovereignty
which the people have assigned to it; nor can it ever be independent while the people possess the right and power to change,
modify, or abolish it. *The federal and State governments, in
this point of view, are alike possessed of sovereign powers: but
the State government can no more be denominated sovereign and
independent in relation to the powers vested in the federal
government than the latter can be so denominated in relation to
the powers vested in the former, or reserved to the people. The
truth is (a political truth that ought never to be overlooked in
the collisions that may arise between State and federal authorities) that the constitutions of the Union and of the State must
be regarded and construed as instruments formed and executed
by the same party, the sovereign people, delegating powers to
different agents, but upon the same trusts and for the same uses.*
The instruments manifest the powers of the constituent and prescribe the duties of the representative. And thus you hear the
mighty voice of the people announcing in a solemn and formal
preface to the work that THEY (not that the sovereign and independent States) ordain and establish the federal, as well as the
State, constitution for their government. The people of Penn-

sylvania, acting as a portion and in concert with all the rest of
the people of the United States, ordained and established the
federal constitution in the year 1787 for their national government; and, subject to the plighted faith of that compact, the
people of Pennsylvania, acting for themselves alone, ordained
and established the State constitution in the year 1790 for their
territorial government. To the national government they gave
all the national attributes of judicial as well as of executive and
legislative power; and on the State government they devolved
the exercise of every other power necessary for the public welfare, with the exceptions and qualifications contained in the
declaration of rights.

"Upon this basis, I trust it will be perceived that, without
derogating from the dignity of organized governments or impairing their legitimate authority, the sovereignty of the people, the
federal jurisdiction, and the State rights may harmoniously and
securely rest. *But to assert an absolute sovereignty and independence in a State, is either to deny any sovereignty and independence in the Union, or to contend for the existence of a
solecism in the science of politics—the existence of two absolute,
sovereign, and independent governments in the same nation!*
Nor is it possible that the subject should have been misunderstood by the people when they adopted the federal constitution;
for General Washington, in the letter of the convention which
accompanied the proposed constitution, proclaimed the effect of
its adoption upon State jurisdiction in these memorable words:
'*It is obviously impracticable, in the federal government of
these States, to secure all rights of independent sovereignty to
each, and yet provide for the interest and safety of all. Individuals entering into society give up a share of liberty to
preserve the rest. The magnitude of the sacrifice must depend
as well on situation and circumstances as on the object to be obtained. It is at all times difficult to draw with precision the
line between those rights which must be surrendered, and those
which may be reserved; and, on the present occasion, this difficulty was increased by a difference among the several States as
to their situation, extent, habits, and particular interests.*'

"That the constitution, adopted with this knowledge of its
design and operation, was indispensable to the duration of the
Union, to the harmony of the States, to the prosperity of the
people, and to the character of the nation, every man will admit,
who saw or felt, who has read or heard, what was the situation
of the country at the crisis of the adoption. That the practical
blessings of the constitution have surpassed all that its most
zealous advocates predicted, even its once jealous opponents
gratefully see and candidly avow. For all know that the infirmities of the old confederation were so extreme, that the Union

had scarcely consummated its independence, when it seemed to touch the period of its dissolution. The necessity of resorting to some principle of resuscitation agitated every heart and exercised every head. Let the Union be dissolved, and what was then to dissipate the gloom that hung over the internal and external prospects of America! In a foreign view, where was the resource of population, or of revenue, to enable a single State to command the respect of the world, to reciprocate the benefits of commerce, or to repel the violence of other nations! In a domestic view, where was *the common umpire to reconcile the jarring interests of the rival States, to regulate the terms of social intercourse, to avert the calamities of civil war, to destroy the hydra of anarchy, or to subdue the efforts of despotism!* But, turning from those lamentable views of the subject, let us ask what, under the auspices of the federal constitution, is now wanting to our honor abroad or to our prosperity at home? The rights, the interests, the treasure, and the power of *all* the States constitute an inheritance and a name, a shield and a sword, for *each* State, in all the pursuits of its enterprise and industry abroad; while a uniform system of national legislation, and an impartial administration of national justice, serve to produce and perpetuate equality, confidence, and concord at home.

"At all times, and under all circumstances, from the dawn of American independence to the splendor of its meridian, the sovereignty of the people has been displayed in the formation of our political compacts.

"The latent sovereignty of the American people was kindled into action so early as the year 1774. Under a sense of wrong (not perhaps of actual oppression, but of meditated usurpation) the Congress of the colonies was formed. The sublime idea of national independence had not then been conceived, or it was carefully repressed. The object of the association was simply petition and remonstrance; and for that object the people, through their colonial representatives, delegated to Congress all the necessary powers of deliberation and agency. But petitions were neglected, remonstrances were despised, insult was added to injury, and upon the preparation of an invading military force to compel obedience to the usurped authority of the British parliament, nothing remained for America but to encounter arms with arms. (Mr. INGERSOLL: '*Then the people, or a colony of the people, may resist by force the encroachments of the paramount government upon their rights?*' Mr. DALLAS: '*If you can find an analogy in the situation of the country now, and then; if you can find in the conduct of the federal government acts of usurpation, contumely, and outrage such as Britain exhibited at that time; and if you conceive that the extreme case of lawful resistance to the constituted authorities of the Union has oc-*

curred, you are welcome to all the benefit of the question. But let it be well considered whether the conflict is likely to terminate in rebellion or revolution.') Even, therefore, before independence was the object, the people had delegated to Congress the powers of resistance and war, and a civil war was actually waged under their authority. It is true, there existed no formal, written compact among the colonies, but each delegation carried to Congress the authority of their immediate constituents to deliberate and to act for the success of the common cause ; and if the maintenance of the common cause required the existence of any particular power of government, the investment of that power in Congress was necessarily implied in the object of the association, without more. Hence it is that the powers of peace and war were derived in the first instance ; and the principal powers carried with them all their incidents. Still, although the Congress regularly possessed the powers, there would have been a difficulty, if not an impossibility, to apply them, had not the patriotism and the good faith of that memorable epoch proved an efficient substitute for all the means of coercion enjoyed by the strongest and oldest political establishments. At length, however, the opposition of *subjects* to the tyranny of their government suddenly taken up (without a disciplined force, without arms, ammunition, or any military supply, and without a common treasury) became too severe and too hazardous to be sustained ; and it was necessary to change the cause into the cause of *freemen* contending for independence, in order to rivet the pride, the valor, and the hope of the people to the glorious object of the war, as well as to inspire confidence in those nations of Europe who had already manifested a desire to espouse the interests of America. With these motives the Declaration of Independence was suggested and announced to the world as the solemn and deliberate act of the American people. It has been erroneously alleged that the Declaration of Independence was the act of the individual States ; but the character of the *States* was first created by that celebrated instrument, under the authority of the people at large, who, if they did not form it originally, voluntarily adopted and confirmed it. It has been erroneously alleged that there was no express, written compact between the people of the different States until the ratification of the articles of confederation ; but the Declaration of Independence is an express and written compact of union for every national purpose. Here, however, let the declaration speak emphatically for itself : ' We, the representatives of the United States of America in Congress assembled, appealing to the Supreme Judge of the world for the rectitude of our intentions, do, *in the name and by the authority of the good people of these colonies*, solemnly declare that *these united* colonies are, and of right ought to be, *free and independent States;* that they are absolved from all allegiance to the British crown, and that all political connection between them and the State of Great Britain is and ought to be totally dissolved; and that as *free and independent States they* have full power *to levy war, conclude peace, contract alliances, establish commerce, and do all other acts which independent States may of right do.* And, for the support of this declaration, with a firm reliance on the protection of Divine Providence, *we mutually pledge to each other our lives, our fortunes, and our sacred honor.*'

"Thus, it is perceived, that the Declaration of Independence was made, not in the corporate capacity of States, or of colonies, but *in the name and by the authority of the people;* and in declaring the freedom and independence of the States, no idea of individuality is introduced, but the declaration is applied to the *united* colonies in their collective and national character. Thus also it is perceived that, in their collective or national character, the *United States* are declared to have full power to *levy war, conclude peace, contract alliances, establish commerce, etc. All objects of national policy, which it will not be pretended an individual State could pursue for the whole, nor even for herself, upon the express and implied conditions of the compact.*

"The Declaration of Independence having provided for the *national* character and the *national* powers, it remained in some mode to provide for the character and powers of the States individually as a consequence of the dissolution of the colonial system. Accordingly the people of each State set themselves to work, under a recommendation from Congress, to erect a local government for themselves; *but in no instance did the people of any State attempt to incorporate into their local system any of those attributes of national authority which the Declaration of Independence had asserted in favor of the United States.* From this conclusive evidence, as well as from every other concomitant and cotemporaneous occurrence, it is obvious that the people approved and ratified the distribution of powers between the federal and the State government; so that, from this period at least, the people of America were bound to each other by an express, written compact, recognizing nothing more, however, in favor of Congress than was necessarily, as I contend, implied in the principle and object of the previous voluntary association of the colonies.

"But the investment of power in Congress, from the generality of the terms of the Declaration of Independence, was soon found inconvenient in practice; and hence arose the necessity of the organization, arrangement, and details contemplated by the articles of confederation, which were proposed to the individual States so early as the 9th of July, 1778, but were not finally ratified by all the States until the 1st day of March, 1781. These articles, however, can only be considered as declaratory of the pre-existing national authority on the great subjects of war and peace, of treaties and commerce, with all their natural and necessary incidents. The States and the people of the States so considered them, for the exercise of the authority (which in such a case is some evidence of its legitimate existence) continued without opposition, complaint, or denial, throughout the whole of the most interesting period of the revolution that passed between the Declaration of Independence and the ratification of the articles of confederation. The struggle of the revolution was indeed almost over before the articles were ratified; treaties of alliance and commerce had been formed with France and other nations; British armies had been beaten and captured, and the day of peace rapidly approached. And no sooner were the articles ratified than it was discovered that they were miserably defective in all the energies requisite to an efficient system of government.

"The termination of the war did not terminate the labors or solicitudes of your patriots. The debts of the nation were to be paid; but Congress had neither the money to pay them nor the means to exact an equitable contribution from the States. The dignity of a national character, acquired by the noble exertions of a seven years' battle, was to be maintained; but Congress was without the power to attract or to command respect at home or abroad. The harmony of the States was to be preserved under the most trying diversity of habits and interests; but Congress could not dictate, and the day of persuasion had fled. The appeal to the gratitude, the justice, and the policy of the States for empowering Congress, under these circumstances of federal obligation, to levy a trifling impost was rendered abortive by the negative of a single (almost of the smallest) member of the Union. And, in short, every feeling of triumph for the past glories of America was superseded in the minds of the good and the wise, by a sense of shame and alarm, at the dreadful prospect of her future destiny. But a ray of hope at length darted through the gloom of the political horizon. The active patriotism of Virginia led to a partial convention of delegates at Annapolis to consider the state of the nation; and, although the deliberations of that body did not produce an immediate remedy for the evils that were suffered, it is enough for the fame and honor of its members that the general convention, from which we eventually received the Constitution of the United States, was assembled upon their recommendation.

"The general convention, it must be allowed, was not composed of delegates elected by the people themselves, but of delegates appointed by the legislatures of the respective States. *The important fact, however, in relation to the adoption of their great*

8

work, is that it was not reported to the State governments; but that, on the express recommendation of the convention, it was submitted to the people of the States respectively for their assent and ratification. The people accordingly assembled, deliberated, assented, and ratified; and in that way alone the Constitution of the United States acquired all its authority as a social compact, as a bond of confederation, and as an instrument of government. The people, perfectly apprised of the nature and operation of the act, were, above all things, anxious that it should not be annulled or evaded. Hence, it is provided not only that the *officers of the federal government, but that 'the members of the several State legislatures, and all executive and judicial officers of the several States shall be bound by oath or affirmation to support the constitution.'* Nay, that no doubt or ambiguity should rest upon the claim of *paramount allegiance for the federal government,* it is imperatively declared in this act of the people themselves, that 'the constitution and the laws of the United States which shall be made in pursuance thereof, and all treaties made or which shall be made under the authority of the United States, *shall be the supreme law of the land, and the judges in every State shall be bound thereby,* ANYTHING IN THE CONSTITUTION OR LAWS OF ANY STATE TO THE CONTRARY NOT-WITHSTANDING.' Whether you contemplate the federal or State institutions, the judicial or the legislative and executive department of government, you have hitherto seen the work come uniformly from the hand of the people; and now (I pray you, gentlemen, to listen, with particular attention, to this authoritative expression of the public will), you hear the direct and unequivocal declaration of the people that the constitution and laws of the United States shall be supreme; that in every collision between the constitution and laws of the United States and the constitution and laws of an individual State, the latter shall yield, the former shall prevail, and that every State functionary shall, by the most solemn pledge of fidelity, undertake, before his God and his country, to support the supremacy of the constitution of the United States.

"It is not, however, by general declarations alone that the people, in establishing the federal constitution, have chosen to limit and restrain the jurisdiction of the individual States. It would be tedious, and is not necessary, to enter into the details; but, by way of illustration, I will suggest two subjects intimately connected with the present trial: 1. The people have limited and restrained the State jurisdiction in matters of war and peace. By a direct investment of power, Congress can alone declare war, grant letters of marque and reprisal, raise and support armies, provide and maintain a navy, make rules for the regulation of the land and naval forces, provide for calling forth the militia to execute the laws of the Union, suppress insurrections, and repel invasions, and provide for organizing, arming, and disciplining the militia. And, by a positive prohibition, no State can enter into any treaty, alliance, or confederation, grant letters of marque and reprisal, keep troops or ships of war in time of peace, nor engage in war unless actually invaded, or in such imminent danger as will not admit of delay. Now, if it shall ever appear that Massachusetts or Virginia, Pennsylvania or Connecticut, have kept troops in time of peace, without the consent of Congress, the act will be a flagrant violation of the constitution ; and, if the force thus unconstitutionally kept shall be arrayed against the constituted authorities of the Union, it must, upon every rational principle of jurisprudence, be an offence in every agent, civil or military, who is engaged in the opposition. 2. The people have also limited and restrained the State jurisdiction in matters of judicial cognizance. By a direct investment, the judicial power of the United States embraces (with various other objects) all cases *in law and equity* arising under the constitution, laws, and treaties (other than suits by individuals *against a State*), *all cases of admiralty and maritime jurisdiction*, all controversies between citizens of different States, between citizens of the same State claiming lands under grants from different States, and between foreigners and citizens. And by the act of Congress which distributes this mass of judicial power among the several courts of the Union, it is expressly declared that the district court '*shall have exclusive original cognizance of all civil causes of admiralty and maritime jurisdiction.*' Now, if it shall ever appear that the legislative, executive, or judicial department of a State government, or that a combination of all the departments has attempted to divest or defeat the jurisdiction of a federal court *in a controversy between citizens of different States*, or has attempted to control the federal courts *in a case of admiralty and maritime jurisdiction*, it will be an act of complicated usurpation, notoriously unconstitutional, and utterly void ; it can never create a right for itself, nor confer an authority upon others."

At the close of this masterly *development of the principles of our social compact in its federal and State characteristics*, the district attorney opened the particular facts he contemplated proving against the prisoners, and examined his witnesses. The evidence was unexceptionable, clear, and conclusive. Nothing to rebut it was attempted. " *There is no dispute*," said Judge Washington in charging the jury, " *about the facts*." The defence, however, was taken upon two general positions of law : 1. The district court, whose writ was resisted, had no jurisdiction, because the court of appeals established by Congress having no authority to determine the case, the decree of that appellate tribunal was a nullity which the district court could not enforce. The court of appeals could not reverse the verdict of the jury. 2. The district court had no jurisdiction because the State of Pennsylvania was a party in interest and the court was therefore prohibited by the constitution from deciding it. The defendants acted in obedience to the laws of the State and the orders of her governor. The argument on these grounds was conducted with great ability by Mr. *Walter Franklin,* the attorney-general of Pennsylvania, and by Mr. *Jared Ingersoll,* specially retained by the Commonwealth to assist him. They were elaborately answered in conclusion by Mr. Dallas.

As we have deemed the only interest and importance of the trial to have been the relation it bore to the collision between the national and local authorities, it may be well to refer to what was said by Judge WASHINGTON on that score.

"*The governor of Pennsylvania had no power to order the defendants to array themselves against the United States, acting through its judicial tribunals; and the legislature of the State was equally incompetent to clothe him with such a power, had it so intended. The defendants were bound by a paramount duty to the government of the Union, and ought not to have obeyed the mandate.* There were but two modes by which the general government could assert the supremacy of its power on this occasion : *by the peaceful interference of the civil authority, or by the sword.* The first has been tried, and the defendants are now called to answer for their conduct before a jury of their country. Will any man be found bold enough to condemn this mode of proceeding, or complain that this alternative has been chosen? But, if the accused can plead the orders of the governor, as a justification of their conduct, and if the sufficiency of such a plea is established, the civil authority is done away, its means are inadequate to its end, and force must be resorted to. Are we prepared for such a state of things? *The doctrine appears to us monstrous, the consequences of it terrible. We regret that it was broached. It was contended that in a case where a State government authorizes resistance to the process of a federal court, though in a cause wherein the court had competent jurisdiction, the only remedy in such an emergency is negotiation. If there were no federal, no common head, this position might be admitted, and on the failure of the negotiations, the ultima ratio must be resorted to. But under our constitution of government which declared the laws of the United States made in pursuance of that instrument the supreme law of the land, and which vests in the courts of the United States jurisdiction to try and decide particular cases, I am altogether at a loss to conceive how, in the case stated, negotiations between the general and paramount government, in relation to the powers granted to it, and a State government, can be necessary and could ever be proper."*

There was much and prolonged difficulty among the jurors in determining the form of their verdict. They would not assent to a *general* one, and were obviously anxious to shield the defendants, if possible, by *specially* finding that in obstructing and resisting the marshal, the accused had acted under the orders of the constituted authorities of the Commonwealth. They attempted to put this impression on paper, but when examined it was thought to be somewhat contradictory and irregular,—whereupon the three counsel agreed each to draft a finding which would exactly convey the conclusion attained by the jury, leaving its effect to be decided by subsequent argument. The draft made by Mr. Dallas was preferred, adopted, and filed as the verdict, and Judge Washington directed the discussion as to its legal character to proceed on the morrow. But when called upon in the morning to proceed, Mr. Ingersoll observed, " for our parts, we shall say nothing upon it;" and the district attorney added that "the discussion had been already so extensive and the attention of the court so intent," that he submitted the point with entire confidence. The judge then ordered judgment for the United States and "that the defendants and every of them are GUILTY."

In calling for sentence, the prosecuting officer made a few remarks, from among which, as illustrative of his temperate disposition and the novelty of his attitude, the following are extracted:

" In all the vicissitudes of a public life (not short in duration nor free from difficulty) I have hitherto been able to discharge the duty of my station, without grief of heart or personal repugnance. But while performing the last act of the present prosecution, while calling upon the court to pronounce the sentence of the law against General Bright and his companions, I confess that I feel a regret the most sincere, a pang the most acute. It would be useless at this time to dwell upon the pernicious nature of the offence, or to urge the necessity and benefit of the example.

"It has been often said by the counsel for the defendants that this was not to be regarded as a common case, and they have endeavored to make a deep impression of its importance on our minds by reiterated appeals to the power and dignity of '*the constituted authorities of Pennsylvania!*' It is indeed an extraordinary case; but while I distinguish it, in its nature and importance, from every other prosecution which has occurred, I can only perceive in that distinction additional motives for a firm and energetic course of conduct on the part of all (judges, jurors, and prosecution) who are intrusted with a share in the administration of justice. *If it shall be deemed sufficient for the purposes of impunity, in the commission of offences against the laws of the United States, to obtain or to allege the sanction of a State law, or a State magistrate, the national authority and the national independence will be no more.*

"But I am still willing to admit that when the jury placed, for the first time, the fact judicially upon the record that the defendants had committed the offence with which they are charged under the direction of the constituted authorities of the Commonwealth, a fair occasion occurred to reciprocate those offices of kindness and respect which are so well calculated to promote and to preserve harmony between governments as well as individuals. I should therefore have listened with eagerness to the first overture from the defendants, acknowledging and regretting the error that has been committed; or even at this moment I would most cheerfully assume the responsibility of abstaining, without the previous authority of the federal government, from demanding the sentence of the court, if the attorney-general, who represents the constituted authorities of Pennsylvania, would intimate the slightest wish that this should be done. But, alas! the defendants seem rather to exult than to grieve at their situation; and all the solicitude that I have expressed, in public or in private, for an amicable arrangement has been treated by the law officer of Pennsylvania with cold and constant indifference.

"It would then be derogatory to the government as well as useless any longer to suspend a performance of my duty. Feeling, as I do (and I derive a satisfaction from the repetition of the sentiment), unaffected good will towards the defendants, and sensible as I am of the great debt of gratitude and reverence which I owe to Pennsylvania, I make undoubtedly a sacrifice of the most interesting personal considerations to the most imperious official obligations. But I look to the future with hope and confidence for gratification and reward. Nay, if I do not mistake the character of some of the defendants, connected as they are with society by all the ties of family, of property, and of patriotism, the time is not far distant when they will themselves rejoice that they have suffered for the laws: deeming it a day of triumph and not of sorrow on which the principle so dear to every freeman that '*the military shall in all cases and at all times be in strict subordination to the civil power*' was practically illustrated and permanently established."

The sentences were then (the 2d of May, 1809) pronounced: against Michael Bright, an imprisonment for three months and a fine of two hundred dollars; against each of the others, an imprisonment of one month and a fine of fifty dollars. The judge, in addressing the defendants, had used the phrase "*it is obvious that you have mistaken a supposed duty*," which being promptly reported to President Madison by Mr. Dallas, A PARDON was at once obtained, and the prisoners were discharged without delay.

When Congress assembled for the first time at *Washington*, on the 17th November, 1800, the House of Representatives found devolved upon it by the second article of the constitution the duty to choose* a President. The aggregate votes of the electoral conventions in the several States exhibited the result of 73 for Mr. Jefferson, 73 for Mr. Burr, 65 for Mr. Adams, 64 for Mr. Pinckney, and 1 for Mr. Jay. The Republican party had triumphed: but in triumphing, they had not discriminated on their ballots which of their candidates had been voted for as President and which for Vice-President. The clause of the constitution, shortly afterwards amended, did not require that they should. To be sure everybody knew the universal intention, but the record did not show it, and the equality of the number of votes respectively for Mr. Jefferson and Mr. Burr therefore gave the power of preference between the two to the house. The complication was exceedingly delicate and dangerous; and, taking into view the virulent condition of party politics, great disaster to the country might well be and was apprehended from factious intrigue and reckless audacity.

Mr. Albert Gallatin was one of the representatives from Pennsylvania; a warm personal friend of Mr. Dallas, and aware of his constant labors and solicitudes in the field of politics. He kept him advised, by short and rapid notes,

---

* *Sic* in constitution.

almost from day to day, of the progress in balloting. Of these notes the following only were preserved :

"*Washington*, 11*th Feb.* 1801, *half-past three, afternoon.*—We have balloted seven times, and no choice is yet made. Eight States for Jefferson, six for Burr, Vermont and Maryland divided. No change in our prospect since my last letter. As to individual votes, we had on the first ballot 55 to 49. We have this minute suspended the ballot for one hour in order to eat a mouthful."

"*Washington*, 12*th Feb.* 1801, *three o'clock in the morning.*— We are still sitting : have balloted twenty-two times, and made no choice, the result on every ballot the same. By all means preserve the city quiet. A report is already here that the Democrats have seized the public arms in Philadelphia. Anything which could be construed into a commotion would be fatal to us."

"*Washington*, 13*th Feb.* 1801, *twelve o'clock.*—I wrote you yesterday by mail that, after twenty-eight ballots, the house had agreed at one o'clock in the afternoon to suspend balloting till this day at eleven, the interval being considered a virtual though not a formal adjournment. To-day we met accordingly, and have balloted once. Result the same. They speak of bringing in a bill in the Senate to appoint a person to administer the government, and of making in this house a motion to rescind that rule which prevents our doing other business than balloting. They appear rather elated than otherwise. An overture was made by —— to —— stating that the Federalists had proposed to him to go over provided New York did. He was, as he said, to give them an answer this morning. The answer from New York was decisive, and so has been his to the other party. This shows a man whom they think they may tamper with. I believe, however, he is decided and will not yield. With this exception, I do not apprehend the most distant danger of defection on our side. I do not expect any on their part until they shall have seen the effect of their proposed law on our side in the house, and on the people. The judiciary bill is signed by the President."

"*Same day*, 1 *o'clock.*—Thirtieth ballot over ; same result. The Senate have adjourned till to-morrow without doing anything. We have this moment suspended the ballot till to-morrow at 12 o'clock. Our expectations of their yielding are better now than one hour ago, from some information we have just received, which I have not time to relate, as the bearer waits."

"16 *Feb.* 1801.—We have balloted this day for the 34th time, and the result is still the same. It is said that Mr. Bayard is decidedly in our favor, but that his vote is delayed in order to attempt to persuade the whole party to come over at once.—The ballot is suspended till to-morrow."

"17 *Feb.* 1801, 2 *o'clock, afternoon.*—We have balloted twice to-day. The result was still the same on the 35th ballot; on the 36th Mr. Jefferson was chosen, ten States voting for him, Maryland and Vermont included. Four States voted for Aaron Burr; two, supposed to be South Carolina and Delaware, put in blank ballots. Morris absented himself. The four other Marylanders put in their State ballot-boxes blanks. Mr. Bayard is this moment nominated Minister Plenipotentiary to France."

"18 *Feb.* 1801.—We consider the manner in which the opposition to Mr. Jefferson suffered him to be elected as an avowed declaration of war. Not one man of the party voting for him shows a determination that the phalanx ought to remain unbroken, and be ready to oppose whenever opportunity shall offer."

What would probably have been the consequence of Aaron Burr's election? He had been a gallant and faithful officer in the revolutionary army. He was of New York,—a man of acknowledged ability, less cultivated but more practical than his Virginia competitor; an ardent Republican, persuasive and conciliatory in speech and deportment. His standing was such, on the scores of service, integrity, and talents, as led Mr. Jefferson to meditate offering him an invitation to undertake the administration of the Department of War,—a project only dismissed because of his unexpected nomination as Vice-President.

Aaron Burr's master-passion was fanned by his disappointment on this occasion into a consuming fire. It may be said of him as of John C. Calhoun: had he been President, he would have remained and died a sound conservative patriot. Like the great Carolinian, his ambition wanted ballast, became ungovernable, and finally wrecked him. Of the two, the wild schemist for a western empire did his country far less injury than the author of such pernicious sorceries as nullification and secession, seen now to have gradually spell-struck and withered, in a large section, the ligaments of union.

Mr. Burr suddenly felt himself, by an accidental complication, within reach of the chief magistracy. The prospect dazzled and shook him. Undoubtedly, as a loyal Republican, it was his duty to refuse promptly and firmly to be made the instrument of faction. Unequal to so obvious and just a part, he allowed the known adversaries of his principles to seize him as a weapon and turn him against his friends,—thus, and by that alone, entering upon a descent which ultimately precipitated him into crime. Had the Federalists placed him in the chair, he must have commissioned "the midnight judges;" he must have retained in their posts all the proscriptive and implacable appointees of John Adams; he must have maintained unimpaired, perhaps enlarged, the Hamiltonian systems of excise and of public debt; he must have retained the fourteen years of novitiate before naturalization; he must, in a word, have kept the government on the *anti republican tack.* They did not succeed in placing him in the chair, but he had voluntarily incurred the odium of this possible course, and his party turned their backs upon him forever.

The functions of the professional post which he had accepted from Mr. Jefferson in the spring of 1801, gradually drew Mr. Dallas into close contact with the cabinet at Washington. He had long been on terms of the kindest intimacy with its chief members, especially during their periodical visits, as public men, to the city of Philadelphia, where his house was their hospitable rendezvous for consultation or enjoyment. He possessed their unbounded confidence and respect. Mr. Madison, Mr. Gallatin, and Mr. Robert Smith were his warm personal friends and admirers, and with them he was in the habit of constant and frank communication. From a few letters interchanged during that period may be collected the topics which engaged attention and possess in themselves a certain interest.

We have already referred to the effort made in 1805 to change the constitution of Pennsylvania. On that subject Mr. Gallatin, under date of the 30th March, 1805, says:

"I heard of you by Mr. Nicholson, who arrived here yesterday, and I hear every day by the newspapers. Will both houses agree to the call of a convention? and if they agree, what will be the consequence? There is certainly a defect in our (State) constitution arising from the omission of a mode to introduce amendments. It is absurd to suppose that any species of laws, whether constitutional or ordinary, ought to be unalterable; and, when no mode is provided, any mode may be adopted, and the security resulting from written constitutions is at an end. In fact it may become more easy to alter the constitution than a law, since legislative forms and restrictions may be considered as inapplicable to the proceedings of the sovereigns, who, reserving to themselves the nominal power of alter'ng the instrument, have neglected to specify the manner in which their will should be ascertained. As the matter stands, I can perceive but two principles to which to resort. The first is to insist that the call of a convention to be legal must be a legislative act. If you depart from this, it must be an invitation, and any self-created meeting of individuals have as much right to make the invitation as the individuals who compose either or both branches of the General Assembly. If it be an invitation, and not an order in the nature of a law, how can it be ascertained whether the people really want any alteration? And how are they to act on the day of election? If they or a majority shall refuse to appoint delegates to the convention, and a number of counties, or portions of counties, or even a number of individuals, perhaps a few in each county, shall appoint, where shall the criterion be found by which to determine whether the convention be a legal body? or, in other words, whether it shall be the true representation of the majority of the people? And by what means are we to avoid the confusion and anarchy which must result from such uncertainty? But if the people, as is probable, will think themselves compelled, in self-defence, and in order to avoid the greater evil, to elect delegates, will not the invitation of the two houses become actual usurpation?

" If, however, it is not practicable to persuade the Assembly that they have not a right to call a convention, unless it be by legislative resolution, and that a recommendation is big with danger, there is another principle which perhaps may be listened to more readily. If the people, reserving the inherent right to amend the constitution, have provided no mode in the instrument itself to introduce amendments, does it not follow that no amendment, nor call of a convention with power to amend, can be effected without their actual assent? If they have not delegated in any manner the power to amend, or to propose amendments to representatives, we must conclude that they intended to reserve the powers to themselves, and that the true and only legal mode of introducing amendments, or of calling a convention, is to submit, in the first instance, the question to them. It is perfectly easy to ascertain the fact;—a ticket, headed ' Convention,' and filled on the day of election with '*Yes*' or '*No*,' will give the result with equal certainty and facility. If a majority shall say they want a convention, they have a right to one; if a majority shall answer in the negative, the *friends of the people* would not dare to assert that a convention ought to have been called contrary to the wish of the majority. Whether amendments shall be introduced or not, I consider but as a secondary question; and there are some of the amendments proposed for which I would vote, if that were the question; although I would live and die perfectly satisfied with the present constitution. But I consider it as of primary importance, both as it relates to myself and posterity, to Pennsylvania, and the cause of republicanism in the United States and elsewhere, that we should have a security against confusion and against the usurpations of a minority. And for that purpose I see no safer remedy than to submit the question to the people by a legislative act, to which I cannot perceive, under existing circumstances, that the governor ought to refuse his assent. This idea, though expressed hastily and loosely, is the result of my most serious reflections. I invite your attention to it, because it seems to me that, as a substitute to the immediate call of a convention, it might have a better chance of succeeding in one of the two houses, than an absolute rejection. But you are on the spot and better able to judge of the question of practicability than I can be."

Mr. Robert Smith, Secretary of the Navy, also wrote to him, three days subsequently, on the 2d of April, 1805, in relation to the same subject:

"Men of consideration throughout the country view with great solicitude the proceedings of your State. Are they to eventuate in the discomfiture of the Jacobins, and in a union of the sensible, virtuous, and honorable? If the turbulent faction should be able to make head against you, and should accomplish their wild projects, then will the United States soon exhibit an additional instance of the incompetency of men to self-government. God forbid that our efforts should terminate thus ingloriously."

In answer to Mr. Smith, Mr. Dallas, on the 11th of April, 1805, says:

"I received with great pleasure your letter on the state of our politics. It convinced me that every man of consideration and reflection in the community must be opposed to the ruinous projects which, commenced in Pennsylvania, will, sooner or later, overthrow our republican institutions throughout the Union. I had determined to recede from the political scene; but, reflecting on the share I had taken in the successful effort to place the powers of government in Republican hands, it became an affair of conscience to resist the abuse of those powers by the influence of a band of wild and unprincipled zealots on our State legislature. It was equally my wish to prevent anarchy, to avoid a coalition with Federalists, and to preserve the dignity and authority of the administration. The inclosed papers will show you the preliminary means that have been employed ; and I trust that I shall receive the advice and countenance of the wise, the virtuous, and the liberal of the Republican party in every other State as well as in our own. The undertaking is arduous, and the event doubtful. But, after doing all that we can do to save the last hope of republicanism from annihilation, it will be a precious consolation that even defeat cannot be accompanied with disgrace.

"The movements in Pennsylvania *apparently* originate with a few notorious characters. But I believe the impulse will eventually be found to proceed from a combination of the disappointed and the desperate of our party, under the auspices of certain ambitious individuals whose heads and whose hearts gave a better promise. The object is to reduce government to its elements, rendering the immediate agency of the people perpetually necessary to every executive, legislative, elective, and judicial purpose. After effecting the object here, it will be enforced by the additional weight of a precedent in the other States ; and we have already seen that the federal constitution is, upon the same ground, the butt of active hostility. It is avowed here, and it will be in practice by the reformers everywhere, that lawyers, men of talents and education, men of fortune and manners, ought not to participate in the formation, or in the administration of a democratic government. The framers of the federal constitution, as well as of the State constitution, are denounced because they were of that description. And, in short, every occurrence indicates a spirit and a scheme to involve our country in all the revolutionary passions and sufferings of the first convulsive throes of France, which have subsided in the lethargy of despotism.

"The design of the conventionalists was to persuade the legislature to call a convention at the last session. This, however, was abandoned when they found that the people were roused to resentment and opposition, and a considerable majority of remonstrants appeared on the files of the House of Representatives. You will observe that we have never denied the power of the citizens to call a convention, nor the expediency of making the call through the medium of the legislature, when they have decided upon it ; but we object to a clandestine attempt to subvert the constitution, in the name of the people before they were consulted or heard upon the subject. Our success is, therefore, so far ascertained ; and although we shall vote against a convention, if a majority of the citizens deem it requisite, we shall cheerfully acquiesce. The object will then be to elect our best men for so important and so confidential a service."

Every excess of every kind is more or less injurious and alarming. Excess of liberty breaks through the necessary restraints of law and order, and excess of repression engenders discontent and explosion. The golden mean, which gives ample freedom, and yet preserves peace and justice, is scarcely attained before it is disturbed by human passions. Had the well reasoned reforms with which Mr. Jefferson cured the reactionary and proscriptive tendencies of Mr. Adams's policy been correctly appreciated by all of his party, serious mischiefs would have been avoided, and the last years of his administration remained as unclouded as the first. But the "*zealots*" were not few who thought their chief tame and hesitating, who looked into the inaugural for something more trenchant than the philosophic phrase, "We are all republicans, we are all federalists," and who, sincerely but unwisely, were for quickly forcing forward changes which could only be safely accomplished gradually and by time. The views of these men were perhaps too strongly sketched in this private letter; but Mr. Dallas could not write otherwise, for he had obviously no confidence whatever in their public virtue, very little respect for their intelligence, though much dread of their plausibility and zeal.

During the following year (1806) the public mind was excited by the development of two criminal cases affecting the national interests and relations. These were the cases of Aaron Burr organizing a military expedition against the United States or against Mexico, and of General Miranda, of Caraccas, making a like organization preparatory to wresting his country from colonial dependence on the crown of Spain. Both involved, if nothing more, misdemeanors or violations of our neutrality statutes, and were attended by circumstances which perplexed the cabinet of Mr. Jefferson. Early in the year the Secretary of the Navy wrote to Mr. Dallas that, "strange as it may seem, Burr is certainly at the head of a military expedition. The object is yet not known, and it is probable that he has completely masked his ultimate design. A few days will ascertain whether the measures taken will be sufficient to support the enterprise. This small affair will,

I fear, too severely test the energies of the government. There is, indeed, some cause to apprehend that a foreign power has a finger in the business."

With regard to the proceeding of Miranda, it involved, as agents in his operations, two citizens of New York,— William S. Smith and Samuel G. Ogden. They had provided him a vessel, stores, and armament for the enterprise. Upon being prosecuted at the April Sessions, 1806, of the circuit court of the United States, in their defence they alleged the scheme of the Spanish patriot to have been countenanced by President Jefferson and the members of his cabinet, and they took the legal steps necessary to compel Mr. Madison and Mr. Robert Smith, official advisers of the national executive, to attend the trial as witnesses on their behalf. The liability of these constitutional and confidential functionaries to be drawn away by judicial process from their public duties, and to be made to disclose consultations with their colleagues, was thought open to question. Mr. Robert Smith, on the 29th May, 1806, wrote to Mr. Dallas:

"Yesterday, in great form, the heads of department were summoned to appear in New York on the fourteenth of July, as witnesses in the cases against Ogden and Smith. These two defendants say they want much the benefit of our testimony. We will be, I suspect, not a little puzzled as to the course proper to be pursued. The attorney-general has, I am this moment informed, given to the President an opinion that the members of his cabinet *are not amenable to such process, and that we ought not to attend.* On the one hand, we see the supremacy of the law; on the other hand, we see the inconveniences and injuries to the nation from the suspension of the operations of government. Will your numerous and important professional engagements allow you some time to look into the books for cases applicable to the question and to give me the result? I would not, my good sir, ask you to take for me such trouble if I had here a library.* In your communication you will be pleased to state to me the duties of the marshal of this district, in case he should have an attachment against us, and the legal consequences to him in case he should, from the orders of the President, verbal or written, not execute it."

---

* Mr. Smith, in addition to the secretaryship of the navy, had held the office of attorney-general of the United States from March to December, 1805.

The attorney-general referred to in this letter was John Breckenridge, the grandfather of the recent Vice-President of the United States. He was a lawyer of acknowledged ability and eminence. Mr. Robert Smith says that he had been that moment "*informed*" that the attorney-general's opinion was that the members of the President's cabinet are "not amenable to such process and that we ought not to attend." This was probably a misapprehension, as to the precise point involved in the inquiry. The attorney-general had undoubtedly as early as the 18th of March preceding looked upon the meditated defence of Smith and Ogden as "wholly inadmissible," or "if admissible, as wholly ineffectual;" and the informant of Mr. Robert Smith remembering *this*, erroneously deemed it equivalent to advice against the process and against obedience to it. See Gilpin's Opinions of the Attorneys-General, p. 98.

Mr. Dallas replied to Mr. Robert Smith by transmitting the following:

NOTES.

"*The U. S. vs. Smith & Ogden.*

"I. This is a criminal prosecution under the act of the 5th June, 1794.

"1. In all *criminal prosecutions* the accused has a right to *compulsory process* for obtaining witnesses in his favor.*

"2. The writ of *subpœna*, with an *attachment*, if it is personally served and not obeyed, is the *compulsory process* generally contemplated by the law on such occasions; but it also has been decided in the circuit court of the Pennsylvania district, that the accused has a right as well as the prosecutor to exact a recognizance from his witnesses, binding them to appear and testify.

"3. And subpœnas for witnesses who may be required to attend a court of the United States, in any district, may run into any other district.

"4. There are statute provisions for taking the depositions of witnesses *in civil cases* instead of compelling their personal attendance when they reside at certain distances from the proper seat of justice, or are about to leave the United States, or are ancient and infirm. These provisions do not, however, extend to *criminal cases*.

"II. This being a criminal prosecution, and the party accused being entitled to a subpœna, it necessarily follows, as a general rule,

---

* Am. Const., Art. 8.

that every person, within the jurisdiction of the court, who is duly served with the process is bound to obey it.

" 1. Subpœnas for witnesses who may be required to attend a court of the United States in any district, may run into any other district, with a limitation applicable only to civil cases. Every person residing within any district of the United States is, therefore, in criminal prosecutions, amenable by a subpœna to the jurisdiction of every federal court of every district.

" 2. There is a dictum in Mathews *vs.* Post that 'witnesses may be examined before a judge by leave of court, as well in criminal cases as in civil, where a sufficient reason appears, as going to sea, etc., and then the other side may cross-examine them ;' but the dictum is not satisfactory in itself, imports the consent of the party who requires the evidence ; and the depositions could not be read if the witnesses remained within the jurisdiction of the court at the time of the trial.

" 3. In Moystin *vs.* Fabrigas,* Lord Mansfield states the only accommodation that can be afforded in a criminal prosecution where a material witness for the defendant resides out of the jurisdiction of the court. 'If,' says the judge, ' the defendant wants the testimony of witnesses whom he cannot compel to attend, the court may do what the court did in the case of the criminal prosecution of a woman who had received a pension as an officer's widow, and it was charged in the indictment that she never was married to him. She alleged a marriage in Scotland, but that she could not compel her witnesses to come up and give evidence. The court obliged the prosecutor to consent that the witnesses might be examined before any of the judges of the court of session, or any of the barons of the court of exchequer in Scotland, and that the depositions so taken should be read at the trial. And they declared that they would put off the trial of the indictment from time to time unless the prosecutor had so consented.'

" 4. The above shows the remedy for the defendant. A case decided in the circuit court of the Pennsylvania district shows that similar terms will be imposed on a defendant applying for the postponement of his trial. A. B. was indicted for murder on the high seas. He had neglected to bind his witnesses over, and moved for the postponement upon an affidavit of their materiality and their absence. The court granted the motion with the express condition that the depositions of the witnesses for the prosecution (seafaring men) should be taken, to be read at all events in evidence at the trial.

---

* Cowp., 174, 175.

"III. Such being the general rule, is there any positive privilege, or implied exemption, which furnishes an exception to it?

"1. The senators and representatives of the United States are privileged in all cases, except treason, felony, and breach of the peace, from *arrest* during their attendance in Congress. This privilege, however, has never been deemed to operate as a dispensation from the obligations of a witness. The comity of one department of the government towards another may, indeed, induce a court of justice to send a letter to the speaker or the witness, instead of a subpœna; and if a collision of public duties should prevent an immediate attendance, the trial would probably for that cause be postponed. But in a criminal prosecution no other expedient could be adopted without the consent of the party accused. The practice in England, and the practice in the United States, correspond substantially on this point.*

"2. There is not any constitutional or legislative provision declaratory of a similar privilege in favor of the President or the auxiliary officers of the executive department, any more than in favor of the judges. Whether it is not implied on principles of public policy, and on a parity of reasoning, that the President (chosen by the people and constantly occupied with public business which no one else can perform) should be privileged to the same extent as the senators and representatives, is a question not easy, nor necessary, for the present to be decided; but his case is certainly distinguishable from the case of the auxiliary officers whom he voluntarily constituted a cabinet council, and whose places, whether in their own departments or in his council, he can, at pleasure, vacate and supply. On principle, and from experience, such officers cannot be considered as exempted even from the ordinary process of law, in suits for debts or torts.

"3. In England there is no such exemption claimed for the privy council or the cabinet of the monarch. From many instances take the following: In the King *vs.* Horne, for a libel on the government, in the year 1774, Lord George Germaine and other cabinet ministers were subpœnaed by the defendant. In the King *vs.* Horn Tooke, for high treason, in 1794, Mr. Pitt, the prime minister, was subpœnaed and examined by the defendant.†

"In the case of the ship Columbus, the judge of the high court of admiralty, speaking of an order of the privy council dispensing with the operation of a statute (for a copy of which order frequent applications had been made to government), uses the fol-

---

* See United States *vs.* T. Cooper, pp. 8, 9, 14, 15.
† 11 State Trials.

lowing strong language applicable perhaps in principle to the present question : ' In any cause where the crown is a party, it is to be observed that the crown can no more withhold evidence of documents in its possession than a private person. If the court thinks proper to order the production of any public instrument, that order must be obeyed. It wants no insignia of an authority derived from the crown. The order will enforce itself; for, if a party suing refuses to produce a necessary document, what follows ?—he shall take nothing by his petition.'

" 4. But in America there is likewise some judicial authority upon the subject. In the United States *vs.* Cooper, the defendant issued a subpœna for a number of members of Congress, for Timothy Pickering, then Secretary of State, and for Jacob Wagner, his chief clerk, who attended in obedience to the process. In the same case, the court refused to issue a subpœna to the President ; but not on the ground of privilege, or exemption. On the contrary, the judge expressly stated : ' It is not upon the objection of privilege that we have refused this subpœna. This court will do its duty against any man, however elevated his situation may be. You have mistaken the ground. We are of opinion that in the case of a prosecution for a libel to bring the President of the United States into contempt, he cannot be compelled to appear at all. When the clerk of the court applied for advice he was informed that he acted very properly in refusing the subpœna, and that Mr. Cooper ought to know that the President could not be subpœnaed, he being a party in the cause.'

" IV. Thus, every person within the United States is amenable, in a criminal prosecution, by subpœna, to the jurisdiction of a federal court, whatever may be his office in the legislative, executive, or judicial departments. But, independent of the remarks already made relative to members of Congress, these considerations must not be omitted :

" 1. The court issuing the subpœna will exercise its judgment upon any reasons offered for the witnesses not attending at the time of trial, or for their not attending at all. If there exist a temporary collision of public duties, legislative, executive, or judicial, on the information of the attorney of the district, the disobedience would not be regarded as a contempt. If the competency and materiality of the witnesses on the issue to be tried did not sufficiently appear, the subpœna might be deemed irregular, and an attachment would not issue for disobedience.

" 2. The necessity of obeying the subpœna does not involve a necessity of giving evidence on points of a political and confidential character, arising from the official relation between the heads of departments and the President. ' Where the heads of the departments are the political or confidential agents of the executive, merely to execute the will of the President, or rather to act in cases in which the executive possesses a constitutional or legal discretion, nothing can be more perfectly clear than that their acts are only politically examinable. But where a specific duty is assigned by law, and individual rights depend upon the performance of that duty, it seems equally clear that the individual who considers himself injured, has a right to resort to the laws of his country for a remedy.'"

These "notes" were highly acceptable to Mr. Smith, who, in a subsequent letter of the 9th of June, 1806, spoke of them as ably supporting the attitude he alone had taken in the cabinet on the question they reviewed. He seems to have been so much strengthened by their clear and systematic result that he was unable to avoid an additional call upon their author in a series of questions respecting other legal points.

It would be difficult to imagine a state of political party more fierce and unchecked than the one which raged about this time. The intemperance which characterized the epoch of what has been known as our "*Reign of Terror*," at the close of Mr. John Adams's presidency, was augmented by the bitterness always incident to the sudden alienation of former associates. During the struggle to stem the torrent, sustained gallantly by the Constitutional Republicans, the unbridled licentiousness of the press seems to have spurned all limit or restraint. An audacious wholesale libel, called "*The Quid Mirror*," set an example of private personal defamation altogether exceeding former experience. How far these malignant slanders affected Mr. Dallas, it is difficult to say. Undoubtedly of a warm temperament and occasionally irritable, he was yet never heard to utter an expression of hatred or a wish for revenge. His surprise at the inventive hardihood of the calumniator was generally the only apparent reception it obtained from him; yet, sometimes mortification, and sometimes scornful defiance, shaded his countenance. Few men have endured a greater amount of virulent attack, and in relation to very few was it ever less warranted by personal demeanor or official conduct. Although himself incapable of degrading his pen, his speech, or his heart to anything of the sort, he knew well the detraction to which inferior souls were prone to lend their narrow powers. Into his proceedings

as a public agent he challenged scrutiny, and was deaf to
invective. Yet, though perhaps still brighter in the family
circle, he vibrated with acute sensibility at the least insinuation against his domestic character. This seeming
contrariety needs no explanation to generous minds. It
is a simple and not an unpleasant task to vindicate official
probity and skill; but no one can, without extreme reluctance, even for the mere purpose of exculpation, osten-
tatiously parade his own social virtues, or expose the
tender privacy of his home. As the servant of the people
he could point at once, and with pride, to the vouchers
of his purity; but as a husband, father, or friend, the
evidences of his value were too delicate to be so treated.
Fortunately, he was known and respected in these relations so extensively and well, that his unscrupulous assail-
ants rarely felt encouragement for attacks whose falsity
and malice would be glaring.

Mr. Madison was inaugurated President on the 4th of
March, 1809. Although any attempt to delineate the
measures of his administration would be misplaced here,
and will be avoided, yet, as Mr. Dallas, at a subsequent
period, became a member of his cabinet, it would seem
indispensable to a just appreciation of that step that at
least a cursory recurrence to leading circumstances should
be had.

A very general belief prevailed among the people of
the United States that a war with Great Britain had become necessary to maintain the national interests and
honor. Mr. Jefferson had gone, in a policy of forbearance
and seclusion, steadily pursued for eight years, as far as
the public spirit could bear. He accomplished nothing.
The aggressions upon our rights were as numerous and
as arrogant as ever. It was time to turn and stand at
bay.

Hence, soon after Congress had convened on the 27th
of November, 1809, a calm observer could not fail to note
a tendency towards military preparation. The joint legislative resolution, too, which denounced as " highly indecorous and insolent," and as "a direct and aggravated
insult and affront to the American people and their
government," certain conduct of the minister plenipotentiary of his Britannic Majesty, coupled with a pledge "to
call into action the whole force of the nation should it

become necessary," strongly evinced the universal sensibility. While the President was directed to announce by proclamation any revocation or modification of the orders in council which violated our neutral commerce, acts were passed to raise more regular forces, to organize fifty thousand volunteers, to equip new vessels of war, to call upon the State executives to hold in readiness an aggregate of one hundred thousand militia, to enlarge the corps of engineers, and to establish an ordnance department.

Notwithstanding these manifestations, which in truth, though publicly, were also quietly made, when Congress, on the 18th of June, 1812, declared war to exist, our enemy was measurably taken by surprise. The campaigns of 1813 and 1814, marked by alternations of success and defeat, were on the whole calculated to gratify the pride of our people, and to abate the despondency incident to an empty treasury, aggravated by plots of secession at Hartford. On the ocean, the theatre of our chief grievances, we had dispelled the pretension of British invincibility; the Great Lakes had witnessed several signal triumphs of our flag; and the gallantry of our officers and soldiers had ceased to be doubted. In another campaign, with finances resolutely handled, and means vigorously applied to the exigencies of the struggle, we might accomplish still more.

When Mr. Gallatin and Mr. Bayard left the United States, in May, 1813, to associate themselves with Mr. J. Q. Adams in forming a joint embassy at St. Petersburg, having for its purpose the negotiation of a peace under the mediation of the Czar Alexander, the Treasury Department, according to what was then understood to be legally permitted, had been placed in charge of the Secretary of the Navy, in the expectation of Mr. Gallatin's early return to it. His protracted detention abroad, however, led Mr. Madison earnestly to invite Mr. Dallas to that important post by letter dated the 1st of February, 1814. Among other reasons for declining the proffer, he seems to have thought that as yet the measure of delay was not adequate to the delicacy with which Mr. Gallatin might, under all the circumstances, expect to be treated. The resignation of Mr. William Pinkney, attorney-general, was mentioned at the same time, and his choice between the two stations urgently requested.

"My dear Sir,—I hasten to acknowledge the receipt of your letter of the 1st current. I feel with unaffected sensibility the proofs which your letter affords of the President's confidence and kindness; nor could ambition lead me to any higher gratification than that of being associated in public business with Mr. Madison, Mr. Monroe, and yourself.

"But, notwithstanding my disposition to meet a wish so obligingly expressed, by the sacrifice of every personal consideration, I must at once decline the secretary's office. Many of the reasons which enforce this decision you already know; and you will give me credit for others which it would, perhaps, be improper to express.

"In the office of attorney-general I might hope to serve the government, and to indulge my domestic and professional views, if a permanent residence at Washington had not been made indispensable. Upon that condition it is impossible that I should accept the office.

"I pray you, therefore, my dear sir, to present an apology for me to the President, and to impress on his mind a conviction of the sincerity of my grateful acknowledgments.

"You will believe me on all occasions to be

"Your affectionate friend and servant,

"A. J. Dallas.

"Hon. W. Jones, Secretary of the Navy.

"3d February, 1814."

Mr. George W. Campbell was appointed on the 9th of February, 1814; but this gentleman soon desired to be relieved from so arduous and augmenting a responsibility. It was then that Mr. Dallas was apprised, for the second time, that the President was more anxious than ever for his co-operation in the cabinet. He hesitated. Our finances have, almost without exception, been superintended by distinguished members of the bar. And yet there is no occupation of civil life more injuriously affected by a prolonged intermission than legal practice. He had no fortune. His generous hospitality precluded accumulation even from the profits of his profession, although they exceeded annually twenty thousand dollars. The salary attached to the offered department was comparatively insignificant. He looked around upon his family, and, as has been said, he hesitated.

But he was too buoyant to continue depressed by personal considerations. The national ones weighed heavily and persuasively upon his reflections. He had early identified himself with the eminent statesmen of the Republican party, whose course of measures he upheld; and he was reluctant to disclaim the duty of standing loyally by them on so emergent an occasion. Only two years before, the expediency of invigorating the government by drawing Mr. Jefferson into its circle again had been devised, and he had then written eagerly in approval:

"19 September, 1812.

"The times are critical. Nothing could be more *apropos* than the appearance of Mr. Jefferson once more upon the field of active politics. The event would demonstrate the highest sense of patriotism on his part, and on the part of the people would insure confidence and energy. There is at present an evident anxiety among the best friends of the administration; and a mere change of men seems to promise relief to our feverish Republicans, as a change of posture flatters the pains of the bedridden patient. The re-election of Mr. Madison is, under any circumstances, certain; but, with the aid of Mr. Jefferson's popularity, we shall make assurance double sure, and take a bond of fate. I do not, however, relish the retreat of Mr. Monroe from the cabinet. He has not only the talents but the good fortune to command general esteem and approbation as a patriot and a statesman. My consolation will be that he continues in the public service, and that when his sword has triumphed his pen will be resumed. Of the other departments of government, you see what is written, but you do not perhaps hear all that is said. Our friends Eustis and Hamilton must do something great and brilliant to meet the public demand, and to redeem the pledges of their own character. If the woods should not soon present us with an antidote for the cowardice or defection of a general, and the waters should not shine with the effects of the glorious example of our *naval* Hull, depend upon it the people will complain that the capacity to wage war does not correspond with the spirit that declared it. Do think *well*, and think *always*, on this subject at Washington."

He was much affected too, in his decision, by discovering, through a host of correspondents in the chief marts of business, money, and commerce, that, as soon as Mr. Madison's disposition to summon him was rumored, great anxiety prevailed lest he should decline the appointment. Capitalists at that juncture, not numerous but vastly important,—the Grays, Primes, Astors, Barkers, Girards, Parrishes, Olivers, Buchanans,—eagerly expressed their

confidence in his character and ability, and augured the
most favorable results to the public credit and securities
if he entered the treasury. It was impressive to be told,
as he was told, by those whose fortunes were at hazard
and whose feelings were keenest, that he had it in his
power to reanimate the federal finances and to rekindle
their own inclination to contribute, at that gloomy period,
to the support of government.

He was not blind to the herculean nature of the task.
With all its obvious dangers and embarrassments, it was
also to him novel and untried. To ward off anticipated
bankruptcy; to satisfy the public creditors, alarmed and
clamorous; to meet the numberless demands of the military establishment, with coffers already drained and a
currency depreciated, dishonored, and worthless,—seemed
to require the attainments and skill of an adept. How
was the raw recruit to encounter and overcome terrors
which had driven the veteran from the field? It was,
nevertheless, the forlorn-hope, whose hazard and difficulty faded when contrasted with the glory of possible
success; and on the event of which it seemed a sacred
duty of patriotism to risk fame, fortune, and life.

A few days after he had communicated his determination to the President, he wrote to Mr. Rush (then attorney-
general) the following letter:

"7 October, 1814.

"My dear Sir,—The kindness of my friends affords the only
relief from the consciousness of the very hazardous and perhaps indiscreet step which I have consented to take. Those
who consider my present situation in the profession, and who
know the superlative enjoyments of my domestic scene, will not
ascribe to me a motive of interest or ambition. But even they
will doubt the correctness of my judgment while they approve
the public motives which can alone account for my conduct.
There are others who will arraign me in every way from party,
possibly from personal excitements. These must be answered by
my actions; and I will not despair, but that with good intentions,
and the co-operation of good men, I may, through toil and
trouble, perform some service for the State. On your attachment I implicitly rely.

"My son George surprised the family last night on his way
from Ghent to Washington. We passed only an hour with him;
and he proceeded, if not to surprise, to animate the legislative
patriots, who are fortunately assembled on the Potomac.

" Tell our friend Ingersoll that I expect great comfort and support from him.

" I am, dear sir, very sincerely and affectionately yours,

"A. J. DALLAS."

His nomination had been confirmed by the Senate on the day of the date of this letter.

Congress had met on the nineteenth of September, and were engaged in perfecting measures connected with the war. Notwithstanding the conciliatory disposition manifested by the American cabinet, who had embraced, without hesitation, the proffered mediation of the Russian emperor, and who subsequently sent a numerous embassy to Ghent, little or no hope was entertained of an early termination of hostilities. The latest information, indeed, reaching this country immediately prior to the departure of Mr. Dallas for Washington, gave reason to believe that the British ministry were resolved to prolong the strife, in the expectation of ultimately triumphing through our fomented dissensions or by our fiscal debility. In general opinion, peace seemed farther removed than ever; and the necessity of raising additional armies and launching additional fleets became as obvious as was the total incapacity of the treasury to supply their wants. The dismal disorder of the currency, the panic of impending bankruptcy pervading our moneyed corporations and introducing evils worse than those they desired to avoid, the impracticability of forwarding funds from and to distant points, and the consequent failure on the part of the executive everywhere to meet the public engagements, inspired a dread that our finances were beyond the reach of extrication, and must soon plunge into chaotic ruin. The solid resources of a rich and patriotic people were as yet undiminished, almost untouched; but it was evident that circumstances had conspired to obstruct their flow, keeping them stagnant and useless.

The spirit and practice of economy were fastened upon the federal government under the auspices of Mr. Jefferson. He strove hard so to reduce the taxation of this republican country that it should be almost insensible to its citizens. For many years the far greater portion of our national income was drawn from the charges upon alien commerce; and while the pacific inclinations of the

President were allowed to remain undisturbed, the industry and enterprise of the mercantile class made this item of receipt adequate to the wants and objects of our political union. A system, however, founded upon foreign trade, was dependent upon the continuation of peace. This great Democratic statesman took with him into the presidential office theories and plans admirably adapted to the United States at the time of his election. Alike the scrutinizing philosopher and the forecasting patriot, he was inflexible against every expenditure not plainly indispensable, and against the disturbing and impoverishing complications of external war. All his financial arrangements bore this stamp. His success was followed by applause and by increased popularity. His Republican disciples perceived in the course adopted the true means for extending and perpetuating their party ascendency, as the people at large could not but feel and own the blessings it diffused. Nevertheless, they who had the wisdom and virtue to inculcate and exemplify such a principle of administration might well depart from it on a coerced change of circumstances, without fearing to be taunted with inconsistency, and without endangering in the least their acquired reputation. History teems with political epochs at which wealth lost its value, or retained it only by being lavished on superior objects. War always creates such an epoch. But the magical results achieved by Mr. Jefferson had produced too deep an impression, and even Mr. Gallatin, whose ability and skill no one doubted or doubts, acknowledged a faltering reluctance, resembling superstitious dread, at every step deviating from his accustomed path.

The new secretary had reflected and decided upon his course. It was exceedingly at variance with current prejudices and plans. On the 17th of October, 1814, "at the moment," he says, "of entering upon the duties of office," he addressed a letter to the Committee of Ways and Means, of which the son-in-law of Mr. Jefferson, Mr. Eppes, was chairman, and then, at the very start, he unfolded distinctly the scheme of vigorous action he intended to pursue. (*Appendix No. 4.*) He told them that the state of the finances could not be ascribed to the want of resources or of integrity in the nation, but arose clearly from *inadequate taxation* and from *an absence of the means adapted to anticipate, collect, and distribute revenue;* that the *wealth* of the nation had been untouched by government, and its *faith,* heretofore relied upon; and that a prompt and resolute application of its resources would relieve every embarrassment.

"It would be vain to attempt to disguise, and it would be pernicious to palliate the difficulties which are now to be overcome. The exigencies of the government require a supply of treasure for the prosecution of the war beyond any amount which it would be politic, even if it were practicable, to raise by an immediate and constant imposition of taxes. There must therefore be a resort to credit for a considerable portion of the supply. But the public credit is at this juncture so depressed that no hope of adequate succor on moderate terms can safely rest upon it. Hence it becomes the object, first and last, in every practical scheme of finance, to reanimate the confidence of the citizens, and to impress on the mind of every man, who for the public account renders services, furnishes supplies, or advances money, a conviction of the punctuality as well as of the security of the government."

He then proceeded to press upon the committee the establishment of a national bank, operating upon credit, combined with capital, as the only efficient remedy for the immensely disordered condition of the circulating medium. And after fully detailing, under six heads of substantive *propositions,* the specific measures from which relief might be certainly and speedily derived, he strives to remove from the project of a bank the constitutional objection by the following course of remark, subsequently, in one of his messages, adopted and repeated by President Madison as entirely just and satisfactory:

"In making a proposition for the establishment of a national bank, I cannot be insensible to the high authority of the names which have appeared in opposition to that measure upon constitutional grounds. It would be presumptuous to conjecture that the sentiments which actuated the opposition have passed away; and yet it would be denying to experience a great practical advantage were we to suppose that a difference of times and circumstances would not produce a corresponding difference in the opinions of the wisest as well as of the purest men. But in the present case, a change of private opinion is not material to the success of the proposition for establishing a national bank. In the administration of human affairs there must be a period when discussion shall cease, and decision shall become absolute.

A diversity of opinion may honorably survive the contest; but upon the genuine principles of a representative government, the opinion of the majority can alone be carried into action. The judge who dissents from the majority of the bench changes not his opinion, but performs his duty, when he enforces the judgment of the court, although it is contrary to his own convictions. An oath to support the constitution and laws is not, therefore, an oath to support them under all circumstances according to the opinion of the individual who takes it, but it is emphatically an oath to support them according to the interpretation of the legitimate authorities. . . . When, therefore, we have marked the existence of a national bank for a period of twenty years, with all the sanctions of the legislative, executive and judicial authorities; when we have seen the dissolution of one institution. and heard a loud and continued call for the establishment of another; when, under these circumstances, neither Congress nor the several States have resorted to the power of amendment,—can it be deemed a violation of the right of private opinion to consider the constitutionality of a national bank as a question forever settled and at rest? But, after all, I should not merit the confidence which it will be my ambition to acquire, if I were to suppress the declaration of an opinion that, in these times, the establishment of a national bank will not only be useful in promoting the general welfare, but that it is necessary and proper for carrying into execution some of the most important powers constitutionally vested in the government."

This paper, submitted immediately to Congress and the country, produced a powerful impression. Its combined ability, courage, and directness were universally extolled. Some, to be sure, would have wished the weakness of the situation less nakedly exposed, while others deemed that very intrepidity of development a rare official excellence. A few timid Republicans winced under its demand for taxation and a bank, but the great body of their party gave a cheerful adhesion to what was so necessary to the success of the war and the credit of the government. The secretary's position as a financier, full of the resources of talent and of high moral energy, could not, after this act, be shaded by the slightest doubt or misgiving. What was said of William Pitt when, in February, 1781, he made his first speech in the House of Commons, may be thought to apply: "Never were higher expectations formed of any person upon his first coming into Parliament, and never were expectations more completely fulfilled. Not only did he please,—it may be said that he astonished the House."*

Having thus taken his attitude, Mr. Dallas hastened to send to Congress a series of admirable papers, facilitating and expediting the measures he had recommended. That usually slow body seems to have been suddenly roused, as by the sound of a trumpet, into activity and confidence, for in six weeks—on the second of December—he felt himself justified in alluding to the promising change already achieved:

"I derive great satisfaction in reflecting upon the inevitable and immediate effect of the legislative sanction (even so far as it has already been given) to a settled and productive system of taxes for defraying the expenses of government and maintaining the public credit. This policy, embracing in its course the introduction of a national circulating medium and the proper facilities for anticipating, collecting, and distributing the public revenue, will at once enliven the public credit, and even the existing resources of the present quarter must ripen and expand under an influence so auspicious."

During the months of November and December, 1814, Mr. Dallas gave a remarkable proof of the facility with which he could transfer the powers of his mind from one important subject to another; while he was straining every nerve at the department to secure within his grasp the means indispensable to the military operations of the next campaign, he quietly devoted nearly all the hours of every night at Mrs. Wilson's boarding-house in writing a manifesto or appeal to the world against the conduct of Great Britain. (*Appendix No. 5.*) This justly celebrated paper obtained the unqualified praise of President Madison, who proposed its adoption by the cabinet as the act of the American government. It would soon have issued under this high sanction (and indeed some copies of it had already left the printer's), when, in the early part of January, 1815, the news that a peace had been signed at Ghent reached the country. Mr. Madison, always prudent and forbearing, then deemed it wiser to withhold from the publication any official stamp. The production, now entitled "*An Exposition of the Causes and Character of*

---

* Stanhope's Life of Pitt.

the War," reviewed, in reference to all the points in controversy between the two nations, the uniform and consistent positions and pretensions of the United States, from the administration of Washington through those of his three successors. It is untinged by the slightest coloring of political party; its statements of fact are verified with exactness by citations at the foot of every page; its diction is of the calm and clear style of Sir William Temple's diplomacy; and its reasoning, though not allowed to stop short of conclusiveness, is never pushed beyond its fair and legitimate limits. Even on the glowing topics of impressment at sea and the barbarities which marked the track of British warfare, on land or water, there is evidently a jealous exclusion of zeal or temper. This great work may be said to have closed in argument, as the battle at New Orleans closed in arms, the war of 1812. No attempt, we believe, has ever been made at refutation. We are told, with what truth we cannot say, that when one of the escaped copies reached London it was read by the author's veteran and inveterate detractor, William Cobbett, who exclaimed, as he threw the pamphlet on his desk, "It is unanswerable; I challenge any British statesman or author to answer it."

Mr. Monroe, the Secretary of State, had been assigned to fill also the Department of War, when General Armstrong withdrew immediately after the defeat at Bladensburg and the arson of the capitol. As soon as the treaty of peace was ratified by the Senate, on the 17th of February, 1815, Congress hastened to invest the President with authority to reduce the army, then consisting of 60,000 men, to a peace establishment of 10,000, and to direct that he should so "*arrange*" the existing officers and privates as out of them to form and complete the new force, discharging all others from the service. This reduction must unavoidably be a matter alike delicate and perplexing. Our soldiers, during two campaigns, had fought their way to popular favor. The nation was proud of the prowess and skill exhibited both north and south. Many of the gallant men were really incapacitated by their wounds from further military duty, and yet would bravely refuse to be so regarded. Conflicts as to rank, lineal and brevet, had to be permanently settled. However, be the responsibility what it might, the task must be performed. The law had begun to operate on the 4th of March, 1815. In about ten days afterwards, Mr. Monroe left Washington for his residence in Albemarle to recover his impaired health; and on the fifteenth, by appointment of the President, Mr. Dallas formally entered the War Department, at once and resolutely beginning the painful operation.

The generous dispositions with which this new labor was assumed are attested by the following brief preliminary notes :

To the President.

" DEAR SIR,—Conversing with Mr. Monroe and Mr. Crowninshield,* we agreed that some attention should be paid to our gallant officers, when vacancies in civil stations occurred.

" I have just suggested to Mr. Monroe that it would be well to offer General Brown the rank in the army and the vacant naval office in New York at the same time. If he declines the latter, then to offer it to General Wilkinson as a comfortable retreat. I send Mr. Monroe's answer. Mr. Crowninshield concurs with us. In this course I think your feelings will be gratified, on many occasions, while the organization of the army will be rendered more easy and satisfactory.

" The naval officer has nothing to do with money.

" I am very faithfully, sir, your most obedient servant,

"A. J. DALLAS.

" 13 March, 1815."

To Mr. Dallas.

" DEAR SIR,—I approve most cordially your suggestion in both its aspects. By offering both offices to Brown, at the same time, you enlist him in support of the *veteran* for the naval office, in case he accepts the other.

" Sincerely your friend,

"JAMES MONROE.

" March 13, 1815.

" Approved (after conclusion of the court-martial at Troy).

"J. M."

With a view to secure the best information as to the merits and services of individuals, and to keep the proceeding as far as possible within the line of military action, a board of officers high in rank and character was formed

---

* On the resignation of Mr. Jones, he had been appointed Secretary of the Navy the 17th of December, 1814.

by the secretary. He instructed them as to the points on which they were to confer and investigate; and he required from them a full report of their acts and conclusions in reference to the new organization. The results of these joint labors were made known to the country by publication, on the 23d May, 1815. These documents we have esteemed worthy of preservation (*Appendix No.* 6), for they best show the skill and justice with which an ungracious but necessary operation was conducted. Some discontent vented itself in clamorous appeals by disarranged sufferers,—that was unavoidable and anticipated; but the sentiment of the nation sympathized with the considerate delicacy exhibited towards patriotic defenders, and the judgment of the nation was satisfied. Mr. Madison appreciated as it deserved the great public service thus rendered, and used in a letter addressed to Mr. Dallas on the 24th of May, 1815, from Montpelier, language of warm approval.

"The *Military Budget* makes its appearance in the *National Intelligencer*. I cannot refer to it without expressing my obligations for the laborious task it has cost you, and my gratification that you are at length relieved from it. Besides the labor, the task has been distinguished by the delicate questions involved in it touching the comparative pretensions of meritorious individuals. That there will be an unanimous approbation of what has been done is not to be expected. But I persuade myself that the candid and reasonable part of the public, taking into view the arduous nature of the duty, and the propriety of blending with a reward for past services a provision for future ones, will be more than merely satisfied with the execution of the law."

As the summer of 1815 advanced, Mr. Dallas prepared to effect two other official objects of much interest. On the 23d of February, the House of Representatives had called, by an adopted resolution, upon the Secretary of the Treasury to report at the next session a digested *tariff* of duties upon imported merchandise. He felt too the necessity of great labor in order perfectly to command and methodically to arrange the multifarious subjects for the elaborate view of the national finances he contemplated taking in his *annual report* to Congress. These two matters engaged every moment of his time not occupied by the current routine of business. To perfect the first,

10

a tariff, he invited and obtained a flood of communications
from merchants and manufacturers in all parts of the
country,—a flood which he discovered to be unmanageable
within the period allowed to it, and which he determined,
after settling in his own mind its leading deductions,
should be postponed for completion to an early day subsequent to the annual report. The papers* described are
among the most eloquent as well as useful ones of his pro-
lific pen. The annual report attracted almost unqualified
eulogy. One correspondent, an eminent manufacturer,
says: "Few papers I have seen are entitled to rank with
the treasury report. It is a perspicuous statement of an
immense and intricate subject of primary importance to
the nation; in short, those who read can understand it,
and it will receive approbation from minds prone to find
fault; indeed, as the good folks say, 'those who come to
scoff' will stay to pray.'" Another correspondent, distinguished for abilities, writes: "I have read and considered
with very great pleasure your treasury report. It is the
only opportunity I could have had to obtain a clear and
distinct idea of the state of the national debt and financial
system. I, for one, am much indebted to you for the full
development of an intricate subject, which must have required immense labor and great talents to avoid confusion
and preserve perspicuity." And a third: "I have studied,
I assure you, this last volume of your reports with great
pleasure and profit, and I doubt, not to flatter, whether
the arid annals of finance can show a production uniting
so much style with so much substance."

In this paper, distinguished not more by beauty of
"style" than by distinctness and precision, Mr. Dallas renewed to Congress generally the recommendation he had
made by letter to the Committee of Ways and Means the
year before for the establishment of a national bank. His
prior *projet* had been displaced by an essentially different
scheme, pushed hastily into favor under the ardent eloquence of Mr. Calhoun. For a short time he thought
this failure released him from the duty of any further
effort to remedy the financial evils incident to the war,
and he frankly stated his determination to withdraw from

---

* See Niles' Register, February 24, 1816, page 437, etc.; December 21,
1816, page 261, etc.

the treasury. But the President had, by message to Congress on the 30th of January, 1815, refused his assent to the measure of Mr. Calhoun; that measure was not strong enough to enlist a two-thirds vote against the veto; and when the secretary warmed amid the details of his annual report, he resolved on another trial to accomplish what he had repeatedly declared to be necessary. It will be remembered that the charter of this moneyed corporation became a law on the 10th of April, 1816, and expired, by its own limitation, on the 4th of March, 1836. A similar success attended the new tariff of duties on imports, which he presented to the consideration of the House of Representatives on the 12th of February, 1816, and which became law on the 27th of April. It is observable that this act was voted for by all the Southern States, on the ground that, having supported the war, they were under a corresponding obligation to sustain establishments which grew out of it.*

The election of a President for the eighth term was now approaching. Shortly before the adjournment of Congress on the 30th of April, the then customary caucus of its Republican members was convened, and Mr. Monroe selected for nomination as the candidate of his party. The choice was in every respect most agreeable to Mr. Dallas, and he drew from it the happy augury for the country suggested by an intimate knowledge of Mr. Monroe's experience in public affairs, well-balanced judgment, and manly integrity of character. He had, however, determined to withdraw from public life; perfectly satisfied that peace being restored and all the necessary measures adopted, the tide of prosperity would rapidly swell in. Early in April he conveyed his purpose by letter to Mr. Madison:

"As it is not my intention to pass another winter in Washington, I think it a duty to give you an opportunity to select a successor for the office of Secretary of the Treasury, during the present session of Congress. I will cheerfully remain, however, if you desire it, to put the national bank into motion,—presuming that this object can be effected before the 1st of October next. Permit me, therefore, to tender my resignation, to be accepted on that day, or at any earlier period which you may find more con-

---

* Calhoun, in Senate on 15th February, 1833.

venient to yourself, or more advantageous to the public. With every affectionate wish for your honor, health, and happiness,

"I am," etc.

The President's reply was as follows:

"DEAR SIR,—I have received your letter of yesterday, communicating your purpose of resigning the department of the treasury. I need not express to you the regret at such an event which will be inspired by my recollection of the distinguished ability and unwearied zeal with which you have filled a station at all times deeply responsible in its duties, through a period rendering them peculiarly arduous and laborious. Should the intention you have formed be nowise open to reconsideration, I can only avail myself of your consent to prolong your functions to the date and for the object which your letter intimates. It cannot but be advantageous that the important measure in which you have had so material an agency should be put into its active state by the same hands. Be assured, sir, that whatever may be the time of your leaving the department, you will carry from it my testimony of the invaluable services you have rendered your country, my thankfulness for the aid they have afforded in my discharge of the executive trust, and my best wishes for your prosperity and happiness.

"JAMES MADISON.

"April 9, 1816."

Mr. Dallas did not leave his residence on Capitol Hill for his home in Philadelphia until the month of July; nor did he cease his superintendence of the Treasury Department before the day chosen for assuming it by his successor, Mr. W. H. Crawford, the 20th of October. Indeed, even after that date, and until the meeting of Congress, he was in active correspondence with the President in relation to the finances, and prepared several official papers for his use, especially one, obviously designed to be incorporated in the forthcoming annual message, and another, called "Sketches," of which Mr. Madison says in a letter, "it cannot fail to be acceptable to Congress, useful to the public, and honorable under every aspect;" in truth, it constituted an elaborate and lucid exposition of the actual and gratifying condition of the treasury on the 1st of August, 1816.* During this period he felt himself free

* See Niles' Register, December 16, 1815, page 261, etc.

to engage once more in professional practice, and he was impelled to do so by considerations too powerful to be resisted. His expenses on "the Hill" had exhausted his means. He had lived with lavish hospitality, without allowing one thought of his private interests to disturb his public preoccupations. He writes to Mr. Rush on the 6th of August:

"I will not disguise from you that I tremble as the period approaches for my return to the business of the bar. Two years have produced great changes in the profession, and I feel as if I were about to begin the world again. However, my health and spirits continuing, I must leave the issue to Providence, and console myself, whatever it may be, with the consciousness of good motives in the exertion which carried me to Washington."

To Mr. Madison he wrote, on the 11th of September:

"Of myself I can only speak with care and doubt, when I reflect upon the effect of two years' absence from the bar to obstruct and embarrass my return."

On the 18th of September, finding that he had been nominated by the Democratic conferees for Congress, he says to Mr. Leiper, chairman of that body:

"Be so good as to express my best thanks for this mark of esteem and confidence, and to inform the conferees that as the acceptance of a seat in Congress will be incompatible with the arrangement which I have made for resuming the practice of my profession, I must respectfully decline being a candidate for that honor."

His apprehensions were soon proved to be unfounded, for on the 7th of December he was able to tell his correspondent, the attorney-general, in a tone of revived confidence:

"I have once more become the drudge of the bar; and since my arrival in Philadelphia I have been engaged in all the important causes tried by Washington and by our supreme court. The German cause,* after a trial of four weeks, ended last night, and this day I take up my pen to salute you."

Putting the finishing touch to the radiance of a career of enlightened patriotism, the President in his message,

---

* Reported in 3 Serg. and Rawle, 29.

sent to Congress on the 3d of December, 1816, spoke of "the late secretary" as follows:

"For a more enlarged view of the public finances, with a view of the measures pursued by the Treasury Department previous to the resignation of the late secretary, I transmit an extract from the last report of that officer. *Congress will perceive in it ample proofs of the solid foundation on which the financial prosperity of the nation rests; and will do justice to the distinguished ability and successful exertions with which the duties of the department were executed during a period remarkable for its difficulties and its peculiar perplexities.*"

These few sentences filled the measure of Mr. Dallas's ambition: they convinced him that he had realized the hope expressed two years before, "I will not despair but that with good intentions and the co-operation of good men, I may, through toil and trouble, perform some service to the State;" and so, in a letter to the same gentleman on the 7th of December, 1816, he exclaims, with warmth:

"I cannot salute you in terms more grateful to you as well as to myself than by speaking of the generous notice which the President has taken of me in his message. To be so praised by such a man! upon such an occasion! I am content. My family are content. And we will say no more of the sacrifice and the slavery of my two years' devotion at Washington."

He had, for many years, been liable to the sudden and severe attacks of a complaint the precise nature of which his two medical advisers failed to penetrate or determine. It would cause immediate and excruciating pain, prostrating as by a resistless blow; and yet, in five or ten minutes, he ceased moaning, accepted an anodyne, and was fully restored. Dr. Wistar, the devoted friend as well as the enlightened physician, conceived it to arise from internal injury referable to the fact of his having been dragged, apparently lifeless, when about seventeen years of age, from the river Thames, and perhaps awkwardly renovated under the auspices of the Humane Society; Dr. Chapman, no less affectionately attached, suspected, but would not pronounce, the disorder to be an irregular form of gout.

While occupied in arguing an important suit at Tren-

ton, before the then governor, and *ex-officio* chancellor, of
New Jersey, Mahlon Dickerson, he became conscious of
the approach of his old and implacable enemy; asked a
short delay, but was obliged to proceed; and concluding
his address, hurriedly drove to his home in Philadelphia,
and on the night of his arrival, the 16th of January, 1817,
died tranquilly while his two sons watched, unaware of
the crisis, at his bedside.

My recollections of my father are still, after the lapse
of near half a century, very vivid, accompanied by the
warmest attachment and deepest veneration. All his
children regarded him as their most delightful companion, instructor, and pride. His labors, in scenes of
business, professional or political, were arduous and unceasing; but his happiness was centred in his domestic
circle. Deriving great pleasure from social intercourse,
he nevertheless preferred that it should be under his own
roof and shared by his family. One of the established
institutions of his household was the "cold cut," or frag-
mentary pretence of supper, which, between ten and
eleven, rallied all the inmates for a lively chat and a
gay "good-night."

He had no hatreds, at least none of which I became
aware, or of whose existence any evidence can be discovered in his multitudinous relics. Certainly, there
were some men whom he disliked and avoided,—whether
owing to contrariety of taste, a wrong suffered, or a
calumny uttered; but the "*odium in longum jacens*" was
foreign to his nature. His irritations were quick and
fugitive.

His facility of thinking, at command, was remarkable.
It did not vary the expression of his countenance, and
was undisturbed by present crowds or noises. He prepared for it by no special posture, no chair of contemplation, no concentrating arrangement of pen, ink, and
paper, no choice even of place; he desired to think, and
the operations of his mind were at once disembarrassed
of all external distraction. He turned from intellectual
toil to mere amusement with equal quickness. Mr. Robert
C. Dallas, writing to me under date of the 18th of August,
1817, mentions an indomitable and perennial vivacity as
his peculiar trait. No labors, however prolonged and
oppressive, kept down the elasticity of his spirits:

"He left the pondering brow in his study, and his overpowering eloquence was reserved for public occasions; when with his family or friends, he seemed as if he had nothing to do but to amuse himself and others; extremely playful, versifying with great facility, and descending even to the merriment of puns. I have known him writing and making up accounts for his uncle, Mr. Gray, during the holidays and after he left school, for the greater part of the twenty-four hours, often up till five o'clock in the morning and getting sleep only by snatches, yet all alive, keeping up the ball of gaiety and mirth throughout the household."

This delightful characteristic never left him. Shortly before his death, in writing to a friend at Washington on a matter of grave import, he yet concludes his letter: "And tell Maria that when we meet I have a budget of conundrums for her!"

He had a perceptible, though never an obtrusive, pride of personal appearance and movement. To this the fashions of the day and his own figure contributed. Very little, if at all, short of six feet in height, and erect without stiffness, he patiently underwent every morning the careful curling of his silvered hair, stiffened with pomatum and white powder, and hanging behind, some eight inches over his coat-collar, in a rose-knotted " club." With such a structure upon the shoulders, though lighted by a bright blue eye, it was impossible to indulge in modern briskness and ease; quietude of bearing was alone inculcated, if not compelled. Besides, there were the drab-colored shorts, with small gold knee-buckles; the white-topped boots, leaving exposed an inch or so of the white silk stocking within; the white and ample vest, relieved by a gairish crimson roll of velvet forming the edge of an interior flannel; and the unvarying white cravat. The close-bodied coat was a deep brown; the surtout a flowing drab. He walked lightly, but with a natural dignity, which riveted the inquiring gaze of a stranger.

My father's written composition was finely wrought. His "style" (for we must remember that we are commenting upon fifty years ago) was liquid, clear, and winning; yet he was fastidious in selecting words and turning periods. Erasures and insertions, without stint, defaced his autographs. They sometimes remain quite illegible, until the idea intended for expression is first detected.

His vocabulary was little less copious than that of his early applauder, Dr. Johnson; yet this great author marshalled his diction at once and unalterably,—a mental tact as enviable as rare.

There was something eminently effective in his addresses at the bar and before legislative bodies. His elder brother, whom I have just mentioned, a critic of admitted authority, came to the United States in 1796, and having heard several of his speeches, was of opinion that in voice, manner, and general persuasiveness, his elocution bore many of the characteristics of Lord Mansfield's. Others have esteemed it somewhat diffuse, marked by repetitions, and clothed in diction too choice for public harangues. He was often fortunate in turning to account the accidents of the moment. On one occasion, in 1807, greatly excited by the attack of the Leopard upon the Chesapeake, he led an immense crowd of fellow-citizens to a town-meeting at Independence Hall, and, while denouncing the aggression, let fall inadvertently the invocation, "Gentlemen of the jury!" Instantly perceiving a general smile, he exclaimed: "Yes, I say gentlemen of the jury, now empanelled in the presence of your country to hear and determine the issue thus violently forced upon us by Great Britain," etc. So it was that on the trial of General Michael Bright, a pertinent and friendly interruption by the opposite counsel drew from him the prompt, pointed, and appropriate distinction between a causeless rebellion and a defensible revolution.

The intellectual power and moral firmness always shown by Mr. Dallas in his politics, had unavoidably exposed him to the censure of the party against which, from the birth-hour of his American citizenship, he argued, wrote, and acted. It is, however, often said, and is confessedly just, that no man, especially no public man, can be correctly appreciated until he has ceased to live. It is death alone that closes the record alike to flattery and abuse; and then perhaps it may be that startled candor momentarily reopens it, to inscribe, as with a sigh of compunction, a hasty memorandum of reality and truth. On the very afternoon of the day upon which he expired, the journal which had most persistently assailed him contained the following:

"DIED, early this morning, after the short illness of twenty-four hours, the Honorable ALEXANDER JAMES DALLAS. Disapproving, as we have done, the tenor of his public conduct, we have never ceased the less to admire the talents and esteem the private virtues of this distinguished man. As a husband, a parent, and a friend, he was confessedly most amiable and exemplary. But it was by the sweet amenity of his disposition, his open hospitality, and the general courtesy of his deportment, that he conciliated, even in the worst times of party contention, so large a portion of the community, and that his death has now covered, as it were, with a pall the spirits of our city."

After all, amid the endless controversies of speculative opinion, there is nothing more persuasive, and oftener triumphant, than the practical argument of a good, indefatigable, intelligent, and honorable life. Everything else is capable of perversion, and is therefore questionable. It is the best light that can shine before men, approaching the widest disagreements to mutual concession, and cementing, without confounding, the tessellations of honest diversities of judgment. As perhaps in religion, so it may be in politics.

> "For modes of faith, let graceless zealots fight;
> His can't be wrong whose life is in the right."

APPENDICES.

APPENDICES.

No. 1.

COMMUNICATIONS

FROM MR. DALLAS, IN THE NAME OF GOVERNOR MIFFLIN, TO THE PRESI-
DENT OF THE UNITED STATES, RESPECTING THE WESTERN INSURREC-
TION.

I.

PHILADELPHIA, 5 August, 1794.

SIR,—The important subject which led to our conference on Saturday last, and the interesting discussion that then took place, having since engaged my whole attention, I am prepared, in compliance with your request, to state with candor the measures which, in my opinion, ought to be pursued by the Commonwealth of Pennsylvania. The circumstances of the case evidently require a firm and energetic conduct on our part, as well as on the part of the general government; but, as they do not preclude the exercise of a prudent and humane policy, I enjoy a sincere gratification in recollecting the sentiment of regret with which you contemplated the possible necessity of an appeal to arms; for I confess that in manifesting a zealous disposition to secure obedience to the constitution and laws of our country, I too shall ever prefer the instruments of conciliation to those of coercion, and never, but in the last resort, countenance a dereliction of judiciary authority for the exertion of military force.

Under the influence of this general sentiment, I shall proceed, sir, to deliver my opinion relatively to the recent riots in the county of Alleghany, recapitulating in the first place the actual state of the information which I have received. It appears, then, that the marshal of the district having, without molestation, served certain process that issued from a federal court on various citizens who reside in the county of Fayette, thought it proper to prosecute a similar duty in the county of Alleghany, with the assistance and in the company of General Neville, the

(149)

inspector of the excise for the Western District of Pennsylvania; that, while thus accompanied, he suffered some insults and encountered some opposition; that considerable bodies of armed men having, at several times, demanded the surrender of General Neville's commission and papers, attacked and ultimately destroyed his house; that the rioters (of whom a few were killed and many wounded) having taken the marshal and others prisoners, released that officer, in consideration of a promise that he would serve no more processes on the western side of the Alleghany Mountains; that, under the apprehension of violence, General Neville, before his house was destroyed, applied to the judges of Alleghany County for the protection of his property, but the judges, on the 17th day of July, the day on which his house was destroyed, declared that they could not, in the present circumstances, afford the protection that was requested, though they offered to institute prosecutions against the offenders; and that General Neville and the marshal, menaced with further outrage by the rioters, had been under the necessity of withdrawing from the country. To this outline of the actual information respecting the riots, the stoppage of the mail may be added as matter of aggravation, and the proposed convention of the inhabitants of the neighboring counties of Pennsylvania and Virginia as matter of alarm.

Whatever constructions may be given, on the part of the United States, to the facts that have been recited, I cannot hesitate to declare, on the part of Pennsylvania, that the incompetency of the judiciary department of her government to vindicate the violated laws, has not at this period been made sufficiently apparent, and that the military power of the government ought not to be employed until its judiciary authority, after a fair experiment, has proved incompetent to enforce obedience or to punish infractions of the law.

The law having established a tribunal and prescribed a mode for investigating every charge, has likewise attached to every offence its proper punishment. If an opponent of the excise system refuses or omits to perform the duty which that system prescribes to him, in common with his fellow-citizens, his refusal or omission exposes him to the penalty of the law; but the payment of the penalty expiates the legal offence. If a riot is committed in the course of a resistance to the execution of any law, the rioters expose themselves to prosecution and punishment; but the sufferance of their sentence extinguishes their crime. In either instance, however, if the strength and audacity of a lawless combination shall baffle and destroy the efforts of the judiciary authority to recover a penalty or to inflict a punishment, that authority may constitutionally claim the auxiliary intervention of a military power; but still the intervention cannot commence until the impotency of the judicial authority has been proved by experiment, nor continue a moment longer than the occasion for which it was expressly required. That the laws of the Union are the laws of the State is a constitutional axiom that will never be controverted; that the authority of the State ought to be exerted in maintaining the authority of the Union, is a patriotic position which I have uniformly inculcated; but in executing the laws, or in maintaining the authority of the Union, the government of Pennsylvania can only employ the same means by which the more peculiarly municipal laws and authority of the State are executed and maintained. Till the riot was committed, no offence had occurred which required the aid of the State government. When it was committed, it became the duty of the State government to prosecute the offenders as for a breach of the public peace and the laws of the Commonwealth; and if the measures shall be precisely what would have been pursued had the riot been unconnected with the system of federal policy, all, I presume, will be done which good faith and justice can require. Had the riot been unconnected with the system of federal policy, the vindication of our laws would be left to the ordinary course of justice, and only in the last resort, at the requisition, and as an auxiliary of the civil authority, would the military force of the State be called forth.

Experience furnishes the strongest inducements to my mind for persevering in this lenient course. Riots have heretofore been committed in opposition to the laws of Pennsylvania, but the rioters have invariably been punished by our courts of justice. In opposition to the laws of the United States, in opposition to the very laws now opposed, and in the very counties supposed to be combined in the present opposition, riots have likewise formerly occurred; but in every instance, supported by legal proof, the offenders have been indicted, convicted, and punished before the tribunals of the State. This result does not announce a defect of jurisdiction—a want of judicial power or disposition to punish infractions of the law—a necessity for an appeal from the political to the physical strength of the nation.

But another principle of policy deserves some consideration. In a free country it must be expedient to convince the citizens of the necessity that shall, at any time, induce the government to employ the coercive authority with which it is invested. To convince them that it is necessary to call forth the military power for the purpose of executing the laws, it must be shown that the judicial power has in vain attempted to punish those who violate them; and therefore thinking, as I do, that the incompetency of the judicial power of Pennsylvania has not yet been sufficiently ascertained, I remarked, in the course of our late conference, that I did not think it would be an easy task to embody the militia on the present occasion. The citizens of Pennsylvania (however a part of them may for awhile be deluded) are the friends of law and order; but when the inhabitants of one district shall be required to take arms against the inhabitants of another, their general character does not authorize me to promise a passive obedience to the mandates of government. I believe that, as freemen, they would inquire into the cause and nature of the service proposed to them; and I believe that their alacrity in performing, as well as in accepting it, would essentially depend on their opinion of its justice and necessity.

Upon great political emergencies, the effect of every measure should be deliberately weighed. If it shall be doubted whether saying that the judicial power is yet untried, is enough to deter us from the immediate use of military force, an anticipation of the probable consequences of that awful appeal will enable us perhaps satisfactorily to remove or overlook the doubt. Will not the resort to force inflame and cement the existing opposition? Will it not associate, in a common resistance, those who have hitherto peaceably as well as those who have riotously expressed their abhorrence of the excise? Will it not collect and combine every latent principle of discontent arising from the supposed oppressive operations of the federal judiciary, the obstruction of the western navigation, and a variety of other local sources? May not the magnitude of the opposition, on the part of the ill-disposed, or the dissatisfaction at a premature resort to arms on the part of the well-disposed citizens of this State, eventually involve the necessity of employing the militia of other States? And the accumulation of discontent which the jealousy engendered by that movement may produce, who can calculate, or who may be able to avert? Nor, in this view of the subject, ought we to omit paying some regard to the ground for suspecting that the British government has already, insidiously and unjustly, attempted to seduce the citizens on our western frontier from their duty; and we know that in a moment of desperation and disgust men may be led to accept that as an asylum which, under different impressions, they would shun as a snare. It will not, I am persuaded, sir, be presumed, from the expression of these sentiments, that I am insensible to the indignation which the late outrages ought to excite in the mind of a magistrate intrusted with the execution of the laws. My object at present is to demonstrate that, on the principles of policy as well as of law, it would be improper in me to employ the military power of the State while its judiciary authority is competent to punish the offenders. But should the judiciary authority prove insufficient, be assured of the most vigorous co-operation of the whole force which the constitution and laws of the State intrust to me, for the purpose of compelling a due obedience to the government;

and in that unfortunate event, convinced that every other expedient has been resorted to in vain, the public opinion will sanctify our measures, and every honest citizen will willingly lend his aid to strengthen and promote them.

The steps which under my instructions were taken, as soon as the intelligence respecting the riots was received, will clearly indeed manifest the sense that I entertain upon the subject. To every judge, justice, sheriff, brigade inspector, in short, to every public officer residing in the western counties, a letter was addressed expressing my indignation and regret, and requiring an exertion of their influence and authority to suppress the tumults and punish the offenders.

The attorney-general of the State was likewise desired to investigate the circumstances of the riot, to ascertain the names of the rioters, and to institute the regular process of the law for bringing the leaders to justice. In addition to these preliminary measures, I propose issuing a proclamation, in order to declare (as far as I can declare them) the sentiments of the government; to announce a determination to prosecute and punish the offenders; and to exhort the citizens at large to pursue a peaceable and patriotic conduct. I propose engaging three respectable citizens to act as commissioners for addressing those who have embarked in the present combination, upon the lawless nature and ruinous tendency of their proceedings, for inculcating the necessity of an immediate return to the duty which they owe to their country; and for promising (as far as the State is concerned) a forgiveness of their past transgressions, upon receiving a satisfactory assurance that in future they will submit to the laws: and I propose, if all these expedients should be abortive, to convene the legislature, that the ultimate means of subduing the spirit of insurrection, and of restoring tranquillity and order, may be prescribed by their wisdom and authority.

You will perceive, sir, that throughout my observations I have cautiously avoided any reference to the nature of the evidence from which the facts that relate to the riots are collected, or to the conduct which the government of the United States may pursue on this important occasion. I have hitherto, indeed, only spoken as the executive magistrate of Pennsylvania, charged with a general superintendence and care that the laws of the Commonwealth be faithfully executed, leaving it, as I ought, implicitly to your judgment to choose, on such evidence as you approve, the measures for discharging the analogous trust which is confided to you in relation to the laws of the Union. But, before I conclude, it is proper, under the impression of my federal obligations, to add a full and unequivocal assurance that whatever requisition you may make, whatever duty you may impose, in pursuance of your constitutional and legal powers, will, on my part, be promptly undertaken and faithfully discharged.

I have the honor to be, etc.

II.

Philadelphia, 12 August, 1794.

Sir,—The Secretary of State has transmitted to me, in a letter dated the 7th of August (but only received yesterday), your reply to my letter of the 5th instant.

For a variety of reasons, it might be desirable at this time to avoid an extension of our correspondence upon the subject to which those letters particularly relate; but the nature of the remarks contained in your reply, and the sincerity of my desire to merit, on the clearest principles, the confidence which you are pleased to repose in me, will justify, even under the present circumstances of the case, an attempt to explain any ambiguity, and to remove any prejudice that may have arisen, either from an inaccurate expression, or an accidental misconception of the sentiments and views which I meant to communicate.

That the course which I have suggested as proper to be pursued, in relation to the recent disturbances in the western parts of Pennsylvania, contemplates the State in a light too separate and unconnected, is a position that I certainly did not intend to sanction in any degree that could wound your mind with a sentiment of regret. In submitting the construction of the facts, which must regulate the operation of the general government, implicitly to your judgment; in cautiously avoiding any reference to the nature of the evidence from which those facts are collected, or to the conduct which the government of the United States might pursue; in declaring that I spoke only as the executive magistrate of the State charged with the general superintendence and care that its laws be faithfully executed; and above all, in giving a full and unequivocal assurance that whatever requisition you might make, whatever duty you may impose, in pursuance of your constitutional and legal powers, would, on my part, be promptly undertaken and faithfully discharged,—I thought that I had manifested the strongest sense of my federal obligations; and that, so far from regarding the State in a separate and unconnected light, I had expressly recognized the subjection of her individual authority to the national jurisdiction of the Union.

It is true, however, sir, that I have only spoken as the executive magistrate of the State; but in that character it is a high gratification to find that, according to your opinion likewise, " the propriety of the course which I suggested would, in most if not in all respects, be susceptible of little question." Permit me, then, to ask in what other character could I have spoken, or what other language did the occasion require to be employed? If the co-operation of the government of Pennsylvania was the object of our conference, your constitutional requisition, as the executive of the Union, and my official compliance as the executive of the State, would indubitably insure it; but if a preliminary, a separate, an unconnected conduct was expected to be pursued by the executive magistrate of Pennsylvania, his separate and unconnected power and discretion must furnish the rule of proceeding; and by that rule, agreeably to the admission which I have cited, "the propriety of my course would, in most if not in all respects, be susceptible of little question." It must, therefore, in justice, be remembered, that a principal point in our conference related to the expediency of my adopting, independent of the general government, a *preliminary* measure (as it was then termed), under the authority of an act of the legislature of Pennsylvania, which was passed on the 22d of September, 1783, and which the attorney-general of the United States thought to be in force, but which had in fact been repealed on the 11th of April, 1793.

Upon the strictest ideas of co-operative measures, however, I do not conceive, sir, that any other plan could have been suggested consistently with the powers of the executive magistrate of Pennsylvania, or with a reasonable attention on my part to a systematic and energetic course of proceeding. The complicated nature of the outrage which was committed upon the public peace gave a jurisdiction to both governments; but in the mode of prosecuting, or in the degree of punishing the offenders, the circumstance could not, I apprehend, alter or enlarge the powers of either. The State, as I observed in my last letter, could only exert itself in executing the laws or maintaining the authority of the Union by the same means which she employed to execute and maintain her more peculiarly municipal laws and authority; and hence I inferred, and still venture to infer, that if the course which I have suggested is the same that would have been pursued had the riot been unconnected with the system of federal policy, its propriety cannot be rendered questionable merely by taking into our view (what I never have ceased to contemplate) the existence of a federal government, federal laws, federal judiciary, and federal officers. But would it have been thought more consonant with the principle of co-operation had I issued orders for an immediate, a separate, and an unconnected call of the militia under the special authority which was supposed to be given by a law, or under the general authority which may be presumed to result from the constitution? Let it be considered that you had already determined to exercise your legal powers in drafting a competent force of the militia; and it will be allowed, if I had undertaken not only to comply with your requisition, but to embody a distinct corps for the same service, a useless expense would have been incurred by the State, an unnecessary burthen would have been imposed on the citizens, and embarrassment and confusion would probably have been introduced instead of system and co-operation. Regarding it in this point of light, indeed, it may be natural to think that, in the judiciary as well as the military department, the subject should be left entirely to the management either of the State or of the general government; for "the very important difference which is supposed to exist in the nature and consequences of the offences that have been committed, in the contemplation of the laws of the United States and of those of Pennsylvania," must otherwise destroy that uniformity in the distinction of crimes and the apportionment of punishments which has always been deemed essential to a due administration of justice.

But let me not, sir, be again misunderstood. I do not mean by these observations to intimate an opinion or to express a wish that "the care of vindicating the authority or of enforcing the laws of the Union should be transferred from the officers of the general government to those of the State;" nor, after expressly avowing that I had cautiously avoided any reference to the conduct which the government of the United States might pursue on this important occasion, did I think an opportunity could be found to infer that I was desirous of imposing a suspension of your proceedings for the purpose of waiting the issue of the process which I designed to pursue. If, indeed, "the government of the United States was at that point, where it was admitted, if the government of Pennsylvania was, the employment of force by its authority would be justifiable," I am persuaded that, on mature consideration, you will do more credit to my candor than to suppose I meant to condemn or to prevent the adoption of those measures on the part of the general government which, in the same circumstances, I should have approved and promoted on the part of Pennsylvania.

The extracts that are introduced into the letter of the Secretary of State, in order to support that inference, can only be justly applied to the case which was immediately in contemplation—the case of the State of Pennsylvania, whose judiciary authority had not then, in my opinion, been sufficiently tried. They ought not surely to be applied to a case which I had cautiously excluded from my view—the case of the United States, whose judiciary had, in your opinion, proved inadequate to the execution of the laws and the preservation of order. And if they shall be thus limited to their proper object, the justice and force of the argument which flows from them can never be successfully controverted or denied. While you, sir, were treading in the plain path designated by a positive law, with no other care than to preserve the forms which the legislature had prescribed, and relieved from a weight of responsibility by the legal operation of a judge's certificate, I was called upon to act not in conformity to a positive law, but in compliance with the duty which is supposed to result from the nature and constitution of the executive office.

The legislature had prescribed no forms to regulate my course, —no certificate to inform my judgment; every step must be dictated by my own discretion; and every error of construction or conduct would be charged on my own character. Hence arose an essential difference in our official situations; and I am confident that on this ground alone you will perceive a sufficient motive for my considering the objection, in point of law, to forbear the use of military force till the judiciary authority has been tried, as well as the probable effects, in point of policy, which that awful appeal might produce. For, sir, it is certain that, at the time of our conference, there was no satisfactory evidence of the incompetency of the judicial authority of Pennsylvania to vindicate the violated laws; I therefore could not, as executive magistrate, proceed upon a military plan ; but, actuated by the genuine spirit of co-operation, not by a desire to sully the dignity or to alienate the powers of the general government, I still hoped and expected to be able, on this as on former occasions, to support the laws of the Union, to punish the violators of them, by an exertion of the civil authority of the State government, the State judiciary, and the State officers. This hope prompted the conciliatory course which I determined to pursue, and which, so far as respects the appointment of commissioners, you have been pleased to incorporate with your plan. And if, after all, the purposes of justice could be attained, obedience to the laws could be restored, and the horrors of a civil war could be averted by the auxiliary intervention of the State government, I am persuaded you will join me in thinking that the idea of placing the State in a separate and unconnected point of view, and the idea of making a transfer of the powers of the general government, are not sufficiently clear and cogent to supersede such momentous considerations.

Having thus generally explained the principles contained in my letter of the fifth instant, permit me (without adverting to the material change which has since occurred in the state of our information relatively to the riots, and which is calculated to produce a corresponding change of sentiments and conduct) to remark that many of the facts that are mentioned by the Secretary of State, in order to show that the judiciary authority of the Union, after a fair and full experiment, had proved incompetent to enforce obedience or punish infractions of the laws, were, before that communication, totally unknown to me. But still, if it shall not be deemed a deviation from the restriction that I have determined to impose upon my correspondence, I would offer some doubts which, in that respect, occurred to my mind on the evidence as it appeared at the time of our conference. When I found that the marshal had, without molestation, executed his office in the county of Fayette, that he was never insulted or opposed till he acted in company with General Neville, and that the virulence of the rioters was directly manifested against the person and property of the latter gentleman, and only incidentally against the person of the former, I thought there was ground yet to suppose (and as long as it was reasonable I wished to suppose) that a spirit of opposition to the officers employed under the excise law, and not a spirit of opposition to the officers employed in the administration of justice, was the immediate source of the outrages which we deprecate. It is true that these sources of opposition are equally reprehensible, and that their effects are alike unlawful; but on a question respecting the power of the judiciary authority to enforce obedience or to punish infractions of the law, it seemed to be material to discriminate between the cases alluded to, and to ascertain with precision the motives and the object of the rioters. Again: as the associate judge had not at that time issued his certificate, it was proper to scrutinize with strict attention the nature of the evidence on which an act of government was to be founded. The Constitution of the Union, as well as of the State, had cautiously provided, even in the case of an individual, that "no warrant should issue but upon probable cause, supported by oath or affirmation, and particularly describing the place to be searched and the persons or things to be seized." And a much higher degree of caution might reasonably be exercised in a case that involved a numerous body of citizens in the imputation of treason or felony, and required a substitution of the military for the judicial instruments of coercion. The only affidavits that I recollect to have appeared at the time of our conference were those containing the hearsay of Colonel Mentges and the vague narrative of the postrider. The letters that had been received from a variety of respectable citizens, not being written under the sanction of an oath or affirmation, could not acquire the legal force and validity of evidence from a mere authentication of the signatures of the respective writers. Under such circumstances, doubts arose, not whether the means which the laws prescribe for effectuating their own execution should be exerted, but whether the existence of a specific case, to which specific means of redress were appropriated by the laws, had been legally established; not whether the laws, the constitution, the government, the principles of social order, and the bulwarks of private right and security should be sacrificed, but whether the plan proposed was the best calculated to preserve those inestimable blessings. And recollecting a declaration which was made in your presence that "it would not be enough for a military force to disperse the insurgents and to restore matters to the situation in which they were two or three weeks before the riots were committed, but that the force must be continued for the purpose of protecting the officers of the revenue and securing a perfect acquiescence in the obnoxious law," I confess, sir, the motives to caution and deliberation strike my mind with accumulated force. I hope, however, that it will never seriously be contended that a military force ought now to be raised with any view but to suppress rioters; or that if raised with that view, it ought to be employed for any other. The dispersion of the insurgents is, indeed, obviously the sole object for which the act of Congress has authorized the use of military force on occasions like the present; for, with a generous and laudable precaution, it expressly provides that even before that force may be called forth a proclamation shall be issued commanding the insurgents to disperse and retire peaceably to their respective abodes within a limited time.

But the force of these topics I again refer implicitly to your decision, convinced, sir, that the goodness of your intentions now, not less than heretofore, merits an affectionate support from every description of your fellow-citizens. For my own part, I derive a confidence from the heart-felt integrity of my views, the sincerity of my professions, which renders me invulnerable by any insinuation of practising a sinister or deceitful policy.

I pretend not to infallibility in the exercise of my private judgment, or in the discharge of my public functions; but in the ardor of my attachment and in the fidelity of my services to our common country I feel no limitations. And your Excellency, therefore, may justly be assured that in every way which the Constitution of the United States and of Pennsylvania shall authorize and present, or future exigencies may require, you will receive my most cordial aid and support.

I am, with perfect respect, etc.

No. 2.

(FROM THE AMERICAN DAILY ADVERTISER.)

" MESSRS. DUNLAP & CLAYPOLE,—The following sketch of ' The Features of Mr. Jay's Treaty' was made, originally, with a view to ascertain for private satisfaction the principles and operation of an instrument which has excited such extensive curiosity and is calculated to produce such important effects. It is published, however, at the instance of several persons, who think that the subject should be placed in every possible light; and that no citizen can be justified at this crisis in suppressing his opinions, or in withholding his share of information from the common stock. But while it is committed to the press, I wish it to be considered merely as a text, which may hereafter be extended by commentary or explained by illustration; and though it will give me pleasure (since my sole object on this occasion is the investigation of political truth) to see it become a source of candid animadversion, I trust it will not, according to the custom of contending parties, be regarded as an instrument of faction, nor be made the foundation of slander and abuse."

FEATURES OF MR. JAY'S TREATY,

TO WHICH IS ANNEXED A VIEW OF THE COMMERCE OF THE UNITED STATES AS IT STANDS AT PRESENT AND AS IT IS FIXED BY MR. JAY'S TREATY.

I. *The origin and progress of the negotiation for the treaty are not calculated to excite confidence.*

1. The administration of our government have, seemingly at least, manifested a policy favorable to Great Britain and adverse to France.

2. But the House of Representatives of Congress, impressed with the general ill conduct of Great Britain towards America, were adopting measures of a mild, though retaliating nature, to obtain redress and indemnification. The injuries complained of were, principally,—1st, the detention of the western posts; 2dly, the delay in compensating for the negroes carried off at the close of the war; and 3dly, the spoliations committed on our commerce. The remedies proposed were, principally,—1st, the commercial regulations of Mr. Madison; 2dly, the non-intercourse proposition of Mr. Clarke; 3dly, the sequestration motion of Mr. Dayton; 4thly, an embargo; and 5thly, military preparation.

3. Every plan of the legislature was, however, suspended, or rather annihilated, by the interposition of the executive authority; and Mr. Jay, the chief justice of the United States, was taken from his judicial seat to negotiate with Great Britain, under the

influence of the prevailing sentiment of the people, *for the redress of our wrongs.* Query—Are not his commission and the execution of it at variance? Is any one of our wrongs actually redressed? Is not an atonement to Great Britain, for the injuries she *pretends* to have suffered, a preliminary stipulation?

4. The political dogmas of Mr. Jay are well known; his predilection, in relation to France and Great Britain, has not been disguised, and even on the topic of American complaints, his reports, while in the office of secretary for foreign affairs, and his adjudications while in the office of chief justice, were not calculated to point him out as the single citizen of America fitted for the service in which he was employed. Query—Do not personal feelings too often dictate and govern the public conduct of ministers? But whatever may have been his personal disqualifications, they are absorbed in the more important consideration of the apparent violence committed by Mr. Jay's appointment, on the essential principles of the constitution. That topic, however, has already been discussed, and we may pass to the manner of negotiating the treaty in England, which was at once obscure and illusory. We heard of Mr. Jay's diplomatic honors; of the royal and ministerial courtesy which was shcwn to him, and of the convivial boards to which he was invited; but, no more! Mr. Jay, enveloped by a dangerous confidence in the intuitive faculties of his own mind, or the inexhaustible fund of his diplomatic information, neither possessed nor wished for external aid; while the British negotiator, besides his own acquirements, entered on the points of negotiation fraught with all the auxiliary sagacity of his brother ministers, and with all the practical knowledge of the most enlightened merchants of a commercial nation. The result corresponds with that inauspicious state of things. Mr. Jay was driven from the ground of an injured, to the ground of an aggressing party; he made atonement for imaginary wrongs before he was allowed justice for real ones; he converted the *resentments* of the American citizens (under the impressions of which he was avowedly sent to England) into *amity and concord;* and seems to have been so anxious to rivet a commercial chain about the neck of America that he even forgot, or disregarded, a principal item of her own produce (cotton), in order to make a sweeping sacrifice to the insatiable appetite of his maritime antagonist. But the idea of the treaty, given by Mr. Pitt in answer to Mr. Fox, who, before he had seen, applauded it as an act of liberality and justice towards America, was the first authoritative alarm to our interests and our feelings. "When the treaty is laid before the Parliament (said the minister), you will best judge whether any improper concession has been made to America!"

5. The treaty being sent here for ratification, the President

and the Senate pursue the mysterious plan in which it was ne
gotiated. It has been intimated that, till the meeting of the
Senate, the instrument was not communicated even to the most
confidential officers of the government; and the first resolution
taken by the Senate was to stop the lips and ears of its members
against every possibility of giving or receiving information.
Every man, like Mr. Jay, was presumed to be inspired. In the
course of the discussion, however, some occurrences flashed from
beneath the veil of secrecy; and it is conjectured that the whole
treaty was, at one time, in jeopardy. But the rhetoric of a
minister (not remarkable for the *volubility of his tongue*) who
was brought post-haste from the country; the danger of exposing
to odium and disgrace the distinguished American characters
who would be affected by a total rejection of the treaty; and
the feeble, but operative, vote of a member transported from the
languor and imbecility of a sick-room to decide in the Senate a
great national question, whose merits he had not heard discussed,
triumphed over principle, argument, and decorum!

6. But still the treaty remains *unratified;* for, unless the
British government shall assent to suspend the obnoxious twelfth
article (in favor of which, however, many *patriotic* members
declared their readiness to vote), the whole is destroyed by the
terms of the ratification; and if the British government shall
agree to add an article allowing the suspension, the whole must
return for the reconsideration of the Senate. But the forms of
mystery are still preserved by our government; and attempts to
deceive the people have been made abroad upon a vain presumption that the treaty could remain *a secret* till it became obligatory
as *a law.*

For instance, in *Fenno's* paper of the 25th of June, it is
unequivocally declared, "the treaty of amity, commerce, and
navigation was ratified yesterday by the Senate of the United
States;" and, even while he corrects that mistake in the paper of
the following day, he commits *an error* of a more extraordinary
kind (particularly when we consider that he is the confidential
person who printed the treaty for the use of the Senate) by
asserting that, in the twelfth article, "the United States are
prohibited from exporting to Europe from the said States sugar,
coffee, cotton, and cocoa, *the produce of any of the West India
Islands.*" The fact must have been known to Mr. Fenno that
the prohibition operates universally, whether the prohibited
articles are the produce of the West India Islands, of the East
Indies, of the United States, or of any other part of the world.
The next essay to render the envelopments of the treaty still more
opaque, appeared in the *American Daily Advertiser* of the 27th
of June. The writer (who is said to be a member of the Senate)
likewise regards the ratification, in his introduction, as a perfect

one; and, after giving a gloss to the general texture of the treaty, he ascribes the obnoxious principle of the twelfth article *to an error which, it appears, has been inadvertently introduced.* An error inadvertently introduced into an instrument which was under the consideration of the chief justice of the United States and the British minister for a term of eight months! and introduced, too, into a part of that very article which is made the sole foundation of the whole commercial superstructure! Whenever the twelfth article ceases, the treaty declares every other article, except the ten first articles, shall also cease! But the author of that sketch proceeds one step further,—he says "that *every cause of offence or collision* towards the French seems to have been studiously avoided in the progress of the negotiation;" for, "no article of the treaty *clashes in the smallest degree* with the obligations and engagements contracted with that gallant nation!" Let the treaty speak for itself,—it is more to be hoped than expected, that the voice of France should not likewise be heard in opposition to so bold an assertion.

II. *Nothing is settled by the treaty.*

1. The western posts are *to be given up.*

2. The northern boundary of the United States is *to be amicably settled.*

3. The river meant by St. Croix River in the treaty, is *to be settled.*

4. The payment for spoliations is *to be adjusted and made.*

5. The ultimate regulation of the West India trade is to depend on a negotiation *to be made* in the course of two years after the termination of the existing war.

6. The question of neutral bottoms making neutral goods is *to be considered* at the same time.

7. The articles that may be deemed contraband are *to be* settled at the same time.

8. The equalization of duties laid by the contracting parties on one another is *to be hereafter treated of.*

9. All the commercial articles depend on the existence of the twelfth article, which may continue twelve years, if it is so agreed within two years after the expiration of the war; but if it is not so agreed, it expires, and with it all the dependent parts of the treaty. Query—Does not the Senate's suspension of the twelfth article bring us to the same ground?

10. The whole business of Mr. Jay's negotiation is left open by the twenty-eighth article, for alteration, amendment, and addition, by new articles, which, when agreed upon and ratified, *shall become a part of this treaty.*

Query — Does not the history of treaties prove that whenever commissioners have been appointed by the parties, to take all the subjects of their dispute *ad referendum,* for the sake of getting rid of an immediate pressure, and patching up a peace, the matter terminates in *creating,* not in *settling,* differences?

III. *The treaty contains a colorable, but no real, reciprocity.*

1. The second article provides for the surrender of the western posts in June, 1796; but it stipulates that, in the mean time, the citizens of the United States shall not settle within the precincts and jurisdiction of those posts; that the British settlers there shall hold and enjoy all their property of every kind, real and personal; and that when the posts are surrendered, such settlers shall have an election either to remain British subjects or to become American citizens. Query—Were not the western posts, and all their precincts and jurisdiction, the absolute property of the United States by the treaty of peace? Query—What equivalent is given for this cession of the territory of the United States to a foreign power? Query—How far do the precincts and jurisdiction of the posts extend? Query—Does not the treaty give an implied assent to Major Campbell's claim, by adopting its language, as far as the falls of the Miami, and to the northern claim upon the territories of New York and Vermont?

2. The third article stipulates that the two contracting parties may frequent the ports of *either party* on the eastern banks of the Mississippi. Query—What ports has Great Britain on the eastern banks of the Mississippi?

3. The third article likewise opens an amicable intercourse on the lakes; but excludes us from their seaports and the limits of the Hudson's Bay Company; and excludes them from navigating our Atlantic rivers higher than the highest port of entry in each. Query—What are the limits of the Hudson's Bay Company? Query—What equivalent do the United States obtain for the general freedom of navigation, portage, and passage? For it must be remembered that the British rivers penetrate the heart of the country,—but of those we can take no advantage; while Great Britain is in fact admitted to all the advantages of which our Atlantic rivers are susceptible.

4. The sixth and seventh articles provide for satisfying every demand which Great Britain has been able, at any time, to make against the United States (the payment of the British debts due before the war, and the indemnification for vessels captured within our territorial jurisdiction); but the provision made for the American claims upon Great Britain is not equally explicit or efficient in its terms, nor is it coextensive with the object. Query—Why is the demand for the negroes carried off by the British troops suppressed, waived, or abandoned? The preamble to the treaty recites an intention to *terminate the differences*

between the nations : was not the affair of the negroes a difference between the nations ? and how has it been terminated ?

5. The ninth article stipulates that the subjects of Great Britain and the citizens of the United States, respectively, who now hold lands within the territories of either nation, shall hold the lands in the same manner as natives do. Query—What is the relative proportion of lands so held ? Query—The effect to revive the claims of British subjects who, either as traitors or aliens, have forfeited their property within the respective States ? Query—The operation of such a compact on the internal policy of the Union, combined with the solemn recognition of a colony of British subjects, professing and owing allegiance to the British crown, though settled within the acknowledged territory of the United States, by virtue of the second article ?

6. The tenth article declares that neither party shall sequester or confiscate the debts or property in the funds, etc. belonging to the citizens of the other in case of a war or of national differences. Great Britain has fleets and armies : America has none. Query—Does not this, supported by other provisions, which forbid our changing the commercial situation of Great Britain, or imposing higher duties on her than on other nations, deprive the United States of their best means of retaliation and coercion ? Query—Is it not taking from America her only weapon of defence ; but from Great Britain the least of two weapons which she possesses ? What is the relative proportion held by the citizens of the contracting nations, respectively, in the funds, etc. of each other ?

7. The twelfth article opens to our vessels, not exceeding seventy tons, an intercourse with the British West India Islands during the present war, and for two years after ; but it prohibits our exporting from the United States, molasses, sugar, cocoa, coffee, or cotton to any part of the world, whether those articles are brought from British, French, or Spanish islands, or even raised (as cotton is) within our own territory. Query—Are vessels of seventy tons equal to maintain the most beneficial part of our trade with the West Indies, the transportation of lumber, etc. ? Query—Do we not *in the time of war* (and the continuance of the privilege for more than two years after the war depends on the situation in which his Majesty of Great Britain shall then find himself in relation to the islands) enjoy a greater privilege, under the temporary proclamations of the colonial governors, than this article admits ? Query—Have not the articles which we are prohibited from exporting formed, of late, a valuable part of our trade ? Is not cocoa chiefly cultivated by the Spaniards ? Is not cotton a staple of America ? Is our own consumption equal to our importation or growth of the prohibited articles ? Will not the want of a vent for any surplus quantity

affect the other branches of our commerce, diminish the demand for ship-building, and injure our agriculture? If we are now thrown out of this branch of the carrying trade, shall we be ever able to recover it? and, in short, will not the loss be of lasting detriment to all our maritime exertions?

8. The thirteenth article admits us to trade in the British settlements in the East Indies; but it excludes us from any share in the coasting trade of that country; it forbids our penetrating the interior of the country, or holding an intercourse with the natives, unless under a license from the local British government; and it compels us to land all the articles that are there shipped in the United States. Is not China the independent territory of the emperor? Is not Canton an open port accessible to all nations? Do we not obtain there, and at independent places in the East Indies with which we have, at present, an uninterrupted communication, tea, porcelain, nankeens, silk, etc., upon the principles of a free trade? Does not a very advantageous part of the trade in that quarter of the globe consist in the exchange of the products and manufactures of the East Indies for those of China, and *vice versa?* Do not our importations of East India goods far exceed our consumption? Is not the trade which we carry on with those goods in Europe, highly beneficial? Are not sugar and coffee a part of our importations from India? and does not the twelfth article prohibit our re-exporting them? Does our trade to Europe, founded on the previous intercourse with India, depend on the British license? and can it be maintained under the disadvantage of a double voyage? Are we not, every voyage, making favorable impressions on the natives of China? Do we not participate, at present, in the carrying trade of that country? Does not our interest in it increase rapidly?

9. The several articles that regulate the rights and privileges of the contracting parties within their respective territories, in case either of them is engaged in a war, may cease in two years after the present war is terminated, and cannot be protracted beyond twelve years. Query—Are not all these advantages, in effect, *exclusively favorable to Great Britain,* a principal maritime power of Europe, often engaged in wars, and interested to obtain for her ships, her colonies, and herself the ports and supplies of this extensive continent?

Is it probable that, during the longest possible existence of this treaty (twelve years), America will be engaged in maritime wars, will want English ports as a refuge for men-of-war or as a retreat for prizes? Or, that it will, during that period, be of importance to her objects, to prevent her enemies from arming in English ports or selling their prizes there?

10. The twenty-second article provides for ships of war being

hospitably treated in the ports of the respective contracting parties ; and that officers shall be treated with the respect that is due to the commissions which they bear. Query—Could not the principle of reciprocity, as well as humanity, suggest to Mr. Jay that some provision should be made to protect our citizen-sailors from the fangs of British press-gangs in England, and from the horrors of their prison-ships in the West Indies? Were the commissions of his Britannic Majesty of more regard than the liberties of American freemen? Or, was it unknown that thousands of our sailors have been occasionally enslaved by the impress tyranny of the British government? Or, that thousands have lost their lives in noxious prisons, while their vessels were carried into British ports for " LEGAL ADJUDICATION?"

11. The fourteenth article provides for a perfect liberty of commerce and navigation, and for the accommodation of traders ; but subject always to the laws and statutes of the two countries respectively. Query—Are not the laws and statutes of England infinitely more rigid, on the subjects of this article, than the laws and statutes of America?

IV. *The treaty is an instrument of party.*

1. The discussions, during the session of Congress in which Mr. Jay's mission was projected, evinced the existence of two parties upon the question,—whether it was more our interest to be allied with the republic of France than with the monarchy of Great Britain. Query—Does not the general complexion of the treaty decide the question in favor of the alliance with Great Britain? Query—Whether that complexion does not manifestly arise from the provisions, for admitting a British colony within our territory, in the neighborhood of the western posts ; for admitting the whole British nation, without an equivalent, into a participation of our territory on the eastern bank of the Mississippi ; for naturalizing all the holders of lands ; for opening a general intercourse with their traders on the lakes, in the interior of our country, rendering (as it is idly said) the local advantages of each party common to both ; for regulating the external trade of the two nations with each other ; for admitting citizens to be punished as pirates who take commissions, etc. from a belligerent power adverse to either contracting party ; for fettering the operations of our treaty with France ; for surrendering criminals, etc. etc. etc.

2. The measures proposed by one party to retaliate the injuries offered by Great Britain to our territorial, commercial, and political rights, were opposed by the other, precisely as the treaty opposes them. For instance :

(1) Mr. Madison projects a regulation of our commerce with Great Britain, by which the hostile spirit of that nation might

be controlled on the footing of its interest. The treaty legitimizes the opposition, which was given to the measure in Congress, by declaring, in article fifteen, "that no other or higher duties shall be paid by the ships or merchandise of the one party in the ports of the other than such as are paid by the like vessels or merchandise of all other nations; nor shall any other or higher duty be imposed in one country on the importation of any articles of the growth, produce, or manufactures of the other than are, or shall be, payable on the importation of the like articles of the growth, etc. of any foreign country."

(2) Mr. Clarke proposes to manifest and enforce the public resentment by prohibiting all intercourse between the two nations. The treaty destroys the very right to attempt that species of national denunciation by declaring, in the same article, that "no prohibition shall be imposed on the exportation or importation of any articles to or from the territories of the two parties, respectively, which shall not equally extend to all other nations."

(3) But Mr. Dayton moves, and the House of Representatives supports his motion, for the sequestration of British debts, etc., to insure a fund for paying the spoliations committed on our trade. The treaty (without regarding the respect due to the commission which is borne by our members of Congress) not only despoils the government of this important instrument to coerce a powerful, yet interested adversary into acts of justice, but enters likewise into a commentary, which, considering the conduct of one of the branches of our legislature, Lord Grenville, consistently with decorum, could not have expressed, or at least, Mr. Jay, for the sake of our national dignity, ought not to have adopted. The tenth article declares, that "neither the debts due from individuals of the one nation to individuals of the other, nor shares nor moneys which they may have in the public funds, or in the public or private banks, shall ever, in any event of war or national difference, be sequestered or confiscated, *it being unjust and impolitic* that debts and engagements contracted and made by individuals having confidence in each other and in their respective governments, should ever be destroyed or impaired by national authority on account of national differences and discontents." The terms are very similar to those that gave Mr. Dayton offence in a speech pronounced by Mr. Ames; and certainly it will be deemed no mitigation that the charge of committing "*an unjust and impolitic* act," has been wantonly engrafted upon the most solemn of all instruments — a public treaty! Query—Would Lord Grenville have consented to brand his royal master with the title of *Great Sea Robber* if Mr. Jay's urbanity could have permitted him to borrow the epithet from another member of Congress, in order to insert it in the article that relates to the British spoliations on our trade? But perhaps

Mr. Jay forgot that the commentary operated as a reflection on the government of the United States, and only meant it as a reproach to Great Britain, for sequestering, during the late war, and retaining at this moment, the property belonging to Maryland lying in the Bank of England. It might, likewise, be intended as a satire upon the parliamentary sequestration of French property in the famous "Intercourse Act;" or perhaps Mr. Jay anticipated the revolution in Holland, and designed his commentary as a warning against the seizing of Dutch property, public and private; which, however, has since taken place, in spite of his solemn admonition.

3. The trials that had occurred relative to the equipment of French privateers in our ports, and the enlistment of our citizens in the service of the republic, had produced some embarrassment in the course of party pursuits. These are obviated by the treaty. The British nation, by which the empress of Russia has always been supplied with naval officers, and whose fleets and armies are always crowded with volunteers from other nations, consents that her subjects shall not serve against us, and stipulates that our citizens shall not serve against her. This contract is made with a power actually engaged in a war—and seldom more than seven years clear of one—by a power at peace, not liable, from her local position and political constitution, to be involved in war, and in strict alliance with the nation against whom the stipulation will immediately operate Captain Barney and the other Americans who have joined the arms of France, are thus involved in the most serious dilemma. If they expatriate themselves they may possibly escape the vengeance of the American government; but will that save them from the vengeance of Great Britain, whose concessions on the doctrine of expatriation are not quite so liberal? By-the-by, it may here be seasonably repeated, that while Mr. Jay was so willing to prevent American citizens from *entering* into the service of France, he might surely have taken some pains to secure them from being *pressed* into the service of England. He would have found, on inquiry, that the instances of the latter kind are infinitely more numerous than of the former. But it is enough that the measure will be introductory of a law favorable to the view of a party which reprobates every idea of assisting the French, and cultivates every means of conciliating the British.

4. It has, likewise, been thought by some politicians that the energies of our executive department require every aid that can be given to them, in order more effectually to resist and control the popular branches of the government. Hence we find the treaty-making power employed in that service ; and Congress cannot exercise a legislative discretion on the prohibited points

(though it did not participate in making the cession of its authority) without a declaration of war against Great Britain. George the Third enjoys by the treaty a more complete negative to bind us as States than he ever claimed over us as colonies.

V. *The treaty is a violation of the general principles of neutrality, and is in collision with the positive previous engagements which subsist between America and France.*

1. It is a general principle of the law of nations that during the existence of a war neutral powers shall not, by favor or by treaty, so alter the situation of one of the belligerent parties as to enable him more advantageously to prosecute hostilities against his adversary. If, likewise, a neutral power shall refuse or evade treating with one of the parties, but eagerly enter into a treaty with the other, it is a partiality that amounts to a breach of neutrality. These positions may be supported by the authority of the most esteemed writers on the subject; but it will be sufficient in the present case to cite the conduct of Great Britain herself. Thus, it has been adjudged by Lord *Mansfield* "that if a neutral ship trades to a French colony, with all the privileges of a French ship, and *and is thus adopted and naturalized*, it must be looked upon as a French ship liable to be taken." (See Judge *Blackstone's Reports*, vol. i. pp. 313, 314.) According to the principle on which this judgment was given, the act of issuing the memorable orders of the 6th of November, 1793, and the consequent seizure of all our vessels, are attempted to be justified. Great Britain alleges (when it is injurious to France) that trading with the French islands, *on a footing not allowed before the war*, is a breach of neutrality, and cause of confiscation; and therefore Great Britain must also admit, at least America will not deny, that trading with the British Islands, on a footing not allowed before the war; or, in different words, altering and enlarging the commercial relations of the two countries, is equally a breach of our neutrality towards France. When the sword is found to cut both ways, the party who uses it has no right to complain.

2. That we have, on the one hand, evaded the overtures of a treaty with France, and on the other hand, solicited a treaty from Great Britain, are facts public and notorious. Let us inquire, then, what Great Britain has gained on the occasion, to enable her more advantageously to prosecute her hostilities against France.

(1) *Great Britain has gained time.* As nothing is settled by the treaty, she has it in her power to turn all the chances of the war in her favor, and, in the interim, being relieved from the odium and embarrassment of adding America to her enemies, the current of her operations against France is undivided, and will of course flow with greater vigor and certainty. We have been

for so many years satisfied with *the promises of the treaty of peace* that Great Britain has cause to expect, at least, an equal period of credit for *the promises of the treaty of amity.* If, indeed, it is true that the reasons assigned by Lord Grenville to Mr. Jay for declining an immediate surrender of the posts were, *first,* that the British traders might have time to arrange their outstanding business,—*a privilege that is expressly granted by the treaty,* and could not, therefore, furnish a real excuse for delay ; and *secondly,* that the British government might be able to ascertain what would be the probable effect of the surrender, on the Indians,—*a reservation that demonstrates an intention to be governed by events ;* we can very well accourt for the late extensive shipment of artillery and ammunition to Canada ; and may easily calculate the importance of *gaining time,* in order to promote the American, as well as European, objects of Great Britain.

(2) *Great Britain gains supplies for her West India colonies ;* and *that* for a period almost limited to the continuance of the war, under circumstances which incapacitate her from furnishing the colonial supplies herself; and, indeed, compel her to invite the aid of all nations in furnishing provisions for her own domestic support. The supplies may be carried to the islands either in *American* bottoms *not exceeding seventy tons,* or in *British* bottoms of *any tonnage.*

(3) *Great Britain gains an advantage over France by prohibiting the exportation of* sugar, etc., in consequence of which the colonies of France must, in a great measure, remain unsupplied with provisions, etc., as they can only in general pay for them in those articles *whose use is confined to the American consumption.* It will be remembered that the produce of the French islands has of late constituted a great part of our European remittances. If, therefore, that trade is cut off, and at the same time, besides employing *our own small craft* of seventy tons, Great Britain is allowed, *to any extent of tonnage,* to be our West India factor, it is obvious that our consumption of sugar, coffee, etc. etc. will be abundantly supplied, without maintaining an intercourse with the French, or even with the East Indies, to procure any of those articles. Perhaps this method, though less bold, will be more effectual to prevent our furnishing the French islands with provision, than declaring them to be in a state of blockade, and seizing the vessels that attempt to visit them.

(4) *It is another important gain to Great Britain* (which might likewise have been adverted to under feature of reciprocity), *that to any extent of tonnage her vessels may carry on the West India trade for us,* either to supply our domestic consumption or European engagements, *subject to no other or higher duties than our own vessels ;* while our own vessels are

restricted to a pitiful size, and circumscribed to a particular voyage. But whatever may be thought of the benefit of acquiring for America even this scanty participation in the West India trade, no one (after the rejection of the twelfth article) will deny that the whole measure changes the relative situation of the two countries avowedly in favor of Great Britain and operatively injurious to France; and every such change is derogatory to our boasted neutral character.

(5) *The admission of Great Britain to all the commercial advantages of the most favored nation, and the restraints imposed upon our legislative independence*, as stated in the *party feature* of the treaty, are proofs of predilection and partiality in the American government which cannot fail to improve the resources of Great Britain and to impair the interests as well as the attachments of France.

(6) *The assent to the seizure of all provision ships*, and that, in effect, upon any pretext, at a period when Great Britain is distressed for provisions as well as France, and when the system of *subduing by famine* has been adopted by the former against the latter nation, is clearly changing our position as an independent republic in a manner detrimental to our original ally. That our merchants will be paid a reasonable profit for their cargoes, etc. may render the measure more palatable to us,—even under the loss of the return cargo, the derangement of the voyage, and the destruction of the spirit of commercial enterprise; but that consideration cannot render it less offensive to France. It may properly be here remarked, that Sweden and Denmark have obtained, by a spirited resistance, an actual indemnification for the seizures which have heretofore taken place, and an exemption from all such outrages in future; while America has only put those which are past *in a train of negotiation*, and has given a *legitimate effect* to those which are to come. The order which, the English gazettes say, has recently been issued for seizing American provision ships on their passage to France, ought not, therefore, to be complained of, as it is merely an exercise, by anticipation, of the right granted by the treaty.

(7) *Great Britain has gained the right of preventing our citizens from being volunteers in the armies or ships of France.* This is not simply the grant of a new right to Great Britain, but is, at the same time, a positive deprivation of a benefit hitherto enjoyed by France. Neither the laws of nations, nor our municipal constitution and laws, prohibited our citizens from *going to another country*, and *there*, either for the sake of honor, reward, or instruction, serving in a foreign navy or army. Colonel *Oswald* and many others have done it; Captain *Barney* and many others are doing it. But a proclamation must issue to recall all such volunteers, and punishment must follow dis-

obedience, if the twenty-first article of the treaty is to be effect-
uated as the supreme law of the land.

(8) *Great Britain has gained a right to treat and punish as
pirates any of our citizens who shall accept, even while they
are in France, any commission* to arm a privateer or letter of
marque. It is true that a similar provision is contained in other
treaties; but we are now only considering *the alterations* which
are made by the treaty under discussion in favor of Great
Britain and injurious to France. How far there exists a power
to define piracy, *by treaty*, will be remarked in delineating
another feature of Mr. Jay's diplomatic offspring.

(9) *Great Britain has doubly gained, by obtaining in our
ports an asylum for her ships of war, privateers, prizes, etc.,
stipulating for an exclusion of those of her enemies other (it
is admitted) than France.* The twenty-fourth and twenty-fifth
articles of the projected treaty are nearly copied from the subsisting treaty with France. It would be curious, however, to
reflect on the very different motives which must justify (if the
idea of justification could, in the late instance, be at all admissible) these analogous grants. The concession to France was
made *when we were at war and she was not;* it was made upon
a certainty of *reciprocal advantage;* and it was made *as a price*
for obtaining the aid of *that gallant nation* in the establishment
of our independence. The concession is made to Great Britain
*when she is at war and we are not; without any rational pros-
pect of deriving any reciprocal advantage from it;* and under
such circumstances of injury and insult as might have admonished us to *reserve it as the price for obtaining aid from other
nations in resisting her hostilities,* instead of paying it for
smiles without affection, and promises without sincerity. When
we were making treaties with Holland, Prussia, etc., did we not
expressly exclude them from such important, and, as we have
already seriously experienced, such dangerous privileges?

But it will be asked, perhaps, what mighty benefit has Great
Britain gained, in this case, at the expense of France, since the
prior similar privileges of France are exclusive? *Answer:*
That as the privilege of Great Britain will operate against every
other nation, it will immediately affect the French republic's alliance, offensive and defensive, with the United Provinces, which
preceded the ratification, at least, of the treaty; and it may,
eventually, have the same pernicious influence in relation to
Prussia, Spain, and Portugal, whose disposition to change sides,
in the present war, has been unequivocally expressed. Thus,
though Holland and Prussia made treaties with us long before
Great Britain would admit the idea of a negotiation, and though
Spain and Portugal are the only customers who furnish us with
the ready money balance for the very purpose of paying our

annual accumulation of debt to Britain, the harbors of America are open to their vessels *as prizes*, but shut to them as *friends*. They may be brought hither and sold by their enemies; but if they have captured their enemy, all but common necessaries shall be denied to them! The habits, bias, and opinions of a people ought not to be altogether disregarded in making a treaty. What honest, feeling American could patiently see an Englishman, *our sunshine ally*, bringing into our ports, *as prizes*, the ships of Holland, *our ally in the times that tried men's souls;* a republic, indissolubly united with France,—that earliest, latest, best of friends? What honest, feeling American, even submitting to a scene so painful, would willingly assist in expelling from our ports the ships of Holland, *which had merely retaliated* by the capture of their foe?

3. But it is time to advert to *the cases of collision* between the two treaties; and these are of such a nature as to produce a violation of the spirit, though not a positive violation of the words, of the previous engagements that subsist between France and America,—*they are causes of offence, and clash in the highest degree.*

(1) *By the ninth article of the treaty of alliance with France we guarantee the possessions of that nation in America.* It is true that our situation is such as to incapacitate, and of course to excuse us, from a *direct* fulfilment of this guarantee; but it is equally true that we violate our faith whenever we do anything that will, either directly or indirectly, endanger those possessions. Query — Whether facilitating the means of supplying the British forces in the West Indies will not be the effect of the arrangements relative to the trade with the British Islands? Query—Whether restraining our intercourse with the French islands, as a consequence of the treaty already predicated, will not expose them to want, and of course to the necessity of yielding to their enemies? Does not every such advantage given to Great Britain *clash* with our engagements to France?

(2) By our treaty with France, and, indeed, with several other nations, *it is expressly stipulated that free vessels* shall *make free goods.* At the time of entering into the stipulation, and even at this moment, the maritime strength of France (always superior to that of Denmark and Sweden, which has, under similar circumstances, been successful) could command the respect of the world for her engagements. It is true America neither was, nor is, in a situation to produce the same complaisance; and, on the ground of that weakness, France has, hitherto, candidly dispensed with a strict performance of the treaty. But though America cannot *enforce*, she ought not to *abandon* her engagements; she may submit to imperious necessity, but *she cannot voluntarily bring into question* the right of protecting, as a neu-

tral power, the property of France; while France is not only ready and able to afford her property the stipulated protection, but, in conformity to the stipulation, actually *allows the property of Great Britain to pass free, under the sanction of the American flag.* When, therefore, the treaty with Great Britain *agrees* that within two years after the termination of the existing war *it shall be discussed,* "whether in any, and in what cases, neutral vessels shall protect enemies' property,"—*does it not clash with our previous promise to France that free ships shall make free goods?* And when the treaty with Great Britain, in formal and explicit terms, *further agrees,* " that in all cases where vessels shall be captured or detained, on suspicion of having on board enemies' property, etc., *the part which belongs to the enemy shall be made prize,*"—is not this *an evident collision with our previous agreement with France,* and with the security which British property enjoys in consequence of it? While France adheres to her treaty, by permitting *British goods* to be protected by American bottoms, is it honest, honorable, or consistent on our part *to enter voluntarily into a compact with the enemies of France* for permitting them to take *French goods* out of our vessels? We may not be able *to prevent,* but ought we to *agree* to the proceeding? Let the question be repeated—Does not such an *express agreement* clash with our express, as well as implied, obligations to France?

(3) By enumerating, as contraband articles, in the treaty with Great Britain, certain articles which are declared free in the treaty with France, *we may, consistently with the latter, supply Great Britain; but, consistently with the former, we cannot supply France.*

Thus, *our treaty with France* (and, indeed, every treaty which we have) expressly declares that, "in general, all provisions which serve for the nourishment of mankind and sustenance of life; furthermore, all kinds of cotton, hemp, flax, tar, pitch, ropes, cables, sail cloths, anchors, and any part of anchors, also ships, masts, planks, boards, and beams of what trees soever, and all other things proper either for building or repairing ships, and all other goods whatever, which have not been worked into the form of any instrument for war, by land or by sea, *shall not be reputed contraband.*"

The treaty with Great Britain expressly declares, "that timber for ship-building, tar, or rosin, copper in sheets, sails, hemp, and cordage, and generally whatever may serve directly to the equipment of vessels,—unwrought iron and fir planks only excepted,— *shall be objects of confiscation whenever they are attempted to be carried to an enemy.*"

Whether this stipulation can be considered as founded on a principle of *reciprocity,* since the articles declared to be contraband are *among our principal exports,* but *among the principal imports of Great Britain*, might have been adverted to in tracing a former feature of the treaty; but let it be now candidly answered, whether it is not *in collision* with our previous engagements with France? The right to make such a stipulation is not, at present, controverted; but only the assertion that *exercising the right does not clash in any degree* with the terms and spirit of the French treaty. France exempts those important materials of our commerce from confiscation in favor of all the world; Great Britain condemns them to confiscation whenever they shall be carried to her enemies; and the compact is made while France is one of her enemies!

VI. *The treaty with Great Britain is calculated to injure the United States in the friendship and favor of other foreign nations.*

1. That the friendship and favor of France will be affected by the formation of so heterogeneous an alliance with her most implacable enemy cannot be doubted, if we reason upon any scale applicable to the policy of nations or the passions of man. From that republic, therefore, if not an explicit renunciation of all connection with the United States, we may at least expect an alteration of conduct; and, finding the success which has flowed from the hostile treatment that Great Britain has shown towards us, she may be at length tempted to endeavor at *extorting from fear* what she has not been able to obtain *from affection.* She will probably declare Great Britain in a state of blockade, for the purpose of seizing our vessels in Europe; and she may institute courts for "legal adjudication," in order to confiscate our vessels in the West Indies. *Great Britain will then chuckle at the scene.* No one can doubt that our embarrassments will gratify not only the avowed objects, but the latent resentments of that nation. Even if she could obliterate the memory of our Revolution, she cannot, with pleasure, behold the successful experiment of a republican system of government, nor the rapid advances of a commercial competitor. The moment she has produced a quarrel between America and France she may exclaim, "*Delenda est Carthago!*" America is again a colony! How different were the interests and dispositions of our tried friend! That our government should preserve its purity and independence—that our commerce and agriculture should attain their zenith—were views *once* congenial with the policy and affections of the French nation; heart, head, and hand she would have joined in promoting them against the arts and enmities of all the rest of the world! What a change, then, have we made!

> "Look on *this* picture, and on *that:*
> The counterfeit presentment of two *allies!*
> Who would on this fair mountain leave to feed,
> To batten on that moor!"

2. During the war we, likewise, formed a seasonable and serviceable treaty with the United Netherlands; and shortly after the war treaties were established with Sweden, Prussia, etc. But in order to avoid *even the appearance of clashing or collision* with the French treaty, the powers thus early in courting our alliance were not allowed those privileges of asylum for themselves, and of excluding their enemies from our ports, which are conceded in the projected treaty to Great Britain. Have those nations no cause for jealousy and reproach? What principle of policy or justice can vindicate the partiality and predilection that has been thus shown?

3. But the projected treaty (after an affected recognition of pre-existing public treaties) declares that while Great Britain and America continue in amity, no future treaty shall be made inconsistent with the articles that grant the high and dangerous privileges that have been mentioned. Every nation of the earth (except France) is thus sacrificed to the pride and interest of Great Britain. And with what motive, or upon what consideration, is the sacrifice made? It has been stated in a former, and will be more fully shown in a future, feature of Mr. Jay's treaty, that the United States do not enjoy any equivalent for this, nor for any other, concession, which is made to Great Britain. But the mischief does not end with the folly of a lopsided bargain. By granting these exclusive privileges to Great Britain, by declaring that no commercial favor shall be conferred on other nations without her participating in them, we have thrown away the surest means of purchasing, on any emergency, the good will and good offices of any other power. We cannot even improve the terms of our old treaty with France. For all the advantages of trade that Spain, Portugal, Holland, etc. might, and probably would, upon a liberal footing of reciprocity, have given us,—what have we now left to offer as the basis of negotiation and compact?

4. The alteration which the treaty makes in the relative situation of several nations with America, and the conduct that is likely to be pursued by those nations, in order to counteract its effect, merit serious reflection. Will Spain see, without some solicitude, the partition which we have made with Great Britain of our territory on the eastern bank of the Mississippi? How would our projected treaty work if France should recover Pondicherry, etc., in the East Indies, should subdue and retain the West India Islands, should stipulate with Spain for the cession of Louisiana, and should conquer Nova Scotia? The curious *cordon* with which we have allowed Great Britain to circumvent us (and of which more will be said hereafter) being thus broken, how are we to calculate the consequences?

5. Considering the Indians as a foreign nation, is not the

treaty calculated to exalt the character of Great Britain, and to depreciate the character of America, throughout the savage world? What right has Great Britain to negotiate for Indians within the limits of our jurisdiction? Suppose the existing western posts surrendered, may not Great Britain establish other posts in a contiguous or more advantageous station? Is she not left at liberty to pursue the fur trade in our territory as well as her own? Will not her enterprise in traffic, superior capital, and experience enable her to monopolize that trade? And will she not in future have the same motives and the same means to foment Indian hostilities, that have hitherto been indulged and employed at the expense of so much American blood and treasure?

VII. *The treaty with Great Britain is impolitic and pernicious in respect to the domestic interests and happiness of the United States.*

1. If it is true, and incontrovertibly it is true, that the *interest* and *happiness* of America consist, as our patriotic President, in his letter to Lord *Buchan,* declares, "in being little heard of in the great world of politics; in having nothing to do in the political intrigues or the squabbles of European nations; but, on the contrary, in exchanging commodities, and living in peace and amity with all the inhabitants of the earth, and in doing justice to and in receiving it from every power we are connected with;" it is likewise manifest that all the wisdom and energy of those who administer our government should be constantly and sedulously employed to preserve or to attain for the United States that enviable rank among nations. To *refrain from forming hasty and unequal alliances*, to let commerce flow in its own natural channels, to afford every man, whether alien or citizen, a remedy for every wrong, and to resist, on the first appearance, every violation of our national rights and independence, are the means best adapted to the end which we contemplate. It may be objected that we are already involved in some alliances that have had a tendency rather to destroy our public tranquillity than to promote our public interest. But a difference of circumstances will require and justify a difference of conduct. For instance, it was necessary and politic, in the state of our affairs at the commencement of the Revolution, to pay a premium for the friendship and alliance of France; we could not have insured success without the co-operation of that nation; and, as *the price* that we paid for it was not greater than *the benefit* that we derived from it, we cannot now with justice cavil at our bargain. But was the inducement to form an alliance with Great Britain of a nature equally momentous? Is the advantage flowing from the sacrifices that are made equally compensatory? Why should we, at this auspicious season of our

affairs, venture to undermine the fundamental maxim of our domestic happiness *by wilfully obtruding on the great world of
politics, or wantonly involving ourselves in the political intrigues
and the squabbles of European nations?* Suppose, as it is often
alleged and sometimes proved, that our treaty with France is
productive of inconveniences, will it happen in the political any
more than in the physical or moral world that, by multiplying
the sources of evil, we shall get rid of the evil itself? If, according to the *quondam* opinion of the friends of a British alliance,
our commerce has been restrained in its operations, or if our
government has been menaced in its peace and stability by a
practical development of *the terms* of our treaty with France,
shall we better our situation because we make *another* treaty
upon the same terms with Great Britain, and furnish *two* nations
instead of *one* with an opportunity to perplex and distress us in
pursuing our natural and laudable policy—*the policy of exchanging commodities and living in peace and amity with all
the inhabitants of the earth, doing justice to and in receiving
it from every power we are connected with?*

2. But even if the question was at large, and we were now
under a necessity of deciding, for the first time, whether we
would be allied to the monarchy of Great Britain or to the republic of France, how would a rational estimate of *the interests
and happiness* of the United States (the true and only touch-
stone for solving, *in the mind of an American*, such an inquiry)
lead us to decide? To *those members of the Senate* who could
regard *the twelfth article* of the treaty *as a mark of parental
care and wisdom, by which Great Britain was fondly desirous
of restraining the excesses of our commercial ardor; excesses
that might eventually and prematurely debilitate and destroy us!*
to *those members of the Senate* who could, with filial gratitude,
declare *that an alliance with Great Britain was natural; that
an alliance with France was artificial; since, although we were
partially indebted to France for our independence, we were entirely indebted to Great Britain for our being!*—to all who can
cherish such ideas, or utter such language, these strictures will be
ungracious and unprofitable; but they claim a candid attention
from *the patriot,* who remembers that when *the parent* sought to
destroy, *the friend* interposed to save; and from *the statesman,*
who possesses too much wisdom to be influenced by prejudice,
and too much fortitude to be controlled by fear.

Are the *interests and happiness* of the United States involved
in the permanent establishment of a republican government?
Yes. Then she ought rather to cultivate the friendship of a republic, actuated by a fellow-feeling, than the alliance of a monarchy impressed with jealousy and apprehension. Are the
interests and happiness of the United States connected with her

territorial and political independence? Yes. Then she ought
rather to fortify herself by an alliance with a nation whose
territorial jurisdiction and physical characteristics preclude the
possibility of collision, than attach herself to a nation whose
language, manners, and habits facilitate the execution of every
attempt to encroach, and whose territorial possessions are in an
irritating and dangerous contact with our own. Are *the interest
and happiness* of America to be promoted by an active employment of the vast store of *materials of the first necessity* which
nature has bestowed on her, by the extension of her commerce,
and by the freedom of her navigation? Yes. Then she ought
rather to court the countenance and protection of a nation whose
occasions of envy are comparatively few; whose temptations
are to foster, not to counteract, our schemes of commercial opulence and enterprise; and whose imperial glory and existence
do not depend upon a claim of universal maritime superiority;
rather than consent to bask beneath the baneful shade of an
alliance with a nation whose very existence is, probably, the
tremendous stake in opposition to our prosperity; and whose
embraces, like the embraces of the tyrant's image, may be rendered the most effectual instruments of torture and destruction.
Are the *interest and happiness* of the United States dependent
on the cordiality of their union and the permanency of their
government? And again—Do that cordiality and that permanency depend upon the confidence and mutual good understanding which subsist between the people who formed the government
and the officers whom the people have appointed to administer
it? Yes. Then it would be the part of duty, as well as policy,
in those officers to follow *the unanimous sentiment of the people,*
by preferring a liberal and faithful alliance with France to a con-
strained and hypocritical alliance with Great Britain.

3. The first striking effect of the treaty *to endanger the interests and disturb the happiness* of the United States may be
detected by a geographical sketch of the *cordon, or line of circumvallation, with which it enables Great Britain to fetter and
inclose us.* The proximity of Canada and the western posts
has heretofore been a cause of great uneasiness; but that is a
trifling source of vexation compared with what we shall have in
future to encounter. Suppose ten thousand *radii* were drawn
diverging from the centre of the United States; not one of them
could escape the conventional circle of British territory, jurisdiction, and occupancy. Has an American occasion to travel to the
east or the north, *the barriers of Nova Scotia and Canada* present themselves. Is it his wish to penetrate the great western wilderness, *a new set of British posts* will intercept his progress,
even if he shall be allowed peaceably to pass *the British colony*
within the precincts and jurisdiction of Detroit. Does business

require him to cross, or float down, the Mississippi, he may evade the vigilance of the Spaniard, but he will find the eastern bank of the river monopolized by British traders, and probably protected by British gunboats. He is in hopes, however, to avoid all difficulty by a passage on the ocean. Alas! our Atlantic harbors are crowded with prizes to British privateers, and our seacoast is lined with British cruisers! Yet let us for a moment imagine that this ill-fated traveller has surmounted his *domestic* obstacles, whither can he fly to be emancipated from the *foreign* jurisdiction of Great Britain? In the West Indies, his *cock-boat* is measured and steered according to the scale and course prescribed by the treaty. In the East Indies, he can hardly exchange a commodity, or make a single acquaintance, without the British license. In Europe, if, during a British war, he carries goods belonging to an enemy of Great Britain, they will be seized as prize; if he takes ship-timber, tar, rosin, etc., they are liable to be confiscated as contraband; and if his cargo consists of provisions, the British may take it, *by treaty, at their own market price!*

One idea more about the boundary of the United States. Before the Revolution, Great Britain had projected that general arrangement and division of her colonial possessions in America which she has since, upon a smaller scale, carried into execution with respect to Canada. The territory then intended to be allotted to the government of the Canadas was extended by a line running along the northern boundaries of the eastern colonies, along the western boundary of Pennsylvania, and along the courses of the Ohio, into the Mississippi. Since we are left at a loss for a positive definition of *the precincts and jurisdiction of the western posts as ceded by the treaty to the settlers under British titles*, may we not conjecture that Great Britain contemplates the territorial extent of her original project? Does not Major Campbell's unexpected pretension, and the constant claim of the Indians, *at the instigation of the British*, to establish the Ohio as a boundary between them and the United States, give some countenance to such a conjecture?

4. But should an American, not stimulated by the desire of travelling into foreign countries, be content to prosecute the objects of his honest industry within the British territorial circle bounding and constituting *his own home*, will his condition be much better than the condition of his itinerant fellow-citizen? What with the establishment of British colonies and British warehouses, the naturalization of British landholders, and, in short, the *unqualified admission* of Englishmen, owing allegiance to the British crown, throughout our lakes, rivers, and territory, while we are *excluded* from their seaports, company-lands, etc., an American will hardly be able to find elbow-room for himself

and family. Their pecuniary capital being larger; their means being easier; their experience being greater,—they must, inevitably, under such circumstances, become our merchants, manufacturers, farmers, etc. etc. They will import for us, *in their vessels*, all the products and fabrics of Europe, Asia, and Africa. They will export for us, *in their vessels*, every article that our soil can furnish ; our merchants will dwindle into clerks; our husbandmen will degenerate into the condition of the feudal villienage; and thus, in a short course of years, *America will probably exhibit the astonishing spectacle of a country possessed, cultivated, and enjoyed by aliens !* The ancient inhabitants of Great Britain, in a similar manner, invited those Saxons to their island as *friends and allies* who soon afterwards became their *conquerors and masters.*

5. In such a state of things *the interest and happiness* of the United States must languish and expire ! At first the American mind will be corroded, by contrasting the elevation of *the guest* with the depression of *the host.* A struggle will probably ensue; but the influence of wealth, and the patronage of extensive commercial and manufactural institutions, etc. *will even divide the Americans themselves ;* and, *by dividing,* capacitate the British settlers to rule them. Is this an idle phantom, a visionary suggestion? No! For, is not a great part of our trade, at this moment, monopolized by British subjects, under *the mask* of American citizenship? Has not the influence of British credits and British politics already formed a considerable party in our government and among our merchants? Disguise it as you will,—let pride deny and shame suppress the sentiment,—still, it is too evident to every candid and discerning observer, that the only subsisting difference in the opinions and conduct of the citizens of America arises from this fatal cause. Why, at the moment of reprobating *self-created societies for civil purposes,* do we gladly see the formation of *self-created societies for military purposes,*—the city cohorts and Prætorian bands? Why are our merchants, who so anxiously called forth the voice of their fellow-citizens in applauding the proclamation of neutrality, so circumspect and so torpid in giving their testimony about the treaty? How comes it that amidst the acclamations of the 4th of July the treaty is *toasted* in the little circle of English manufacturers on the banks of the Passaic, and at the convivial tables of the English emigrants on the plains of the Genesee? How comes it that every man who prefers France to Great Britain—republicanism to monarchy—is denominated *anti-Federalist,* Jacobin, Disorganizer, Miscreant, etc., while men of another humor arrogantly and exclusively assume the titles of *Federalists, Friends to Order,* etc. etc.? But let every honest American reflect seriously and seasonably upon the means of promoting *the*

interest and happiness of the United States, and he will disdain, as well as dread, to augment, by the adventitious force of treaties, that paramount interest which Great Britain has already insidiously acquired in our commerce, navigation, manufactures, territory, and government.

6. Besides the injury eventually to be apprehended from these causes, the treaty is calculated to impair *the interest and happiness* of the United States by producing an immediate and violent concussion in the federal atmosphere. For,

It ransacks the archives of our revolutionary transactions, and rejudges the solemn judgments of our courts of justice.

It condemns individuals to the payment of debts from which they had previously been discharged by law.

It makes the government of the Union responsible for the contracts of private citizens and the defalcations of bankrupts.

It disregards the freedom of our commerce and navigation, and it restrains the use of our staple commodities.

It does *not* exact a just indemnification for the detention of the western posts.

It does *not* require the payment, stipulated by the preceding treaty, *for the value* of the negroes carried off at the close of the war.

It does *not* provide for the freedom and safety of our seamen in their intercourse with the British dominions.

Let any one of these propositions be separately analyzed, and sufficient cause will be found to excite and justify popular dissatisfaction; but view them combined, and the mind is shocked with an apprehension that *the ratification of the treaty may be the death-warrant of the Union!*

VIII. *The British treaty and the Constitution of the United States are at war with each other.*

1. Self-preservation is the first law of society as well as of individuals; it is the radical principle of all political compacts. Nations, says Vattel, are bound to guard *their own preservation and to pursue their own perfection.* We have incessant opportunities, indeed, of observing the operation of this universal rule—in animals of *instinct* as well as in animals of *reason;* in the world of *things* as well as in the world of *beings.*

2. Self-preservation, however, is a relative idea; it relates to the nature of the animal—to the constitution of the society. A man may lose his *human character* without destroying his *vital existence;* and a government may be changed *in its essence* without being subverted *in its forms.*

3. So likewise, without open assault or positive violence, the sources of animal life may be poisoned by the imperceptible contaminations of a luxurious habit; so, without the aid of terror

or force, the legitimate foundations of government may be undermined by the insidious encroachment of the rulers, and by the sedative acquiescence of the people. Governments, indeed, have too generally proved to be a kind of *political chrysalis*, passing, by progressive transmutations, from the grub of pure democracy to the butterfly of absolute monarchy.

4. But it will not *yet* be denied in America that, as the people have the sole right to constitute their government, the rule of *self-preservation* requires that the government should be maintained in practice as well as in theory, *such as they have constituted it.* To render it, by any construction of the written articles of our social compact, *other than a republican government*, would be as fatal a subversion as daring usurpation or military conquest could achieve. For what real difference does it make to a nation whether its constitution is *seized upon* by an enterprising individual, as in the Swedish revolution of 1770, or *overthrown* by a triumphant warrior, as in the recent extinction of the Polish monarchy, or *voted out of doors*, as in the disorganizing edicts of the Long Parliament of England? Thus, likewise, for one department of the government to assume the authority of another, or, by constructive amplifications of its own jurisdiction, so to monopolize the attributes of government as to render the other departments useless and inefficient, must ever be deemed an effectual subversion of any constitution. The mode of distributing and organizing the powers of government, as well as the consideration of the nature and extent of the powers to be delegated, essentially belongs to the people; and, in the body politic as well as in the body natural, whenever any particular member absorbs more than its allotted portion of the aliment that is destined to vivify and invigorate the whole, debility and disease will infallibly ensue. After the emperors had usurped the functions, privileges, and powers of the Senate, and of the popular magistrates of Rome, they preserved the formalities of the commonwealth, but they trampled on the liberties of the people. Though the parliaments of France had long been deprived of every deliberative faculty as the representatives of the people, they were summoned to the last as the ministerial officers of the monarch for the purpose of registering his edicts.

5. The government of the United States being, then, theoretically a *republican government*, and with great propriety denominated a *government of departments*, let us proceed to examine how far the *principles of self-preservation*, and the duty of *pursuing the perfection* of our political system, are involved in the ratification of the projected treaty with Great Britain.

The second section of the second article of the constitution says that "the President shall have power, by and with the advice and consent of the Senate, to make treaties, provided two-thirds of the senators present concur."

To the exercise of this power no immediate qualification or restriction is attached; but must we, therefore, suppose that the jurisdiction of the President and Senate, like the jurisdiction ascribed to the British Parliament, is omnipotent? To place the authority of our President and Senate on the same footing with the prerogative of the king of Great Britain will not be commensurate with the objects to which the treaty extends. It must be remembered that the treaty of peace, by which the rights of sovereignty and soil were ceded by the king of Great Britain to the United States, was negotiated and ratified under the positive sanction of an act of Parliament; and it is expressly stated in *Vattel* that the king of Great Britain cannot, by *treaty*, confer the rights of citizenship on an alien. (B. i. c. 19, f. 214.) Now, Mr. Jay's treaty does both these things (as will be hereafter demonstrated) without the intervention of the legislative authority of the Union.

6. The consequence of admitting this unqualified claim to omnipotence, in transacting the business of the nation, would be so hostile to the principle and preservation of our government that it is an indispensable duty (*obsta principiis*) to controvert and resist it. Whenever the President and two-thirds of the Senate shall be desirous to counteract the conduct of the House of Representatives; whenever they may wish to enforce a particular point of legislation; or whenever they shall be disposed to circumscribe the power of a succeeding Congress,—a treaty with a foreign nation, nay, a talk with a savage tribe, affords the ready and effectual instrument for accomplishing their views; since the treaty or the talk will constitute the supreme law of the land. That *such things may happen*, let the history of Mr. Jay's mission and negotiation testify.

7. If the extraordinary *treaty-making power* is paramount to the ordinary *legislative power*, — supersedes its exercise,—and embraces all its objects, let us endeavor to trace whither the proposition will carry us.

The fifth article of the constitution vests a power in two-thirds of both houses of Congress to *propose amendments to the constitution*.

Let us suppose that a defect in our judiciary, or in any other department, operated injuriously to a foreign nation,—could the Senate and President, uniting with that foreign nation, and excluding the House of Representatives, *propose an amendment upon the subject?* If they could by these means *originate*, might they not by other means *effectuate*, alterations in the fundamental points of our government, and make, in fact, a new constitution for us?

13

By the eighth section of the first article, *Congress is* empowered to *borrow money* on the credit of the United States.

Suppose it was deemed expedient to subsidize Portugal, instead of building frigates, to keep the Algerines within the straits of the Mediterranean,—could two-thirds of the Senate and the President either borrow, or guarantee, a loan for that purpose *by treaty?*

The same section empowers *Congress* to establish uniform laws on *the subject of bankruptcies.*

Suppose Great Britain had remarked that, as her subjects were constantly the creditors of the citizens of the United States, she was deeply interested in our system of bankrupt laws,—had the President and two-thirds of the Senate a right to incorporate such a system with the projected treaty?

The same section empowers *Congress* to *coin money,* to regulate the value thereof, and of *foreign coin,* and fix the *standards of weights and measures.*

Suppose the Birmingham manufacturers offered, on a cheap plan, to supply us with coin; suppose Great Britain were pleased to insist upon our receiving her guineas at their English value, and upon our promising not to sweat, deface, or clip them, according to the current practice of the Union; suppose France were desirous that we should adopt the fanciful project of that republic respecting weights and measures;—could all, or any, of these propositions be acceded to and established *by treaty?*

The ninth section of the same article declares "that the migration or importation of such persons as the States now existing shall think proper to admit, shall not be prohibited by the Congress *prior* to the year eighteen hundred and eight."

Suppose Mr. Wilberforce had negotiated on the part of Great Britain, instead of Lord Grenville, and had made the prohibition of the importation of slaves into the United States, in the year eighteen hundred and eight, *sine qua non,*—could the President and two-thirds of the Senate admit and legitimize the stipulation *by treaty?*

By the constitution, *Congress* has the power to constitute tribunals inferior to the supreme court.

Suppose Great Britain desired, for the future, as well as for the past, to establish a tribunal of her own judges in America, for deciding controversies between British subjects and American citizens,—could this be accomplished through the medium of a treaty?

By the constitution, *Congress* is endowed with the power of declaring war.

Suppose Lord Grenville had insisted, and Mr. Jay had approved, that the treaty should be an offensive and defensive alliance, and that we should forthwith join Great Britain in her hostilities against France,—could the President and Senate thus *negotiate* us into a war ?

By the constitution it is declared "that no person holding any office, etc. under the United States shall, without the consent of Congress, accept of any present, emolument, office, or title, of any kind whatsoever, from any king prince, or foreign state."

Suppose our envoy had been offered a present or a title by the British monarch,—would the consent of the treaty be tantamount to the consent of Congress for the purpose of approving and justifying his acceptance ?

By the constitution it is provided that all bills for raising revenues shall originate in the House of Representatives, and that no money shall be drawn from the treasury but in consequence of appropriations made by law.

Suppose Great Britain had stipulated that, as soon as the commissioners had fixed the sum due to her subjects for old debts, the President should draw a warrant for the amount, and that the same should be paid out of all public moneys in the treasury of the United States prior to the payment of any antecedent appropriation by law,—would this be the proper subject for a treaty or for an impeachment ?

8. But, fatigued and disgusted with displaying thus hypothetically the monstrous consequences which will inevitably flow from *the jurisdiction claimed on behalf of the President and Senate to bind the United States by any treaty, and in all cases whatsoever*, let us particularly examine *the numerous and extravagant infractions* of the constitution *which the projected treaty actually commits.* Recent as is the establishment of the federal constitution, it is, indeed, to be lamented that the possibility of violating it, is not a matter of floating and fluctuating popular opinion, but a matter susceptible of fixed and positive proof. For, who does not recollect that a bill touching the fundamental principle of the government (its representative quality), *after having passed both houses of Congress, was declared by the President to be unconstitutional, and therefore undeserving of his official approbation and signature?* Who can forget that a law touching the essential properties of the judicial department of our government, *after being ratified by every organ of legislative authority* (the President, Senate, and House of Representatives), *was declared by Chief Justice Jay and his associate judges to be unconstitutional, and therefore incapable of being executed and enforced?* With such authoritative precedents (and there are many others that might be adduced from the transactions of individual States) of the possibility of deviating from the rule and meaning of our constitution, are we to be damned for political heresy merely because we doubt, or deny, *the infallibility of*

Mr. Jay's negotiating talents? And must every man be *accursed* (to use, for a moment, the intolerant language of the late Secretary of the Treasury, in his character of *the New York Camillus*) who thinks that *the American envoy and the British minister were at least as likely to mistake, or misconstrue, the constitutional boundaries of the American government as the President, Senate, and House of Representatives of the United States?* It is certainly, upon the whole, more candid and more convincing to put "the defence" of the treaty upon the *true trading ground* taken by the New York Chamber of Commerce; to wit—"*That we have made as good a market as such pedlars had a right to expect on the royal exchange; and that we cannot afford to fight, though we must submit to be plundered.*"

9. Let us proceed, however, in examining the points on which *the British treaty is at war with the American constitution.*

(1) *By the Constitution of the United States, the* JUDICIAL POWER is vested in one supreme court, and in such inferior courts as *the Congress* may from time to time establish; and its jurisdiction embraces, among other things, "*controversies between a state, or citizens thereof, and foreign states, citizens, or subjects.*"

By the treaty, a tribunal other than the supreme court, or any inferior court established by Congress, is erected, with a jurisdiction to ascertain the amount of any losses or damages sustained "by *divers British* merchants and others, his Majesty's subjects, *on account of debts,* etc. that still remain owing to them *by citizens or inhabitants* of the United States;" and it is agreed, "that in all such cases, where full compensation for such losses and damages cannot, *for whatever reason,* be actually had and received by the said creditors, in the ordinary course of justice, the United States will make full and complete compensation for the same to the creditors," etc.

Remarks.—1. It is the right of every independent nation to establish and maintain a judicial authority coextensive with its territorial possessions. The principle is indisputable, and it is incidentally recognized by Lord Mansfield and other great lawyers in the celebrated controversy between the king of Prussia and Great Britain relative to the Silesia Loan. 2. The constitutional tribunals of the United States were adequate to the administration of complete justice in the very cases for which the treaty provides a special tribunal. 3. If it is possible in any case, with any nation, and at any time, to stipulate, *by treaty,* for the erection of a tribunal, in order to ascertain and liquidate debts due from citizens to foreigners, may it not be done in every case, with every nation, and at every time? 4. Is not the court of commissioners, in effect, an high court of errors and appeals for the United States, with power to revise and reverse every judgment that has been given since the year 1783, *either in a federal or State court,* in every cause between a British subject and an American citizen ? 5. Wherever the recovery of the principal debt has been protracted by *the forms of law*—wherever there has been *an abatement of interest,* by the compromise of the parties, or the verdict of a jury—wherever *the debtor has become insolvent,*—this high court of commissioners may sustain an appeal, and can award damages for the detention or loss of the debt. It is true, the treaty adds that this " provision is to extend to such losses only as have been occasioned by *lawful impedi-ments ;*" but the *extent* of the discretion of the commissioners, in adjudging what constitutes a *lawful* impediment, is without limitation or control ; and the nature of the evidence, by which their minds are to be informed, is without rule or definition ; since (in the language of the treaty) it may be "either according to the legal forms now respectively existing in the two countries, or in such other manner as the said commissioners shall see cause to require or allow." Thus not only erecting a court unknown to our constitution, but admitting a species of proof not recognized by the legal forms of our country. 6. Let us appeal to Mr. Jay himself upon the constitutionality of such proceedings. By an act of Congress, the judges of the circuit courts were required to take, and report to the Secretary at War, certain proofs in the case of invalids and pensioners. The judges refused (as we have already noticed) to execute the act, declaring it to be *unconstitutional,* as well on account of the nature of the duty imposed upon them as on account of the re-visionary power which was vested in the Secretary at War. *By the treaty,* the President and Senate will appoint commissioners, in conjunction with the king of Great Britain, to hold a court of appeals from every court in the Union ; and to determine judicial questions, upon private controversies, between British subjects and American citizens. Now, let us ask, whether it is more un-constitutional *for the legislature* to impose new and extraordinary duties upon a court, *existing according to the constitution,* than *for the executive* to create a new and extraordinary tribunal, *incompatible with the constitution,*—inasmuch as it can only act upon the alienation of the jurisdiction *previously and exclusively* vested in our domestic courts :—the jurisdiction of hearing and deciding judicial questions, upon private controversies, between British subjects and American citizens ? 7. But this is not the only infraction of the constitution involved in the arrangement alluded to—*the obligation of private contracts is transferred from individuals to the public.* The framers of the constitution, in declaring that " all debts contracted, and engagements entered into, before its adoption, shall be as valid against the United States under the constitution as under the confederation," could hardly anticipate that they charged the treasury of the Union with the payment of all the outstanding debts of the individual citizens of America! And when Congress was vested with a power "to lay and collect taxes, *to pay the debts,* and provide for the common defence and general welfare of the United States," it certainly never was contemplated that the government of America became the insurer of every British merchant against litigious delays and fraudulent or accidental bankruptcies! It cannot be suggested that Great Britain acts in a similar manner upon our complaints of the spoliations on our trade. For the injury that we have sustained originated *in an act of government,*—the injured individuals are, in the *first* instance, bound to apply *to the British courts of justice,*—and the public are only responsible in the *last* resort for the individual aggressors.

(2) By the Constitution of the United States, Congress is empowered to establish "an uniform rule of naturalization," and that power has accordingly been exercised in an act that provides, among other things, that "no person heretofore proscribed by any State shall be admitted a citizen except by an act of the legislature of the State in which such person was proscribed."

By the treaty, all the British settlers and traders within the precincts or jurisdiction of the western posts are allowed an election either to remain British subjects or to become citizens of the United States; and it is agreed "that *British subjects* who now hold lands in the territories of the United States may hold, grant, sell, or devise the same to *whom they please* in like manner *as if they were natives;* and that neither they *nor their heirs or assigns* shall, so far as may respect the said lands and the legal remedies incident thereto, be regarded *as aliens.*"

Remarks.—Is not the *treaty* at war with the *constitution* in this great and delicate point of *naturalization?* A British colony is *ipso facto,* by the magic of Mr. Jay's pen, converted into an American settlement! Every *British subject* who now holds lands (and when we recollect the recent speculations for the sale of lands, how can we calculate the extent of the adoption?) is, without ordeal or restraint, endowed with all the rights of a *native American!* If it is possible by treaty to give the rights of property to aliens, may not the *civil rights* of the community be disposed of by the same potent instrument? If it is possible by treaty to confer citizenship on the British garrison at Detroit and its contiguous settlers, why may we not by treaty also confer an instantaneous citizenship on *every flight of emigrants* that shall hasten to our shores from Germany or Ireland? It may not be amiss here to intimate a doubt of *the power* of the federal government to regulate the tenure of real estates; it is nowhere expressly given, and therefore cannot be constitutionally implied; and it seems to be among the necessary and natural objects of State legislation. But let us presume (what is highly probable) that there are amongst the settlers within the precincts or jurisdiction of the western posts certain *proscribed persons*,—can the treaty, in spite of *the law*, restore them to the rights of citizenship without the authoritative assent of the State that proscribed them? Again: is every man whose estate was liable to confiscation as a traitor or as an alien, in consequence of the Revolution, entitled *now to hold lands as a native?* The Fairfax claim in Virginia, the claim of the Penns in Pennsylvania, and the claims of Galloway, Allen, etc., may hence derive a dangerous principle of resuscitation. *Look to it well.*

(3) By the constitution, Congress is empowered to regulate commerce with foreign nations.

By the treaty, the commerce of the United States, not only directly with Great Britain, but incidentally with *every* foreign nation, is regulated.

Remarks.—There is not a source of *legislative jurisdiction* upon the subject of commerce which is not absorbed by this *executive compact.* The power of regulating commerce with foreign nations is expressly and specifically given *to Congress.* Can a power so given to one department be divested by implication in order to amplify and invigorate another power given in general terms to another department? But more of that hereafter.

(4) By the constitution, Congress is empowered to regulate commerce with the Indian tribes.

By the treaty, it is agreed that "it shall at all times be free to British subjects, etc., and also to the Indians dwelling on either side of the boundary line of the United States, freely to pass and repass by land or inland navigation into the respective territories and countries of the two parties on the continent of America, etc., and freely to carry on trade and commerce with each other." The treaty likewise provides that "no duty of entry shall ever be levied by either party *on peltries* brought by land or inland navigation into the said territories respectively; nor shall the Indians, passing or repassing with their own proper goods and effects of whatever nature, pay for the same any impost or duty whatever.

Remarks.—It is easy to perceive that the stipulations in favor of the Indians were introduced at the instance of Great Britain; and her motives are not even attempted to be disguised. Her traders will boast of the favor and security which she has compelled America to grant to the Indians, and so engage their confidence and attachment; while the privilege of free passage and the exemption from duties will inevitably throw the whole fur-trade into the hands of the British. The surrender of the western posts under such circumstances can produce no loss to Great Britain, and will certainly be of no advantage to America: it will not add a shilling to the profits of our Indian traffic, nor insure us a moment's suspension of Indian hostilities! But, to prosecute our *constitutional* inquiry,—what right is there, by *treaty*, to regulate our commerce with the Indian tribes? Whenever a treaty of peace and amity has *heretofore* been concluded with the Indians, it has been the constitutional practice of the President to call on Congress to regulate the commerce with them. Such calls were totally unnecessary, if the same thing might as well and as lawfully be done by treaty; and if it could not be done by treaty in the case of the *Indians*, neither could it be done by treaty in the case of a *foreign nation;* for both are expressed in the *same terms*, and included in the *same member* of the section. " Congress shall have power (says the constitution) to regulate commerce with foreign nations, and among the several States, and with the Indian tribes." What right is there, by *treaty*, to declare that *no duty* of entry shall ever be levied by either party *on peltries*, etc. (and a similar promise is made in cases that more immediately affect Great Britain), since *Congress* has the sole power to lay and collect taxes, *duties*, etc. to pay the debts and provide for the common defence and general welfare of the United States? If we may, *negatively*, say, *by treaty*, that certain duties shall not be laid, may we not *affirmatively* say, *by treaty*, that certain other duties shall be laid? And then, what becomes of that part of our constitution which declares "that all bills for raising revenue shall originate in the House of Representatives?" But let us imagine for a moment that it is in the power of the President and Senate to regulate our commerce with the Indian tribes,—*ought not the regulation to be made with the Indians themselves?* Why suffer Great Britain to negotiate and stipulate for Indians actually residing within the territory of the United States? Is such a concession consistent with the dignity and independence of our government—with the peace and interest of the nation? Let Mr. Randolph's letter to Mr. Hammond, on the conduct of General Simcoe and Major Campbell, be referred to as an answer to this question. It is not, at present, within reach to be quoted; but its contents were too important to have already escaped the memory of any reflecting American.

(5) By the constitution, Congress is empowered "to define and punish piracies and felonies committed on the high seas, and offences against the law of nations."

By the treaty, the definition and punishment of certain offences not known by any law of the Union, are declared and permitted; to wit:—1st. For accepting commissions or instructions from any foreign prince or state to act against Great Britain. 2d. For accepting any foreign commission or letter of marque for arming any privateer, etc., Great Britain may punish an American citizen, *as a pirate.* 3d. For not treating British officers *with that respect which is due to the commissions they bear,* and for offering any insult to such officers, the offenders shall be punished *as disturbers of the peace* and amity *between America and Great Britain.* 4th. For making a prize upon the subjects of Great Britain, the people of every other belligerent nation (except France) shall be punished *by a denial of shelter or refuge in our ports.*

Remarks.—To define crimes and apportion punishments is the peculiar province of the *legislative authority* of every free government; but it is obvious, from the foregoing recapitulation, that the *executive authority* has likewise encroached upon that province, by the instrumentality of its *treaty-making* power. Can a citizen be surrendered *by treaty* to all the pains and penalties of *piracy?* Then, *by treaty,* he might be subjected to all the pains and penalties of *treason.* It is true that the constitution reserves to itself *the exclusive right* of declaring what shall constitute *treason;* but it is equally true that it bestows on Congress the *exclusive right* to define and punish *piracy:* and the invasion of *the right to define* in one case, is as unconstitutional as the invasion of *an actual definition* in the other. But what legitimate authority can *a treaty* suggest in order to justify the restraint upon that right of expatriation which Congress itself has not ventured to restrain while legislating on subjects of a similar class? It is not intended to convey the slightest doubt of the power and propriety of controlling our citizens in their conduct towards *foreign nations* while they are within the reach of *domestic coercion;* but to prohibit an American freeman from going whither he pleases in quest of fortune and happiness, to restrict him from exercising, *in a foreign country and in a foreign service,* his genius, talents, and industry; to denounce him for seeking honor, emolument, or instruction, by enlisting *within the territory, and under the banners,* of another nation—to do such things, is to condemn the principle of our own policy, by which we invite all the world to fill up the population of our country: to do such things is, in fact, to prostrate the boasted rights of man. It is hardly worth a pause to ask, what proportion of respect is due to the commission of a British officer? and what degree of punishment the refusal or neglect to pay it may deserve?

(6) By the constitution, it is declared "that no tax or duty shall be laid *on articles exported from any State.*"

By the treaty, "it is expressly agreed and declared, that the United States will prohibit and restrain the carrying any molasses, sugar, coffee, cocoa, or cotton, in American vessels, either from his Majesty's islands *or from the United States,* to any part of the world."

Remarks.—This is an extract, it is true, from the twelfth article of the treaty ; but it equally serves to show the probability of attempts to violate the constitution. Besides, the advocates for the treaty are hasty and premature when they desire to throw the twelfth article entirely out of consideration; for, by that proposition, *though they should save the treaty, they effectually destroy its author.* They are hasty and premature for another reason : the twelfth article is to be *suspended for the declared purpose of negotiating something as a substitute ;* and therefore we must consider its principle in order to ascertain how far *any modification* of it could be rendered palatable. But, *on constitutional ground,* when it is declared that *no duty* shall *by law* be laid on articles exported from any State, is it not absurd, or wicked, to suppose that *by treaty* the exportation of *the articles themselves* can be prohibited ? The obvious intention of *the constitution* is to encourage *our export trade ;* the immediate effect of *the treaty* is to obstruct and annihilate it.

(7) There are many other points in which *a collision occurs between the constitution and the treaty,* but to which the scope and nature of these strictures will not admit a full attention. It may be cursorily remarked, however, that a *cession of territory,* which will, probably, be the consequence of *settling anew the boundaries* of the United States, and even the actual cession of the precincts of the western posts, *though in favor of individuals,* are subjects for serious reflection. If a part of the United States may be ceded, if a whole State may be ceded,—what becomes of the guarantee of a republican form of government to every State? The propriety of presenting this consideration to the public mind will be allowed by those who know that, *in the course of the senatorial debate, the* right of ceding by treaty *a whole State,* nay, any number *of the States short of a majority, was* boldly asserted *and* strenuously argued !!!

(8) It may not be amiss, likewise, to add that our government has no more right to *alienate powers that are given* than it has to *usurp powers that are not given.* For instance, *an act of Congress* could not (and can a treaty?) surrender the right of sequestering the property of a hostile nation, — the right of giving commercial preferences to a friendly nation, — and the right of suspending a ruinous intercourse with any nation. Great clamors have been raised against *the exercise* of these rights ; and, undoubtedly, they should only be used *in the last resort ;* but they are rights *recognized by the law of nations ;* and they are rights often essential to the duties of *self-preservation,* and sometimes necessary to the accomplishment of *reciprocal justice.*

10. Having taken this *review of the actual warfare between the constitution and Mr. Jay's diplomatic work*, and of the destructive consequences of the claim of *the executive to bind the United States, in all cases whatsoever, by treaty*, let us recur to the position with which the present feature was introduced, namely, *the duty of preserving the constitution, such as it was made and intended by the people*, and we shall find, by a faithful comparison of theory with practice, that *the government of the United States may be transformed, through the medium of the treaty-making power, from a republic to an oligarchy,—from a free government of several departments*, legislative, judicial, and executive, *to the simple aristocratical government of a* President and Senate.

11. This fatal effect, however, of converting our government from the system which the people *love* to a system which they *abhor*,—from what it was made in theory, to what it was never intended to be made by practice,—can only proceed from *error* or *corruption*. It would ill become the writer of these strictures, who so freely, but, it is hoped, so fairly, expresses an opinion, to impute to any man, or set of men, a sinister and traitorous design against the constitution of our common country. The denunciations fulminated by *the New York Camillus* and his small circle of coadjutors, harmlessly expend themselves in the violence of their explosion; like the denunciations of *the Tiara*, they spring from *an arrogant claim of infallibility ;* and like them, too, will only excite *the derision or the disgust of an enlightened nation*. Is it credible that every citizen of the United States, from Georgia to New Hampshire, who reprobates Mr. Jay's treaty must either be *an enemy to our government* or *a rancorous incendiary ?* Is it to be presumed that no man can utter a sentence of disapprobation respecting *the principles* of the treaty, without feeling a sentiment of animosity respecting *the person* of the negotiator ? Are we really such slaves to faction, so trammelled with party, so insensible to virtue, truth, and patriotism, that every thought which we conceive, every expression which we use, on this momentous occasion, must be connected with the possible (but, it is ardently hoped, the distant) event *of electing a successor to the present chief magistrate of the Union ?* Yet such are the base and sordid motives passionately and wantonly ascribed by *Camillus*, and the scanty troop of advocates who follow him *in supporting the treaty*, to the *great host of the American people, rising* (as it were) *in mass to condemn it*.

If it could be thought a convenient, a reputable, or a necessary task, how successfully might *the argument of recrimination* be employed ! Who, it could be asked, are *the persons* that support the treaty ? What are *the motives* that actuate them ? Is it surprising that *the men who advised* the treaty, or that THE MAN *who composed it*, should endeavor, by the force of ingenuity, art, or defamation, to rescue it from general malediction and impending ruin ? Was it not to be expected that a *faction, uniformly eager to establish an alliance with Great Britain at the expense of France*, would strenuously attempt to procure the ratification of *any instrument* calculated to accomplish that object ? Does not consistency require from *him who openly projected in the federal convention*, and from those *who secretly desire, in the execution of public offices*, the establishment of an aristocracy under the insidious title of *an energetic scheme of government*, that they should approve and countenance every practical application of *any medium* by which the barriers that separate our constitutional departments may be overthrown, and the occasions for interposing the popular sanction of the legislature may be superseded or avoided ? Is it not *natural* that British merchants and British agents,—is it not *necessary* that British debtors and British factors,—should clamorously unite or tacitly acquiesce in the applause bestowed upon a compact which, however detrimental to America, is beneficial to Great Britain, the nation of chief importance to the allegiance and affections of some of those characters, and to the opulence and subsistence of all ? Or, if the paltry idea of an *electioneering* plan must be forced upon our consideration, is it not at least as likely that *the party which aims at making a President of Mr. Jay will, on that ground alone, exert itself in "*The Defence*" of the treaty* as that the party which is desirous of conferring the same elevated office on Mr. Jefferson will, for no other reason, attempt to blast the fruits of his competitor's negotiation ? Considering, indeed, that *Camillus* himself, by confining his " Defence " *to the treaty as advised to be ratified by the Senate*, virtually abandons the treaty as negotiated and concluded by *Mr. Jay;* and also considering that a part of *Camillus's* defence of the *present treaty* arises from the *ambiguity* that Mr. Jay had left in the *former treaty* with Great Britain (upon which, however, his character as a negotiator was founded), we might be led to suppose that Mr. Jay's pretensions to the wisdom of a statesman and to the station of a President were not deemed, *even by his own party*, to be any longer tenable; but that *Camillus* still condescends, on the obvious presumption of a subsisting rivalship, to impeach the ministerial character and to depreciate the official performances of Mr. Jefferson.

But why should we arbitrarily *abuse*, instead of endeavoring rationally to *convince*, each other ? We all have the same right, from natural and from social law, *to think and to speak*. It is true that we do not all possess the same powers of reason, nor the same charms of eloquence ; but when men are on *an equality in the possession* as well as in *the right of exercising* those endowments, there can be no amicable way of adjusting a difference of opinion but that which is adopted for adjusting all the other differences of a free people—*an appeal to the voice of the majority!* Now, let it be allowed (and so far ought it to be allowed, but no farther) that Mr. Jay who negotiated the treaty, the twenty members of the Senate who assented to a conditional ratification, and Mr. Hamilton and the New York Chamber of Commerce who have appeared in support of it (an enumeration that comprises, it is believed, all that have hitherto *avowed a perfect approbation*), are in the possession of as great a proportion of information, integrity, and talents as a *like number* of citizens selected for their approved wisdom, virtue, and patriotism from the aggregate of those who have publicly condemned the treaty, and then let it be candidly answered which scale in the balance must of right preponderate. After such a selection there will still remain the great body of the community in opposition to a ratification, and as members of that community thousands of individuals who honorably served during the late war in the field and the cabinet, and many of whom at this moment serve with zeal, fidelity, and wisdom in the various departments of government. Is it not, then, the symptom of an arrogant vanity, of a tyrannical disposition, to stigmatize such an opposition to *a projected measure* with the name of *"Faction?"* The violence offered to Mr. Hamilton's person in New York and to Mr. Bingham's house in Philadelphia has justly excited the indignation of every sincere Republican; but even that reprehensible and odious conduct is not to be compared to the enormous guilt of endeavoring to *force* the opinion of a *few* individuals upon the *people* as the ultimate test of political truth, and to cast an *odium* upon the late conventions in which, according to the language of the constitution, "the people were peaceably assembled to petition the government for the redress (or rather the prevention) of a grievance."

But let the pardon of the reader be granted for *this digression*, and we will return to a delineation of the feature that lies before us.

12. Declining, then, either to create or to follow a bad example, let us ascribe the deviation from the principles of our constitution to an *erroneous construction* rather than to a *wilful perversion*, and let us exert our skill in averting the evil that threatens rather than indulge our resentment in convicting those who labor to produce it.

Our government, therefore, being a *government of departments*, it is, as we have already observed, inconsistent with *the duty of self-preservation*; or, in other words, it must proceed from an error in *construction*, that *one* department shall assume and exercise all or any of the powers of all or any of the other departments. "The departments of government (to adopt the elegant figure used by an excellent judge in a late admirable charge to a Philadelphia jury) are planets that revolve each in its appropriate orbit round the constitution as the sun of our political system." Thus, if the legislative, executive, or judicial departments shall encroach one upon the orbit of the other, the destruction of the order, use, and beauty of the political system must as inevitably ensue as the destruction of the order, use, and beauty of the planetary system would follow from a subversion of the essential principles of attraction, repulsion, and gravity.

13. It was necessary, however, that the power of making treaties with foreign nations should be vested in one of the departments of the government; but the power of making treaties is not, in its nature, paramount to every other power; nor does the exercise of that power naturally demand an exclusive jurisdiction. A nation may carry on its *external commerce* without the aid of *the treaty-making power*, but it cannot manage its *domestic concerns* without the aid of the *legislative power;* the legislative power is, consequently, of superior importance and rank to the treaty-making power. Again: *the legislative power, exercised conformably to the constitution*, must be direct, universal, and conclusive in its operation and force upon the people; but *the treaty-making power* is scarcely in any instance independent of legislative aid to effectuate its efforts and to render its compacts obligatory on the nation. A memorable occurrence in English history will serve to illustrate both of these positions. It is the fate of *the commercial part of the famous treaty of Utrecht*, concluded between France and England in the year 1712. "The peace," says Russell in his History of Modern Europe, vol. iv. p. 457, "was generally disliked by the people, and all impartial men reprobated the treaty of commerce with France as soon as the terms were known. Exception was particularly taken against the 8th and 9th articles, importing that Great Britain and France should mutually enjoy all the privileges in trading with each other which either granted to the most favored nation; that all prohibitions should be removed, and no higher duties imposed on the French commodities than on those of any other people." The ruinous tendency of these articles was perceived by the whole trading part of the kingdom. It was accordingly urged, when a bill was brought into the House of Commons for confirming them, that the trade with Portugal, the most beneficial of any, would be lost should the duties on French and Portuguese wines be made equal, etc. These and similar arguments induced the more moderate Tories to join the Whigs, *and the bill was rejected by a ma-*

jority of nine votes. In relating the same transaction, Smollett's History of England, vol. ii. pp. 242, 246, contains some passages too remarkable to be omitted on the present occasion : "Against the 8th and 9th articles," says the historian, "the Portuguese minister presented a memorial declaring that should the duties on French wines be lowered to the same level with those that were laid on the wines of Portugal, his master would renew the prohibition of the woollen manufactures and other products of Great Britain. Indeed all the trading part of the nation exclaimed against the treaty of commerce, which seems to have been concluded in a hurry, before the ministers fully understood the nature of the subject. This precipitation was owing to the fears that their endeavors after peace would miscarry, from the intrigues of the Whig faction and the obstinate opposition of the confederates." "Another bill," continues the same writer in a subsequent page, "being brought into the House of Commons for rendering the treaty of commerce effectual, *such a number of petitions were delivered against it,* and so many solid arguments advanced by the merchants who were examined on the subject, that even a great number of Tory members were convinced of the bad consequence it would produce to trade, and voted against the minister on this occasion."

Perhaps there cannot, in the annals of all the nations of the earth, be found two cases more parallel than the one which is thus recorded in English history, and the one which at present agitates the American nation. 1. All impartial men reprobated both treaties as soon as the terms were known. 2. The admission of the opposite contracting party to an unqualified participation in trade with the most favored nation is, in both cases, a principal source of complaint. 3. The removal of all prohibitions, and the surrender of the right to impose higher duties on the commodities of the opposite contracting party than on those of any other people, are, in both cases, condemned. 4. The good and the intelligent of all parties have united their influence in both cases to prevent a confirmation of articles of so ruinous a tendency. 5. The whole nation, in both cases, have exclaimed against the treaty. 6. Both treaties were concluded in a hurry, before the ministers fully understood the nature of the subject. 7. Innumerable petitions (and who will NOW deny the propriety of exercising the American right to petition?) were delivered against both treaties. 8. And the Portuguese minister declared, in effect, of the treaty of Utrecht (*mutalis mutandis*) what the minister of France will, probably, declare of the treaty of London (but what America surrenders the right of saying at any time to Great Britain), "If you ratify your alliance with the British, you must surrender your alliance with France." If such a wonderful similarity of circumstances concur *in the negotiation, terms, and reception* of these memorable instruments, let us hope that the guardian angel of American liberty and prosperity has also doomed them finally to experience a *merited similarity of fate!*

14. But having thus shown that, *even in Great Britain* the treaty-making prerogative is *neither paramount nor exclusive* (though *the generality* of Judge Blackstone's expressions on the subject would, perhaps, lead to that preposterous conclusion), we might be satisfied to presume, on general principles, that so high a claim of jurisdiction could not be maintained, at least, on the part of our President and Senate. Yet let us endeavor, by the infallible test of the constitution, to put the matter, if possible, beyond doubt and controversy; and having established that each department of the government should be confined to its proper orbit, let us endeavor to ascertain what that orbit is in relation to the *treaty-making power.*

(1) The power of the President and Senate to make treaties is given (as we have already stated) *in general and unrestricted terms.*

But the powers given to Congress (except in an instance to be hereafter noticed) are *definite in their terms and appropriated in their objects.*

Let us ask, then, by what rule of construction a power *primarily and specifically* given to one body can be assumed and exercised by another to which, *in a subsequent clause,* a mere *general* authority is given?

Upon the common-law principles of construction, *the specific powers* would clearly, in such a case, be deemed a reservation and exception out of *the general grant.* But even according to a rule furnished by the constitution itself, the same result will be produced. Thus, the twelfth ratified amendment declares "that the powers not delegated to the United States by the constitution, are reserved to the States respectively, or to the people." Now, if the general power granted for the purpose of making treaties can set at naught the jurisdiction specifically given to Congress for the purpose of making laws, may it not, with equal propriety and effect, overleap the boundary thus interposed between popular rights and constituted powers? In the one case, the reservation is expressly declared,—in the other, it is necessarily implied.

(2) But if the delegation of a *general power* does, *ipso facto,* convey a right to embrace, in the exercise of that power, every authority not incompatible with its objects, the consequence will be that *Congress may enter into treaties as well as the President and Senate;* for Congress is vested with a jurisdiction "to make all laws which shall be necessary and proper for carrying into execution their own powers;" and what laws are, in that respect,

necessary and proper, they must, from the nature of the thing, be the judge.

Suppose, therefore, that Congress was desirous of forming *an alliance, offensive and defensive, with France*, but could not obtain the constitutional number of two-thirds of the Senate for accomplishing the measure *by treaty,—an act of Congress, in order to regulate commerce with that nation*, would afford as effectual a mode (according to the new doctrine), since the act, on the pretext of an equivalent for commercial advantages, might *legislate* us into the coveted alliance. The temptation and facility of proceeding in this way is obvious,—the passing of a law requiring but a majority of the Senate ; whereas the ratification of a treaty requires the concurrence of two-thirds of the members of that body.

(3) It is not, however, necessary to mingle and confuse the departments of our government, contrary to the first principles of a free republic; nor to make *a part* of our political system *equal to the whole*, contrary to the soundest axioms of demonstrative philosophy, in order to give a just, efficient, and salutary effect to the treaty-making power of the President and Senate. For although,

In the *first* place, the *treaty-making* power cannot bind the nation by *a decision* upon any of the subjects which the constitution expressly devolves upon the *legislative power ;*

Yet, in the *second* place, the treaty-making power may *negotiate conditionally* respecting the subjects that constitutionally belong to *the decision of the legislative power ;*

And, in the *third* place, *every other subject*, proper for the national compact of a republic, may be *negotiated and absolutely concluded by the treaty-making power.*

(4) That such a distinction was intended by the framers of our present excellent constitution, the reasons that have been glanced at must, it is thought, sufficiently prove to every ingenuous mind. But let one argument more be adduced.

By the ninth article of the old confederation, it was declared " that the United States in Congress assembled shall have *the sole and exclusive right and power of determining on peace and war.*"

By the existing constitution of the United States, it is provided "that Congress shall have power *to declare war*, grant letters of marque and reprisal," etc.

Now, it is evident that by omitting to deposit *with Congress* the power of *making peace*, in addition to the power of *declaring war*, the framers of our present government had in full view the division of its department and the corresponding distribution of its powers.

Congress, *under the confederation*, was a *single* body, and

14

therefore necessarily possessed of all the little legislative, executive, and judicial authority which *the States* had been pleased to delegate *to the Union.*

The government of the United States, on the contrary, is a compound system, of which the Congress is only *the legislative department:* and, therefore, the executive and judicial functions are elsewhere to be sought for and exercised.

Hence it is that although the power of *declaring war is* (as it ought to be) *left with Congress,* the power of making peace is (as it ought to be) *transferred to the executive;* being a natural appendage of the general power of *making treaties.*

This deduction serves likewise to demonstrate that the framers of the constitution did not intend to leave the powers that are *specifically* given to Congress at the mercy of the power that is *generally* given to the President and Senate. By expressing a positive jurisdiction in favor of the former, it excludes a claim of jurisdiction in favor of the latter.

(5) Nor is it in *the power of making treaties only* that the constitution has abridged *the executive department* of its customary attributes in order to augment the sources of *legislative jurisdiction.*

In Great Britain (for instance), *the executive* possesses the power of making peace; of granting letters of marque and reprisal; of regulating weights and measures; of coining money, regulating the value thereof, and of foreign coins; of erecting courts of judicature; of conferring the rights of denizenship on aliens, etc. etc.

In the United States, the power for all those purposes is absolutely vested *in the legislature.*

15. On reviewing the various positions that have been taken in the course of these strictures, a desire is felt to exhibit the corroborative opinions of men who have been justly valued by the public. It will be useful to the reader, as well as pleasing to the writer, to indulge the disposition in a few instances and in a brief manner.

(1) It has been said that *the power of regulating commerce belonged to Congress.*

The report of Mr. Mason (a member of the federal convention) on that subject was delivered in the convention of Virginia as follows: "With respect to commerce and navigation, I will give you, to the best of my information, the history of that affair. This business was discussed (in the convention) at Philadelphia for four months, during which time the subject of commerce and navigation was often under consideration; and I assert that eight out of twelve, for more than three months, voted for requiring two-thirds of the members present in each house to pass commercial and navigation laws. True it is that afterwards it was carried by a majority as it stands. If I am right, there was a great majority for two-thirds of the States in this business, till a compromise took place between the northern and southern States; the northern States agreeing to the temporary importation of slaves, and the southern States conceding, in return, that navigation and commercial laws should be on the footing in which they now stand."

(2) It has been said that *the treaty-making power could not cede a part of the Union, nor surrender a citizen to be punished as a pirate.*

The opinion of Mr. Randolph (a member of the federal convention, and now Secretary of State), delivered in the same convention, contains the following passage : "I conceive that neither the life nor the property of any citizen, nor the particular right of any State, can be affected by a treaty."

Mr. Madison, also, justifying and recommending the adoption of the constitution to his fellow-citizens, says, with respect to *the treaty-making power:* "I am persuaded that when this power comes to be thoroughly and candidly viewed it will be found right and proper. Does it follow, because this power is given to Congress, that it is absolute and unlimited? I do not conceive that power is given to the President and Senate to dismember the empire or to alienate any great, essential right. I do not think the whole legislative authority have this power. The exercise of the power must be consistent with the object of the delegation."

(3) It has been said *the right of suspending a commercial intercourse with any nation, and the right of sequestering an enemy's property, etc.,* were rights *essential to an independent government and recognized by the law of nations.*

Vattel contains the following, among many other passages, on those subjects :

"Every state has a right to prohibit the entrance of foreign merchandise, and the people who are interested have no right to complain of it as if they had been refused an office of humanity." (B. i. c. 8, f. 90.)

"It depends on the will of any nation to carry on commerce with another, or to let it alone." (*Ibid.*, f. 92.)

"The goods even of the individuals in their totality ought to be considered as the goods of the nation in regard to other states. From an immediate consequence of this principle, if one nation has a right to any part of the goods of another it has a right indifferently to the goods of the citizens of that part till the discharge of the obligation." (*Ibid.*, f. 81, 82.)

"It is not always necessary to have recourse to arms in order to punish a nation : the offended may take from it, by way of punishment, the privileges it enjoys in his dominions; seize, if he has an opportunity, on some of the things that belong to it, and detain them till it has given him a just satisfaction." (B. ii. c. 28, f. 340.)

" When a sovereign is not satisfied with the manner in which his subjects are treated by the laws and customs of another nation, he is at liberty to declare that he will treat the subjects of that nation in the same manner that his are treated." (*Ibid.*, f. 341.)

(4) It has been said that the constitution ought to be preserved *such as the people have made it;* that, of course, the departments of government ought to be kept separate and distinct, *each revolving in its proper orbit,* and that *no other judicial tribunal* could be erected by *a law of the legislative power,* much less by *a treaty of the executive power than what the constitution prescribes or expressly permits.*

On this interesting subject we fortunately possess the opinions of the judges of the supreme court and of the judges of some of the district courts in the case of the act of Congress (already more than once alluded to), *which they have unanimously adjudged to be unconstitutional and void.*

Extract from the opinion of *Judges* IREDELL and SITGREAVES :

"*First.* That the legislative, executive, and judicial departments are each formed in a separate and independent manner, and that the ultimate basis of each is the constitution only, within the limits of which each department can alone justify any act of authority.

"*Secondly.* That the legislature, among other important powers, unquestionably possesses that of establishing courts in such a manner as to their wisdom shall appear best, limited by the terms of the constitution only; and to whatever extent that power may be exercised, or however severe the duty they may think proper to require, the judges, when appointed in virtue of any such establishment, owe implicit and unreserved obedience to it.

"*Thirdly.* That at the same time such courts cannot be warranted, as we conceive, by virtue of that part of the constitution delegating *judicial power,* for the exercise of which any act of the legislature is provided in exercising (even under the authority of another act) any power not in its nature judicial, or, if judicial, *not provided for upon the terms the constitution requires.*

"*Fourthly.* That whatever doubts may be suggested, whether the power in question is properly of a judicial nature, yet, inasmuch as the decision of the court is not made final, but may be at least suspended in its operation by the Secretary at War, if he shall have cause to suspect imposition or mistake, this subjects the decision of the court to a mode of revision which we consider to be unwarranted by the constitution. For, though Congress may certainly establish, in instances not yet provided for, courts of appellate jurisdiction, yet such courts must consist of judges appointed in the manner the constitution requires, and holding their offices by no other tenure than that of their good behavior, by which tenure the office of Secretary at War is not held; and we beg leave to add, with all due deference, that no decision of any court of the United States can, under any circumstances, in our opinion, agreeably to the constitution, be liable to a reversion, or even suspension, by the legislature itself, in whom no judicial power of any kind appears to be vested but the important one relative to impeachments."

Extract from the opinion of *Judges* WILSON, BLAIR, and PETERS:

"The people of the United States have vested in Congress all *legislative* powers granted in the constitution.

"They have vested in one supreme court, and in such inferior courts as the Congress shall establish, the *judicial* power of the United States.

"It is worthy of remark that in Congress the *whole* legislative power of the United States is not vested; an important part of that power was exercised by the people themselves when they 'ordained and established the constitution.'

"This constitution is the 'supreme law of the land.' This supreme law 'all judicial officers of the United States are bound by oath or affirmation to support.'

"It is a principle important to freedom that, in government, the *judicial* should be distinct from and independent of the legislative department. To this important principle the people of the United States, in forming their constitution, have manifested the highest regard.

"They have placed their *judicial* power not in Congress, but in 'courts.' They have ordained that 'the judges of those courts shall hold their offices during good behavior; and that 'during their continuance in office their salaries shall not be diminished.'

"Congress have lately passed an act 'to regulate (among other things) the claims to invalid pensions.'

"Upon due consideration, we have been unanimously of opinion that, under this act, the circuit court, held for the Pennsylvania district, could not proceed:

"*First.* Because the business directed by this act is not of a judicial nature. It forms no part of the power vested by the constitution in the courts of the United States; the circuit court must, consequently, have proceeded without constitutional authority.

"*Secondly.* Because if, upon that business, the court had proceeded, *its judgments* (for its opinions are its judgments) *might, under the same act, have been revised and controlled by the legislature and by an officer in the executive department.* Such revision and control we deemed radically inconsistent with the independence of that judicial power which is vested in the courts; and, consequently, with that important principle which is so strictly observed by the Constitution of the United States."

Extract from the opinion of *Chief Justice* JAY, and Judges CUSHING and DUANE:

"The court were unanimously of opinion,

"*First.* That by the Constitution of the United States, the government thereof is divided into *three* distinct and independent branches; and *that it is the duty of each to abstain from and oppose encroachments on either.*

"*Secondly.* That neither the *legislative* nor *the executive branches* can constitutionally assign to the *judicial* any duties, but such as are properly judicial, and to be performed in a judicial manner.

"*Thirdly.* That the duties assigned to the circuit court by the act in question are not of that description; and that the act itself does not appear to contemplate them as such; inasmuch as it subjects the decision of these courts, made pursuant to those duties, first to the consideration and suspension of the Secretary at War, and then to the revision of the legislature; *whereas, by the constitution, neither the Secretary at War nor any other executive officer, nor even the legislature, are authorized to sit as a court of errors on the judicial acts or opinions of this court.*"

SUCH, upon the whole, are "THE FEATURES OF MR. JAY'S TREATY." It was not intended to protract this sketch of them to so great a length; and yet more circumstances are recollected that might have been inserted than could, upon a fair reconsideration, be retrenched. If it shall, in any degree, serve the purposes of truth, by leading, through the medium of a candid investigation, *to a fair, honorable, and patriotic decision,* the design with which it was written will be completely accomplished, *whether* RATIFICATION *or* REJECTION *is the result.*

But before the subject is closed, let the citizens of the Union be warned from too credulous an indulgence of *their prejudices* and *their fears.* The discordant cry of party is loud; and the phantoms of war assail the imagination; yet, let us not be deluded by stratagem nor vanquished by terror. The question is not a question between party and party, but between nation and nation; it is not a question of war or peace between military powers, but a question of policy and interest between commercial rivals. The subject is too momentous to be treated as the football of contending factions,—it appeals from the passions to the judgment, from the selfishness to the patriotism, of every citizen!

That *the British treaty, or a British war, is a necessary alternative,* will be more fully controverted if the writer's present intention of delineating "FEATURES OF THE DEFENCE" shall be carried into effect. But, in the mean time, let a few self-evident propositions contribute to relieve the public mind from the weight of that apprehension.

1. The *disposition of Great Britain*, manifested by the order of the 6th of November, 1793, by the speech of Lord Dorchester to the Indians, and by the repeated invasions made, under General Simcoe's authority, upon our territory, *is naturally hostile to the United States.*

2. Even if the United States could, by any means, soothe and convert that disposition into amity and peace, *the projected treaty is too high a price to pay for such a change.*

3. The refusal to enter into the projected treaty with Great Britain is *not a just cause of war;* and if a *pretence* only is wanting, it may be found in the toasts at our festivals as well as in the acts of our government.

4. But the ratification of the treaty will assuredly give umbrage to *another nation*—to an ancient ally.

5. If war is inevitable *either with Great Britain or with France,* it would be more politic for the state, more congenial to the sentiments of the people, to engage the former than the latter power.

6. In case of a war with Great Britain, we have assurance *that France will aid us with all the energy of her triumphant arms.*

7. In case of a war with France, we ought not to count upon *the affections,* and we cannot rely upon the power, of Great Britain to befriend us.

———

(FROM THE PHILADELPHIA GAZETTE.)

View of the Commerce of the United States as it stands at present and as it is fixed by Mr. Jay's Treaty.

1. ACTUAL STATE.—American ships from Europe enjoy a protecting duty of ten per cent. on the amount of duties on goods, wares, and merchandises imported into the United States in foreign bottoms from Europe, and of 30 to 50 per cent. on teas imported in foreign bottoms from Asia or Europe, paid by foreign bottoms more than is paid on such goods imported in our own vessels. Foreign bottoms pay also 44 cents a ton on every voyage more than is paid by American shipping; all which had been allowed by the federal government to encourage American ship-builders, mariners, mechanics, merchants, and farmers.

1. STATE BY TREATY.—By treaty America cedes to Great

Britain the right of laying duties on our ships in Europe, the West Indies, and Asia to countervail these, and engages not to increase her duties on tonnage on this side so as to check the exercise of this right; in consequence British ships may be put, at the discretion of the British government, on exactly the same footing as American ships in the carrying trade of Europe and Asia.

2. ACTUAL STATE.—American ships of any size now go freely to all the British West Indies, sell their cargoes, and bring returns, as it suits them.

2. STATE BY TREATY.—By treaty American ships are to be reduced to *seventy tons*, in order to be admitted in the British West Indies.

3. ACTUAL STATE.—American ships may now freely load molasses, sugar, coffee, cocoa, or cotton to any part of the world from the United States.

3. STATE BY TREATY.—By treaty American ships are to be totally prohibited this commerce, which is to be carried on under any flag but theirs.

4. ACTUAL STATE.—American citizens can now go supercargoes to India, settle and reside, and do their business there.

4. STATE BY TREATY.—By treaty no American citizen can settle or reside in these ports, or go into the interior country, without special license from the local government, who may, under color of this, impose what obstacles they please to the commerce.

5. ACTUAL STATE.—America now enjoys the right of regulating commerce, so as to encourage one nation and discourage another, in proportion to benefits received or injuries felt respectively.

5. STATE BY TREATY.—All this abandoned by the treaty so far as respects Great Britain; no duties can be laid on British goods but what must apply to all other nations from whom we import goods; no embargoes on exports to British ports but what must apply to all nations alike.

6. ACTUAL STATE.—American ships now freely navigate to the British dominions in India, and from thence proceed with cargoes to any part of the world.

6. STATE BY TREATY.—By treaty American ships are admitted as usual into the British ports of India, but prohibited carrying any return cargoes except to the United States; prohibited also from the coasting trade in the British ports of India, from which they were not, that I know of, before excluded.

7. ACTUAL STATE.—Timber for ship-building, tar or rosin, copper in sheets, sails, hemp, cordage, and generally whatever may serve directly to the equipment of vessels not contraband by former treaties of the United States.

7. STATE BY TREATY.—All these articles made contraband by this treaty.

8. ACTUAL STATE.—American ships carrying provisions, by America claimed as having a free right of passage to the ports of their destination.

8. STATE BY TREATY.—This claim now apparently waived; such American ships, when taken, to be allowed indemnity of freight, demurrage, and a reasonable mercantile profit, the amount whereof not ascertained.

9. ACTUAL STATE.—American ports open to prizes made on Britain by France, and America possessed of the liberty to grant similar douceurs to other nations, as she sees fit in future compacts with them.

9. STATE BY TREATY.—American ports now opened to prizes taken by Britain from any nation except France, but shut to prizes taken from Britain by Spain, or any other power not favored in this way by treaties already made; of course discouraging to our future negotiations with all powers, France and Britain excepted.

10. ACTUAL STATE.—American ships allowed at present freely to enter British ports in Europe, the West Indies, and Asia, but shut out from the seaports of Nova Scotia and Canada.

10. STATE BY TREATY.—American ships allowed to go into these ports, but under new restrictions of size in the West Indies, and of latitude of trade in the East Indies; the ports of Halifax, Quebec, etc. still shut to America.

11. ACTUAL STATE.—American ships thus partially allowed entrance into British ports.

11. STATE BY TREATY.—British ships allowed universal entrance into all our ports.

12. ACTUAL STATE —American ships now sail, though not under naval protection, under guarantee of all the British effects possessed here, which might be made answerable for our floating property, if unjustly seized on by Great Britain in case of a war, so much apprehended by the Chamber of Commerce of New York.

12 STATE BY TREATY.—By treaty American ships deprived of this guarantee; sequestrations or confiscations being declared impolitic and unjust when applied to stocks, or banks, or debts, though nothing said about them when applied to ships or cargoes.

13. ACTUAL STATE.—British debts now recoverable in the federal courts of the United States, but reposing on the solvency of the debtors only.

13. STATE BY TREATY.—By treaty a new court of commissioners opened on this subject, with immense power and guarantee of the United States, who must meet, indeed, at Philadelphia, but may adjourn where they please. Nothing said of

debts due to Americans in England, if, by legal impediments, prevented from recovery there.

14. ACTUAL STATE —America sends Mr. Jay to recover redress for spoliations on our commerce actually sustained.

14. STATE BY TREATY.—By treaty a court of commissioners opened, who are to sit in London, without power of adjournment, as in the case of the commission for debts. Americans must, therefore, transport themselves and claims to London, and employ counsel there, to recover what the commissioners shall think fit to allow them. Admirable compensation, indeed !

15. ACTUAL STATE —American ships much plagued by British privateers.

15. STATE BY TREATY.—By treaty the privateersmen are to give £1500 to £3000 sterling security for their good behavior.

16. ACTUAL STATE —American citizens may now expatriate and serve in foreign countries.

16. STATE BY TREATY.—By treaty they are declared pirates if serving against Great Britain ; but no provision made to guard American seamen from being forced to serve in British ships.

17. ACTUAL STATE. — America possesses claims to a large amount on account of negroes carried off, and the western posts detained in violation of the treaty of 1783.

17. STATE BY TREATY.—These claims all waived by the treaty, without reference to the merits of these pretensions.

The casting up of the above is submitted to the Chamber of Commerce of New York.

Errors, outstandings, and omissions excepted.

PHILADELPHIA, July 27, 1795.

No. 3.

MEMORIAL TO LEGISLATURE AGAINST CALLING A CONVENTION.

To the Honorable the Senate and House of Representatives of the Commonwealth of Pennsylvania, the memorial of the subscribers, citizens of the said Commonwealth, most respectfully represents :

That your memorialists have seen with alarm and regret proposals recently and suddenly sent forth and pressed upon your consideration for calling a convention with the avowed intention of altering the constitution of this State.

Your memorialists who, in common with their fellow-citizens, have for nearly fifteen years enjoyed the benefits resulting from our present system of government, framed by the wisdom, adopted by the choice, and suited to the character of the people, are unable to discover what new or formidable evils have arisen to require even deliberation or a change.

We now enjoy personal liberty; freedom of religion, of speaking, and of writing; property and reputation are protected. Some inconveniences may exist; but they are within the reach of remedy from the constitutional power of the legislature.

Believing the constitution to be so composed and organized as fully to secure all the objects of good government, and seeing no prospect but of danger in a project of innovation which, when required by no evident necessity, can lead to no useful end, your memorialists, solemnly protesting against a measure the pernicious consequences of which they sincerely deprecate, rely on the virtue and patriotism of the Senate and House of Representatives to preserve their country from the impending evil, and confidently hope they will firmly reject whatever application may be made for assembling a convention having for its object any change in the Constitution of Pennsylvania.

And your memorialists, etc.

ADDRESS TO THE REPUBLICANS OF PENNSYLVANIA.

FRIENDS AND FELLOW-CITIZENS,—After an arduous contest in support of those principles of civil liberty to which the Revolution gave birth, during the first period of a triumph that conferred the executive and legislative authority of the nation upon patriots of our own choice, while the character of the American people and of their government is rising, with unrivalled lustre, in the estimation of the wise and the good throughout the world, and in the ripe season of domestic prosperity, presenting its blessings as the reward of virtue and industry, without distinction of persons, places, and pursuits, who can hear without surprise the cry of social discontent, or view without apprehension a spirit of political innovation? But the painful crisis has arrived! Amidst all our inducements to preserve harmony and peace, the standard of discord has been wantonly unfurled. By specious tales of imaginary wrongs, you have been urged to doubt the reality of the happiness you enjoy. In the hope of substituting the glitter of impracticable theories for the steady light of experience, the fundamental laws and constitutions of the land are assailed. The

wreath of honor placed by yourselves upon the brow of sages
and of chiefs is rudely violated by strange and obtrusive hands.
And the Republican party of Pennsylvania, outrunning the opprobrious predictions of its enemies, seems eager to become the
speedy instrument of its own destruction.

The evil, thus distinctly traced, is great; but, fellow-citizens, it is not incurable. Reflecting upon the origin and process
of the schemes to subvert our government and to degrade our
patriots; the motives, the means, and the number of its authors
and supporters; the very nature of the influence which has be-
guiled some honest and respectable citizens to its aid; and the
irresistible force of reason and truth in developing the fatal consequences with which it teems, you will be convinced that there
is yet safety by an appeal to the virtue, intelligence, and power
of the people. In countries whose overgrown population is
tainted with crimes and enervated by want, where the inequali-
ties of property and of rank produce envy on the one hand and contumely on the other, where labor has no excitement for its movements nor any security for its accumulations, and where, in a
struggle to be emancipated from oppression, the end is deemed a
sufficient sanction for all the means that can be employed to attain it, the smallest spark of political enthusiasm naturally kin-
dles into a blaze, and the public tranquillity is forever held at
the mercy of individuals sanguine, bold, and aspiring. Far different, however, is the condition of Pennsylvania, where no material change can be projected without involving the hazard of a
material injury; and the people, neither insensible to the bounties of Providence nor regardless of the dictates of prudence,
will hear, examine, and decide for themselves. Encountering
this ordeal, the clamor which has been suddenly raised must as
rapidly pass away, and, like a summer's storm, serve only, by its
concussion, to purify and enliven the political atmosphere.

Behold, then, fellow-citizens, in the history of the existing
crisis, as well the ground of consolation as the source of your
affliction. During the memorable period in which the Republican party strove to rescue our civil institutions from danger,
and to enforce the right of participation in the service and honors
of our country, a principle of concert and conciliation gave life
and confidence and effect to all our plans and operations. But
no sooner were the stations of power and patronage occupied by
distinguished Republicans; scarcely had the auspicious inaugu-
ration of 1801 been celebrated, nor indeed had the toils of the
recent conflict ceased to require relaxation and repose, when
symptoms of ambition and intrigue, of jealousy and discontent,
of disunion and disorder, awakened the patriotic mind to a sense
of new troubles and new sorrows. The distinction, then, became
obvious between those Republicans who had fought for the cause

and those who had only fought for themselves. With some merit, on the score of service, but with more pretension, from the desire of remuneration, a small but active *combination of malcontents* was formed to influence or control the measures of government; and these men (in their career presumptuous, intrepid, and persevering) have deemed no claim too extravagant to be advanced ; no artifice too mean to be employed ; no obstacle too great to be surmounted. While they have marked, for popular scorn and suspicion, every other citizen in public employment, their business and pleasure and pride have been the designation of offices for themselves and the hungry circle of their adherents. The highest have not been above the soarings of their vanity, nor are the lowest beneath the cravings of their indigence. The cabinet of state and the direction of a bank, the desk of the customs and the bench of a court, the magistracy of a city and the clerkships of a department, contracts for public supplies and agencies for charitable institutions, military commissions and medical appointments, have been alike the aim, the hope, or the solace of their labors.

Although the objects of the combination which we deprecate may be thus regarded as single (the self-aggrandizement of its members), the arts that have been practised to accomplish it have been numerous and diversified. When the issue of our elections had destined the reins of government for Republican hands, it was seen and felt by the genuine friends of the rising administration that a dignified execution of the trust would be embarrassed by expectations which justice could not warrant, by solicitations which reason was unable to satisfy, and by suggestions which an enlightened policy could not fail to condemn. The indications of this perturbed and prowling spirit preceded the first official act of the new administration; and measures *to be adopted* were delineated by a bold and specious anticipation, that offered, in the form of a conjecture, what was meant to be prescribed as a task. While the great body of the Republicans, aware that their position did not afford a view of the whole of the political ground, left the arrangements of state and the work of reformation implicitly to their illustrious chief and his associates, the malcontents pressed with increasing vehemence on the councils of the nation. Sometimes they endeavored to attract attention by florid representations of their own personal worth and civic popularity. At other times they have sought to elevate themselves by depreciating the character of every real or supposed competitor. On one occasion you have seen them magnify the hasty opinion of a few inhabitants of a few wards of the city into a deliberate expression of the wish of the people. On another occasion they have been detected in divulging plots which were never conceived, and in branding as conspirators against the fame and fortunes of the chief magistrate men who would cheerfully expose their lives for the vindication of his principles and the advancement of his happiness. The whole machinery of confidential letters, essays upon the state of parties, anonymous hints, admonitions, and accusations has been set in motion. The petty incidents of private life and the momentary asperities of private altercation, mutilated scraps of conversation and sudden ebullitions of passion have been obtruded, from the recesses of a malignant memory, upon the public ear; and indeed it was once vainly thought that favor might be achieved by an attempt to sow the seeds of disunion, even within the hallowed precincts of the capitol.

But, baffled in every scheme and disappointed in every wish, mortified with contempt and exasperated by despair, the malcontents resolved to coerce whom they could not persuade, and to ruin what they could not enjoy. They quickly, therefore, exchanged the arts of solicitation and deception for the weapons of denunciation and terror, transferring their principal scene of action from Washington to Philadelphia, where the *Press*, which had obtained a matchless celebrity under the guidance of its able and upright founder, was devoted by its present proprietor to all their passions and projects. A few leading members of the General Assembly, honest perhaps, fascinated by the mischievous and glowing speculations of Godwin, were also enlisted in their cause, and undertook sometimes to act in the name of the legislature, just as the malcontents themselves have always presumed to act in the name of the people. The plausible pretext of redress of grievances and a reformation of abuses naturally operated upon weak though worthy men in a small degree to augment their numbers, while the desperate and the dissolute (to whom any change is preferable to the continuance of order) listened with delight to the sound of the revolutionary tocsin.

Thus composed and thus prepared, the malcontents commenced the work of devastation upon our public characters and public institutions, boasting, without shame or compunction, that in the prosecution of their designs the merit of past services should be obliterated; the hope of future usefulness should be blighted; every feeling of friendship, every claim of gratitude, every tie of domestic affection, should be disregarded and subdued. Although they still wore a mask of respect towards the chief magistrate of the Union, the members of his cabinet (the inmates of his heart as well as the partners of his toil) have been successively libelled by their newspaper squibs or stigmatized in their toasts at a festival. They have sentenced a Republican majority in Congress to the grossest imputations of corruption. In terms of unequivocal import they have charged eleven Republican senators of Pennsylvania with perjury while deciding in a judicial capacity. An opposition to the candidate whom they delight to honor, or to a measure which they are pleased, without consultation, to propose, has never failed to open the sluices of scurrility and defamation upon veterans of the Revolution and Republicans of the day of trial. In the lust of power, in the rage of proscription, the exercise of the equal right of opinion at political meetings has either been overawed by boisterous menaces or frustrated by clandestine combinations. The essential rules of discipline have been violated in the military corps to which they belong; while men wearing the garb and claiming the name of soldiers have refused obedience, on a political pretext, to the orders of their commander, leaving him no refuge from intolerable disgrace but an indignant resignation of his commission. For maintaining the freedom of election (that vital principle of a republican government guaranteed by the constitution and laws against every species of influence and outrage) Republicans have been deprived of petty offices under the city corporation. Nay, descending to the humble sphere of persecution, a long list of tried and inflexible Republicans have been expelled without a hearing from a popular society, charged with the inexplicable crime of suspicion or attainted of a contumacious opposition to the election of the member of Congress presiding at their expulsion. In short, who has not felt, or does not fear to feel, the goad and the lash of the present usurpation? To the elevation of bad men, the prostration of good men has always been found a necessary prelude. The Gironde of Brissot formed a base for the mountain of Robespierre. The worst views of faction, too, are generally pursued under professions of the best. And the citizens of America begin at length to perceive that advantage has been taken of their just veneration for the liberty of the press to shackle them with the tyranny of printers.

But it early occurred to the malcontents that this system of denunciation could not be supported by the mere weight of their own authority. Many citizens who were the objects of their enmity bore honorable marks of service in the war of independence; many had grown gray with the solicitudes of public council; most of them were attached to the soil by the ties of parentage, of offspring, or of property; and all of them had contributed to the triumph of republicanism. A generous people may be vigilant, but they cannot be suspicious; before they decide they will examine; before they inflict punishment they must be convinced that there exists guilt. It was natural, therefore, to expect an inquiry why men who had been firm and faithful throughout the gloomy season of privation and suffering, should abruptly abandon their principle and their party when all was sunshine, hilarity, and enjoyment. To escape from the difficulty of answering this question, the malcontents dexterously raised the phantom of a

third party! It is obvious, however, that while the rapid progress of their denunciation presents numbers sufficient to constitute an independent political corps, their ingenuity has been
exerted in vain to assign an adequate motive for its formation ;
nor has their zeal been more successful in discovering any proofs
of its existence. For though the public have been long amused
by a succession of promises to unveil "treasons, stratagems, and
spoils," what has been heard in performance of those promises
except the ravings of ambition and the ribaldry of nicknames ?
Thus to oppose a candidate pertinaciously nominated by the leading malcontents has been deemed an inexpiable *heresy*, although
a Republican was his competitor. A refusal to acquiesce in the
decision of the malcontents at a popular meeting has been arraigned as *apostasy*, although the decision was surreptitiously
obtained. A verdict for the acquittal of judges whom the malcontents had foredoomed to conviction has been stigmatized as
political defection, although it was delivered in favor of innocence
under the solemnity of an oath. In short, every freeman who
was unwilling to yield passive obedience to the mandates of a
secret tribunal and to sacrifice substantial benefits for airy novelty ; who would not applaud characters that he did not approve,
nor vindicate measures that he never advised ; who disdained to
carry the prejudices of party into the circles of social life, or to
declare all learning, learned men, and good manners hostile to
the dignity of republican virtue,—the malcontents have arbitrarily
enrolled as a *Quid* or a *Federalist*, a *traitor* or a *Tory;* involving
them all at last (under the auspices of General Steele and Mr.
Mitchell) in a comprehensive proscription of "*the Constitutional
Republicans.*" But here let it be explicitly announced, that if
to differ at this period in opinion and feeling, in theory and practice, from the malcontents can furnish the foundation of a *third
party*, we shall rather boast than blush at the imputation of belonging to it. For, as the malcontents have widely wandered
from the political ground on which we once acted together, our
last great hope (repeating the sentiment of 1801) is "an union
of honest men on the principles which led *Washington* to the field
and placed Jefferson in the cabinet."

Having traced the malcontents through the windings of sinister intrigue and personal detraction, we proceed, with increasing
indignation, to review their daring and sacrilegious efforts against
the civil institutions of our country. On a vain presumption
that the establishment of their own influence had been the necessary consequence of undermining the influence of others, it was
thought easy to consummate the work of destruction by employing the same arts to decry principles which they had hitherto
employed to disgrace men. Resorting, therefore, to all that
could excite passion or rivet prejudice ; to all that could stimu-

late fear or attract credulity, they have exposed the form and substance of our government, the code of our laws, the system of our jurisprudence, and the administration of justice, through a false and deceptive medium, to the scorn and detestation of the world. Whatever was prepared for us by our venerable ancestors is ridiculed as obsolete; whatever is the production of cotemporary wisdom is branded with corruption. The patriots of America are supposed to have been ignorant of the true interests of their country, and her statesmen are reproached with a treacherous contempt of the rights of man; while the impious and visionary standard of *human perfectibility* is proclaimed to be the only rational guide in the formation of a free government, and the malcontents themselves to be the only qualified rulers of a free people.

Under the impulse of these dogmas, and with a view to the introduction of wild, pernicious, and unheard-of schemes of legislation and politics,

The malcontents have endeavored to deprive us of the inestimable right of the trial by jury in cases of trespass and damages, as well as in cases of debt and contract.

They have endeavored to deprive us of the security of independent judges; of judges independent of popularity and persecution, as well as of power and patronage.

They have endeavored to deprive us of the sanctuary of the courts of justice where publicity will always insure impartiality; substituting the private chamber of an individual justice where secrecy too often encourages oppression and begets impunity.

They have endeavored to deprive us of the freedom of election by a display of the terrors of denunciation and proscription, threatening the good man with the loss of character, and the poor man with the loss of office.

They have endeavored to deprive us of the liberty of the press by denying to Republicans the usual channels of public communication.

They have endeavored to deprive us of the honors of a well-organized militia by flagrant examples of disobedience, contumacy, and disorder.

They have endeavored to deprive us of the benefits of the common law of Pennsylvania, as recognized, approved, and confirmed by the Whigs of 1776.

They are endeavoring to overthrow the State constitution, involving in its ruins the order of society and the principle of republicanism.

And finally, they are endeavoring, through the influence and example of *Pennsylvania*, to subvert the federal constitution at the hazard of civil war and a dissolution of the Union.

Such, fellow-citizens, is the crisis at which your decision is required upon the great questions—

15

Whether a convention shall be called? and whether the present governor shall be re-elected?

The inalienable right of the people to assemble for the alteration or abolition of their form of government, and the absolute authority of the citizens to select whom they please for their chief magistrate, have never been denied, and ought not to be resisted. But the possession of the right and the authority bespeaks discretion and justice in using them; and it would be disgraceful as well as destructive to yield that obedience to the cry of faction which is due alone to the legitimate voice of the people.

Here, then, let us ask what is the evidence of the public sentiment, what is the test of the public interest, on the important subjects before you? As the late session of the General Assembly was drawing to a close, the ultimate plot to subvert the constitution of the State was deemed mature for execution, and measures were accordingly taken to obtain signatures to a petition for the call of a convention. But this petition (and we appeal to the inhabitants of every county for a corroboration of the fact) did not originate with the people in thought, word, or deed; nor has any individual been yet bold enough to avow himself the presumptuous author. Issuing, however, from the *secret tribunal* of the malcontents, it was clandestinely and partially circulated in the remote districts of Cumberland, Washington, Franklin, Northumberland, and Mifflin; while in the city and the populous middle counties it was seen only by a few confidential persons, until the publication of the eighteenth of February last made a full disclosure of its contents to the astonished and insulted community. The object being merely to catch the semblance of a popular wish for a convention, and the snare for that purpose being thus artfully set, the malcontents seemed for awhile to be devoid of every apprehension of a defeat, and openly made arrangements for the enjoyment of a victory. In the House of Representatives a grand committee was appointed to receive the *solicited petitions.* Before a single petition was presented, legislative business of great moment (particularly a bill to alter the law respecting contempts of court) was laid aside, under the declaration of a leading character that "the approaching convention superseded the necessity of acting upon it." The correspondence of the members in favor of a convention invited support from their friends, evidently contemplating an immediate call, and forgetting that their sacred trust was conferred to preserve, not to destroy, the constitution; while the correspondence of their opponents anxiously claimed an expression of the sense of their constituents to avert the danger of an immediate dissolution of the government. The press likewise prematurely considered the event as realized; for there the time of assembling the convention was actually referred to the month of August,—the place of meeting was designated at Harrisburg, and merchants and lawyers, men of education and men of wealth, were indiscriminately excluded from the honors of the sitting.

But these visions of disturbed and sickly imaginations were suddenly dispelled. Our fellow-citizens, of every political description, feeling, at length, the necessity of a prompt interposition, hastened to rally round the constitution as the ark of their common safety; and now the malcontents beheld, with terror and dismay, the people, whose name they had craftily assumed and whose indignation they had justly excited, rising in the native majesty of their power and their virtue to vindicate the dominion of the laws. In the course of a few days, by a spontaneous subscription, the list of remonstrants considerably exceeded the list of names which had been collected during a long, industrious, and secret circulation of the petition; and when the report of the grand committee was discussed, the comparative numbers were 4944 petitioners and 5590 remonstrants, exhibiting to the actual view of the legislature a majority of 646 against the call of a convention, independent of thousands who could not transmit their remonstrances to the seat of government before the termination of the session.

Though the malcontents had themselves appealed to the community, though they had loudly deprecated every species of resistance to the sense of a majority, and though they did not dare, under such circumstances, to summon a convention upon their own responsibility or under the authoritative name of the people, yet they could not patiently acquiesce in a result so fatal to their personal and political speculations. The recent expression of the public sentiment could not be revoked or suppressed, but they thought it might be evaded. The freemen of Pennsylvania did not wish to alter their government as a benefit to themselves, but it was thought that they might be induced to alter it as a favor to *their friends.* The gratitude, as well as the policy of the State, forbade the degradation of her chief magistrate; but it was thought that the inconstancy and credulity of human nature would furnish instruments to accomplish it. To these and similar suggestions can alone be ascribed the extraordinary transactions which succeeded the failure of the project for an immediate call of a convention. The same principle that commands obedience to the sovereignty of the people must always insure respect towards the depositaries of their authority; but we can no more regard a few members of the legislature as the legislature itself than we can regard a few malcontents as the body of the nation. We saw, therefore, with regret—but, we repeat, without apprehension—that even some men, who wore the legislative honors of their country, appeared at that time to undertake the direction of the revolutionary engine. The House of

Representatives, too, under their influence, assumed a tone of superiority, and eventually monopolized the legislative character of the State; for the memorials, recommending as well as opposing the call of a convention, were addressed to both branches of the General Assembly (to the Senate as well as to the House of Representatives); but the House of Representatives alone received and considered, approved or condemned, denying to the Senate all information upon the subject and all participation in the decision. In this paroxysm of revolutionary zeal, the report of the grand committee was produced, bearing indelible marks of the disappointment and chagrin of its authors. Contrary to the approved maxims of republican legislation, and in contempt of the exclusive right of the people to originate every change in their government, the report controverts and derides the sentiments of the majority, applauds and enforces the sentiments of the minority, propounds abstract principles which no honest man will dispute, draws practical conclusions which no wise man can admit, repudiates the constitution for supposititious abuses or imaginary defects, and finally, solicits the agency of a convention to organize a political *millennium* upon the ideal scale of human perfectibility!

But here let us pause for awhile to recapitulate the various pretexts which have been used as a cover for the real designs of the malcontents, and as an excuse for the unauthorized interposition of a majority of one of the legislative chambers.

1. It has been said, in general terms of reprobation, that the constitution is defective; but as it would be idle to expect a perfect work from the hands of imperfect man, the remark carries with it neither censure nor information. It may certainly be applied to every other form of government, past or present; and we shall only indulge a pernicious vanity if we suppose that it will not be equally applicable to every future effort of human invention. But the Constitution of Pennsylvania was constructed on the model of the Constitution of the United States, and has itself become a model for the constitutions of several of our sister States. Its basis and its superstructure are, however, pre-eminently democratic; for, while other constitutions exact the qualification of property from electors as well as candidates, and transfer the choice of a governor from the people to a department of the government, the Constitution of Pennsylvania establishes the right of universal suffrage, declares every freeman eligible to every office, and reserves for the people themselves the appointment of their chief magistrate. It embraces, likewise, every principle of liberty, every security for life, reputation, and property, every means of knowledge by the freedom of the press, and every guard against the encroachments of delegated power upon popular rights or co-ordinate departments which the wisest statesmen could devise and the most anxious patriots could desire. Still, the Constitu-

tion of Pennsylvania may be defective; but are the defects such as demand the corrective of a convention? Have they generated calamity, oppression, or disorder? Is there a coincidence of opinion on the points of defect or the modes cf reparation? and do we not incur the risk of losing a constitution positively good for the mere chance of obtaining a constitution hypothetically better? The formation of every social compact depends upon mutual deference and conciliatory sacrifices of individual opinion.

No system of government was ever approved in all its parts by those who framed or by those who adopted it. And we venture to affirm that no system of government, no scheme of modification or amendment, will ever unite so great a portion of public sentiment and attachment in its favor as are united in favor of the constitution under which the people of Pennsylvania now live and flourish.

2. It has been said in the indefinite expressions of jealousy and alarm, that the delegated powers of the constitution may be perverted and abused; but this also is a remark so general (embracing equally the legislative, the executive, and the judicial power) that it strikes at the very existence of civil government. In truth, the use of power is essential to the order and peace of society; and the hazard of its being abused must therefore be encountered. But every well-regulated system, while it confers power, exacts responsibility; and no government can, consistently with the other important objects and operations of its institution, be more efficient in this respect than the government of Pennsylvania. Thus the members of the House of Representatives must annually account to their constituents. The Senate annually sends one-fourth of its members in regular rotation to the ordeal of an election. The executive magistrate undergoes a triennial investigation of his conduct at the bar of the people; nor can he enjoy the favors of popularity beyond a limited period. The judges are constantly subject to the censorial power of impeachment and to legislative addresses for their removal; while the subordinates of the State are amenable to the governor, and (in common with himself and the judges) may be impeached and dismissed for misconduct in office. If, with such precautions, there is not safety in the delegation of power, to what substitutes can we more confidently resort? Let it not be answered to the direct and constant agency of the people; for that is impracticable. Let it not be answered to the exclusive authority of the legislative agents of the people; for we know that legislative agents may feel power and forget right as well as executive and judicial magistrates. But, rather let us bow with reverence to the decrees of Providence, thus mingling with all its bounties to mankind a portion of bitterness and alloy.

3. It has been said, in terms of indignation and disgust, that

the constitution tolerates the common law, and is, therefore, inconsistent with true liberty and genuine republicanism. On no occasion has the declamation of the malcontents betrayed more ignorance or more wickedness than in the attempt to despoil this venerable code of the affections and confidence of the people. In depicting the common law they have ransacked the cells of monks; they have pillaged the lumber of colleges; they have revived the follies of a superstitious age; and they have brandished the rigors of a military despotism; but in all this rage of research they have forgotten or concealed that such things enter not into the composition of the common law of Pennsylvania; for the constitution tolerates only that portion of the common law which your ancestors voluntarily brought with them to the wilderness as a birthright, and which the patriots of the Revolution bestowed upon us as a charter of privilege and benevolence. Let us not, therefore, be ensnared by prejudices nor be deceived by the mere similitude of names. Every nation has its common law. The common law of every nation is the accumulated wisdom of its best men through a succession of ages settled into known rules, maxims, and precedents. The common law of England, stripped of its feudal trappings, is the admiration of the world. The common law of Pennsylvania is the common law of England as stripped of its feudal trappings; as originally suited to a colonial condition; as modified by acts of the General Assembly, and as purified by the principles of the constitution. For the varying exigencies of social life, for the complicated interests of an enterprising nation, the positive acts of the legislature can provide little; and, independent of the common law, rights would remain forever without remedies and wrongs without redress. The law of nations, the law of merchants, the customs and usages of trade, and even the law of every foreign country in relation to transitory contracts originating there but prosecuted here, are parts of the common law of Pennsylvania. It is the common law, generally speaking, not an act of Assembly, that assures the title and the possession of your farms and your houses, and protects your persons, your liberty, your reputation from violence; that defines and punishes offences; that regulates the trial by jury; and (in a word, comprehending all its attributes) that gives efficacy to the fundamental principles of the constitution. If such are the nature and the uses of the common law, is it politic, or would it be practicable, to abandon it? Simply because it originated in Europe cannot afford a better reason to abandon it than to renounce the English and the German languages, or to abolish the institutions of property and marriage, of education and religion, since they, too, were derived from the more ancient civilized nations of the world. Messrs. Jefferson, Wythe, and Pendleton declared, in reference to a revision of the code of Virginia (for all our sister States have adopted the common law of England, differing only in the degree and the manner of the adoption), that " the *common law* of England, by which is meant that part of the English law which was anterior to the date of the oldest statutes extant, is made the *basis of the work. It was thought dangerous to attempt to reduce it to a text;* it was therefore left to be collected from the usual monuments of it." (*Notes on Virginia*, p. 226.) How chimerical, then, must be the project of calling a convention to reduce the common law, not to a statutory detail, but to a constitutional text! How superfluous the trouble and the expense, since the legislature itself already possesses a competent authority to reform every abuse, to remedy every defect, and to control every operation of the common law!

4. It has been said that the judges, "under color of the common law, have exercised the most daring tyranny and violated the constitution and laws of the State," and hence the necessity of a convention has also been inferred. This assertion appears under the signature of Mr. Steele, *the president of the Senate.* It involves eleven of his fellow-senators (Republicans of inflexible political and personal integrity) in the imputation of perjury in voting in favor of the impeached judges; and it charges those judges with a crime for which they had been fairly tried, and of which they had been lawfully acquitted. But we will not enter into a discussion of the question to which the charge refers,— whether the judges of the supreme court have a constitutional power to punish *contempts of court* by the summary process of attachment,—nor will we even state the essential distinction between a wilful violation of the constitution, which could alone be criminal, and an honest error in judgment, which cannot be imputable or punished upon impeachment as a crime. These might be proper grounds of inquiry in estimating the *truth* as well as the *decency* of Mr. Steele's publication; but in the abstract inquiry, whether the conduct of the judges furnishes an adequate cause for calling a convention, it is sufficient to observe, that if contempts of court ought no longer to be punished by attachment, the legislature may, by their own authority, modify or abolish the process without any additional sanction from a constituent assembly; and we presume that the malcontents will not avow the design to render a bare majority of the Senate competent to a conviction on impeachment, lest it should be seen that the unanimity of a jury in other criminal prosecutions is also obnoxious to their views and equally the object of revolutionary reform.

5. It has been said that the constitutional power of appointment to office bestows on the executive the means of acquiring a dangerous influence, and that the constitutional negative of the

governor, upon legislative propositions, has been employed to retard the progress of political improvement. But the power of appointment to office can only produce a dangerous influence when those who enjoy it may be served by gratitude, yet cannot be injured by resentment. In a free, republican government, the power of appointment to office can never be made a dangerous instrument of personal ambition; since those who exercise it are as dependent upon the candidates whom they reject as upon the candidates whom they accept, and the number and activity of the former will forever exceed the number and activity of the latter. The transactions of the day evince the truth of this political position. The clamor of discontent is loud and virulent against the present distribution of offices, and an exercise of the power of appointment, in opposition to particular interests, has obviously furnished a signature for invective, and a certificate for imposture. But when it is said that the executive ought to be deprived of this power, we should likewise be told where it can more safely, more usefully, be deposited. The secret has not yet been divulged; but, fellow-citizens, beware! there is not an honest politician who, hearing the cabals of elections for federal senators, for State treasurer, for bank directors, will readily consent to endanger the purity of the legislative character, by enlarging the sphere of its patronage, in the appointment to office.

Nor can the qualified negative, upon legislative proceedings, however beneficial to the public, advance the popularity or influence of the chief magistrate. It is a power wisely created as an additional security for the preservation of the constitution from the encroachments of a popular assembly, whose numbers serve at once to abate caution and to diminish responsibility; for the protection of the co-ordinate departments of government from the absorbing tendencies of legislative authority; and for the prevention of sudden and dangerous innovations upon the laws and habits of the community. For all these purposes you have seen a firm and honorable interposition of the power during the present administration; but you have also seen that (raising a host, in opposition to an individual) no respect for the power, as vested by the constitution; no deference for the claims of conscience, as involved in exercising it; no consideration of personal wisdom and worth, as due to the magistrate himself; nor any sense of decorum, as inspired by his constituents,—could deter the malcontents from resorting to this ground as the stronghold of their operations against the official reputation of the governor. Let it be asked, however, in what instance the power has been found injurious or inconvenient to the rights and interests of the people? It has, indeed, sometimes suspended an important decision till the sense of the people could be ascertained. It has sometimes embarrassed an attack upon the principles of the constitution. It has often produced useful deliberation; and once, at least, it has prevented the disgrace of legislating upon subjects that belong exclusively to the jurisdiction of another country. But are these effects of a constitutional power that we should approve and encourage? or, on the contrary, that we should demand a convention to condemn and to prohibit? Let the honest and intelligent freemen of Pennsylvania reflect and determine.

These, then, fellow-citizens, are the pretexts for raising an artificial tempest in a season of calm and fruitful prosperity. With these pretexts, men deranged by Utopian theories or corrupted by foreign arts; men formed turbulent by nature, or become so from necessity; men who delight in confusion, and subsist upon defamation; idlers, without social attachments; and politicians by trade—gathering their scanty numbers into a malignant circle, have scattered envy and malice, fear and suspicion, throughout the land. It was not to be expected that indulging a more than Gothic fury for the demolition of our public institutions, the malcontents would permit the venerable McKean (who had long labored for their establishment and preservation) to close his patriotic life in peace. His services and his renown are indeed coeval with the dawn of American independence; for he is among the few (the lamentably few) surviving members of the illustrious Congress of 1765; and in every vicissitude of the war of 1776 he was the firm and efficient servant of his country. But neither these testimonials, nor all the assiduity since displayed by an enlightened mind for the public good, nor the gratitude which bounty should command, have furnished a shield to protect him from obloquy the most unjust, or from insult the most cruel. A new order of things required a new character of men. Those who had contributed to rear the fabric of civil government could never sincerely be beloved by those who seek to undermine and destroy it. The first election of Governor McKean was espoused with a zeal that graced the noblest motives, and the second election was distinguished by an unprecedented majority of the suffrages of a free people. In these movements, however, the malcontents (as far as their co-operation extended) contemplated their own interests, and not the interests of the community. The well-known name of the patriot gave assurance of success on the day of election, and it was imagined the unsuspecting nature of the man would render him an easy victim to the arts of solicitation and intrigue. For awhile, too, the malcontents seemed to reap the fruits of their speculation. Much was obtained for personal gratification, but no more to indulge the vanity of a reflected patronage. To prove the first part of our assertion we refer to the evidence of commissions and contracts, of petitions and testimonials, on the public files of

the secretary's office; and as to the second part, the lapse of time
is too short to have impaired the recollection of the pains which
were taken to create a popular opinion that the recommendation
of the leading malcontents was a certain, but an indispensable,
passport to executive favor. During that period, every act that
the governor performed, every sentiment that he uttered, furnished a theme for adulation and applause. But the pressure
of incessant importunity, the insatiable thirst for place and
patronage, could not be forever tolerated or supplied. The leading malcontents were often here, as at Washington, solicitors for
the same office, or advocates for different candidates; all could
not succeed, and all, by alternate disappointment, became discontented and hostile. Under these impressions, the designs
against the fundamental institutions of our country were conceived; and at length the governor had no other alternative
but openly to renounce the favor of the malcontents, or tacitly
to permit the constitution to be violated and supplanted by successive acts of unauthorized legislation. The decision, prompt
and unequivocal, was worthy of the chief magistrate of Pennsylvania; but, from that moment, his downfall was deemed by
the malcontents to be a necessary concomitant of the downfall
of our government. The proper instruments for so ungracious
an undertaking were speedily put into operation. Because bills
have been sometimes presented for his approbation which he
could not, in his conscience, approve, they have endeavored to
provoke an unwarrantable rupture between the legislative and
executive departments. Because the execution of the laws has
been sometimes difficult, and the administration of justice has
long been obstructed, they have endeavored to involve him in the
odium of such defects, concealing that the legislature alone can
supply an adequate remedy. Those who before extolled him are
now industrious to debase him, and without enjoying the merit
of invention or feeling the shame of inconsistency, they assail
him with a repetition of the very slanders which, on a former
occasion, they had themselves refuted and condemned. He has
been surrounded with spies and informers, who, crossing him in
his walks of exercise, or obtruding upon his hours of domestic
retirement, distort all his actions and falsify all his words. In
this progressive course, the malcontents finally reached the
ground of action; and the borough of Lancaster witnessed in
the same week the invocation for a convention to abolish our
constitution and the cabal of a ballot to degrade our governor!

It must be remembered that before the re-election of Governor
McKean, in 1802, the malcontents had actually calculated the
chances in favor of another candidate; but, however sanguine
and bold they are in their political temperament, nothing, at that
time, had occurred which could afford the slightest encourage-

ment for the attempt. Nor can it be precisely stated when their confidence had so increased as to produce a determination to make an experiment at the ensuing election; since, in the very petition for calling a convention, they accompany their general objections to *the executive power* with these remarkable declarations: "We wish not to be understood as *insinuating, in the remotest degree, that this power has been abused* by the present executive magistrate, etc. All we mean is that this dangerous power does exist, and may be exercised when a less upright and virtuous governor is in office," etc. It was manifest, however, as soon as the malcontents were defeated in the scheme for an immediate call of a convention, that their leaders, in a conclave at Lancaster, had resolved upon the opposition to Governor McKean. After the resolution was taken, the members of the legislature, who were also members of the cabal, appeared more than usually solicitous to procure justices' commissions for their friends and partisans; and it may be fairly presumed, that the visit of Messrs. McKenney, Montgomery, Steele, etc., of the 21st March (to which the public are indebted for the exploded tale of the clodhoppers), was connected with the secret plot to supersede the executive magistrate. But the first open display of hostility is to be found in the extraordinary spectacle which almost instantaneously followed the adjournment of the General Assembly. The legislature had acquired a habit of electing some of its own body to the offices of federal senator, State treasurer, and bank director; and now the members, who had conspired with the malcontents on the present occasion (being repulsed in their repeated applications for permission to use the respectable name of Muhlenberg or of Hiester), boldly determined likewise to make one of themselves a governor,—an example more dangerous to the rights of the people, more destructive to the purity and independence of the legislature, than all the imputed imperfections of the constitution. A meeting of the Republican members generally was accordingly called. Several of the friends of Governor McKean had previously left Lancaster, but many of them attended the meeting. A request was urged, on their part, for information of the cause and design of the meeting, but none was communicated. It was suggested that an open nomination of candidates should be made, but the suggestion was disregarded. It was proposed that the vote should be taken *viva voce*, and not by ballot, but the proposition was overruled. The truth is that the members who were parties to the conspiracy went to the meeting with their tickets prepared; and although they intended to give to the proceeding the influence of their legislative character, they were so ashamed of the act, or so fearful of its consequences, that they could not be induced to add to it the pledge of their legislative responsibility.

The body of Governor McKean's friends retired in disgust from this mockery and usurpation; this premeditated outrage upon legislative decorum and the freedom of election. Though reason, as well as constitutional authority, requires that every vote given in a representative capacity should be openly given; and though the vote on this occasion is described as the vote of forty-two representatives of the people, the members who remained delivered a prepared and secret ballot for a new candidate to fill the executive chair; leaving their constituents little more than a conjecture to designate by whom the injury and the insult had been given.

Having furnished this insidious instrument for promoting the designs of the malcontents, the members dispersed; but the sanction of the legislative character was still necessary to complete the spell for ruin and detraction. A libel was prepared under the specious title of "An Address of the Members of the General Assembly," and circulated in the form of a pamphlet, subscribed only by John Steele and Jacob Mitchell. It was accompanied, too, with certificates of a conversation, noted the very day that it occurred, with a view to the present use; but both of the certificates are inaccurate, and one of them is of doubtful authenticity, as it purports to be written and signed by a member of the House of Representatives, though it contains a material variance from another representation of that member (asserting here, that the governor said he would consult "*his own convenience*," while it is asserted elsewhere that the governor said, "he would consult his own conscience"); and as the certificate itself presents no character of similitude with the signature, or style, of a general letter from the same member now in possession of the public. On the 20th of May, 1805, this libel was ushered into public notice by a Philadelphia newspaper, with a preface declaring "that it had been reported and *unanimously* agreed to on Thursday evening," the 4th of April last; and plainly intending to convey the idea that it had been *so unanimously* agreed to at a second meeting of the persons assembled the preceding day, when General John Steele was appointed chairman, and Presley Carr Lane (who, as a senator, voting for the acquittal of the impeached judges, is himself an object of the very slander which, it is alleged, he approved) and Jacob Mitchell were appointed tellers. But we beseech you, fellow-citizens, to peruse this extraordinary composition with attention, in order to be convinced, from the profligacy of its principles and the scurrility of its language (as well as from the notoriety of other opposing facts), that it ought not to be deemed the work of any association of your representatives. In the face of the recent declaration of the malcontent petition, that there was no fault to be found with the official conduct of the governor, the jaundiced author has represented his whole administration as a tissue of tyranny, favoritism, and error. In contempt of a majority of 30,000 free suffrages, which gave the stamp of merit and approbation to his first period, nay, in immediate contradiction to the concession of the address itself, "that the administration of that period promised upon the whole to be beneficial to the State," the governor's transactions, from the first to the last day, are brought into a faithless and malignant review, to decorate the black book of the malcontents. Not only important facts have been suppressed, but the reasons assigned for his conduct on particular occasions have been garbled, perverted, and misconstrued. Not only his public agency, but his private honor, has been impeached. Not only his distribution of public offices, but his intercourse in social life, has been invidiously scrutinized. The temper of his mind, and the habit of his manners (long fixed, and known and respected by his fellow-citizens), have been made topics of public discussion and reproach. Nay, epithets have been formed, and words have been selected, for the inhuman purpose of torturing his sensibility as a parent and a friend, till, in fine, the address of the malcontents has deemed the veteran patriot to lament (and others are yet doomed to feel) that, although the carcass of Callander is no more, his spirit, ungrateful and vindictive, still survives!

We emphatically repeat, fellow-citizens, that such a composition ought not, without an express and individual avowal, to be ascribed to any set of men who are honored with the confidence of the people. We believe that the address never was seen or read, before it was published, by twenty members of the legislature; we believe that there never were ten members assembled at any meeting which approved and adopted it; and we are confident that there is not one member who is prepared to substantiate the criminal charges which it contains. We speak not here of charges which impute to the governor as a crime the conscientious exercise of a constitutional power. We speak not of charges which, on the presumption, as it would seem, that the legislature has already absorbed all the powers of government, treat as a menace against legislative authority the simple declaration that the judgment of the supreme court upon a point of law would be an *authoritative* decision. We speak not of charges which convert a deference for legislative opinion into a contempt of legislative dignity, where the governor has tacitly acquiesced in the enactment of a law, though he could not positively affix the signature of approbation. We speak not here of charges which arraign the executive for not returning bills with his approbation or dissent, where the bills were only presented for his consideration on the eve of an adjournment of the legislature. We speak not of charges which decry a wish to transmit the constitution unimpaired to his successor as a symptom of aristocracy and despotism. We speak not of charges which clamorously condemn the distribution of offices, manifestly because the authors of the charge were not the persons appointed. We speak not of charges which (forgetting that to be a governor is not to lose the affections of a man, nor to be the relation of a governor a forfeiture of the equal rights of a citizen) stigmatize as extravagant the grant of three commissions to connexions by blood and marriage, out of the unbounded patronage which the executive, for another purpose, is idly said to possess. We speak not of charges in which Messrs. McKinney and Montgomery appear as arbiters of elegant manners and polite conversation. But we speak of *gross charges of official delinquency and corruption*, for which we trust the libellous authors will be compelled, at a proper time and in a proper place, to answer to the offended laws and justice of their country.

1. It is alleged that an election-ticket "was distributed from the governor's coach by two officers of executive appointment, who accompanied him, and daily held him up as the patron of faction. The attempt was frustrated by the force of popular suffrage, and he was driven to disavow, only after a defeat, what he had really taken pains to promote without success." The charge is denied. We demand the informer and the proof.

2. It is alleged that the author and abettors of the address have seen the governor "employing the whole weight of his opinion and the influence of the officers of his appointment, besides an interference with private citizens, to procure the extrication of three judges of the supreme court from an impeachment, who had, under color of the common law, exercised the most daring tyranny, and violated the constitution and laws of the State." The charge is denied. We demand the informer and the proof.

3. It is alleged that the governor asserted that "he would not suffer a convention to take place;" and it is insinuated that he meant "to employ arms or corruption to prevent it." The charge is denied. Let it be said that the honorable and enlightened informers, Messrs. Montgomery and McKinney, seem to prove that he reprobated (as most honest men do) the call of a convention, and that he said (as every citizen has a right to say) he would firmly resist it; but still we demand the proof that, as an executive magistrate, he threatened the use of arms or corruption.

4. It is alleged that "an address for the removal of Judge *Brackenridge* from office was presented *by more than two-thirds of each branch of the legislature*, and that the executive has not even deigned to make any communication in reply." The charge is unfounded; for we answer:

1. That the extraordinary nature of the case merited a very

serious consideration. Judge *Brackenridge* informed the House of Representatives that he had concurred in the punishment of the offender (who had complained to the House) for a contempt of court, and observed that it might be thought an effect of the bias of party by others (not that he thought so himself) if his name was not comprehended with the names of other judges in the meditated impeachment. The House of Representatives considered the letter of Judge *Brackenridge* on this subject as a contempt. They admitted his own acknowledgment as sufficient proof to involve him in the only punishment which could follow on a conviction on impeachment, the removal from office; but they would not admit it to be sufficient to give him the opportunity of explanation or defence, which, upon impeachment, they could not refuse. At the very time, therefore, that the House of Representatives was instituting a prosecution against the judges of the supreme court for punishing a private individual's contempt of court by attachment, after a full defence, with a small fine and a short imprisonment, the Senate and the House of Representatives concurred in the design to punish Judge Brackenridge without a notice or a hearing, or a trial by jury, or a trial by impeachment, for a contempt of the legislature, degrading him from office, stripping an aged man and his family of their subsistence, and fining him to the amount of two thousand dollars per annum during his life! Let Mr. Steele or Mr. Mitchell, or all or any of the authors of the address, who have called the conduct of the supreme court "the most daring tyranny and violation of the constitution and laws of the State," find out a precedent or a name for such an act as this! But let us not be surprised, fellow-citizens, that Governor McKean, who had long administered justice upon the maxim "that no man should be condemned unheard," deliberated before he would acquiesce in an address under such circumstances for the removal of a judicial officer

2. That the governor possesses a constitutional discretion whether he will comply with an address for the removal of a judge, and is no more responsible to the legislature for the exercise of that discretion than the legislature is responsible to him for the motives of the application.

3. That the application for the removal of Judge Brackenridge was not constitutionally made, and therefore could not be lawfully granted. It is true that the address asserts the application to have been made *by two-thirds of each branch of the legislature;* and it is also true that the constitution requires the application to be so made; but, in point of real fact, *two-thirds of each branch of the legislature did not make the application.* Two-thirds of *a house* and two-thirds of *a branch* of the legislature are distinct things in the language of the constitution and

in the meaning of the convention, as conveyed by their own journals. The branch is composed of all its members; but a majority of the members of a branch constitutes *a house* for the ordinary branches of legislation. For special purposes, however (an impeachment or an address for removal from office), *the branch*, and not *the house*, is appealed to, and for this plain reason, that the rule of decision should be uniform. For instance, two-thirds of the Senate, considered as *a branch* of the legislature, will invariably amount to sixteen; but two-thirds of the Senate, considered as *a house*, may vibrate from nine, which is two-thirds of the quorum of thirteen, to sixteen, which is two-thirds of the whole branch of twenty-four members. In the case of Judge Brackenridge, the votes for his removal amounted to two-thirds of each *house*, but did not amount to two-thirds of each *branch* of the legislature. The governor could not, therefore, violate the constitution to gratify the wishes, or to resent the injuries, which occasioned the address.

But, fellow-citizens, it is a more laudable, a more just, a more salutary task, to turn your attention from this loathsome and ungrateful scene of defamation to a contemplation of the important services of the executive magistrate. It was not manly or decent to break open the tomb of departed worth and to repudiate the memory of a patriot to whose honor the legislature itself had decreed a public funeral and monument. But if it is true that the governor succeeded to a chair shattered, tottering, and feeble from the indiscretion of his predecessor, to whom are we to ascribe its present efficient and impressive character? There is no State that boasts a more prompt, faithful, and beneficial execution of its laws; while, as a member of the Union, Pennsylvania has maintained, through the medium of its executive, with exemplary dignity, the principles of federate harmony and confidence. The militia has been an object of our governor's most assiduous and successful attention. The discipline, the supplies of artillery, of arms, and of other military equipments, which render our militia pre-eminently respectable and efficient, may be ascribed to his indefatigable zeal for the preservation of an institution on which he well knows the people can alone safely rely for their peace, liberty, and independence. By his care the Wyoming controversy, which has so long annoyed the peace of Pennsylvania, will, probably, be soon terminated to the satisfaction of all the parties and to the honor of the State. The actual settlers on the western frontier owe much to his sympathy and protection during the litigation of their claims. Agriculture has received his aid in exertions to extend our roads and improve our navigable communication. Commerce has been advanced by his assiduity in employing the best means to preserve the health of our capital. Of mechanics and manufacturers he has been the unaffected friend and patron,

and, feeling himself all the blessings of knowledge, he inces
santly labors to disseminate the means of education. But why
should we advance in this pleasing, though superfluous, delineation of his merit? After fifty years of public life, you must
understand the value of such a man; and you will not easily
submit to be deprived of his services, to see his virtues unjustly
obscured, or his honors ungratefully despoiled.

We have now, fellow-citizens, traced the original of the present
crisis. We have developed the motives, plans, and operations
of the malcontents. The trespass upon your time has been
great; but the importance of the occasion must be our excuse.
It is an effort to preserve institutions and men we know and approve against projects which we cannot comprehend, proposed
by men whom we cannot trust, whose object cannot be good,
since the means that they employ are evidently bad. It is a
cause of principle independent of party. Every man has an
interest in the issue, and every man is bound to bear a part in
the contest. For ourselves, we think that it is time to evince to
the world that a democratic republic can enjoy energy without
tyranny, and liberty without anarchy. It is time to brush from
the skirts of the Republican party the moths that stain the purity
of its color and feed upon the consistency of its texture. It is
time to convince the malcontents that their machinations are
detected, that their influence is lost, and that their denunciations
are despised. For these purposes the Society of Constitutional
Republicans was formed, and when these purposes shall be accomplished, the society will cheerfully cease to exist.

The epoch of their accomplishment, we confidently refer to the
next general election. Let us, then, fellow-citizens, implore your
co-operation. Prepare with vigilance and act with firmness.
Re-elect our venerable governor. Exclude from the legislature
all who have avowed a disposition hostile to the constitution.
Circulate and transmit to the secretary's office remonstrances in
opposition to a convention. Communicate your information on
the crisis of our public affairs in repeated meetings and in every
private conversation. Rescue your country from the impending
evil, and deserve to be happy.

GEORGE LOGAN, *President.*
ISRAEL ISRAEL, *Vice-President.*

SAMUEL WETHERILL, *Secretary.*

A. J. DALLAS,
I. B. SMITH,
ISAAC WORRELL,   } *Corresponding Committee.*
SAMUEL WETHERILL,
BLAIR MCCLENACHAN,

PHILADELPHIA, June 10, 1805.

16

No. 4.

OFFICIAL LETTERS

TO THE COMMITTEE OF WAYS AND MEANS.

Washington, Oct. 14, 1814.

Sir,—The Committee of Ways and Means have had under their consideration the support of public credit by a system of taxation more extended than the one heretofore adopted. They have determined to suspend proceeding on their report at present before the House of Representatives, with a view to afford you an opportunity of suggesting any other or such additional provisions as may be necessary to revive and maintain unimpaired the public credit.

I have the honor to be your most obedient,

John W. Eppes.

Honorable Mr. Dallas, *Secretary of the Treasury.*

Treasury Department, October 17, 1814.

Sir,—I have the honor to acknowledge the receipt of your letter dated the 14th inst., and aware of the necessity for an early interposition of Congress on the subject to which it relates, I proceed, at the moment of entering upon the duties of office, to offer to the consideration of the Committee of Ways and Means an answer on the several points of their inquiry.

Contemplating the present state of the finances, it is obvious that a deficiency in the revenue and a depreciation in the public credit exist from causes which cannot in any degree be ascribed either to the want of resources or to the want of integrity in the nation. Different minds will conceive different opinions in relation to some of those causes; but it will be agreed on all sides that the most operative have been the inadequacy of our system of taxation to form a foundation for public credit; and the absence even from that system of the means which are best adapted to anticipate, collect, and distribute the public revenue.

The wealth of the nation in the value and products of its soil, in all the acquisitions of personal property, and in all the varieties of industry, remains almost untouched by the hand of government; for the national faith and not the national wealth has hitherto been the principal instrument of finance. It was reasonable, however, to expect that a period must occur in the course of a protracted war when confidence in the accumulating public engagements could only be secured by an active demonstration both of the capacity and the disposition to perform them. In the present state of the treasury, therefore, it is a just consolation to reflect that a prompt and resolute application of the resources of the country will effectually relieve from every pecuniary embarrassment and vindicate the fiscal honor of the government.

But it would be vain to attempt to disguise, and it would be pernicious to palliate, the difficulties which are now to be overcome. The exigencies of the government require a supply of treasure for the prosecution of the war beyond any amount which it would be politic, even if it were practicable, to raise by an immediate and constant imposition of taxes. There must, therefore, be a resort to credit for a considerable portion of the supply. But the public credit is at this juncture so depressed that no hope of adequate succor on moderate terms can safely rest upon it. Hence it becomes the object first and last in every practical scheme of finance to reanimate the confidence of the citizens, and to impress on the mind of every man who, for the public account, renders services, furnishes supplies, or advances money, a conviction of the punctuality as well as of the security of the government. It is not to be regarded, indeed, as the case of preserving a credit which has never been impaired, but rather as the case of rescuing from reproach a credit over which doubt and apprehension (not the less injurious, perhaps, because they are visionary) have cast an inauspicious shade. In the former case the ordinary means of raising and appropriating the revenue will always be sufficient; but in the latter case no exertion can be competent to attain the object which does not quiet in every mind every fear of future loss or disappointment in consequence of trusting to the pledges of the public faith.

The condition of the circulating medium of the country presents another copious source of mischief and embarrassment. The recent exportations of specie have considerably diminished the fund of gold and silver coin; and another considerable portion of that fund has been drawn by the timid and the wary from the use of the community into the private coffers of individuals. On the other hand, the multiplication of banks in the several States has so increased the quantity of paper currency that it would be difficult to calculate its amount, and still more difficult to ascertain its value with reference to the capital on which it has been issued. But the benefit of even this paper currency is in a great measure lost, as the suspension of payments in specie at most of the banks has suddenly broken the chain of accommodation that previously extended the credit and the circulation of the notes which were emitted in one State into every State of the Union. It may in general be affirmed, therefore, that there exists at this time no adequate circulating medium common to the citizens of the United States. The moneyed transactions of private life are at a stand, and the fiscal operations of the government labor with extreme inconvenience. It is impossible that such a state of things should be long endured; but, let it be fairly added, that with legislative aid it is not necessary that the endurance should be long. Under favorable circumstances and to a limited extent an emission of treasury notes would probably afford relief; but treasury notes are an expensive and precarious substitute either for coin or for bank-notes, charged as they are with a growing interest productive of no countervailing profit or emolument, and exposed to every breath of popular prejudice or alarm. The establishment of a national institution operating upon credit combined with capital and regulated by prudence and good faith is, after all, the only efficient remedy for the disordered condition of our circulating medium. While accomplishing that object, too, there will be found under the auspices of such an institution a safe depository for the public treasure and a constant auxiliary to the public credit. But whether the issues of a paper currency proceed from the national treasury or from a national bank, the acceptance of the paper in a course of payments and receipts must be forever optional with the citizens. The extremity of that day cannot be anticipated when any honest and enlightened statesman will again venture upon the desperate expedient of a tender law.

From this painful but necessary development of existing evils we pass with hope and confidence to a more specific consideration of the measures from which relief may be certainly and speedily derived. Remembering always that the objects of the government are to place the public credit upon a solid and durable foundation; to provide a revenue commensurate with the demands of a war expenditure, and to remove from the treasury an immediate pressure, the following propositions are submitted to the committee with every sentiment of deference and respect:

PROPOSITIONS.

I. It is proposed that during the war, and until the claims contemplated by the proposition are completely satisfied or extinct, there shall be annually raised by taxes, duties, imposts, and excises, a fund for these purposes:

1. For the support of government............................ $1,500,000
2. For the principal and interest of the public debt existing before the declaration of war and payable according to the contract.. 8,500,000
3. For the interest of the public debt contracted and to be contracted by loans or otherwise from the commencement to the termination of the war, calculated upon an annual principal of $72,000,000.............................. 4,320,000
4. For the payment of treasury notes, with the accruing interest... 7,400,000
5. For the payment of debentures to be issued (as is hereinafter proposed) for liquidated balances due to individuals on account of services or supplies authorized by law, but either not embraced by a specific appropriation or exceeding the sum appropriated............................. 280,000
6. For a current addition to the sums raised by loan or issues of treasury notes towards defraying the general expenses of the war.. 2,000,000
7. For the gradual establishment of a sinking fund to extinguish the debt incurred during the war...................... 500,000
8. For a contingent fund to meet sudden and occasional demands upon the treasury.................................... 1,500,000

$21,000,000

II. It is proposed that during the war, and until the claims contemplated by the preceding proposition are completely satisfied, or other adequate funds shall be provided and substituted by law, there shall be annually raised by the means here specified the following sums :

1. By the customs (which cannot be safely estimated during the war at a higher product)............................... $4,000,000
2. By the existing internal duties............................ 2,700,000
3. By the existing direct tax................................ 2,500,000
4. By the sales of public lands (which cannot be safely estimated during the war at a higher product)................ 800.000
5. By an addition to the existing direct tax of 100 per cent. 2,850.000
6. By an addition of 100 per cent. on the present auction duties... 150,000
7. By an addition of 100 per cent. on the existing duties upon carriages... 200,000
8. By an addition of 50 per cent. on the existing duties on licenses to retail wines, spirituous liquors, and foreign merchandise.. 300,000
9. By an addition of 100 per cent. on the existing rate of postage.. 500,000
10. By the proceeds of the new duties specified in the annexed schedule, marked A, making in the aggregate... 7,000,000

$21,000,000

III. It is proposed that a national bank shall be incorporated for a term of twenty years, to be established at Philadelphia, with a power to erect offices of discount and deposit elsewhere, upon the following principles :

1. That the capital of the bank shall be $50,000,000, to be divided into 100,000 shares of $500 each. Three-fifths of the capital, being 60,000 shares, amounting to $30,000,000, to be subscribed by corporations, companies, or individuals; and two-fifths of the capital, being 40,000 shares, amounting to $20,000,000, to be subscribed by the United States.

2. That the subscriptions of corporations, companies, and individuals shall be paid for in the following manner:

One-fifth part, or $6,000,000, in gold or silver coin.

Four-fifth parts, or $24,000,000, in gold or silver coin, or in six per cent. stock issued since the declaration of war, and treasury notes, in the proportion of one-fifth in treasury notes and three-fifths in six per cent. stock.

3. That the subscriptions of corporations, companies, and individuals shall be paid at the following periods:

$20 on each share, to be paid at the time of subscribing, in gold or silver coin	$1,200,000
40 on each share, to be paid in gold or silver coin one month after the subscription	2,400,000
40 on each share, in two months after the subscription, in gold or silver coin	2,400,000
$100 specie	$6,000,000
100 on each share, in gold or silver coin, or in six per cent. stock, or in treasury notes, according to the preceding apportionment, to be paid at the time of subscribing	6,000,000
150 on each share, to be paid in like manner in two months after subscribing	9,000,000
150 on each share, to be paid in like manner in three months after subscribing	9,000,000
$500	$30,000,000

4. That the subscription of the United States shall be paid in six per cent. stock, at the same periods and in the same proportions as the payments of private subscriptions in stock and treasury notes.

5. That the United States may substitute six per cent. stock for the amount of the treasury notes subscribed by corporations, companies, and individuals, as the notes respectively become due and payable.

6. That the bank shall loan to the United States $30,000,000, at an interest of six per cent., at such periods and in such sums as shall be found mutually convenient.

7. That no part of the public stock, constituting a portion of the capital of the bank shall be sold during the war, nor at any subsequent time, for less than par; nor at any time to an amount exceeding one moiety, without the consent of Congress.

8. That provision shall be made for protecting the bank-notes

from forgery; for limiting the issue of bank-notes; and for receiving them in all payments to the United States.

9. That the capital of the bank, its notes, deposits, dividends, or profits (its real estate only excepted), shall not be subject to taxation by the United States or by any individual State.

10. That no other bank shall be established by Congress during the term for which the national bank is incorporated.

11. That the national bank shall be governed by fifteen directors, being resident citizens of the United States and stockholders. The President of the United States shall annually name five directors, and designate one of the five to be the president of the bank. The other directors shall be annually chosen by the qualified stockholders, in person or by proxy, if resident within the United States, voting upon a scale graduated according to the number of shares which they respectively hold. The cashier and other officers of the bank to be appointed as is usual in similar institutions.

12. That the directors of the national bank shall appoint seven persons, one of whom to preside, as the managers of each office of discount and deposit, and one person to be the cashier.

13. That the general powers, privileges, and regulations of the bank shall be the same as are usual in similar institutions; but with this special provision, that the general accounts shall be subject to the inspection of the Secretary of the Treasury.

IV. It is proposed that, after having thus provided for the punctual payment of the interest upon every denomination of public debt; for raising annually a portion of the annual expense by taxes; for establishing a sinking fund, in relation to the new debt as well as in relation to the old debt; and for securing to the public the efficient agency of a national bank,—the only remaining object of supply shall be accomplished by annual loans and issues of treasury notes, if, unexpectedly, such issues should continue to be necessary or expedient.

1. The amount of annual expenditure during the war exceeding the sums provided for, does not admit of a prospective estimate beyond the year 1815; but for that year it may be estimated with sufficient accuracy for the general purposes of the present communication, at $28,000,000.

2. Then for the year 1815 an additional provision must be made, authorizing a loan and the issue of treasury notes to an equal amount, $28,000,000.

V. It is proposed that the accounts for authorized expenses being duly stated and settled, a certificate or debenture shall issue to the accountant specifying the balance; and that in all cases where there has been no specific appropriation, or the claim exceeds the amount of the sum appropriated, the balance shall bear an interest of three per cent. until provision is made by law for paying the amount.

VI. And finally, it is proposed to relieve the treasury from an immediate pressure upon the principles of the following statement:

1. The amount of demands upon the treasury (exclusively of balances of appropriations for former years unsatisfied) was stated in the report of the late Secretary of the Treasury of the 23d of September, 1814, to be on the 30th of June.. $27,576,391 19

2. The accounts of the third quarter of 1814 are not yet made up, and the precise sums paid during that quarter cannot now be ascertained; but they amount to nearly... 8,400,000 00

Leaving to be paid in the 4th quarter of 1814...... $19,176,391 19

3. This balance payable during the 4th quarter of 1814 consists of the following items:

Civil, diplomatic, and miscellaneous expenses, about.. $353,292 99
Military, about................................. 8,792,688 00
Naval, about.................................... 2,382,010 97
Public debt, about............................. 7,648,419 23
————————— $19,176,391 19

4. The existing provisions by law for the payment of this balance of $19,176,391 19, may be stated as follows:
The act of the 24th of March, 1814, authorized a loan for $25,000,000 00
The act of the 4th of March, 1814, authorized an issue of treasury notes for................................. 5,000,000 00
————————— $30,000,000 00

Under these authorities there have been borrowed on loan about................ $10,895,000
There has been sent to Europe in six per cent. stock....................................... 6,000,000
There has been issued in treasury notes, 3,504,000
————————— 20,399,000 00
————————— $9,601,000 00

There remains therefore an unexecuted authority to borrow.......................... $8,105,000
To issue treasury notes....................... 1,496,000
————————— 9,601,000 00

The demands of the fourth quarter being then.. 19,176,391 19
There may be applied to meet them the revenue accruing during the quarter from all sources, about..................... $2,900,000
Also, payments to be made on account of loans already contracted for, according to the authority above stated, about.. 2,500,000
————————— 5,400,000 00

Leaving a balance to be provided for................ $13,776,391 19

By the authority remaining to borrow. $8,105,000 00
By the authority remaining to issue
  treasury notes.................................... 1,496,000 00
By an additional authority to be granted
  by law, to borrow and to issue treasury
  notes.. 4,175,391 19
                        ——————— $13,776,391 19

These estimates, however, it will be observed, are made with a view, simply, to the appropriations by law for the expenses of the year 1814, and do not embrace a provision to satisfy balances of appropriations made for the expenses of preceding years which have not been called for at the treasury. But it will, probably, be deemed expedient to make such provision by extending the new authority to borrow from the above balance, to $6,000,000. If the six per cent. stock which has been sent to Europe should be there disposed of, it will form an item in the estimates of the ensuing year.

As a portion of the amount to be provided during the present quarter consists of treasury notes which will soon be due, it will be advisable to make them receivable in subscriptions to the loan.

It is proper to accompany these propositions with a few explanatory remarks:

1. The first proposition contemplates a permanent system; but the estimate of the particular items of claims and demands upon the public must be regarded as immediately applying to the year 1815. In every subsequent year there will necessarily be some variation; as, for instance, the item of interest on the old debt will annually sink, while the item of interest on the new debt will annually rise, during the continuance of the war.

The items for annually raising a portion of the public expenses by taxes, and for applying to the new debt a sinking fund (gradually increasing, until it becomes commensurate to its object) are essential features in the plan suggested with a view to the revival and maintenance of public credit. The extinguishment of the old debt is already in rapid operation by the wise precaution of a similar institution.

2. The second proposition will, doubtless, generate many and very various objections. The endeavor has been, however, to spread the general amount of the taxes over a wide surface with a hand as light and equal as is consistent with convenience in the process and certainty in the result.

All the opportunities of observation, and all the means of information that have been possessed, leave no doubt upon the disposition of the people to contribute generously for relieving the necessities of their country; and it has been thought unworthy of that patriotic disposition to dwell upon scanty means of supply, or short-lived expedients. Whenever the war shall be happily terminated in an honorable peace, and the treasury shall be again replenished by the tributary streams of commerce, it will be at once a duty and a pleasure to recommend an alleviation, if not an entire exoneration, of the burthens which necessarily fall at present upon the agriculture and manufactures of the nation.

3. In making a proposition for the establishment of a national bank, I cannot be insensible to the high authority of the names which have appeared in opposition to that measure upon constitutional grounds. It would be presumptuous to conjecture that the sentiments which actuated the opposition have passed away; and yet it would be denying to experience a great practical advantage, were we to suppose that a difference of times and circumstances would not produce a corresponding difference in the opinions of the wisest as well as of the purest men. But in the present case a change of private opinion is not material to the success of the proposition for establishing a national bank. In the administration of human affairs, there must be a period when discussion shall cease and decision shall become absolute. A diversity of opinion may honorably survive the contest; but, upon the genuine principles of a representative government, the opinion of the majority can alone be carried into action. The judge who dissents from the majority of the bench changes not his opinion, but performs his duty, when he enforces the judgment of the court, although it is contrary to his own convictions. An oath to support the constitution and the laws is not, therefore, an oath to support them under all circumstances, according to the opinion of the individual who takes it, but it is, emphatically, an oath to support them according to the interpretation of the legitimate authorities. For the erroneous decisions of a court of law there is the redress of a censorial as well as of an appellate jurisdiction. Over an act founded upon an exposition of the constitution made by the legislative department of the government, but alleged to be incorrect, we have seen the judicial department exercise a remedial power. And even if all the departments—legislative, executive, and judicial—should concur in the exercise of a power which is either thought to transcend the constitutional trust or to operate injuriously upon the community, the case is still within the reach of a competent control, through the medium of an amendment to the constitution, upon the proposition not only of Congress but of the several States. When, therefore, we have marked the existence of a national bank for a period of twenty years, with all the sanctions of the legislative, executive, and judicial authorities; when we have seen the dissolution of one institution, and heard a loud and continued call for the establishment of another; when, under these circumstances, neither Congress nor the several States

have resorted to the power of amendment,—can it be deemed a violation of the right of private opinion to consider the constitutionality of a national bank as a question forever settled and at rest?

But, after all, I should not merit the confidence which it will be my ambition to acquire, if I were to suppress the declaration of an opinion that, in these times, the establishment of a national bank will not only be useful in promoting the general welfare, but that it is necessary and proper for carrying into execution some of the most important powers constitutionally vested in the government.

Upon the principles and regulations of the national bank it may be sufficient to remark that they will be best unfolded in the form of a bill, which shall be immediately prepared. A compound capital is suggested, with a design equally to accommodate the subscribers and to aid the general measures for the revival of public credit; but the proportions of specie and stock may be varied, if the scarcity of coin should render it expedient, yet not in so great a degree as to prevent an early commencement of the money operations of the institution.

4. The estimates of receipts from established sources of revenue and from the proposed new duties, and the estimates of expenditures on all the objects contemplated in the present communication, have been made upon a call so sudden, and upon materials so scattered, that it is not intended to claim a perfect reliance on their accuracy. They are, however, believed to be sufficiently accurate to illustrate and support the general plan for the revival of the public credit, the establisment of a permanent system of revenue, and the removal of the immediate pressure on the treasury.

Upon the whole, sir, I have freely and openly assumed the responsibility of the station in which I have the honor to be placed. But, conscious of the imperfections of the judgment that dictates the answer to the important inquiries of the Committee of Ways and Means, I derive the highest satisfaction from reflecting that the honor and safety of the nation, for war or for peace, depend on the wisdom, patriotism, and fortitude of Congress during times which imperiously demand a display of those qualities in the exercise of the legislative authority.

I have the honor to be, very respectfully, sir, your most obedient servant,

A. J. DALLAS.

J. W. EPPES, Esq., *Chairman of the Committee of Ways and Means.*

LETTER

To whom was recommitted, on the twenty-fifth instant, the bill, entitled "An Act to Incorporate the Subscribers to the Bank of the United States of America," to the Secretary of the Treasury, requesting his opinion on the provisions of the said bill, particularly their effects upon the prospects of a loan for 1815, with the answer of the Secretary of the Treasury.

WASHINGTON, November 27, 1814.

SIR, — The committee of the House of Representatives, to which the bank bill was recommitted on Friday last, have directed me to request you to communicate your opinion in relation to the effect which a considerable issue of treasury notes (to which should be attached the quality of being receivable in subscriptions to the bank) might have upon the credit of the government, and particularly upon the prospects of a loan for 1815.

As the bill, as it was referred to the committee, provides for the subscription of forty-four millions of treasury notes to form, with six millions of specie, the capital of the bank, any information which you may think proper to give, either in relation to the practicability of getting them into circulation without depreciation, or in regard to their operation on any part of our fiscal system afterwards, will be very acceptable.

I am, sir, very respectfully, your obedient servant,

WM. LOWNDES.

To the Honorable the Secretary of the Treasury.

TREASURY DEPARTMENT, November 27, 1814.

SIR,—I have the honor to acknowledge the receipt of your letter, requesting, for a committee of the House of Representatives, an opinion upon the following inquiries:

1. The effect which a considerable issue of treasury notes, with the quality of being receivable in subscriptions to a national bank, will have upon the credit of the government, and particularly upon the prospects of a loan for 1815?

2. The practicability of getting forty-four millions of treasury notes (forming, with six millions of specie, the capital for a national bank) into circulation without depreciation?

The inquiries of the committee cannot be satisfactorily answered in the abstract; but must be considered in connection with the state of our finances and the state of the public credit.

When I arrived at Washington, the treasury was suffering under every kind of embarrassment. The demands upon it were great in amount, while the means to satisfy them were comparatively small; precarious in the collection, and difficult in the application. The demands consisted of dividends upon old and new funded debt, of treasury notes, and of legislative appropriations for the army, the navy, and the current service,—all urgent and important. The means consisted,—First of the fragment of an authority to borrow money when nobody was disposed to lend, and to issue treasury notes which none but necessitous creditors, or contractors in distress, or commissaries, quartermasters, and navy agents, acting, as it were, officially, seemed willing to accept. Second, of the amount of bank credits scattered throughout the United States, and principally in the southern and western banks, which had been rendered in a great degree useless by the stoppage of payments in specie, and the consequent impracticability of transferring the public funds from one place to meet the public engagements in another place. And third, of the current supply of money from the imposts, from internal duties, and from the sales of public land, which ceased to be a foundation of any rational estimate, or reserve, to provide even for the dividends on the funded debt, when it was found that the treasury notes (only requiring, indeed, a cash payment at the distance of a year), to whomsoever they were issued at the treasury, and almost as soon as they were issued, reached the hands of the collectors in payments of debts, duties, and taxes; thus disappointing and defeating the only remaining expectation of productive revenue.

Under these circumstances (which I had the honor to communicate to the Committee of Ways and Means), it became the duty of this department to endeavor to remove the immediate pressure from the treasury; to endeavor to restore the public credit; and to endeavor to provide for the expenses of the ensuing year. The only measures that occurred to my mind for the accomplishment of such important objects have been presented to the view of Congress. The act authorizing the receipt of treasury notes in payment of subscriptions to a public loan was passed, I fear, too late to answer the purpose for which it was designed. It promises, at this time, little relief either as an instrument to raise money or to absorb the claims for treasury notes, which are daily becoming due. From this cause, and from other obvious causes, the dividend on the funded debt has not been punctually paid; a large amount of treasury notes has already been dishonored, and the hope of preventing further injury and reproach in transacting the business of the treasury is too visionary to afford a moment's consolation.

The actual condition of the treasury, thus described, will serve to indicate the state of the public credit. Public credit depends essentially upon public opinion. The usual test of public credit is, indeed, the value of the public debt. The faculty of borrowing money is not a test of public credit: for a faithless government, like a desperate individual, has only to increase the premium, according to the exigency, in order to secure a loan. Thus public opinion, manifested in every form, and in every direction, hardly permits us, at the present juncture, to speak of the existence of public credit; and yet, it is not impossible that the government, in the resources of its patronage and its pledges, might find the means of tempting the rich and the avaricious to supply its immediate wants. But when the wants of to-day are supplied, what is the new expedient that shall supply the wants of to-morrow? If it is now a charter of incorporation, it may then be a grant of land; but, after all, the immeasurable tracts of the western wild would be exhausted in successive efforts to obtain pecuniary aids, and still leave the government necessitous, unless the foundations of public credit were re-established and maintained. In the measures, therefore, which it has been my duty to suggest, I have endeavored to introduce a permanent plan for reviving the public credit; of which the facility of borrowing money in anticipation of settled and productive revenues, is only an incident, although it is an incident as durable as the plan itself. The outline seemed to embrace whatever was requisite, to leave no doubt upon the power and the disposition of the government, in relation to its pecuniary engagements; to diminish, and not to augment, the amount of the public debt in the hands of individuals, and to create general confidence, rather by the manner of treating the claims of the present class of creditors than by the manner of conciliating the favor of a new class.

With these explanatory remarks, sir, I proceed to answer, specifically, the questions which you have proposed:

I. I am of opinion, that a considerable issue of treasury notes, with the quality of being receivable in subscriptions to a national bank, will have an injurious effect upon the credit of the government, and also upon the prospects of a loan for 1815.

Because, it will confer, gratuitously, an advantage upon a class of new creditors over the present creditors of the government, standing on a footing of at least equal merit.

Because, it will excite general dissatisfaction among the present holders of the public debt, and general distrust among the capitalists, who are accustomed to advance their money to the government.

Because, a quality of subscribing to the national bank attached to treasury notes exclusively, will tend to depreciate the value of all public debt not possessing that quality; and whatever depreciates the value of the public debt, in this way, must necessarily impair the public credit.

Because, the specie capital of the citizens of the United States, so far as it may be deemed applicable to investments in the public

stocks, has already, in a great measure, been so vested ; the holders of the present debt will be unable to become subscribers to
the bank (if that object should, eventually, prove desirable)
without selling their stock at a depreciated rate, in order to procure the whole amount of their subscriptions in treasury notes ;
and a general depression in the value of the public debt will
inevitably ensue.

Because, the very proposition of making a considerable issue
of treasury notes, even with the quality of being subscribed to a
national bank, can only be regarded as an experiment, on which
it seems dangerous to rely ; the treasury notes must be purchased at par, with money ; a new set of creditors are to be
created ; it may, or it may not, be deemed an object of speculation by the money-holders to subscribe to the bank ; the result
of the experiment cannot be ascertained until it will be too late
to provide a remedy in case of failure ; while the credit of the
government will be affected by every circumstance which keeps
the efficacy of its fiscal operations in suspense or doubt.

Because, the prospect of a loan for the year 1815, without the
aid of a bank, is faint and unpromising ; except, perhaps, so far
as the pledge of a specific tax may succeed ; and then, it must
be recollected, that a considerable supply of money will be required, for the prosecution of the war, beyond the whole amount
of the taxes to be levied.

Because, if the loan for the year 1815 be made to depend upon
the issue of treasury notes, subscribable to the national bank, it
will probably fail for the reasons which have already been suggested ; and if the loan be independent of that operation, a considerable issue of treasury notes, for the purpose of creating a
bank capital, must, it is believed, deprive the government of
every chance of raising money in any other manner.

II. I am of opinion, that it will be extremely difficult, if not
impracticable, to get forty-four millions of treasury notes (forming, with six millions of specie, the capital of a national bank)
into circulation, with or without depreciation.

Because, if the subscription to the bank becomes an object of
speculation, the treasury notes will probably be purchased at the
treasury and at the loan-offices, and never pass into circulation
at all.

Because, whatever portion of the treasury notes might pass
into circulation, would be speedily withdrawn, by the speculators
in the subscription to the bank, after arts had been employed to
depreciate their value.

Because, it is not believed that, in the present state of the
public credit, forty-four millions of treasury notes can be sent
into circulation. The only difference between the treasury notes
now issued and dishonored and those proposed to be issued,

consists in the subscribable quality; but reasons have been already assigned for an opinion, that this difference does not afford such confidence in the experiment, as seems requisite to justify a reliance upon it, for accomplishing some of the most interesting objects of the government.

I must beg you, sir, to pardon the haste with which I have written these general answers to your inquiries. But knowing the importance of time, and feeling a desire to avoid every appearance of contributing to the loss of a moment, I have chosen rather to rest upon the intelligence and candor of the committee than to enter upon a more labored investigation of the subject referred to me.

I have the honor to be, very respectfully, sir, your most obedient servant,

A. J. DALLAS.

WILLIAM LOWNDES, Esquire.

WASHINGTON, Dec. 2, 1814.

SIR,—Your letter of the 27th of November has been referred to the Committee of Ways and Means, and I am instructed to ask for the amount of the payments to be made during the present quarter on account of the public debt, the funds prepared to meet those payments, and any other information which may enable the committee to decide as to the necessity of adopting additional measures for meeting the public engagements during the present quarter of the year.

I have the honor to be your most obedient,

JOHN W. EPPES.

Honorable Mr. DALLAS, *Secretary of the Treasury.*

TREASURY DEPARTMENT, December 2, 1814.

SIR,—I have the honor to acknowledge the receipt of your letter, dated this morning, stating that mine of the 27th of November, addressed to the Committee on a National Bank, has been referred to the Committee of Ways and Means.

In my communications to the committees of Congress, I have never been disposed to disguise the embarrassments of the treasury. A frank and full development of existing evils will always, I hope, be best calculated to secure the attention and exertion of the public authorities, and, with legislative aid, I am still confident that all the difficulties of a deficient revenue, a suspended circulating medium, and a depressed credit may be speedily and completely overcome. My only apprehension arises from the lapse of time, as a remedy which would be effectual to-day will, perhaps, only serve to increase the disorder to-morrow.

In answering the inquiries of your letter, permit me to state, 1st, the amount of the payments which were to be made during the whole of the present quarter on account of the public debt, and the funds prepared, or applicable, to meet those payments; 2d, the payments that remain to be made and the funds that remain to meet them for the residue of the quarter; and 3d, general information in relation to additional measures for meeting the public engagements.

FIRST POINT.

It is respectfully stated, agreeably to an estimate which was formed on the 4th of October, 1814:

DR.

1. That, during the quarter commencing the 1st of October, 1814, and ending the 1st of January, 1815, including both days, there was payable for the principal and interest of treasury notes during the whole quarter, chiefly at Boston, New York, and Philadelphia, a sum of..$4,457,069 80

2. That, during the same period, there was payable for the principal and interest of temporary loans at Boston, Baltimore, and Charleston the sum of...................... 771,125 00

3. That, during the same period, there was payable in dividends upon the public funded debt at the several loan offices the sum of... 1,900,000 00

$7,128,194 80

CR.

1. That there were bank credits scattered throughout the United States, on the 1st of October, 1814, amounting by estimate to.. 2,500,000 00

2. That there was receivable from the customs during the whole quarter the sum of...................................... 1,800,000 00

3. That there was receivable on account of the sales of public lands during the same period a sum of............ 160,000 00

4. That there was receivable on account of internal duties and direct taxes during the same period a sum of........ 900,000 00

5. That there was receivable on account of loans during the same period a sum of.. 1,700,000 00

6. That there might be obtained upon an issue of treasury notes during the same period a sum of about.............. 2,500,000 00

$9,560,000 00

From which it results,—

1. That the amount of the whole payments for dividends of public debt for temporary loans and for treasury notes during the whole of the current quarter was.............. 7,128,194 80

2. That the amount of the whole of the estimated receipts of the treasury was.. 9,560,000 00

Leaving a surplus of receipts of.........................$2,431,805 20

It is believed that this estimate, formed upon official facts and experience, would have been substantially realized in the event if the banks had not suddenly determined to suspend their pay-

17

ments in specie. But for that occurrence the dividend on the public debt would have been punctually paid to the individual creditors of Boston on the 1st of October last, the transfer of the public funds from one place to another place, in order to meet the public engagements, would have continued easy and certain, the credit and use of treasury notes (limited to the specified amount) would probably have been preserved, and the revenue arising from duties and taxes would not have been materially intercepted, if at all, in its passage to the treasury by payments in treasury notes.

SECOND POINT.

Dr.

1. That of the principal and interest of the treasury notes, payable during the present quarter, and which have already fallen due, there remains on this day unpaid at the places mentioned in the schedule A, the sum of... $1,902,680 80

2 That the principal and interest of the treasury notes, which will become due on or before the 1st of January, 1815, at the places mentioned in the schedule B, amount to............ 1,243,720 00

3. That the dividends on the public debt, payable on the 1st of January, 1815, at the places mentioned in schedule C, amount to the sum of............ 1,873,000 00

4. That the principal and interest of temporary loans, payable during the present quarter and contracted at the treasury, in part execution of the authority granted by the act of Congress, passed the 14th of March, 1812, and payable at Boston on the 15th and 31st of December, amount to............ 506,875 00

$5,526,275 80

Cr.

1. That on the twenty-eighth ultimo there were bank credits in the banks, specified in the schedule D, applicable to the payment of the public debt during the present quarter, deducting the amount of bank credits ($813,000), which, as it could not be transferred for the payment of public debt, has been recently applied to the appropriations for the War and Navy Departments, amounting to............ 2,372,287 13

2. That the amount, receivable during the remainder of the present year, on account of the loan of six millions, applicable also to the payment of the public debt, if no failure in payment occurs, will be about............ 450,000 00

3. That the estimated amount, receivable during the remainder of the present year, on account of customs, applicable also to the payment of the public debt, subject, however, to various contingencies, such as the non-payment of bonds, the payment of bonds in treasury notes, etc., may be stated at............ 350,000 00

4. The estimated amount, receivable during the remainder of the present year, on account of the sales of public lands, subject, however, to contingent payments in treasury notes, may be stated at............ 150,000 00

5. The estimated amount, receivable during the remainder of the present year, for internal duties and direct tax, subject, however, to contingent payments in treasury notes, may be stated at $450,000 00

$3,772,287 13

From this second view of the debit and credit of the account, limited merely to the payment of the public debt, becoming due for the residue of the present quarter, it appears,—

1. That the debt amounts to the sum of 5,526,275 80
2. That the resources to pay the debt, excluding the sum applied to the Army and Navy Departments as before stated, and excluding the possible proceeds of new loans and new issues of treasury notes, for the single purpose of paying public debt, amount to................ 3,772,287 13

$1,753,988 67

The difference between the results of the statements, under the first and the second points, will be accounted for by the unexpected effect of payments in treasury notes on account of duties, taxes, and land; by the total cessation of the use of treasury notes either to pay the public creditors or to raise money; and by an unavoidable variance in estimates, depending upon a variance in the state of information at the treasury. A priority of payment may be justly claimed by the holders of the funded debt; and, therefore, it is proper to add,—

1. That the amount of public credits, as estimated in the preceding statements, is the sum of........................$3,772,287 13
2. That the amount of the dividend on the old and new funded debt, payable on the 1st of January, 1815, is the sum of... 1,873,000 00

3. And that, consequently, the surplus of the resources, after satisfying that single object, is the sum of.........$1,899,287 13

It will be observed that these estimates do not include, as an item of the debt, the dividend on the funded debt, amounting to $200,000, which was not actually paid to the individual creditors at Boston on the 1st of October last. But it is omitted, because an adequate fund in the State bank was seasonably provided for the occasion, and the usual treasury draft was issued in favor of the commissioner of loans, so as to deduct a corresponding amount from the bank credits of the government. The State bank declined, for several reasons (which it is unnecessary to repeat), paying in coin or in bank-notes, and most of the public creditors refused to accept the treasury notes, which the bank offered to them as an alternative payment. It is not considered that under these circumstances, connected with the general state of the circulating medium (which places the power of the government to meet its engagements on the same footing with the power of the most opulent of its citizens), there can exist any just reproach upon the public credit or resources. But, nevertheless, efforts have been anxiously made by this department, and are still in operation, to satisfy the public creditors independent of the fund which was originally set apart, and which still remains on deposit at the State bank, by all the remaining means, at the disposal of the treasury.

Nor, on the other hand, have I included in the statement of our resources to pay the public debt the unexecuted authority to borrow upon public loans, and to issue treasury notes. I have only included the items of revenue, which, in ordinary times, would be deemed certain and effective ; reserving any surplus of those items, with the loan and the treasury notes, to meet the general appropriations for the public service.

THIRD POINT.

It is respectfully stated that the non-payment of the treasury notes, and the hazard of not being able to pay the dividend on the public debt, according to the respective contracts, was chiefly (I believe entirely) owing to the suspension of specie payments at the banks, and the consequent impracticability of transferring the public funds, from the place in which they were deposited, to the place in which they were wanted. I have endeavored, therefore, to induce the banks, as the performance of an act of justice, not inconsistent with their interest or their policy, to assist in alleviating the fiscal embarrassments of the government, which they have thus contributed to produce. The answers to my last proposition (of which a copy is annexed in schedule E) have not been received.

But the danger of depending upon gratuitous aids (of depending, indeed, upon anything but the wisdom and the vigilance of Congress) makes, with every day's experience, a deeper impression upon the mind. In speaking, therefore, of additional measures for meeting the public engagements during the present quarter of the year, I derive great satisfaction in reflecting upon the inevitable and immediate effect of the legislative sanction (even so far as it has already been given) to a settled and productive system of taxes, for defraying the expenses of government and maintaining the public credit. This policy, embracing in its course the introduction of a national circulating medium, and the proper facilities for anticipating, collecting, and distributing the public revenue, will at once enliven the public credit; and even the existing resources of the present quarter must ripen and expand under an influence so auspicious. But something may be conveniently and usefully added. For instance,—

1. A discretionary authority may be given, by law, to issue treasury notes for the amount of the sums now authorized to be raised by law.

2. An authority may be given, by law, to transfer bank credits from one place to another place, in order to meet the public engagements, allowing a reasonable rate of exchange.

3. Appropriations may be made, by law, to defray the extra expenses of the War and Navy Departments during the present year; and a general authority may be given to borrow or to issue treasury notes, to supply any deficiencies in former appropriations for those departments, and for the payment of the public debt, the treasury notes, and the civil list.

The present opportunity enables me to assure you, sir, that I am preparing, with all possible diligence, to report to the Committee of Ways and Means upon the subjects which they have been pleased to confide to me.

1. The tax bills are numerous, new in some of their principles, and complicated in most of their details; nor are the best sources of information at hand. They will, however, be drafted, and sent to the committee in succession.

2. The plan for establishing a competent sinking fund is under consideration, and will, probably, be ready to be reported before the tax bills are passed.

3. The estimates for the expenses of 1815, the annual appropriation bill, and the bills to authorize a loan, and an issue of treasury notes for that year, are also objects of attention.

I have the honor to be, very respectfully, sir, your obedient servant,

A. J. DALLAS.

JOHN W. EPPES, Esq., *Chairman of the Committee of Ways and Means.*

A.

Schedule of Treasury Notes which have already fallen due and remain unpaid this 2d Day of December, 1814.

Where Payable.	When Payable. 1814.	Principal.	Interest.	Total.
Philadelphia	November 1,	$269,000	$14,526 00	$283,526 00
"	December 1,	366,200	19,774 80	385,974 80
New York		570,000	30,780 00	600,780 00
Boston		600,000	32,400 00	632,400 00
		$1,805,200	$97,480 80	$1,902,680 80

B.

Schedule of Treasury Notes becoming due on or before the 1st of January,
1815.

Where Payable.	When Payable.	Principal.	Interest.	Total.
	1814.			
New York......................	December 11,	$100,000	$5,400	$105,400
Philadelphia	....	600,000	32,400	632,400
Boston	December 21,	30,000	1,620	31,620
	1815.			
New York......................	January 1,	400,000	21,600	421,600
Philadelphia......................	....	50,000	2,700	52,700
		$1,180,000	$63,720	$1,243,720

C.

*Estimated Amount of the Dividends on the Domestic Funded Debt of the
United States, Payable on the 1st of January, 1815.*

At Portsmouth, N. H.	$12,000	At Wilmington, Del....	$1.000
Boston......................	320,000	Baltimore	125,000
Providence...............	20,000	Richmond	20,000
Hartford	37,000	Raleigh..................	5,000
New York.................	625,000	Charleston...............	85,000
Trenton.	8,000	Savannah................	5,000
Philadelphia, includ-		Treasury at Washingt'n,	
ing stocks on treas-		exclusive of dividends	
ury books...............	545,000	payable at Philad'a...	65,000
			$1,873,000

Note.—From the daily transfers of stock from one loan-office
to another, it is impossible at this time to estimate with precision
the amount which will be payable at each loan-office on the 1st
of January next. The above may be considered as near the
sums which will be payable, unless the removal of stock should,
in the mean time, be unusually large.

D.

Cash in the several banks, according to the state of the information at the treasury, on the 28th of November, 1814, after
deducting moneys in the southern and western banks, assigned
to the Secretaries of the War and Navy Departments, in consequence of their being transferable from the places of deposit to
the places of payment of the public debt, amounting to $813,000.

Bath Bank.....................	$9,723 18	Union Bank,	
Lincoln Bank, Bath.....	5,750 00	Georgetown	$87,561 45
Cumberland Bank, Portland........................	24,217 79	Mechanics' Bank of Alexandria	5,000 00
Portland Bank............	12,043 18	Bank of Potomac,	
New Hampshire Union Bank	12,807 39	Alexandria..........	15,000 00
		Bank of Virginia ...	35,020 35
Saco Bank..................	1,435 83	Branch of Bank of	
Merchants' Bank, Salem	34,376 82	Virginia, at Norfolk	372 24
Roger Williams' Bank.	12,365 57	State Bank, Raleigh	366 93
Newport Bank............	42,738 99	Branch of do. Salisbury	6,263 88
New Haven Bank.......	15,081 12		
New York State Bank, Albany....................	40,730 17	Branch of do. Wilmington..............	5,502 33
Mechanics' and Farmers' Bank, Albany..........	18,369 08	Bank of Cape Fear ..	1,697 26
		Planters' and Mechanics' Bank,	
Manhattan Company ...	378,788 46	Charleston	101,235 28
Branch Bank of Manhattan Company, at Utica	15,433 59	Bank of South Carolina.....................	22,712 50
Mechanics' Bank, New York	222,896 14	Union Bank, South Carolina	14,028 47
City Bank, New York..	34,254 08	Planters' Bank, Savannah	102 98
Bank of Pennsylvania..	94,668 63	Bank of Kentucky..	9,174 70
Farmers' and Mechanics' Bank, Philadelphia...	376 67	Branch of Bank of Kentucky, at Russellville	1,247 61
Branch Bank, Pittsburg	910 59		
Bank of Baltimore	65,288 16	Branch of Bank of Kentucky, at Louisville.................	699 01
Commercial and Farmers' B'k, Baltimore	18,212 19		
Mechanics' Bank, Baltimore	628,594 51	Bank of Chillicothe	9,866 08
Washington...............	67,067 82	Miami Exporting Company, Cincinnati	30,110 89
Metropolis	11,609 60		
Columbia..................	241,974 26	Louisiana Bank......	66,514 92
Farmers' and Mechanics' Bank, Georgetown	596 48		$2,372,287 13

SCHEDULE E.

(*Circular.*)

TREASURY DEPARTMENT,
November 25, 1814.

SIR,—The sudden determination of most of the banks in which the deposits of public money were made to refuse payment of their notes and of drafts upon them, in specie, deprived the government of the use of its gold and silver, without any act or assent on the part of the treasury. The equally sudden determination of the banks of each State to refuse credit and circulation to the notes issued in other States, deprived the government, without its participation, of the only means that were possessed for transferring its funds from the places in which they lay inac-

tive to the places in which they were wanted for the payment of
the dividends on the funded debt and the discharge of treasury
notes. It was the inevitable result of these transactions that the
bank credits of the government should be soon exhausted in
Boston, New York, Philadelphia, etc., where the principal loan-
offices for the payment of the public debt were established, and
that the government should be unable to satisfy its engagements
in those cities, unless the public creditors would receive drafts on
banks in other States, or would subscribe the amount of their
claims to a public loan, or would accept a payment in treasury
notes. It was not unreasonable, indeed, to hope that the banks,
whose conduct had produced the existing embarrassment, would
cheerfully afford some alleviating accommodation to the government; but every attempt to realize that hope has hitherto failed.
Even, however, if the present application should also be unsuccessful, I think I may rely on the intelligence and candor of our
fellow-citizens to vindicate the government from any reproach for
a want of good faith or of essential resources to maintain the
public credit. The events which have occurred, the government
could neither avert nor control.

Under these circumstances, I have deemed it a duty to the
public and to myself to request the attention of the banks which
have acted as agents of the treasury in the receipt and distribution of public money, to the following propositions:

1. That the banks shall assist the government with the means
of discharging the treasury notes and paying the dividends of
public debt during the present quarter at the loan-office of their
respective States. A great portion both of the treasury notes
and public debt belongs to the banks respectively; and so far
nothing more than a protracted credit will be required. The
balance of the demand will be payable, of course, in the notes of
the respective banks.

2. That to secure and satisfy the advances thus to be made by
the banks respectively, the banks shall be admitted on reasonable
terms to subscribe to the loan of three millions of dollars; or
they shall receive treasury notes, or they shall receive bank-notes,
or drafts upon banks in other States. If any bank should prefer
accommodating the treasury with a temporary loan on a legal
interest, this course may be pursued.

I will thank you, sir, for an early answer to this proposition,
and if it should be accepted I will immediately make the necessary arrangements to carry it into effect.

I have the honor to be, sir, very respectfully, your most obedient servant,

A. J. DALLAS.

LETTER

FROM THE SECRETARY OF THE TREASURY

To the Chairman of the Committee of Ways and Means, accompanying the Bill entitled "An Act to prohibit intercourse with the enemy, and for other purposes."

TREASURY DEPARTMENT, Nov. 19, 1814.

SIR,—I have the honor to acknowledge the receipt of your letter requesting, on behalf of the Committee of Ways and Means, "any information which the Treasury Department can furnish as to the defects of the present revenue laws, and the best mode of correcting the evils arising from an intercourse with the enemy."

Although the expediency of a general revision of the revenue laws, with the view contemplated by the committee, is acknowledged, I fear it will be impracticable at this time to undertake and to execute satisfactorily so extensive a task. The pressure of the current business upon the department is severe, and precludes an application of the secretary's time to any object which is not of immediate importance. The inconveniences that are suggested in the documents from Vermont, accompanying the reference of the committee, require, however, an early attention; and the following views of the subject are respectfully submitted to your consideration:

I. The representations from Vermont present various causes of complaint:

1. That smuggling is extensively prosecuted on the northern frontier by citizens of the United States, sometimes with and sometimes without the cover of a neutral character, in the course of which the enemy obtains important intelligence; he is furnished with cattle and other essential supplies; and he is enabled to introduce his merchandise surreptitiously into our markets.

2. That the powers of the revenue officers are inadequate to the detection and prosecution of these offences, because the right of search is not extended to every vehicle that may be employed; because the prohibitory laws do not sufficiently define and enumerate the subjects of an illicit trade; because no efficient act of prevention is authorized to be performed even upon the strongest ground of suspicion; and because there is no force, civil or military, provided to aid the revenue officers in the execution of their duty when cases of violent opposition occur.

3. That limited as the general powers of the revenue officers appear to be, they are rendered still more inadequate by the terror which the officers now feel of being exposed to suits for damages under the authority of recent decisions in the courts of

law; for it has been adjudged in Vermont that the inspectors of the customs are not authorized in any case to make seizures; and that actions may be maintained against them to recover the whole value of the property seized, even when the property itself has been duly condemned as forfeited by law.

II. The actual state of the laws in relation to these subjects of complaint may be sufficiently seen in the following analysis:

Of the power and privileges of inspectors and other officers of the customs.

1. The inspectors of the customs are persons employed by the collector, with the approbation of the principal officer of the Treasury Department, and their duties are entirely directed to guard against frauds upon the revenue by smuggling or any other kind of illicit trade. They are described and considered throughout the acts of Congress as officers of the customs, though not as chief officers.

2. On the arrival or the approach of ships or vessels, the inspectors, as well as the chief and other officers of the customs, are empowered to go on board (whether in or out of their respective districts) for the purpose of demanding manifests of their cargoes and of examining and searching the ships and vessels. This act is to be performed *ex officio*, by way of precaution, without any special deputation from a collector, naval officer, or surveyor. (Vol. iv. 367, s. 54.)

3. If, however, there be reason to suspect that any goods subject to duty are concealed in any ship or vessel, an inspector cannot enter such ship or vessel to search for, seize, and secure such goods without being specially appointed for that purpose by the collector, naval officer, or surveyor. And if there be cause to suspect a concealment of such goods in any particular dwelling-house, store, building, or other place, a search-warrant must be obtained from a justice of the peace to authorize a search and seizure. The cases here provided for are cases of suspicion only,—when probable information has been received of a concealment of goods, either on water or on land, with a design to evade the payment of duties. The act to be performed is not in the ordinary course of an inspector's official duty; it is not an act of precaution, but of detection; it is not an act authorized for seizing goods which are notoriously liable to seizure, but for entering a ship or a house in a doubtful case to ascertain whether any goods liable to seizure are there concealed. (Vol. iv. 389, s. 68.)

4. But any ship or vessel, goods, wares, or merchandise which are liable to seizure by virtue of any act respecting the revenue, it is the duty of the several officers of the customs (including by general description and practical construction the inspectors of

the customs) to seize and secure as well without as within their respective districts. The act to be performed in this case is founded on the fact that the property is liable to seizure; but that it is not necessary to enter either a ship or a house to ascertain whether such goods are so liable and are there concealed. (Vol. iv. 390, s. 70.)

5. In the performance of their duties the inspectors, in common with the other officers of the customs, are protected by the law when unjustly sued or molested, in actions for damages; and when any prosecution is commenced on account of the seizure of any ship or goods in which judgment is given for the claimant, the inspectors are released from all responsibility on showing that there was a reasonable cause of seizure. (Vol. iv. 391, s. 71; ibid. 429, s. 89.) This last provision, indeed, has been extended generally for the protection of any collector or other officer, under any act of Congress authorizing a seizure of any ship or vessel, goods, wares, or merchandise, where the seizure has been made on probable cause, although restitution should be decreed. (Vol. viii. 255, s. 1.)

6. The "Act to prohibit any American from proceeding to, or trading with, the enemies of the United States, and for other purposes," declares that "if any person shall transport or attempt to transport, overland or otherwise, in any wagon, cart, sleigh, boat, or otherwise, naval or military stores, arms, or the munitions of war, or any article of provision from any place of the United States to Upper or Lower Canada, Nova Scotia, or New Brunswick," certain forfeitures and penalties shall be incurred. And authority is given "to the collectors of the several ports of the United States to seize and stop naval or military stores, arms, or the munitions of war, or any articles of provision, and ship or vessel, wagon, cart, sleigh, boat, or thing by which any article prohibited as aforesaid is shipped or transported, or attempted to be shipped or transported." It seems to be a strained and impracticable construction of the provision to confine the exercise of the authority for stopping and seizing the contraband articles to the personal agency of the collectors. A collector in this case, as in every other case where a positive restriction is not imposed, must act through the vigilance and co-operation of the inspectors and other officers of the customs.

Of the existing auxiliary means to execute the revenue laws, and the laws prohibiting trade and intercourse with the enemy.

1. In addition to the means which the preceding statements will suggest, the judges of the supreme court, and of the several district courts of the United States, and all judges and jus-

tices of the courts of the several States (having authority, by the laws of the United States, to take cognizance of offences against the constitution and laws thereof), have the like power to hold to security of the peace and for good behavior, in cases arising under the constitution and laws of the United States, as may or can be lawfully exercised, by any judge or justice of the peace of the respective States, in cases cognizable before them. (Vol. iv. 231.)

2. Whenever the laws of the United States are opposed, or the execution thereof obstructed, in any State by combinations too powerful to be suppressed by the ordinary course of judicial proceedings or the powers of the marshal, the President is authorized to call forth a competent force of the militia to cause the laws to be executed. (Vol iv. 188, s. 2, 9.) And by a subsequent act, the President is authorized to employ the land or naval force of the United States for the same purpose. (Vol. viii. 311.)

3. A final judgment or decree, in any suit, in the highest court of law or equity of a State in which a decision of the suit could be had, where is drawn in question the validity of an authority exercised under the United States (as in the case of an officer of the customs), and the decision is against the validity, may be re-examined, and reversed or affirmed, in the supreme court of the United States, upon a writ of error; but the matter in dispute must exceed the value of two thousand dollars, exclusive of costs. (Vol. i. s. 61, 63.)

III. From these views of the subject of complaint, and of the state of the law in relation to them, we are led to consider the best modes of amending the defects and correcting the evils which exist.

1. An habitual respect for the judicial authority does not permit me to controvert any further the decisions of the courts of law, in the State of Vermont, respecting the official character and powers of the inspectors and other officers of the customs. It is recommended, therefore, that the law should be so amended as to place the inspector upon the footing of officers within the meaning of the revenue laws and laws prohibiting trade and intercourse with the enemy; and that the collectors should be authorized to employ a competent number of inspectors, with authority to stop, search, detain, and seize all cattle, live stock, and other supplies; all goods and money; and, generally, all other articles whatsoever, howsoever carried and transported, by land or by water, on the way to or from the British Provinces, subject to such regulations as will secure, with as little embarrassment as possible, the rights of a lawful or neutral trade.

2. The officers of the customs should be entitled, in proper cases, and on proper proofs, to obtain from any magistrate a

warrant to search dwelling-houses and other buildings; to demand the assistance of the marshal of the district and his deputies, with the posse of the district, if necessary, for the execution of their duties; and to hold any person to security for his good behavior, stating, on oath, that they have probable and just cause for believing that such person is carrying on an unlawful trade or intercourse with the enemy.

3. No citizen, or person, usually residing within the United States, should be allowed to cross the frontier into the British Provinces without a passport from the Secretary of State or from the Secretary of War, or from the officer commanding the military district in which such person usually resides. All persons coming from the British Provinces into the United States should be required to report themselves, within a reasonable time, to the military commander, or the collector, of the district within which they shall, respectively, first arrive. And any person hovering upon the frontier, at a distance from his usual place of residence, without any business requiring his attendance there, and without a passport, should be held to security for his good behavior, as a person suspected, upon probable cause, to be engaged in an unlawful trade or intercourse with the enemy.

4. The militia and army of the United States on the frontier should be authorized, under proper regulations, to co-operate with the civil magistrates and officers of the customs in seizing and securing persons engaged in an unlawful trade, or intercourse with the enemy, together with the articles and vehicles employed in such trade or intercourse.

5. A more effectual provision should be made for transferring from the State courts to the federal courts suits brought against persons exercising an authority under the United States, so that such suits may be transferred, as soon as conveniently may be, after they are commenced.

6. Treason being defined by the constitution, and misprision of treason being an offence which is necessarily founded upon that definition, many practices of a treasonable nature and effect, which cannot be constitutionally classed with treason, are unnoticed in our penal code. An act of Congress declaring such practices to be misdemeanors, and punishing them with fine and imprisonment, would, perhaps, be the most effectual mode of correcting the evils arising from an intercourse with the enemy.

The papers that were received from the committee are now returned; and I embrace the opportunity to repeat the assurances of the sincere respect with which I have the honor to be,

Sir, your most obedient servant,

A. J. DALLAS.

J. W. EPPES, Esq., *Chairman of the Committee of Ways and Means.*

LETTER

FROM THE SECRETARY OF THE TREASURY

To the Chairman of the Committee of Ways and Means, exhibiting a view of the state of the treasury at the close of the year 1814; also a view of the situation of the treasury for the year 1815, with propositions relative to the ways and means for the same.

TREASURY DEPARTMENT, January 17, 1815.

SIR,—I have deemed it hitherto my duty to wait, with deference and respect, for a decision upon the measures which I had the honor to suggest to the Committee of Ways and Means on the 17th of October last. But the rapid approach to the termination of the session of Congress induces me again to trespass upon your attention, earlier, perhaps, than is consistent with a satisfactory view of the situation of the treasury, as some important plans are still under legislative discussion. I have now, however, the honor to submit to the consideration of the Committee of Ways and Means the following additional statements and propositions :

STATEMENTS.

I. Statement of the situation of the treasury at the close of the year 1814.

1. *The charges on the treasury for* 1814.

It appears, that at the close of the year 1813 there was a general balance of the appropriations for that year remaining unsatisfied, and subject to be called for at the treasury in the year 1814, amounting to about $8,131,313 03, and composed of the following items :

Of the appropriation for the civil department, about.........	$390,499 07
Of the appropriation for the military department............	2,666,230 33
Of the appropriation for the naval department...............	3,611,240 75
Of the appropriation for the diplomatic department.........	253,846 62
Of the appropriations for miscellaneous services.............	1,209,496 26
	$8,131,313 03

The annual appropriations for the year 1814 amounted to the sum of.............. $38,003,691 28
The sum necessary to meet the engagements, in relation to the public debt, was about..................................... 11,560,586 39
        49,563,277 67

The gross charge on the treasury for the year 1814 was...... $57,694,590 70

2. *The ways and means of the treasury for* 1814.

The gross charge upon the treasury for the year 1814, amounting to $57,694,590 70, included, as above stated, the balance of the appropriations of 1813 remaining unsatisfied at the close of that year. It is, therefore, proper to place to the credit of the treasury the outstanding revenue and resources at the commencement of the year 1814; and these consisted of the following items:

Of cash in the treasury on the 1st of January, 1814.........		$5,196,482 00
Of revenue received at the treasury in the 1st quarter of 1814....	$4,286,062 28	
Of revenue received in the second quarter..	2,822,108 05	
Of revenue received in the third quarter....	2,313,183 20	
Of revenue received in the fourth quarter, by estimate...	1,920,000 00	
		11,311,353 53
Of the proceeds of loans contracted for in 1813, and paid in 1814...........................	$3,592,665 00	
Of the proceeds of treasury notes issued under the act of 1813, and received in 1814........	1,070,000 00	
		4,662,665 00
Of the amount of the loan authorized by the act of the 24th of March, 1814........	$25,000,000 00	
Of the amount of the loan authorized by the act of the 15th of November, 1814.........	3,000,000 00	
		28,000,000 00
Of the amount of treasury notes authorized to be issued by the act of the 4th of March, 1814.....................................	$5,000,000 00	
Of the amount of treasury notes authorized to be issued by the act of December 26, 1814..	3,000,000 00	
		8,000,000 00
		$57,170,500 53

From this statement, therefore, it appears,—

That the charges on the treasury for 1814 amounted to...	$57,694,590 70
That the ways and means of the treasury for 1814 amounted to..	57,170,500 53
	$524,090 17

And this excess of charges on the treasury, amounting to $524,090 17, beyond the ways and means actually appropriated, will be payable out of the revenue uncollected on the 31st of December, 1814.

But, independent of the general view thus taken of the existing charges on the treasury, and of the ways and means designated, by law, for the service of 1814, it is necessary to present a statement of the actual receipts and disbursements for that year.

The *actual receipts* at the treasury, during the year 1814, amounted to the sum of $40,007,661 53, and consisted of the following items:

The cash in the treasury on the 1st of January, 1814, amounted, as above stated, to		$5,196,482 00
The revenue received at the treasury, during the year 1814, amounted, as above stated, to		11,311,353 53
The cash received at the treasury in the year 1814, on account of the loans and issues of treasury notes authorized in 1813, amounted, as above stated, to		4,662,665 00
The cash received at the treasury on account of the loans authorized in 1814, amounted, in the second quarter, to	$6,087,011	
In the third quarter, to	2,815,060	
In the fourth quarter, by estimate	2,707,810	
		11,609,881 00
The cash received at the treasury on account of the issues of treasury notes, authorized in 1814, amounted, in the second quarter, to	$1,392 100	
In the third quarter, to	1,603,900	
In the fourth quarter, to	4,231,280	
		7,227,280 00
		$40,007,661 53

The actual disbursements at the treasury, during 1814 (taking a part of the fourth quarter by estimate), amounted to the sum of $38,273,619 28, and consisted of the following payments:

For the civil department	$933,327 97	
For miscellaneous services	1,207,492 30	
For the diplomatic department	206,306 52	
For the military department	20,510,238 00	
For the naval department	7,312,899 90	
For the public debt	8,103,354 59	
		$38,273,619 28

The estimated balance of cash in the treasury on the 31st of December, 1814, being	$1,734,042 25

To these views, however, 1st, of the general charges on the treasury, and of the ways and means designated, by law, for the service of 1814; and 2d, of the actual receipts and disbursements at the treasury, during that year, it is proper to add a statement of the result, showing the condition of the treasury at the end of 1814, in relation to the unsatisfied demands, and to the unexpended ways and means.

The unsatisfied demands on the treasury, at the close of 1814, amounted to $19,420,971 42, and consisted of the balances of appropriations for the following objects:

For the civil department......................... .... $519,967 11
For miscellaneous services............................ 1,285,682 36
For the diplomatic department.................... 230,540 10
For the military department...................... 9,458,898 33
For the naval department........................ 4,468.251 72
For the public debt........................... .... 3,457,231 80
                                              $19,420,971 42

The unexpended amount of the ways and means provided for 1814 was $23,396,881 25, and consisted of the following items :

Cash in the treasury on the 1st of January, 1814, estimated at.............................. $1,734,042 25

Revenue uncollected and outstanding, estimated at.................................... 4,500,000 00

Authority to borrow money and to issue treasury notes, not executed, or not yet productive, under acts of the 4th and 24th of March, 1814...................... 8,162,839 00

    Stock sent to Europe... $3,000,000
    Under act of November
      15, 1814.................. 3,000,000
    Under act of December
      26, 1814.................. 3,000,000
                             9,000,000 00
                                     $23,396,881 25

The surplus of ways and means, in reference to the service of 1814, including revenue and the unexecuted authority to borrow and to issue treasury notes, is, therefore $3,975,909 83

The conclusion from this statement of the situation of the treasury at the close of 1814, under the different views which have been presented, would seem to establish that the ways and means provided for the service of that year were considerably more than the demands on the treasury would require. But it must always be recollected that the demands are positive and urgent; while a great portion of the ways and means rests upon a precarious foundation. Thus:

The unsatisfied demands on the treasury for the service of 1814, positive and urgent in their nature, amount to $19,420,971 42
The cash in the treasury and the outstanding revenue, only amount to.. 6,234,042 25
                                     $13,186,929 17

And, consequently, the payment of the difference, amounting to $13,186,929 17, for the service of 1814, must depend on the success of raising money by loan, or by issues of treasury notes, under the unexecuted authority constituting the remaining ways and means designated for the same year.

18

II. Statement of the situation of the treasury for the year 1815.

1. *The charges upon the treasury for the year 1815, as already ascertained.*

The estimates for the annual appropriations amount to $40,538,889 39, consisting of the following items:

For civil, diplomatic, and miscellaneous
expenses... $1,979,289 39
For the military department.................... 30,342,238 00
For the naval department....................... 8,217,362 00
                                      ————— $40,538,889 39

The public debt will call for a sum of $15,493,145 30, to answer the following claims:

For interest and reimbursement of stocks
existing before the war......................... $3,452,775 46
For interest on the funded debt created
since the war....................................... 2,922,816 72
For the interest on loans to be effected in
1815, by estimate................................. 1,500,000 00
For the principal and interest of treasury
notes falling due in 1815, and on the 1st
of January, 1816................................... 7,617,553 12
                                       ————— $15,493,145 30

                                         $56,032,034 69

From this view it appears, that ways and means must now be provided for an expenditure of $56,032,034 69, in the year 1815, independent of such additions as may arise from the contemplated establishment of a sinking fund, in relation to the public debt created since the war, and from any other new object of expense, which shall be authorized during the present year.

2. *The ways and means of the treasury for 1815.*

The outstanding and uncollected revenue, at the commencement of 1815, has been considered as applicable to the payment of the unsatisfied balances of the appropriations for the preceding year; and, consequently, only such parts of the revenue as shall accrue, and be actually received at the treasury, during 1815, can be embraced in the resources for the current service. But it also follows, from that view of the subject, that the treasury is entitled to be credited in 1815 for the excess, in the provision of ways and means, to meet the expenditure of 1814.

This excess, consisting of cash, of outstanding revenue, and of an authority to borrow or to issue treasury notes, amounts, as above stated, to the sum of...................... $3 975,909 83

The net sum receivable into the treasury in the year 1815, for duties on goods imported during that year, cannot be safely estimated at a greater sum than................... 1,000,000 00

The direct tax will probably give to the treasury during the year 1815, a sum of.. 2,000,000 00

The internal duties, old and new, and postage, on an estimate which is stated in the schedule A, will probably produce, in the year 1815, a sum of 7,050,000 00

The sales of public lands will probably produce in the year 1815, a sum of 1,000,000 00

The amount of incidental receipts, from miscellaneous sources, will probably be................................... 100,000 00

$15,125,909 83

But it appears, that the single item of public debt will require in the year 1815, a sum of.. .... $15,493,145 30

And that the revenue (independent of the excess of the authority to borrow, etc. brought from the last year's ways and means) will only be.............................. 11,150,000 00

Leaving a deficiency, in that respect alone, of...... $4,343,145 30

In a more general view, however, it is to be stated,—

That the charges upon the treasury for the year 1815, amount to the sum of... $56,032,034 69

That the existing sources of supply amount only to......... 15,125,909 83

And that ways and means must be provided to raise the deficit of... $40,906,124 86

It will be readily seen, that the estimates of the product of the direct tax, and of the new internal duties, are applicable only to the present year; and that in every succeeding year the amount will be greatly augmented.

It must also be repeated, that in the statements now presented no provision is inserted for the contemplated sinking fund; nor for the payment of a considerable amount of unliquidated claims upon the government for services and supplies; as these objects seem to require a distinct consideration.

PROPOSITIONS.

I. It is respectfully proposed, that provision be made to raise a sum of $40,906,124 86, in addition to the amount of the existing revenue, for the service of the year 1815; partly by taxes, partly by an issue of treasury notes, and partly by an authority to procure money upon loan.

II. It is respectfully proposed, that an additional sum be raised by taxes, to the amount of $5,000,000; and that the following objects, or a selection from these objects of taxation, graduated in the amount to produce that sum, to be made equally productive, shall form the basis of the additional levy:

1. A **tax** upon inheritances and devises, to be paid by the heirs or devisees, may be made to produce.................. $900,000
2. A **tax** upon bequests, legacies, and statutory distribution, to be paid by the legatees or legal representatives, may be made to produce.................................... 500,000
3. An auxiliary **tax** upon all testamentary instruments and letters of administration, to be paid by the executors or administrators, may be made to produce.............. 200,000
4. A **tax** upon legal process and proceedings in the courts of the United States, to be paid by the parties at the time of taking out the process or entering the proceedings, may be made to produce...................................... 250,000
5. A **tax** upon conveyances, mortgages, and leases, to be paid by the grantees, mortgagees, and lessees, may be made to produce.. 300,000
6. A stamp **tax** upon bonds, penal bills, warrants of attorney, notarial instruments, policies of insurance, all negotiable notes, protests of bills of exchange, and promissory notes, bills of sale, and hypothecations of vessels, bottomry and respondentia bonds, may be made to produce 400,000
7. A **tax** of one dollar upon every barrel of wheaten flour, to be paid by the miller, may be made to produce..... 3,500,000
8. A **tax** upon the dividends (other than the dividends of banks) and upon the sale and transfer of the stocks of banks, insurance companies, and other corporations, operating for profit, upon a money capital, may be made to produce.. 600,000
9. An income **tax** may easily be made to produce............. 3,000,000

III. It is respectfully proposed, that the additional sum to be raised, by the specified taxes, shall be appropriated as follows:

1. Towards establishing a sinking fund, in relation to the public debt, created since the war ....
2. Towards the payment of principal and interest of the treasury notes, to be issued in the manner hereafter suggested...
3. Towards defraying the expenses of the present year........

IV. It is respectfully proposed, that there shall be an emission of treasury notes, for the service of the year 1815, to the amount of $15,000,000, on the following plan:
1. The denominations of the notes shall be such as the Secre-

tary of the Treasury, with the approbation of the President, may direct.

2. The notes of the denomination of $100 and upwards, shall be made payable to order, and shall bear an interest of five and two-fifths per centum per annum.

3. The notes of a denomination less than $100, and not less than $20, shall be payable to order, and bear an interest at the same rate; or shall be payable to bearer, and bear no interest; as the Secretary of the Treasury, with the approbation of the President of the United States, shall direct.

4. The notes of a denomination under $20, shall be made payable to bearer, and shall be circulated without interest.

5. The notes shall be issued, and be made payable at the treasury only; but any portion of them may be deposited with the loan officers or banks throughout the United States, for the purpose of being put into general circulation.

6. The holders of the treasury notes, not bearing an interest, may, at any time, exchange them, in sums not less than $100, for certificates of public stock, bearing an interest of seven per cent. per annum, and irredeemable for twelve years, from the date of the certificates respectively.

7. The notes shall be receivable in all payments to the United States; but, in such cases, they may be reissued.

8. The notes shall be payable by annual instalment, according to their dates, and in the manner to be notified by the treasury, to wit:

In 1816, the sum of (one-fifth)	$3,000,000
In 1817, the sum of (one-fifth)	3,000,000
In 1818, the sum of (one-fifth)	3,000,000
In 1819, the sum of (one-fifth)	3,000,000
In 1820, the sum of (one fifth)	3,000,000
	$15,000,000

9. The reimbursement of the notes shall be effected, according to the instalments, either by the payment of the principal and interest to the holders; or by taking out of circulation, and destroying the amount of the instalment, in notes, which have been paid to the United States for duties, taxes, or other demands.

10. There shall be an appropriation of such a portion of the taxes, above specified, as will be adequate to the payment of the successive instalments of the notes; and the faith of the United States shall be pledged to make good any deficiency.

11. There shall be no additional issue of treasury notes, except upon a specific pledge of the same taxes, or of other competent taxes, to an amount equal to the reimbursement of the notes, according to the stipulated instalments.

V. It is respectfully proposed, that authority should be given to the President to borrow the sum of $25,000,000 on the faith of the United States.

1. The loan to be accepted on the most advantageous terms that can be obtained.

2. The amount of the loan, for the payment and security of principal and interest, to be placed on the same footing as the rest of the funded debt created since the war.

If the propositions submitted to the consideration of the Committee of Ways and Means should be adopted, the treasury will be placed on the following footing for the year 1815:

1. The ascertained demands upon the treasury amount to..			$56,032,034 69
2. The existing sources of revenue and supply will produce.............................	$11.150,000 00		
3. The excess of outstanding revenue, and of authority to borrow money and to issue treasury notes for the service of 1814, beyond the demand, is estimated at...................	3,975,909 83		
4. The taxes now proposed, are estimated to produce for 1815............................	5,000,000 00		
5. The issue of treasury notes for the service of 1815, will produce...................	15,000,000 00		
6. The authority to raise money by loan, for the service of 1815, extends to......	25,000,000 00		
			60,125,909 83
Surplus of ways and means..........................			$4,093,875 14

The surplus of ways and means for the year 1815 will be applicable to the establishment of the contemplated sinking fund, and to the payment of any additional expenses that Congress may authorize.

In making the present communication, I feel, sir, that I have performed my duty to the legislature and to the country; but when I perceive that more than $40,000,000 must be raised for the service of the year 1815, by an appeal to public credit, through the medium of treasury notes and loans, I am not without sensations of extreme solicitude. The unpromising state of the public credit, and the obstructed state of the circulating medium, are sufficiently known. A liberal imposition of taxes, during the session, ought to raise the public credit, were it not for counteracting causes; but it can have no effect in restoring a national circulating medium. It remains, therefore, with the wisdom of Congress to decide, whether any other means can be applied to restore the public credit, to re-establish a national circulating medium, and to facilitate the necessary anticipations of the public revenue. The humble opinion of this department on the subject has been respectfully, though frankly, expressed on former occasions, and it remains unchanged.

I have the honor to be, with great consideration, sir, your most obedient servant,

A. J. DALLAS.

J. W. EPPES, Esq., *Chairman of the Committee of Ways and Means.*

SCHEDULE A.

TREASURY DEPARTMENT. REVENUE OFFICE,
December 1€, 1814.

SIR,—I have the honor, in compliance with your request, to submit the annexed estimates of the products of the existing internal duties, and of the additional duties proposed to be laid by the bills now before Congress; the first statement exhibiting the products for an entire year after the respective duties shall be in full operation; and the last statement showing the amounts that may be expected to be received from each duty during the year 1815. It may be proper to add that the materials do not exist for forming estimates with regard to the new duties, on which a perfect reliance should be reposed.

I am, very respectfully, your obedient servant,

S. H. SMITH, *Commissioner of the Revenue.*

Hon. Secretary of the Treasury.

No. 1.

Estimates of the Products of the existing Internal Duties and of the proposed additional Duties for an entire Year after they shall be in full operation.

Stamps	$510.000	Boots	$75,000
Carriages	300,000	Saddles and bridles	66,000
Sales at auction	300,000	Paper	50,000
Refined sugar	150,000	Candles	200,000
Licenses to retailers	900,000	Playing-cards	80,000
Licenses for stills with the		Tobacco and snuff	200,000
duty on spirits	4,000,000	Hats	400,000
Postage	250,000	Iron	350,000
Lotteries	150,000	Nails	200,000
Furniture	1,238,000	Beer, ale, and porter	60,000
Horses for the saddle and		Leather	600,000
carriage	70,000		
Gold watches	60,000		$10,379,000
Silver watches	170,000		

No. 2.

Estimate of the Amounts that may be expected to be received from the fore-
going Duties during the Year 1815.

Stamps	$510,000	Boots,		
Carriages	300,000	Saddles and bridles,		
Sales at auction	210,000	Paper,		
Refined sugar	150,000	Candles,		
Licenses to retailers	875,000	Playing-cards,		
Licenses for stills with the		Tobacco and snuff,	... $570,000	
duty on spirits	2,600,000	Hats,		
Postage	250,000	Iron,		
Lotteries	50,000	Nails,		
Furniture	1,238,000	Beer, ale, and porter,		
Horses for the saddle and		Leather,		
carriage	70,000			
Gold watches	60,000		$7,053,000	
Silver watches	170,000			

This estimate has been made on the supposition that the bills
laying the new duties will be passed previous to the 1st of
January next.

LETTER.

TREASURY DEPARTMENT, Feb. 20, 1815.

SIR,—I have the honor to acknowledge the receipt of your
letter, dated the 15th instant, which, in consequence of the termination of the war, requests, in behalf of the Committee of
Ways and Means, "a view of the probable receipts from imports
and tonnage during the year 1815, and any other information
that may enable the committee to decide on the measures necessary to meet the unexpected and fortunate change, which peace
must produce, in the resources of the United States." It has
hitherto been my arduous and painful employment to suggest to
your consideration measures for relieving the embarrassments of
the treasury with a view to the expenditures of a protracted war.
And you will readily believe that, on every account, personal as
well as public, I join you most sincerely in rejoicing at an event
which brings with it an immediate alleviation of the pressure
upon this department, as well as a general assurance of national
honor and prosperity.

The objects which claimed the attention of the committee in
my former communications were,—1st, the state of the public
credit; 2d, the state of the circulating medium; and 3d, the
ways and means to defray the various expenses of the government.

1. The public credit was depressed during the war, owing to

several causes that must now cease to operate. All the circumstances, internal and external, which were calculated to excite doubt as to the duration, or as to the issue, of the contest in the minds of the cautious and the timid have passed away, and in their place the proofs of confidence begin already to appear with practical advantage. While it was doubtful to what extent the public exigencies would require the aid of loans, those persons who retained the means of lending, either feared, or affected to fear, the eventual security of the government; and even the exemplary display of the national resources, which has been made during the present session of Congress, for the benefit of the public creditors, was curtailed of its natural effect in the resuscitation of public credit by the countervailing influence of causes which it is unnecessary to specify. But when the whole amount of the public debt incurred during the war is fixed and ascertained; when it is known that ample provision is made for the punctual payment of the interest, and for the gradual extinguishment of the principal, of the debt; and when, above all, it is seen that Congress is inflexible in its adherence to the faith and policy of the legislative pledges, the public credit of the United States will stand upon a basis the most durable and the most honorable.

2. The difficulties of the national circulating medium remain, however, to be encountered under circumstances which the government cannot control. The effects of the peace will certainly restore a metallic medium; but until that result be produced, the only resource for all the pecuniary transactions of the treasury, as well as of individuals, will be the issues of treasury notes and the notes of the State banks. If, indeed, the State banks were soon to resume their payments in specie, or if they were again to give credit and circulation to the notes of each other throughout the United States; and if they were, moreover, able and willing to accommodate the fiscal views of the government (which I do not permit myself for a moment to doubt), a total dependence upon those institutions, however impolitic in the abstract, would be practically safe and beneficial. But if, on the other hand, the notes of the State banks shall continue limited in circulation and use to the city, the town, or the State in which they are issued, it must be obvious that they cannot answer the purposes of a national medium; and that the receipt of such notes in payments for duties of import or internal duties, will convert the public revenue, which is destined for general uses abroad as well as at home, into a local fund that may not be wanted where it exists, and cannot be applied where it is wanted. It is, nevertheless, in the power of Congress to obviate, in a considerable degree, this difficulty, by authorizing the payment of a reasonable rate of exchange upon the transfer

of its revenue from the places of collection and deposit to the places of demand and employment; and I respectfully recommend the expedient to the consideration of the Committee of Ways and Means.

The alternative, or concurrent resource of treasury notes for a national circulating medium, has, on other occasions, been considered. The security of the government must always, upon every reasonable and candid estimate, be deemed superior to the security of any private corporation, and, so far as treasury notes bear an interest and are receivable in the payment of duties and taxes, they are evidently more valuable than bank-notes, which do not possess those characteristics. But the machinery of a bank is calculated to give an impulse and direction to its issues of paper which cannot be imparted by the forms of the treasury, or any merely official institution, to the paper of the government. In the operations of a bank, too, the facilities of bank credits supply the place, in a very important degree, of the issues of notes; so that a bank loan of $30,000,000, for instance, would probably require no greater issue than $6,000,000 in notes. On the contrary, the whole amount of whatever sum is to be raised by an issue of treasury notes must be actually sent, in the form of treasury notes, into the market, through the various channels of credit or demand. It is, however, to be admitted that an issue of treasury notes, not greatly exceeding in amount the demand created for them by the duties and taxes for which they are receivable, can be annually sustained; but if the amount exceeds, or even equals, the amount of that demand, the revenue will generally be absorbed by the notes before it reaches the treasury; the holder of the treasury notes being thus paid in preference, and often to the exclusion, of every other public creditor, and the other branches of the public service being thus deprived of the contemplated means for their support.

It is proper here to observe that the actual issue of treasury notes on this day (including those due and unpaid, those which are daily becoming due, and those which have been ordered but are not yet signed) amounts to the sum of $18,637,436 80, and the amount will be constantly augmenting. If, therefore, the revenue for the year 1815, enriched by the duty on imports, and by the other beneficial effects of the peace, should amount to $20,000,000, it is still evident that the whole of the revenue might be expended in the single purpose of paying the treasury-note debt, leaving every other object of the government to be provided for by loans, or by new issues of treasury notes.

Having suggested the difficulty and the danger, I cannot presume to dwell upon any expedient for relief which Congress has already refused to adopt; but I take the liberty, with deference and respect, to renew the recommendation of the plan that was submitted to your consideration in my letter of the 17th of January last, under a belief that, considering the outstanding amount of treasury notes, any new issue should be made to rest upon a basis that will enable the government to employ it both as a circulating medium and as the means of raising money in aid of the revenue. How far a power given to fund the treasury notes upon an advanced interest, or to pass them in payment of taxes and duties, will be sufficient for the purposes contemplated, without providing other means of payment by regular instalments, I must submit to the judgment of the committee.

3. The ways and means to defray the various expenses of the government for 1815, will consist of the revenue which will be actually received at the treasury during that year. It is not intended, on the one hand, to take into view the balances due upon the appropriations of preceding years, nor, on the other hand, to take into view the revenue which will accrue in the present year, but which will not be payable until the year 1816.

The direct amelioration of the resources of the country, in consequence of the peace, applies principally to the item of the duties on import and tonnage. The effect, however, must be confined, with immaterial exceptions, for 1815, to two-thirds, or the eight concluding months, of the year. The West India trade will produce little, and the European trade nothing, by way of revenue, before the 1st of May next. Some outstanding adventures beyond the Cape of Good Hope will hardly be brought home, upon the intelligence of peace, before the present year has expired. Considering, therefore, that a credit of eight, ten, and twelve months is allowed for the duties on merchandise imported from Europe, and that a credit of three and six months is allowed for the duties on merchandise imported from the West Indies, it is evident that, whatever may be the amount accruing on merchandise imported from Europe for the year 1815, the actual receipts at the treasury cannot be great; that the whole of the duties accruing on merchandise imported from the West Indies before the 1st of July will be actually received at the treasury in the year 1815; and that one moiety of the amount of the duties on merchandise imported from the West Indies between the 1st of July and the 1st of October will also be received at the treasury in the year 1815.

The average of the net revenue of the customs which accrued for the three years 1806, 1807, and 1808, was more than $14,000,000 for each year; and a similar average for the three succeeding years, 1809, 1810, and 1811, was about $9,000,000 for each year. But the first period was one of uncommon commercial prosperity, when the United States were the only neutral nation, and cannot be taken as the basis of an estimate for the present time, when the other nations of the world are also at peace. The second period was embarrassed by commercial restrictions; but probably the effect of those embarrassments upon the revenue were counterbalanced by the advantages of our neutrality. It is thought, therefore, upon the whole, that in a state of general peace the customs operating upon the single duties would not have produced, before the American war, more than a sum between $9,000,000 and $10,000,000 annually. But the comparatively small quantity of foreign merchandise at present in the American market would probably give rise to an extraordinary amount of importations during the first year of peace, equal at least to the supply of two years, if the fact that the double duties are limited in their continuance to a year after the termination of the war did not operate as a check upon importations beyond what may be requisite for the consumption of the current year. These counteracting causes may, therefore, be reasonably supposed to neutralize the force of each other, and, consequently, to refer and confine any estimate of the double duties upon merchandise imported in the year 1815 to the amount of the importations for the consumption of a single year.

Under these views it is estimated that the produce of the customs during the first twelve months of peace will amount, with double duties, to a sum between $18,000,000 and $20,000,000. Of that period, ten months occur in the year 1815; but as the importations can only partially commence for the space of two months, and cannot reach their average extent for three or four months, the fair proportion of time to form the ground of an estimate will be (as already suggested) eight months of the year 1815. Upon this scale of computation, the product of the customs which will *accrue* from the 1st of May to the 31st of December, 1815, will, probably, be $13,500,000; but there must be added to that sum the estimated amount of customs accruing, independent of the effects produced by the peace, from the first of January to the 1st of May, to wit, $1,500,000; making the aggregate of the revenue of the customs accruing in the year 1815 about $15,000,000.

It remains, however, to present an estimate of the amount of the customs which will not only accrue but which will be actually received at the treasury in the year 1815. The extent of the commerce which is expected to be opened, and the effect of the credits which are allowed for the payment of duties for the year 1815, have been already explained. The estimate, therefore, assumes the following form:

1. The total revenue of the customs accruing in the year 1815, being, as above stated $15,000,000
   It is estimated that of that sum there will become payable and will actually be received into the treasury, in the

year 1815, in the manner exhibited in the annexed
schedule, marked A, about...................... .... $3,500,000
2. That on account of custom-house bonds outstanding at the
end of the year 1814, which, in the letter from this department, dated the 17th of January, 1815, was reserved
to meet the unsatisfied appropriations of that year, there
will be received during the year 1815 near.................. 3,000,000

Making the total amount of the actual receipts into the
treasury from the customs for the year 1815.................. $6,500,000

The ways and means of the treasury for 1815, provided and
payable during the year, may now be presented in a view essentially different from that which was necessarily taken in the letter
from this department, dated the 17th of January last, while contemplating a continuance of the war.

1. The duties on imports and tonnage will, probably, produce
a sum, inclusive of that receivable for duties which accrued prior to the present year, of about................... $6,500,000
2. The direct tax, instead of a sum of $2,000,000, will prob-
ably give to the treasury in the year 1815, in consequence of the facilities of the peace, a sum of about...... 2,500,000
3. The internal duties, old and new, and postage, instead of a
sum of $7,050,000, will probably give to the treasury in
the year 1815, in consequence of the facilities of the
peace, a sum of about......... 8,000,000
4. The sales of the public lands will probably produce in the
year 1815... 1,000,000
5. The amount of incidental receipts from miscellaneous
sources will probably be about......... 200,000

$18,200,000

While the revenue is thus materially augmented, the charges
upon the treasury will be considerably reduced. It is not in the
power of this department at the present time to advert to the
estimates of the expenses of the peace establishment for the War
and Navy Departments; but with the aid of the public credit and
the legislative sanction for the measures which will be proposed,
it is believed that the treasury will be competent in that respect
to meet the most liberal views of the government. Independent,
therefore, of the estimates of the War and Navy Departments,
the charges on the treasury for the year 1815 will consist of the
following items:

1. Civil, diplomatic, and miscellaneous expenses, as stated
in the general estimates for 1815............................. $1,979,289 39
2. The public debt will call for a sum of $14,723,808 58,
to answer the following claims:
For interest and reimbursement of the
funded debt created before the war (the
amount of principal unredeemed on the

31st of December, 1814, being about
$39,005,183 60) $3,452,775 46
For interest of the funded debt created
since the war (the amount of principal
on Dec. 31st, 1814, being $48,580,812 26,
to which little has been since added),
about.. 3,000,000 00
For the principal and interest of treas-
ury notes falling due in 1815, and the 1st
of January, 1816, including $620,000
of notes issued under the act of February 25th, 1813, falling due within this
period... 8,271,033 12
                                          —————— $14,723,808 58
                                          —————————
                                             $16,703,097 97

It is to be observed, however, that the preceding estimate does
not include a sum of $2,799,200, being the principal of the treas-
ury notes which became due in 1814 and remain unpaid, because the unexecuted authority to raise money by loan for that
year is sufficient to cover the amount, if a loan can now be obtained, independent of the custom-house debt ($3,000,000) which
accrued in 1814, but is payable in 1815, and which is now considered as part of the excess of $3,975,909 83, stated in the letter
of the 17th of January, 1815, for the purpose of being specifically transferred in the present estimates from the ways and
means of last year to the credit of the ways and means for the
present year.

Upon the whole, then, it appears that the revenue for the year
1815 will probably amount to $18,200,000, and that ways and
means are now to be devised to provide for the difference between that sum and the aggregate amount of the demands for
the service of the year 1815, which will be ascertained by adding
the amount of the estimates for the peace establishment of the
War and Navy Departments to the amount of the demands for
the expenses of government, and the public debt being, as above
stated, the sum of $16,703,097 97.

It only remains to suggest some additional measures, which
appear to be required at this time, for the support of the public
credit and the supply of the treasury

1. It is respectfully suggested that all the holders of treasury
notes issued or to be issued under the authority of any existing
law, should be allowed to fund them at an interest of seven per
cent., and that interest be allowed on all treasury notes which
have not been punctually paid until the day of funding or of payment.

2. It is respectfully suggested that a new issue of treasury
notes should be authorized upon the principles suggested in the
letter from this department dated the 17th of January, 1815.

3. It is respectfully suggested that a loan should be authorized to the amount necessary, upon a view of all the estimates, to complete the ways and means for the year 1815.

4. It is respectfully suggested that the exportation of specie should be prohibited for a limited period.

I am, very respectfully, sir, your most obedient servant,

A. J. DALLAS.

J. W. EPPES, Esq., *Chairman of the Committee of Ways and Means.*

LETTER

FROM THE SECRETARY OF THE TREASURY

To the Chairman of the Committee of Ways and Means, submitting a proposition to provide for paying the interest, and gradually reducing the stock debt, created during the late war.

TREASURY DEPARTMENT, February 24, 1815.

SIR,—I have the honor to submit to the consideration of the Committee of Ways and Means a proposition to provide for paying the interest, and gradually reducing the stock debt, which has been created during the late war. It was my intention to have accompanied this communication with tables, illustrating, in detail, the operation of the sinking fund, as well as the effect of the present proposition; but various causes render the performance of this task impracticable before the adjournment of Congress; and I cannot do better than to refer to the report which was made by the Treasury Department to the House of Representatives on the 9th of April, 1808, exhibiting explanatory statements and notes of the public debt, its increase or decrease, from the 1st of January, 1791, to the 1st of January, 1808. I shall, therefore, confine my views to—1st, the general state of the public debt before the war; 2d, the general state of the public debt contracted since the war; and 3d, the particular provision to be now made for the last description of the public debt.

I. On the 31st of December, 1814, the amount of the public debt, created before the war, may be estimated at $39,905,183 66, and it consisted of the following particulars:

1. Old six per cent. stock, the nominal
    amount being........................... $17,250,871 39
    Of which there had been reimbursed.... 12,879,283 78

    Leaving due on the 31st December, 1814............... $4,371,587 61

2. Deferred six per cent. stock, the nominal amount being.............................. $9,358,320 85
Of which there had been reimbursed..... 3,971,148 36

Leaving due on the 31st December, 1814.............. $5,887,171 99
3. Three per cent stock... 16,158,177 84
4. Exchanged six per cent. stock under the act of 1812.... 2,984,746 72
5. Six per cent. stock of 1796................................... 80,000 00
6 Louisiana six per cent. stock................................... 10,923,500 00

Estimated amount of the whole of the public debt, contracted before the war, due on the 31st of December, 1814... 39,905,183 66

Upon the principles and estimates of the treasury report of the 9th of April, 1808, it was computed,—

1. That on the 1st of January, 1808, the public debt amounted to.................... .... $64,700,000 00
2. If, therefore, the amount of the public debt, computed to be due on the 31st of December, 1814, be deducted, to wit:... 39,905,188 66

The amount redeemed between the 1st of January, 1808, and the 31st of December, 1814, may be estimated at.... $24,794,816 34

The establishment of a sinking fund to redeem the principal of the public debt was coeval with the funding system of 1790; but the payment of the interest of the debt was not charged upon that fund until 1802. The amount of the public debt was increased during several of the years that intervened between January, 1791, and January, 1803, and the sinking fund was enriched at various periods by the assignment of additional revenues. The acts of the 8th of May, 1792, the 3d of March, 1795, the 29th of April, 1802, and the 10th of November, 1803, form, however, the principal basis of the present sinking fund, providing for the annual payment of the interest, as well as for the gradual redemption of the debt.

Under the authority of these acts of Congress, the sinking fund amounts to the sum of $8,000,000 annually, which, at this time, is supplied from the following sources:

1. From the interest on such parts of the public debt as have been reimbursed, or paid off, and which, at present, amounts to the sum of..................................... $1,969,577 64
2. From the net proceeds of the sales of public lands (exclusive of lands sold in the Mississippi territory, which, as yet, belong to the State of Georgia), estimated annually at the sum of........ .... 800,000 00
3. From the proceeds of duties on imports and tonnage, to make the annual sum of $8,000,000, estimated at about... 5,230,422 36

$8,000,000 00

II. On the 31st of December, 1814, the amount of the public debt, created since the war (independent of temporary loans and issues of treasury notes), may be estimated at $49,780,322 13.

And it consisted of the following particulars:

1. Six per cent. stock of 1812 (the eleven million loan)....	$7,710,000 00
2. Six per cent. stock of 1813 (the sixteen million loan)...	18,109,377 51
3. Six per cent. stock of 1813 (the seven million five hundred thousand loan).......................................	8,498,583 50
4. Six per cent. stock of 1814 (the loan of ten millions, part of the loan authorized for twenty-five millions)	9,919,476 25
5. Six per cent. stock of 1814 (the loan of six millions, part of the loan authorized for twenty-five millions)	4,342,875 00
	$48,580,312 26

But it is proper to bring into view here the additional six per cent. stock which will be created in consequence of contracts depending on the 31st of December, 1814, to be completed in 1815, to wit:

1. The Committee of Defence of Philadelphia contracted to loan $100,000, to fortify the island in the river Delaware called the Pea Patch, for six per cent. stock at par, which will be issued under the act of March, 1812............	$100,000 00	
2. The corporation of New York contracted to advance money for fortifications, supplies, etc., at New York, on the terms of the six million loan, and the amount being liquidated, six per cent. stock has been ordered for.....	1,100,009 87	1,200,009 87
		$49,780,322 13

There are, however, other contracts for loans, made through the medium of the War Department, which have been recognized at the treasury, to be paid in six per cent. stock, but which have not been so liquidated, as to furnish a ground to estimate their amount.

The six per cent. stock, which was issued under the act of the 24th of March, 1814, amounting to $3,000,000, and sent to Europe, has not been, and probably will not be, sold. It is, therefore, omitted in the present estimates.

Besides the funded debt, above stated, there have been contracted debts to the amount of $19,002,800, upon temporary loans, and upon the issues of treasury notes, consisting of the following particulars:

19

1 Temporary loans have been obtained under the act of
March, 1812 (of which the sum of $500,000 became
due in December, 1814, and remains unpaid ; and of
which $50,000 will be payable in the year 1817), for. $550,000 00
2. Treasury notes had been issued or ordered on the 20th
of February, 1815.
  (1) Payable on or before the 1st of January,
    1815. due and unpaid, principal.......... $2,799,200
  (2) Payable since the 1st of January, 1815,
    due and unpaid................. 620,000
  (3) Payable almost daily, from the 11th of
    March to, and including, the 1st of
    January, 1816........................ 7,227,280
  (4) Payable from the 11th of January to,
    and including, the 1st of March, 1816 7,806,320
                —— $18,452,800 00

Making floating public debt in temporary loans and
  issues of treasury notes............. ....$19,002,800 00
To which add the amount of funded debt.................. 49,780,322 13

And the whole of the ascertained amount of debt created
  during the war is the sum of............................... $68,783,122 13

The general claims for militia services and supplies arising
under the authority of the individual States, as well as of the
United States, have been partially exhibited, but neither the
principle of settlement, nor the amount of the claims, can at this
time be stated.

III. In suggesting provisions to pay the interest and gradually to reduce the principal of the public debt, contracted since
the declaration of war, the inconvenience which has been introduced by making the payment of the principal and interest of
the treasury notes a charge upon the sinking fund is greatly to
be lamented. The treasury notes were in their design, and
ought to be in their use, a species of circulating medium ; but it
is evident that a sinking fund of $8,000,000 could never supply
the means of paying the prior claims, and also of discharging
punctually the whole of the principal as well as the interest of
annual issues of treasury notes, amounting to $8,000,000 or
$10,000,000. It is indispensable, therefore, to the free and bene-
ficial operation of the sinking fund that it should be disengaged
as soon as possible from this burden. The means of disengaging
it are,—1st, by the payment of the treasury notes out of the current revenue ; or 2d, by funding them upon reasonable terms
under the act by which it is proposed to authorize a loan for the
service of the year 1815 ; and these means, it is believed, will be
effectual.

The sinking fund, being thus emancipated from the treasury-
note debt, would be sufficient, in 1815, for the interest and reimbursement of the stock created before the war, for the interest

of the stock created since the war, and for the interest of the
loan to be raised for the present year, either in money or by converting the treasury-note debt into stock debt. Thus,—

1. The sinking fund amounts to $8,000,000 00
2. The interest and reimbursement of stocks
      created before the war will require a
      sum of... $3,452,775 46
3. The interest on the stocks created since the
      war (computed on the above sum of
      $49,780,322 13), and including $7,968,
      payable for annuities, will require a
      sum of... 2,994,787 32
4. The interest on the loan for 1815 (com-
      puted to average a half year's interest
      on the sum of $11,500,000, being the
      estimated amount of the treasury notes,
      which may be converted into stocks)
      will require a sum of........................... 345,000 00
5. But there must be added the interest and
      principal of the temporary loans due
      and unpaid, which were obtained under
      the authority to borrow, granted by the
      act of the —— March, 1812, amounting
      for 1815 to the sum of........................ 583,000 00
                                              7,825,562 78

       And would leave a surplus of $674,437 22

It appears, on this view of the sinking fund, independent of
the operation of the past year, that there will be a surplus of
$674,437 22, to be further applied to the reduction of the prin-
cipal both of the old and the new public debt. But this can
only be now done by purchases in the market

The proposition to be at this time submitted to the consideration of the Committee of Ways and Means in relation to the
stock debt created since the war involves the following points:

1. That provision be made for the payment or for the funding
of the treasury-note debt, so as to relieve the sinking fund from
that charge.

2. That the sinking fund be applied in the *first* place to the
interest and reimbursement of the old six per cent. stock, according to the existing laws.

3. That the sinking fund be applied in the *second* place to the
payment of the principal and interest of the temporary loans
obtained under the act of March, 1812.

4. That the sinking fund be applied in the *third* place to the
payment of the interest accruing upon the stock debt created
since the war.

5. That the annual surplus of the sinking fund, after satisfying
the above objects, be applied to the purchase of the stock created
since the war; and that the interest upon the stock annually pur-

chased be added from time to time to that appropriation for the purpose of making new purchases.

After the present year, there is reason to presume that the public revenue will considerably exceed the public expenditure, and, consequently, that the necessity of borrowing will cease. At that period a more satisfactory view may be taken of the subject than can be taken while the amount of the public debt remains in some measure unascertained; the operation and product of the new taxes, as well as of the impost upon the revival of commerce, are conjectural, and the legislative intentions respecting a peace establishment have not been declared.

Since, therefore, the existing sinking fund (being relieved in the manner before intimated from the incumbrance of the treasury-note debt) is already charged with the payment of the interest on the stock created since the war, and will be sufficient for that purpose, besides paying the interest and the annual reimbursement of the stock created before the war, I respectfully propose that no further step be taken during the present session of Congress than to authorize the subscription of treasury notes to the loan which is now under legislative consideration, and to direct the surplus of the sinking fund to be applied to purchases of the stock created since the war for the emolument of the fund. But it will be proper to confine the benefit of subscribing to the loan to such treasury notes only as have been, or may be, issued under the acts which render them a charge upon the sinking fund, namely, the acts of the 30th of June, 1812, of the 25th of February, 1813, and of the 4th of March, 1814; and the Secretary of the Treasury should be authorized to designate the notes to be received in subscription, from time to time, according to the date of the issues.

I have the honor to be, very respectfully, sir, your most obedient servant,

A. J. DALLAS.

The Honorable J. W. EPPES, Esq., *Chairman of the Committee of Ways and Means.*

LETTER TO THE STATE BANKS.

TREASURY DEPARTMENT, March 18, 1815.

SIR,—The restoration of peace, the revival of commerce, and the liberal provision made by Congress, at the last session, for raising a permanent revenue from internal duties and taxes, will furnish the treasury with ample means to meet all the demands upon it, and to re-establish the public credit upon the surest foundations. It will be a favorite object with this department to connect the prosperity of such of the State banks as are deserving of confidence with the fiscal operations of the government; and acting upon the principles of mutual interest and good will, there can be no doubt of the decisive effect of the joint efforts of those institutions and of the treasury in relieving every part of the community from the embarrassments which the want of a competent circulating medium has produced.

The treasury can, at this time, offer great advantages to the State banks which shall be connected with it; for instance,—

1. Such banks as hold treasury notes which are due and unpaid, may fund them, upon equal and liberal terms, with other holders under the existing laws.

2. The banks connected with the treasury may be made exclusively the depositaries of the public revenue arising from every source.

3. The notes of the banks connected with the treasury may be made receivable, exclusively of the notes of other banks, in all payments to the United States; placing them upon the same footing, in that respect, as treasury notes.

4. For loans in anticipation of the revenue, the direct tax and the duty upon distilled spirits and stills may be specifically pledged to the banks, which shall make temporary advances for the accommodation of the government.

The treasury requires, at this time, the co-operation of the State banks, principally for the purpose of facilitating the transfer of the public money from place to place; for the purpose of circulating the new issues of treasury notes, intended for general convenience, throughout the United States; and for the purpose of anticipating a part of the revenues of the present year to discharge the public engagements, which are of immediate urgency.

Upon these views, I have deemed it a duty, frankly and cordially, to submit to your consideration the outline of a plan which is designed, in some degree, to connect the State banks specified in the subjoined list with each other, and all of them with the treasury, upon safe, beneficial, and patriotic principles.

The terms may be modified so as to be rendered generally satisfactory; and the details can easily be thrown into form.

1. That the State banks, acceding to this plan, shall be the depositaries, in fair proportions, of the public revenue; and that their notes shall be receivable in all payments to the United States for revenue; both privileges to be enjoyed in exclusion of banks which are not parties to the arrangement.

2. That such of the banks, acceding to this plan, as are holders of treasury notes, due and unpaid, shall be permitted to subscribe the same to the loan proposed under the act of the 3d of March, 1815, upon just and liberal terms, to be settled between the Secretary of the Treasury and the banks respectively.

3. That the banks, acceding to this plan, shall open accounts, each with the rest of them, for the purpose of accommodating the treasury in the manner hereafter stated.

4. That the banks, acceding to this plan, shall open and keep accounts with the Treasurer of the United States, under the following heads:

(1) "Cash Account." To embrace all deposits of money; of the notes of the proper bank; of the notes of the other banks acceding to this plan; and of such bank-notes, or treasury notes bearing an interest, as the bank may assent to take to its own account.

(2) "Special Deposit." To embrace all deposits of bank-notes, and of treasury notes bearing an interest, which the bank may not assent to take to its own account.

(3) "Small Treasury Notes." To embrace all deposits of treasury notes not bearing an interest.

5. That the drafts of the treasurer shall specify on which account he draws, and the entries shall be made accordingly.

6. That the drafts of the treasurer upon any of the banks acceding to this plan shall be received by the bank to which it is sent, and shall be forthwith credited in the specified account: thus enabling the treasury to transmit the public revenue from one place to another. But in relation to this part of the plan, the treasury will take special care to consult the convenience and safety of the banks.

7. That the banks acceding to this plan shall furnish the treasurer and the Secretary of the Treasury with weekly statements of the treasurer's accounts. And they shall transmit to the secretary, in confidence, a monthly statement of the general affairs of the bank.

8. That the banks acceding to this plan shall afford the usual

accommodations to the treasury, for the payment of the dividend on the public debt and for negotiating public loans.

9. That the Secretary of the Treasury may add to or diminish the number of the banks, parties to this plan ; or he may entirely annul the plan ; whenever he shall think that the public interest requires such interpositions.

10. That any of the banks may, at their pleasure, cease to be parties to the present arrangement.

As soon as the sense of the banks, on these propositions, shall be received, the proper measures will be adopted to give effect to the general plan ; and I have to request the favor of an early answer from your institution.

It only remains, sir, to inquire whether your bank is disposed to accommodate the government, by an advance of any, and of what proportion, of the direct tax assessed upon   for the year 1815, upon an adequate pledge of that tax ? or whether you would make a reasonable advance upon a similar pledge of the duty on distilled spirits and stills ?

I shall proceed immediately to Philadelphia and New York upon the business of the treasury ; and your answer, if written within ten days, may be addressed to me at the latter place.

I am, very respectfully, sir, your most obt. servt.,
A. J. DALLAS.

Boston.—State Bank, Union Bank, Massachusetts Bank.

Hartford.—Phœnix Bank.

New York.—Manhattan Company, Mechanics' Bank, City Bank, Bank of America.

Philadelphia.—Bank of Pennsylvania, Bank of North America, S. Girard's Bank, Bank of Philadelphia, Farmers' and Mechanics' Bank.

Baltimore.—Bank of Baltimore, Commercial and Farmers' Bank.

Washington.—Bank of Washington, Bank of the Metropolis, Bank of Columbia.

Richmond.—Bank of Virginia, Farmers' Bank of Virginia.

Charleston.—Planters' and Mechanics' Bank.

Raleigh.—State Bank of North Carolina.

Savannah.—Planters' Bank.

LETTER

FROM THE SECRETARY OF THE TREASURY

To the Chairman of the Committee on that part of the President's Message which relates to an uniform National Currency; inclosing an outline of a plan for a National Bank, accompanied with some explanation of the principles upon which the system is founded.

TREASURY DEPARTMENT, 24th December, 1815.

SIR,—I have the honor to acknowledge the receipt of your letter, dated the 23d instant, informing me "that the committee on so much of the President's message as relates to the national currency, had determined that a national bank is the most certain means of restoring to the nation a specie circulation;" and had directed you to obtain the opinion of this department on the following points :

1st. The amount and composition of the capital of the bank.

2d. The government of the bank.

3d. The privileges and duties of the bank.

4th. The organization and operation of the bank.

5th. The bonus to be required for the charter of the bank.

6th. The measures which may aid the bank in commencing and maintaining its operations in specie.

It affords much satisfaction to find that the policy of establishing a national bank has received the sanction of the committee ; and the decision, in this respect, renders it unnecessary to enter into a comparative examination of the superior advantages of such an institution for the attainment of the objects contemplated by the legislature. Referring, therefore, to the outline of a national bank, which is subjoined to this letter, as the result of an attentive consideration bestowed upon the subjects of your inquiry, I proceed, with deference and respect, to offer some explanation of the principles upon which the system is founded.

I. It is proposed that, under a charter for twenty years, the capital of the national bank shall amount to $35,000,000 ; that Congress shall retain the power to raise it to $50,000,000 ; and that it shall consist of three-fourths of public stock and one-fourth of gold and silver.

1st. *With respect to the amount of the capital.* The services to be performed by the capital of the bank are important, various, and extensive. They will be required through a period almost as long as is usually assigned to a generation They will be required for the accommodation of the government in the collection and distribution of its revenue, as well as for the uses of commerce, agriculture, manufactures, and the arts throughout the Union. They will be required to restore and maintain the national currency. And, in short, they will be required, under every change of circumstances, in a season of war as well as in the season of peace, for the circulation of the national wealth; which augments with a rapidity beyond the reach of ordinary calculation.

In the performance of these national services the local and incidental co-operation of the State banks may undoubtedly be expected ; but it is the object of the present measure to create an independent, though not a discordant, institution ; and while the government is granting a monopoly for twenty years, it would seem to be improvident and dangerous to rely upon gratuitous or casual aids for the enjoyment of those benefits which can be effectually secured by positive stipulation.

Nor is it believed that any public inconven'ence can possibly arise from the proposed amount of the capital of the bank with its augmentable quality. The amount may, indeed, be a clog upon the profits of the institution ; but it can never be employed for any injurious purpose (not even for the p irpose of discount accommodation beyond the fair demand), w thout an abuse of trust, which cannot, in candor, be anticipated ; or which, if anticipated, may be made an object of penal responsibility.

The competition which exists, at present, among the State banks will, it is true, be extended to the national bank ; but competition does not imply hostility. The commercial interests, and the personal associations of the stockholders, will generally be the same in the State banks and in the national bank. The directors of both institutions will naturally be taken from the same class of citizens And experience has shown not only the policy, but the existence of those sympathies by which the intercourse of a national bank and the State banks has been, and always ought to be, regulated for their common credit and security. At the present crisis it will be peculiarly incumbent upon the national bank, as well as the treasury, to conciliate the State banks ; to confide to them, liberally, a participation in the deposits of public revenue; and to encourage them in every reasonable effort to resume the payment of their notes in coin. But, independent of these considerations, it is to be recollected that when portions of the capital of the national bank shall be transferred to its branches, the amount invested in each branch will not, probably, exceed the amount of the capital of any of the principal State banks ; and will certainly be less than the amount of the combined capital of the State banks operating in any of the principal commercial cities. The whole number of the banking establishments in the United States may be stated at 260, and the aggregate amount of their capitals may be estimated at $85,000,000 ; but the services of the national bank are also required in every State and Territory; and the capital proposed is $35,000,000, of which only one-fourth part will consist of gold and silver.

2d. *With respect to the composition of the capital of the bank.* There does not prevail much diversity of opinion upon the proposition to form a compound capital for the national bank, partly of public stock and partly of coin. The proportions now suggested appear, also, to be free from any important objections. Under all the regulations of the charter, it is believed that the amount of gold and silver required will afford an adequate supply for commencing and continuing the payments of the bank in current coin; while the power which the bank will possess to convert its stock portion of capital into bullion or coin, from time to time, is calculated to provide for any probable augmentation of the demand. This object being sufficiently secured, the capital of the bank is next to be employed, in perfect consistency with the general interests and safety of the institution, to raise the value of the public securities by withdrawing almost one-fifth of the amount from the ordinary stock market. Nor will the bank be allowed to expose the public to the danger of a depreciation, by returning any part of the stock to the market, until it has been offered, at the current price, to the commissioners of the sinking fund; and it is not an inconsiderable advantage, in the growing state of the public revenue, that the stock subscribed to the capital of the bank will become redeemable at the pleasure of the government.

The subscription to the capital of the bank is opened to every species of funded stock. The estimate that the revenues of 1816 and 1817 will enable the treasury to discharge the whole of the treasury-note debt, furnishes the only reason for omitting to authorize a subscription in that species of debt. Thus,—

The old and the new six per cent. stocks are receivable at par.

The seven per cent. stock, upon a valuation referring to the 30th of September, 1816, is receivable at $106 51 per cent.

The three per cent. stock, which can only be redeemed for its nominal or certificate value, may be estimated, under all circumstances, to be worth about sixty-two per cent. when the six per cent. stock is at par; but as it is desirable to accomplish the redemption of this stock, upon equitable terms, it is made receivable at sixty-five per cent.,—the rate sanctioned by the government, and in part accepted by the stockholders, in the year 1807.

Of the instalments for paying the subscriptions, it is only necessary to observe that they are regulated by a desire to reconcile an early commencement of the operations of the bank with the existing difficulties in the currency and with the convenience of the subscribers. In one of the modes proposed for discharging the subscription of the government, it is particularly contemplated to aid the bank with a medium which cannot fail to alleviate the first pressure for payments in coin.

II. It is proposed that the national bank shall be governed by twenty-five directors, and each of its branches by thirteen directors; that the President of the United States, with the advice and consent of the Senate, shall appoint five of the directors of the bank, one of whom shall be chosen as president of the bank by the board of directors; that the resident stockholders shall elect twenty of the directors of the national bank, who shall be resident citizens of the United States; and that the national bank shall appoint the directors of each branch (being resident citizens of the United States), one of whom shall be designated by the Secretary of the Treasury, with the approbation of the President of the United States, to be president of the branch bank.

The participation of the President and Senate of the United States in the appointment of directors, appears to be the only feature in the proposition for the government of the national bank which requires an explanatory remark.

Upon general principles, wherever a pecuniary interest is to be affected by the operations of a public institution, a representative authority ought to be recognized. The United States will be the proprietors of one-fifth of the capital of the bank, and in that proportion, upon general principles, they should be represented in the direction. But an apprehension has sometimes been expressed, lest the power of the government thus inserted into the administration of the affairs of the bank should be employed eventually to alienate the funds and to destroy the credit of the institution. Whatever may have been the fate of banks in other countries, subject to forms of government essentially different, there can be no reasonable cause for the apprehension here. Independent of the obvious improbability of the attempt, the government of the United States cannot by any legislative or executive act impair the rights or multiply the obligations of a corporation constitutionally established, as long as the independence and integrity of the judicial power shall be maintained. Whatever accommodation the treasury may have occasion to ask from the bank can only be asked under the license of a law; and whatever accommodation shall be obtained must be obtained from the voluntary assent of the directors, acting under the responsibility of their trust.

Nor can it be doubted that the department of the government which is invested with the power of appointment to all the important offices of the State, is a proper department to exercise the power of appointment in relation to a national trust of incalculable magnitude. The national bank ought not to be regarded simply as a commercial bank. It will not operate upon the funds of the stockholders alone, but much more upon the funds of the nation. Its conduct, good or bad, will not affect the corporate credit and resources alone, but much more the credit and resources of the government. In fine, it is not an institution created for the purposes of commerce and profit alone, but much more for the purposes of national policy, as an auxiliary in the exercise of some of the highest powers of the government. Under such circumstances the public interest cannot be too cautiously guarded, and the guards proposed can never be injurious to the commercial interests of the institution. The right to inspect the general accounts of the bank may be employed to detect the evils of a maladministration; but an interior agency in the direction of its affairs will best serve to prevent them.

III. It is proposed that, in addition to the usual privileges of a corporation, the notes of the national bank shall be received in all payments to the United States, unless Congress shall hereafter otherwise provide by law; and that, in addition to the duties usually required from a corporation of this description, the national bank shall be employed to receive, transfer, and distribute the public revenue under the directions of the proper department.

The reservation of a legislative power on the subject of accepting the notes of the national bank in payments to the government is the only new stipulation in the present proposition. It is designed not merely as one of the securities for the general conduct of the bank, but as the means of preserving entire the sovereign authority of Congress relative to the coin and currency of the United States. Recent occurrences inculcate the expediency of such a reservation, but it may be confidently hoped that an occasion to enforce it will never arise.

It is not proposed to stipulate that the bank shall in any case be bound to make loans to the government; but, in that respect, whenever a loan is authorized by law the government will act upon the ordinary footing of an applicant for pecuniary accommodation.

IV. It is proposed that the organization of the national bank shall be effected with as little delay as possible; and that its operations shall commence and continue upon the basis of payments in the current coin of the United States, with a qualified power under the authority of the government to suspend such payments.

The proposition now submitted necessarily implies an opinion that it is practicable to commence the operations of the national bank upon a circulation of gold and silver coin; and in support of the opinion a few remarks are respectfully offered to the consideration of the committee.

1. The actual receipts of the bank at the opening of the subscription will amount to the sum of $8,400,000, of which the

sum of $1,400,000 will consist of gold and silver, and the sum of $7,000,000 will consist of public stock convertible by sale into gold and silver. But the actual receipts of the bank, at the expiration of six months from the opening of the subscription, will amount to the sum of $16,800,000, of which the sum of $2,800,000 will be in gold and silver, and the sum of $14,000,000 will be in public stock convertible by sale into gold and silver. To the fund thus possessed by the bank, the accumulations of the public revenue and the deposits of individuals being added, there can be little doubt, from past experience and observation in reference to similar establishments, that a sufficient foundation will exist for a gradual and judicious issue of bank-notes payable on demand in the current coin; unless, contrary to all probability, public confidence should be withheld from the institution, or sinister combinations should be formed to defeat its operations, or the demands of an unfavorable balance of trade should press upon its metallic resources.

2. The public confidence cannot be withheld from the institution. The resources of the nation will be intimately connected with the resources of the bank. The notes of the bank are accredited in every payment to the government, and must become familiar in every pecuniary negotiation. Unless, therefore, a state of things exist in which gold and silver only can command the public confidence, the national bank must command it. But the expression of the public sentiment does not, even at this period, leave the question exposed to difficulty and doubt; it is well known that the wealth of opulent and commercial nations requires for its circulation something more than a medium composed of the precious metals. The incompetency of the existing paper substitutes to furnish a national currency is also well known. Hence, throughout the United States, the public hope seems to rest at this crisis upon the establishment of a national bank; and every citizen, upon private or upon patriotic motives, will be prepared to support the institution.

3. Sinister combinations to defeat the operations of a national bank ought not to be presumed and need not be feared. It is true that the influence of the State banks is extensively diffused; but the State banks and the patrons of the State banks partake of the existing evils; they must be conscious of the inadequacy of State institutions to restore and maintain the national currency; they will perceive that there is sufficient space in the commercial sphere for the movement of the State banks and the national bank; and, upon the whole, they will be ready to act upon the impulse of a common duty and a common interest. If, however, most unexpectedly a different course should be pursued, the concurring powers of the national treasury and the national bank will be sufficient to avert the danger.

4. The demand of an unfavorable balance of trade appears to

be much overrated. It is not practicable at this time to ascertain either the value of the goods imported since the peace or the value of the property employed to pay for them. But when it is considered that a great proportion of the importations arose from investments of American funds previously in Europe; that a great proportion of the price has been paid by American exports; that a great proportion has been paid by remittances in American stocks; and that a great proportion remains upon credit, to be paid by gradual remittances of goods as well as in coin, it cannot be justly concluded that the balance of trade has hitherto materially affected the national stock of the precious metals. So far as an opportunity has occurred for observation, the demand for gold and silver to export appears rather to have arisen from the expectation of obtaining a higher price in a part of Europe, and from the revival of commerce with the countries beyond the Cape of Good Hope, than from any necessity to provide for the payment of the recent importations of goods into the United States. The former of these causes will probably soon cease to operate; and the operation of the latter may, if necessary, be restrained by law.

The proposition now under consideration further provides for a suspension of the bank payments in coin upon any future emergency. This is merely a matter of precaution; but if the emergency should arise, it must be agreed on all hands that the power of suspension ought rather to be confided to the government than to the directors of the institution.

V. It is proposed that a bonus be paid to the government by the subscribers to the national bank, in consideration of the emoluments to be derived from an exclusive charter during a period of twenty years.

Independent of the bonus here proposed to be exacted, there are undoubtedly many public advantages to be drawn from the establishment of the national bank; but these are generally of an incidental kind, and (as in the case of the deposits and distribution of the revenue) may be regarded in the light of equivalents, not for the monopoly of the charter, but for the reciprocal advantages of a fiscal connection with the public treasury.

The amount of the bonus should be in proportion to the value of the charter grant; or, in other words, to the net profits which the subscribers will probably make in consequence of their incorporation. The average rate of the dividends of the State banks before the suspension of payments in coin was about eight per cent. per annum. It appears by a report from this department to the House of Representatives, dated the 3d of April, 1810, that the annual dividends of the late Bank of the United States averaged throughout the duration of its charter the rate of $8\frac{13}{80}$ per cent. But under all the circumstances which will attend the establishment and operations of the proposed national bank, its enlarged capital, and the extended field of competition, it is not deemed reasonable, for the present purpose, to rate the annual dividends of the institution higher than seven per cent. upon its capital of $35,000,000.

Allowing, therefore, two, three, and four years for the payment of the bonus, a sum of $1,500,000 would amount to about four per cent. upon the capital of the bank, and would constitute a just equivalent for the benefits of its charter.

VI. It is proposed that the measures suggested by the following considerations be adopted, to aid the national bank in commencing and maintaining its operations upon the basis of payments in the current coin.

1. To restore the national currency of gold and silver, it is essential that the quantity of bank paper in circulation should be reduced; but this effort alone will be sufficient to effect the object. By reducing the amount of bank paper, its value must be proportionably increased; and as soon as the amount shall be contracted to the limits of a just proportion in the circulating medium of the country, the consequent revival of the uses for coin, in the business of exchange, will insure its reappearance in abundance. The policy, the interest, and the honor of the State banks, will stimulate them to undertake and to prosecute this salutary work. But it will be proper to apprise them that after a specified day the notes of such banks as have not resumed their payments in the current coin will not be received in payments, either to the government or to the national bank.

2. The resumption of payments in current coin, at the State banks, will remove every obstacle to the commencement of similar payments at the national bank. The difficulty of commencing payments in coin is not, however, to be considered as equal to the difficulty of resuming them. The national bank, free from all engagements, will be able to regulate its issues of paper with a view to the danger as well as to the demand that may be found to exist. But in addition to the privileges granted by the charter, it will also be proper to apprise the State banks, that after the commencement of the operations of the national bank the notes of such banks as do not agree to receive, reissue, and circulate the notes of that institution shall not be received in payments either to the government or to the national bank.

3. The possibility that the national currency of coin may not be perfectly restored at the time of organizing the bank, has induced the proposition that the payment of the government subscription to the capital shall be made in treasury notes, which will be receivable in all payments to the government, and to the national bank, but which will not be demandable in coin. The principle of this proposition might perhaps be usefully extended

to authorize the national bank to issue notes of a similar character for a limited period: and it will be proper further to apprise the State banks, that the notes of such banks as do not agree to receive, reissue, and circulate these treasury notes or national bank notes shall not be received in payments either to the government or to the national bank.

I have the honor, very respectfully, sir, to be your most obedient servant,

A. J. Dallas.

The Hon. John C. Calhoun, *Chairman of the Committee on the National Currency.*

OUTLINE OF A PLAN FOR THE NATIONAL BANK.

I. The charter of the bank.
1. To continue twenty-one years.
2. To be exclusive.
II. The capital of the bank.
1. To be $35,000,000—at present.
2. To be augmentable by Congress to $50,000,000, and the additional sum to be distributed among the several States.
3. To be divided into 350,000 shares of $100 each, on the capital of $35,000,000, and to be subscribed,—

By the United States, one-fifth, or 70,000 shares....	$7,000,000
By corporations and individuals, four-fifths, or 280,000,000 shares.......................	28,000,000
	$35,000,000

4. To be compounded of public debt and of gold and silver; as to the subscriptions of corporations and individuals, in the proportions—

Of funded debt, three-fourths, equal to.............................	$21,000,000
Of gold and silver, one-fourth, equal to............................	7,000,000
	$28,000,000

The subscriptions of six per cent. stock to be at par.

The subscriptions of three per cent. stock to be at sixty-five per cent.

The subscriptions of seven per cent. stock to be at $106 51 per cent.

5. The subscriptions in public debt may be discharged at pleasure by the government at the rate at which it is subscribed.

6. The subscriptions of corporations or individuals to be payable by instalments.

(1.) *Specie,* at subscribing:

On each share, $5		$1,400,000
At 6 months, 5		1,400,000
At 12 months, 5		1,400,000
At 18 months, 10		2,800,000
		$7,000,000

(2) *Public debt*, at subscribing :

Each share, $25		$7,000,000
At 6 months, 25		7,000,000
At 12 months, 25		7,000,000
		$28,000,000

7. The subscription of the United States to be paid in instalments, not extending beyond a period of seven years; the first instalments to be paid at the time of subscribing, and the payments to be made at the pleasure of the government, either in gold and silver, or in six per cent. stock, redeemable at the pleasure of the government, or in treasury notes not fundable nor bearing interest, nor payable at a particular time, but receivable in all payments to the government, and also in all payments to the bank, with a right on the part of the bank to reissue the treasury notes so paid from time to time, until they are discharged by payments to the government.

8. The bank shall be at liberty to sell the stock portion of its capital, to an amount not exceeding   in any one year; but if the sales are intended to be effected in the United States, notice thereof shall be given to the Secretary of the Treasury that the commissioners of the sinking fund may, if they please, become the purchasers at the market price, not exceeding par.

III. The government of the bank.

1. The bank shall be established at Philadelphia, with power to erect branches, or to employ State banks as branches elsewhere.

2. There shall be twenty-five directors for the bank at Philadelphia, and thirteen directors for each of the branches where branches are erected, with the usual description and number of officers.

3. The President of the United States, with the advice and consent of the Senate, shall annually appoint five of the directors of the bank at Philadelphia.

4. The qualified stockholders shall annually elect twenty of the directors of the bank at Philadelphia; but a portion of the directors shall be changed at every annual election, upon the principle of rotation.

5. The directors of the bank at Philadelphia shall annually, at their first meeting after their election, choose one of the five directors appointed by the President and Senate of the United

20

States, to be president of the bank; and the president of the bank shall always be re-eligible if reappointed.

6. The directors of the bank at Philadelphia shall annually appoint thirteen directors for each of the branches where branches are erected, and shall transmit a list of the persons appointed to the Secretary of the Treasury.

7. The Secretary of the Treasury, with the approbation of the President of the United States, shall annually designate from the list of the branch directors, the person to be the president of the respective branches.

8. None but resident citizens of the United States shall be directors of the bank, or its branches.

9. The stockholders may vote for directors in person or by proxy; but no stockholder, who is not resident within the United States at the time of election, shall vote by proxy; nor shall any one person vote as proxy a greater number of votes than he would be entitled to vote in his own right, according to a scale of voting to be graduated by the number of shares which the voters respectively hold.

10. The bank and its several branches, or the State banks employed as branches, shall furnish the officer at the head of the Treasury Department with statements of their officers, in such form and at such period as shall be required.

IV. The privileges and duties of the bank.

1. The bank shall enjoy the usual privileges, and be subject to the usual restrictions of a body corporate and politic, instituted for such purposes, and the forgery of its notes shall be made penal.

2. The notes of the bank shall be receivable in all payments to the United States, unless Congress shall hereafter otherwise provide by law.

3. The bank and its branches, and State banks employed as branches, shall give the necessary aid and facility to the treasury for transferring the public funds from place to place, and for making payments to the public creditors, without charging commissions, or claiming allowances on account of differences of exchange, etc.

V. The organization and operation of the bank.

1. Subscriptions to be opened with as little delay as possible, and at as few places as shall be deemed just and convenient. The commissioners may be named in the act or be appointed by the President.

2. The bank to be organized and commence its operations in specie as soon as the sum of $1,400,000 has been actually received from the subscriptions in gold and silver.

3. The bank shall not at any time suspend its specie payments, unless the same shall be previously authorized by Congress, if

in session, or by the President of the United States if Congress be not in session. In the latter case, the suspension shall continue for six weeks after the meeting of Congress, and no longer, unless authorized by law.

VI. The bonus for the charter of the bank.

The subscribers to the bank shall pay a premium to the government for its charter. Estimating the profits of the bank from the probable advance in the value of its stock, and the result of its business when in full operation, at seven per cent., a bonus of $1,500,000, payable in equal instalments of two, three, and four years after the bank commences its operations, might, under all circumstances, be considered as about four per cent. upon its capital, and would constitute a reasonable premium.

No. 5.

Note.—This Exposition of the Causes and Character of the War was prepared and committed to the press before any account had been received in the United States of the signature of a treaty of peace by the American and the British negotiators; and it would have been difficult, even if it were desirable, to withhold the exposition from the public.

But the charges which have been solemnly exhibited against the American government, in the face of the world, render an exposition of its conduct necessary, in peace as much as in war, for the honor of the United States and the unsullied reputation of their arms, lest those charges should obtain credit with the present generation, or pass for truth into the history of the times, upon the evidence of a silent acquiescence.

AN EXPOSITION

OF THE CAUSES AND CHARACTER OF THE WAR.

Whatever may be the termination of the negotiations at Ghent, the despatches of the American commissioners, which have been communicated by the President of the United States to the Congress during the present session, will distinctly unfold to the attentive and impartial of all nations the objects and dispositions of the parties to the present war.

The United States, relieved by the general pacification of the treaty of Paris from the danger of actual sufferance under the evils which had compelled them to resort to arms, have avowed their readiness to resume the relations of peace and amity with

Great Britain upon the simple and single condition of preserving their territory and their sovereignty entire and unimpaired. Their desire of peace, indeed, " upon terms of reciprocity, consistent with the rights of both parties, as sovereign and independent nations,"* has not, at any time, been influenced by the provocations of an unprecedented course of hostilities, by the incitements of a successful campaign, or by the agitations which have seemed again to threaten the tranquillity of Europe.

But the British government, after inviting "a discussion with the government of America for the conciliatory adjustment of the differences subsisting between the two states, with an earnest desire on their part (as it was alleged) to bring them to a favorable issue upon principles of a perfect reciprocity not inconsistent with the established maxims of public law and with the maritime rights of the British Empire,"† and after "expressly disclaiming any intention to acquire an increase of territory,"‡ have peremptorily demanded, as the price of peace, concessions calculated merely for their own aggrandizement and for the humiliation of their adversary. At one time they proposed, as their *sine qua non,* a stipulation, that the Indians inhabiting the country of the United States, within the limits established by the treaty of 1783, should be included as the allies of Great Britain (a party to that treaty) in the projected pacification ; and that definite boundaries should be settled for the Indian territory, upon a basis which would have operated to surrender to a number of Indians, not probably exceeding a few thousands, the rights of sovereignty, as well as of soil, over nearly one-third of the territorial dominions of the United States, inhabited by more than one hundred thousand of their citizens.§ And, more recently (withdrawing, in effect, that proposition), they have offered to treat, on the basis of the *uti possidetis,* when, by the operations of the war, they had obtained the military possession of an important part of the State of Massachusetts, which, it was known, could never be the subject of a cession, consistently with the honor and faith of

---

* See Mr. Monroe's letter to Lord Castlereagh, dated January, 1814.
† See Lord Castlereagh's letter to Mr. Monroe, dated the 4th of November, 1813.
‡ See the American despatch, dated the 12th of August, 1814.
§ See the American despatches, dated the 12th and 19th of August, 1814 ; the note of the British commissioners, dated the 19th of August, 1814 ; the note of the American commissioners, dated the 21st of August, 1814 ; the note of the British commissioners, dated the 4th of September, 1814 ; the note of the American commissioners of the 9th of September, 1814 ; the note of the British commissioners, dated the 19th of September, 1814 ; the note of the American commissioners, dated the 26th of September, 1814 ; the note of the British commissioners, dated the 8th of October, 1814 ; and the note of the American commissioners of the 13th of October, 1814.

the American government.* Thus it is obvious that Great Britain, neither regarding "the principles of a perfect reciprocity" nor the rule of her own practice and professions, has indulged pretensions, which could only be heard in order to be rejected. The alternative, either vindictively to protract the war or honorably to end it, has been fairly given to her option; but she wants the magnanimity to decide, while her apprehensions are awakened for the result of the congress at Vienna, and her hopes are flattered by the schemes of conquest in America.

There are periods in the transactions of every country, as well as in the life of every individual, when self-examination becomes a duty of the highest moral obligation; when the government of a free people, driven from the path of peace, and baffled in every effort to regain it, may resort for consolation to the conscious rectitude of its measures; and when an appeal to mankind, founded upon truth and justice, cannot fail to engage those sympathies, by which even nations are led to participate in the fame and fortunes of each other. The United States, under these impressions, are neither insensible to the advantages nor to the duties of their peculiar situation. They have but recently, as it were, established their independence, and the volume of their national history lies open at a glance to every eye. The policy of their government, therefore, whatever it has been, in their foreign as well as in their domestic relations, it is impossible to conceal, and it must be difficult to mistake. If the assertion that it has been a policy to preserve peace and amity with all the nations of the world be doubted, the proofs are at hand. If the assertion that it has been a policy to maintain the rights of the United States, but at the same time to respect the rights of every other nation, be doubted, the proofs will be exhibited. If the assertion that it has been a policy to act impartially towards the belligerent powers of Europe be doubted, the proofs will be found on record, even in the archives of England and of France. And if, in fine, the assertion that it has been a policy, by all honorable means, to cultivate with Great Britain those sentiments of mutual good will which naturally belong to nations connected by the ties of a common ancestry, an identity of language, and a similarity of manners, be doubted, the proofs will be found in that patient forbearance, under the pressure of accumulating wrongs, which marks the period of almost thirty years that elapsed between the peace of 1783 and the rupture of 1812.

The United States had just recovered, under the auspices of

---

* See the note of the British commissioners, dated the 21st of October, 1814; the note of the American commissioners, dated the 24th of October, 1814; and the note of the British commissioners, dated the 31st of October, 1814.

their present constitution, from the debility which their revolutionary struggle had produced, when the convulsive movements of France excited throughout the civilized world the mingled sensations of hope and fear—of admiration and alarm. The interest which those movements would in themselves have excited was incalculably increased, however, as soon as Great Britain became a party to the first memorable coalition against France and assumed the character of a belligerent power, for it was obvious that the distance of the scene would no longer exempt the United States from the influence and the evils of the European conflict. On the one hand, their government was connected with France by treaties of alliance and commerce, and the services which that nation had rendered to the cause of American independence had made such impressions upon the public mind as no virtuous statesman could rigidly condemn and the most rigorous statesman would have sought in vain to efface ; on the other hand, Great Britain, leaving the treaty of 1783 unexecuted, forcibly retained the American posts upon the northern frontier, and, slighting every overture to place the diplomatic and commercial relations of the two countries upon a fair and friendly foundation,* seemed to contemplate the success of the American Revolution in a spirit of unextinguishable animosity. Her voice had indeed been heard from Quebec and Montreal, instigating the savages to war.† Her invisible arm was felt in the defeats of General Harmar‡ and General St. Clair,§ and even the victory of General Wayne‖ was achieved in the presence of a fort which she had erected far within the territorial boundaries of the United States to stimulate and countenance the barbarities of the Indian warrior.¶ Yet the American government, neither yielding to popular feeling nor acting upon the impulse of national resentment, hastened to adopt the policy of a strict and steady neutrality, and solemnly announced that policy to the citizens at home and to the nations abroad by the proclamation of the 22d of April, 1793. Whatever may have been the trials of its pride and of its fortitude—whatever may have been the imputations upon its fidelity and its honor—it will be demonstrated in the sequel that the American government, throughout the European contest and amidst all the changes of the objects and the parties that have been involved in that con-

---

* See Mr. Adams's correspondence.
† See the speeches of Lord Dorchester.
‡ On the waters of the Miami of the lakes, on the 21st of October, 1790.
§ At Fort Recovery, on the 4th of November, 1791.
‖ On the Miami of the lakes, in August, 1794.
¶ See the correspondence between Mr. Randolph, the American Secretary of State, and Mr. Hammond, the British plenipotentiary, dated May and June, 1794.

test, has inflexibly adhered to the principles which were thus authoritatively established to regulate the conduct of the United States.

It was reasonable to expect that a proclamation of neutrality, issued under the circumstances which have been described, would command the confidence and respect of Great Britain, however offensive it might prove to France, as contravening essentially the exposition which she was anxious to bestow upon the treaties of commerce and alliance. But experience has shown that the confidence and respect of Great Britain are not to be acquired by such acts of impartiality and independence. Under every administration of the American government the experiment has been made, and the experiment has been equally unsuccessful; for it was not more effectually ascertained in the year 1812 than at antecedent periods, that an exemption from the maritime usurpation and the commercial monopoly of Great Britain could only be obtained upon the condition of becoming an associate in her enmities and her wars. While the proclamation of neutrality was still in the view of the British minister, an order of the 8th of June, 1793, issued from the cabinet, by virtue of which "all vessels loaded wholly or in part with corn, flour, or meal, bound to any port in France, or any port occupied by the armies of France," were required to be carried forcibly into England, and the cargoes were either to be sold there or security was to be given that they should only be sold in the ports of a country in amity with his Britannic Majesty.* The moral character of an avowed design to inflict famine upon the whole of the French people was at that time properly estimated throughout the civilized world, and so glaring an infraction of neutral rights as the British order was calculated to produce did not escape the severities of diplomatic animadversion and remonstrance. But this aggression was soon followed by another of a more hostile cast. In the war of 1756, Great Britain had endeavored to establish the rule that neutral nations were not entitled to enjoy the benefits of a trade with the colonies of a belligerent power, from which, in the season of peace, they were excluded by the parent state. The rule stands without positive support from any general authority on public law. If it be true that some treaties contain stipulations by which the parties expressly exclude each other from the commerce of their respective colonies, and if it be true that the ordinances of a particular state often provide for the exclusive enjoyment of its colonial commerce, still Great Britain cannot be authorized to deduce the rule of the war of 1756 by implication from such treaties and such ordinances, while it is

---

* See the order in council of the 8th of June, 1793, and the remonstrance of the American government.

not true that the rule forms a part of the law of nations, nor that it has been adopted by any other government, nor that even Great Britain herself has uniformly practised upon the rule, since its application was unknown from the war of 1756 until the French war of 1792, including the entire period of the American war. Let it be argumentatively allowed, however, that Great Britain possessed the right as well as the power to revive and enforce the rule ; yet the time and the manner of exercising the power would afford ample cause for reproach. The citizens of the United States had openly engaged in an extensive trade with the French islands in the West Indies, ignorant of the alleged existence of the rule of the war of 1756, or unapprised of any intention to call it into action, when the order of the 6th of November, 1793, was silently circulated among the British cruisers, consigning to legal adjudication " all vessels loaden with goods, the produce of any colony of France, or carrying provisions or supplies for the use of any such colony."* A great portion of the commerce of the United States was thus annihilated at a blow, the amicable dispositions of the government were again disregarded and contemned, the sensibility of the nation was excited to a high degree of resentment by the apparent treachery of the British order, and a recourse to reprisals or to war for indemnity and redress seemed to be unavoidable. But the love of justice had established the law of neutrality, and the love of peace taught a lesson of forbearance. The American government, therefore, rising superior to the provocations and the passions of the day, instituted a special mission to represent at the court of London the injuries and the indignities which it had suffered, " to vindicate its rights with firmness and to cultivate peace with sincerity."† The immediate result of this mission was a treaty of amity, commerce, and navigation between the United States and Great Britain, which was signed by the negotiators on the 19th of November, 1794, and finally ratified, with the consent of the Senate, in the year 1795. But both the mission and its result serve also to display the independence and the impartiality of the American government in asserting its rights and performing its duties, equally unawed and unbiased by the instruments of belligerent power or persuasion.

On the foundation of this treaty the United States, in a pure spirit of good faith and confidence, raised the hope and the expectation that the maritime usurpations of Great Britain would cease to annoy them; that all doubtful claims of jurisdiction would be suspended; and that even the exercise of an incontest-

---

* See the British order of the 6th of November, 1793.
† See the President's message to the Senate of the 16th of April, 1794, nominating Mr. Jay as envoy extraordinary to his Britannic Majesty.

able right would be so modified as to present neither insult, nor outrage, nor inconvenience to their flag, or to their commerce. But the hope and the expectation of the United States have been fatally disappointed. Some relaxation in the rigor, without any alteration in the principle, of the order in council of the 6th of November, 1793, was introduced by the subsequent orders of the 8th of January, 1794, and the 25th of January, 1798; but from the ratification of the treaty of 1794 until the short respite afforded by the treaty of Amiens, in 1802, the commerce of the United States continued to be the prey of British cruisers and privateers, under the adjudicating patronage of the British tribunals. Another grievance, however, assumed, at this epoch, a form and magnitude which cast a shade over the social happiness as well as the political independence of the nation. The merchant vessels of the United States were arrested on the high seas while in the prosecution of distant voyages; considerable numbers of their crews were impressed into the naval service of Great Britain; the commercial adventures of the owners were often, consequently, defeated; and the loss of property, the embarrassments of trade and navigation, and the scene of domestic affliction became intolerable. This grievance (which constitutes an important surviving cause of the American declaration of war) was early, and has been incessantly, urged upon the attention of the British government. Even in the year 1792 they were told of "the irritation that it had excited, and of the difficulty of avoiding to make immediate reprisals on their seamen in the United States."* They were told "that so many instances of the kind had happened that it was quite necessary that they should explain themselves on the subject, and be led to disavow and punish such violence, which had never been experienced from any other nation."† And they were told "of the inconvenience of such conduct, and of the impossibility of letting it go on, so that the British ministry should be made sensible of the necessity of punishing the past and preventing the future."‡ But after the treaty of amity, commerce, and navigation had been ratified, the nature and the extent of the grievance became still more manifest; and it was clearly and firmly presented to the view of the British government, as leading unavoidably to discord and war between the two nations. They were told "that unless they would come to some accommodation which

---

* See the letter of Mr. Jefferson, Secretary of State, to Mr. Pinckney, minister at London, dated the 11th of June, 1792.

† See the letter from the same to the same, dated the 12th of October, 1792.

‡ See the letter from the same to the same, dated the 6th of November, 1792.

might insure the American seamen against this oppression, measures would be taken to cause the inconvenience to be equally felt on both sides."* They were told "that the impressment of American citizens, to serve on board of British armed vessels, was not only an injury to the unfortunate individuals, but it naturally excited certain emotions in the breasts of the nation to whom they belonged, and of the just and humane of every country; and that an expectation was indulged that orders would be given, that the Americans so circumstanced should be immediately liberated, and that the British officers should in future abstain from similar violences."† They were told "that the subject was of much greater importance than had been supposed; and that instead of a few, and those in many instances equivocal cases, the American minister at the court of London had, in nine months (part of the years 1796 and 1797), made applications for the discharge of two hundred and seventy-one seamen, who had, in most cases, exhibited such evidence as to satisfy him that they were real Americans, forced into the British service, and persevering generally in refusing pay and bounty."‡ They were told "that if the British government had any regard to the rights of the United States, any respect for the nation, and placed any value on their friendship, it would facilitate the means of relieving their oppressed citizens."§ They were told "that the British naval officers often impressed Swedes, Danes, and other foreigners from the vessels of the United States; that they might with as much reason rob American vessels of the property or merchandise of Swedes, Danes, and Portuguese as seize and detain in their service the subjects of those nations found on board of American vessels; and that the President was extremely anxious to have this business of impressing placed on a reasonable footing."‖ And they were told "that the impressment of American seamen was an injury of very serious magnitude, which deeply affected the feelings and honor of the nation; that no right had been asserted to impress the natives of America, yet, that they were impressed; they were dragged on board British ships of war, with the evidence of citizenship in their hands, and forced by violence there to serve until conclusive testimonials of their

---

* See the letter from Mr. Pinckney, minister at London, to the Secretary of State, dated the 13th of March, 1793.

† See the note of Mr. Jay, envoy extraordinary, to Lord Grenville, dated the 30th of July, 1794.

‡ See the letter of Mr. King, minister at London, to the Secretary of State, dated the 13th of April, 1797

§ See the letter from Mr. Pickering, Secretary of State, to Mr. King, minister at London, dated the 10th of September, 1796.

‖ See the letter from the same to the same, dated the 20th of October, 1796.

birth could be obtained; that many must perish unrelieved, and all were detained a considerable time in lawless and injurious confinement; that the continuance of the practice must inevitably produce discord between two nations which ought to be the friends of each other; and that it was more advisable to desist from, and to take effectual measures to prevent, an acknowledged wrong than by perseverance in that wrong, to excite against themselves the well-founded resentments of America, and force the government into measures which may very possibly terminate in an open rupture."*

Such were the feelings and the sentiments of the American government, under every change of its administration, in relation to the British practice of impressment; and such the remonstrances addressed to the justice of Great Britain. It is obvious, therefore, that this cause, independent of every other, has been uniformly deemed a just and certain cause of war; yet, the characteristic policy of the United States still prevailed: remonstrance was only succeeded by negotiation; and every assertion of American rights was accompanied with an overture to secure, in any practicable form, the rights of Great Britain.† Time seemed, however, to render it more and more difficult to ascertain and fix the standard of the British rights according to the succession of the British claims. The right of entering and searching an American merchant ship for the purpose of impressment was, for awhile, confined to the case of British deserters; and even so late as the month of February, 1800, the minister of his Britannic Majesty, then at Philadelphia, urged the American government "to take into consideration, as the only means of drying up every source of complaint and irritation upon that head, a proposal which he had made two years before in the name of his Majesty's government, for the reciprocal restitution of deserters."‡ But this project of a treaty was then deemed inadmissible by the President of the United States, and the chief officers of the executive departments of the government, whom he consulted, for the same reason specifically which, at a subsequent period, induced the President of the United States to withhold his approbation from the treaty negotiated by the American ministers at London, in the year 1806, namely, "that it did not sufficiently provide

---

* See the letter from Mr. Marshall, Secretary of State (now Chief Justice of the United States), to Mr. King, minister at London, dated the 20th of September, 1800.

† See particularly Mr. King's propositions to Lord Grenville and Lord Hawkesbury of the 13th of April, 1797, the 15th of March, 1799, the 25th of February, 1801, and in July, 1813.

‡ See Mr. Liston's note to Mr. Pickering, the Secretary of State, dated the 4th of February, 1800.

against the impressment of American seamen ;"* and "that it is better to have no article, and to meet the consequences, than not to enumerate merchant vessels on the high seas among the things not to be forcibly entered in search of deserters."† But the British claim, expanding with singular elasticity, was soon found to include a right to enter American vessels on the high seas, in order to search for and seize all British seamen ; it next embraced the case of every British subject; and finally, in its practical enforcement, it has been extended to every mariner who could not prove upon the spot that he was a citizen of the United States.

While the nature of the British claim was thus ambiguous and fluctuating, the principle to which it was referred for justification and support appeared to be at once arbitrary and illusory. It was not recorded in any positive code of the law of nations; it was not displayed in the elementary works of the civilian ; nor had it ever been exemplified in the maritime usages of any other country in any other age. In truth, it was the offspring of the municipal law of Great Britain alone; equally operative in a time of peace and in a time of war; and, under all circumstances, inflicting a coercive jurisdiction upon the commerce and navigation of the world.

For the legitimate rights of the belligerent powers, the United States had felt and evinced a sincere and open respect. Although they had marked a diversity of doctrine among the most celebrated jurists upon many of the litigated points of the law of war ; although they had formerly espoused, with the example of the most powerful government of Europe, the principles of the armed neutrality, which were established, in the year 1780, upon the basis of the memorable declaration of the empress of all the Russias ; and although the principles of that declaration have been incorporated into all their public treaties, except in the instance of the treaty of 1794, yet, the United States, still faithful to the pacific and impartial policy which they professed, did not hesitate, even at the commencement of the French revolutionary war, to accept and allow the exposition of the law of nations as it was then maintained by Great Britain ; and, consequently, to admit, upon a much-contested point, that the property of her enemy in their vessels might be lawfully captured as prize of

---

* See the opinion of Mr. Pickering, Secretary of State, inclosing the plan of a treaty, dated the 3d of May, 1800, and the opinion of Mr. Wolcott, Secretary of the Treasury, dated the 14th of April, 1800.

† See the opinion of Mr. Stoddert, Secretary of the Navy, dated the 23d of April, 1800, and the opinions of Mr. Lee, Attorney-General, dated the 26th of February, and the 30th of April, 1800.

war.* It was, also, freely admitted that a belligerent power had a right, with proper cautions, to enter and search American vessels for the goods of an enemy, and for articles contraband of war; that if, upon a search, such goods or articles were found, or if, in the course of the search, persons in the military service of the enemy were discovered, a belligerent had a right of transhipment and removal; that a belligerent had a right, in doubtful cases, to carry American vessels to a convenient station for further examination; and that a belligerent had a right to exclude American vessels from ports and places under the blockade of an adequate naval force. These rights the law of nations might reasonably be deemed to sanction; nor has a fair exercise of the powers necessary for the enjoyment of these rights been, at any time, controverted or opposed by the American government.

But it must be again remarked that the claim of Great Britain was not to be satisfied by the most ample and explicit recognition of the law of war, for the law of war treats only of the relations of a belligerent to his enemy, while the claim of Great Britain embraced also the relations between a sovereign and his subjects. It was said that every British subject was bound by a tie of allegiance to his sovereign, which no lapse of time, no change of place, no exigency of life could possibly weaken or dissolve. It was said that the British sovereign was entitled at all periods and on all occasions to the services of his subjects. And it was said that the British vessels of war upon the high seas might lawfully and forcibly enter the merchant vessels of every other nation (for the theory of these pretensions is not limited to the case of the United States, although that case has been almost exclusively affected by their practical operation) for the purpose of discovering and impressing British subjects.† The United States presume not to discuss the forms or the principles of the governments established in other countries. Enjoying the right and the blessing of self-government, they leave implicitly to every foreign nation the choice of its social and political institutions. But, whatever may be the form or the principle of government, it is a universal axiom of public law among sovereign and independent states that every nation is bound so to use and enjoy its own rights as not to injure or destroy the rights of any other nation. Say, then, that the tie of allegiance cannot be severed or relaxed as respects the sovereign and the subject, and say that

---

* See the correspondence of the year 1792 between Mr. Jefferson, Secretary of State, and the ministers of Great Britain and France. See, also, Mr. Jefferson's letter to the American minister at Paris, of the same year, requesting the recall of Mr. Genet.

† See the British declaration of the 10th of January, 1813.

the sovereign is at all times entitled to the services of the subject, still there is nothing gained in support of the British claim, unless it can also be said that the British sovereign has a right to seek and seize his subject while actually within the dominion or under the special protection of another sovereign state. This will not, surely, be denominated a process of the law of nations for the purpose of enforcing the rights of war; and if it shall be tolerated as a process of the municipal law of Great Britain for the purpose of enforcing the right of the sovereign to the service of his subjects, there is no principle of discrimination which can prevent its being employed, in peace or in war, with all the attendant abuses of force and fraud, to justify the seizure of British subjects for crimes or for debts, and the seizure of British property for any cause that shall be arbitrarily assigned. The introduction of these degrading novelties into the maritime code of nations it has been the arduous task of the American government, in the onset, to oppose; and it rests with all other governments to decide how far their honor and their interests must be eventually implicated by a tacit acquiescence in the successive usurpations of the British flag. If the right claimed by Great Britain be indeed common to all governments, the ocean will exhibit, in addition to its many other perils, a scene of everlasting strife and contention. But what other government has ever claimed or exercised the right? If the right shall be exclusively established as a trophy of the naval superiority of Great Britain, the ocean, which has been sometimes emphatically denominated "the highway of nations," will be identified, in occupancy and use, with the dominions of the British crown, and every other nation must enjoy the liberty of passage upon the payment of a tribute or the indulgence of a license. But what nation is prepared for this sacrifice of its honor and its interests? And if, after all, the right be now asserted (as experience too plainly indicates) for the purpose of imposing upon the United States, to accommodate the British maritime policy, a new and odious limitation of the sovereignty and independence which were acquired by the glorious Revolution of 1776, it is not for the American government to calculate the duration of a war that shall be waged in resistance of the active attempts of Great Britain to accomplish her project; for where is the American citizen who would tolerate a day's submission to the vassalage of such a condition?

But the American government has seen with some surprise the gloss which the prince regent of Great Britain, in his declaration of the 10th of January, 1813, has condescended to bestow upon the British claim of a right to impress men on board of the merchant vessels of other nations, and the retort which he has ventured to make upon the conduct of the United States relative to the controverted doctrines of expatriation. The American government, like every other civilized government, avows the principle and indulges the practice of naturalizing foreigners. In Great Britain, and throughout the continent of Europe, the laws and regulations upon the subject are not materially dissimilar, when compared with the laws and regulations of the United States. The effect, however, of such naturalization upon the connection which previously subsisted between the naturalized person and the government of the country of his birth has been differently considered at different times and in different places. Still, there are many respects in which a diversity of opinion does not exist, and cannot arise. It is agreed on all hands that an act of naturalization is not a violation of the law of nations, and that, in particular, it is not, in itself, an offence against the government whose subject is naturalized. It is agreed that an act of naturalization creates between the parties the reciprocal obligations of allegiance and protection. It is agreed that while a naturalized citizen continues within the territory and jurisdiction of his adoptive government he cannot be pursued or seized or restrained by his former sovereign. It is agreed that a naturalized citizen, whatever may be thought of the claims of the sovereign of his native country, cannot lawfully be withdrawn from the obligations of his contract of naturalization by the force or the seduction of a third power. And it is agreed that no sovereign can lawfully interfere to take from the service or the employment of another sovereign persons who are not the subjects of either of the sovereigns engaged in the transaction. Beyond the principles of these accorded propositions, what have the United States done to justify the imputation of "harboring British seamen, and of exercising an assumed right to transfer the allegiance of British subjects?"* The United States have, indeed, insisted upon the right of navigating the ocean in peace and safety, protecting all that is covered by their flag, as on a place of equal and common jurisdiction to all nations, save where the law of war interposes the exceptions of visitation, search, and capture; but in doing this they have done no wrong. The United States, in perfect consistency it is believed with the practice of all belligerent nations, not even excepting Great Britain herself, have, indeed, announced a determination, since the declaration of hostilities, to afford protection as well to the naturalized as to the native citizen who, giving the strongest proofs of fidelity, should be taken in arms by the enemy; and the British Cabinet well know that this determination could have no influence upon those councils of their sovereign which preceded and produced the war.- It was not, then, to "harbor British seamen,"

---

* See the British declaration of the 10th of January, 1813.

nor to "transfer the allegiance of British subjects," nor to "cancel the jurisdiction of their legitimate sovereign," nor to vindicate "the pretension that acts of naturalization and certificates of citizenship were as valid out of their own territory as within it,"* that the United States have asserted the honor and the privilege of their flag by the force of reason and of arms. But it was to resist a systematic scheme of maritime aggrandizement which, prescribing to every other nation the limits of a territorial boundary, claimed for Great Britain the exclusive dominion of the seas, and which, spurning the settled principles of the law of war, condemned the ships and mariners of the United States to suffer upon the high seas, and virtually within the jurisdiction of their flag, the most rigorous dispensations of the British municipal code, inflicted by the coarse and licentious hand of a British press-gang.

The injustice of the British claim and the cruelty of the British practice have tested, for a series of years, the pride and the patience of the American government; but still every experiment was anxiously made to avoid the last resort of nations. The claim of Great Britain, in its theory, was limited to the right of seeking and impressing its own subjects on board of the merchant vessels of the United States, although, in fatal experience, it has been extended (as already appears) to the seizure of the subjects of every other power sailing under a voluntary contract with the American merchant; to the seizure of the naturalized citizens of the United States, sailing also under voluntary contracts, which every foreigner, independent of any act of naturalization, is at liberty to form in every country; and even to the seizure of the native citizens of the United States, sailing on board the ships of their own nation, in the prosecution of a lawful commerce. The excuse for what has been unfeelingly termed "partial mistakes and occasional abuse,"† when the right of impressment was practised towards vessels of the United States is, in the words of the prince regent's declaration, "a similarity of language and manners;" but was it not known, when this excuse was offered to the world, that the Russian, the Swede, the Dane, and the German; that the Frenchman, the Spaniard, and the Portuguese; nay, that the African and the Asiatic, between whom and the people of Great Britain there exists no similarity of language, manners, or complexion, had been, equally with the American citizen and the British subject, the victims of the impress tyranny?‡ If, however, the excuse

---

* See these passages in the British declaration of the 10th of January, 1813.

† See the British declaration of the 10th of January, 1813.

‡ See the letter of Mr. Pickering, Secretary of State, to Mr. King,

be sincere; if the real object of the impressment be merely to secure to Great Britain the naval services of her own subjects, and not to man her fleets, in every practicable mode of enlistment, by right or by wrong; and if a just and generous government, professing mutual friendship and respect, may be presumed to prefer the accomplishment even of a legitimate purpose by means the least afflicting and injurious to others, why have the overtures of the United States, offering other means as effectual as impressment for the purpose avowed, to the consideration and acceptance of Great Britain, been forever eluded or rejected ? It has been offered that the number of men to be protected by an American vessel should be limited by her tonnage ; that British officers should be permitted, in British ports, to enter the vessel, in order to ascertain the number of men on board ; and that, in case of an addition to her crew, the British subjects enlisted should be liable to impressment * It was offered, in the solemn form of a law, that American seamen should be registered ; that they should be provided with certificates of citizenship ;† and that the roll of the crew of every vessel should be formally authenticated.‡ It was offered that no refuge or protection should be given to deserters; but that, on the contrary, they should be surrendered.§ It was " again and again offered to concur in a convention, which it was thought practicable to be formed, and which should settle the questions of impressment in a manner that would be safe for England and satisfactory to the United States."‖ It was offered that each party should prohibit its citizens or subjects from clandestinely concealing or carrying away from the territories or colonies of the other any seaman belonging to the other party.¶ And conclusively, it has been offered and declared by law that " after the termination of the present war it should not be lawful to employ on board of any of the public or private vessels of the United States any persons

---

minister at London, of the 26th of October, 1796, and the letter of Mr. Marshall, Secretary of State, to Mr. King, of the 20th of September, 1800.

* See the letter of Mr Jefferson, Secretary of State, to Mr. Pinckney, minister at London, dated the 11th of June, 1792, and the letter of Mr. Pickering, Secretary of State, to Mr. King, minister at London, dated the 8th of June, 1796.

† See the act of Congress passed the 28th of May, 1796.

‡ See the letter of Mr. Pickering, Secretary of State, to Mr. King, minister at London, dated the 8th of June, 1796

§ See the project of a treaty on the subject, between Mr. Pickering, Secretary of State, and Mr. Liston, the British minister, at Philadelphia, in the year 1800.

‖ See the letter of Mr. King, minister at London, to the Secretary of State, dated the 15th of March, 1799.

¶ See the letter of Mr. King to the Secretary of State, dated in July, 1803.

except citizens of the United States, and that no foreigner should be admitted to become a citizen hereafter who had not for the continued term of five years resided within the United States, without being at any time during the five years out of the territory of the United States."*

It is manifest, then, that such provision might be made by law, and that such provision has been repeatedly and urgently proposed, as would, in all future times, exclude from the maritime service of the United States, both in public and in private vessels, every person who could possibly be claimed by Great Britain as a native subject, whether he had or had not been naturalized in America.† Enforced by the same sanctions and securities which are employed to enforce the penal code of Great Britain, as well as the penal code of the United States, the provision would afford the strongest evidence that no British subject could be found in service on board of an American vessel ; and, consequently, whatever might be the British right of impressment in the abstract, there would remain no justifiable motive—there could hardly be invented a plausible pretext—to exercise it at the expense of the American right of lawful commerce. If, too, as it has sometimes been insinuated, there would, nevertheless, be room for frauds and evasions, it is sufficient to observe that the American government would always be ready to hear and to redress every just complaint ; or, if redress were sought and refused (a preliminary course that ought never to have been omitted, but which Great Britain has never pursued), it would still be in the power of the British government to resort to its own force by acts equivalent to war for the reparation of its wrongs. But Great Britain has, unhappily, perceived in the acceptance of the overtures of the American government, consequences injurious to her maritime policy, and therefore withholds it at the expense of her justice. She perceives, perhaps, a loss of the American nursery for her seamen while she is at peace, a loss of the service of American crews while she is at war, and a loss of many of those opportunities which have enabled her to enrich her navy by the spoils of the American commerce without exposing her own commerce to the risk of retaliation or reprisals.

Thus were the United States, in a season of reputed peace, involved in the evils of a state of war ; and thus was the American flag annoyed by a nation still professing to cherish the sentiments of mutual friendship and respect which had been recently

---

* See the act of Congress passed on the 3d of March, 1813.

† See the letter of instructions from Mr. Monroe, Secretary of State, to the plenipotentiaries for treating of peace with Great Britain under the mediation of the Emperor Alexander, dated the 15th of April, 1813.

vouched by the faith of a solemn treaty. But the American government even yet abstained from vindicating its rights and from avenging its wrongs by an appeal to arms. It was not an insensibility to those wrongs, nor a dread of British power, nor a subserviency to British interests that prevailed at that period in the councils of the United States; but under all trials the American government abstained from the appeal to arms then, as it has repeatedly since done in its collisions with France as well as with Great Britain, from the purest love of peace, while peace could be rendered compatible with the honor and independence of the nation.

During the period which has hitherto been more particularly contemplated (from the declaration of hostilities between Great Britain and France in the year 1792 until the short-lived pacification of the treaty of Amiens in 1802), there were not wanting occasions to test the consistency and the impartiality of the American government by a comparison of its conduct towards Great Britain with its conduct towards other nations. The manifestations of the extreme jealousy of the French government and of the intemperate zeal of its ministers near the United States, were coeval with the proclamation of neutrality; but after the ratification of the treaty of London, the scene of violence, spoliation, and contumely opened by France upon the United States became such as to admit, perhaps, of no parallel except in the contemporaneous scenes which were exhibited by the injustice of her great competitor. The American government acted in both cases on the same pacific policy, in the same spirit of patience and forbearance, but with the same determination, also, to assert the honor and independence of the nation. When, therefore, every conciliatory effort had failed, and when two successive missions of peace had been contemptuously repulsed, the American government, in the year 1798, annulled its treaties with France and waged a maritime war against that nation for the defence of its citizens and of its commerce passing on the high seas. But as soon as the hope was conceived of a satisfactory change in the dispositions of the French government, the American government hastened to send another mission to France; and a convention, signed in the year 1800, terminated the subsisting differences between the two countries.

Nor were the United States able, during the same period, to avoid a collision with the government of Spain upon many important and critical questions of boundary and commerce, of Indian warfare, and maritime spoliation. Preserving, however, their system of moderation in the assertion of their rights, a course of amicable discussion and explanation produced mutual satisfaction, and a treaty of friendship, limits, and navigation was formed in the year 1795, by which the citizens of the United

States acquired a right for the space of three years to deposit their merchandise and effects in the port of New Orleans, with a promise either that the enjoyment of that right should be indefinitely continued, or that another part of the banks of the Mississippi should be assigned for an equivalent establishment. But when, in the year 1802, the port of New Orleans was abruptly closed against the citizens of the United States without an assignment of any other equivalent place of deposit, the harmony of the two countries was again most seriously endangered; until the Spanish government, yielding to the remonstrances of the United States, disavowed the act of the intendant of New Orleans, and ordered the right of deposit to be reinstated on the terms of the treaty of 1795.

The effects produced, even by a temporary suspension of the right of deposit at New Orleans, upon the interests and feelings of the nation, naturally suggested to the American government the expediency of guarding against their recurrence by the acquisition of a permanent property in the province of Louisiana. The minister of the United States at Madrid was accordingly instructed to apply to the government of Spain upon the subject; and, on the 4th of May, 1803, he received an answer, stating, that "by the retrocession made to France of Louisiana, that power regained the province, with the limits it had, saving the rights acquired by other powers; and that the United States could address themselves to the French government to negotiate the acquisition of territories, which might suit their interest."* But before this reference, official information of the same fact had been received by Mr. Pinckney from the court of Spain in the month of March preceding, and the American government, having instituted a special mission to negotiate the purchase of Louisiana from France, or from Spain, whichever should be its sovereign, the purchase was accordingly accomplished for a a valuable consideration (that was punctually paid), by the treaty concluded at Paris, on the 30th of April, 1803.

The American government has not seen, without some sensibility, that a transaction, accompanied by such circumstances of general publicity and of scrupulous good faith, has been denounced by the prince regent, in his declaration of the 10th of January, 1813, as a proof of the "ungenerous conduct" of the United States towards Spain.† In amplification of the royal charge, the British negotiators at Ghent have presumed to impute "the acquisition of Louisiana, by the United States, to a

---

* See the letter from Don Pedro Cevallos the minister of Spain, to Mr. C. Pinckney, the minister of the United States, dated the 4th of May, 1803, from which the passage cited is literally translated.

† See the prince regent's declaration of the 10th of January, 1813.

spirit of aggrandizement, not necessary to their own security;"
and to maintain "that the purchase was made against the known
conditions on which it had been ceded by Spain to France;"*
that "in the face of the protestation of the minister of his Catholic Majesty at Washington, the President of the United States
ratified the treaty of purchase;"† and that "there was good
reason to believe that many circumstances attending the transaction were industriously concealed."‡ The American government cannot condescend to retort aspersions so unjust, in language so opprobrious; and peremptorily rejects the pretension of
Great Britain to interfere in the business of the United States
and Spain; but it owes, nevertheless, to the claims of truth, a
distinct statement of the facts which have been thus misrepre-
sented.   When the special mission was appointed to negotiate
the purchase of Louisiana from France, in the manner already
mentioned, the American minister at London was instructed to
explain the object of the mission; and, having made the explanation, he was assured by the British government "that the communication was received in good part; no doubt was suggested
of the right of the United States to pursue, separately and alone,
the objects they aimed at; but the British government appeared
to be satisfied with the President's views on this important subject."§ As soon, too, as the treaty of purchase was concluded,
before hostilities were again actually commenced between Great
Britain and France, and previously, indeed, to the departure of
the French ambassador from London, the American minister
openly notified to the British government that a treaty had been
signed "by which the complete sovereignty of the town and
territory of New Orleans, as well as of all Louisiana, as the
same was heretofore possessed by Spain, had been acquired by
the United States of America; and that in drawing up the treaty
care had been taken so to frame the same as not to infringe any
right of Great Britain in the navigation of the river Mississippi."‖
In the answer of the British government, it was explicitly declared by Lord Hawkesbury "that he had received his Majesty's
commands to express the pleasure with which his Majesty had

---

* See the note of the British commissioners, dated the 4th of September,
1814.
† See the note of the British commissioners, dated the 19th of September, 1814.
‡ See the note of the British commissioners, dated the 8th of October,
1814.
§ See the letter from the Secretary of State to Mr King, the American
minister at London, dated the 29th of January, 1803. and Mr. King's
letter to the Secretary of State, dated the 23th of April, 1803.
‖ See the letter of Mr. King to Lord Hawkesbury, dated the 15th of
May, 1803.

received the intelligence ; and to add, that his Majesty regarded the care, which had been taken so to frame the treaty as not to infringe any right of Great Britain in the navigation of the Mississippi, as the most satisfactory evidence of a disposition on the part of the government of the United States, correspondent with that which his Majesty entertained, to promote and improve that harmony which so happily subsisted between the two countries, and which was so conducive to their mutual benefit."* The world will judge whether, under such circumstances, the British government had any cause, on its own account, to arraign the conduct of the United States in making the purchase of Louisiana ; and, certainly, no greater cause will be found for the arraignment on account of Spain. The Spanish government was apprised of the intention of the United States to negotiate for the purchase of that province ; its ambassador witnessed the progress of the negotiation at Paris ; and the conclusion of the treaty, on the 30th of April, 1803, was promptly known and understood at Madrid. Yet the Spanish government interposed no objection, no protestation, against the transaction, in Europe ; and it was not until the month of September, 1803, that the American government heard, with surprise, from the minister of Spain at Washington, that his Catholic Majesty was dissatisfied with the cession of Louisiana to the United States. Notwithstanding this diplomatic remonstrance, however, the Spanish government proceeded to deliver the possession of Louisiana to France in execution of the treaty of St. Ildelfonso ; saw France, by an almost simultaneous act, transfer the possession to the United States in execution of the treaty of purchase ; and finally, instructed the Marquis de Casa Yrujo to present to the American government the declaration of the 15th of May, 1804, acting " by the special order of his sovereign," "that the explanations, which the government of France had given to his Catholic Majesty, concerning the sale of Louisiana to the United States, and the amicable dispositions on the part of the king, his master, towards these states, had determined him to abandon the opposition which, at a prior period, and with the most substantial motives, he had manifested against the transaction."†

But after this amicable and decisive arrangement of all differences in relation to the validity of the Louisiana purchase, a question of some embarrassment remained in relation to the boundaries of the ceded territory. This question, however, the American government always has been, and always will be, willing

---

* See the letter of Lord Hawkesbury to Mr. King, dated the 19th of May, 1803.
† See the letter of the Marquis de Casa Yrujo to the American Secretary of State, dated the 15th of May, 1804.

to discuss in the most candid manner, and to settle upon the most liberal basis, with the government of Spain. It was not, therefore, a fair topic with which to inflame the prince regent's declaration, or to embellish the diplomatic notes of the British negotiators at Ghent.* The period has arrived when Spain, relieved from her European labors, may be expected to bestow her attention more effectually upon the state of her colonies; and, acting with the wisdom, justice, and magnanimity of which she has given frequent examples, she will find no difficulty in meeting the recent advances of the American government for an honorable adjustment of every point in controversy between the two countries, without seeking the aid of British mediation or adopting the animosity of British councils.

But still the United States, feeling a constant interest in the opinion of enlightened and impartial nations, cannot hesitate to embrace the opportunity, for representing, in the simplicity of truth, the events by which they have been led to take possession of a part of the Floridas, notwithstanding the claim of Spain to the sovereignty of the same territory. In the acceptation and understanding of the United States, the cession of Louisiana embraced the country south of the Mississippi territory, and eastward of the river Mississippi, and extending to the river Perdido; but "their conciliatory views, and their confidence in the justice of their cause and in the success of a candid discussion and amicable negotiation with a just and friendly power, induced them to acquiesce in the temporary continuance of that territory under the Spanish authority."† When, however, the adjustment of the boundaries of Louisiana, as well as a reasonable indemnification on account of maritime spoliations, and the suspension of the right of deposit at New Orleans, seemed to be indefinitely postponed on the part of Spain, by events which the United States had not contributed to produce, and could not control; when a crisis had arrived subversive of the order of things under the Spanish authorities, contravening the views of both parties, and endangering the tranquillity and security of the adjoining territories, by the intrusive establishment of a government, independent of Spain, as well as of the United States; and when, at a later period, there was reason to believe that Great Britain herself designed to occupy the Floridas (and she has, indeed, actually occupied Pensacola for hostile purposes),

---

* See the prince regent's declaration of the 10th of January, 1813. See the notes of the British commissioners, dated 19th September and 8th October, 1814.

† See the proclamation of the President of the United States, authorizing Governor Claiborne to take possession of the territory, dated the 27th of October, 1810.

the American government, without departing from its respect for the rights of Spain, and even consulting the honor of that state, unequal, as she then was, to the task of suppressing the intrusive establishment, was impelled by the paramount principle of self-preservation to rescue its own rights from the impending danger. Hence the United States, in the year 1810, proceeding step by step, according to the growing exigencies of the time, took possession of the country in which the standard of independence had been displayed, excepting such places as were held by a Spanish force. In the year 1811, they authorized their President, by law, provisionally to accept of the possession of East Florida from the local authorities, or to preoccupy it against the attempt of a foreign power to seize it. In 1813 they obtained the possession of Mobile, the only place then held by a Spanish force in West Florida, with a view to their own immediate security, but without varying the questions depending between them and Spain in relation to that province. And in the year 1814, the American commander, acting under the sanction of the law of nations, but unauthorized by the orders of his government, drove from Pensacola the British troops, who, in violation of the neutral territory of Spain (a violation which Spain, it is believed, must herself resent, and would have resisted if the opportunity had occurred), seized and fortified that station to aid in military operations against the United States. But all these measures of safety and necessity were frankly explained, as they occurred, to the government of Spain, and even to the government of Great Britain antecedently to the declaration of war, with the sincerest assurances that the possession of the territory thus acquired "should not cease to be a subject of fair and friendly negotiation and adjustment."*

The present review of the conduct of the United States toward the belligerent powers of Europe, will be regarded by every candid mind as a necessary medium to vindicate their national character from the unmerited imputations of the prince regent's declaration of the 10th of January, 1813, and not as a medium, voluntarily assumed, according to the insinuations of that declaration, for the revival of unworthy prejudices or vindictive pas-

---

* See the letter from the Secretary of State to Governor Claiborne, and the President's proclamation, dated the 27th of October, 1810. See the proceedings of the convention of Florida, transmitted to the Secretary of State by the Governor of the Mississippi territory in his letter of the 17th of October, 1810, and the answer of the Secretary of State, dated the 15th of November, 1810. See the letter of Mr. Morier, British chargé d'affaires, to the Secretary of State, dated the 15th of December, 1810, and the Secretary's answer. See the correspondence between Mr. Monroe and Mr. Foster, the British minister, in the months of July, September, and November, 1811.

sions in reference to transactions that are past. The treaty of Amiens, which seemed to terminate the war in Europe, seemed, also, to terminate the neutral sufferings of America; but the hope of repose was, in both respects, delusive and transient. The hostilities which were renewed between Great Britain and France in the year 1803, were immediately followed by a renewal of the aggressions of the belligerent powers upon the commercial rights and political independence of the United States. There was scarcely, therefore, an interval separating the aggressions of the first war from the aggressions of the second war; and although in nature the aggressions continued to be the same, in extent they became incalculably more destructive. It will be seen, however, that the American government inflexibly maintained its neutral and pacific policy in every extremity of the latter trial with the same good faith and forbearance that in the former trial had distinguished its conduct, until it was compelled to choose from the alternative of national degradation or national resistance. And if Great Britain alone then became the object of the American declaration of war, it will be seen that Great Britain alone had obstinately closed the door of amicable negotiation.

The American minister at London, anticipating the rupture between Great Britain and France, had obtained assurances from the British government "that, in the event of war, the instructions given to their naval officers should be drawn up with plainness and precision; and, in general, that the rights of belligerents should be exercised in moderation, and with due respect for those of neutrals."[*] And in relation to the important subject of impressment, he had actually prepared for signature, with the assent of Lord Hawkesbury and Lord St. Vincent, a convention to continue during five years, declaring that "no seaman nor seafaring person should, upon the high seas, and without the jurisdiction of either party, be demanded or taken out of any ship or vessel belonging to the citizens or subjects of one of the parties, by the public or private armed ships or men of war belonging to or in the service of the other party; and that strict orders should be given for the due observance of the engagement."[†] This convention, which explicitly relinquished impressments from American vessels on the high seas, and to which the British ministers had at first agreed, Lord St. Vincent was desirous afterwards to modify, "stating that, on further reflection, he was of opinion that the narrow seas should be expressly excepted, they having been, as his lordship remarked, immemorially con-

---

[*] See the letter of Mr. King to the Secretary of State, dated the 16th of May, 1803.
[†] See the letter of Mr. King to the Secretary of State, dated July, 1803.

sidered to be within the dominion of Great Britain." The American minister, however, "having supposed, from the tenor of his conversations with Lord St. Vincent, that the doctrine of *mare clausum* would not be revived against the United States on this occasion, but that England would be content with the limited jurisdiction or dominion over the seas adjacent to her territories, which is assigned by the law of nations to other states, was disappointed on receiving Lord St. Vincent's communication, and chose rather to abandon the negotiation than to acquiesce in the doctrine it proposed to establish."[*] But it was still some satisfaction to receive a formal declaration from the British government, communicated by its minister at Washington, after the recommencement of the war in Europe, which promised, in effect, to reinstate the practice of naval blockades upon the principles of the law of nations, so that no blockade should be considered as existing "unless in respect of particular ports, which might be actually invested, and then that the vessels bound to such ports should not be captured unless they had previously been warned not to enter them."[†]

All the precautions of the American government were, nevertheless, ineffectual; and the assurances of the British government were in no instance verified. The outrage of impressment was again indiscriminately perpetrated upon the crew of every American vessel, and on every sea. The enormity of blockades, established by an order in council, without a legitimate object and maintained by an order in council, without the application of a competent force, was more and more developed. The rule, denominated "the rule of the war of 1756," was revived in an affected style of moderation, but in a spirit of more rigorous execution.[‡] The lives, the liberty, the fortunes, and the happiness of the citizens of the United States, engaged in the pursuits of navigation and commerce, were once more subjected to the violence and cupidity of the British cruisers. And, in brief, so grievous, so intolerable, had the afflictions of the nation become, that the people, with one mind and one voice, called loudly upon their government for redress and protection;[§] the Congress of the United States, participating in the feelings and resentments

---

[*] See the letter of Mr. King to the Secretary of State, dated July, 1803.

[†] See the letter of Mr. Merry to the Secretary of State, dated the 12th of April, 1804, and the inclosed copy of a letter from Mr. Nepean, the Secretary of the Admiralty, to Mr. Hammond, the British Undersecretary of State for Foreign Affairs, dated Jan. 5th, 1804.

[‡] See the orders in council of the 24th of June, 1803, and the 17th of August, 1805.

[§] See the memorials of Boston, New York, Philadelphia, Baltimore, etc., presented to Congress in the end of the year 1805 and the beginning of the year 1806.

of the time, urged upon the executive magistrate the necessity of an immediate demand of reparation from Great Britain,* while the same patriotic spirit which had opposed British usurpation in 1793 and encountered French hostility in 1798 was again pledged, in every variety of form, to the maintenance of the national honor and independence during the more arduous trial that arose in 1805.

Amidst these scenes of injustice on the one hand and of reclamation on the other, the American government preserved its equanimity and its firmness. It beheld much in the conduct of France and of her ally, Spain, to provoke reprisals. It beheld more in the conduct of Great Britain, that led, unavoidably (as had often been avowed), to the last resort of arms. It beheld in the temper of the nation all that was requisite to justify an immediate selection of Great Britain as the object of a declaration of war. And it could not but behold in the policy of France the strongest motive to acquire the United States as an associate in the existing conflict. Yet these considerations did not then, more than at any former crisis, subdue the fortitude or mislead the judgment of the American government; but in perfect consistency with its neutral as well as its pacific system, it demanded atonement by remonstrances with France and Spain; and it sought the preservation of peace by negotiation with Great Britain.

It has been shown that a treaty proposed emphatically by the British minister resident at Philadelphia, "as the means of drying up every source of complaint and irritation upon the head of impressment," was "deemed utterly inadmissible" by the American government, because it did not sufficiently provide for that object.† It has also been shown that another treaty, proposed by the American minister at London, was laid aside because the British government, while it was willing to relinquish expressly impressments from American vessels on the high seas, insisted upon an exception in reference to the narrow seas claimed as a part of the British dominion; and experience demonstrated that, although the spoliations committed upon the American commerce might admit of reparation by the payment of a pecuniary equivalent, yet, consulting the honor and the feelings of the nation, it was impossible to receive satisfaction for the cruelties of impressment by any other means than by an entire discontinuance of the prac-

---

* See the resolutions of the Senate of the United States of the 10th and 14th of February, 1806, and the resolution of the House of Representatives of the 26th of January, 1806.

† See Mr. Liston's letter to the Secretary of State, dated the 4th of February, 1800, and the letter of Mr. Pickering, Secretary of State, to the President of the United States, dated the 20th of February, 1800.

tice. When, therefore, the envoys extraordinary were appointed in the year 1806 to negotiate with the British government, every authority was given for the purposes of conciliation; nay, an act of Congress prohibiting the importation of certain articles of British manufacture into the United States was suspended in proof of a friendly disposition ;* but it was declared that "the suppression of impressment and the definition of blockades were absolutely indispensable ;" and that " without a provision against impressments no treaty should be concluded." The American envoys accordingly took care to communicate to the British commissioners the limitations of their powers. Influenced at the same time by a sincere desire to terminate the differences between the two nations; knowing the solicitude of their government to relieve its seafaring citizens from actual sufferance; listening with confidence to assurances and explanations of the British commissioners in a sense favorable to their wishes; and judging from a state of information that gave no immediate cause to doubt the sufficiency of those assurances and explanations, the envoys, rather than terminate the negotiation without any arrangement, were willing to rely upon the efficacy of a substitute for a positive article in the treaty to be submitted to the consideration of their government, as this, according to the declaration of the British commissioners, was the only arrangement they were permitted at that time to propose or to allow. The substitute was presented in the form of a note from the British commissioners to the American envoys, and contained a pledge "that instructions had been given, and should be repeated and enforced, for the observance of the greatest caution in the impressing of British seamen ; that the strictest care should be taken to preserve the citizens of the United States from any molestation or injury ; and that immediate and prompt redress should be afforded upon any representation of injury sustained by them."†

Inasmuch, however, as the treaty contained no provision against impressment, and it was seen by the government when the treaty was under consideration for ratification that the pledge contained in the substitute was not complied with, but, on the contrary, that the impressments were continued with undiminished violence in the American seas so long after the alleged date of the instructions which were to arrest them, that the practical inefficacy of the substitute could not be doubted by the government here, the ratification of the treaty was necessarily declined ; and it has since appeared that after a change in the British ministry had

---

* See the act of Congress passed the 18th of April, 1806, and the act suspending it, passed the 19th of December, 1806.

† See the note of the British commissioners, dated 8th of November, 1806.

taken place it was declared by the Secretary for Foreign Affairs that no engagements were entered into on the part of his Majesty as connected with the treaty except such as appear upon the face of it.*

The American government, however, with unabating solicitude for peace, urged an immediate renewal of the negotiations on the basis of the abortive treaty, until this course was peremptorily declared, by the British government, to be "wholly inadmissible."†

But, independent of the silence of the proposed treaty, upon the great topic of American complaint, and of the view which has been taken of the projected substitute; the contemporaneous declaration of the British commissioners, delivered by the command of their sovereign, and to which the American envoys refused to make themselves a party, or to give the slightest degree of sanction, was regarded by the American government as ample cause of rejection. In reference to the French decree, which had been issued at Berlin, on the 21st of November, 1806, it was declared that if France should carry the threats of that decree into execution, and "if neutral nations, contrary to all expectation, should acquiesce in such usurpations, his Majesty might probably be compelled, however reluctantly, to retaliate in his just defence, and to adopt, in regard to the commerce of neutral nations with his enemies, the same measures which those nations should have permitted to be enforced against their commerce with his subjects;" "that his Majesty could not enter into the stipulations of the present treaty without an explanation from the United States of their intentions, or a reservation on the part of his Majesty, in the case above mentioned, if it should ever occur;" and "that without a formal abandonment or tacit relinquishment of the unjust pretensions of France, or without such conduct and assurances upon the part of the United States as should give security to his Majesty that they would not submit to the French innovations in the established system of maritime law, his Majesty would not consider himself bound, by the present signature of his commissioners, to ratify the treaty or precluded from adopting such measures as might seem necessary for counteracting the designs of the enemy."‡

The reservation of a power to invalidate a solemn treaty at the pleasure of one of the parties, and the menace of inflicting punishment upon the United States for the offences of another

---

* See Mr. Canning's letter to the American envoys, dated 27th October, 1807.

† See the same letter.

‡ See the note of the British commissioners, dated the 31st of December, 1806. See, also, the answer of Messrs. Monroe and Pinkney to that note.

nation, proved in the event a prelude to the scenes of violence which Great Britain was then about to display, and which it would have been improper for the American negotiators to anticipate. For if a commentary were wanting to explain the real design of such conduct, it would be found in the fact that within eight days from the date of the treaty, and before it was possible for the British government to have known the effect of the Berlin decree on the American government; nay, even before the American government had itself heard of that decree, the destruction of American commerce was commenced by the order in council of the 7th of January, 1807, which announced "that no vessel should be permitted to trade from one port to another, both which ports should belong to, or be in possession of, France or her allies; or should be so far under their control as that British vessels might not trade freely thereat."*

During the whole period of this negotiation, which did not finally close until the British government declared in the month of October, 1807, that negotiation was no longer admissible, the course pursued by the British squadron, stationed more immediately on the American coast, was, in the extreme, vexatious, predatory, and hostile. The territorial jurisdiction of the United States, extending, upon the principles of the law of nations, at least a league over the adjacent ocean, was totally disregarded and contemned. Vessels employed in the coasting trade, or in the business of the pilot and the fisherman, were objects of incessant violence; their petty cargoes were plundered, and some of their scanty crews were often either impressed, or wounded, or killed by the force of British frigates. British ships of war hovered in warlike display upon the coast, blockaded the ports of the United States so that no vessel could enter or depart in safety, penetrated the bays and rivers, and even anchored in the harbors of the United States to exercise a jurisdiction of impressment, threatened the towns and villages with conflagration, and wantonly discharged musketry, as well as cannon, upon the inhabitants of an open and unprotected country. The neutrality of the American territory was violated on every occasion, and at last the American government was doomed to suffer the greatest indignity which could be offered to a sovereign and independent nation, in the ever-memorable attack of a British fifty-gun ship, under the countenance of the British squadron, anchored within the waters of the United States, upon the frigate Chesapeake peaceably prosecuting a distant voyage. The British government affected from time to time to disapprove and condemn these outrages, but the officers who perpetrated them were generally applauded; if tried, they were acquitted; if removed from

---

* See the order in council of January 7, 1807.

the American station, it was only to be promoted in another station ; and if atonement were offered, as in the flagrant instance of the frigate Chesapeake, the atonement was so ungracious in the manner, and so tardy in the result, as to betray the want of that conciliatory spirit which ought to have characterized it.*

But the American government, soothing the exasperated spirit of the people by a proclamation, which interdicted the entrance of all British armed vessels into the harbors and waters of the United States,† neither commenced hostilities against Great Britain, nor sought a defensive alliance with France, nor relaxed in its firm, but conciliatory efforts, to enforce the claims of justice upon the honor of both nations.

The rival ambition of Great Britain and France now, however, approached the consummation, which, involving the destruction of all neutral rights upon an avowed principle of action, could not fail to render an actual state of war comparatively more safe and more prosperous than the imaginary state of peace to which neutrals were reduced. The just and impartial conduct of a neutral nation ceased to be its shield and its safeguard when the conduct of the belligerent powers towards each other became the only criterion of the law of war. The wrong committed by one of the belligerent powers was thus made the signal for the perpetration of a greater wrong by the other; and if the American government complained to both powers, their answer, although it never denied the causes of complaint, invariably retorted an idle and offensive inquiry into the priority of their respective aggressions ; or each demanded a course of resistance against its antagonist, which was calculated to prostrate the American right of self-government, and to coerce the United States against their interest and their policy into becoming an associate in the war. But the American government never did, and never can, admit that a belligerent power, "in taking steps to restrain the violence of its enemy, and to retort upon them the evils of their own injustice,"‡ is entitled to disturb and to destroy the rights of a neutral power as recognized and established by the law of nations. It was impossible, indeed, that the real features of the miscalled retaliatory system should be long masked from the world, when Great Britain, even in her acts of professed retaliation, declared that France was unable to

---

* See the evidence of these facts reported to Congress in November, 1806. See the documents respecting Captain Love, of the Driver, Captain Whitby, of the Leander, and Captain   . See, also, the correspondence respecting the frigate Chesapeake, with Mr. Canning at London, with Mr. Rose at Washington, with Mr. Erskine at Washington, and with   .

† See the proclamation of the 2d of July, 1807.

‡ See the orders in council of the 7th of January, 1807.

execute the hostile denunciations of her decrees,* and when Great Britain herself, unblushingly, entered into the same commerce with her enemy (through the medium of forgeries, perjuries, and licenses) from which she had interdicted unoffending neutrals. The pride of naval superiority, and the cravings of commercial monopoly, gave, after all, the impulse and direction to the councils of the British cabinet, while the vast, although visionary, projects of France, furnished occasions and pretexts for accomplishing the objects of those councils.

The British minister, resident at Washington in the year 1804, having distinctly recognized, in the name of his sovereign, the legitimate principles of blockade, the American government received with some surprise and solicitude the successive notifications of the 9th of August, 1804, the 8th of April, 1806, and more particularly of the 16th of May, 1806, announcing, by the last notification, "a blockade of the coast, rivers, and ports from the river Elbe to the port' of Brest, both inclusive."† In none of the notified instances of blockade were the principles that had been recognized in 1804 adopted and pursued; and it will be recollected by all Europe, that neither at the time of the notification of the 16th of May, 1806, nor at the time of excepting the Elbe and Ems from the operation of that notification,‡ nor at any time during the continuance of the French war, was there an adequate naval force, actually applied by Great Britain, for the purpose of maintaining a blockade from the river Elbe to the port of Brest. It was then, in the language of the day, "a mere paper blockade," a manifest infraction of the law of nations, and an act of peculiar injustice to the United States, as the only neutral power against which it could practically operate. But whatever may have been the sense of the American government on the occasion, and whatever might be the disposition to avoid making this the ground of an open rupture with Great Britain, the case assumed a character of the highest interest when, independent of its own injurious consequences, France, in the Berlin decree of the 21st of November, 1806, recited as a chief cause for placing the British islands in a state of blockade, "that Great Britain declares blockaded, places before which she has not a single vessel of war, and even places which her united forces would be incapable of blockading, such as entire coasts and a whole empire; an unequalled abuse of the right of blockade, that had no other object than to interrupt the communications of dif-

---

* See the orders in council of the 7th of January, 1807.

† See Lord Harrowby's note to Mr. Monroe, dated the 9th of August, 1804, and Mr. Fox's notes to Mr. Monroe, dated respectively the 8th of April and the 16th of May, 1806.

‡ See Lord Howick's note to Mr. Monroe, dated the 25th of September, 1806.

ferent nations, and to extend the commerce and industry of England upon the ruin of those nations."* The American government aims not, and never has aimed, at the justification, either of Great Britain or of France, in their career of crimination and recrimination; but it is of some importance to observe, that if the blockade of May, 1806, was an unlawful blockade, and if the right of retaliation arose with the first unlawful attack made by a belligerent power upon neutral rights, Great Britain has yet to answer to mankind, according to the rule of her own acknowledgment, for all the calamities of the retaliatory warfare. France, whether right or wrong, made the British system of blockade the foundation of the Berlin decree, and France had an equal right with Great Britain to demand from the United States an opposition to every encroachment upon the privileges of the neutral character. It is enough, however, on the present occasion, for the American government to observe that it possessed no power to prevent the framing of the Berlin decree, and to disclaim any approbation of its principles or acquiescence in its operations; for it neither belonged to Great Britain nor to France to prescribe to the American government the time or the mode, or the degree of resistance to the indignities and the outrages with which each of those nations in its turn assailed the United States.

But it has been shown that, after the British government possessed a knowledge of the existence of the Berlin decree, it authorized the conclusion of the treaty with the United States, which was signed at London on the 31st of December, 1806, reserving to itself a power of annulling the treaty, if France did not revoke, or if the United States, as a neutral power, did not resist, the obnoxious measure. It has also been shown that before Great Britain could possibly ascertain the determination of the United States in relation to the Berlin decree, the orders in council of the 7th of January, 1807, were issued, professing to be a retaliation against France, " at a time when the fleets of France and her allies were themselves confined within their own ports by the superior valor and discipline of the British navy,"† but operating in fact against the United States, as a neutral power, to prohibit their trade " from one port to another, both which ports should belong to, or be in the possession of, France or her allies, or should be so far under their control as that British vessels might not trade freely thereat."† It remains, however, to be stated that it was not until the 12th of March, 1807, that the British minister, then residing at Washington, communicated to the American government, in the name of his sovereign, the

---

* See the Berlin decree of the 21st of November, 1806.
† See the order in council of the 7th of January, 1807.

22

orders in council of January, 1807, with an intimation that stronger measures would be pursued unless the United States should resist the operations of the Berlin decree.* At the moment the British government was reminded "that within the period of those great events which continued to agitate Europe, instances had occurred in which the commerce of neutral nations, more especially of the United States, had experienced the severest distresses from its own orders and measures, manifestly unauthorized by the law of nations," assurances were given "that no culpable acquiescence on the part of the United States would render them accessary to the proceedings of one belligerent nation, through their rights of neutrality, against the commerce of its adversary," and the right of Great Britain to issue such orders, unless as orders of blockade, to be enforced according to the law of nations, was utterly denied.†

This candid and explicit avowal of the sentiments of the American government upon an occasion so novel and important in the history of nations did not, however, make its just impression upon the British cabinet ; for, without assigning any new provocation on the part of France, and complaining merely that neutral powers had not been induced to interpose with effect to obtain a revocation of the Berlin decree (which, however, Great Britain herself had affirmed to be a decree nominal and inoperative), the orders in council of the 11th of November, 1807, were issued, declaring "that all the ports and places of France and her allies, or of any other country at war with his Majesty, and all other ports or places in Europe, from which, although not at war with his Majesty, the British flag was excluded, and all ports or places in the colonies belonging to his Majesty's enemies should, from thenceforth, be subject to the same restrictions in point of trade and navigation, as if the same were actually blockaded by his Majesty's naval forces in the most strict and rigorous manner ;" that "all trade in articles which were the produce or manufacture of the said countries or colonies should be deemed and considered to be unlawful ;" but that neutral vessels should still be permitted to trade with France from certain free ports, or through ports and places of the British dominions.‡ To accept the lawful enjoyment of a right as the grant of a superior, to prosecute a lawful commerce under the forms of favor and indulgence, and to pay a tribute to Great Britain for the privileges of a lawful transit on the ocean, were concessions

---

* See Mr. Erskine's letter to the Secretary of State, dated the 12th of March, 1807.

† See the Secretary of State's letter to Mr. Erskine, dated the 20th of March, 1807.

‡ See the orders in council of the 11th of November, 1807.

which Great Britain was disposed insidiously to exact by an appeal to the cupidity of individuals, but which the United States could never yield consistently with the independence and the sovereignty of the nation. The orders in council were therefore altered in this respect at a subsequent period ;* but the general interdict of neutral commerce, applying more especially to American commerce, was obstinately maintained against all the force of reason, of remonstrance, and of protestation employed by the American government when the subject was presented to its consideration by the British minister residing at Washington. The fact assumed as the basis of the orders in council was unequivocally disowned, and it was demonstrated that so far from its being true, "that the United States had acquiesced in an illegal operation of the Berlin decree, it was not even true that at the date of the British orders of the 11th of November, 1807, a single application of that decree to the commerce of the United States on the high seas could have been known to the British government;" while the British government had been officially informed by the American minister at London "that explanations, uncontradicted by any overt act, had been given to the American minister at Paris, which justified a reliance that the French decree would not be put in force against the United States."†

The British orders of the 11th of November, 1807, were quickly followed by the French decree of Milan, dated the 17th of December, 1807, "which was said to be resorted to only in just retaliation of the barbarous system adopted by England," and in which the denationalizing tendency of the orders is made the foundation of a declaration in the decree "that every ship, to whatever nation it might belong, that should have submitted to be searched by an English ship, or to a voyage to England, or should have paid any tax whatsoever to the English government, was thereby and for that alone declared to be denationalized, to have forfeited the protection of its sovereign, and to have become English property, subject to capture as good and lawful prize; that the British islands were placed in a state of blockade both by sea and land, and every ship, of whatever nation or whatever the nature of its cargo might be, that sails from the ports of England or those of the English colonies, and of the countries occupied by English troops, and proceeding to England or to the English colonies, or to countries occupied by English troops, should be good and lawful prize; but that the pro-

---

* See Mr. Canning's letter to Mr. Pinkney, 23d February, 1808.

† See Mr. Erskine's letter to the Secretary of State, dated the 22d of February, 1808, and the answer of the Secretary of State, dated the 25th of March, 1808.

visions of the decree should be abrogated and null in fact as soon as the English should abide again by the principles of the law of nations, which are also the principles of justice and honor."* In opposition, however, to the Milan decree, as well as to the Berlin decree, the American government strenuously and unceasingly employed every instrument except the instruments of war. It acted precisely towards France as it acted towards Great Britain on similar occasions; but France remained for a time as insensible to the claims of justice and honor as Great Britain, each imitating the other in extravagance of pretension and in obstinacy of purpose.

When the American government received intelligence that the orders of the 11th of November, 1807, had been under the consideration of the British cabinet, and were actually prepared for promulgation, it was anticipated that France, in a zealous prosecution of the retaliatory warfare, would soon produce an act of, at least, equal injustice and hostility. The crisis existed, therefore, at which the United States were compelled to decide either to withdraw their seafaring citizens and their commercial wealth from the ocean, or to leave the interests of the mariner and the merchant exposed to certain destruction, or to engage in open and active war for the protection and defence of those interests. The principles and the habits of the American government were still disposed to neutrality and peace. In weighing the nature and the amount of the aggressions which had been perpetrated, or which were threatened, if there were any preponderance to determine the balance against one of the belligerent powers rather than the other as the object of a declaration of war, it was against Great Britain, at least, upon the vital interest of impressment and the obvious superiority of her naval means of annoyance. The French decrees were indeed as obnoxious in their formation and design as the British orders; but the government of France claimed and exercised no right of impressment, and the maritime spoliations of France were comparatively restricted not only by her own weakness on the ocean, but by the constant and pervading vigilance of the fleets of her enemy. The difficulty of selection, the indiscretion of encountering at once both of the offending powers, and, above all, the hope of an early return of justice, under the dispensations of the ancient public law, prevailed in the councils of the American government; and it was resolved to attempt the preservation of its neutrality and its peace, of its citizens and its resources, by a voluntary suspension of the commerce and navigation of the United States. It is true that for the minor outrages committed, under the pretext of the rule of war of 1756, the citizens of every denomination had de-

---

* See the Milan decree of the 17th of December, 1807.

manded from their government, in the year 1805, protection and redress; it is true that for the unparalleled enormities of the year 1807 the citizens of every denomination again demanded from their government protection and redress; but it is also a truth conclusively established by every manifestation of the sense of the American people, as well as of their government, that any honorable means of protection and redress were preferred to the last resort of arms. The American government might honorably retire for a time from the scene of conflict and collision, but it could no longer with honor permit its flag to be insulted, its citizens to be enslaved, and its property to be plundered on the highway of nations.

Under these impressions the restrictive system of the United States was introduced. In December, 1807, an embargo was imposed upon all American vessels and merchandise,* on principles similar to those which originated and regulated the embargo law, authorized to be laid by the President of the United States in the year 1794; but soon afterwards, in the genuine spirit of the policy that prescribed the measure, it was declared by law "that, in the event of such peace, or suspension of hostilities, between the belligerent powers of Europe, or such changes in their measures affecting neutral commerce as might render that of the United States safe, in the judgment of the President of the United States, he was authorized to suspend the embargo in whole or in part."† The pressure of the embargo was thought, however, so severe upon every part of the community that the American government, notwithstanding the neutral character of the measure, determined upon some relaxation; and, accordingly, the embargo being raised as to all other nations, a system of non-intercourse and non-importation was substituted in March, 1809, as to Great Britain and France, which prohibited all voyages to the British or French dominions, and all trade in articles of British or French product or manufacture.‡ But still adhering to the neutral and pacific policy of the government, it was declared "that the President of the United States should be authorized, in case either France or Great Britain should so revoke or modify her edicts as that they should cease to violate the neutral commerce of the United States, to declare the same by proclamation; after which the trade of the United States might be renewed with the nation so doing."§ These appeals to the justice and the interests of the belligerent powers proving ineffectual, and the necessities of the country increasing, it was finally re-

---

* See the act of Congress, passed the 22d of December, 1807.
† See the act of Congress, passed the 22d of April, 1808.
‡ See the act of Congress, passed the 1st day of March, 1809.
§ See the 11th section of the last-cited act of Congress.

solved by the American government to take the hazards of a war; to revoke its restrictive system; and to exclude British and French armed vessels from the harbors and waters of the United States; but, again, emphatically to announce "that in case either Great Britain or France should, before the 3d of March, 1811, so revoke or modify her edicts as that they should cease to violate the neutral commerce of the United States, and if the other nation should not, within three months thereafter, so revoke or modify her edicts in like manner," the provisions of the non-intercourse and non-importation law should, at the expiration of three months, be revived against the nation refusing, or neglecting, to revoke or modify its edict.*

In the course which the American government had hitherto pursued relative to the belligerent orders and decrees, the candid foreigner, as well as the patriotic citizen, may perceive an extreme solicitude for the preservation of peace; but, in the publicity and impartiality of the overture that was thus spread before the belligerent powers, it is impossible that any indication should be found of foreign influence or control. The overture was urged upon both nations for acceptance, at the same time and in the same manner; nor was an intimation withheld from either of them that "it might be regarded, by the belligerent first accepting it, as a promise to itself and a warning to its enemy."† Each of the nations, from the commencement of the retaliatory system, acknowledged that its measures were violations of public law; and each pledged itself to retract them whenever the other should set the example.‡ Although the American government, therefore, persisted in its remonstrances against the original transgressions, without regard to the question of their priority, it embraced with eagerness every hope of reconciling the interests of the rival powers, with a performance of the duty which they owed to the neutral character of the United States; and when the British minister, residing at Washington, in the year 1809, affirmed, in terms as plain and as positive as language could supply, "that he was authorized to declare that his Britannic Majesty's orders in council of January and November, 1807, will have been withdrawn, as respects the United States, on the 10th day of June, 1809," the President of the United States hastened, with approved liberality, to accept the declaration as conclusive evidence that the promised fact would exist at the stipulated period; and, by an immediate proclamation, he announced "that

---

* See the act of Congress, passed the 1st of May, 1810.

† See the correspondence between the Secretary of State and the American ministers at London and Paris.

‡ See the documents laid before Congress from time to time by the President, and printed.

after the 10th day of June next the trade of the United States with Great Britain, as suspended by the non-intercourse law, and by the acts of Congress laying and enforcing an embargo, might be renewed."* The American government neither asked, nor received, from the British minister, an exemplification of his powers, an inspection of his instructions, nor the solemnity of an order in council; but executed the compact, on the part of the United States, in all the sincerity of its own intentions, and in all the confidence which the official act of the representative of his Britannic Majesty was calculated to inspire. The act, and the authority for the act, were, however, disavowed by Great Britain; and an attempt was made by the successor of Mr. Erskine, through the aid of insinuations, which were indignantly repulsed, to justify the British rejection of the treaty of 1809, by referring to the American rejection of the treaty of 1806; forgetful of the essential points of difference, that the British government, on the former occasion, had been explicitly apprised by the American negotiators of their defect of power, and that the execution of the projected treaty had not, on either side, been commenced.†

After this abortive attempt to obtain a just and honorable revocation of the British orders in council, the United States were again invited to indulge the hope of safety and tranquillity, when the minister of France announced to the American minister at Paris that, in consideration of the act of the 1st of May, 1809, by which the Congress of the United States "engaged to oppose itself to that one of the belligerent powers which should refuse to acknowledge the rights of neutrals, he was authorized to declare that the decrees of Berlin and Milan were revoked, and that after the 1st of November, 1810, they would cease to have effect; it being understood that, in consequence of that declaration, the English should revoke their orders in council, and renounce the new principles of blockade, which they had wished to establish, or that the United States, conformably to the act of Congress, should cause their rights to be respected by the English."‡ This declaration, delivered by the official organ of the government of France, and in the presence, as it were, of the French sovereign, was of the highest authority according to all the rules of diplomatic intercourse; and certainly far surpassed any claim of credence which was possessed by the British

---

* See the correspondence between Mr. Erskine, the British minister, and the Secretary of State, on the 17th, 18th, and 19th of April, 1809, and the President's proclamation of the last date.

† See the correspondence between the Secretary of State and Mr. Jackson, the British minister.

‡ See the Duke de Cadore's letter to Mr. Armstrong, dated the 5th of August, 1810.

minister residing at Washington, when the arrangement of the
year 1809 was accepted and executed by the American government. The President of the United States, therefore, owed to
the consistency of his own character, and to the dictates of a
sincere impartiality, a prompt acceptance of the French overture;
and, accordingly, the authoritative promise that the fact should
exist, at the stipulated period, being again admitted as conclusive
evidence of its existence, a proclamation was issued on the 2d
of November, 1810, announcing "that the edicts of France had
been so revoked as that they ceased, on the first day of the same
month, to violate the neutral commerce of the United States, and
that all the restrictions, imposed by the act of Congress, should
then cease and be discontinued in relation to France and her de-
pendencies."* That France, from this epoch, refrained from all
aggressions on the high seas, or even in her own ports, upon the
persons and the property of the citizens of the United States
never was asserted; but, on the contrary, her violence and her
spoliations have been unceasing causes of complaint. These
subsequent injuries, constituting a part of the existing reclama-
tions of the United States, were always, however, disavowed by
the French government; whilst the repeal of the Berlin and
Milan decree has, on every occasion, been affirmed, insomuch
that Great Britain herself was, at last, compelled to yield to the
evidence of the fact.

On the expiration of three months from the date of the President's proclamation the non-intercourse and non-importation law
was, of course, to be revived against Great Britain, unless, during that period, her orders in council should be revoked. The
subject was, therefore, most anxiously and most steadily pressed
upon the justice and the magnanimity of the British government;
and even when the hope of success expired by the lapse of the
period prescribed in one act of Congress, the United States
opened the door of reconciliation by another act, which, in the
year 1811, again provided, that in case at any time "Great
Britain should so revoke or modify her edicts as that they shall
cease to violate the neutral commerce of the United States, the
President of the United States should declare the fact by proclamation; and that the restrictions previously imposed should,
from the date of such proclamation, cease and be discontinued."†
But, unhappily, every appeal to the justice and magnanimity of
Great Britain was now, as heretofore, fruitless and forlorn.
She had, at this epoch, impressed from the crews of American
merchant vessels, peaceably navigating the high seas, not less
than six thousand mariners who claimed to be citizens of the

---

* See the President's proclamation of the 2d of November, 1810.
† See the act of Congress, passed the 2d of March, 1811.

United States, and who were denied all opportunity to verify their claims. She had seized and confiscated the commercial property of American citizens to an incalculable amount. She had united in the enormities of France to declare a great proportion of the terraqueous globe in a state of blockade, chasing the American merchant flag effectually from the ocean. She had contemptuously disregarded the neutrality of the American territory, and the jurisdiction of the American laws, within the waters and harbors of the United States. She was enjoying the emoluments of a surreptitious trade, stained with every species of fraud and corruption, which gave to the belligerent powers the advantages of peace, while the neutral powers were involved in the evils of war. She had, in short, usurped and exercised, on the water, a tyranny similar to that which her great antagonist had usurped and exercised upon the land. And, amidst all these proofs of ambition and avarice, she demanded that the victims of her usurpations and her violence should revere her as the sole defender of the rights and liberties of mankind.

When, therefore, Great Britain, in manifest violation of her solemn promises, refused to follow the example of France by the repeal of her orders in council, the American government was compelled to contemplate a resort to arms as the only remaining course to be pursued for its honor, its independence, and its safety. Whatever depended upon the United States themselves the United States had performed for the preservation of peace, in resistance of the French decrees as well as of the British orders. What had been required from France in its relation to the neutral character of the United States, France had performed by the revocation of its Berlin and Milan decrees. But what depended upon Great Britain for the purposes of justice in the repeal of her orders in council, was withheld, and new evasions were sought when the old were exhausted. It was at one time alleged that satisfactory proof was not afforded that France had repealed her decrees against the commerce of the United States; as if such proof alone were wanting to insure the performance of the British promise.* At another time it was insisted that the repeal of the French decrees, in their operation against the United States in order to authorize a demand for the performance of the British promise, must be total. applying equally to their internal and their external effects; as if the United States had either the right or the power to impose upon France the law of her domestic institutions.† And it was finally insisted, in a despatch from Lord Castlereagh to the British minister residing at Washington, in the year 1812, which was officially communi-

---

* See the correspondence between Mr. Pinkney and the British government.
† See the letters of Mr. Erskine.

cated to the American government, "that the decrees of Berlin and Milan must not be repealed singly and specially in relation to the United States, but must be repealed, also, as to all other neutral nations; and that in no less extent of a repeal of the French decrees had the British government ever pledged itself to repeal the orders in council;"* as if it were incumbent on the United States not only to assert her own rights, but to become the coadjutor of the British government in a gratuitous assertion of the rights of all other nations.

The Congress of the United States could pause no longer. Under a deep and afflicting sense of the national wrongs and the national resentments, while they "postponed definite measures with respect to France in the expectation that the result of unclosed discussions between the American minister at Paris and the French government would speedily enable them to decide with greater advantage on the course due to the rights, the interests, and the honor of the country,"† they pronounced a deliberate and solemn declaration of war between Great Britain and the United States on the 18th of June, 1812.

But it is in the face of all the facts which have been displayed in the present narrative that the prince regent, by his declaration of January, 1813, describes the United States as the aggressor in the war. If the act of declaring war constitutes in all cases the act of original aggression, the United States must submit to the severity of the reproach; but if the act of declaring war may be more truly considered as the result of long suffering and necessary self-defence, the American government will stand acquitted in the sight of Heaven and of the world. Have the United States, then, enslaved the subjects, confiscated the property, prostrated the commerce, insulted the flag, or violated the territorial sovereignty of Great Britain? No; but in all these respects the United States had suffered for a long period of years previously to the declaration of war the contumely and outrage of the British government. It has been said, too, as an aggravation of the imputed aggression, that the United States chose a period for their declaration of war when Great Britain was struggling for her own existence against a power which threatened to overthrow the independence of all Europe; but it might be more truly said that the United States, not acting upon choice but upon compulsion, delayed the declaration of war until the persecutions of Great Britain had rendered further delay destructive and disgraceful. Great Britain had converted the commercial

---

* See the correspondence between the Secretary of State and Mr. Foster, the British minister, in June, 1812.

† See the President's message of the 1st of June, 1812, and the report of the Committee of Foreign Relations, to whom the message was referred.

scenes of American opulence and prosperity into scenes of comparative poverty and distress; she had brought the existence of the United States as an independent nation into question; and surely it must have been indifferent to the United States whether they ceased to exist as an independent nation by her conduct while she professed friendship or by her conduct when she avowed enmity and revenge. Nor is it true that the existence of Great Britain was in danger at the epoch of the declaration of war. The American government uniformly entertained an opposite opinion; and at all times saw more to apprehend for the United States from her maritime power than from the territorial power of her enemy. The event has justified the opinion and the apprehension. But what the United States asked as essential to their welfare and even as beneficial to the allies of Great Britain in the European war, Great Britain, it is manifest, might have granted without impairing the resources of her own strength or the splendor of her own sovereignty, for her orders in council have been since revoked; not, it is true, as the performance of her promise to follow in this respect the example of France, since she finally rested the obligation of that promise upon a repeal of the French decrees as to all nations, and the repeal was only as to the United States; nor as an act of national justice towards the United States, but simply as an act of domestic policy for the special advantage of her own people.

The British government has also described the war as a war of aggrandizement and conquest on the part of the United States; but where is the foundation for the charge? While the American government employed every means to dissuade the Indians, even those who lived within the territory and were supplied by the bounty of the United States, from taking any part in the war,* the proofs were irresistible that the enemy pursued a very different course,† and that every precaution would be necessary to prevent the effects of an offensive alliance between the British troops and the savages throughout the northern frontier of the United States. The military occupation of Upper Canada was, therefore, deemed indispensable to the safety of that frontier in the earliest movements of the war, independent of all views of extending the territorial boundary of the United States. But when war was declared in resentment for injuries which had been suffered upon the Atlantic, what principle of public law, what modification of civilized warfare, imposed upon the United States the duty of abstaining from the invasion of the Canadas? It

---

* See the proceedings at the councils held with the Indians during the expedition under Brigadier-General Hull, and the talk delivered by the President of the United States to the Six Nations at Washington, on the 8th of April, 1813.

† See the documents laid before Congress on the 13th of June, 1812.

was there alone that the United States could place themselves
upon an equal footing of military force with Great Britain ; and
it was there that they might reasonably encourage the hope of
being able, in the prosecution of a lawful retaliation, "to restrain
the violence of the enemy and to retort upon him the evils of his
own injustice." The proclamations issued by the American commanders on entering Upper Canada have, however, been adduced
by the British negotiators at Ghent as the proofs of a spirit of
ambition and aggrandizement on the part of their government.
In truth, the proclamations were not only unauthorized and disapproved, but were infractions of the positive instructions which
had been given for the conduct of the war in Canada. When
the general commanding the northwestern army of the United
States received, on the 24th of June, 1812, his first authority to
commence offensive operations, he was especially told that " he
must not consider himself authorized to pledge the government
to the inhabitants of Canada further than assurances of protection in their persons, property, and rights." And on the ensuing
1st of August it was emphatically declared to him " that it had
become necessary that he should not lose sight of the instructions
of the 24th of June, as any pledge beyond that was incompatible with the views of the government."* Such was the nature
of the charge of American ambition and aggrandizement, and
such the evidence to support it.

The prince regent has, however, endeavored to add to these
unfounded accusations a stigma at which the pride of the American government revolts. Listening to the fabrications of British
emissaries, gathering scandals from the abuses of a free press,
and misled, perhaps, by the asperities of a party spirit common
to all free governments, he affects to trace the origin of the war
to "a marked partiality in palliating and assisting the aggressive
tyranny of France," and " to the prevalence of such councils as
associated the United States in policy with the government of
that nation."† The conduct of the American government is now
open to every scrutiny, and its vindication is inseparable from a
knowledge of the facts. All the world must be sensible, indeed,
that neither in the general policy of the late ruler of France nor
in his particular treatment of the United States, could there exist
any political or rational foundation for the sympathies and associations, overt or clandestine, which have been rudely and un-
fairly suggested. It is equally obvious that nothing short of the
aggressive tyranny exercised by Great Britain towards the United
States could have counteracted and controlled those tendencies

---

* See the letter from the Secretary of the War Department to Brigadier-General Hull, dated the 24th of June and the 1st of August, 1812.
† See the British declaration of the 10th of January, 1813.

to peace and amity which derived their impulse from natural
and social causes, combining the affections and interests of the
two nations. The American government, faithful to that principle of public law which acknowledges the authority of all governments established *de facto*, and conforming its practice in this
respect to the example of Europe, has never contested the validity
of the governments successively established in France, nor refrained from that intercourse with either of them which the just
interests of the United States required. But the British cabinet
is challenged to produce, from the recesses of its secret or of its
public archives, a single instance of unworthy concession or of
political alliance and combination throughout the intercourse of
the United States with the revolutionary rulers of France. Was
it the influence of French councils that induced the American
government to resist the pretensions of France in 1793, and to
encounter her hostilities in 1798? that led to the ratification of
the British treaty in 1795? to the British negotiation in 1805,
and to the convention with the British minister in 1809? that
dictated the impartial overtures which were made to Great Britain as well as to France during the whole period of the restrictive system? that produced the determination to avoid making
any treaty, even a treaty of commerce, with France until the
outrage of the Rambouillet decree was repaired?* that sanctioned the repeated and urgent efforts of the American government to put an end to the war almost as soon as it was declared?
or that, finally, prompted the explicit communication which, in
pursuance of instructions, was made by the American minister
at St. Petersburg to the court of Russia, stating "that the principal subjects of discussion which had long been subsisting between the United States and France remained unsettled; that
there was no immediate prospect that there would be a satisfactory settlement of them; but that whatever the event in that
respect might be, it was not the intention of the government of
the United States to enter into any more intimate connexions
with France; that the government of the United States did not
anticipate any event whatever that could produce that effect; and
that the American minister was the more happy to find himself
authorized by his government to avow this intention, as different
representations of their views had been widely circulated as well
in Europe as in America."† But, while every act of the American government thus falsifies the charge of a subserviency to

---

* See the instructions from the Secretary of State to the American
minister at Paris, dated the 29th of May, 1813.

† See Mr. Monroe's letter to Mr. Adams, dated the 1st of July, 1812,
and Mr. Adams's letter to Mr. Monroe, dated the 11th of December,
1812.

the policy of France, it may be justly remarked, that of all the governments maintaining a necessary relation and intercourse with that nation from the commencement to the recent termination of the revolutionary establishments, it has happened that the government of the United States has least exhibited marks of condescension and concession to the successive rulers. It is for Great Britain, more particularly as an accuser, to examine and explain the consistency of the reproaches which she has uttered against the United States with the course of her own conduct; with her repeated negotiations during the republican as well as during the imperial sway of France; with her solicitude to make and to propose treaties; with her interchange of commercial benefits so irreconcilable to a state of war; with the almost triumphant entry of a French ambassador into her capital amidst the acclamations of the populace; and with the prosecution instituted, by the orders of the king of Great Britain himself in the highest court of criminal jurisdiction in his kingdom, to punish the printer of a gazette for publishing a libel on the conduct and character of the late ruler of France! Whatever may be the source of these symptoms, however they may indicate a subservient policy, such symptoms have never occurred in the United States throughout the imperial government of France.

The conduct of the United States, from the moment of declaring the war, will serve, as well as their previous conduct, to rescue them from the unjust reproaches of Great Britain. When war was declared, the orders in council had been maintained, with inexorable hostility, until a thousand American vessels and their cargoes had been seized and confiscated under their operation; the British minister at Washington had, with peculiar solemnity, announced that the orders would not be repealed but upon conditions which the American government had not the right nor the power to fulfil; and the European war, which had raged with little intermission for twenty years, threatened an indefinite continuance. Under these circumstances, a repeal of the orders, and a cessation of the injuries which they produced, were events beyond all rational anticipation. It appears, however, that the orders, under the influence of a parliamentary inquiry into their effects upon the trade and manufactures of Great Britain, were provisionally repealed on the 23d of June, 1812, a few days subsequent to the American declaration of war. If this repeal had been made known to the United States before their resort to arms, the repeal would have arrested it; and that cause of war being removed, the other essential cause, the practice of impressment, would have been the subject of renewed negotiation, under the auspicious influence of a partial yet important act of reconciliation. But the declaration of war having announced the practice of impressment as a principal cause, peace could only be the result of an express abandonment of the practice, of a suspension of the practice for the purposes of negotiation, or of a cessation of actual sufferance in consequence of a pacification in Europe, which would deprive Great Britain of every motive for continuing the practice.

Hence, when early intimations were given, from Halifax and from Canada, of a disposition on the part of the local authorities to enter into an armistice, the power of these authorities was so doubtful, the objects of the armistice were so limited, and the immediate advantages of the measure were so entirely on the side of the enemy that the American government could not consistently with its duty embrace the propositions.* But some hope of an amicable adjustment was inspired when a communication was received from Admiral Warren, in September, 1812, stating that he was commanded by his government to propose, on the one hand, "that the government of the United States should instantly recall their letters of marque and reprisal against British ships, together with all orders and instructions for any acts of hostility whatever against the territories of his Majesty or the persons or property of his subjects," and to promise, on the other hand, if the American government acquiesced in the preceding proposition, that instructions should be issued to the British squadrons to discontinue hostilities against the United States and their citizens. This overture, however, was subject to a further qualification, "that should the American government accede to the proposal for terminating hostilities, the British admiral was authorized to arrange with the American government as to the revocation of the laws which interdict the commerce and ships of war of Great Britain from the harbors and waters of the United States; but that in default of such revocation within the reasonable period to be agreed upon, the orders in council would be revived."† The American government at once expressed a disposition to embrace the general proposition for a cessation of hostilities with a view to negotiation; declared that no peace could be durable unless the essential object of impressment was adjusted; and offered as a basis of the adjustment, to prohibit the employment of British subjects in the naval or commercial service of the United States; but, adhering to its determination of obtaining a relief from

---

* See the letters from the Department of State to Mr. Russell, dated 9th and 10th August, 1812, and Mr. Graham's memorandum of a conversation with Mr. Baker, the British Secretary of Legation, inclosed in the last letter. See, also, Mr. Monroe's letter to Mr. Russell, dated the 21st of August, 1812.

† See the letter of Admiral Warren to the Secretary of State, dated at Halifax, the 20th of September, 1812.

actual sufferance, the suspension of the practice of impressment pending the proposed armistice, was deemed a necessary consequence; for "it could not be presumed, while the parties were engaged in a negotiation to adjust amicably this important difference, that the United States would admit the right, or acquiesce in the practice of the opposite party, or that Great Britain would be unwilling to restrain her cruisers from a practice which would have the strongest effect to defeat the negotiation."* So just, so reasonable, so indispensable, a preliminary, without which the citizens of the United States navigating the high seas would not be placed by the armistice on an equal footing with the subjects of Great Britain, Admiral Warren was not authorized to accept; and the effort at an amicable adjustment, through that channel, was necessarily abortive.

But long before the overture of the British admiral was made (a few days, indeed, after the declaration of war), the reluctance with which the United States had resorted to arms was manifested by the steps taken to arrest the progress of hostilities and to hasten a restoration of peace. On the 26th of June, 1812, the American chargé d'affaires at London was instructed to make the proposal of an armistice to the British government, which might lead to an adjustment of all differences, on the single condition, in the event of the orders in council being repealed, that instructions should be issued suspending the practice of impressment during the armistice. This proposal was soon followed by another admitting, instead of positive instructions, an informal understanding between the two governments on the subject.† But both of these proposals were unhappily rejected.‡ And when a third, which seemed to leave no plea for hesitation, as it required no other preliminary than that the American minister at London should find in the British government a sincere disposition to accommodate the difference, relative to impressment, on fair conditions, was evaded, it was obvious that neither a desire of peace, nor a spirit of conciliation, influenced the councils of Great Britain.

Under these circumstances the American government had no choice but to invigorate the war; and yet it has never lost sight of the object of all just wars, a just peace. The emperor of Russia having offered his mediation to accomplish that object, it was instantly and cordially accepted by the American govern-

---

* See the letter of Mr. Monroe to Admiral Warren, dated the 27th of October, 1812.

† See the letters from the Secretary of State to Mr. Russell, dated the 26th of June and 27th of July, 1812.

‡ See the correspondence between Mr. Russell and Lord Castlereagh, dated August and September, 1812, and Mr. Russell's letters to the Secretary of State, dated September, 1812.

ment;* but it was peremptorily rejected by the British government. The emperor, in his benevolence, repeated his invitation: the British government again rejected it. At last, however, Great Britain, sensible of the reproach to which such conduct would expose her throughout Europe, offered to the American government a direct negotiation for peace, and the offer was promptly embraced; with perfect confidence that the British government would be equally prompt in giving effect to its own proposal. But such was not the design, or the course, of that government. The American envoys were immediately appointed, and arrived at Gottenburg, the destined scene of negotiation, on the 11th of April, 1814, as soon as the season admitted. The British government, though regularly informed that no time would be lost on the part of the United States, suspended the appointment of its envoys until the actual arrival of the American envoys should be formally communicated. This pretension, however novel and inauspicious, was not permitted to obstruct the path to peace. The British government next proposed to transfer the negotiation from Gottenburg to Ghent. This change, also, notwithstanding the necessary delay, was allowed. The American envoys, arriving at Ghent on the 24th of June, remained in a mortifying state of suspense and expectation, for the arrival of the British envoys, until the 6th of August. And from the period of opening the negotiations to the date of the last despatch of the 31st of October, it has been seen that the whole of the diplomatic skill of the British government has consisted in consuming time without approaching any conclusion. The pacification of Paris had suddenly and unexpectedly placed at the disposal of the British government a great naval and military force; the pride and passions of the nation were artfully excited against the United States; and a war of desperate and barbarous character was planned at the very moment that the American government, finding its maritime citizens relieved by the course of events from actual sufferance, under the practice of impressment, had authorized its envoys to waive those stipulations upon the subject, which might, otherwise, have been indispensable precautions.

Hitherto the American government has shown the justice of its cause, its respect for the rights of other nations, and its inherent love of peace. But the scenes of the war will, also, exhibit a striking contrast between the conduct of the United States and the conduct of Great Britain. The same insidious policy, which taught the prince regent to describe the American government as the aggressor in the war, has induced the British

---

* See the correspondence between Mr. Monroe and Mr. Daschkoff, in March, 1813.

government (clouding the daylight truth of the transaction) to call the atrocities of the British fleets and armies a retaliation upon the example of the American troops in Canada. The United States tender a solemn appeal to the civilized world against the fabrication of such a charge; and they vouch, in support of their appeal, the known morals, habits, and pursuits of their people; the character of their civil and political institutions; and the whole career of their navy and their army, as humane as it is brave. Upon what pretext did the British admiral, on the 18th of August, 1814, announce his determination "to destroy and lay waste such towns and districts upon the coast as might be found assailable?"* It was the pretext of a request from the governor-general of the Canadas for aid to carry into effect measures of retaliation; while, in fact, the barbarous nature of the war had been deliberately settled and prescribed by the British cabinet. What could have been the foundation of such a request? The outrages and the irregularities which too often occur during a state of national hostilities, in violation of the laws of civilized warfare, are always to be lamented, disavowed, and repaired by a just and honorable government; but if disavowal be made, and if reparation be offered, there is no foundation for retaliatory violence. "Whatever unauthorized irregularity may have been committed by any of the troops of the United States, the American government has been ready, upon principles of sacred and eternal obligation, to disavow, and, as far as it might be practicable, to repair."† In every known instance (and they are few) the offenders have been subjected to the regular investigation of a military tribunal; and an officer, commanding a party of stragglers, who were guilty of unworthy excesses, was immediately dismissed, without the form of a trial, for not preventing those excesses. The destruction of the village of Newark, adjacent to Fort George, on the 10th of December, 1813, was long subsequent to the pillage and conflagration committed on the shores of the Chesapeake, throughout the summer of the same year, and might fairly have been alleged as a retaliation for those outrages; but, in fact, it was justified by the American commander, who ordered it, on the ground that it became necessary to the military operations at that place;‡ while the American government, as soon as it heard of the act, on the 6th of January, 1814, instructed the general commanding the northern

---

* See Admiral Cochrane's letter to Mr. Monroe, dated the 18th of August, 1814, and Mr. Monroe's answer of the 6th Sept. 1814.
† See the letter from the Secretary at War to Brigadier-General M'Lure, dated the 4th of October, 1813.
‡ General M'Lure's letter to the Secretary at War, dated Dec. 10 and 13, 1813.

army, "to disavow the conduct of the officer who committed it; and to transmit to Governor Prevost a copy of the order under color of which that officer had acted."* This disavowal was accordingly communicated; and on the 10th of February, 1814, Governor Prevost answered, "that it had been with great satisfaction he had received the assurance that the perpetration of the burning of the town of Newark was both unauthorized by the American government and abhorrent to every American feeling; that if any outrages had ensued the wanton and unjustifiable destruction of Newark, passing the bounds of just retaliation, they were to be attributed to the influence of irritated passions, on the part of the unfortunate sufferers by that event, which, in a state of active warfare, it has not been possible altogether to restrain; and that it was as little congenial to the disposition of his Majesty's government as it was to that of the government of the United States, deliberately to adopt any plan of policy which had for its object the devastation of private property."† But the disavowal of the American government was not the only expiation of the offence committed by its officer; for the British government assumed the province of redress in the indulgence of its own vengeance. A few days after the burning of Newark, the British and Indian troops crossed the Niagara for this purpose; they surprised and seized Fort Niagara, and put its garrison to the sword; they burnt the villages of Lewistown, Manchester, Tuscarora, Buffalo, and Black Rock; slaughtering and abusing the unarmed inhabitants; until, in short, they had laid waste the whole of the Niagara frontier, levelling every house and every hut, and dispersing, beyond the means of shelter, in the extremity of the winter, the male and the female, the old and the young. Sir George Prevost himself appears to have been sated with the ruin and the havoc which had been thus inflicted. In his proclamation of the 12th of January, 1814, he emphatically declared, that for the burning of Newark "the opportunity of punishment had occurred, and a full measure of retaliation had taken place;" and "that it was not his intention to pursue further a system of warfare so revolting to his own feelings and so little congenial to the British character, unless the future measures of the enemy should compel him again to resort to it."‡ Nay, with his answer to the American general, already mentioned, he transmitted "a copy of that proclamation,

---

* See the letter from the Secretary at War to Major-General Wilkinson, dated the 26th of January, 1814.

† See the letter of Major-General Wilkinson to Sir George Prevost, dated the 28th of January, 1814, and the answer of Sir George Prevost, dated the 10th of February, 1814.

‡ See Sir George Prevost's proclamation, dated at Quebec, the 12th of January, 1814.

as expressive of the determination as to his future line of conduct;" and added, "that he was happy to learn that there was
no probability that any measures on the part of the American
government would oblige him to depart from it."* Where, then,
shall we search for the foundation of the call upon the British
admiral, to aid the governor of Canada in measures of retaliation? Great Britain forgot the principle of retaliation, when her
orders in council were issued against the unoffending neutral, in
resentment of outrages committed by her enemy; and, surely,
she had again forgotten the same principle, when she threatened
an unceasing violation of the laws of civilized warfare, in retaliation for injuries which never existed, or which the American
government had explicitly disavowed, or which had been already
avenged by her own arms, in a manner and a degree cruel and
unparalleled. The American government, after all, has not hesitated to declare, that "for the reparation of injuries, of whatever
nature they may be, not sanctioned by the law of nations, which
the military or naval force of either power might have committed
against the other, it would always be ready to enter into reciprocal arrangements; presuming that the British government would
neither expect nor propose any which were not reciprocal."†

It is now, however, proper to examine the character of the
warfare which Great Britain has waged against the United States.
In Europe it has already been marked, with astonishment and
indignation, as a warfare of the tomahawk, the scalping-knife,
and the torch; as a warfare incompatible with the usages of
civilized nations; as a warfare that, disclaiming all moral influence, inflicts an outrage upon social order, and gives a shock
to the very elements of humanity. All belligerent nations can
form alliances with the savage, the African, and the bloodhound;
but what civilized nation has selected these auxiliaries in its hostilities? It does not require the fleets and armies of Great
Britain to lay waste an open country, to burn unfortified towns
or unprotected villages, nor to plunder the merchant, the farmer,
and the planter, of his stores; these exploits may easily be
achieved by a single cruiser or a petty privateer; but when have
such exploits been performed on the coasts of the continent of
Europe or of the British islands by the naval and military force
of any belligerent power, or when have they been tolerated by
any honorable government, as the predatory enterprise of armed
individuals? Nor is the destruction of the public edifices which

---

* See the letter of Sir George Prevost to General Wilkinson, dated the
10th of February, 1814, and the British general orders of the 22d of
February, 1814.

† See Mr. Monroe's letter to Admiral Cochrane, dated the 6th of September, 1814.

adorn the metropolis of a country, and serve to commemorate the taste and science of the age, beyond the sphere of action of the vilest incendiary as well as of the most triumphant conqueror. It cannot be forgotten, indeed, that in the course of ten years past the capitals of the principal powers of Europe have been conquered and occupied alternately by the victorious armies of each other,* and yet there has been no instance of a conflagration of the palaces, the temples, or the halls of justice. No ; such examples have proceeded from Great Britain alone,—a nation so elevated in its pride, so awful in its power, and so affected in its tenderness for the liberties of mankind ! The charge is severe ; but let the facts be adduced.

1. Great Britain has violated the principles of social law, by insidious attempts to excite the citizens of the United States into acts of contumacy, treason, and revolt against their government. For instance :

No sooner had the American government imposed the restrictive system upon its citizens, to escape from the rage and depredation of the belligerent powers, than the British government, then professing amity towards the United States, issued an order which was, in effect, an invitation to the American citizens to break the laws of their country, under a public promise of British protection and patronage " to all vessels which should engage in an illicit trade, without bearing the customary ship's documents and papers."†

Again : During a period of peace between the United States and Great Britain, in the year 1809, the governor-general of the Canadas employed an agent (who had previously been engaged in a similar service, with the knowledge and approbation of the British cabinet) " on a secret and confidential mission" into the United States, declaring " that there was no doubt that his able execution of such a mission would give him a claim not only on the governor-general but on his Majesty's ministers." The object of the mission was to ascertain whether there existed a disposition in any portion of the citizens " to bring about a separation of the Eastern States from the general Union, and how far, in such an event, they would look up to England for assistance, or be disposed to enter into a connexion with her." The agent was instructed " to insinuate that if any of the citizens should wish to enter into a communication with the British government, through the governor-general, he was authorized to receive such communication, and that he would safely transmit it to the

---

* See Mr. Monroe's letter to Admiral Cochrane, dated the 6th of September, 1814.

† See the instructions to the commanders of British ships of war and privateers, dated the 11th of April, 1808.

governor-general."* He was accredited by a formal instrument, under the seal and signature of the governor-general, to be produced "if he saw good ground for expecting that the doing so might lead to a more confidential communication than he could otherwise look for;" and he was furnished with a cipher "for carrying on the secret correspondence."† The virtue and patriotism of the citizens of the United States were superior to the arts and corruption employed in this secret and confidential mission, if it ever was disclosed to any of them ; and the mission itself terminated as soon as the arrangement with Mr. Erskine was announced.‡ But in the act of recalling the secret emissary, he was informed "that the whole of his letters were transcribing to be sent home, where they could not fail of doing him great credit, and it was hoped they might eventually contribute to his permanent advantage."§ To endeavor to realize that hope, the emissary proceeded to London ; all the circumstances of his mission were made known to the British minister ; his services were approved and acknowledged, and he was sent to Canada for a reward, with a recommendatory letter from Lord Liverpool to Sir George Prevost, "stating his lordship's opinion of the ability and judgment which Mr. Henry had manifested on the occasions mentioned in his memorial (his secret and confidential missions), and of the benefit the public service might derive from his active employment in any public situation in which Sir George Prevost might think proper to place him."‖ The world will judge, upon these facts, and the rejection of a parliamentary call for the production of the papers relating to them, what credit is due to the prince regent's assertion "that Mr. Henry's mission was undertaken without the authority or even knowledge of his Majesty's government." The first mission was certainly known to the British government at the time it occurred, for the secretary of the governor-general expressly states "that the information and political observations heretofore received from Mr. Henry were transmitted by his Excellency to the Secretary of State, who had expressed his particular approbation of them ;"¶ the second mission was approved when it was known ; and it remains for the British government to explain, upon any established prin-

---

* See the letter from Mr. Ryland, the secretary of the governor-general, to Mr. Henry, dated the 26th of January, 1809.
† See the letter of Sir James Craig to Mr. Henry, dated February 6, 1809.
‡ See the same letter, and Mr. Ryland's letter of the 26th of January, 1809.
§ See Mr. Ryland's letter, dated the 26th of June, 1809.
‖ See the letter from Lord Liverpool to Sir George Prevost, dated the 16th of September, 1811.
¶ See Mr. Ryland's letter of the 26th of January, 1809.

ciples of morality and justice, the essential difference between ordering the offensive acts to be done and reaping the fruit of those acts, without either expressly or tacitly condemning them.

Again : These hostile attempts upon the peace and union of the United States, preceding the declaration of war, have been followed by similar machinations subsequent to that event. The governor-general of the Canadas has endeavored occasionally, in his proclamations and general orders, to dissuade the militia of the United States from the performance of the duty which they owed to their injured country ; and the efforts at Quebec and Halifax to kindle the flame of civil war have been as incessant as they have been insidious and abortive. Nay, the governor of the island of Barbadoes, totally forgetful of the boasted article of the British Magna Charta in favor of foreign merchants found within the British dominions upon the breaking out of hostilities, resolved that every American merchant within his jurisdiction at the declaration of war should at once be treated as a prisoner of war, because every citizen of the United States was enrolled in the militia, because the militia of the United States were required to serve their country beyond the limits of the State to which they particularly belonged, and because the militia of " all the States which had acceded to this measure were, in the view of Sir George Beckwith, acting as a French conscription."*

Again: Nor was this course of conduct confined to the colonial authorities. On the 26th of October, 1812, the British government issued an order in council authorizing the governors of the British West India Islands to grant licenses to American vessels for the importation and exportation of certain articles enumerated in the order ; but in the instructions which accompanied the order it was expressly provided that " whatever importations were proposed to be made from the United States of America should be, by licenses, confined to the ports in the Eastern States exclusively, unless there was reason to suppose that the object of the order would not be fulfilled if licenses were not granted for importations from the other ports in the United States."†

The President of the United States has not hesitated to place before the nation, with expressions of a just indignation, " the policy of Great Britain thus proclaimed to the world, introducing into her modes of warfare a system equally distinguished by the deformity of its features and the depravity of its character, and having for its object to dissolve the ties of allegiance and the

---

* See the remarkable state paper issued by Governor Beckwith, at Barbadoes, on the 13th of November, 1812.

† See the proclamation of the governor of Bermuda, dated the 14th of January, 1814, and the instructions from the British Secretary for Foreign Affairs, dated November 9, 1812.

sentiments of loyalty in the adversary nation, and to seduce and separate its component parts the one from the other."*

2. Great Britain has violated the laws of humanity and honor by seeking alliances, in the prosecution of the war, with savages, pirates, and slaves.

The British agency in exciting the Indians at all times to commit hostilities upon the frontier of the United States is too notorious to admit of a direct and general denial. It has sometimes, however, been said that such conduct was unauthorized by the British government; and the prince regent, seizing the single instance of an intimation alleged to be given on the part of Sir James Craig, the governor of the Canadas, that an attack was meditated by the Indians, has affirmed that "the charge of exciting the Indians to offensive measures against the United States was void of foundation; that, before the war began, a policy the most opposite had been uniformly pursued; and that proof of this was tendered by Mr. Foster to the American government."† But is it not known in Europe as well as in America that the British Northwest Company maintain a constant intercourse of trade and council with the Indians; that their interests are often in direct collision with the interests of the inhabitants of the United States, and that by means of the inimical dispositions and the active agencies of the company (seen, understood, and tacitly sanctioned by the local authorities of Canada) all the evils of an Indian war may be shed upon the United States, without the authority of a formal order emanating immediately from the British government? Hence the American government, in answer to the evasive protestations of the British minister residing at Washington, frankly communicated the evidence of British agency which had been received at different periods since the year 1807, and observed "that, whatever may have been the disposition of the British government, the conduct of its subordinate agents had tended to excite the hostility of the Indian tribes towards the United States; and that, in estimating the comparative evidence on the subject, it was impossible not to recollect the communication lately made respecting the conduct of Sir James Craig in another important transaction (the employment of Mr. Henry, as an accredited agent, to alienate and detach the citizens of a particular section of the Union from their

---

* See the message from the President to Congress, dated the 24th of February, 1813.

† See the prince regent's declaration of the 10th of January, 1813. See, also, Mr. Foster's letters to Mr. Monroe, dated the 28th of December, 1811, and the 7th and 8th of June, 1812, and Mr. Monroe's answer, dated the 9th of January, 1812, and the 10th of June, 1812, and the documents which accompanied the correspondence.

government), which, it appeared, was approved by Lord Liverpool."*

The proof, however, that the British agents and military officers were guilty of the charge thus exhibited becomes conclusive when, subsequent to the communication which was made to the British minister, the defeat and flight of General Proctor's army on the   of   placed in the possession of the American commander the correspondence and papers of the British officers. Selected from the documents which were obtained upon that occasion, the contents of a few letters will serve to characterize the whole of the mass. In these letters, written by Mr. M'Kee, the British agent, to Colonel England, the commander of the British troops, superscribed "On his Majesty's service," and dated during the months of July and August, 1794, the period of General Wayne's successful expedition against the Indians, it appears that the scalps taken by the Indians were sent to the British establishment at the rapids of the Miami;† that the hostile operations of the Indians were concerted with the British agents and officers;‡ that when certain tribes of Indians "having completed the belts they carried with scalps and prisoners, and being without provisions resolved on going home, it was lamented that his Majesty's posts would derive no security from the late great influx of Indians into that part of the country should they persist in their resolution of returning so soon;"§ that "the British agents were immediately to hold a council at the Glaze, in order to try if they could prevail on the Lake Indians to remain ; but that without provisions and ammunition being sent to that place it was conceived to be extremely difficult to keep them together;"‖ and that "Colonel England was making great exertions to supply the Indians with provisions."¶ But the language of the correspondence becomes, at length, so plain and direct that it seems impossible to avoid the conclusion of a governmental agency on the part of Great Britain in advising, aiding, and conducting the Indian war while she professed friendship and peace towards the United States. "Scouts are sent," says Mr. M'Kee to Colonel England, "to view the situation of the American army, and *we now muster one thousand Indians.* All the Lake Indians, from Sagana downwards, should not lose one moment in joining their brethren, as every

---

* See Mr. Monroe's letter to Mr. Foster, dated the 10th of June, 1812.
† See the letter from Mr. M'Kee to Colonel England, dated the 2d of July, 1794.
‡ See the letter from the same to the same, dated the 5th of July, 1794.
§ See the same letter.
‖ See the same letter.
¶ See the same letter.

accession of strength is an addition to their spirits."* And again: "I have been employed several days in endeavoring to fix the Indians, who have been driven from their villages and corn-fields, between the fort and the bay. Swan Creek is generally agreed upon, and will be a very convenient place for the delivery of provisions, etc."† Whether, under the various proofs of the British agency in exciting Indian hostilities against the United States in a time of peace, presented in the course of the present narrative, the prince regent's declaration that, "before the war began, a policy the most opposite had been uniformly pursued" by the British government,‡ is to be ascribed to a want of information or a want of candor, the American government is not disposed more particularly to investigate.

But, independent of these causes of just complaint, arising in a time of peace, it will be found that when the war was declared, the alliance of the British government with the Indians was avowed upon principles the most novel, producing consequences the most dreadful. The savages were brought into the war upon the ordinary footing of allies without regard to the inhuman character of their warfare, which neither spares age nor sex, and which is more desperate towards the captive at the stake than even towards the combatant in the field. It seemed to be a stipulation of the compact between the allies that the British might imitate, but should not control, the ferocity of the savages. While the British troops behold, without compunction, the tomahawk and the scalping-knife brandished against prisoners, old men and children, and even against pregnant women, and while they exultingly accept the bloody scalps of the slaughtered Americans,§ the Indian exploits in battle are recounted and applauded by the British general orders. Rank and station are assigned to them in the military movements of the British army, and the unhallowed league was ratified, with appropriate emblems, by intertwining an American scalp with the decorations of the mace, which the commander of the northern army of the United States found in the legislative chamber of York, the capital of Upper Canada.

---

* See the letter from Mr. M'Kee to Colonel England, dated the 13th of August, 1794.

† See the letter from the same to the same, dated the 30th of August, 1794.

‡ See the prince regent's declaration of the 10th of January, 1813.

§ See the letter from the American General Harrison to the British General Proctor. See a letter from the British Major Muir, Indian agent, to Colonel Proctor, dated the 26th of September, 1812, and a letter from Colonel St. George to Colonel Proctor, dated the 28th of October, 1812, found among Colonel Proctor's papers.

In the single scene that succeeded the battle of Frenchtown, near the river Raisin, where the American troops were defeated by the allies, under the command of General Proctor, there will be found concentrated, upon indisputable proof, an illustration of the horrors of the warfare which Great Britain has pursued and still pursues in co-operation with the savages of the South as well as with the savages of the North. The American army capitulated on the 22d of January, 1813; yet, after the faith of the British commander had been pledged in the terms of the capitulation, and while the British officers and soldiers silently and exultingly contemplated the scene, some of the American prisoners of war were tomahawked, some were shot, and some were burnt. Many of the unarmed inhabitants of the Michigan territory were massacred; their property was plundered and their horses were destroyed.* The dead bodies of the mangled Americans were exposed, unburied, to be devoured by dogs and swine, "because, as the British officers declared, the Indians would not permit the interment;"† and some of the Americans who survived the carnage had been extricated from danger only by being purchased at a price, as a part of the booty belonging to the Indians. But, to complete this dreadful view of human depravity and human wretchedness, it is only necessary to add that an American physician, who was despatched with a flag of truce to ascertain the situation of his wounded brethren, and two persons, his companions, were intercepted by the Indians in their humane mission; the privilege of the flag was disregarded by the British officers; the physician, after being wounded, and one of his companions were made prisoners, and the third person of the party was killed.‡

But the savage, who had never known the restraints of civilized life, and the pirate, who had broken the bonds of society, were alike the objects of British conciliation and alliance for the purposes of an unparalleled warfare. A horde of pirates and outlaws had formed a confederacy and establishment on the island of Barrataria, near the mouth of the river Mississippi. Will Europe believe that the commander of the British forces addressed the leader of the confederacy from the neutral territory of Pensacola, "calling upon him, with his brave followers, to enter into the service of Great Britain, in which he should have

---

* See the report of the committee of the House of Representatives on the 31st of July, 1812, and the depositions and documents accompanying it.

† See the official report of Mr. Baker, the agent for the prisoners, to Brigadier-General Winchester, dated the 26th of February, 1813.

‡ In addition to this description of savage warfare under British auspices, see the facts contained in the correspondence between General Harrison and General Drummond.

the rank of captain, promising that lands should be given to them all in proportion to their respective ranks, on a peace taking place, assuring them that their property should be guaranteed and their persons protected, and asking, in return, that they would cease all hostilities against Spain or the allies of Great Britain, and place their ships and vessels under the British commanding officer on the station, until the commander-in-chief's pleasure should be known, with a guarantee of their fair value at all events?"* There wanted only, to exemplify the debasement of such an act, the occurrence that the pirate should spurn the proffered alliance; and, accordingly, Lafitte's answer was indignantly given by a delivery of the letter containing the British proposition to the American governor of Louisiana.

There were other sources, however, of support which Great Britain was prompted by her vengeance to employ in opposition to the plainest dictates of her own colonial policy. The events which have extirpated or dispersed the white population of St. Domingo are in the recollection of all men. Although British humanity might not shrink from the infliction of similar calamities upon the Southern States of America, the danger of that course, either as an incitement to a revolt of the slaves in the British islands or as a cause for retaliation on the part of the United States, ought to have admonished her against its adoption. Yet, in a formal proclamation issued by the commander-in-chief of his Britannic Majesty's squadrons upon the American station, the slaves of the American planters were invited to join the British standard in a covert phraseology that afforded but a slight veil for the real design. Thus Admiral Cochrane, reciting "that it had been represented to him that many persons now resident in the United States had expressed a desire to withdraw therefrom with a view of entering into *his Majesty's service*, or of being received *as free settlers* into some of his Majesty's colonies," proclaimed that "all those who might be disposed to emigrate from the United States would, with their families, be received on board of his Majesty's ships or vessels of war, or at the military posts that might be established upon or near the coast of the United States, when they would have their choice of either entering into his Majesty's sea or land forces, or of being sent *as free settlers* to the British possessions in North America or the West Indies, where they would meet with all due encouragement."† But even the negroes seem, in contempt or disgust,

---

* See the letter addressed by Edward Nichols, lieutenant-colonel commanding his Britannic Majesty's forces in the Floridas, to Monsieur Lafitte, or the commandant at Barrataria, dated the 31st of August, 1814.

† See Admiral Cochrane's proclamation, dated at Bermuda, the 2d of April, 1814.

to have resisted the solicitation; no rebellion or massacre ensued; and the allegation, often repeated, that in relation to those who were seduced or forced from the service of their masters, instances have occurred of some being afterwards transported to the British West India Islands and there sold into slavery for the benefit of the captors, remains without contradiction. So complicated an act of injustice would demand the reprobation of mankind. And let the British government, which professes a just abhorrence of the African slave-trade, which endeavors to impose in that respect restraints upon the domestic policy of France, Spain, and Portugal, answer, if it can, the solemn charge against their faith and their humanity.

3. Great Britain has violated the laws of civilized warfare by plundering private property; by outraging female honor; by burning unprotected cities, towns, villages, and houses; and by laying waste whole districts of an unresisting country.

The menace and the practice of the British naval and military force "to destroy and lay waste such towns and districts upon the American coast as might be found assailable," have been excused upon the pretext of retaliation for the wanton destruction committed by the American army in Upper Canada;"* but the fallacy of the pretext has already been exposed. It will be recollected, however, that the act of burning Newark was instantaneously disavowed by the American government; that it occurred in December, 1813; and that Sir George Prevost himself acknowledged, on the 10th of February, 1814, that the measure of retaliation for all the previously imputed misconduct of the American troops was then full and complete.† Between the month of February, 1814, when that acknowledgment was made, and the month of August, 1814, when the British admiral's denunciation was issued, what are the outrages upon the part of the American troops in Canada to justify a call for retaliation? No; it was the system, not the incident, of the war; and intelligence of the system had been received at Washington from the American agents in Europe, with reference to the operations of Admiral Warren upon the shores of the Chesapeake, long before Admiral Cochrane had succeeded to the command of the British fleet on the American station.

As an appropriate introduction to the kind of war which Great Britain intended to wage against the inhabitants of the United States, transactions occurred in England under the avowed direction of the government itself that could not fail to wound the moral sense of every candid and generous spectator. All the

---

* See Admiral Cochrane's letter to Mr. Monroe, dated August 18, 1814.
† See Sir George Prevost's letter to General Wilkinson, dated the 10th of February, 1814.

officers and mariners of the American merchant ships who, having lost their vessels in other places, had gone to England on the way to America, or who had been employed in British merchant ships but were desirous of returning home, or who had been detained in consequence of the condemnation of their vessels under the British orders in council, or who had arrived in England through any of the other casualties of the seafaring life, were condemned to be treated as prisoners of war; nay, some of them were actually impressed while soliciting their passports, although not one of their number had been in any way engaged in hostilities against Great Britain, and although the American government had afforded every facility to the departure of the same class, as well as of every other class, of British subjects from the United States for a reasonable period after the declaration of war.* But this act of injustice, for which even the pretext of retaliation has not been advanced, was accompanied by another of still greater cruelty and oppression. The American seamen who had been enlisted or impressed into the naval service of Great Britain were long retained, and many of them are yet retained, on board of British ships of war, where they are compelled to combat against their country and their friends; and even when the British government tardily and reluctantly recognized the citizenship of impressed Americans to a number exceeding one thousand at a single naval station, and dismissed them from its service on the water, it was only to immure them as prisoners of war on the shore. These unfortunate persons, who had passed into the power of the British government by a violation of their own rights and inclinations as well as of the rights of their country, and who could only be regarded as the spoils of unlawful violence, were nevertheless treated as the fruits of lawful war. Such was the indemnification which Great Britain offered for the wrongs that she had inflicted, and such the reward which she bestowed for services that she had received.†

Nor has the spirit of British warfare been confined to violations of the usages of civilized nations in relation to the United States. The system of blockade, by orders in council, has been revived, and the American coast from Maine to Louisiana has been declared by the proclamation of a British admiral to be in a state of blockade, which every day's observation proves to be practically ineffectual, and which, indeed, the whole of the British

---

* See Mr. Beasley's correspondence with the British government, in October, November, and December, 1812. See, also, the act of Congress, passed the 6th of July, 1812.

† See the letter from Mr. Beasley to Mr. M'Leny, dated the 13th of March, 1815.

navy would be unable to enforce and maintain.* Neither the orders in council, acknowledged to be generally unlawful and declared to be merely retaliatory upon France, nor the Berlin and Milan decrees, which placed the British islands in a state of blockade without the force of a single squadron to maintain it, were in principle more injurious to the rights of neutral commerce than the existing blockade of the United States. The revival, therefore, of the system, without the retaliatory pretext, must demonstrate to the world a determination on the part of Great Britain to acquire a commercial monopoly by every demonstration of her naval power. The trade of the United States with Russia and with other northern powers, by whose governments no edicts violating neutral rights had been issued, was cut off by the operation of the British orders in council of the year 1807 as effectually as their trade with France and her allies, although the retaliatory principle was totally inapplicable to the case. And the blockade of the year 1814 is an attempt to destroy the trade of those nations, and, indeed, of all the other nations of Europe, with the United States; while Great Britain herself, with the same policy and ardor that marked her illicit trade with France when France was her enemy, encourages a clandestine traffic between her subjects and the American citizens wherever her possessions come in contact with the territory of the United States.

But approaching nearer to the scenes of plunder and violence, of cruelty and conflagration, which the British warfare exhibits on the coast of the United States, it must be again asked, what acts of the American government, of its ships of war, or of its armies had occurred or were even alleged as a pretext for the perpetration of this series of outrages? It will not be asserted that they were sanctioned by the usages of modern war, because the sense of all Europe would revolt at the assertion. It will not be said that they were the unauthorized excesses of the British troops, because scarcely an act of plunder and violence, of cruelty and conflagration, has been committed except in the immediate presence, under the positive orders, and with the personal agency, of British officers. It must not be again insinuated that they were provoked by the American example, because it has been demonstrated that all such insinuations are without color and without proof. And, after all, the dreadful and disgraceful progress of the British arms will be traced as the effect of that animosity arising out of recollections connected with the American Revolution, which has already been noticed, or as the effect of that jealousy which the commercial enterprise and native

---

* See the successive blockades announced by the British government and the successive naval commanders on the American station.

resources of the United States are calculated to excite in the councils of a nation aiming at universal dominion upon the ocean.

In the month of April, 1813, the inhabitants of Poplar Island, in the bay of Chesapeake, were pillaged, and the cattle and other live stock of the farmers, beyond what the enemy could remove, were wantonly killed *

In the same month of April, the wharf, the stores, and the fishery at Frenchtown Landing were destroyed, and the private stores and storehouses in the village of Frenchtown were burnt.†

In the same month of April, the enemy landed repeatedly on Sharp's Island, and made a general sweep of the stock, affecting, however, to pay for a part of it.‡

On the 3d of May, 1813, the town of Havre de Grace was pillaged and burnt by a force under the command of Admiral Cockburn. The British officers being admonished "that with civilized nations at war, private property had always been respected," hastily replied, "that, as the Americans wanted war, they should now feel its effects; and that the town should be laid in ashes." They broke the windows of the church, they purloined the houses of the furniture, they stripped women and children of their clothes; and when an unfortunate female complained that she could not leave her house with her little children, she was unfeelingly told "that her house should be burnt with herself and her children in it."§

On the 6th of May, 1813, Fredericktown and Georgetown, situated on Sassafras River, in the State of Maryland, were pillaged and burnt, and the adjacent country was laid waste by a force under the command of Admiral Cockburn; and the officers were the most active on the occasion.‖

On the 22d of June, 1813, the British forces made an attack upon Craney Island, with a view to obtain possession of Norfolk, which the commanding officers had promised, in case of success, to give up to the plunder of the troops.¶ The British were repulsed; but, enraged by defeat and disappointment, their course was directed to Hampton, which they entered on the   of June. The scene that ensued exceeds all power of description; and a detail of facts would be offensive to the feelings of decorum as

---

* See the deposition of William Sears.

† See the depositions of Frisby Anderson and Cordelia Pennington.

‡ See Jacob Gibson's deposition.

§ See the depositions of William T. Killpatrick, James Wood, Rosanna Moore, and R. Mansfield.

‖ See the depositions of John Stavely, William Spencer, Joshua Ward, James Scanlan, Richard Barnaby, F. B. Chandlear, Jonathan Greenwood, John Allen, T. Robertson, M. N. Cannon, and J. T. Vearey.

¶ See General Taylor's letter to the Secretary at War, dated the 2d of July, 1813.

well as of humanity. " A defenceless and unresisting town was given up to indiscriminate pillage, though civilized war tolerates this only as to fortified places carried by assault, and after summons. Individuals, male and·female, were stripped naked; a sick man was stabbed twice in the hospital; another sick man was shot in his bed and in the arms of his wife, who was also wounded, long after the retreat of the American troops; and females—the married and the single—suffered the extremity of personal abuse from the troops of the enemy and from the infatuated negroes, at their instigation."* The fact that these atrocities were committed, the commander of the British fleet, Admiral Warren, and the commander of the British troops, Sir Sidney Beckwith, admitted without hesitation;† but they resorted, as on other occasions, to the unworthy and unavailing pretext of a justifiable retaliation. It was said by the British general "that the excesses at Hampton were occasioned by an occurrence at the recent attempt upon Craney Island, when the British troops, in a barge sunk by the American guns, clung to the wreck of the boat; but several Americans waded off from the island, fired upon, and shot these men." The truth of this assertion was denied; the act, if it had been perpetrated by the American troops, was promptly disavowed by their commander; and a board of officers appointed to investigate the facts after stating the evidence, reported " an unbiased opinion, that the charge against the American troops was unsupported; and that the character of the American soldiery for humanity and magnanimity had not been committed, but, on the contrary, confirmed."‡ The result of this inquiry was communicated to the British general; reparation was demanded; but it was soon perceived that, whatever might personally be the liberal dispositions of that officer, no adequate reparation could be made, as the conduct of his troops was directed and sanctioned by his government.§

---

* See the letters from General Taylor to Admiral Warren, dated the 29th of June, 1813; to General Sir Sidney Beckwith, dated the 4th and 5th of July, 1813; to the Secretary of War, dated the 2d of July, 1813; and to Captain Myers, of the last date. See, also, the letter from Major Crutchfield to Governor Barbour, dated the 20th of June, 1813; the letters from Captain Cooper to Lieutenant-Governor Mallory, dated in July, 1813; the report of Messrs. Griffin and Lively to Major Crutchfield, dated the 4th of July, 1813; and Colonel Parker's publication in the "Enquirer."

† See Admiral Warren's letter to General Taylor, dated the 29th of June, 1813; Sir Sidney Beckwith's letter to General Taylor, dated the same day; and the report of Captain Myers to General Taylor, of July 2, 1813.

‡ See the report of the proceedings of the board of officers appointed by the general order of the 1st of July, 1818.

§ See General Taylor's letter to Sir Sidney Beckwith, dated the 5th of July, 1813; and the answer of the following day.

During the period of these transactions the village of Lewistown, near the capes of the Delaware, inhabited chiefly by fishermen and pilots, and the village of Stonington, seated upon the shores of Connecticut, were unsuccessfully bombarded. Armed parties, led by officers of rank, landed daily from the British squadron, making predatory incursions into the open country, rifling and burning the houses and cottages of peaceable and retired families, pillaging the produce of the planter and the farmer (their tobacco, their grain, and their cattle); committing violence on the persons of the unprotected inhabitants, seizing upon slaves, wherever they could be found, as booty of war; and breaking open the coffins of the dead in search of plunder, or committing robbery on the altars of a church at Chaptico, St. Inagoes, and Tappahannock with a sacrilegious rage.

But the consummation of British outrage yet remains to be stated, from the awful and imperishable memorials of the capitol at Washington. It has been already observed that the massacre of the American prisoners at the river Raisin occurred in January, 1813; that throughout the same year the desolating warfare of Great Britain, without once alleging a retaliatory excuse, made the shores of the Chesapeake, and of its tributary rivers, a general scene of ruin and distress; and that, in the month of February, 1814, Sir George Prevost himself acknowledged that the measures of retaliation, for the unauthorized burning of Newark, in December, 1813, and for all the excesses which had been imputed to the American army, was at that time full and complete. The United States, indeed, regarding what was due to their own character, rather than what was due to the conduct of their enemy, had forborne to authorize a just retribution; and even disdained to place the destruction of Newark to retaliatory account for the general pillage and conflagration which had been previously perpetrated. It was not without astonishment, therefore, that, after more than a year of patient suffering, they heard it announced in August, 1814, that the towns and districts upon their coast were to be destroyed and laid waste in revenge for unspecified and unknown acts of destruction which were charged against the American troops in Upper Canada. The letter of Admiral Cochrane was dated on the 18th, but it was not received until the 31st of August, 1814. In the intermediate time, the enemy debarked a body of about five or six thousand troops at Benedict, on the Patuxent, and, by a sudden and steady march through Bladensburg, approached the city of Washington. This city has been selected for the seat of the American government; but the number of its houses does not exceed nine hundred, spread over an extensive site; the whole number of its inhabitants does not exceed eight thousand; and the adjacent country is thinly populated. Although the necessary precautions had been ordered, to assemble the militia for the defence of the city, a variety of causes combined to render the defence unsuccessful; and the enemy took possession of Washington on the evening of the 24th of August, 1814. The commanders of the British force held, at that time, Admiral Cochrane's desolating order, although it was then unknown to the government and the people of the United States; but conscious of the danger of so distant a separation from the British fleet, and desirous by every plausible artifice to deter the citizens from flying to arms against the invaders, they disavowed all design of injuring private persons and property, and gave assurances of protection wherever there was submission. General Ross and Admiral Cockburn then proceeded in person to direct and superintend the business of conflagration, in a place which had yielded to their arms, which was unfortified, and by which no hostility was threatened. They set fire to the capitol, within whose walls were contained the halls of the Congress of the United States, the hall of their highest tribunal for the administration of justice, the archives of the legislature, and the national library. They set fire to the edifice which the United States had erected for the residence of their chief magistrate. And they set fire to the costly and extensive buildings erected for the accommodation of the principal officers of the government in the transaction of the public business. These magnificent monuments of the progress of the arts, which America had borrowed from her parent, Europe, with all the testimonials of taste and literature which they contained, were, on the memorable night of the 24th of August, consigned to the flames, while British officers of high rank and command united with their troops in riotous carousals by the light of the burning pile.

But the character of the incendiary had so entirely superseded the character of the soldier, on this unparalleled expedition, that a great portion of the munitions of war, which had not been consumed when the navy-yard was ordered to be destroyed upon the approach of the British troops, were left untouched; and an extensive foundry of cannon, adjoining the city of Washington, was left uninjured; when, in the night of the 25th of August, the army suddenly decamped, and returning with evident marks of precipitation and alarm to their ships, left the interment of their dead and the care of their wounded to the enemy, whom they had thus injured and insulted in violation of the laws of civilized war.

The counterpart to the scene exhibited by the British army was next exhibited by the British navy. Soon after the midnight flight of General Ross from Washington, a squadron of British ships of war ascended the Potomac, and reached the town of Alexandria on the 27th of August, 1814. The magistrates, presuming that the general destruction of the town was intended, asked on what terms it might be saved. The naval commander declared "that the only conditions in his power to offer were such as not only required a surrender of all naval and ordnance stores (public and private), but of all the shipping, and of all the merchandise in the city, as well as such as had been removed since the 19th of August." The conditions, therefore, amounted to the entire plunder of Alexandria, an unfortified and unresisting town, in order to save the buildings from destruction. The capitulation was made, and the enemy bore away the fruits of his predatory enterprise in triumph.

But even while this narrative is passing from the press, a new retaliatory pretext has been formed to cover the disgrace of the scene which was transacted at Washington. In the address of the governor-in-chief to the provincial parliament of Canada, on the 24th of January, 1815, it is asserted, in ambiguous language, "that as a just retribution, the proud capitol at Washington has experienced a similar fate to that inflicted by an American force *on the seat of government* in Upper Canada." The town of York, in Upper Canada, was taken by the American army, under the command of General Dearborn, on the 27th of April, 1813,* and it was evacuated on the succeeding 1st of May, although it was again visited for a day by an American squadron, under the command of Commodore Chauncy, on the 4th of August.† At the time of the capture, the enemy, on his retreat, set fire to his magazine, and the injury produced by the explosion was great and extensive; but neither then nor on the visit of Commodore Chauncy, was any edifice which had been erected for civil uses destroyed by the authority of the military or the naval commander; and the destruction of such edifices by any part of their force would have been a direct violation of the positive orders which they had issued. On both occasions, indeed, the public stores of the enemy were authorized to be seized, and his public storehouses to be burnt; but it is known that private persons, houses, and property were left uninjured. If, therefore, Sir George Prevost deems such acts inflicted on "the seat of government in Upper Canada" similar to the acts which were perpetrated at Washington, he has yet to perform the task of tracing the features of similarity; since at Washington, the public edifices which had been erected for civil uses were alone destroyed, while the munitions of war and the foundries of cannon remained untouched.

---

* See the letters from General Dearborn to the Secretary of War, dated the 27th and 28th of April, 1813.

† See the letter from Commodore Chauncy to the Secretary of the Navy, dated the 4th of August, 1813.

If, however, it be meant to affirm that the public edifices, occupied by the legislature, by the chief magistrate, by the courts of justice, and by the civil functionaries of the province of Upper Canada, with the provincial library, were destroyed by the American force, it is an occurrence which has never been before presented to the view of the American government by its own officers, as matter of information, nor by any of the military or civil authorities of Canada, as matter of complaint; it is an occurrence which no American commander had in any degree authorized or approved, and it is an occurrence which the American government would have censured and repaired with equal promptitude and liberality.

But a tale told thus out of date, for a special purpose, cannot command the confidence of the intelligent and the candid auditor, for even if the fact of conflagration be true, suspicion must attend the cause for so long a concealment with motives so strong for an immediate disclosure. When Sir George Prevost, in February, 1814, acknowledged that the measure of retaliation was full and complete for all the preceding misconduct imputed to the American troops, was he not apprised of every fact which had occurred at York, the capital of Upper Canada, in the months of April and August, 1813? Yet, neither then, n,or at any antecedent period, nor until the 24th of January, 1815 was the slightest intimation given of the retaliatory pretext which is now offered. When the admirals Warren and Cochrane were employed in pillaging and burning the villages on the shores of the Chesapeake, were not all the retaliatory pretexts for the barbarous warfare known to those commanders? And yet "the fate inflicted by an American force on the seat of government in Upper Canada" was never suggested in justification or excuse? And finally, when the expedition was formed in August, 1814, for the destruction of the public edifices at Washington, was not the "similar fate which had been inflicted by an American force on the seat of government in Upper Canada" known to Admiral Cochrane as well as to Sir George Prevost, who called upon the admiral (it is alleged) to carry into effect measures of retaliation against the inhabitants of the United States? And yet both the call and the compliance are founded (not upon the destruction of the public edifices at York, but) upon the wanton destruction committed by the American army in Upper Canada upon the inhabitants of the province, for whom alone reparation was demanded.

An obscurity, then, dwells upon the fact alleged by Sir George Prevost which has not been dissipated by inquiry. Whether any public edifice was improperly destroyed at York, or at what period the injury was done, if done at all, and by what hand it was inflicted, are points that ought to have been stated when the charge was made; surely it is enough, on the part of the American government, to repeat that the fact alleged was never before brought to its knowledge for investigation, disavowal, or reparation. The silence of the military and civil officers of the provincial government of Canada indicates, too, a sense of shame, or a conviction of the injustice of the present reproach. It is known that there could have been no other public edifice for civil uses destroyed in Upper Canada than the house of the provincial legislature, a building of so little cost and ornament as hardly to merit consideration, and certainly affording neither parallel nor apology for the conflagration of the splendid structures which adorned the metropolis of the United States. If, however, that house was indeed destroyed, may it not have been an accidental consequence of the confusion in which the explosion of the magazine involved the town? Or perhaps it was hastily perpetrated by some of the enraged troops in the moment of anguish for the loss of a beloved commander and their companions, who had been killed by that explosion, kindled, as it was, by a defeated enemy, for the sanguinary and unavailing purpose. Or, in fine, some suffering individual, remembering the slaughter of his brethren at the river Raisin, and exasperated by the spectacle of a human scalp, suspended in the legislative chamber, over the seat of the speaker, may, in the paroxysm of his vengeance, have applied, unauthorized and unseen, the torch of vengeance and destruction.

Many other flagrant instances of British violence, pillage, and conflagration, in defiance of the laws of civilized hostilities, might be added to the catalogue which has been exhibited; but the enumeration would be superfluous, and it is time to close so painful an exposition of the causes and character of the war. The exposition had become necessary to repel and refute the charges of the prince regent, when, by his declaration of January, 1813, he unjustly states the United States to be the aggressors in the war, and insultingly ascribes the conduct of the American government to the influence of French councils. It was also necessary to vindicate the course of the United States in the prosecution of the war, and to expose to the view of the world the barbarous system of hostilities which the British government has pursued. Having accomplished these purposes, the American government recurs with pleasure to a contemplation of its early and continued efforts for the restoration of peace. Notwithstanding the pressure of the recent wrongs, and the unfriendly and illiberal disposition which Great Britain has at all times manifested towards them, the United States have never indulged sentiments incompatible with the reciprocity of good will and an intercourse of mutual benefit and advantage. They can never repine at seeing the British nation great, prosperous,

and happy, safe in its maritime rights, and powerful in its means
of maintaining them; but, at the same time, they can never
cease to desire that the councils of Great Britain should be
guided by justice and a respect for the equal rights of other
nations. Her maritime power may extend to all the legitimate
objects of her sovereignty and her commerce, without endangering the independence and peace of every other government. A
balance of power, in this respect, is as necessary on the ocean
as on the land; and the control that it gives to the nations of the
world over the actions of each other, is as salutary in its operation to the individual government which feels it as to all the
governments by which, on the just principles of mutual support
and defence, it may be exercised. On fair and equal and honorable terms, therefore, peace is at the choice of Great Britain;
but if she still determine upon war, the United States, reposing
upon the justness of their cause, upon the patriotism of their
citizens, upon the distinguished valor of their land and naval
forces, and, above all, upon the dispensations of a beneficent
Providence, are ready to maintain the contest for the preservation of the national independence with the same energy and fortitude which were displayed in acquiring it.

Washington, February 10, 1815.

No. 6.

ORGANIZATION OF THE MILITARY PEACE ESTAB-
LISHMENT OF THE UNITED STATES.

Department of War, May 17th, 1815.

The act of Congress of the 3d of March, 1815, declares "that
the military peace establishment of the United States shall
consist of such proportions of artillery, infantry, and riflemen,
not exceeding, in the whole, ten thousand men, as the President
of the United States shall judge proper; that the corps of engineers, as at present established, be retained; and that the President of the United States cause to be arranged the officers, non-
commissioned officers, musicians, and privates of the several
corps of troops in the service of the United States, in such
manner as to form and complete out of the same the corps authorized by this act; and that he cause the supernumerary officers,
non-commissioned officers, musicians, and privates to be discharged from the service of the United States, from and after the
first day of May next, or as soon as circumstances may permit."

The President of the United States, having performed the duty which the law assigned to him, has directed that the organization of the military peace establishment be announced in general orders; and that the supernumerary officers, non-commissioned officers, musicians, and privates be discharged from the service of the United States, as soon as the circumstances which are necessary for the payment and discharge of the troops will permit.

But on this important and interesting occasion, the President of the United States is aware that he owes to the feelings of the nation, as well as to his own feelings, an expression of the high sense entertained of the services of the American army. Leaving the scenes of private life, the citizens became the soldiers of the United States; the spirit of a genuine patriotism quickly pervaded the military establishment; and the events of the war have conspicuously developed the moral as well as the physical character of an army, in which every man seems to have deemed himself the chosen champion of his country.

The pacific policy of the American government, the domestic habits of the people, and a long sequestration from the use of arms will justly account for the want of warlike preparation, for an imperfect state of discipline, and for various other sources of embarrassment or disaster which existed at the commencement of hostilities; but to account for the achievements of the American army in all their splendor, and for its efficient acquirements in every important branch of the military art during a war of little more than two years' continuance, it is necessary to resort to that principle of action which, in a free country, identifies the citizen with his government, impels each individual to seek the knowledge that is requisite for the performance of his duty, and renders every soldier in effect a combatant in his own cause.

The President of the United States anticipated from the career of an army thus constituted all the glory and the fruits of victory; and it has been his happiness to see a just war terminated by an honorable peace, after such demonstrations of valor, genius, and enterprise as secure for the land and naval forces of the United States an imperishable renown; for the citizens the best prospect of an undisturbed enjoyment of their rights; and for the government the respect and confidence of the world.

To the American army, which has so nobly contributed to these results, the President of the United States presents this public testimonial of approbation and applause, at the moment when many of its gallant officers and men must unavoidably be separated from the standard of their country. Under all governments, and especially under all free governments, the restoration of peace has uniformly produced a reduction of the military establishment. The United States disbanded, in 1800, the troops which had been raised on account of the differences with France, and the memorable peace of 1783 was followed by a discharge of the illustrious Army of the Revolution. The frequency or the necessity of the occurrence does not, however, deprive it of its interest; and the dispersion of the military family at this juncture, under circumstances peculiarly affecting, cannot fail to awaken all the sympathies of the generous and the just.

The difficulty of accomplishing a satisfactory organization of the military peace establishment has been anxiously felt. The act of Congress contemplates a small but an effective force, and, consequently, the honorable men, whose years or infirmities or wounds render them incapable of further service in active warfare, are necessarily excluded from the establishment. The act contemplates a reduction of the army from many to a few regiments, and, consequently, a long list of meritorious officers must inevitably be laid aside. But the attempt has been assiduously made to collect authentic information from every source as a foundation for an impartial judgment on the various claims to attention; and, even while a decision is pronounced, the President of the United States desires it may be distinctly understood, that from the designation of the officers who are retained in service, nothing more is to be inferred than his approbation of the designated individuals, without derogating in any degree from the fame and worth of those whose lot it is to retire.

The American army of the war of 1812 has hitherto successfully emulated the patriotism and the valor of the army of the war of 1776. The closing scene of the example remains alone to be performed. Having established the independence of their country, the Revolutionary warriors cheerfully returned to the walks of civil life; many of them became the benefactors and ornaments of society in the prosecution of various arts and professions; and all of them, as well as the veteran few who survive the lapse of time, have been the objects of grateful recollection and of constant regard. It is for the American army now dissolved to pursue the same honorable course, in order to enjoy the same inestimable reward. The hope may be respectfully indulged that the beneficence of the legislative authority will beam upon suffering merit; an admiring nation will unite the civic with the martial honors which adorn its heroes, and posterity, in its theme of gratitude, will indiscriminately praise the protectors and the founders of American independence.

By order of the President of the United States.

A. J. DALLAS,
Acting Secretary of War.

DEPARTMENT OF WAR, 8th of April, 1815.

GENTLEMEN,— The President of the United States has requested your attendance at Washington with a view to the aid which your experience and information enable you to afford, in forming the military peace establishment, according to the directions of the act of Congress passed on the 3d of March, 1815. I have the honor, therefore, of calling your attention to this interesting and important business; and to request an early report upon the following points, premising that your report will be considered as an authentic source of information, to which a just respect will be paid in all future deliberations upon the subject:

    1. The organization of the army.
    2. The selection of the officers.
    3. The military stations.

I. *The Organization of the Army.*

The act of Congress declares that the military peace establishment of the United States shall consist of proportions of artillery, infantry, and riflemen, not exceeding in the whole ten thousand men; and that the corps of engineers as at present established be retained.

Upon full consideration of the terms of the act and of the military interpretation given to similar terms on other occasions, the President is of opinion that the military peace establishment, so far as it is composed of artillery, infantry, and riflemen, is to consist of the number of ten thousand men, exclusively of officers, non-commissioned officers, and musicians; and you will be pleased to conform in your report to that opinion.

The proportions of artillery, infantry, and riflemen to compose the military peace establishment of ten thousand men are referred to your consideration; and you will be pleased in your report to furnish the necessary details for forming the establishment into brigades, regiments, battalions, and companies. But it is proper to observe that special provision is made by law for the organization of the corps of artillery as prescribed in the act of the 30th of March, 1814; for the organization of the regiment of light artillery as prescribed in the act of the 12th of April, 1808; and for the organization of the regiments of infantry and riflemen as prescribed in the act of the 3d of March, 1815.

The law has also specially provided that there shall be four brigade inspectors, four brigade quartermasters, and such number of hospital surgeons and surgeons' mates as the service may require,—not exceeding five surgeons and fifteen mates,—with one steward and one wardmaster, to each hospital. But the brigade inspectors are to be taken from the line, and the brigade quartermasters, as well as adjutants, regimental quartermasters, and paymasters, are to be taken from the subalterns of the line.

II. *The Selection of the Officers.*

The reduction of the military establishment to the number of ten thousand men indicates the intention of Congress to be, that the officers, non-commissioned officers, and privates should be selected and arranged in such a manner as to form and complete an effective corps. It is, undoubtedly, a painful task to make a discrimination which affects the interest and possibly the subsistence of honorable men whose misfortune it is by age, by infirmities, or by wounds to be disabled from rendering further service to their country ; but the task must be performed by those who are charged with the execution of the law, leaving the relief which may be justly claimed by suffering merit to the beneficent care of the legislative authority.

It is the opinion of the President, therefore, that in the selection of the officers to be retained upon the military peace establishment, those only should be recommended in your report for his approbation who are at this time competent to engage an enemy in the field of battle.

The number of field officers now in service amounts to two hundred and sixteen, and the number of regimental officers now in service amounts to two thousand and fifty-five. Of the former about thirty-nine, and of the latter about four hundred and fifty, can be retained in service according to the provisions of the act of Congress for fixing the military peace establishment. In every grade of appointment almost every officer has gallantly performed his duty. It is obvious, therefore, that with respect to the field officers and the regimental officers, as well as with respect to the general officers, men of high military merit must unavoidably be omitted in the present organization of the army. It has not been, and it never can be, under such circumstances, a mark of disrespect or a subject of reproach to omit the name of any officer ; and the President wishes it may be distinctly understood that from the selection of officers nothing more ought to be inferred than his approbation of the selected individuals, without derogating in any degree from the reputation and worth of others.

It is the President's desire upon this important point that distinguished military merit and approved moral character should form the basis of all the selections which your report shall submit to his consideration. Where, in these respects, the claims of officers are equal, length of service, a capacity for civil pursuits, and the pecuniary situation of the parties may justly furnish considerations to settle the question. And where neither direct nor collateral circumstances exist by which your judgment can be fixed, you will find a reasonable satisfaction, perhaps, in referring the decision in this case, as is done in many similar cases, to the chance of a lottery ; or you may submit a recommendatory list, leaving the selection entirely to the executive. Great pains have been taken to collect and preserve the testimonials of military merit; and these, with all the other documents of the department which can assist your inquiries, will be confidentially placed before you. It is not doubted, therefore, that your report will be as advantageous to the government as it will be just to the army. A result at once impartial and effective will not only correspond with the President's views, but must command the approbation of every honorable mind; and it is, in particular, believed that an appeal may be confidently made in the performance of so arduous a duty to the candor of your military brethren, whatever may be their personal disappointment or regret.

III. *The Military Stations.*

The general division of the United States into a department of the north and a department of the south, with a subdivision into convenient districts, including in each department a major-general, two brigadier-generals, and a proper proportion of the army, will probably be attended with practical advantages, and it is therefore referred to your consideration.

The assignment of a competent garrison to the existing forts and military stations, and an apportionment of the troops to the districts according to the service which may be required, will engage your particular attention. But it has been suggested that some of the regiments have obtained a local character from the residence of the officers, the enlistment of the men, and the scene of service during the war. If, therefore, you should deem it practicable and useful both in the selection of officers and in the assignment of stations to the troops, to regard that character of locality, you will be pleased to report accordingly.

There are other important subjects connected with the execution of the act of Congress of the 3d of March, 1815, which I may hereafter have occasion to lay before you; but the points of this communication being of immediate urgency, I shall at present close the general views which I have taken of them with an assurance that you may command all the information and assistance that it is in my power to give.

I have the honor to be, very respectfully, gentlemen, your most obedient servant,

A. J. DALLAS, *Acting Secretary of War.*

Major-Generals BROWN, JACKSON, SCOTT, GAINES, MACOMB, and RIPLEY.

DEPARTMENT OF WAR. April 17, 1815.

GENTLEMEN,—I proceed to state some additional views connected with the execution of the act of Congress fixing the military peace establishment.

I. Corps belonging to the army which are not expressly retained by the provisions of the act are to be discharged.

The corps expressly provided for are :

1. The corps of artillery.
2. The regiment of light artillery.
3. The corps of engineers.
4. Regiments of infantry and riflemen.

The corps not provided for are :

1. The regiment of light dragoons.
2. The Canadian volunteers.
3. The sea fencibles.

II. The officers of the general staff employed in the command, discipline, and duties of the army who are not expressly retained by the provisions of the act, are to be discharged.

The officers provided for are :

1. Two major-generals, with two aids-de-camp each.
2. Four brigadier-generals, with one aid-de-camp each.
3. Four brigade inspectors.
4. Four brigade quartermasters.

The officers not provided for are :

1. All the general officers except the six above mentioned.
2. All the officers of the adjutant-general's department.
3. All the officers of the inspector-general's department, four brigade inspectors being substituted.
4. All the officers of the quartermaster's department, four brigade quartermasters being substituted.
5. All the officers of the topographical department.

III. Departments which do not form a constituent part of the army are preserved, except so far as the act of Congress, by express provision or by necessary implication, introduces an alteration.

1. The *Ordnance Department* is preserved. It is a distinct establishment, with a view to a state of peace as well as a state of war. It is not affected by any express provision in the act of Congress, and it is an object of the appropriations made for the military peace establishment.

2. The *Purchasing Department* is preserved for similar reasons.

3. The *Pay Department* is preserved with specific modifications. The act of Congress expressly provides for the appointment of regimental paymasters. The office of district paymaster

and assistant district paymaster is abolished; but the act of the 18th of April, 1814, which continues in force for one year after the war, is not repealed, nor affected in any other manner than has been mentioned by the act of the 3d of March, 1815. It is seen, therefore, that the act of the 16th of March, 1802, fixing the military establishment, constituted the office of paymaster of the army, seven paymasters, and two assistants; and that the act of the 18th of April, 1814, recognizes the office of paymaster of the army, and, in lieu of a monthly compensation, allows the paymaster an annual salary of two thousand dollars, payable quarterly at the treasury. The former act is of indefinite continuance, and the latter will continue in force until the 17th of February, 1816. Nor does the act of the 3d of March, 1815, affect the office of deputy paymaster-general; the act of the 6th of July, 1812, providing that to any army of the United States, other than that in which the paymaster of the army shall serve, the President may appoint one deputy paymaster-general, to be taken from the line of the army, and each deputy shall have a competent number of assistants.

4. The *Office of Judge Advocate* is preserved. The act of the 11th of January, 1812, provides that there shall be appointed to each division a judge advocate. The act of the 3d of March, 1815, neither expressly nor by necessary implication repeals that provision.

5. The *Chaplains* are preserved. The act of the 11th of January, 1812, provides that there shall be appointed to each brigade one chaplain. The act of the 3d of March, 1815, neither expressly nor by necessary implication repeals that provision.

6. The *Hospital Department* is not preserved. The act of the 3d of March, 1815, provides for regimental surgeons and surgeons' mates, and for such number of hospital surgeons and surgeons' mates as the service may require, not exceeding five surgeons and fifteen mates, with one steward and one wardmaster to each hospital. From this specific arrangement it is necessarily implied that the physician and surgeon-general, the assistant apothecaries' general, and all the hospital surgeons and surgeons' mates, except the above specified number, are to be discharged. The physician and surgeon-general and the apothecary-general were appointed the better to superintend the medical and hospital establishment of the army of the United States under the act of the 3d of March, 1813; and the act of the 30th of March, 1814, authorized the President to appoint so many assistant apothecaries as the service might in his judgment require. The occasion for the appointments under both acts has ceased; and the act of the 3d of March, 1815, meant to provide a substitute for the whole department, according to the demands of the peace establishment.

7. The *Military Academy* is preserved. The act of the 3d of March, 1815, provides that the corps of engineers, as at present established, shall be retained. By the act of the 16th of March, 1802, ten cadets were assigned to the corps of engineers; by the act of the 29th of April, 1812, the cadets, whether of artillery, cavalry, riflemen, or infantry, were limited to the number of two hundred and fifty, who might be attached by the President as students to the military academy; but the act of the 3d of March, 1815, declares that the regiment of light artillery shall have the same organization as is prescribed by the act passed the 12th of April, 1808, and by that act two cadets are to be attached to each company. It is therefore to be considered that there are two hundred and fifty cadets attached to the military academy under the establishment of the act of the 29th of April, 1812, and twenty cadets attached to the regiment of light artillery.

Upon this analysis of the act of Congress for fixing the military peace establishment, the President wishes to receive any information which you think will tend to promote the public service in reference to the following inquiries :

1. The best arrangements to adapt to the peace establishment the ordnance department, the purchasing department, the pay department, and the military academy.

2. The arrangements best adapted to render the medical establishment competent to the garrison as well as to the regimental service.

It is obvious that considerable difficulty will arise if the adjutant-general's and the quartermaster-general's departments should be immediately and entirely abolished, and if the garrison surgeons should be immediately discharged. The President is desirous to execute the act of Congress, as far as it is practicable and safe, on the 1st of May next; but he is disposed to take the latitude which the act allows in cases that clearly require a continuance of the offices for the necessary public service. You will be pleased therefore to state,—

1. Whether, in your judgment, the continuance of the office of adjutant and inspector-general is necessary for the public service.

2. Whether, in your judgment, the continuance of any and which of the offices in the quartermaster's department is necessary for the public service.

3. Whether, in your judgment, the continuance of any and which of the offices in the medical department, not expressly provided for by the law, is necessary for the public service.

I have the honor to be, gentlemen, very respectfully, your most obedient servant,

A. J. DALLAS, *Acting Secretary of War.*

Major-Generals BROWN, JACKSON, SCOTT, GAINES, MACOMB, and RIPLEY.

DEPARTMENT OF WAR, 12th of May, 1815.

The Acting Secretary of War has the honor to submit to the President of the United States the following report:

That the act of Congress, entitled "An act fixing the military peace establishment of the United States," passed on the 3d of March, 1815, provided that, after the corps constituting the peace establishment was formed and completed, the supernumerary officers, non-commissioned officers, musicians, and privates should be discharged from the service of the United States from and after the first day of May ensuing the date of the act, or as soon as circumstances might permit. But it was soon found impracticable to obtain from all the military districts the information which was requisite to do justice to the army and to the nation in reducing the military establishment from a force of (sixty?) thousand men to a force of ten thousand men so early as the first of May. And it is obvious that circumstances do not even yet permit the entire reduction contemplated by the act of Congress with regard to the settlement of the numerous accounts depending in the quartermaster, commissary, and pay departments, and the medical care of the troops at the many military stations to which they must be apportioned.

That having, however, diligently collected from every proper source of information the necessary materials for deciding upon the various subjects involved in the execution of the act of Congress, and having obtained from the board of general officers convened at Washington the most valuable assistance, the Acting Secretary of War respectfully lays the result before the President of the United States in the form of four general orders, to be issued from this department:

No. 1. A general order announcing the military divisions and departments of the United States, the corps and regiments constituting the military peace establishment, and the distribution and apportionment of the troops.

No. 2. A general order announcing the army register for the peace establishment, including the officers provisionally retained in service, until circumstances shall permit their discharge.

No. 3. A general order directing the supernumerary officers non-commissioned officers, musicians, and privates to be paid, and discharging them from the service of the United States, on the 15th day of June next, or as soon thereafter as the payment can be completed, provided, 1st, that such officers of every rank as may be necessary to supply vacancies created by resignations on the first organization of the corps and regiments for the peace establishment shall be deemed to be in service for that purpose alone; and 2d, that paymasters, quartermasters, commissaries, and other officers who have been charged with the disbursement of public money, shall be deemed to be in service for the single purpose of rendering their accounts for settlement within a reasonable time.

No. 4. A general order requiring the major-generals to assume the command of their respective divisions, and to proceed to form and distribute the corps and regiments for their respective commands, according to the system announced for the military peace establishment.

All which is respectfully submitted.

A. J. DALLAS, *Acting Secretary of War.*

The President of the United States.

JAMES MADISON.

Approved May 15, 1815.

LETTERS OF MR. STEPHEN DUPONCEAU.

1.

PHILADELPHIA, 23 October, 1814.

DEAR SIR,—Permit me to offer you my most sincere congratulations on the brilliant manner in which you have entered on the duties of your new office. I expected it of you, and my hopes have not been disappointed. Genius is always in its proper place where there are difficulties to overcome and resources to be created. The plan contained in your excellent report does both. As far as I have been able to see, it meets with the approbation of all reflecting men. It is traced with the steadiness of a master's hand. You have probed to the quick the festering wounds of our financial system, and discarding palliatives and nostrums, you have pointed out a severe, but the only remedy, from which success may be reasonably hoped. Your reasoning on the indispensable necessity of adopting the bank system is conclusive, and were the point of constitutionality still doubtful, it must be practically construed. And who can hesitate to adopt that construction which the safety of the state imperiously requires? I hope the subject, after so fatally encountering theoretical difficulties, will not now strike on practical ones. You have a sea full of shoals to steer your bark through, and I trust in the skill of the pilot and in the good sense of the moneyed men of the nation.

25

II.

DEAR SIR,—To the pleasure which I always feel in receiving a letter from you, you have added flattering expressions of esteem which elevate my pride, and a full and satisfactory answer to my little personal requests: so that you have made the favor as complete as it could be. I feel it as I ought, and, "*cum tot sustineas et tanta negotia,*" I shall not expect, nay, as a good patriot, I shall not wish to divert you from the important affairs trusted to your care to advert to my idle correspondence. I shall only not despair that at some of the least busy moments (if such there are) you will recollect that the great Frederick sometimes relaxed his mind by writing to his literary friends.

For my part, if I occasionally address you, it will be principally to remind you of my constant attachment. You are polite enough to ask for my opinions and advice. The latter you do not want, and as for my *opinions*, you must first "commit some faults," and then they will be at your service. A continued strain of approbation would be so much like flattery that it would be as disgusting to you as irksome to me. It will not be, I hope, considered in that light, when I tell you with the greatest truth that the measures of the administration in general, and those which are more peculiarly to be ascribed to you, appear to me to be well adapted to, and commensurate with, the exigencies of the times, and bear that stamp of decision and grandeur which becomes the nation which has honored you with its most important trusts. As to the war and its concerns, you have very properly considered that a powerful enemy is only to be resisted by force, and that force consists of men and money. As to the mere internal concerns of the state, you have also been convinced that the intrigues of faction are to be counteracted only by the exertion of the legal authority, in the form of great and comprehensive measures affecting all the citizens alike, but calculated to operate on the malcontents so as ultimately to defeat their purposes. I therefore wish success to all your plans, convinced as I am that it is by them, and by them only, that the country is to be saved.

You do not expect, I imagine, to find your path strewed with roses. I am told that your bank system is to meet with opposition from a quarter whence it should not be expected. I hope it will not be so, and that the casuists will dispel their ill-timed scruples. Here I have heard of no objections to the plan, except to such of its details as seem most particularly to affect party feelings, such as the nomination by our executive of the president of the institution. Candid Federalists acknowledge that the administration has a right to be represented in the direction, though some have expressed a wish that provision should be made for the case of government parting with all its stock, as it has done once before. Then, say they, the administration, ceasing to be a stockholder, would cease to be entitled to a representation. There are obvious answers to this reasoning, drawn from other parts of the system; but I give you the objection as it is made. The public debt rose some days ago to 80. I have not heard of its having risen since. I believe it is at present at a stand. There will be intrigues, no doubt, to prevent the moneyed men from subscribing, but if I can venture an opinion, a firm and decided perseverance in the plan will defeat them.

In reading over the treaty of Utrecht, I find that France has indirectly acknowledged the territorial jurisdiction, or rather the marine jurisdiction, of England to extend to the distance of thirty leagues from the coast of Nova Scotia for the purpose of the fisheries. France, I think, by the fifteenth article, cedes Nova Scotia to Great Britain, and at the same time stipulates that her subjects shall not fish within thirty leagues from the coast of that colony, beginning from Cape Sable. I have seen much more in various places that points to a different extent of marine jurisdiction for different purposes, say, for instance, three miles or one league to preserve the peace, four leagues to prevent smuggling, a greater distance, perhaps, to fix buoys, lighthouses, etc., and lastly, for the purpose of fisheries. This may, hereafter, make a subject of controversy between us and Great Britain unless fixed by treaty.

I am sorry to observe that the reasonings of Pacificus (who is said to be Mr. Lowell, of Boston) produce more effect here than I should have imagined. I have no doubt that it will be reprinted in England in a pamphlet as an American work, and scattered through the continent, where it will not fail to produce a strong impression against us, for you cannot estimate too low the information of European cabinets on American affairs. The elegant piece on the Silesia loan, which we all know, made even the great Montesquieu call it a "réponse sans réplique," though England was clearly wrong under the circumstances of the case, without affecting at all the general principles which the document involves. When Great Britain first broached her rule of 1756, her writings on the subject were not answered by any writer of eminence on the continent, not even in France, who was so much affected by it. Even Hubner, who wrote at Paris in 1759, under the influence, and, I believe, in the pay of France, was at a loss what to say upon the subject, and more than half approved of the measure. All this is lamentably true, and points to the necessity of counteracting the effects of the publication of Pacificus.

III.

7 December, 1814.

DEAR SIR,—I cannot lose sight of you, though I have nothing to write that is worth reading. Information I cannot give, entertainment less. But if I can cheer you for a moment on your Ixionic wheel, I shall have answered my purpose.

I have read with a dreadful pleasure your letter to the Chairman of the Committee of Ways and Means on the subject of treasury notes. I cannot compare the sensations which it excited in me to anything else than to those I feel on reading Dante's *Inferno.* Scenes of horror ably and beautifully described, but still scenes of horror. And these are the scenes to which you have wedded yourself for your country's sake! I admire your self-devotion and your fortitude, and ardently wish that you may infuse it into others. But there are those who will not sacrifice even the little pride of a miserable opinion, often not their own. You will persist, I hope, for all your powers are wanted at this critical moment. Perseverance is the mother of wonders. We stand here in trembling expectation of something to be done for the relief of our financial embarrassments; the negotiations at Ghent and Vienna are of minor consequence compared with this great object; the result of the bank measure will determine the fate of our preparations for the next campaign, of the campaign itself, of the war, perhaps, and who knows how far it may yet influence the future destinies of this nation?

Our militia has been disbanded this morning for the season. I am told they are gone home without pay. Great fears are entertained here by the public stockholders for *next quarter-day.* All business is at a stand No goods hardly of any description bought or sold. The speculators are in a perfectly torpid state.

This state of complete apathy is to me incomprehensible. There are many who entertain hopes of peace from the apparently improved state of the negotiations at Ghent. Those who were frightened by *sine qua non* are lulled asleep by *uti possidetis;* as if one bugbear was not as good as another for our enemy's purposes. I believe it is indifferent to them which of the hard terms of the science of negotiation they make use of, provided it has the effect of keeping the apparent discussion on foot as long as they please. If the time should come when it will be expedient for them to conclude a peace, they will not be at a loss for a jump which will bring them precisely to the ground that will suit them. They know how to dance on the tight as well as on the slack rope. I have never seen such an *harlequinade* as this negotiation exhibits on their part.

Our negotiators have exhibited in their diplomatic correspondence the greatest ability. Their letters are admirable when con-

sidered in the light of an appeal to the impartial world, and the
British negotiators will have reason to blush for their glaring
inconsistency, and will be laid under the necessity of either
avowing that they have been all the while trifling with us, or of
submitting to imputations which no government that respects
itself will be willing to deserve.

IV.

14 December, 1814.

DEAR SIR,—Your unexpected favor of the 10th instant has
given me great pleasure. I say "unexpected," for I knew all
the burthens that you labor under, and when I hesitate to give
you the additional trouble of reading a letter from me, it is peculiarly gratifying to me to receive an answer from you.

I hope you begin with me to anticipate the triumph which, to
a mind like yours, will be an ample reward for your patriotic
labors. The confusion produced by the astonishment, and other
passions, excited by your first official acts, is beginning to sub-
side; by repeated strokes you have commanded and received an
attention less and less disturbed by the meaner feelings. You
have even in a great measure tamed the Cerberus of party, and
the happiest general results may be expected from the union of
the patriots and judicious men of both the great political denominations, which has manifested itself in favor of your financial
plans. Of all the departments of government, yours has singly,
as yet, obtained that triumph. For I consider Mr. Hanson's
speech of the 29th ult. as a brilliant trophy of victory. You will
hear with pleasure that it has given the tone to the leading Federalists of this State, and that it is now evident that the Eastern
projectors are to receive no support from this quarter. Indeed,
their measures are now openly blamed, nay, deprecated by men
who, not long ago, sought, at least, to palliate them.

I have no hesitation in ascribing all these favorable appear-
ances to your masterly exertions. If the country will unite in
strong constitutional measures there will be no necessity for
extra-constitutional ones. You know that our constitution can
do much under skilful hands. Continue, then, to strike home,
excite and vivify all around you. I may be partial, I may be
sanguine, but I think your success inevitable.

When you went into office there were many who did not believe that a *lawyer* could become suddenly a *financier*. It would
have been in vain to ask those men where Gallatin, Wolcott,
Hamilton, Pitt had served their apprenticeship, and why the
great nations of Europe did not put the first clerks in their offices

at the head of their respective departments. Such men must see to be convinced; but I have heard lately no more of this stuff.

V.

4 January, 1815.

DEAR SIR,—In complying with the desire, which you have in so friendly a manner expressed, that I should occasionally write to you, I have no object in view but to divert your mind from the oppressive burthens under which, in times like these, and in a situation like yours, it must, of necessity, incessantly labor. Although you are endowed with more than ordinary fortitude, this virtue has its bounds, and humanity now and then will claim its rights. Still, I hope you will persevere, *tenax propositi*, as I have always known you to be, and who knows but success will at last crown your honorable efforts? *Tume quod optanti*, etc.

Availing myself of the ample leisure with which the circumstances of the times have liberally favored me, I have thought that I could not employ my time better than in studying such parts of our history as might tend to elucidate the events of the day; I therefore turned my attention to the war of 1755. In the public library of this city, and in my own, I found sufficient materials to gratify my utmost wishes. My curiosity was first arrested by the correspondence of General Braddock with his own government, from the time of his arrival in Virginia to that of his defeat. He had been sent, you know, to make war upon the French in America while the ministry kept up the appearance of negotiation in Europe. I was peculiarly struck with what he said respecting the dispositions of the different colonies to aid in the projected operations. Those of *New England* alone, it seems, joined heartily with him, and evinced zeal for the cause of the mother country. New York gave her assistance, but only *for the defence of her own frontier*. Pennsylvania and Maryland refused to give any aid. He even complains that Pennsylvania assisted the enemy and supplied them with provisions. Virginia openly resisted the efforts of her governor to make her co-operate in the cause. She, however, voted £20,000 for the war, but when the general made contracts on the credit of that money for the supply of the army, she refused to carry them into execution. Of the Carolinas no mention is made. "On the whole," he says (only a few days after his arrival in Williamsburg), "the jealousy of the people and the disunion of the colonies, as well of all in general as of each in particular, makes me almost despair. Indeed, I am sorry to tell you that, according to all appearance, I shall have much difficulty to obtain from these colonies the succors his Majesty expects, and the common interest requires."

The disputes in the proprietary governments between the governors and the legislatures account, in some degree, but not sufficiently in my opinion, for these results. The Quaker spirit, also, in Pennsylvania may be supposed to have produced them, but I am not satisfied that it was not used as a means, instead of being itself a primary cause. However that may be, it is certain that about that time a leading Quaker, who was Speaker of the Assembly of Pennsylvania, used these remarkable words in debate: "I had rather see Philadelphia sacked three times by the French than vote a single copper for the war." This is not related in Braddock's letter, but is drawn from other monuments of the times.

This feeble sketch is not, perhaps, sufficient to produce the same chain of ideas in your mind which has occurred to me in the course of my study of the historical documents from which it is drawn; you are, however, welcome to two conclusions, which have appeared to me necessarily to flow from the facts above stated:

1. That the primary cause of the disunion which manifests itself at present between the different States is to be sought for in things existing, not only antecedently to the present war, but to the Revolution.

2. That this disunion was so great in those early times that common danger, instead of allaying, rather seemed to increase it.

To which we may add a third.

3. That the unwillingness to aid in the war was greater in those colonies that were the most exposed to the enemy than in those that were less so, or rather, indeed, not at all exposed.

Thus far my reflections have carried me, but no farther. To discover the true cause of the effects alluded to would require much more study,—and more reflection. This cause is, no doubt, complicated; but I am apt to believe that there must exist some master principle which, if sought for and discovered, would lead to unravel the whole clue. Some great master in politics will probably discover it, as Sir Isaac Newton did the principle of gravitation, by accident. In the mean time we shall go on ascribing everything to secondary causes; and, in seeking a variety of remedies, we may, perhaps, stumble upon the right one.

If you are tired of my lucubrations you may throw this letter by, for I am going unmercifully to proceed to another point.

In pursuing my study of the history of the war of 1755, I did not overlook the negotiations that took place between the two great contending powers. Those of 1750, 1753, 1755, and of 1761 (the last referred to by our commissioners at Ghent), were all open to my view in the original documents. I sought, of course, for the principles maintained from time to time by Great Britain and France, but particularly by Great Britain, respecting the Indians, and my curiosity was amply rewarded by the discoveries I made. These discoveries have lost much of their interest by the abandonment of the *sine qua non*, but in one point of view, at least, they are not altogether devoid of it. You will recollect that our commissioners, in their note to those of Britain of the 26th of September last, argued in favor of our doctrine respecting the Indians from the conduct of the elder Pitt, in the negotiation of 1761. The British commissioners in their reply told them that they were not well acquainted with the course of that negotiation, otherwise it would have led them to a different conclusion. They afterwards attempt to give a statement of what then took place, which, however, in spite of their equivocations, of their confounding facts and dates, and of the liberal use which they make of the utmost resources of diplomacy, does not seem to help them much. You will recollect, also, that our ministers, finding the principle abandoned, did not think it worth their while to enter into a contest with their opponents on the point of historical accuracy, but left Mr. Pitt and his negotiation to shift for themselves, satisfied with having so far succeeded in their own. Where their labor ends, therefore, that of the historical inquirer begins, and the patriot feels pleasure in being able to vindicate our commissioners from the charge of misrepresentation, which is strongly implied, if not directly made, in the statement of the British ministers, which they have disdained to answer.

You will see, by the inclosed copy of the fifteenth article of the treaty of Utrecht, the ideas which were entertained both by Great Britain and France respecting the Indians. I inclose also, by-the-by, an extract from an answer of Shirley and Mildmay, the British commissioners, to La Galissonière and Sithouette, commissioners of France, for the settlement of their controversy respecting the Caribbee Islands. The French claimed St. Lucia as their own, and argued from some act of the Indians in favor of their title. You will see what opinion the British government then entertained of the independence of those nations. The memorial is dated 15th November, 1751.

The negotiations of 1750–1703 related solely to the Caribbee Islands and to the boundaries of Nova Scotia or Acadia. France had ceded the latter country to Britain by the treaty of Utrecht, with its ancient limits, which were altogether undefined. According to Great Britain, it included not only the peninsula of Acadia proper but the whole of what is now the Province of Maine, at least from the Kennebec eastward (the remainder being clearly part of the British provinces), the whole of what is now

New Brunswick, and all Lower Canada south of the St. Lawrence to somewhere above Quebec. The discussions respecting these boundaries are foreign to our purpose, except so far that not a word was said on either side respecting the Indians, who still at that time inhabited parts of those territories. It had not, probably, occurred to either party to draw an argument from their pretended sovereignty and independence.

In the year 1755 a new negotiation was set on foot, not merely for the limits of the province of Nova Scotia but for those of all the French and British colonies as far as Virginia; for the boundaries of the more southern parts do not seem to have been yet thought of. Britain claimed to extend her limits to the west beyond the Ohio, and towards the north she insisted on the boundary of the Great Lakes. Here, for the first time, France offered that the Indian nations should form an independent barrier between the possessions of the two countries. Britain rejected the offer with disdain, on the ground that the Indians, and particularly the Five Nations, were her *subjects*, and were recognized as such by the treaty of Utrecht. At any rate, she said, France had so acknowledged them, and her acknowledgment must operate as an estoppel against her. I inclose, for your satisfaction, some extracts from the arguments of the respective ministers, which I hope you will not think altogether uninteresting.

But, while Britain was thus affecting to negotiate, she did not mean to remain at peace. Braddock had already sailed for America, armed with ample instructions to make war against the French in this country. And on the 7th of June, the very day of the date of the last British memorial,—of which an extract is sent to you,—the most unequivocal hostilities had begun on the American coast by the capture of the two French ships of war L'Alcide and Le Lys by the British fleet, under the command of Admiral Boscawen.

Thus negotiation was put an end to, and was not resumed until the year 1761, and with no better effect. This is the negotiation to which our ministers particularly allude. It ended, you know, by producing the family compact on the one side, and on the other the most vigorous efforts on the part of Great Britain, and, in the end, that most complete humiliation of France and Spain together which was consummated by the peace of 1763.

Great Britain now (in 1761) had conquered Canada, and France had no hopes of regaining it. She was, therefore, disposed to sanction the conquest of that province by a formal cession. Hence France immediately offered to cede Canada, but required that its limits should be clearly fixed, as well as those of Louisiana and Virginia. Britain,—who wanted all, or nearly all, that she got afterwards by the treaty of 1763, that is to say, the whole left bank of the Mississippi, but was not yet willing to avow it,—took fire at the proposition, said it was insidious, inasmuch as it involved the principle, which she was not disposed to admit, that all that was not Canada was Louisiana, *whereby*, she said, all the *intermediate nations*, the true barrier to each province, would be given up to France. In consequence, she sent her instructions to Mr. Stanley, divulged for the first time in the note of the British commissioners at Ghent. Stanley immediately despatched a note, which he declared to be the *ultimatum* of England, in which he insisted,—

1. That Canada should be ceded by France, *without any new limits.*

2. That Louisiana should not extend to Virginia, nor to the British possessions on the Ohio, giving as a reason that "the nations and countries which lie intermediate, and which form the true barrier between the said provinces, were not proper, on any account, to be *ceded*, directly or by any consequence, to France, even admitting them to be included within the limits of Louisiana."

"Here," observes the Duke de Choiseul in his *Mémoire justificatif* of the conduct of France, " one might infer that England pretended not only to keep exclusive possession of all Canada but also to make herself mistress of all the *neutral* countries between Canada and Louisiana, to be nearer at hand to invade the last colony when she should think proper."

Thus Great Britain, by a necessary implication, though without saying so, expressly claimed, under the name of Canada, the whole of the country north and east of the Ohio; and, although that country was at that time peopled with savages even as far as the Alleghany Mountains, not a word is said about their neutrality or their being a necessary barrier between the possessions of the two countries : this demand is confined to the most southern Indians, most of whom were clearly within the limits of France. As to her pretension respecting the boundary of Canada, it is well known that all the country southward and westward of Lake Erie, except the Territory of Michigan and a narrow border to the southward of that lake, was always considered by the French, when in possession of the two countries, to belong to Louisiana, and not to Canada. I believe the line of boundary was drawn from some point in the Miami River.

However this may be, the Duke de Choiseul took the British minister at his word, and immediately agreed to the *neutrality* of the Indian nations (observe that the word "*independence*" is never mentioned by either party), provided it should be reciprocal on both sides. He therefore gave in his *ultimatum*, expressly by him so entitled ; and you will also observe that the British commissioners at Ghent deny this fact ; and in this *ultimatum* he agreed at once to the proposal of Great Britain. His words are worthy of observation :

"The king," says he, "has in no part of his memorial of propositions affirmed that all which did not belong to Canada appertained to Louisiana. On the contrary, France *demands* that the intermediate nations *between Canada and Louisiana*, as also between Virginia and Louisiana, shall be considered as *neutral nations, independent* of the sovereignty of the two crowns, and serve as a barrier between them."

Britain was now taken in her own snare. To get rid of the proposal for the independence of the Indians north of the Ohio she was driven to the wretched resource of a false allegation. She asserted in her reply that Mr. de Vaudreuil, the governor of Canada, had, when he capitulated, given up the country by metes and bounds to the whole extent of the limits claimed. This Mr. de Vaudreuil solemnly and peremptorily denied, and his denial, published in the *Annual Register* for the year 1761, was never replied to. It is accompanied with such details of particular facts as impress it with the stamp of truth, and of course fix direct and downright falsehood on the British ministry of that day.

As to the southern Indians, Great Britain now declared her views, which till then had been obscurely expressed, in the clearest and most explicit manner. They were to be neither neutral nor independent, but to be, as she pretended they had been before, under the *protection* of the British government. Here are the words of Mr. Pitt, to which our commissioners more particularly allude in their letter above referred to :

"The line proposed to fix the bounds of Louisiana (a line to be drawn northward from the Perdido) cannot be admitted, because it would comprise on the side of the Carolinas very extensive countries and numerous nations who have always been reputed to be *under the protection of the king*, A RIGHT which his Majesty *has no intention of renouncing ;* and then the king, for the advantage of peace, might consent *to leave the intermediate countries under the protection of Great Britain*, and particularly the Cherokees, the Creeks, the Chickasaws, the Choctaws, and another nation situate between the British settlements and the Mississippi."

After receiving this note, France made another and a last effort for peace. She offered to cede Canada with the utmost extent claimed by Great Britain, and that the Indian nations should be neuter and independent,—those within the British line under the protection of England, the others under the protection of France. Great Britain answered this note by sending to M. Bussy, the French commissioner, his passports, and breaking suddenly the negotiation, because *France had refused to agree to the ulti-matum proposed by Great Britain.*

With this statement of facts you may now have a complete view of the merits of the discussion between our ministers and those of Great Britain on the subject of the negotiation of 1761, and the inference which the former drew from it.

VI.

5 January, 1814.

DEAR SIR,—The bank bill I find has been rejected by a ma-jority of one vote. I hope you will make one more effort to defeat the intrigues of your opponents. Your majority must take heart, give up their ridiculous scruples, and unite under the single motto, *Fill the ranks: fill the purse.* This is extremely plain, and requires not to be elucidated by long speeches.

It seems to me that the war made upon us both by our internal and external enemies is a war of bugaboos. At home the buga-boos are *conscription* and *unconstitutionality,* supported by the great bugaboo of bugaboos, the Hartford Convention. Abroad the bugaboos of last campaign were Lord Hill and his paper army. Afterwards came the *sine qua nons,* the *uti possidetis,* and all the host of diplomatic magical words. The bugaboo of the day is the New Orleans expedition on the one hand, and Gen-eral Packenham and his officers on the other. Amidst all this I see very little effective physical force. The real force—the force that I dread, and of which the power is among us terribly felt— is the *vis inertiæ* which at Washington holds the seat of its pow-erful empire. This is the *superior force, the vis major,* as Judge P—— would call it, that paralyzes the noble spirit of this noble nation. It cannot be too often repeated that the nation south of Connecticut River at least is disposed to submit to any strong measures that its representatives may think proper to adopt for the common defence. Congress have the power in their hands ; if they let it escape by their own indecision and weakness, it does not require the spirit of prophecy to foretell that they will severely rue the day ; and if they once let go the stirrup, they will be rid thereafter with a whip and a spur that shall never tire. Then they will understand to their sorrow the constitutionality of con-scriptions and of banks, and of many other things that they do not yet dream of.

It is a fact that the islands of Martinique and Guadaloupe were on the 2d of December still in the hands of the British, who delayed delivering those colonies up to the French. This does not argue great cordiality between the two powers. I wish the French naval and land commanders could have taken it upon themselves to come at once to this country as to a safe neighboring spot, where they might have quietly waited until it suited the British commanders to give up the islands, or at least that they had immediately returned to France. Their remaining where they are, encamped in their own country, while strangers are in possession of the barracks and the forts, appears to me a weak measure, and, what is more, a dangerous one. I fear there is also a *vis inertiæ* in the royal head of the French government.

I long to hear something more from our commissioners at Ghent. I wish they could have been enabled to put the British commissioners to the test by offering to them at once that foolish triangle of the Province of Maine, which they wish to have, it seems, for a road. I well know the great sea of prejudice that there is against the measure, and what effects might be feared from such a cession in this country. At the same time I am convinced that it would be an advantage to us if the British were possessed of that territory (exclusive of the seaports). Our population will always increase in a greater ratio than theirs, and a good military road from Halifax to Quebec would be of more use to us in a future war than to them. I fear also that the powers of Europe will think us unreasonable if we persist in refusing that cession. I see no real difficulties but this, supposing both parties well disposed in the way of an honorable treaty. For the fisheries, etc. we have some good things also to give or withhold; for instance, the liberty to trade with our Indians. I am glad to find that our commissioners have very skilfully and delicately hinted at this point, for it is certainly a principle of the law of nations between powers who possess colonies or settlements in America, that they cannot trade with the Indians within each other's limits without permission or the sanction of a treaty.

As you have desired me to give you my opinions frankly on every subject, I have tried it for once; but as I am not in a situation to take a view of the whole ground, you will of course make allowances.

I inclose the extracts from the negotiations of 1755 which I have promised. You will consider, I fear, my long lucubrations on the subject of these antiquated discussions as *de la moutarde après diner;* yet, as the extent of the powers of the greatest minds is but limited, I should think it can never come amiss even to a Pitt or a Talleyrand, to have the result of long and attentive studies communicated to them in the space of a few pages. You have read, I make no doubt, all that is contained in my letter of yesterday, and its addenda, but you never had occasion to consider it together in the point of view of its application to recent events. Therefore I have some apology for having troubled you with that long letter; but I should have none if I were to abuse the privilege any longer.

VII.

10 February, 1815.

DEAR SIR,—I am too well aware of the importance of your time to the public to misinterpret your omitting to answer my insignificant letters. I am satisfied that you receive them, and perhaps read them with more pleasure than certain petitions, or even than certain *lengthy* debates, which, for obvious reasons, shall not be here more particularly described. I have even the vanity to think that my scraps find sometimes more favor in your eyes than all the eloquence of Mr. C——h——n.

I have seen the President's objections to the late bank bill. They appeared to me very strong, and will be stronger still, I think, if they produce a bill of a different character. This I am strongly inclined to hope, perhaps because I wish it; but if I am not mistaken, the late law for preventing intercourse with the enemy gives indications of a better spirit than has prevailed heretofore. It seems to me to be fraught with much decision and strength.

The newspaper editors tell us again that you have it in serious contemplation to resign. I hope it will not be so; for if it should happen, the whole machine will be wonderfully relaxed, and God knows what will next take place. My hero Frederick desponded sometimes, and indulged himself in writing it to his friends; but he never despaired; he persevered, and at last succeeded. There is one remarkable trait in your as yet short political career which ought to encourage you to the same perseverance. Your measures have, indeed, been attacked by party opponents, but as far as I have seen (and I have taken pains to be as well informed as I could) their attacks have been comparatively mild, and your personal feelings have been spared beyond what any of your predecessors have, and any of your successors, perhaps, will ever experience. This mark of universal respect ought to be as grateful as, surely, it is honorable to you. And yet it was not so in former situations; I have tried to account to myself for this difference, and I can find no reason for it but that you were not then in your proper place, and that now you are.

The glorious defence at New Orleans, if it ends, as I hope it will, in the final expulsion of the enemy, will be a decisive event, like the captures of Burgoyne and Cornwallis, and the flight of

Bonaparte from Moscow. In point of character I do not think it inferior to any of these, and I believe with you that it will give us an honorable peace next spring. But you must be one of the peace-making administration. You have had the thorns of office: wait but a little while, and the rose-gathering will soon begin. You may lose patience; but depend upon it, you have lost, and will lose, no fame.

Excuse these warm expressions of friendly anxiety. I anticipate the day when you may retire with glory, and when it will not merely be said that you *would* do good to your country, but that you could and did do it, in spite of obstacles by which men of ordinary minds would have been deterred.

VIII.

13 February, 1815.

DEAR SIR,—I congratulate you with all my heart on the glorious news of an honorable peace, and the retreat of the British from before New Orleans. I am so overjoyed, that you must excuse me if I trace zigzag lines with my pen, as I surely do with my feet. The war administration have conferred upon us invaluable blessings; among which, not the least, are the knowledge and consciousness of our national strength, the conviction not only of the enemy, but of the world, that we are not that peddling, speechifying, special-pleading nation which they believed us to be, an immense store of experience, by which I hope we shall profit to the utmost, and, as to the objects of the war itself, we have satisfaction (in blood, at least) for the past, and ample security for the future. Not the paper security of treaties, but the security of the Scotch motto, which we have nobly appropriated to ourselves, and by means of which we have killed in the egg future orders in council and future Milan decrees. If we improve as we ought this interval of universal peace, we shall find belligerent rights considerably modified in the event of a future European maritime war. *Magnum est jus canonicum et prævalebit.*

You may well indulge an honorable pride, as one of the authors of this glorious peace. For I make no doubt that the firm countenance which the administration showed in October last, has not a little contributed to produce it. The British could not foresee the ridiculous difficulties which subsequently impeded the execution of your bold and energetic plans. They fancied them already adopted by Congress, and carried into execution with all the spirit of a brave and indignant people. You retorted the bugaboo war upon them, but with more success.

I have heard you blamed for laying open the wounds of the country in your famous letter to the Committee of Ways and Means. I never thought so. You exhibited us to the world as a nation that dares to look its situation in the face, and from that moment we became truly formidable. My life for it, this letter, and the conscription plan, have greatly contributed to produce the peace.

Your situation will now become comparatively easy, and your burthen considerably lightened. I hope you will continue in it, or go to some other more suited to your inclination, but equally important. Once a statesman, always a statesman. You are now spoiled for everything else.

IX.

17 February, 1815.

DEAR SIR,—Mr. I—— oins me in thanks to you for your early and full communication of the important features of the lately concluded treaty, and in the opinion that it deserves all the encomiums that you have bestowed upon it. The British ministry will find it difficult to make it palatable to their nation, particularly after having raised their expectations in such a manner as betrays their utter incapacity. There is not a single bright spot to which they can point with honest pride, not a favor sullenly refused by them that is not compensated by advantages at least of equal magnitude withheld from them by ourselves. The treaty is a vast blank on which the relations of the two countries are to be inscribed at a future day, and he who can do best without the favors of the other will have the advantage. The navigation of our inland waters, for the purposes of the Indian trade, is a boon of such immense importance to the British nation, that I have no doubt that they will come down very handsomely to obtain it.

Thank God, the ball is again in our hands, and I rejoice at the prospects of our national ascendency and influence on the general affairs of the world; in which hope, I think, with proper management, we can hardly be too sanguine.

Although the state of affairs on the continent of Europe has no doubt contributed in part to bring about this treaty, yet I cannot give up my favorite hypothesis that the firm attitude of our government in October contributed at least as much to it. The enemy then saw that all hopes of overturning Mr. Madison's administration were over, as it had stood the shock of the Washington fire, and now reared its crest higher than ever. This *demonstration* (for which I give you an ample share of the credit) could not possibly be without a corresponding effect in Europe, where, when the treaty was signed, it appears they as yet knew nothing of our unhappy C——niads. Several London paragraphs confirm me in this opinion, and I am not disposed to give it up.

X.

30 May, 1815.

DEAR SIR,—I had read already in the newspapers the documents which you have had the goodness to send to me; and you may see whether I duly appreciate the trouble which you have had in raising this fair, regular edifice out of the chaos of its details, when I tell you that I have not yet done studying its contents. For you have excited in me an emulation at least to understand what you have been able to perform. I perceive upon the whole that you have made the most of our *exiguous* army, and that if you could not make it large, you have at least made it efficient, by exhausting all the resources of organization, selection, and loco-position. You have had a most invidious task to perform, and government must feel under peculiar obligations to you for assuming at such a critical moment a burthen not less delicate than it is heavy. Nor have you lost sight of the main object committed to your care,—I mean the Department of Finance. The elevated ground on which the credit of the nation stands at this moment is the best eulogium upon your measures, as it is one that everybody can feel and understand. The want of a national bank, however, still places you under momentary difficulties; but you can see through them, and they will not arrest the course of your exertions. I hope Congress will give you a bank at their next session, and such an one as you ought to have, or that they will find some other mode to prevent the stagnation of the public moneys, and give them the degree of circulation necessary, and indispensably so, for the operations of your department.

I fear our prize courts will always embarrass the government until they are organized as in Europe; that is to say, taken out of the line of the ordinary judiciary establishment, to which they no more belong than courts-martial. In England, you know, the Court of Appeals consists of a board of privy counsellors, and the judge of the admiralty does not sit as judge of prize, *virtute officii*, but by virtue of a special commission from the king. Prize courts are temporary instruments of war; it is therefore absurd to constitute them in a permanent manner and vest their powers permanently in judges appointed for life. This subject is susceptible of a much greater development, but *sapienti verbum*

26

sat. I ought to add, however, that Mr. Gallatin, to whom I once suggested these ideas at your house, asked me how I would connect my board of commissioners of prize with the supreme court of the United States. Precisely as in England, by the superintending and restrictive power exercised by writs of mandamus, prohibition, and the like; and that would, it seems, be enough to satisfy so much of the constitution as makes the supreme court paramount to all other courts. As to that which declares that all judges shall be appointed during good behavior, I do not know, I acknowledge, how to satisfy it, except by saying that nothing can be meant to be applied where it is inapplicable. This principle never was applied to courts-martial, and I contend that prize courts are *ejusdem generis.*

You see I am perfectly sensible of the difficulties attending a correct organization of the prize courts; yet, difficult as it is, you must sooner or later come to it, and the earlier the public mind is prepared for this, in my opinion, indispensable arrangement, the better. The executive is responsible for the acts of its prize courts, therefore they ought not to be independent of the executive. You have felt it already; you will feel it more in a maritime war of some years' continuance.

XI.

20 June, 1815.

DEAR SIR,—I cannot resist the inclination to communicate to you the strong feeling which has been excited in me by your late measure on the subject of treasury notes. It is as well-timed as it is happily conceived. It cannot fail of producing a most salutary effect. I entertain the most sanguine hopes that it will bring our jarring mediums to a proper level, and establish true republican equality in the commonwealth of bank-notes. The haughty *Easterlings* will no longer reign supreme over the commerce of America as their namesakes and prototypes did some centuries ago over that of Europe. Had their supremacy continued we would have had *sterling* (Easterling) bank-notes as we have sterling money. Their pride would not have overlooked the analogy, and they might have assumed the name, as they had the thing. You have availed yourself with great skill and decision of the high ground on which you have placed the credit of the government; you have issued your commands from the *mountain,* and I hope they will be obeyed.

XII.

11 December, 1815.

DEAR SIR,—I have read with great pleasure the first part of your able and luminous report to Congress on the state of the finances, which has appeared in the *National Intelligencer.* I long to see the remainder. I had never read a financial report till you came to office ; I thought them too dry and uninteresting, never having in my life turned my thoughts to that abstruse subject. Now I read them with as much pleasure as a young girl does novels.

My correspondents in France write to me that we may expect many emigrants here of two descriptions,—the first rich revolutionists, and the second poor but ingenious manufacturers. Of the latter class, one called on me this morning, recommended by our consul at Bordeaux. He is a dyer of linen, silk, and cotton, and draws his own patterns. He showed me borders of merino shawls designed and colored by him, which are really beautiful. He says he possesses the secret of fixing all the colors at once, and that he was the only person in France that had it. Mr. L—— in his letter to me concludes thus: "Had I the means I could send hundreds of such men yearly to the United States."

XIII.

16 December, 1815.

DEAR SIR,—I have received with very great pleasure your letter of the 14th inst., with its valuable inclosure, the printed copy of your last financial report. I mean to have it bound in a separate volume, as its folio size does not admit of its being bound with other things, and which its contents will amply justify.

The first thought that struck me when I read the first part of it in a newspaper was, as you well say, that it would be a complete manual of American finance. It will not only instruct society at large and the members of the legislature of what every one ought to know, but by condensing in one view all the requisite data, will save much discussion and research in committees and on the floor of Congress, and will expedite business. For my part, long as the report is, I would not wish one word left out. The results appear to me incontrovertible, and the plans wisely thought and presented in a luminous view.

You know you have promised the American Philosophical Society, of which you are a worthy member, to send them your reports from time to time for the use of their historical committee. You, who may now say with Prince Henry of Prussia, "*J'appartiens tout entier à l'histoire*," will not forget a pledge given to a body of men in any way connected with that awful tribunal. I therefore solicit for them the fulfillment of that promise, which will be very gratefully received.

XIV.

23 February, 1816.

DEAR SIR,—Accept again my sincere thanks for the valuable present of your late report on the new tariff. As I do not understand the subject I can only join in the general approbation. One thing I well understand, that I shall be able to drink claret cheaper than before. I am not sorry for the circumstance, though I would have paid a higher duty with great pleasure for the good of the nation. On the whole, it is evident that you have determined to promote the complete independence of the country by protecting its manufactures. I hope that you and I will live to see some of the wonderful effects which this system will produce.

XV.

15 April, 1816.

DEAR SIR,—I again intrude upon you to request a copy of your letter of the 19th of March to the Chairman of the Committee on the National Currency. Called to the head of our finances at the beginning of the paper age, I was sure you would not quit them without restoring to us the golden age, which I fondly anticipate from the measures you propose. I congratulate you and the country on the final passage of the bank bill, though it is not all that you would have wished. This you may be sure of, that your administration will be long remembered; its features are strongly marked, and will produce decisive results. Adopted sooner and with a better grace, the country would by this time have been sensible of blessings produced by your conceptions.

I hear with pain that you are going to quit the ministry. This measure of yours I cannot be brought to approve, and you will excuse me for being a strong oppositionist. Certain it is, however, that the impulse is given, and there is now nothing to do but follow it. You will leave an easy task to your successors.

Having done thus much, you are certainly entitled to retire

from the labors of public life, and no man will be more pleased than I to see you again among us. Yet if I had any influence upon you I could entreat you to remain where you are for the public good. But your talents are so various that I console myself with the hope, if you should cease to be our purse-holder, of seeing you benefit the nation in some other equally important branch of government which wants to be set in motion, as you have done the department of finance.

LETTERS BETWEEN THE PRESIDENT AND THE SECRETARY.

1815.

DEAR SIR,—I inclose the draft of a letter to the general officers, on the execution of the act of the 3d of March, 1815, with a copy of the act. You will see by a memorandum from Mr. Monroe that he thinks the peace establishment is to be composed of ten thousand men, exclusive of officers. General Scott agrees in that opinion, and I shall be very glad to adopt it with your approbation. I shall write to you again to-morrow, and have only to request the favor of an early instruction upon the present communication.

I am, dear sir, faithfully and respectfully, your obedient servant,

A. J. DALLAS.

The President.

11 April, 1815.

DEAR SIR,—The result of the conference of the heads of departments on General Jackson's case will be seen in the inclosed draft of a letter to the general, which is submitted to your consideration. Be so good as to return it with your instructions to alter it or to send it in its present shape. There is no other copy of the letter. The fact of the release of Judge Hale and Mr. Dick is stated in a second communication from the latter to Mr. Monroe.

There are no accounts from Generals Macomb, Brown, Jackson, or Gaines further than I have already mentioned. General Ripley arrived this afternoon, but I have not seen him. It is said, from several quarters, that he would prefer a civil appointment to a continuance in the army; but the intimation seems to proceed originally from interested parties. I can easily ascertain it from himself.

The inclosed recommendation from General Scott to Brevet Captains Pentland and Smith is submitted to your decision. These recommendations will probably so multiply as to deprive the brevet of its complimentary character.

I am, dear sir, most faithfully, your obedient servant,

A. J. DALLAS.

The President.

13 April, 1815.

———

MONTPELIER, April 14, 1815.

DEAR SIR,—I received by the mail of this morning your two letters of the 11th and 12th instant, with the several papers to which they refer. That of the 9th came to hand yesterday.

The construction of the fifth section of the act fixing the military establishment is not without difficulty. Do not the terms and interpretation of former acts of Congress determine the question whether "men" means privates, etc. only, or includes commissioned officers also? Not having a copy of the laws at hand, I am not able to form an opinion. If the construction, excluding officers, be not forbidden by precedents or clear analogy, I take the more obvious meaning to be that officers should not be included in the "ten thousand" men specified in the act.

I feel all the delicacy and magnitude of the task imposed by the law which your communications express, and regret that there is not less room for erring in the execution of it. In choosing the general officers, I do not see that we can do better, on the whole, than adhere to the individuals first agreed on, unless indeed something should be finally ascertained in the proceedings at New Orleans, which, I trust, will not be the case, compelling us to relinquish the preference given to the general commanding there. With respect to the fourth brigadier also, the door is not understood to be finally closed, unless something has passed with him having that effect, as was authorized. If serious difficulties are in his way, or there be decisive grounds of preference in favor of another, and there be commitment on the subject, I wish you to consult your judgment freely, and give me an opportunity of sanctioning it. Nor do I see that we can advantageously vary the course marked out for discriminating between the officers to be retained and to be discharged. I approve the idea, however, of considering the report of the board of officers as imposing no fetters on the authoritative decision. How would it do to prescribe a recommendatory list, giving to the executive an option among several candidates? I ask the question without intending to arrest the progress of the business. If the expedient should be entirely approved, and not otherwise, the form of the report required may be changed without the delay of a communication with me. If it were admissible to have the opinions of the most respectable officers of high rank, General Dearborn for example, who will have no future connection with the army, either as associates in the Board or otherwise, it might be useful in different views. But I see so many difficulties in the way that I do not press it even on my own thoughts.

As neither Jackson nor Gaines can attend, I think you will do well to obtain the presence of Colonel H. in the mode which has occurred to you.

The scope of your letters in general appears to be the just one. I wish you to make the final decision on the selection of officers as distinctly that of the President as you deem suitable and consistent with respect and confidence due to and felt for the head of the War Department.

I am engaged with the proceedings of the court-martial on General Wilkinson. It is so extremely voluminous that I shall not be able to get through it for some days. The court acquit him, I perceive, with honor on every charge, and, of course, strengthens his claims and expectations from the public. What has become of the chance presented by the appointment of the naval officers at New York to the mayoralty?

I was not unaware of some of the difficulties which you would encounter in your fiscal arrangements. The steps you have taken and contemplate accord with the best judgment I can form on the business. Whilst the money market in Europe continues as it is indicated by the present state of the English stocks, the United States will not be able to realize the advantages due to the merit of theirs.

I observe that the "exposition," etc. is finding its way to the public here and to the world in different ways, and I have not yet seen that the government is charged by its opponents, as it could not justly be, with any indelicate participation. The idea of Mr. Jefferson, therefore, of publishing the work officially in a different dress, could not be excuted without more difficulty than occurred to him. Whether it ought to go out from the government at all is another question. If the truths it contains can be otherwise sufficiently promulgated, and with sufficient credibility, it will be best, I continue to think, to let them speak for themselves.

Accept my great esteem and my affectionate respects,

JAMES MADISON.

Mr. DALLAS.

MONTPELIER, April 16, 1815.

DEAR SIR,—I received by the mail of this morning your two letters of the 13th and 14th. The letter for General Jackson cannot be improved, and I lose no time in returning it. The cases recommended by General Scott for brevets are strong ones, and I suppose cannot well be rejected. I am aware with you, however, that these honorary commissions, already so much multiplied, are in danger of losing their value. If you think it advisable, the cases may lie over till a fuller estimate can be made of this danger.

Affectionate respects,

JAMES MADISON.

Mr. DALLAS.

MONTPELIER, April 18, 1815.

DEAR SIR,—I have received your two letters of the 15th and 16th inst I approve the transfers you propose in the army appropriations, and will give the formal sanction to them as soon as I receive the usual documents for signature.

I approve, also, the course you have in view for winding up the affairs of the army, and am glad to find that you will be able so far to overcome the pecuniary difficulties. I have left it with you and Mr. Monroe to make the definitive arrangement of the case of General Ripley in all its relations.

Affectionate respects,

JAMES MADISON.

Mr. DALLAS.

MONTPELIER, April 19, 1815.

DEAR SIR,—I have at length run through the trial of General Wilkinson, and send it to you, with an approbation of the sentence of the court. I send, also, the trial of Captain Hanson, with a decision conformable to the sentence and recommendation of the court in his case.

Affectionate respects,

JAMES MADISON.

The Secretary of War.

DEAR SIR,—I am obliged to trouble you again on Mr. Lesborough's business. He has mistaken my expression, which was, "that if the claim is not legal, still it appears to me to be equitable." However, recollecting your view of the subject, I do not wish to give a formal decision without your sanction; and

I will thank you to say whether I shall leave it as it stands or submit it to the comptroller on equitable principles.

General Macomb arrived last night; and I hope General Brown will be here to-morrow. The business is now so digested that I think it will not cost the Board three days to pass upon it.

If General Ripley conforms to my view of propriety, as to the court of inquiry, I shall act on your authority in issuing the brevet, as well as in writing a letter to retain him in service.

In this morning's *National Intelligencer* I have published a general order to restrain some abuses, and to quiet the minds of the soldiers as to their pay and discharge. The collection of military documents which are in the hands of officers who may be deranged is also attempted.

I am, dear sir, most respectfully and faithfully yours,

A. J. DALLAS.

The President.

19 April, 1815.

MONTPELIER, April 20, 1815.

DEAR SIR,—I have just received yours of ――. I wish the arrival of Brown may have been followed by a compromise satisfactory to Ripley. If it should not, the case of the latter becomes unpleasant in several respects. Can a court of inquiry be refused if he insists on it? I am led to believe that, if disappointed altogether, he will think himself bound to lay his case before the public. It must be admitted that the charge in General Brown's letter will be a record against him, if neither revoked, nor explained, nor disproved.

I return the proceedings of the two courts-martial, with my signature to the respective decisions indorsed on them; with O'Connor's charges against Izard, and demand of a trial on them. The charges are of a nature so interesting to General Izard, and involving points interesting in so many other views, that I presume, inconvenient and difficult as a court-martial will be, the prosecutor will not waive it, if justice could dispense with it. Could it be exchanged for a court of inquiry? Be so good as to take the course which right and prudence prescribe, availing yourself of all the lights attainable on the spot.

Affectionate respects,

JAMES MADISON.

Mr. DALLAS.

DEAR SIR,—I have the pleasure to say that the business respecting General Ripley is arranged; and I hope it will be to your satisfaction. I inclose copies of the letters which have passed between us. The selection of general officers being complete, I will announce it; and if General Brown arrives to-day or to-morrow, I think the general plan of organization may be sent for your consideration on Monday.

There is nothing new. I expect Mr. Monroe to-day.

I am, dear sir, most respectfully and faithfully yours,

A. J. DALLAS.

The President.

20 April, 1815.

Mr. Monroe arrived at noon, but not much the better for his ride. He saw and approved the letters in General Ripley's case before I had sent my answer.

MONTPELIER, April 23, 1815.

DEAR SIR,—I have received yours of the 20th, and return the correspondence with General Ripley. I hope it will be followed by all the advantages which it promises. I received yesterday from Mr. Graham a blank brevet commission for him. It was suggested that a reference might be inserted to the resolution of Congress. Unless some valuable purpose would be attained by it, it may be best to decline a precedent which might in unforeseen cases be embarrassing. I leave the decision with yourself, as I do the returned recommendation of Trevett for the vacancy on the revenue cutter at Boston; so also on that stated in Dr. Blake's letter inclosed.

Affectionate respects,

JAMES MADISON.

Mr. DALLAS.

MONTPELIER, April 25, 1815.

DEAR SIR,—The mail due yesterday having failed, I did not receive till this morning your communications dated on the 22d instant.

As it appears that no legal consideration is opposed to the appointment of Bissel and Smith to regiments, their just claims to that arrangement cannot be doubted. The brevets to them may be issued when you choose. It has been mentioned that Smith would gladly accept the Creek agency, which it is supposed Hawkins does not mean longer to hold. Should it be vacated, Smith's wishes may be taken into view, and if his qualifications be of the right sort, of which you have better means of judging than I have, he may be commissioned, unless, indeed, other candidates appear with even superior pretensions. It will be proper, however, not to accept the resignation of Hawkins without knowing that it is the effect of inclination, and not of some cause which ought to be explained and removed. I recollect that he manifested, long ago, an impression that the executive was not satisfied with him, and, on that account, proposed to withdraw himself at the end of the war, if not sooner. I desired the late Secretary of War to drop him a line, expressing my confidence and a continuance of the friendly dispositions I have for many years entertained for him. It is possible that such a communication may never have reached him, and that he may still be under his original misconception. One of your clerks, or General Parker, can collect for you all the circumstances which merit attention. I am thus particular, because I have always regarded Colonel Hawkins as a benevolent and honorable man, and singularly useful and meritorious in the agency committed to him, and because an old and intimate acquaintance with him makes me feel an interest in whatever may concern his welfare or touch his sensibility.

The business of O'Connor and Izard seems to be on a fair footing. The former can the less complain of the delay or uncertainty attending it, as his own delay has contributed to it. It may be well to recur to a former communication from him to the War Department, in which he recited the same or other allegations against General Izard. It was shown to me by Mr. Monroe while acting secretary, but I do not recollect the precise scope of it.

I return, signed, the power for the Yazoo cases, and an approbation of the proposed allowances to the collectors of the direct tax.

The silence of General Jackson on the proceedings which were the subject of your letter to him, cannot be explained but by a failure on the road, or by a difference between the real and reported facts, or some uncommon view which his mind has taken of them. The importance and novelty of the proceedings could not fail, one would suppose, to suggest an official explanation of them. If he should not fill the post in the army allotted to him, it will be necessary to put other pretensions into the scales. Before Mr. Monroe leaves Washington, be so good as to make the proper selection a subject of conversation with him and the other gentlemen.

Mr. McIlvaine's letter may be shown to the Secretary of State.

I shall be absent for a few days on a visit to Mr. Jefferson; but I shall keep hold of the thread of daily communication with Washington.

Affectionate respects,

JAMES MADISON.

Mr. DALLAS.

DEAR SIR,—General Brown will probably be here to-night; and I think the organization of the corps and selection of officers may be completed on Wednesday. Be so good as to put the inclosed into any shape that will answer the purpose intended. I think it of some importance that the feelings of the deranged officers should be soothed; but it would be impolitic, and, indeed, impracticable, to use any but general terms upon the occasion.

I am, dear sir, most respectfully and faithfully yours,

A. J. DALLAS.

The President.

25 April, 1815.

General Brown has arrived.

DEAR SIR,—General Brown has joined the Board; and I have the pleasure to inform you that, so far, everything has been transacted with perfect harmony and unanimity. The selections are of a high and distinguished character, as far as I can judge; and I am assured that the army will itself acknowledge their justness. The field officers at present on the list are these, for infantry and riflemen:

Colonels.	Majors.
T. A. Smith, Brigadier-General.	Jessup.
D. Bissel, Brigadier-General.	Wool.
M. Porter, Brevet Brigadier-Gen'l.	Levensworth.
H. Brady.	McNeil.
W. King.	Chambers.
J. Miller.	Appling.
James McDonald.	Lawrence.
R. C. Nicholas.	Brooke.
J. Mullin, or W. N. Irvine.	Langworth, or Butler.
Lieutenant-Colonels.	Overton transferred from the In-
Not named yet.	fantry to the Artillery.

The selections will probably be complete on Friday; and I will send them to you by express, as it is very desirable to receive your decision before Monday.

The brevet for General Ripley was not designed to refer, as Mr. Graham supposed, to the vote of Congress, but to the same subjects. It will be filled up with " Chippewa, Niagara, and Erie." The insertion will satisfy General Ripley, and cannot displease General Brown.

General Scott has been desirous to construe the act of Congress so as to permit the superseding two captains in the engineers and replacing them with captains from the line. I do not think that the act contemplates the case; and I know that it would create feuds, discontents, and resignations were the attempt made. I have, therefore, stated an opinion to the Board that the corps of engineers is excepted from the special authority of the act fixing the peace establishment, and that no change can be effected in it but on the general law. It seems that there are two officers who are deemed unworthy of their commissions; but their removal may be accomplished at another time and in another way, without exciting dissatisfaction.

I am, dear sir, most respectfully and faithfully yours,

A. J. DALLAS.

The President.

26 April, 1815.

MONTICELLO, April 28, 1815.

DEAR SIR,—I am just favored with yours of the 25th. The paper inclosed in it is returned without delay. It is well adapted to its delicate object. I have merely noted for your consideration a change of expression in page 3, "the enjoyment of undisturbed rights, etc.," not being *secured*, like the renown of the army; and another in page 4, in order to guard against the criticisms of those who may not have been in fact *peculiar* objects of public confidence and favor, and especially of such as may lose the marks of it by the present arrangement. If any change should occur in the closing sentence, page 5, that will lessen the pledge of legislative beneficence without losing sight of it, it may, perhaps, be also well, considering the want of right in the executive and the sensibility to it that may be awakened in the legislative department. I have but a moment to drop these lines, being in danger of missing the present mail and under a necessity of losing the next.

Affectionate respects,

JAMES MADISON.

Mr. DALLAS.

MONTICELLO, April 29, 1815.

DEAR SIR,—The inclosed letter, though anonymous, makes statements and references in a manner which is embarrassing at the present moment. Should the posture of the military arrangements admit nothing further, the location of the officer thus criminated ought at least to be influenced by the representations, unless these be invalidated in some mode or other before the final allotments be made to military stations.

Affectionate respects,

Mr. DALLAS.   JAMES MADISON.

DEAR SIR,—The board of officers still continue industriously at work, but I have no report yet. Perhaps I shall be able to communicate a plan of organization by Monday's mail.

The inclosed letter and extra newspaper were received by me in the mail of yesterday. The letter is certainly written by Mr. T. Biddle, and I presume Mr. Bache threw it into the mail after the bag had been locked, which accounts for the absence of a post-mark. I give credit (and so do Mr. Monroe and Mr. Crown-inshield) to the news; but I have declined being the instrument of publishing it, lest it should turn out to be an imposition. The mail of to-day will clear up all doubts. What a scene for speculation does the event, if true, open upon us!

I am, dear sir, most respectfully and faithfully yours,
A. J. DALLAS.

The President.

29 April, 1815.

———

DEAR SIR,—I inclose recommendations for granting Captain Romayne the vacant appointment of assistant inspector-general. The appointment will be merely nominal, to carry the rank, as the office will be abolished when the army shall be discharged. The reasons for soliciting it, however, are stated in the recommendations, and I will thank you to favor me with your decision on the subject. Captain Romayne has certainly great estimation among his brother officers.

I am, dear sir, most respectfully and faithfully yours,
A. J. DALLAS.

The President.

2 May, 1815.

———

DEAR SIR,—At the request of Colonel Owings the inclosed letter is sent to you. His case has been well considered and well devised. Major Taylor has been placed on the left.

I am, dear sir, your most obedient,

The President.   A. J. DALLAS.

3 May, 1815.

———

MONTPELIER, May 4, 1815.

DEAR SIR,—I have duly received your several letters of ——, and of May 2. The views you have taken of the late intelligence from France will justly claim all our attention. Should war ensue between Great Britain and France, our great objects will be to save our peace and our rights from the effect of it; and whether war ensue or not, to take advantage of the crisis to adjust our interests with both. It is particularly desirable to ascertain as soon as possible their temper and views respectively towards the United States, and many days cannot elapse without communications from Paris and London, which will throw light on the path leading to our objects. In the mean time it becomes us to be in a position to face events whatever may be the turn of them, and consequently to suspend the discharge of the army, with the exception of the part not within our discretion. Prudence suggests also a delay of the expedition to the Mediterranean. It is of great importance in every point of view that we should lose no part of the respect we now command by a precipitate and improvident surrender of the best means of preserving our title to it. It may be hoped that with due precautions on our part, the former competition between those powers in aggressions on us, will be succeeded by rival dispositions to court our good will, or at least to cultivate our neutrality. The lessons afforded by their own experience ought alone to produce wiser councils, and the change in the state of Europe in general in relation to France, and the trial which Great Britain has made of the strength and character of this country, are sources of additional instruction of the same tendency. But in a case of such vast magnitude, we should add to every other motive to do us justice a condition on our part to enforce it.

I return the recommendations in favor of Romayne, on whom you will confer the commission proposed for him. I return also the letter of General B. which is very skilfully framed.

Affectionate respects,
JAMES MADISON.

I have returned the proceedings of the court-martial at Detroit without any decision on the sentence dismissing the militia officers from the service of the United States. As they are actually out of the service, and the confirmation of the sentence by General McArthur, though not within the legal period, was presumably just in itself, the case did not appear to require the formality of my interposition. If there be any circumstances rendering it expedient, be so good as to let me know.

Mr. DALLAS.

MONTPELIER, May 4th, 1815.

DEAR SIR,—The waggons with Mr. Jefferson's library are on their way to Washington, and will expect to be paid on their arrival. Not having the law on the subject of that purchase, I know not whether it includes an appropriation for the expense of transportation, or leaves this to be paid out of any other, and what, fund. I must ask you to decide this point, and have the waggoners paid without delay. They are, I understand, entitled each to $4 per day, for 15 days, with the exception of one, who will not arrive for some time with a few cases of books which did not accompany the others, and who is to receive at the rate of $6 per day. Should my sanction be necessary in any form to close this little transaction, it will be added as soon as I receive notice of it. Mr. Smith (Commissioner of the Revenue) has been so obliging as to give some attention to the arrangement for conveying the library, and will be requested to relieve you from all the trouble not officially essential.

Accept my cordial respects and best wishes,

JAMES MADISON.

Do what you find proper in the case stated in the inclosed letter.

The Secretary of the Treasury.

DEAR SIR,—I transmit to you the concluding Reports of the Board of Officers, and I presume that they will express a wish to be discharged as soon as you have seen their plans. Upon the whole, they have furnished very good materials; and I will prepare from them a general report of the department for your consideration and sanction, which, when approved, will be the proper official document for publication. The necessary arrangements of the peace establishment will still give you time to hear from Europe, without making the events there a specific cause of delay.

I inclose two letters from General Brown. He presses, you will see, Major Gardner for additional honors. If, however, the major's character and conduct are such as have been described to me in conversation by General Ripley, General Scott, and General Wilkinson, I still think Major Butler should be preferred to him. The subject may be kept in suspense for some days without any disadvantage.

In an interview of this morning, General Brown stated that at General Scott's instance, he mentioned the wish of that gentleman to go to Europe in pursuit of professional instruction, etc., retaining only his rank, pay, and emoluments. I declared that so far as my voice went he should be gratified, and that I would submit the question at once to you. General Scott would do us credit abroad; and I do not think that the service would suffer by his temporary absence. If, however, you should assent to General Scott's request, I presume he would not leave us while there is the slightest doubt of the effect of European events upon our military establishment.

General Brown's letter, relative to the purchase of a site for a military station on the waters of the St. Lawrence, merits consideration. He says that he is willing to purchase the necessary tract of land, and to look to Congress for his reimbursement at the next session. There are many things to be considered before the proposed change of situation can be correctly estimated in its consequences of advantages and disadvantages. What can we do with our ships on the stocks at Sackett's Harbor? If the war had commenced on General Brown's plan, we should not have had the troubles nor the glories of the lake conflicts; and if we are to expect war again, his plan is probably the best mode of preparing for it.

The disposition of the troops appears to me to be judicious in its outline. The artillery will be at the Atlantic ports, and the infantry and the riflemen will be on the northern frontier, and particularly in the neighborhood of the Indians and British traders. General Brown has arranged the northern division to his own mind, and it will be right to allow General Jackson to modify the arrangement for the southern division if he wishes to do so.

I am, dear sir, most respectfully and faithfully yours,

A. J. DALLAS.

The President.

———

MONTPELIER, May 7, 1815.

DEAR SIR,—I have this morning received yours of the 5th inst., those of the 3d and 4th having previously come to hand. They are accompanied by the reports of the board of officers on the organization of the army,—on the plan for establishing a N. and S. division, military departments, etc. etc.,—and respecting hospital surgeons, judge advocates, and chaplains.

It were to be wished that the act relating to the peace establishment had been more explicit in some respects and more comprehensive in others. But there can be no doubt as to the authority to substitute the rule of selection for that of seniority, nor to prefer the sound and competent to the wounded and infirm, in retaining the officers for an establishment requiring for its object the most effective services. The appointment of officers of higher grades to fill the lower, with their own consent, can be liable to no objection whatever if it be not a new appointment. On this point there may be room for a difference of opinions. The construction is clearly in favor of the public service; and f it should be found not sufficiently supported by usage or precedents, the error can be amended with the aid of the Senate. The transfer of officers from one corps to another seems also free from objection, as they are both liable to exclusion altogether, and have the resource of resigning. The transfer of the men presents an-

27

other aspect where they have been enlisted into particular corps and are compulsively retained in service. It is more than probable that if the understanding at the time of enlistment impose any restraint in this case, it may be removed by the consent of the individuals, or that the difficulty may be got over with the aid of the supernumerary fund.

The local distribution of the troops and the definition of military departments being at all times alterable, require the less observation. It may deserve consideration whether Maryland and Virginia, as having a common relation to the Chesapeake, would not be advantageously associated with perhaps the northern part of North Carolina. The District of Columbia, omitted, I presume casually, would fall of course into the same department.

I have but slightly glanced at the report on hospital surgeons, etc. etc. I notice only the omission of two hospital surgeons whose pretensions I had considered very strong, if not liable to objections unknown to me, and the selection of one who does not appear with advantage in the proceedings of the court-martial which tried Colonel Coles. Doctors Waterhouse and Shaw are the two first alluded to, and Doctor Bronaugh the last.

With respect to the selection of officers generally for the establishment, I have great confidence in the officers of the Board, and especially where your own judgment coincides. I have thought it incumbent on me, nevertheless, to look over it with attention, and shall note any instances in which my information, or, in a few cases possibly, my personal knowledge may suggest changes. I have been a little embarrassed and retarded by leaving behind me the Army Register sent me by Mr. Parker when I returned from Monticello. I hope, however, to send you the result by the mail of to-morrow or the day after. In the mean time I wish it to be understood, if not sufficiently signified already, that the address prepared for the army had my approbation; that I leave it with you, advising with whom you may think proper, to do what you find best with respect to Majors Butler and Bankhead, and to make any other alterations such as you allude to. You will also make the use of brevets as proposed in your letter, blanks for which I take for granted are already signed; if not, let them be forwarded.

Your intended letter of thanks to the officers of the Board will be very proper. You will decide whether it be necessary or not for them to remain at Washington till a final decision be had on their reports.

The question whether the general discharge of the army contemplated by the act of Congress, ought to be carried into effect under existing circumstances, is a momentous one. On one hand, the measure is urged by the face of the law, by the motive to economy, mingled with the prospects suggesting a delay of the measure, by the number of men, above ten thousand, on whom the deliberation turns,—a number not amounting to a very impressive augmentation,—and by the embarrassments incident to a provisional retention of the officers not required for the establishment, divisible as they would be also into the class allotted to the supernumerary men provisionally retained and the class who would be put on furlough. On the other hand, the danger of a renewal of hostilities, and the tendency of a posture ready for them to prevent so great an evil, are weighty considerations in the other scale. The public opinion also seems to lean to the precautionary side. It is more than probable that a few days will bring us from Europe valuable lights on the subject. Those by the Fingal have not come by the mail of this morning, nor the conversation of Mr. M—— with Mr. Baker. I shall look for them by that of tomorrow, unless a day more should be necessary for him to arrange and comment on the communications.

Affectionate respects,

Mr. DALLAS. JAMES MADISON.

—————

DEAR SIR,—I send inclosed a report in the case of Mr. Eustaphiere, the Russian consul at Boston. The documents are recited verbatim in the report, and therefore I do not trouble you with them. I preferred a recital to a reference, that all who read the report should distinctly understand the facts without being forced to examine the evidence. It appears to me to be a most flagrant case. I submit to you, however, whether it will not be better, considering the European revolution, to act in the manner the most delicate towards the emperor, referring to his justice the punishment of the offender, instead of cancelling at once the consul's exequatur. Mr. Monroe will give it the turn of a compliment to the master, without allowing the servant to escape.

I will attend to your instructions relative to Mr. Jefferson's library.

I am, dear sir, most respectfully and faithfully yours,

A. J. DALLAS.

The President.

8 May, 1815.

—————

MONTPELIER, May 10, 1815.

DEAR SIR,—I now return the General Report of the Military Board on the Organization of the Army. I have not found among the officers retained some whose merits I had supposed would have placed them on the list of selections; but I have great confidence in the intelligence and dispositions of the Board, and am ready to presume that those preferred have titles to distinction better known to them than to me; or that there may be objections known to them, and not to me, against some who had attracted my attention. It may have happened also that some of these did not choose to be included in the peace establishment.

A very anxious desire was expressed to me by the Ex-Gov. Sevier, of the House of Representatives, that his kinsman, colonel 1st Rifle Regiment, should be retained in the service. As his present position must have marked him for consideration, I take for granted that his comparative pretensions were deficient; especially as I understood that the solicitude of his uncle expressed his own, and that of course his omission was not his own choice.

The letter from Colonel Owings and Major Taylor is herewith returned. Of the former I know only that his general standing and connexions in Kentucky are respectable. Whatever merit he may have in his profession, I should suppose that it could not justify the dissatisfaction he expresses. As to Major Taylor, if there be no flaws in his character which have not come to my knowledge, I do not believe that a continuance of him in his present rank would have warranted just complaint in others. He was, if I mistake not, a captain at the commencement of the war, and the first officer that was breveted. The defence of Fort Harrison, that led to it, though on an obscure theatre, has probably not been exceeded in brilliancy by any affair that has occurred. The circumstances of it put to the severest trial the military qualities of the commanding officer, and it appeared that the result was conspicuously favorable to him. But for the haste in which many subsequent appointments were made, and particularly those to the new rifle regiments, the view in which he stood would have obtained for him a higher grade. If the door be not too far closed, which may perhaps be the case, and there be no deficiencies of any sort in his title, it may be worth your while to recur to the account given of the attack of Fort Harrison. I wish not to be understood, however, as pressing a revision of the selections, unless a change can be conveniently and satisfactorily made. Will you be so good, also, as to advert to the case of Chas. Todd, who was in Governor Harrison's family. I do not know how he stands in comparison with others, nor whether it is his desire to be retained. He was understood to be much in favor with General Harrison. My personal acquaintance with his friends will lead them to expect whatever attention may be justly and fairly due to him.

In restricting myself to the number and nature of the observations made, I give a proof of my reliance on the better information and the judgment of others, and that I am prepared to pay every attention to such suggestions from yourself as may be comprised in the general report you are preparing.

I can say nothing of my own knowledge of Major Gardner.

If the opinion of General B. has against it that of the other officers you name, and no conspicuous achievement be referred to, I see no grounds on which he ought to be preferred to Butler.

I believe I have already expressed my concurrence in the expediency of retaining the adjutant and inspector-general, and such of the garrison surgeons and surgeons' mates as may be requisite.

With respect to the hospital surgeons, I have nothing to add to my remarks on that part of the report of the Board, unless it be that if there should be a hospital contemplated at or in the vicinity of Washington, I wish that Dr. Elzy may be selected for it. My personal knowledge of him suggests this intimation in his favor.

The report, received this morning and returned, on the distribution of the troops, appears to be founded on a judicious view of the subject. I should not have disapproved a larger provision for Sackett's Harbor, and some artillery force for Detroit. You are right in reserving for Jackson a revision of the southern disposition. He will probably think more due to the security of New Orleans. Provision for a fort, co-operating with Plaquemine, will be entitled to consideration.

The idea of incorporating the chaplains of brigades with the military academy might be useful; but is so remote from the legal contemplation of their services, that it must at least lie over for consideration.

The change proposed by General Brown, in his letter to you of the 8th, has much to recommend it. It may be well, however, to have the opinion of Chauncey, and of some others, on the subject. The Secretary of the Navy will state to you what has passed on the subject of the ships building at Sackett's Harbor. The subject is embarrassing in several respects. The remark is applicable in some degree to naval possessions on all the lakes.

I requested Mr. Monroe in a letter yesterday, as you will learn from him, to bring into consultation the question of an immediate reduction of the army, which if approved by the result, you will act upon. My reasons in favor of the measure may in part be collected from a late one to you. They are strengthened by the probable removal of the British troops not only from our limits, but in great degree from Canada also. I shall receive a different opinion of the members of the cabinet, nevertheless, with a mind open to the reasons for it. I have asked for a consultation also on the expediency of diplomatic experiments for obviating the tendency of a war in Europe, to renew embarrassments to the United States. The case of Decatur's expedition is another topic for consideration.

Affectionate respects,

Mr. DALLAS.   JAMES MADISON.

DEAR SIR,—In the haste of my last letter to you I omitted to notice the wish of General Scott for permission to visit Europe, without a discontinuance of official emoluments. He is certainly entitled to every admissible indulgence, and in this case the public interests might be promoted by the military instruction he might acquire on that theatre. His departure will of course be under the control, and with his own choice, of the bearing of European events on our military arrangements.

Affectionate respects,

MR. DALLAS.   JAMES MADISON.

May 11, 1815.

———

DEAR SIR,—I send a report on the organization of the peace establishment for your consideration. The first general order proposed is also sent; the second general order will conform, with some slight exceptions, to the report of the Board; and the remaining two general orders will be in substance what the report states. I will forward them to you as fast as I can put them into form; but if you approve the outline, be so good as to sign your approbation at the foot of the report, which will put the whole subject in order for the record, and enable me to begin the publications.

Mr. Monroe left us this morning. Mr. Crowninshield has sent sailing orders to Commodore Decatur, with a confidential instruction, as to any danger that may present itself in Europe.

Colonel George Croghan has resigned. Shall his resignation be accepted and another name substituted? Or shall we wait until we see the effect of his being announced in the Army Register?

I am, dear sir, most respectfully and faithfully yours,

A. J. DALLAS.

The President.

13 May, 1815.

MEMORANDA.

1. The exceptions from the general reduction of the military establishment, as contemplated in the act of Congress, seem to be necessary, and they are few, to wit:

(1) The adjutant and inspector-general.

(2) The quartermaster-general.

(3) The apothecary-general and two assistants.

(4) Two garrison surgeons, and ten garrison surgeons' mates.

(5) Two deputy paymasters-general.

To supply vacancies, created by resignations of the first appointments on the peace establishments, all the officers are declared to be held provisionally in service.

To secure a prompt settlement of accounts, all officers intrusted with public money are held in service until they render their accounts.

2. The brigade inspectors and brigade quartermasters are to be taken by the brigadier-generals from the line, in the usual way, and cannot, therefore, be named in the Register.

3. Dr. Waterhouse and Dr. Elzy are substituted for Dr. Thomas and Dr. Watkins, reported by the Board. Dr. Bronaugh is retained, as Mr. Monroe thinks there would be suggestions of a disagreeable kind were he to be struck off. I find all officers, of all parties, speaking well of him here, and lamenting the affair with Colonel Coles as a personal one.

4. I have substituted H. Wheaton, of New York, as a judge advocate, instead of R. H. Winder, reported by the Board. Mr. Wheaton's talents are unquestionable; and it is desirable, on many accounts, to gratify him.

————

MONTPELIER, May 14, 1815.

DEAR SIR,—Yours of the 12th is duly received. The result of the consultation on the discharge of the army and the expedition against Algiers is entirely satisfactory; that relating to the question of diplomatic measures required by the crisis is so also. My own idea was rather to ripen the subject for decision than to act on it before the intelligence daily expected from Europe, and particularly from our functionaries there, should arrive. In the mean time the ordinary measure of communications, such as will proceed from the Department of State, will be proper and sufficient.

Vessels regularly condemned by a prize court cannot fairly come within the stipulation for restoring private property. If the vessels were captured in places and under circumstances rendering the capture lawful, the case is still clearer. The order you propose to issue is the more proper, as a prompt and liberal attention to the claims of the other party will strengthen ours to a liberal construction of the treaty in favor of American citizens. The more we keep in view the irregularity or unreasonableness of the capture, as the principle of restitution in the case of private property, the more our construction of the treaty will be favored and the restitution extended.

Affectionate respects,

JAMES MADISON.

I have detained the mail for a hasty perusal of the printed defence of General Jackson, which, according to request, is returned.

Mr. DALLAS.

Dear Sir,—I am anxious to make our army arrangement satisfactory, without taking too great a latitude in the discretion left to the executive. I am afraid General Jackson will be mortified if Major Butler and Major Hayne are not noticed in some part of our arrangement; and I think we can manage the matter safely by allowing an adjutant-general (Major Butler) to be provisionally retained for the division of the south, and another (Major Hayne) to be provisionally retained for the division of the north. The appointments are essential in the first movements to organize the peace establishment; and it is clear that Congress must provide more effectually for a general staff. If you approve of this alteration, my only remaining desideratum will be an honorable subsistence for the gallant and unfortunate M'Pherson. Something will, perhaps, occur in the civil line to gratify us in his case.

I am, dear sir, most respectfully and faithfully yours,

A. J. Dallas.

The President.

14 May, 1815.

———

Dear Sir,—On reflection, I have thought it right to recommend some additions and alterations in the plan submitted to you for organizing the army.

1. To transport the troops from place to place before they are formed into brigades will require more assistance in the quartermaster's department. I propose, therefore, retaining provisionally,

Samuel Brown (the general's brother), deputy quartermaster-general for the division of the north.

Abram B. Fannin (highly recommended), deputy quartermaster-general for the division of the south.

2. In the pay department, I propose that the deputies provisionally retained should be located in different divisions:

Washington Lee, deputy paymaster-general for the division of the north.

John T. Pemberton, deputy paymaster-general for the division of the south.

3. The vacancy produced by Colonel Aspinwall's appointment as consul to be supplied by Colonel Joseph L. Smith, leaving Colonel Clemson to fill the vacancy produced by the resignation of Colonel Croghan, if it is persisted in.

4. Captain Wm. O. Allen to be substituted for Captain Wm. O. Wenston in the corps of artillery, upon the request of the board of officers in a supplemental report.

5. The board of officers left a blank for the surgeon of the second regiment. I propose to fill it with the name of Franklin

Bache, surgeon of the twenty-second infantry, a young man of fine talents and amiable character. I think the appointment will have a good effect.

6. The inclosed letter from General Scott will show the mistake that has unfortunately excluded Captain Burd of the light dragoons. He is very anxious to correct it, and I propose to substitute his name as captain in the fourth regiment for the name of Captain J. Hook. Captain Burd was breveted for a gallant affair in Maryland.

7. If Major Bankhead will accept a company with the brevet of major, I propose to substitute his name for the name of B. Peyton as captain of the fourth regiment.

8. Captain George Bender, of the ninth infantry, has been omitted. He is praised as the first captain in the army by Colonel Aspinwall, and I cannot account for the omission. I send a note on his subject from Colonel Aspinwall and General Parker, and I propose to substitute Captain Bender's name instead of Wm. Browning, lately promoted, as captain of the fifth regiment. I will then transfer Browning to the head of the list of lieutenants and leave off the name of the lowest lieutenant on the list.

9. Mr. Monroe informed me that he had reflected much upon the effect of leaving off Major Gardner's name and substituting Major Butler's, and he recommended that the change should not be made. I adopt his opinion, and shall act accordingly, unless you give other instructions. Mr. Monroe left us yesterday.

I am, dear sir, most respectfully and faithfully yours,

A. J. DALLAS.

The President.

14 May, 1815.

DEAR SIR,—I have written to you already by this day's mail; but one more alteration in the army list is desirable. Major Cutler is an excellent officer, a modest man, and much esteemed. He has been in service eight years, but has not enjoyed an opportunity of becoming conspicuous in the field. He will be content with a company and the brevet. I must add that he is very poor. If you approve of it, I can make an arrangement similar to the one proposed in Captain Bender's case, with advantage, I think, to the list.

I hope it will be unnecessary to trouble you further on the general organization of the army. .

I am, dear sir, most respectfully and faithfully yours,

A. J. DALLAS.

The President.

14 May, 1815.

Montpelier, May 15, 1815.

Dear Sir,—Yours of the 13th is received, and I return the outline of what you propose with the approbation desired, which may be acted on or reconsidered in any of its parts as you judge best. This discretion is suggested by a question whether the order relating to the military departments and to the distribution of the corps ought to be combined with that relating to the reduction and organization of the army,—the former being matters of executive regulation and alteration; the last, of a legal and fixed character. It is recollected, also, that the military commanders of districts have been led by such an arrangement into views of their separate and independent authority within their respective precincts, which have embroiled them with one another and embarrassed the War Department, and which may be strengthened by the formality to be given in this case. The commanders of districts have contested the right of a senior officer arriving within them to take the command; and have complained of orders from the War Department given *directly* to inferior officers within their districts, although required by considerations of distance and urgency and made known at the same time to the commanders themselves. Should any deviation from what is proposed be ineligible, these remarks will suggest an explanation, if error on these points be not already sufficiently guarded against, of the real authority conferred by these local arrangements.

The resignation of Colonel Croghan may be accepted or not, as you choose. You understand better than I do the circumstances which ought to decide the question.

Affectionate respects,

, Mr. Dallas.   James Madison.

Montpelier, May 16, 1815.

Dear Sir,—I have received your two letters, both of the 14th. I know of no objection to your proposed additions to or changes in the list of retained officers, unless it may be in the erasure of B. Peyton. If he be the young gentleman who has been employed at or in the neighborhood of Charlottesville (Virginia), I have heard him spoken of as of merit, and much esteemed by some whose esteem would be an evidence of it. I have no personal knowledge of him. You may perhaps have the means of ascertaining the extent of his pretensions in comparison with others standing in the way of Major Bankhead.

Affectionate respects,

Mr. Dallas.   James Madison.

MONTPELIER, May 17, 1815.

DEAR SIR,—The arrangement proposed in yours of the 14th, just received, with respect to Majors Butler and Hayne, appear to be eligible, though the latter may not find it convenient, being, I understand, an inhabitant of South Carolina, to be allotted to the northern division of the army. It is desirable to gratify General Jackson, and it is fortunate that in this case it can be done with an accommodation at the same time to the public service. I know not how to account, unless by faults of the mail, for his long silence on the subject of martial law and the events growing out of it. His printed defence shows the ground on which his explanation will be made, and shows also that he will not be prepared for the view of the subject presented in your letter to him. It is to be regretted that his defence was forbidden by the judge and that it assumed the form it did. The ground on which martial law takes place is that it results from a given military situation; not that it can be introduced or extended in time or place by the authority of a military commander. When the public safety calls for its introduction or extension, the exertion of it rests on the patriotic assumption of an extraordinary responsibility. If this distinction be just, a better course might have been taken than that which the general was led to adopt. All his reasons and views ought, however, to be seen before any final opinion be formed, and if not altogether satisfactory when seen, ought to be judged with a liberality proportioned to the greatness of his services, the purity of his intentions, and the peculiarity of the circumstances in which he found himself.

Affectionate respects,

Mr. DALLAS.   JAMES MADISON.

DEPARTMENT OF WAR, May, 1815.

SIR,—The very difficult and unpleasant task of reducing the army to the number prescribed by the act of Congress fixing the military peace establishment of the United States, has been accomplished, and the proceedings of this department, as well as the result, you will find stated in the inclosed document. It has been a subject of great regret that neither you nor General Gaines could attend at Washington, to afford us the aid of your experience and information, but you may be assured that the merits of the gallant army which you commanded have not been overlooked. Your communications, and those of Colonel Hayne (to whom you referred us), have been regarded as conclusive testimonials of military character, and I hope that yourself as well as your officers will be gratified with the designation that has been made for the military peace establishment. If there are any officers of your army, either among those who are retained, or those who are discharged, to whom you think the honorary distinction of a brevet is due for distinguished services, you will be pleased to name them to the department, with a reference to the nature and date of their services.

You observe, sir, that you are appointed to the command of the division of the south under the new organization of the army. It was proper, in the first instance, to apportion and distribute the troops at military stations, in order to facilitate the formation of the corps and regiments, but you will consider the present apportionment and distribution in your division as subject to any alterations that your observation and judgment may suggest for the benefit of the service.

The defence and security of New Orleans and Mobile are objects of primary interest and importance. The recent events in Europe, and the conflicting claims of the United States and Spain to a part of the Territory of West Florida, recommend every precaution that can be taken to protect our own rights without infringing the rights of others, and I will thank you to favor the department with an early statement of your views on that subject, extending your care to the protection of Charleston, Savannah, and other exposed situations of the southern coast.

The preservation of peace with the Indians, and, indeed, with our neighbors in Canada, whether acting as a company of merchants or as a government, will essentially depend upon the positions which are now to be occupied in the Indian country. The object contemplated in that respect is to establish posts along the course of the British traders from Michilimackinac by Green Bay, the Fox River, and the Ouiscousin River, to Prairie du Chien, and thence up the Mississippi to St. Anthony's Falls. Commissioners have been appointed to hold a treaty with the Indians at St. Louis, and Colonel Miller, with a detachment of men, attending the commissioners, will take position at Prairie du Chien, whence he will be eventually ordered into the division of the north, to which his regiment is assigned. Major-General Brown will be requested to correspond with you on the measures taken for the establishment of the posts falling within his division and to avail himself of your information and experience.

The object of preserving peace may be united with the policy of improving the country and civilizing the Indians by the establishment of competent posts on a lower route from Chicago along the Illinois River to St. Louis. This object is committed to your special care as falling within the duties of your command; but besides communicating your views upon it to this department, you will be pleased to make it the subject of a correspondence with Major-General Brown, so that the measures taken in each division may be known in both, and be the result of a beneficial concert and co-operation.

For the accomplishment of the objects which have been stated, every possible despatch should be used. Castine and Fort Bowyer have been restored, and assurances are given that Fort Niagara and Fort Michilimackinac will be soon restored. Some indulgence is asked at the last place, but it cannot be long allowed, as the season for the Indian trade will soon commence, and, in a single season, the foundation of great evils may be laid.

I inclose an extract from the letter of Governor Sevier, requesting that the commissioners, who are appointed to survey the lands lately ceded by the Creeks to the United States, may have a military escort assigned to them. You will be pleased to comply with this request, if you deem it advisable, and the state of your troops renders it convenient.

The general orders which have been issued this day comprise all the instructions that are deemed necessary to be given by this department for the immediate organization of the army according to the peace establishment, and the most diligent attention is earnestly requested from all the officers in the performance of their respective duties.

I have the honor to be, very respectfully, sir, your most obedient servant,

A. J. DALLAS.

Major-General ANDREW JACKSON,
Nashville.

MONTPELIER, May 19, 1815.

DEAR SIR,—Yours of the 16th is received. The army report was returned some time ago. There have of late been delays between this and Fredericksburg, owing to inattention at the post-office there, which may account for your not having received the report. There must have been a miscarriage altogether of the document transferring appropriations. I now return a duplicate sent me from the War Department.

I am apprehensive that some uneasiness will be produced in Kentucky by the organization and appointments for the army, however unavoidable the causes of it may be. It probably happens that there will be a greater proportion of individual disappointments, and a smaller proportion of selections to the aggregate and acknowledged merits of the people there than elsewhere, and the want of a western member of the Board at Washington will not fail to excite attention. The whole is to be regretted, but no remedy, I presume, can be applied. On reflection, I think it will be best to accept Croghan's resignation, and if there be no special objection to Major Z. Taylor's replacing him, it may be done. A selection from Kentucky or Tennessee seems indispensable.

I am glad to learn that the difficulties in the fiscal department are yielding to your management of them. Should a war not result from the crisis in Europe, which is possible, or our commerce should escape its former rapacities, which may happen, the state of our treasury and our credit will put us out of the reach of domestic intrigue and cupidity.

If Chandler's claim to double rations be not within the scope of the law, or the precedents interpreting it, it must of course be disallowed. If otherwise it appears to be reasonable, and is strengthened by the opinion of General Dearborn, I am not prepared to judge of the extent to which the allowance would open a door for like claims not supported by the same equity. The war office can place the whole subject before you.

Affectionate respects,
JAMES MADISON.

Mr. DALLAS.

———

DEAR SIR,—The inclosed letter from General Jackson shows that Fort Bowyer has been restored, without difficulty; but that the negroes taken near New Orleans are retained. There are no accounts from Niagara.

I have sent by this mail the new Army Register, the general orders for effecting the organization of the peace establishment, and copies of my letters to Generals Jackson and Brown. These, together with your address of thanks, and the instructions to the board of general officers, will appear in the *National Intelligencer* of Monday, and be transferred into a small pamphlet for circulation in the army. A knowledge of the principles which have been adopted on the present occasion must, I think, secure the approbation of the candid, and silence the clamors of the malcontent.

I have thought it best to retain Colonel Croghan's name in the Register, as he constitutes an important feature in the selection from the northwestern army, and the substitute proposed by the Board, Colonel Clemson, comes from the east. If Colonel Croghan perseveres in his resignation, it will be more easy to introduce another name, without being exposed to cavils hereafter. Major Bankhead has declined taking the only place which was open for him; but, as I understood that Mr. Monroe would write to him on the subject, and wished the arrangement to be made, I shall retain Major Bankhead's name for the present.

Commodore Rodgers has received a letter from Dr. Bullus, the navy agent, stating that a vessel had just arrived at New York with accounts of a declaration of war by England against France, and of a battle in Belgium, the issue of which was not known. This day's eastern mail will give more correct information. Our squadron has probably sailed from New York.

Our stocks are rising every day. They are in demand at 93 in Philadelphia. The speculators and brokers are in a rage that I have refused their offers at 85, 87, and 89. That refusal, however, aided by the events in Europe, will probably put six per cents at par in six months. I think Mr. Adams may negotiate the sale in Europe at a higher rate than 95. As soon as the army is paid and the navy provided for, I shall begin to call in the treasury notes which are due and unpaid.

I am, dear sir, most respectfully and faithfully yours,

A. J. DALLAS.

The President.

20 May, 1815.

DEAR SIR,—I have just received your letter, expressing a wish that Colonel Croghan's resignation should be accepted ; but the Army Register has been actually printed, including his name, for the reason which I assigned in my last letter. I think, however, you will not regret the occurrence when you observe that Major Taylor must have been promoted to a higher rank in order to take Colonel Croghan's place, who is a lieutenant-colonel in the line ; and this course would not have corresponded with the general principle of the selections, which admitted of an officer's being reduced with his own consent, but has not been applied to give any officer higher rank in the line. But you will find that both Major Taylor and Major Bradford, who were united in Colonel Owing's protest, are retained as captains, with brevets as majors. Bradford has expressed perfect satisfaction with the arrangement, and he told me that the protest had been written under a misapprehension of the course taken by the board of general officers ; but that he was confident, upon better information, that the selections would be approved and supported in Kentucky. Colonel Jessup and Major Bradford told me that they doubted whether Major Taylor would consent to remain in the army on any terms ; that he was a man of fortune, and that he had long ago expressed a determination to resign. But, viewing the subject in its general aspect, you will find, I believe, that the western country has a full portion of the peace establishment. Generals Jackson, Gaines, Smith, etc., Colonel Miller, Colonel Nicholas, Colonel Croghan, Colonel Jessup, etc., are at the head of a long western list.

I inclose letters from St. Louis on Indian affairs, and a report from Colonel Jessup of his proceedings in Connecticut.

There are no details of the news sent by Dr. Bullus to Commodore Rodgers.

Be so good as to state whether you have received my report in the case of Mr. Eustaphiere, the Russian consul.

I am, dear sir, most respectfully and faithfully yours,
A. J. DALLAS.

The President.

21 May, 1815.

I open my letter to add that letters from New Orleans inform us that provision was made at that place for paying the whole of the regulars and militia, the banks advancing money for drafts on the paymaster of the army, which will be punctually paid here. The northern army is amply provided for; and I think that our funds cannot fail in any quarter.

MONTPELIER, May 21, 1815.

DEAR SIR,—I have received yours, without date, inclosing the letters from Mr. Hall and Mr. Forsyth, which are now returned. A letter was lately sent to the Secretary of State from Governor Early, recommending a successor to Mr. Harris as district attorney for Georgia. I forget whether it was the same gentleman as is the subject of the letters from Messrs. H. and F. If it was, the appointment of Mr. Davis may take place; otherwise, further inquiry may not be amiss.

I have a letter from General Gaines, by which I find that the selection of him is accepted with equal modesty and gratitude.

In my remarks on the resignation of Colonel Croghan, it was not my meaning that Major Taylor should succeed to the vacancy as lieutenant-colonel, but that it might open the way for retaining the latter as major. If the case could be so managed as to advance Jessup to the place of Croghan, it would do no more than justice to that very distinguished officer, and would unite several advantageous considerations. But, if I am right in my recollection, Jessup has risen to the brevet rank of colonel from that of major only in the line.

Affectionate respects,
JAMES MADISON.

Mr. DALLAS.

DEAR SIR,—I have received the inclosed letters from General Jackson and General Gaines. The former does not appear to have received any of our letters; and the latter has only received the letter inviting him to Washington, or his answers have miscarried.

There is a remarkable coincidence between General Gaines'

recommendatory list and the selections made here; and Lieutenant Spotts, who is strongly recommended by General Jackson, and for whom I ask a brevet, says, that the Army Register will give the highest satisfaction to the South. As 'the *National Intelligencer* of to-day contains the whole of the military budget, we shall soon ascertain the feelings of the officers and the printers upon the occasion.

I send a letter from General Dearborn, inclosing Colonel Starke's official report of the surrender of Castine. When you return this communication, I will send a copy of it to the Department of State, that Mr. Monroe may be able to meet Mr. Baker's claim with a knowledge of the facts.

I am, dear sir, most respectfully and faithfully yours,

A. J. DALLAS.

The President.
22 May, 1815.

———

DEAR SIR,—I had prepared a letter to General Brown respecting the surrender of the fort at Michilimackinac before I received your favor of the 24th instant. Every consideration presses that object upon our attention; and an early possession must be insisted on by all means except force. If the delay continues until Mr. Monroe's return, you will, perhaps, think it right to address Mr. Baker on the subject. The views which I have taken of the posts to be introduced into the Indian country contemplate a gradual, but steady, operation, which may be completed in two or three years. We have no answer from Colonel Hawkins.

The Secretary of the Navy, Commodore Chauncey, and myself concur in the view which General Brown has taken of the expediency of transferring the naval and military station from Sackett's Harbor to Henderson's Bay. They concur, too, in the opinion that the ships at Sackett's Harbor should be finished for launching; and, when launched, should be removed to Henderson's Bay, and sunk. If left on the stocks, they will perish in two years; and they cannot be launched and sunk at Sackett's Harbor. The expense of finishing them will amount to a sum of about fifty thousand dollars; and the expense of purchasing a site for the military and naval station at Henderson's Bay will be about two or three dollars per acre. It would, I think, however, be wise to purchase the peninsula included within a line run from the head of the bay to the mouth of Stoney Creek. The subject will remain for your consideration at Washington; but, in the mean time, I will request General Brown to ascertain the quantity of land, the price, etc., and to make a conditional arrangement, so as to avoid binding the government to purchase, but, at the same time, prevent the price being raised upon us.

Mr. Crowninshield has, I presume, mentioned to you the differ-ence of opinion which has arisen between him and the Board of navy commissioners. The occurrence was anticipated, and stated to Mr. Jones when he showed me his plan. It appears to me to be a plain case in favor of the Secretary of the Navy; but a case of some delicacy. The style of the Board was improper, even if their claims were correct. I am afraid that the employment of Goldsborough has been injurious; but I fear still more that our good comptroller's opinion of his own legal learning has laid the foundation of much error.

I have recommended Mr. Wardell's case to the collector of New York.

There is nothing new here. I presumed that you would not return to Washington until some accounts from our commissioners reached us. If your health improves at Montpelier I should be sorry to see you hasten your return, as I am not aware of any immediate pressure of business.

I am, dear sir, most respectfully and faithfully yours,

A. J. DALLAS.

The President.
26 May, 1815.

MONTPELIER, May 24, 1815.

DEAR SIR,—I have received yours of the 20th and 21st, to which the arrival of the mail enables me to add that of the 22d. I return the letter from General Jackson inclosed in the first, and the letters from Forsyth, Russell, Governor Holmes, and Jessup inclosed in the second. The last is a very interesting document, and shows the writer to be a man of excellent sense, as well as a shining warrior. The aspect of things in the Missouri district is rendered much worse than described by Russell, by a melan-choly paragraph in a St. Louis gazette, which, as it may not have reached you, I put under this cover. It furnishes a topic on which the British commander in Canada may be pressed with peculiar force to hasten the delivery of Michilimackinac. That ocular proof only of the honorable termination of the war will extinguish the confidence and hostility with which the savages have been inspired by their allies; especially as the latter, from pride and policy both, will exaggerate the stipulation in the treaty in favor of the former. I am glad you are turning your thoughts systematically to the Indian department of our affairs. It embraces a cordon of posts. Agents political, and agents com-mercial. A cordon, stretching from Michigan to the frontier settlements westward of the Mississippi, and on the back of those settlements southward to a connection with Louisiana, would form an advantageous barrier between the white and the red people, and protect, at the same time, the public lands against lawless occupancies. The military force, however, that can fairly be so applied is inadequate to the whole object. It is questionable whether an adequate portion can be found for the double cordon you have in view for the northwestern quarter, which, being most under the influence of the Canadian traders, evidently requires the strongest precautions, without neglecting too much the defence due to the Missouri territory on the western side. General Mason will be able to afford much useful information on the subject of the commercial agencies. If that mode of supplying the wants of the Indians be continued, some new regulations may be found necessary, as well to prevent abuses at distant factories as to supersede more the resort of the Indians to British supplies. The correspondences and communications on the files of the War Department will throw light on this subject, if they can be selected by any of the remaining clerks. Some valuable information was communicated by Judge Lucas, but whether on paper or verbally I do not recollect. It becomes an interesting question how far we ought at once to shut out the British traders from our limits, not only on this side the Mississippi, but through the whole extent of the Louisiana purchase. Within the latter they never had a right, though they once set up a claim to trade with the Indians, and from the former they may now be excluded by the tenor of the treaty at Ghent; and as to both, a prohibition, at no distant day, will be essential. For the moment, it may perhaps be as well to bring these questions into view as little as possible, as they may increase difficulties on others depending on the treaty of Ghent, taking care, however, that no sanction be given, in any way, to the trade enjoyed of right heretofore with the Indians on this side the Mississippi. It has not yet been decided whether a general superintendency (political), such as was held by Governor Hull, should be established for the northwest Indians, or into whose hands it should be placed. Mr. Monroe had it under consideration as a service for General Wilkinson. Whether it would suit him, and he that, are of course open questions. If Colonel Hawkins should leave the Creek agency, a candidate will be seen in a letter now forwarded. I recollect nothing of his character. If the vacancy be not applied in alleviation of reduced officers, great respect is due to Colonel Hawkins's recommendation. A commission may be issued for Colonel Hinds as brigadier, etc., as recommended by Governor Holmes.

The papers relating to Mr. Eustaphiere were sent to the Secretary of State, with a suggestion that his case should be stated to the emperor in the manner most likely to combine the two objects of conciliating the master and getting rid of the servant.

Issue the brevet you propose for Lieutenant Spotts.

I return the papers relating to Castine and the captured stores, which may await the return of the Secretary of State to Washington, previous to which he will probably hold no further communication with Mr. Baker on the subject.

The military budget makes its appearance, I observe, in the *National Intelligencer.* I cannot refer to it without expressing my obligations for the laborious task it has cost you, and my gratification that you are at length relieved from it. Besides the labor, the task has been distinguished by the delicate questions involved in it, touching the comparative pretensions of meritorious individuals. That there will be a unanimous approbation of what has been done is not to be expected. But I persuade myself that the candid and reasonable part of the public, taking into view the arduous nature of the duty, and the propriety of blending with a reward for past services a provision for future ones, will be more than merely satisfied with the execution of the law.

I return the papers in behalf of B. and I. Bohlen. Be so good as to refer them to the State Department; and if you think the circumstances of the case sufficiently peculiar and strong, without the usual resort for information to the official sources, a pardon may issue. Some countenance to a favorable interposition of the executive in such cases has been generally required from the judges, the jury, or the law officer prosecuting, in order to guard against the liberality and sympathy which so readily furnish private recommendations. I am not prepared to form an opinion on the merits of the question as decided by the supreme court. I presume that they were much influenced by the consideration, that, if the securing the duties, etc. were to stamp imported merchandise with all the rights of circulation, a dangerous door might be opened for collusion. Whatever may have been the ground of the decision, it is but fair to distinguish between cases prior and cases subsequent to it. If you think it requisite that the prosecuting attorney should be applied to, the order indorsed for the pardon may be suspended. The indorsement is on your statement of the case.

The letter of Mr. Sailler and the papers with it were brought to me here by Mr. Buel, the subject of them. I told him they would of course be referred to the Treasury Department, to which he might add any explanations he might have to make. Sailler was formerly a very respectable member of Congress, and, as far as his testimony with the drawback of kindred bias goes, it is entitled to attention. But he is aware of the indiscretion which calls for the executive animadversion. And with respect to the question of interest between Buel and his successor, I understood that it was already in court. If Buel means to lodge charges against Vanness, or his representations suggest inquiry as to the conduct of the latter, you will of course take the usual steps.

The letter recommending Mr. Wardell for an office in the customs at New York is from two of my worthy neighbors. Mr. Monroe, I learn, has been led by his friends in Fredericksburg to write to Mr. Gelston ,with a view to his patronage. I am not acquainted with Wardell, but have much confidence in those recommending him. The great objection arises from the circumstance of his intending to settle in New York without having previously settled there, and which may be pressed by his competitors. If this objection be waived or disregarded by Mr. Gelston, Mr. Wardell may fairly enter into comparison with other candidates.

I have not yet fixed on the time of my return to Washington. It will probably be in the course of next week. I hope to see Mr. Monroe in the course of this or early in the next, and I shall then fix on the day for setting out.

Yours affectionately,

JAMES MADISON.

The letter from General McArthur, now returned, is another proof of the obligation on the British commander to deliver Fort Mackinaw, and of ours to press it on him. You will of course approve the means necessary to make Fort Wayne temporarily secure at least. And unless it be understood that the northwest Indians alluded to are embraced in and will attend the treaty already instituted, another may be set on foot under Governor Cass and General McArthur, or any other commissioners that may be more conveniently employed. Perhaps Worthington might properly be at the head of the commission. The expense and the extent of the proceeding ought, however, to be influenced by the number and the importance of the tribes to be treated with. Query—How would it do to offer General Wilkinson a service on the occasion? He is at home in that quarter.

Mr. DALLAS.

MONTPELIER, May 27, 1815.

DEAR SIR,—It is represented to me from a very respectable source in Kentucky that Messrs. Ward and Taylor (army contractors) are men of real patriotism and integrity; that their services have been particularly critical and meritorious; and that they are threatened with absolute ruin in consequence of their pecuniary exertions unless they can be immediately aided by anticipations of what will be due to them, and which will be justified by their characters and their responsibility. If anything can be done for them I am sure you will not let them suffer unjustly or improperly. The case is doubtless within your command of all the requisite information by which its merits is to be determined.

I am just favored with yours of the 25th instant.

I am commencing my arrangements preparatory to my return to Washington. I hope to reach it about the end of the ensuing week.

Affectionate respects,

Mr. DALLAS.   JAMES MADISON.

DEAR SIR,—I inclose a report upon the expediency of selling a part of the gunpowder, to which you will be so good as to subjoin your approbation.

My friend Colonel Johnstone spares no one on the subject of Ward and Taylor's contract. The truth is that by his assiduity during the session of Congress they fared much better than any other contractors. They have actually received near $500,000 on their old contract, and I have just given them a warrant for $10,000 on their new contract *in advance.* Their accounts are not settled, and the apparent balance of their account for their old contract is about $50,000, liable, however, to an augmentation upon additional vouchers. One of the New York contractors has a balance of more than $500,000 due to him. But in point of fact Mr. Ward himself was with me a day or two ago, and was perfectly satisfied with my arrangements; and in point of law the appropriation for subsistence is exhausted, and unless we can remit it from the ordnance fund we shall be obliged to suspend all payments until Congress meets.

I sent a copy of General McArthur's letter to General Brown as soon as I received it, and I will write to the commanding officer at Fort Wayne to make himself secure at that place. I think you will find it necessary to hold a distinct treaty with the Indians to whom the general's letter relates. Governor Clarke's commission is to treat with the Indians west of the Illinois River and Lake Michigan merely for peace in pursuance of our treaty with England. But the Indians of whom General McArthur speaks inhabit east of the Illinois River and Lake Michigan, in Michigan Territory, etc. etc., and are principally the very Indians with whom Governor Cass and General Harrison concluded the treaty of the 2d July, 1814. As a treaty is certainly better than a war, I submit to you the appointment of Governor Worthington, General Wilkinson, and Mr. John Graham (who in a letter to his brother from Chillicothe expresses a willingness to serve) as the pacific negotiators. In the mean time I will write to Governor Worthington merely to draw his attention to the subject and to request his good offices in preserving harmony. Governor

Cass will also be instructed to use his best endeavors to prevent or to repel hostilities.

As it is probable that I shall see you in a few days, the important objects connected with our Indian country, the posts at Malden and Mackinac, and the arbitration articles of our treaty will be reviewed. But do you not think it would be advisable to appoint at once our arbitrators under each article of the treaty, and to notify the appointment to the British government? The English interest is all on the side of delay; our interest is all on the side of decision; and the moment is favorable to enforce a settlement. I am always afraid of allowing rights or claims to assume the character of being obsolete.

I am, dear sir, most respectfully and faithfully yours,

A. J. DALLAS.

The President.

29 May, 1815.

I inclose Mr. Graham's letter. Provision had been long ago made to pay the troops which he mentions as wanting their pay.

I have just received a letter from Mr. Stickney dated at St. Mary's. It contains very unpleasant accounts, and I am afraid our white men provoke much of the hostility manifested by the Indians. Perhaps you will think it right to send an admonitory proclamation into the several regions of new settlements.

MONTPELIER, May 30, 1815.

DEAR SIR,—Since my last I have received the inclosed from the two western contractors.

I have determined to set out for Washington on the 1st of June, and shall probably have the pleasure of being with you on Monday next, if not sooner. It may be expected that by that time the multiplying arrivals from Europe will put us in possession of the state of things there which ought to influence measures here. Another consideration is, that a decision on the case produced by the act establishing the navy board may be more satisfactory if made with the advantages on the spot than if made without them. I cannot but hope that the constitutional relation of the Secretary of the Navy to the executive, and the legal relation of the Board to the former, will furnish a ground for a decision that will be satisfactory. But I perceive with regret the subject has presented itself to the commissioners in some views that may be embarrassing. Where can be found most conveniently the constitutions of the British admiralty and navy boards? The relations between them might be of use on the occasion.

Be so good as to discontinue communications hither after the receipt of this, and to accept my affectionate respects,

JAMES MADISON.

Mr. DALLAS.

Montpelier, June 1, 1815.

Dear Sir,—I have just received yours of the 29th ult. I return approved your proposition for the sale in the ordnance department; also your recommendation for provisionally retaining Mr. Linnard.

I am under the impression that Mr. Monroe wrote to Governor Cass on the subject of the Indians on that frontier, and took the steps necessary for having the peace notified to them. Be that as it may, it is proper that immediate attention should be given to the matter as it is now represented. General Wilkinson and Mr. Graham will be fit commissioners, and may without loss of time be put on the service. Worthington and Cass are also well adapted. But both will not be wanted, and the appointment of one may not be taken well by the other. McArthur may also have his feelings in the case unless his services be employed in some other way. On the whole, however, I do not know that any selection can be made better than that you have suggested, viz., Worthington, Wilkinson, and Graham. If a different view of the subject should present itself, it may await my arrival at Washington. The subject of General Scott's letter may conveniently do so.

I wrote some time since to Mr. Monroe, calling his attention to the appointment of commissioners for boundary, etc.; one of them has long been designated. There has been a difficulty in choosing among the others brought into view.

I shall set out to-day for Washington, taking the route through Stephanburg and Elkrun Church, and shall probably be in Washington by Monday.

Affectionate respects,

Mr. Dallas.   James Madison.

Washington, July 11, 1815.

Dear Sir,—As the writer of the inclosed letter may possibly call on you, I have thought it proper that you should be previously acquainted with its singular contents. Mr. Graham mistook my intentions in touching the subject of communications between you and myself. He will, in order to put an end to the business, inform Major O'C. definitely that the vacancy in the artillery which he seeks will not be *immediately* filled. One other respectable candidate for it I recollect you named as recommended by General Pinkney, and it is possible that others may be brought into view. There are several vacancies of the same rank in the line for which there are, I believe, candidates also already before the department, and others may be expected to come forward. It will be time enough to decide on the pretensions of Major O'C. after reasonable opportunities are given for

estimating the comparative merits of others. We remain without a ray of intelligence from or of our ministers abroad.

Affectionate respects,

Mr. DALLAS.   JAMES MADISON.

WASHINGTON, July 18, 1815.

DEAR SIR,—That no erroneous impression might be left on Major O'C. by the conversation of Captain Graham, the latter has taken occasion to let him understand that the contents of his letter to you had been mentioned to me, and that the letter itself had been deposited in the war office. It is truly vexatious to have a moment thrown away on such incidents. This importunate suitor for office appears to be reconciled to his present disappointment by his hope of better fortune hereafter. A captaincy in the line will probably be very acceptable, and I am not desirous that he should be excluded from a fair chance of obtaining one, notwithstanding the exceptionable manner in which he has pursued his object.

Written information from Bordeaux of June 2d, and printed, from Paris of May 29, have been received here by the Spartan. Both concur in representing the preparations and prospects of France as flattering to Napoleon. The accounts through those channels from England are not later than, I observe, are brought by a late arrival at New York.

Affectionate respects,

Mr. DALLAS.   JAMES MADISON.

WASHINGTON, July 19, 1815.

DEAR SIR,—I have duly received your two favors of the 15th and 16th. That inclosing the letter from the collector of Barnstable had been previously received. Mr. Monroe has presented this enormity to the attention of Mr. Baker, and will, of course, make it the subject of proper remarks and instructions to Mr. Adams. He has done and will do the same in relation to the Indians Your suggestion in favor of a proclamation on the latter subject will be duly considered. I am not without hopes that the military and conciliatory measures jointly on foot, with the evacuation of Machinac succeeding that of Prairie du Chien, will change the conduct, if not the temper, of the savages towards the frontier settlements.

Not hearing a word yet from our envoys, and perceiving no material disadvantage from my absence, I shall set out to-day for my farm. I leave with the Department of State the communications for Mr. Crawford. Be so good, if you should learn that he will decline his appointment, to ascertain whether Mr. Clay would undertake it, and drop me a line without delay on the subject. I make this request on the supposition that both of them will be destined to Philadelphia. The arrangements with the post-office here will hasten to me whatever you may have occasion to communicate. As your letter to General Jackson did not arrive yesterday, I shall probably receive it on the road.

Be assured of my great esteem and affectionate respects,

JAMES MADISON.

P. S.—Should you fail of an opportunity to ascertain the intentions of Mr. Crawford, it is still desirable that the disposition of Mr. Clay should be sounded.

Mr. DALLAS.

MONTPELIER, July 24, 1815.

DEAR SIR,—I have received from Mr. Monroe your letter to him, with the inclosed, from Governor Nicholas to you, and an intimation of his own wish that the object of the latter may, if practicable, be complied with. I received yesterday a letter from Mr. Jefferson, which has a very material bearing on the subject. I inclose it for your perusal ; after which be so good as to return it. It would afford me much pleasure to gratify Governor Nicholas on a point which he naturally has so much at heart. But the difficulty is not a little increased by the tenor of Mr. Jefferson's letter, and by the fact that previous applications for the consulate at Leghorn have been answered by a reference to the occupancy of it by Appleton. The appointment of A. to another place would remove the difficulty immediately pressing, but no opening occurs which he would prefer and be entitled to ; and to an exchange for a place of inferior value he would not, of course, consent. Not knowing or recollecting the candidates who were rejected on the ground of Appleton's possession, I cannot appreciate their pretensions, and the difficulty of yielding without providing for them, to the appointment of a later candidate. I give you this full view of the subject that you may have an opportunity of suggesting a mode, if any should occur to you, of avoiding its difficulties as well as of explaining them to Governor N.

Mr. Monroe informs me that Mr. Serrurier has received a *copy* of new credentials from Napoleon, the originals being probably in the hands of Mr. Crawford. Mr. M. had heard nothing from abroad on any other subject. He proposed to leave Washington on Sunday (yesterday) to join his family, of whose health he had unfavorable accounts.

We got safe to our home on Saturday last, and are enjoying a respite which would be heightened if extended to all who are equally entitled to it.

Be assured of my great esteem and my affectionate respects,

JAMES MADISON.

If you think it proper to grant the petition of Taft, be so good as to send it to the Department of State with a note for a pardon to be made out and sent to me.

Mr. DALLAS.

———

DEAR SIR,—The business of Fort Washington is a bad one. The inclosed papers will show that there is no plan, no responsibility, no honesty. I do not mean to inculpate Major L'Enfant on the score of honesty, but his strange course of conduct is embarrassing in the extreme, and will render it impossible to give any explanation to Congress. If you approve of my report on the subject, be so good as to return it with an expression of your approbation.

I am, dear sir, most respectfully and faithfully yours,

A. J. DALLAS.

The President.
31 July, 1815.

———

It is very desirable to promote the wishes of Governor Tompkins, and the interest of the State of New York; but there are national views of the subject which must be combined with them. All transactions with the Indians relative to their lands are more or less delicate; a removal of them from one region to another is particularly so as relates to the effect on the Indians themselves and on the white neighbors to their new abode. Governor T. does not refer to any particular part of the western country which he has in view, or which the Indians would probably select, nor does he say whether he means, by lands within the limits of the United States, lands of which the Indian titles have been extinguished, as well as those still in Indian occupancy. If the latter only be meant, the arrangement will essentially lie between the Senecas and the State of New York on the one part, and the Indian occupants on the other. If it be contemplated to transfer the Senecas to lands which have been purchased from other Indians, the national government seems bound to take into view the effect of such an arrangement (1) in shutting the lands against the sales and settlements contemplated by the purchase, or involving the expense of a repurchase from the Senecas; (2) in giving Indian neighbors to white settlements, which might not choose them. When it was proposed to transfer the Indians on the northern frontier of Ohio to a new abode on the Illinois, etc., such a measure was protested against on the part of the neighboring Territories of Illinois and Missouri. It will be proper to assure Governor T. of the accommodating disposition of the executive, and to obtain from him explanations enabling it to decide with the requisite attention to the national interest under its charge. He may be generally informed, at the same time, that a removal of the Indians, should it take place, will not affect the annuities stipulated to them.

J. M.

Mr. Dallas.
July 31, 1815.

———

Dear Sir,—I can gather no news from the officers of the Neptune worth communicating. Mr. Crawford has told you all that is important of our own affairs, and of the affairs of Europe when he left it. The newspapers will tell you, as soon as this letter can reach you, of the dreadful battle of the 15th, 16th, 17th, and 18th of June. The carnage must have exceeded anything in the history of battles. The Duke of Wellington's account claims, but certainly does not prove, a victory on the part of the allies. A few such victories would leave the British without generals, and probably without troops.

The cases of General Wilkinson, General Cushing, and General Boyd are urged upon me. The vacancies at Castine, etc. are too humble for these gentlemen; and I am requested to ask your authority to create vacancies of a higher kind in the collectorships of New York, New London, Newport, etc. There is no delicacy used on the occasion, and I am at a loss how to treat the daily importunity of some of the officers. Mr. Crawford's arrival will relieve me in part; but I wish entirely to relieve you, if I could ascertain your wish as to the mode.

Mr. Todd was in perfect health, with Mr. Gallatin in London, when the Neptune sailed.

I am, dear sir, most faithfully and respectfully yours,

A. J. Dallas.

The President.
3 August, 1815.

———

Dear Sir,—The inclosed paper gives, it is alleged, the sequel of the battle of the 18th of June, between Bonaparte and the allies. The report, in the extent stated, is doubted here; but I think it probable that Bonaparte's repulse will produce something like a test of his popularity at Paris.

I have written to Mr. Crawford, but no answer has been received. It may be that he is on his way to visit you.

I am, dear sir, most respectfully and faithfully yours,

A. J. Dallas.

The President.
6 August, 1815.

The Secretary of the Treasury has the honor to represent to the President of the United States,—

That he has received from the mayor of the city of New York a letter dated the 3d instant, to which the answer dated the 7th instant has been given, relative to the American seamen who have arrived in cartels from England, and are exposed to great want, being destitute of pecuniary funds : and that similar communications have been made from other ports of the United States.

That for the cases thus represented there is no provision made by law ; but, as the corporation of the city of New York offers to afford the necessary relief upon receiving assurances of a reimbursement, the President's sanction is respectfully requested for giving an assurance that the reimbursement will be recommended to Congress at the next session.

A. J. DALLAS.

7 August, 1815.

TREASURY DEPARTMENT, 7 August, 1815.

SIR,—I have received your letter of the 3d instant, and exceedingly regret that it is not in my power to comply immediately with your wish for the relief of our suffering seamen who have recently arrived in cartels at New York. I have sent your letter to the Secretary of the Navy, and I will lay the subject before the President ; but you are perfectly aware that this department has no authority to make advances beyond the appropriations of the law. As soon as I have received the President's instructions I will do myself the honor to address you again upon the subject. In the mean time, I am confident that the humanity and public spirit of the corporation of New York will not relax in the attention which has been bestowed on the distressed mariners.

I am, etc.,   A. J. DALLAS.

The Mayor of the City of New York.

NEW YORK, August 8, 1815.

SIR,—I consider it my duty to mention to you the case of American seamen and others, late prisoners with the British, who have arrived at this port, and are daily arriving, principally from Dartmoor, in England, in considerable numbers. They are landed from cartels, destitute of money, and without the means of subsistence or any provision for conveying them to their homes or places of residence in the different States to which they belong ; and are thus cast upon the charity of the public, and compelled literally to beg in the streets. Their situation is truly distressing, and has become the subject of remark very unfriendly to the government, and our citizens are mortified to find that no one here is authorized or willing, on the part of the government, to afford the necessary assistance to men who have already suffered so much in the cause of their country.

The collector of this port, Mr. Gelston, has been strongly solicited to make the necessary advances for their relief; but he has declined doing it, considering himself unauthorized, and apprehending that the expenditure might not be allowed to him in his accounts.

The corporation of this city have contributed some moneys for this purpose, in confidence that they will be reimbursed by the government of the United States; but, finding the demands upon them to increase, and fearing that some difficulties may arise on this head, and considering it to be out of their province, they have also declined to make any further advances.

We have now a considerable number of men who were such prisoners in town, and who depend for their immediate bread and the means of getting to their families on the charity of individual citizens.

Under such circumstances, I trust you will excuse the liberty I take in mentioning this subject, and requesting that you will, if you consider it proper, direct the collector of this port to provide for all such late prisoners; or, since the corporation have already expended some moneys for this object, that you will authorize the expenditure, and enable me to say that they will be reimbursed by the government, in which case, I have no doubt, they would continue to make the necessary advances, though they would prefer it should be done by the collector.

Your immediate attention to this subject is very much desired, and I trust will be satisfactory to the parties concerned.

> I have, etc.,   JACOB RADCLIFF.

The Hon. ALEX. J. DALLAS.

MONTPELIER, Aug. 10, 1815.

DEAR SIR,—I have received your several favors of the 29th and 31st of July, and of the 1st, 3d, and 6th instant. I have delayed acknowledging them in the daily expectation of receiving something from London which would supply the defect of information at Philadelphia, relative to our affairs and functionaries there. A letter from Mr. Crawford received this morning, contains the agreeable information that he will become a member of the executive family, but he is entirely silent as to everything else. I suspect that he left London before anything like negotiation commenced, and that he had received nothing from Mr. G. or Mr. C. on the subject. The only glimpse of it which has yet reached me is in a letter from J. P. Todd, dated June 10, in which he says that in consequence of some official interviews, a member of the Board of Trade had been added to the Ghent commissioners of Great Britain, and that a negotiation was taking place in form. He adds that the fact was not given out to the public, which may account for the silence of the London prints.

I have received a letter from Governor Nicholas on the subject of his son, and have explained the difficulties arising—first, from the possession of the consulate at Naples by Mr. A.; and secondly, from the rejection on that ground of two other military candidates. One of these I learn was Colonel Fenwick, the other, Colonel Drayton, of South Carolina.

I have sent to Mr. Monroe the communication from Bremen. It is another proof of the incaution of the act of Congress in its existing form. To such states as Bremen, etc., which has nothing to give in return, it not only gives valuable privileges in navigation, but with the moral certainty, that without guards, which a treaty only could provide, the privileges will be fraudulently assumed by our more formidable competitors.

The case of the Barratarians is a puzzling one, especially in the absence of our naval force on foreign service. Be so good as to send me any further information you may receive from New Orleans. Some concert will be necessary between the Navy and War Departments. In the mean time the expediency of proclaiming a reward for apprehending the pirates may be considered.

I have not noticed your publication intended for the first of August, but take for granted it has been in the northern papers.

I foresaw that Mr. Gales's notice of the reappointment of Mr. Serrurier would be caught at and misinterpreted. The truth is that there has been no intention to acknowledge the government of Napoleon during the uncertainty of the issue of the contest. In a consultation with the Secretary of State this was our joint view of the course most becoming.the principle on which the United States have acted, and threatening least embarrassment in the result.

The business of Fort Washington is truly a bad one. As Mr. Monroe had been so much connected with the introduction of L'Enfant into it, and was considered by L'E. as friendly to him, I communicated your report and the other papers to Mr. M. He entirely concurs in the propriety of putting an end to the agony of L'E., but he wishes the mode to be softened as much as may be. This may easily be done by resting the discontinuance of the extra employment on the change of circumstances and the liberation of the regular engineers from other services.

If you think proper, the term "discharge" may be exchanged in the report for a phrase conformable to that idea. The report may retain its date.

I return the draft of a letter to General Jackson. I do not see that one could be framed more advantageously combining the several objects to be attained. I have suggested merely with the pencil one or two slight variations, which you will not adopt if they appear doubtful. You will of course give to the letter as early a date as circumstances will permit.

As this will be among the last aids which I shall receive from you in the provisional station you were so obliging as to accept, I take the occasion of adding to my particular thanks for it a general acknowledgment of my obligations, and still more my sense of those of the nation, for the very arduous and very able services which you so cheerfully added to the important and laborious duties of another department.

The cases of the three generals you name are embarrassing, but the mode of relief merits serious consideration also. The principle of it is entirely new, and the extent of it not easily limited. Boyd, I believe, is not needy, and his case therefore the less pressing. After the language with which General W. met the offer to treat with the Indians, it ought to be well ascertained before another be made that the motives to it will not be misinterpreted. Cushing's situation is probably urgent, and his conduct strengthens his claims. But is not the foundation of them the same with those on which the actual collector of New London received and has retained his appointment? Huntington was a revolutionary officer, with whatever particular merit I do not recollect, but probably with services and sufferings equal to those of General Cushing. It is true, his political conduct has been justly exceptionable, but it is not on that ground that his removal is required. Ellery, of Rhode Island, though not a revolutionary soldier, was a revolutionary patriot in high public trusts, and on that ground also has been retained in his present office, notwithstanding frequent charges of political misconduct. Of Gelston's history I am less possessed. I am disposed to take into fair consideration the mode proposed for rewarding or alleviating the cases to which it would apply; but I should be glad to learn, before it be adopted, some practicable rule for designating the officers to be displaced, and for selecting those to be provided for. If the deciding consideration be the wealth of the former and the poverty of the latter, the rule would probaby not be very correspondent with any preconceived ideas of the public. These remarks do not exclude the resource in favor of meritorious and indigent officers, which may be found in special removals pointed out by legitimate causes for them.

I had received by a line from Mr. Cutts in Boston a sketch

of the news in yours of the 6th instant, but had noticed the report from the *Bramble* met at sea on the 24th July, twenty days from England, and paid but little attention to so improbable a story. The numerous circumstances not seen necessarily vary the aspect of the intelligence. Still, unless there be an error in one or other of those dates, the improbability of it is strengthened into nearly a certainty that it is not true. We cannot be long in suspense.

Affectionate respects,

Mr. DALLAS. JAMES MADISON.

The inclosed letter from Thomas is another mark of the delicacy of the Board, or of one at least of it. Please to return the letter.

———

DEAR SIR,—I have received yours of the 7th instant on the subject of the seamen returning in distress. It is incumbent on the executive to do everything within its province for their relief. Your answer to the mayor of New York was entirely proper. He may be assured of the favorable dispositions of the executive, and that a reimbursement of the advances of the corporation will be recommended to Congress. The same assurance may be given in other cases calling for it. In the mean time it will be proper to consider whether a provision for seamen under such circumstances might not be covered by some of the existing appropriations. Be so good as to look into them with an eye to this question. If that for foreign intercourse, or for prisoners of war, be found inadequate or inapplicable, the contingent fund of government, at least as far as it will go, can be legally resorted to on such an occasion.

Affectionate respects,

Mr. DALLAS. JAMES MADISON.

Aug. 13, 1815.

———

TREASURY DEPARTMENT, 22 August, 1815.

GENTLEMEN,—I have received your letter of the 19th instant, claiming for the vessels lately arrived from Bremen the benefit of entry, on payment of the same duties which the law imposes on American vessels.

The act of Congress of the 3d of March, 1815, on which this claim is founded, depends for its execution upon the sanction and authority of the President of the United States, and not upon the mere regulations of a foreign nation. There are many considerations to be weighed in forming a decision upon the subject;

29

and probably the President may deem it necessary to reduce the arrangements to the form of a compact. For the present, therefore, the collector of the port of Baltimore acts with propriety in demanding the payment of foreign duties from the Bremen vessels.

I am, etc.,

A. J. DALLAS.

Messrs. BRUNE & DANNEMAN, Baltimore.

MONTPELIER, Sept. 2, 1815.

DEAR SIR,—I received this morning yours of the 29th August, covering a copy of the circular complying with Mr. Daschkoff's request, which is precisely what it ought to be, and a newspaper containing the late news from Europe. The political annihilation at least of Napoleon will give play to many springs in the allied powers, which a fear of him had kept in an inert state ; and very important scenes are probably yet to be exhibited. I am very glad to find that the intoxicating triumph of Great Britain has not seduced her from the conciliatory policy commenced towards us whilst the great events on the continent were undecided. The glimpse we have of the treaty of commerce, which appears to have been concluded, is too faint for any estimate of its character. But we cannot doubt that it will contain nothing positively bad, and some things substantially good ; and a conclusion of it at such a moment is itself an evidence that the British government finds in its own situation, and that of Europe, sufficient motives to cultivate and secure the friendly intercourse which we have never ceased to desire.

Having neglected to possess myself of the act of Congress relating to the conditional abolition of discriminating duties, I am at a loss how far the execution of it is imperative or discretionary. If the latter, the case presented by the Bremen vessels is without difficulty ; as will be similar claims from other countries. If the former, no wrong has been yet done, because the Bremen vessels bringing with them the first evidence of their claim, must of necessity have *entered* before a *proclamation* could issue, and this must have been foreseen by those who had the law before them. Future arrivals from Bremen may be more embarrassing. But it will be better to apply a retrospective remedy than to be precipitate in laying down a general rule. Mr. Daschkoff has not renewed his application. If the treaty with Great Britain has equalized the navigation between the two countries, one objection to the execution of the law, in favor of the carrying states, the danger of frauds, will be removed. But it is clear that the United States will be the losers by a voluntary extension of the equality to such powers as are most ready to seek it. Where these have colonies whose ports are shut to our vessels, there can be neither legal nor equitable title to the benefit of the act of Congress.

The case of the cartels bringing seamen from England is certainly entitled to all the liberality, with respect to entrance and tonnage, within the authority of the execut ve, or that can be warranted by the peculiarity of the case.

The case presented by the Commissioner of the Revenue requires more examination than I can now apply to it. With respect to duties on goods imported through Mackinaw, it seems best not to press them on individuals, but to leave them for a diplomatic subject to be pressed or not according to circumstances. In every other respect the revenue laws, as far as applicable to goods imported from Canada or other foreign territories, and as far as practicable in the remote districts, ought not to be relaxed. I suspend a more particular opinion till I have the pleasure of learning the result of your inquiry into the law on the subject.

If fit persons cannot be at present found for the collectorships of Penobscot, we must wait till the meeting of Congress, which always promises information on such points. I am surprised at the change of tone in General Cushing. Whatever rights he may have or suppose, they are certainly not on the executive ; nor against persons possessed of offices, and not charged by him with misfeasance in them.

I hope by the silence of your last letter on the subject of your health that it has been perfectly restored. I hope also that you will be careful not to endanger it by too much mental, and too little bodily, exercise.

Mr. Monroe has not returned from the Springs. He is expected soon, and with re-established health. The arrival of *Mr. Barclay* will call for prompt instructions to the commissioner who is to meet him. It is probable, however, that nothing will be done this year in their business beyond the discussions of the title to Moose Island and the line through Passamaquoddy Bay.

Accept my affectionate respects,

Mr. DALLAS.   JAMES MADISON.

———

MONTPELIER, Sept. 8, 1815.

DEAR SIR,—The commercial convention with Great Britain has just reached me. It abolishes the discriminating and countervailing duties, and establishes the rule of the most favored nation, between the United States and the British dominions in Europe. The equality of the vessels of the two countries extends to the cases of bounties and drawbacks, as well as of duties, with a reservation to the parties of a right to regulate and diminish the amount of the drawbacks, where the re-exportation is to a third country. A trade to enumerated ports in the East Indies is opened to the United States. It is to be *direct* from thence, but is not so restricted from the United States thither. The convention is to become binding on the exchange of ratifications, for which six months are allowed, and is to continue in force four years from the date of signature, which was the 3d of July.

The question to be immediately decided, is whether an anticipated meeting of the Senate, or rather the Legislature, is called for. As the difference between such a meeting and the first Monday in December will be necessarily very inconsiderable, as there will probably be very few arrivals or departures during that short period, and at that season, of vessels which would be affected by the changes made, it may happen that the United States would be gainers, at the treasury at least, rather than losers, by awaiting the regular meeting of Congress; and as the other party cannot reasonably expect that the expense and inconvenience of a previous meeting should be incurred for the sake of its interest, a course which it may fairly be presumed would not be pursued by itself, I am not impressed with an obligation to convene Congress with the sole view of carrying the treaty into effect, for which the time allowed (six months) will enable the Legislature to provide at its regular meeting.

Whilst I take this view of the subject, I am so sensible that a decision on it ought to be governed by facts and calculations, which in your situation you can judge of better than myself, that I cannot do better than refer the case to your inquiry and reflection; and under the existing circumstances to provide for giving effect to the result of them, without waiting for the opinions of the other secretaries, and even without incurring the delay of a previous sanction from myself. I shall accordingly desire Mr. Rush, who remains at Washington, to pay immediate attention to the opinion you may communicate to him, and in case it should be in favor of a call of Congress, to have a proclamation immediately issued in the usual form If a call be made, the precedent which allows the shortest time may be adopted. What that is I do not recollect. If it be two months from the date of the proclamation, it will so far lessen the importance of the measure.

You have noticed a reference in the British House of Commons to a depending bill regulating the trade with the United States. If it should have passed, in a form abolishing the countervailing duties absolutely, or to take effect on the condition which the executive is authorized to comply with, a proclamation abolishing the discriminating duties will substantially meet the occasion without an extra session of Congress. You can probably ascertain the fact as to the bill. Mr. Gallatin or Mr. Clay ought to know something of it.

Affectionate respects,

Mr. Dallas.   James Madison.

Montpelier, Sept. 15, 1815.

Dear Sir,—Yours of the 11th has just come to hand. I return the papers from the Commissioner of the General Land Office, with an acquiescence in the survey ordered in Missouri. I think the condition attached to it the least that will suffice to justify the measure.

I have received a letter from Mr. Gallatin, from which, as well as from his reserve to you, I infer that he has not made up his mind on his appointment to France. Whatever his alternatives may be, I am persuaded the one you mention is not within the scope of them. He intimated his intention to write to the Secretary of State, and may be expected in that letter to say more than he has done to me on some points, though probably not on the question of his diplomatic mission. I do not perceive that he looked to a special meeting of Congress. Indeed, the more I weigh the subject, the more I incline to the persuasion that a special call would be giving a magnified importance to the treaty. In my answer to Mr. G. I have asked him what are the probable intentions of the British cabinet with respect to the coasting fisheries, and whether the mouth of Columbia River was understood at Ghent to be within the objects of restoration.

I was informed, through *confidential* channels several days ago, that Jos. Bonaparte was about to visit me incog. to make a personal report of himself to this government. I immediately wrote to Mr. Rush to have him diverted from his purpose on his arrival at Washington. Protection and hospitality do not depend on such a formality; and whatever sympathy may be due to fallen fortunes, there is no claim of merit in that family on the American nation; nor any reason why its government should be embarrassed in any way on their account. In fulfilling what we owe to our own rights, we shall do all that any of them ought to expect. I was the more surprised at the intended visit as it was calculated to make me a party to the concealment, which the exile was said to study as necessary to prevent a more vigilant pursuit by British cruisers of his friends and property following him. Commodore Lewis consulted his benevolence more than his discretion in the course he took, without, as I presume, any sanction from any superior quarters.

You will have noticed that an order has been published on the point on which I asked your opinion. From the concurrent opinions of others, it is probable that the order may not contradict yours; but the issue of it prior to my hearing from you proceeded from my having asked, at the same time, the opinion of the attorney-general, which, being communicated to the War Department, was acted on. It seems that the case had become urgent.

Ripley and Brown are taking very painful attitudes towards each other; and I regret that your conciliatory efforts are likely to be perverted into fuel for their angry passions. Ripley presses for leave to come to Washington about the middle of October, with a view to settle his accounts. It is easy to see the effect of either a refusal or compliance.

If peace takes place in Europe, it seems probable that the Bank of England will soon resume specie payments, unless the balance of trade should be against her, which is not probable. That example will favor a return here to the original principle. But many circumstances will require the change to be gradual and guarded. I was always pleased with the feature in the bank proposed at the last session of Congress, which required a certain portion of specie to be in the bank, although not demandable by the holders of notes. If the same idea could be applied to the banks generally, it would not only smooth the way to a final reform, but have good effects in the mean time. Might it not be reduced to practice by requiring the banks, within a reasonable period, to draw specie into their vaults, and verified to a competent authority to be kept there? It might also be required that, until specie payments should commence, the notes issued should not exceed a fixed proportion to specie, such as might be an average of the usual proportion in former times. Such a regulation would have the advantage of inspiring confidence in the banks, of preparing them for a return to specie payments, and in the mean time would be an adequate barrier against excessive issues of paper. To make the regulation, if it be founded in solid considerations, complete, the interposition of the State authorities would be essential. The prerogative of the general government as to the medium in paying taxes, might go far in effectuating it by attaching conditions to the receivable paper. But there may be greater difficulties on the subject than strike the first view of it.

I have a letter from Mr. Monroe of the 11th. He had visited several of the more celebrated waters, and thought himself benefited by them. He named this day for his arrival at home.

Affectionate respects,

JAMES MADISON.

Mr. DALLAS.

DEAR SIR,—On my return from New York, I received your favor of the 2d instant, and the copy of Mr. Crawford's letter on the question of brevet rank.

I can add nothing, by way of information on public points, to the last communication of the talk of our commissioners. Mr. Gallatin has probably written to you at large on all that relates to the mission. As to his future pursuits, he has left me completely in the dark. Sometimes I think he looks towards France, then towards Congress, then towards the treasury, and ultimately towards his western farm. Though silent to me, I presume he will speak distinctly to you. Mr. Clay leaves Philadelphia to-morrow or the next day, taking Washington in his way to Kentucky. He seems to be satisfied with the prospect of returning to the chair in the House of Representatives.

Commodore Lewis has just escorted Joseph Bonaparte from New York to Philadelphia. The ex-king travels as Count Survilliers, and is lodged with Mr. Clay at the Mansion House.

I will send an answer to the question on brevet rank by the next mail.

I am, dear sir, most respectfully and faithfully yours,

A. J. DALLAS.

The President.
11 Sept., 1815.

———

DEAR SIR,—The inclosed letters from Mr. Adams show the impracticability of selling the stock in Europe within the limits which were prescribed. It is indispensable, however, to provide for the reimbursement of the heavy advances of Messrs. Baring in London, and for the advances of Messrs. Willinks in Amsterdam. It is time also to make arrangements for paying the dividends on the Louisiana stock in January next. These objects can only be accomplished by the sale of stock in Europe or by the purchase of bills of exchange here. The stock will bring no more than 90 ; but exchange is now twenty per cent. advance, and will, I think, rise higher. Six per cents are between three and four per cent. above par in Philadelphia ; they are above 96, and rising fast, in New York ; and even Boston affords a prospect of an advantageous movement in the value of the public debt. Viewing, then, the whole ground, I am very much indisposed to authorize a sale of stock in Europe at a rate so much below the price here, as Mr. Baring offers, which may not only injure the credit of the government abroad, but materially affect it at home. If, therefore, you approve of it, I will enter upon the purchase of bills on the best terms we can obtain for the whole sum wanted by the treasury, amounting to about $500,000. Indeed, I think it an object of some importance to pay away the bank-notes which we now hold for any effective means of satisfying our debts.

Be so good as to return Mr. Adams's letters with your instructions.

I am, dear sir, most respectfully and faithfully yours,

A. J. DALLAS.

The President.

18 Sept., 1815.

MONTPELIER, September 22, 1815.

DEAR SIR,—Yours of the 18th has just reached me, inclosing two letters from Mr. Adams, which are returned.

Our engagements in Europe must be fulfilled both with a view to justice and to the public credit. In doing this there are so many reasons for preferring the purchase of bills to the sale of stock abroad, where there is an approach to equality of loss, that I concur in your opinion in favor of the former. It is a consideration of much weight in that scale that our calculations can be made with more certainty if the remittance be made in bills than in a paper which will be constantly fluctuating in the market. It is not improbable that the balance of trade now running so high against us will not only keep up but raise the price of bills; but it is not to be doubted that the same cause, whilst it favors the price of stock at home by increasing the demand, will reduce it in the foreign market by glutting the demand there. In making these remarks I wish not to control any new views of the subject into which you may be led by changes in the money state of things, or by further information relating to it.

You will probably better understand the scope of the anonymous letter than I do.

Affectionate respects,

Mr. DALLAS.   JAMES MADISON.

DEAR SIR,—Since writing to you yesterday I have received the inclosed letter from Mr. Baring, which will give you a distinct view of our situation with the bankers in London. Every mail brings me additional accounts of the rise in exchange, and, indeed, of the extreme difficulty of procuring good bills. The importance of reinstating our credit by payment of the advances which have been so handsomely made, will strike you forcibly; and upon reflection I submit to your consideration the propriety of authorizing the sale of at least one million of the stock in Europe, which will put us at ease, on account of every engagement, as far forward as January next. The price must be left, as Mr. Baring suggests, to the state of things when the sale is. effected.

Be so good as to return Mr. Baring's letter. with your instructions on the present proposition.

I am, dear sir, most respectfully and faithfully yours,

A. J. DALLAS.

The President.

19 September, 1815.

————

MONTPELIER, September 23, 1815.

DEAR SIR,—I have just received yours of the 19th, inclosing a letter from Mr. Baring. As the choice between the two modes of providing for our pecuniary wants in Europe depends essentially on a comparison of the rate of exchange here and the price of stock abroad, it must be determined by the information possessed as to the state and prospects of each. My letter of yesterday made a reserve accordingly for any change which further information might suggest. And in sanctioning your present proposal for selling a million of stock abroad I repeat the discretion which I wish you to exercise in carrying it into execution. It is essential that provision be made for meeting the foreign demands on the United States. And if any extra motive were needed it is furnished by the friendly conduct and liberal confidence of Mr. Baring.

Affectionate respects,

JAMES MADISON.

Mr. DALLAS.

————

1816.

The Secretary of the Treasury has the honor to submit to the President a revised copy of the circular addressed to the collectors of the customs for carrying the act of Congress and the commercial convention with Great Britain into effect, together with Mr. Monroe's opinion on the subject. The revisal is made to conform to the suggestions of the President's note, except in relation to the equalization of drawbacks, which is again submitted, with Mr. Monroe's remark upon it.

6 March, 1816.

————

Mr. Dallas respectfully states to the President that Mr. William Gamble has been appointed by the Secretary of War to receive from the British commander a surrender of Fort Michilimackinac, and Mr. Gamble is ready to proceed in the execution of his trust.

Mr. Dallas recommends, also, that Mr. Gamble should be appointed collector at Michilimackinac.

Mr. Abbot, who was formerly collector, has not made any communication to the Treasury Department since August last, and such representations have been made as render his continuance in office inexpedient.

14 March, 1816.

MEMORANDUM IN JACOB BARKER'S CASE.

Mr. Barker seems to think that there is a personal severity shown to him in the treatment of his applications to the treasury. There is no foundation for the opinion. His bills have returned protested for non-payment, and suits are instituted to recover the principal, damages, etc. He offers to pay the principal, interest, and costs if the claim to the damages shall be released. The comptroller and Mr. Fish, the district attorney of New York, consulted me on the subject some time ago. Having expressed a wish that every justifiable indulgence should be shown to Mr. Barker, I examined—first, what it was in the power of the treasury to do; and second, what, under all the circumstances of the case, it was proper to do. The substance of my opinion was as follows :

1. The treasury cannot release the whole or any part of a debt due to the United States. It may exercise a reasonable discretion to enlarge the time of payment, and to secure the principal it may waive the claim of interest; but it has not in cases of debt gone further. In cases of penalty and forfeiture, before they are reduced to a certainty, compromises have been allowed when the law was doubtful or the evidence imperfect.

The damages upon the return of bills protested for non-payment have always been regarded as a part of the debt. It was so decided in Mr. Francis's case (Ambler, i.), and I gave that opinion to Mr. Gallatin several years ago, when Mr. Girard's bills were likely to return under protest in consequence of the failure of the drawer, George Barclay. Mr. Girard had offered to refund the money with interest, or to give new bills, if the claim to the damages were waived, should the first set of bills be returned. The offer was declined, but Mr. Girard was rescued from the loss of the damages by the interposition of Messrs. Baring, who paid the bills for the honor of the drawer.

2. But as Mr. Barker set up various pleas to defeat the demand of the United States either entirely or partially, two propositions were recommended to Mr. Fish:

The first, that if, as the law officer of the government, he thought the suits could not be maintained in point of law or of evidence for the whole or any part of the demand, the suits ought to be discontinued or the demand reduced accordingly.

The second, that if Mr. Barker would pay the amount which his counsel admitted to be recoverable in law, the expense and trouble of prosecuting all the suits should be saved by trying the controverted points upon a writ of error in a single case.

No remarks are made on the extraordinary character of Mr. Barker's pleas,—such as the plea that the government had no right to remit bills to England during the war; that there was an understanding between him and the late Secretary of the Treasury relative to the funds for paying the bills, and that the secretary had failed on his part, etc. etc.

I am desirous to accommodate Mr. Barker as far as it is practicable, and therefore I have referred the subject once more to the comptroller.

A. J. D.

19 March, 1816.

————

The Secretary of the Treasury respectfully submits to the President the answer which he proposes to give to the Committee of Foreign Relations on the reference of the petitions respecting the West India trade, etc. He thinks that it would be premature to commence a commercial warfare; but at all events the facts respecting the British regulations are not sufficiently ascertained to be the foundation of any legislative act.

1 April, 1816.

————

Dear Sir,—As it is not my intention to pass another winter in Washington, I think it a duty to give you an opportunity to select a successor for the office of Secretary of the Treasury during the present session of Congress. I will cheerfully remain, however, if you desire it, to put the national bank into motion, presuming that this object can be effected before the 1st of October next. Permit me, therefore, to tender my resignation, to be accepted on that day, or at any earlier period, which you may find more convenient to yourself or more advantageous to the public.

With every affectionate wish for your honor, health, and happiness, I am, dear sir, most respectfully and faithfully your obedient servant,

A. J. DALLAS.

The President.

8 April, 1816.

———

DEAR SIR,—I have received your letter of yesterday communicating your purpose of resigning the Department of the Treasury. I need not express to you the regret at such an event, which will be inspired by my recollection of the distinguished ability and unwearied zeal with which you have filled a station, at all times deeply responsible in its duties, through a period rendering them peculiarly arduous and laborious.

Should the intention you have formed be nowise open to reconsideration, I can only avail myself of your consent to prolong your functions to the date and for the object which your letter intimates. It cannot but be advantageous that the important measure in which you have had so material an agency should be put into its active state by the same hands.

Be assured, sir, that whatever may be the time of your leaving the department, you will carry from it my testimony of the invaluable services you have rendered your country, my thankfulness for the aid they have afforded in my discharge of the executive trust, and my best wishes for your prosperity and happiness.

JAMES MADISON.

ALEXANDER J. DALLAS, *Secretary of the Treasury.*

April 9, 1816.

———

MONTPELIER, Saturday morning, June 8, 1816.

DEAR SIR,—I have received and thank you for the letters for Hamburg and Bremen, which will be transmitted from the Department of State. We ended our journey last evening. With the exception of a short pelting shower on the day we set out, the weather and the roads were peculiarly favorable. I found the prospects of the farmers generally far better than I had expected; the wheat-fields much better until I reached my own neighborhood, where the Hessian fly has done considerable injury, though much less than was reported, and the injury has been in some degree also mitigated by late rains.

Affectionate respects,

JAMES MADISON.

A. J. DALLAS, Esq.

DEAR SIR,—I return your communications of the 12th inst.,
with my approbation of what you propose in relation to the
Cumberland Road. Perplexing as this business is, it will become more so, I fear, if Mr. Shriver should withdraw from it.
He has, notwithstanding the impatience of some, more of the
public confidence than will probably be enjoyed by a successor.
And if a distrust of the agent be added to the unavoidable difficulties and delays, it is easy to foresee the complaints that will
abound.

The conduct of the banks who refuse or evade the necessary
efforts to restore the specie standard is truly reproachful. This
is the only effectual cure for the diseases of the currency, and the
effect of them on the national character and the morals of the
people. The sense of justice and the respect for contracts are
daily losing force in the public mind. Whilst the banks refuse
to pay their debts, notwithstanding the means they have in the
public stock, which they could dispose of with a profit, or even to
pay interest on their debts, they at once set an example and impose a necessity for injustice and breach of faith between individual
debtors and creditors; at the same time that they distract and
obstruct all the pecuniary transactions of the government.

It is certainly incumbent on the executive to do everything
in its power to promote the salutary object of the resolution
passed near the close of the late session of Congress ; and the
consultation you suggest cannot but be proper. Be so good,
therefore, as to communicate to your colleagues my wish that
they assemble for the purpose, and transmit the result of their
united reflections. You will be best able to present the several
points on which decisions are proper. Unless the national
bank should be both able and willing to afford relief, I see no
resource against the existing policy of the State banks, if supported by the State governments, and for a universal medium,
but in a treasury paper, with the prerogative of being used in
the national taxes and transactions, and an entire exclusion of
the local bank paper. And this cannot be effected without a
dilatory process. At present the abuses growing out of a diversity of currencies, and the discretion exercised by the collectors,
are as provoking as they are mischievous. I just learn, though
the information may not be accurate, that the collectors in some
districts in this State, availing themselves of this discretion, and
of the authorized regulations of the State courts, receive the
national taxes indiscriminately in all the circulating paper, and exchange for their own profit the better for the inferior notes,
particularly those of the District of Columbia. Should this be
the fact, they must calculate on the latter's being receivable from

them into the treasury; and some correction of the error becomes necessary.

Although it may be proper not to act on the result of the cabinet consultation until the bank subscriptions be closed, it will be proper that the consultation be held before the members in Washington be separated. Mr. Crawford, I understand, meditates a visit to Georgia, and Mr. Monroe to Virginia. You will ascertain their precise views, and fix the time for the consultation accordingly.

I return also the letters of Mr. Hassler. I wish his compensation could have been arranged in the manner proposed to him. There is, however, weight in his observations in favor of his own mode. I believe we cannot do better than to acquiesce in it: allowing him $3000 for salary, and $2000 for his estimated expenses. If $1500 for the latter would content him, there would be an advantage in it.

Best respects and regards,

Mr. DALLAS.   JAMES MADISON.

DEAR SIR,—Your instructions relative to Fort Harrison, and the reservation of the land in its neighborhood, have been carried into effect. I hope now to be able to put the business of the Cumberland Road, as well as the business of the survey of the coast, into a course of execution without troubling you again. The consultation on the resolution of Congress respecting the currency will be attended to, as you desire.

The inclosed papers exhibit a general complaint against Mr. Du Plessis, the collector of New Orleans, without specifying any fact of official delinquency. The subject, however, seems to demand attention; and I propose referring it, confidentially, to Mr. Benjamin Morgan and the district attorney for investigation and report. I will also write to Mr. Robertson requesting his attention to the inquiry. The probability is that the present calamitous state of New Orleans will disperse its inhabitants; but it is best to take the chance of a letter's finding Mr. Robertson and Mr. Morgan at that place.

We have no news, foreign or domestic.

I am, dear sir, most respectfully and faithfully yours,

A. J. DALLAS.

The President.

18 June, 1816.

TREASURY DEPARTMENT, 24 June, 1816.

GENTLEMEN,—The President has authorized me to request that you will communicate your opinions upon the questions contained in the inclosed statement, which is founded on the resolution of Congress, passed the 29th of April, 1816, relative to the collection of the public revenue in the legal currency of the United States.

I will do myself the honor to meet you upon the subject of the statement whenever you shall appoint.

I am, very respectfully, your most obedient servant,

A. J. DALLAS.

The Hon. JAMES MONROE, *Secretary of State.*
 WM. H. CRAWFORD, *Secretary of War.*
 B. W. CROWNINSHIELD, *Secretary of the Navy.*
 RICHARD RUSH, *Attorney-General.*

DEAR SIR,—The inclosed report gives you the result of our consultation on the resolution of the 29th of April, 1816. I entertained a doubt for a moment upon the power of the treasury to make a discrimination in the terms of paying different descriptions of public debts and duties. I am satisfied, however, upon reflection, that the arrangement is indispensable for the accommodation of the country; and as the rule is a general one, applying to the kind of debt, and not to the person of the debtor, I perceive no breach of law or of impartiality. As soon as the papers are returned to me with your opinion, I will act upon them.

I am, dear sir, most respectfully and faithfully, your obedient servant,

A. J. DALLAS.

The President.

The Secretary of the Treasury has the honor to submit to the President of the United States the following

REPORT.

That in pursuance of the authority given by the President, the Secretary of the Treasury prepared and submitted to the consideration of the heads of departments and the Attorney-General the statement, founded upon the resolution of Congress of the 29th of April, 1816, relative to the collection of the revenue in the legal currency of the United States, which is hereunto annexed, marked A.

That the Secretary of State, the Secretary of War, and the Attorney-General, assembled at the treasury, after having duly considered the statement, and in answer to the several questions therein proposed, it was unanimously decided,—

1st. That it is not the duty of the Secretary of the Treasury, at this time, nor at any time before the 20th of February, 1817, to demand that all payments to the United States shall be made in the manner specified in the resolution of the 29th of April, 1816.

2d. That it is not the duty of the Secretary of the Treasury, at this time, nor at any time before the 20th of February, 1817, to cause the notes of the State banks, which are not payable and paid on demand in the legal currency of the United States, to be refused in all payments to the United States.

3d. That it will be expedient and proper for the Secretary of the Treasury to adopt the measures which he has suggested,—to wit:

A circular letter to the State banks in the form of the draft marked B.

A proposition to the banks in the form of the notice marked C.

If the State banks, or a considerable number of the most influential banks of the commercial cities, accede to the proposition, it will be advisable to announce and enforce it as a treasury regulation. If there should not be such an accession of the banks, it will be advisable and proper to suspend any further proceedings until the 20th of February, 1817, when it will be the duty of the Secretary of the Treasury to demand that all payments to the United States be made in the manner specified in the resolution of the 29th of April, 1816.

All which is respectfully submitted.

A. J. DALLAS, *Secretary of the Treasury.*

TREASURY DEPARTMENT, 29 June, 1816

MONTPELIER, June 30, 1816.

DEAR SIR,—I return the papers inclosed in yours of the 27th, concurring in the opinion of the comptroller, founded on his statement of the case of the schooner Mary Stiles. I do not think a pardon proper. I am not sure that it would be correct to decide the question of a remission under the act of Congress, which I believe submits it exclusively to the Treasury Department. The case may, therefore, lie over for future decision, or a non-remittitur may be entered, as you think proper. The nature of the case, the opinion of the comptroller, and the refusal to pardon, would doubtless protect the latter alternative against suggestions of indelicacy, if that be the only consideration to be weighed.

I have written to Mr. Monroe on the subject of both Algerian and Spanish misconduct. There is more to be said in excuse of the Dey than of Ferdinand, although it may be fairly suspected that there has been a collusion between them. If the brig was surrendered gratis, it was a gross breach not only of friendship but of a special promise to mitigate, instead of augmenting, the difficulty between the United States and Algers. If a price was paid by Algiers, it was an acknowledgment on both sides that the capture by us was lawful. I have written to the Secretary of State also on the subject of the whaling-vessel, as you will have learned from himself. Our affairs with Spain generally are, as you observe, taking a very critical shape.

I have not yet received the despatch from Mr. Harris. A dispute with Russia, of any sort, would be a very disagreeable incident, especially at this moment. But, having right on our side, we may hope for a favorable result to amicable explanations ; or, these failing, must sustain the national character, for which the government is responsible. If the emperor has taken any hasty and harsh step towards Mr. Harris, who personally stood so well with him, it must have been the effect of shameful misrepresentations to him, such as may reasonably be expected to recoil on the authors.

Gardner's resignation has produced, as you will see, an application from Governor Plumer in behalf of his son. Other candidates may be looked for, having, possibly, superior pretensions; but I have, on other occasions, heard a very favorable account of the talents and amiable qualities of this young man.

I shall direct this to be forwarded to Philadelphia, in the probable event of your having left Washington.

Accept my esteem and cordial regards,

JAMES MADISON.

Mr. DALLAS.

DEAR SIR,—I send, for your consideration, Governor Plumer's recommendation of his son, to succeed Mr. Gardner, whose resignation of the loan-office in New Hampshire was forwarded a few days ago.

Mr. Smith, the marshal of New York, is dead, and you will, I presume, be harassed with applications for the office.

I am, dear sir, most respectfully and faithfully your obedient servant,

A. J. DALLAS.

The President.

1 July, 1816.

The Secretary of the Treasury has the honor to submit to the President a copy of his letter to the auditor of the treasury respecting the settlement of Mr. Hassler's accounts, which will require the President's approbation.

A. J. DALLAS.

TREASURY DEPARTMENT,
5 July, 1816.

Montpelier, July 4, 1816.

Dear Sir,—I have received yours of the 29th of June, with the several papers sent with it.

Under the difficult circumstances of the currency, and the obligation to attempt a remedy, or at least an alleviation of them, the plan you have in view is entitled to a fair experiment. You do right, however, in reserving a discretion to judge of the sufficiency of accessions by the State banks. Should there be a single State in which a failure of its banks to accede should reduce the people to the necessity of paying their taxes in coin, or treasury notes, or a bank paper out of their reach, the pressure and complaint would be intense, and the more so from the inequality with which the measure would operate.

Can the suspension of payments in coin by the principal banks be regarded as the precise cause of the undue depreciation of treasury notes, as intimated in the third paragraph of your circular? A slight modification, if you think it requisite, would obviate the remark.

As your statement to the President will remain an official document, I suggest, for your consideration, the expression that the treasury "cannot discriminate, in the mode of payment, between the revenue of customs and the internal revenue" as liable to be turned against the distinction proposed in the payment of them.

With respect to the validity of this distinction I should yield my doubts, if they were stronger than they are, to the unanimous opinion which has sanctioned it.

I anxiously wish that the State banks may enter promptly and heartily into the means of re-establishing the proper currency. Nothing but their general co-operation is wanting for the purpose; and they owe it to their own character, and ultimately to their own interests, as much as they do to the immediate and vital interests of the nation. Should they sacrifice all these powerful obligations to the unfair gain of the moment, it must remain with the State legislatures to apply the remedy in their hands; and it is to be hoped that they will not be diverted from it either by their share in the gains of the banks or the influence of the banks on their deliberations. If they will not enforce the obligations of the banks to redeem their notes in specie, they cannot, surely, forbear to enforce the alternatives of redeeming them with public stock, or with national bank-notes, or finally, of paying interest on all their notes presented for payment. The expedient, also, of restricting their circulating paper in a reasonable proportion to their metallic fund, may merit attention, as at once aiding the credit of their paper and accelerating a resumption of specie payments.

I inclose the papers A, B, C, to guard against the possibility that you may not have copies of them with you.

Accept my esteem and cordial respects,

JAMES MADISON.

The Secretary of the Treasury.

DEAR SIR,—On the day of my departure from Washington, the heads of departments assembled at Mr. Monroe's office and considered all the subjects which you had referred to them. Mr. Monroe will communicate the result to you, together with a statement of the measures suggested in relation to Mr. Kusloff's case.

There is no business to trouble you with from the treasury; and there is neither foreign nor domestic intelligence beyond the articles to be found in the newspapers. The subscription to the national bank proceeds slowly, but steadily. There is perfect confidence that it will exceed the amount of the capital before the twenty days have expired. The New England Federalists will subscribe freely, and they have already despatched an agent to Philadelphia to negotiate for the election of Mr. James Lloyd as the president of the bank. Mr. Willing declines, and Mr. Jones's pecuniary situation seems to present a serious difficulty in the way of his advancement. If, however, the southern and western interests support him, I think his success probable.

I am, dear sir, most respectfully and faithfully, your obedient servant,

A. J. DALLAS

The President.

7 July, 1816.

DEAR SIR,—The act of the 30th of April, 1816, appropriates $250,000 for custom-house establishments. It will probably be a sum sufficient for the five principal commercial cities; but I have not received satisfactory information from any collector but the collector of Boston, upon whose report I now transmit to you an official statement, which you will be so good as to return with your directions subjoined.

This opportunity is taken to place before you the recommendations for Mr. Plumer and Mr. Wentworth as candidates for the vacant loan-office. I do not hear of any other name; and, on the whole, I think the weight of recommendation is in favor of Mr. Plumer.

I am, dear sir, most respectfully and faithfully, your obedient servant,

A. J. DALLAS.

The President

8 July, 1816.

Dear Sir,—I have received your favor of the 4th instant, and shall alter the circular on the currency in the way which you suggest.

The receipt of several additional recommendations for the loan-office in New Hampshire induces me to suspend an application for the commission in favor of Mr. Plumer, until you have seen the documents now sent. I do not anticipate, however, a change in your instructions.

I am, dear sir, most respectfully and faithfully, your obedient servant,

A. J. DALLAS.

The President.

11 July, 1816.

———

MONTPELIER, July 15, 1816.

Dear Sir,—I have received your several letters of the 5th, 7th, 8th, and 11th. Your statement in the case of Mr. Hassler was sanctioned and sent to the treasury, as was the proposed purchase of a custom-house at Boston. Be so good as have issued a commission for Mr. Plumer as loan-officer for New Hampshire. The recommendations of Mr. Wentworth are very weighty, but, being local, justify the preference of Mr. Plumer, who is called for by those more in a situation to speak for the whole State, and it is a State, not local office.

The accounts from all quarters promise success to the bank commissioners. If there be no hope for Mr. Jones, it is much to be wished that some commanding character might come into view. It will be a real disadvantage both to the bank and the government if a president should be chosen with disaffected views, or even without the entire confidence of the treasury department and the nation.

You will have noticed the return of the Macedonian. I understand Mr. Hughes speaks unfavorably of the prospects, and of the character also, of the revolutionary party in that quarter.

Cordial respects,

Mr. DALLAS.   JAMES MADISON.

———

Dear Sir,—I trouble you with a draft of the agreement with Mr. Hassler relative to the survey of the coast. The work is an important one, and must require both time and money to complete it. I am confident that Mr. Hassler is the only person equal in all respects to the undertaking, within the reach of the government.

The circular to the banks is prepared for issuing, and the prospect of an accumulation of revenue in New York was so favorable that I had drafted a treasury notice assigning funds to pay all the treasury notes, which were payable in New York, during the year 1814 and the early months of 1815, on the first day of September next. The inclosed letter from Mr. Irving has, however, induced me to pause upon both measures. The crisis described by Mr. Irving will not immediately affect Philadelphia and Baltimore, where the banks continue to issue notes, most licentiously, for the accommodation of the merchants. The paper balloon will, nevertheless, explode unless some relief can be afforded to the sufferers in New York, and some reform be introduced at the banks of Philadelphia and Baltimore. I will reflect upon the powers of the treasury, and beg the favor of your views as to the best course to be pursued.

The collector of Philadelphia has sent a report, which accompanies this letter, relative to the site for a custom-house. The apportionment of the sum appropriated by Congress is left to the department under the direction of the President. As we can procure a custom-house at Boston for $29,000, the sum to be applied at Philadelphia may exceed the one-fifth of the appropriation. I think the purchases in the other commercial cities will also be within the amount of an equal distribution.

I am, dear sir, most respectfully and faithfully, your obedient servant,

A. J. DALLAS.

The President.
16 July, 1816.

———

The Secretary of the Treasury has the honor to submit to the President of the United States the inclosed report and estimate of the collector of the port of Philadelphia relative to the purchase of a site and the erection of buildings for a custom-house in that city.

A. J. DALLAS, *Secretary of the Treasury.*
TREASURY DEPARTMENT, 16 July, 1816.

———

MONTPELIER, July 18, 1816.

DEAR SIR,—I have just received yours of the ——, inclosing Mr. Hassler's letter on the subject of the observatory. I had previously received one from Colonel Lane, informing me of the selection made by Mr. Hassler for its site. Although I had no doubt of the fitness of any spot preferred by Mr. H., taken in the abstract, it occurred to me that as the whole square would be required, the expense to the public might be very considerable, and that there might be inconveniences in alienating so much ground in that particular situation from uses to which it might be otherwise applied. On these considerations, I thought it proper to desire Mr. Munroe, the superintendent of the city, to make out an estimate of the value of the grounds in question, with such observations as to the other points as he might think useful; to be furnished to you, or, in your absence, to Mr. Rush, whose attention I asked to the subject. I am glad to find the concurrence in what has been separately done. After all, the question you raise as to the legality of a *purchase* of ground by the public is a material one, and cannot be decided without an accurate view of the case. I suggested to Colonel Lane that it might be well for Mr. Hassler to point out the best substitute for a site, which would be free from the difficulties incident to the square best in itself. From Mr. Hassler's letter I conclude he will have left Washington before the arrival of mine there. Perhaps he can, from memory, refer you to the one he would have named to Colonel Lane.

I return the letter from Mr. H., and the note from Mr. Jones. I have already expressed my wish, in case his prospect for the presidency of the bank should, unfortunately for him, prove hopeless, his place might be taken by one whose standing would insure success. It is of great importance to the nation as well as to the bank itself that the head of it should enjoy the full confidence, in every respect, of the treasury and of Congress. I observe that, notwithstanding the general calculation of success to the subscriptions, their progress is slow and deliberate. Perhaps it results from the very certainty of the successful issue, and a policy, in those who wish as much as they can get, to damp subscriptions, that they may rush in at the last moment.

Accept my esteem and affectionate respects,

JAMES MADISON.

Mr. DALLAS.

———

MONTPELIER, July 21, 1816.

DEAR SIR,—I have received yours of the 16th, inclosing the propositions of Mr. Hassler, the report of the collector of Philadelphia, and the letter from Mr. Irving.

The importance of the object, and the peculiar fitness of Mr. Hassler for it, prescribe an acquiescence in his terms. Will it not be better to throw his paper into the form of instructions and explanations accompanying his appointment, than to let it stand in that of a contract? Some attention will be necessary to the *mode* of subjecting military officers to his orders. The War and Navy Departments will understand it. Mr. Hassler proposes that the chief officer shall be the treasurer, etc. Can this service be forced on him, or will his consent and compensation be requisite ? If there be a difficulty, it may be provided for by an after-arrangement.

Considering the expense of erecting permanent observatories, and the competition of sites for them, to which may be added the question of appropriating an *occasional* fund to permanent objects, it may deserve your consideration whether it may not be advisable to borrow the use of existing establishments, if such can be found, or to erect temporary observatories, if it can be done with a material diminution of expense.

I presume you cannot do better than to secure the site referred to by General Steele for the custom-house in Philadelphia. It must be of peculiar importance that it be located conveniently for the public and for the merchants. Of the reasonableness of the price for the lots I cannot judge. The judgment of General Steele is entitled to much confidence. As it is uncertain what may be the expense called for in New York and Baltimore, it will be fortunate if offers from both should arrive before that at Philadelphia be made unalterable. It is possible that the excess at other places may be greater beyond their proportions than that at Philadelphia. In that case, if economy be impracticable in purchasing the sites, it must be applied to the buildings, unless an increase of the appropriations by Congress can be safely anticipated.

Mr. Irving's letter gives a deplorable picture of the mercantile and moneyed situation of New York. If the evil, however, arises from the excess of imports beyond the wants of the country, a partial and temporary relief only can be administered. The country merchants cannot sell, because the people do not need more of their merchandise ; not selling, they cannot pay the importers ; and these, not receiving, cannot pay their duties to the treasury. Were they enabled to pay the duties, or indulged with time for the purpose, how are they to make their remittances to Europe, amounting to so much more than their duties ? Of the several alleviations stated by Mr. Irving, my first impression is in favor of a renewal of the bonds, with an augmented security, as countenanced by the danger, in case of an extensive explosion, of an actual loss to the public. I suspend my opinion, however, till I can aid it with the result of your reflections on the subject. A memorial from the merchants is desirable, as an authentic groundwork for executive interposition, if it finally take place.

Accept my best wishes,

JAMES MADISON.

Mr. DALLAS.

DEAR SIR,—Having considered the question as to *purchasing* a site for the observatory more attentively, I conclude that it would be deemed probably an extreme latitude of construction to make an expensive purchase of lots as an incident to the authority for a survey of the coast, which is a temporary work. The objection does not arise to occupying lots already belonging to the public, and which would at all times be subject to the directions of Congress. Under that impression, I will address Mr. Hassler upon the subject.

I have received a letter from Mr. Baker complaining of a discrimination between British and American vessels in the port of New York as to pilotage and fees exacted under the State laws. The draft of an answer is submitted for your consideration with the letter itself. It seems, however, to me that subjects of this kind should be discussed in the Department of State.

The bank subscriptions close to-morrow, and I will hasten to communicate the result as soon as the materials are collected to ascertain it. There is a general confidence that the whole capital will be subscribed. Mr. Girard's interest is at the maximum, three thousand shares, or $300,000. He says that he will take a much greater interest if it be necessary. His name is sometimes mentioned as president of the bank; but it is probable that he will support Mr. Jones, whose prospects become more favorable. Except these gentlemen, I do not know a Republican within your description of fitness who would be likely to succeed or be willing to become a candidate.

I trouble you with a case from Bermuda, because it seems to be, in some sort, anomalous. The island is not within the exception of the convention as to the West Indies, nor within the general provision as to the British European dominions; but it is stated that, by an act of Parliament, vessels of the United States are permitted to go to and trade at Bermuda.

I am, dear sir, most respectfully and faithfully, your obedient servant,

A. J. DALLAS.

The President.
23 July, 1816.

DEAR SIR,—I inclose the memorial of the merchants of New York, to which Mr. Irving's letter (already communicated to you) referred. It appears to me that the only proper mode of interfering for the relief of the memorialists would be to authorize the district attorney to stay executions after judgments had been entered, taking, if necessary, additional security. To suspend suits, or to renew the bonds, is an alternative that I am not prepared to recommend.

I send for your perusal a letter, which I have received from Mr. McCall, covering two Spanish documents.

I am, dear sir, most respectfully and faithfully yours,

A. J. DALLAS.

The President.

— July, 1816.

MONTPELIER, July 26, 1816.

DEAR SIR,—I have received yours of the ——, and return the New York memorial inclosed in it. Interpositions for relief in such cases are of a delicate nature when proceeding from the legislature, the most competent authority. When claimed from the executive they are peculiarly delicate. The only ground on which the latter can proceed seems to be that of increasing the security of the revenue by suspending a pressure which might impair the solvency of the debtor to the treasury; and this ground is sanctioned by precedents as well as by its intrinsic policy. Cases of necessity, arising from calamities in a manner preternatural, will provide for themselves.

From this view of the subject, the course you suggest of staying executions in individual cases and guarding effectually against loss from the delay, is the one to be pursued. A lumping relief, which would embrace cases not within the reason of it and authorize expectations so general as to threaten bankruptcy to the treasury, belongs to the deliberations of those who make laws, not of those who are to execute them. The distress of the merchants of New York is much to be regretted; the more so, as far as it is the effect of a laudable co-operation of the banks there with the national system, and there would be the greater pleasure in mitigating their sacrifices, if it were practicable, as these involve with the ruin of the importing merchants an increase of danger to our struggling manufacturers.

Friendly respects,

Mr. DALLAS.   JAMES MADISON.

MONTPELIER, July 27, 1816.

DEAR SIR,—I have received yours of the 23d, inclosing a letter from Mr. Baker, with the draft of an answer, and a letter from Wm. Js. Sears, of Bermuda.

The subject of Mr. Baker's letter regularly belongs to the Department of State. But whether addressed to the Treasury Department or to that, ought to have proceeded from the minister and not from the consul otherwise than through the minister. From courtesy, which, as well as conveniency, sometimes takes the place of strict rule, it may not be amiss to make to Mr. Baker the observations contained in your intended answer, with a reference to the usual channel for such discussions. I send both the papers to Mr. Monroe, who, in speaking with Mr. Bagot, will lead his attention to the diplomatic usage.

I send to Mr. Monroe also the letter from Mr. Sears. If our vessels enjoy in that island the same privileges as in the European ports of Great Britain, the claim stated, though not supported by the convention, seems to be covered by the general terms of the act of Congress referred to. I have, however, but slightly looked into the subject, and the fact and the extent of the trade allowed to our vessels at Bermuda ought to be scrutinized. In describing the British dominions, the convention would seem to include Bermuda in the West Indies, since it is not probable that it was overlooked altogether by both the American and British commissioners. Whether an American consul will be admitted there, is another point to be ascertained. This can probably be done at Washington.

Cordial respects and esteem,

Mr. DALLAS. JAMES MADISON.

DEAR SIR,—Mr. Jones promised to communicate to you a statement of the subscriptions to the Bank of the United States. The deficit will not be great, and will be immediately subscribed at Philadelphia. Mr. Jones's prospect brightens. He is opposed, however, by Major Butler, whose appointment produces all the inconveniences that I apprehended.

The treasury circular seems to be approved by all but the bankers. A convention of delegates from the banks of the Middle States will meet here on the 6th instant, and I am promised a candid and explicit answer.

The custom-house establishment at Boston has been purchased for $29,000. The Baltimore proposition is suspended, as you desired, for further information from other points. The site for the Philadelphia establishment is ordered to be purchased.

I am, dear sir, most respectfully and faithfully yours,

A. J. DALLAS.

The President.

3 August, 1816.

DEAR SIR,—The collector's selection of a site and buildings for the New York custom-house is generally approved, and the price deemed moderate.

The inclosed letter from Mr. Derbigny creates an apprehension that the subscription to the bank has not been opened at New Orleans. The commissioners were named by the Louisiana members of Congress; and as Mr. Brown and Mr. Robertson are on the spot, I hope that they have advised Judge Hall, singly, to open the subscription. There will probably be a deficit in the subscriptions to the amount of $2,000,000 or $3,000,000; but the demand for the shares is increasing. As soon as the sum required by law has been received, I propose, with your approbation, to instruct the commissioners to provide a temporary establishment for transacting the business of the bank, to prepare plates and paper for the bank-notes, and to make such other general arrangements as will enable the directors to commence the operations of the institution without delay.

Mr. Coles left Philadelphia this morning.

I am, dear sir, most respectfully and faithfully yours,

A. J. DALLAS.

The President.

6 August, 1816.

———

MONTPELIER, August 7, 1816.

DEAR SIR,—Colonel McCobb has just handed me yours of the 3d inst. The recommendations of him for the vacant office he seeks, appear to be decisive. I have referred him, however, to you for a communication of the result. That there may be no unnecessary delay, I write by the present opportunity to the Department of State to forward immediately a blank commission to you, if there be one on hand already signed: and if not, to me for signature; and you may let Colonel McCobb understand that his name will be put into it, unless reasons for a different decision should have reached you, which is not probable.

I have retained the two Spanish documents sent by Mr. McCall for the information of the Department of State. Though not of recent date, they are very interesting as authentic keys to the cabinet feelings and views at Madrid towards the United States, and the use it wishes to make of Great Britain against us. If such a treaty exists or was ever entered into with the latter, as Mr. McCall supposes, a knowledge of it would be very desirable. But I doubt the reality of more than some informal understanding on the subject, and that perhaps short of what is supposed.

It was hoped at one time, from interviews between Mr. Bagot and the Secretary of State, that the former had powers adequate to some satisfactory arrangements both as to the fisheries and armaments on the lakes. The latest, though not the final conversations between them, make it probable that he can only receive propositions for the consideration of his government. Whether he can even arrest the progress of naval equipments, is more than doubtful.

I have received from Captain Jones a memorandum of the known subscriptions to the bank. He is perfectly confident that any deficiency will be supplied instantly in Philadelphia. I am very glad to learn by your late letter that his prospect of being at the head of the institution had become favorable, and I should calculate that supplemental subscriptions at Philadelphia would make it rather more so. Besides the personal motives which make me wish his success, I am persuaded that it would accord much better with the interests both of the bank and the public than any other applicant in competition with it.

Accept my esteem and affectionate respects,

JAMES MADISON.

Mr. DALLAS.

MONTPELIER, August 10, 1816.

DEAR SIR,—I have received yours of the 6th instant; I have approved the contemplated purchase of a custom-house in New York, as I do your proposed instructions to the bank commissioners on the subject of preparatory arrangements. It is to be hoped that Judge Hall will have taken the course you allude to. Should he have failed even to ascertain the offers to subscribe within the prescribed period, the delay may be embarrassing, as New Orleans cannot be fairly deprived of an opportunity of sharing in the subscriptions. The best expedient that occurs is to give them a priority in the supplemental shares; explaining to Judge Hall the intentions of the treasury. Should a better course occur to you, pursue it without the delay of further communication with me on the subject. Would it be amiss to send a couple of blank commissions to New Orleans, to be filled by Judge H. or some other functionary on the spot?

Friendly respects,

Mr. DALLAS.   JAMES MADISON.

DEAR SIR,—I find Mr. Jones so infirm in body and mind that I feel uneasy to be longer absent from Washington. I shall, therefore, return next week to finish my treasury report there.

It will give you pleasure to learn that I am able to give notice for payment of the treasury notes due in New York as far down as the month of June, 1816. Indeed, everything but the currency will be in good order. The bank may be organized and active before January next.

I am, dear sir, most respectfully and faithfully yours,

A. J. DALLAS.

The President.

23 August, 1816.

TREASURY DEPARTMENT, 24 August, 1816.

The Secretary of the Treasury has the honor to submit the following statement to the consideration of the President of the United States:

Treasury notes which were issued under acts passed prior to the act of the 24th of February, 1815, were payable at the expiration of a year from their respective dates, with interest at the rate of $5\frac{2}{5}$ per cent. per annum, at the loan-offices respectively specified in the notes. Many of these treasury notes became due and remained unpaid.

By the act of the 24th of February, 1815, it was declared that "it should be lawful for the Secretary of the Treasury to cause to be paid the interest upon the treasury notes which have become due and remain unpaid, as well with respect to the time elapsed before they became due as with respect to the time that shall elapse after they become due, and until funds shall be assigned for the payment of the said treasury notes and notice thereof shall be given."

On the 15th and 22d of June, 1815, notice was given that funds were assigned for the payment of treasury notes due and becoming due at all the loan-offices except those of Massachusetts and New York. The funds assigned consisted of bank-notes, the local currency at the respective places of payment being the only funds possessed by the treasury.

Many of the holders of treasury notes have refused to accept the payment thus offered. And it appears from a communication made by the collector of Portsmouth, in New Hampshire (which accompanies this statement), that "a treasury note for $1000 payable in Philadelphia, dated on the 1st of August, 1814, was tendered to him in payment of a bond for $1109 95, being the amount of said note, with interest from the date to the time of the tender." This note was provided for under the treasury notices of June, 1815. And the tender is now made with a view to try the general question whether the assignment of bank-notes is the assignment of a lawful fund for payment, in consequence of which the interest on the treasury notes shall cease to run.

The collector and the district attorney request that they may receive the instructions of the government upon the occasion; and the Secretary of the Treasury respectfully submits the expediency of instructing them to proceed as if no tender had been made.

A. J. DALLAS, *Secretary of the Treasury.*

MONTPELIER, August 25, 1816.

DEAR SIR,—Since the receipt of your several letters relating to the treasury proposition and the decision of bank deputies at

Philadelphia, my thoughts have been duly turned to the important and perplexing subject.

Although there may be no propriety in recalling the proposition, it seems now certain that it will fail of its effect. Should the banks not represented at Philadelphia come into the measure, the refusal of those represented would be fatal. The want of a medium for taxes in a single State would be a serious difficulty. So extensive a want would forbid at once an enforcement of the proposition.

The banks feel their present importance and seem more disposed to turn it to their own profit than to the public good and the views of the government. Without their co-operation it does not appear that any immediate relief can be applied to the embarrassments of the treasury or of the currency. This co-operation they refuse. Can they be coerced?

Should the State legislatures unite in the means within their power the object may be attained. But this is scarcely to be expected, and in point of time is too remote.

The national bank must for a time at least be on the defensive.

The interposition of Congress remains, and we may hope the best as to a vigorous use of it. But there is danger that the influence of the local banks may reach even that resource. Should this not be the case, the remedy is future, not immediate.

The question then before us is, whether any and what further expedients lie with the executive.

Although we have satisfied, by what has been already attempted, our legal responsibility, it would be still incumbent on us to make further experiments if any promising ones can be devised. If there be such, I have full confidence that they will enter into your views of the subject.

One only occurs to me, and I mention it because no other does, not because I regard it as free from objections which may be deemed conclusive.

The notes on the treasury might be presented to the banks respectively with a demand of the specie due on the face of them. On refusal, suits might be immediately instituted, not with a view to proceed to execution, but to establish a claim to interest from the date of the demand. The notes thus bearing interest being kept in hand, treasury notes bearing interest might be issued in payments from the treasury, and so far injustice to the several classes of creditors might be lessened, whilst a check would be given to the unjust career of the banks.

Such a proceeding ought to be supported by the stockholders, the army, the navy, and all the disinterested and well-informed part of the community. The clamor against it would be from the banks and those having interested connections with them, supported by the honest part of the community misled by their fallacies. And the probability is but too great that the clamor would be overwhelming.

I do not take into view the expedient of requiring a payment of the impost in specie, in part at least, because it could not be extended to the other taxes, and would in that respect as well as otherwise be a measure too delicate for the executive authority; nor could its effect be in time for any very early purpose.

I have been led by the tenor of your letters to put on paper these observations. The report you are preparing will doubtless enlighten my view of the whole subject.

Friendly respects,

Mr. DALLAS.   JAMES MADISON.

DEAR SIR,—It appears that Dr. Flord returned to New Orleans on the 3d of July, and that the bank subscriptions were opened. The amount is not expected to exceed $300,000 at that place. The general deficit will probably be $3,000,000, but it will be immediately supplied by companies already formed. Mr. Girard alone will take $1,000,000, if he can obtain that sum.

I am anxious to receive your sentiments upon the expediency of persevering in the treasury proposition for commencing coin payments of small bank-notes on the 1st of October. I think the banks here would be obliged to acquiesce. There is a danger, however, of a failure of current means of paying taxes in the interior; and the merchants would be glad, at this crisis, to seize any pretence for refusing to pay their bonds.

I am, dear sir, most respectfully and faithfully yours,

A. J. DALLAS.

The President.

DEAR SIR,—The bank subscription is filled. The deficit of the general returns ($3,000,000) was taken by Mr. Girard in a single line, to the great disappointment of the brokers and speculators. I congratulate you upon this event. There is little doubt of the organization of the bank being Republican, and friendly to the government.

The Cumberland Road presents new embarrassments; and I shall have occasion to trouble you upon the subject as soon as I reach Washington, which will probably be on Sunday next.

I am, dear sir, most respectfully and faithfully yours,

A. J. DALLAS.

The President.

27 August, 1816.

Dear Sir,—I inclose Mr. Hassler's letter respecting a site for the observatory. The recommendation of the ground selected is very strong; but it requires consideration whether the authority is sufficient for purchasing that portion of it which does not belong to the public. The appropriation is adequate, regarding it as an incident to the survey of the coast. I have requested from Mr. Monroe and Colonel Lane an estimate of the price of the lot and the cost of the building, which shall be forwarded to you as soon as I receive it.

Mr. Jones has just sent me the inclosed note, which will give you a general idea of the progress of the bank subscription. The institution is becoming every day more popular; and the universal expectation, that it is the only remedy for the disordered currency, must essentially contribute to make it effectual.

I am, dear sir, most respectfully and faithfully your obedient servant,

A. J. DALLAS.

The President.

———

MONTPELIER, September 6, 1816.

Dear Sir,—I return the answers of the banks to the treasury proposition. Some of them, I observe, are sore at the idea of their yielding to the temptation of gain, in prolonging the refusal to resume specie payments. The best mode of repelling the suspicion would be to dispose of their public stock, and thus reduce their dividends. Whilst they refuse to co-operate with the treasury, that circumstance will justify it in not persisting in efforts to anticipate the epoch fixed by Congress for a general reform; and an adherence to that epoch cannot be declined, unless Congress should themselves give way. That great exertions will be used to overcome their firmness, and to substitute the epoch (July next) fixed by the banks, cannot be doubted; and the success of these exertions is not a little to be apprehended, unless the national bank can acquire an activity that will enfeeble the pleas of the State banks, and fortify the good dispositions in that body. This may be hoped for; and the hope is strengthened by the general views you present of the fiscal condition of the United States, which cannot fail to be grateful and encouraging to the nation.

The proposition of Mr. Carroll is a handsome one. It may lie over, however, for the meeting of Congress, or at least till our reassembling at Washington. The sufficiency of the offer, to say nothing of the authority to accept it, cannot be judged of without knowing how far it embraces the ground considered by Mr. Hassler as essential, or what effect it may have on the owners of the residue.

I have not departed from the course intimated to you for filling the vacancy which your determination to retire will produce at a day not very distant. Mr. Crawford signified, lately, his acquiescence in the proposition made to him, and I have written to Mr. Clay in consequence of it. As soon as I receive his answer, you shall be made acquainted with it.

Accept my great esteem and cordial regards,

JAMES MADISON.

Mr. DALLAS.

———

DEAR SIR,—When the report first reached me that Mr. Sheldon was going to Europe, I felt some solicitude that he should not go before the treasurer's accounts were stated and settled; and I released him from all the other duties of the office that he might attend exclusively to that object. I certainly felt no objection, generally, to his departure, as his health really required some relaxation from business; nor was I at all disposed to deprive him of the benefit of Mr. Gallatin's patronage; but, if I had been apprised of your decision to nominate him as secretary of legation, it would have been my duty to recommend a stipulation that he should not leave the office until he had executed the special trust which belonged peculiarly to him. I mention these circumstances merely to introduce the inclosed note from the treasurer on the subject of his accounts, and my answer. The clerks are not familiar with this part of our business; and one of them, who has been charged with it, in consequence of Mr. Sheldon's resignation, has not, I fear, a conciliatory temper or habits of mind suited to the task. Everything that can be done shall be done to recover our leeway. It is proper to add that the aid derived by the treasurer from the secretary's office is an affair of usage and comity, not of legal obligation under the acts of Congress. The law requires the treasurer to render and settle his own accounts.

This opportunity is taken to transmit a letter from Mr. Robertson, recommending the removal of Mr. Du Plessis, and the appointment of Mr. Beverly Chew. There is something in the terms of recommending Mr. Chew which merits reflection. He is an honest man, but he is insolvent, or so I infer from Mr. Robertson's language.

Commodore Porter has written a letter offering a site on Meridian Hill (his late purchase) for an observatory. The terms of the offer are reasonable; but I have answered that the establishment of an observatory is postponed until the meeting of Congress; that another site had been selected by Mr. Hassler; and that Mr. Carroll had offered to sell, or give, it to the government; but, I added, that his letter would be submitted to you, and duly considered.

The pressure of business has continued throughout the summer; and I approach the termination of my official life with a solicitude of which my affectionate attachment to you is the source. I hope, however, to leave the department in a situation of less difficulty to my successor than could well have been expected; and the report (which is copying) will give him all the general views that are necessary to guide him in the commencement of his labors. Of myself, I can only speak with care and doubt, when I reflect upon the effect of two years' absence from the bar, to obstruct and embarrass my return; but when you mentioned my *determination* to retire from the treasury, I am sure you would account for that determination from the necessity of changing my situation for the sake of my family, or from any other cause, rather than from an indisposition to remain with you.

I am, dear sir, most respectfully and faithfully yours,

A. J. DALLAS.

The President.

11 September, 1816.

MONTPELIER, September 15, 1816.

DEAR SIR,—I have duly received yours of the 11th. The difficulty which gave rise to the letter from the treasurer is much to be regretted, and the regret is increased by the cause of it. The condition at which you glance would have been justly imposed on Mr. Sheldon. His nomination to the Senate was postponed to what was considered as the latest date, with reference, in part at least, to a protraction of his duties in the treasury, and was made under the impression that the intention was not unknown. Your answer to Dr. Tucker, and instruction to Mr. Taylor, are certainly the best remedy that the case admits of. I sincerely wish it may terminate the adventitious trouble thrown on you.

The favorable report of the comptroller on the accounts of Mr. Du Plessis, with the pecuniary situation of Mr. Chew, hinted in the recommendation of him by Mr. Robertson, will justify a pause on our part—perhaps till the meeting of Congress.

The offer of Commodore Porter may lie over for a comparison with other sites for an observatory. Your answer to him was the proper one.

I have not yet heard from Mr. Clay. Should he decline the proposal made to him, the delicate considerations attending a completion of the cabinet will not be at an end. Whatever may be the final arrangement, I hope you will be persuaded that I have never contemplated your purpose of retiring from the Treasury Department without doing justice to your motives, or without recollecting the great private sacrifices involved in your acceptance of and continuance in that important public trust; that I feel with full force the expressions in your letter which are personal to myself, and that I take a sincere interest in what may relate to your future welfare and happiness.

If there be no objection within the knowledge of the Treasury Department to a pardon of Augustus Johnson, whose petition is inclosed, be so good as to have one made out.

I took the liberty of requesting, through Mr. Rush, the attention of yourself and the other members of the cabinet at Washington to the difficulties arising in the business superintended by Colonel Lane, who thought, with me, that a decision on them could be better formed on the spot than by myself at this distance. I have just received the inclosed letter from the librarian, which presents a new one. Between the alternatives of a temporary building and a continuance of the library where it is, the option seems to be prescribed by a want of legislative provision for the former. Will you be so good as to obtain from Colonel Lane a full view of the case, and to decide on it as may be found best by yourself and the other gentlemen? Mr. Watterston is informed of this reference of the subject.

We have had a profusion of rain, after an unexampled drought. It will be of great benefit to farmers and planters in several respects; but it is too late to have any material effect on the crops of Indian corn, the great esculent staple in this country, and its excess gives it a bad as well as a good effect on tobacco, the other important crop at stake. This is the tenth day since I have been able to communicate with Mr. Monroe, who is separated from me by a branch of James River. The interruption, however, has been prolonged by the want of exertion in the mail-carrier.

Accept my esteem and affectionate respects,

JAMES MADISON.

Mr. DALLAS.

———

DEAR SIR,—The inclosed sketch will give you a general view of the finances. The item of floating debt is left open until Mr. Nourse, the register, returns, that the amount of treasury notes absorbed by the payments for duties and taxes may be precisely ascertained. It is very great, and may be estimated by the statement which reduces the outstanding treasury notes to something like $6,000,000.

The actual receipts for revenue cannot, I think, fall short of $60,000,000 from January to December, 1816, including the receipts from the old as well as the new rates of duty and taxes.

Be so good as to return the report that the blanks may be

filled. If there are any points on which you wish further information, I will thank you to note them.

There is not any business to detain me here except the business of signing the warrants for the October quarter; but that can be done at Philadelphia, where I will continue to transact the routine until you tell me that you are perfectly prepared to dispense with my services. I propose leaving Washington on this day week, the 28th of September.

I am, dear sir, most respectfully and faithfully yours,

A. J. DALLAS.

The President.
21 Sept., 1816.

———

Sept 27, 1816.

DEAR SIR,—I have received with your two letters of the 20th and 21st the general sketch of the finances to which they refer. That of the 25th has also just come to hand. I return the sketch under an address to Washington, passing it through the hands of Mr Crawford with a request that he would hasten it to the department.

The document embraces all the points occurring to me as requisite to be touched, and contains so many gratifying features that it cannot fail to engage the favorable attention of the public to the ability and success with which the fiscal business has been conducted through the labyrinth into which it had been forced. The facts stated in your letter of the 25th present an additional prospect extremely grateful in several views, and particularly as bearing testimony to the auspicious course which the treasury has pursued.

Mr. Clay declines the War Department. The task now to be fulfilled is not without its delicacies, as you know. I shall avail myself of a conversation with Mr. Monroe, which his journey back to Washington will afford me in a day or two. I could wish for a similar opportunity with others whose sentiments would be valuable on the occasion. I thank you for your kindness in continuing the routine of business, and regret that I cannot more promptly exonerate you from the trouble it imposes. You will hear from me again on the subject the moment I have anything to impart.

Accept my esteem and cordial regards,

JAMES MADISON.

———

DEAR SIR,—I have just received yours of the 1st instant, and anxiously hope that this will find you perfectly recovered from your indisposition and in the bosom of your family in Philadelphia. I repeat my thanks for the kind attention you offer to the routine of the treasury business, from which I calculate on your being speedily released. I have written to Mr. Lowndes on the vacancy approaching in the War Department, and invited him to accept it, and have apprised Mr. Crawford of this step, with an intimation of the expediency of his assuming the Treasury Department as soon as he can make it convenient to do so.

I propose to set out for Washington on Monday, and expect to be there by the middle of the week. Mr. Monroe is now with me, and will probably be a day or two before me.

Be assured, my dear sir, of my best regards,

Mr. Dallas. JAMES MADISON.

———

DEAR SIR,—Colonel Lane seems to think that the librarian has been too officious in making his communication to you; and agrees that there ought not to be a change in the situation of the library until Congress shall decide upon it. This is also the opinion of Mr. Crawford and Mr. Rush.

We have met on Colonel Jessup's letter, and Mr. Crawford will communicate our general views upon the subject. The colonel does not appear in character. His letter is wanting in judgment and discretion. It is impossible to admit that any officer, civil or military, can become the depositary of a secret which involves either treason or invasion under a promise not to reveal it to his government. The Havana enterprise is extravagant, and the scheme of seizing suspected traitors without the interposition of the judicial power, should, I think, be condemned. As to the rest, notice should so far be taken of the intelligence as to set the Departments of War and Navy and the judicial officers in motion for prompt defensive operations.

We have also met on the question raised by Mr. Crawford in the case of the captive Indian agent. Upon every view of it we could not bring it, with any law or principle, to authorize the payment of any compensation during the period of captivity.

I was in hopes to have heard from you by this day's mail, as the newspapers mention that you will return to Washington on the 1st of October. My departure from it will be deferred on account of the absence of Mr. Jones, the chief clerk, whose health required the benefit of a journey.

I am, dear sir, most respectfully and faithfully yours,

A. J. DALLAS.

The President.
27 Sept., 1816.

WASHINGTON, Oct. 15, 1816.

DEAR SIR,—It being finally arranged that Mr. Crawford will enter the Treasury Department on Monday next, I lose no time in apprising you of the day on which the requisition on your kind and protracted attention to its duties will be at an end. The letter offering the War Department to Mr. Lowndes having been sent to New York, missed him altogether; and it unluckily happened that he set out after his return to Washington before I had an opportunity of communicating with him. A letter will follow him, with a chance of overtaking him before he reaches Charleston, but will probably not arrest his journey should the object of it be acceptable to him.

I thank you very much, my dear sir, for the friendly offers in your favor of the 5th instant, and I renew all my acknowledgments and assurances with respect to the past services for which I am personally indebted as well as our country, which is enjoying and awaiting the beneficial fruits of them. Accept my high esteem and my cordial salutations,

JAMES MADISON.

Nothing has occurred diminishing the improbability of Colonel Jessup's intelligence. You will have noticed the occurrence in the Gulf of Mexico, which is producing considerable sensation. We are not able to appreciate all its circumstances, but it is difficult to believe that the conduct of the Spanish squadron is to be ascribed to hostile orders from Madrid.

Mr. DALLAS.

———

DEAR SIR,—The President informs me that you enter the treasury on Monday. I hasten to express my sincere wish that you may enjoy honor, health, and happiness in the station. If in any way you think my experience can be serviceable, you cannot oblige me more than to draw freely upon it.

Permit me to take this opportunity of mentioning the clerks in the secretary's office :

Mr. Jones merits consideration for his long and faithful services.

Mr. Anthony is possessed of very useful information in several branches of the duty of the office, and I am satisfied with his diligence and fidelity.

Mr. Fox is the son of a friend in Philadelphia, and will make an excellent assistant. He is intelligent, assiduous, and correct in his deportment.

Mr. McKean is the son of the late attorney-general, and the grandson of Governor McKean. His talents, application, manners, and morals will recommend him to your attention.

Mr. Dungan was highly recommended, is possessed of very useful talents, and will soon master the whole routine of office.

Mr. Gibson is related to Governor Wright, and was received as a clerk upon the governor's application. He is industrious and capable.

Mr. Taylor,—but the conduct of this clerk has been such as to render it painful to speak of him, and I will leave his character and capacity to develop themselves.

In the fortunes of Messrs. McKean and Fox I take a personal interest, and beg you to patronize them, as well to oblige me as to reward their own merit.

I am, dear sir, with sincere respect and esteem, your most obedient servant,

A. J. DALLAS.

Honorable W. H. CRAWFORD.
18 Oct., 1816.

————

DEAR SIR,—I have received yours of the 27th. Finding that you have been detained at Washington, I regret the more my detention here. I dropped you a few lines on the supposition that you had proceeded to Philadelphia, addressing at the same time your reported view of our finances to Washington, and passing it through the hands of Mr. Crawford as preparing him for his new and arduous trust. Mr. Monroe has not yet arrived on his way to the seat of government, and I cannot well fix the day for setting out thither till I see him. I am hastening my preparations as much as possible, but fear I shall not be able to wind up some necessary business before the last of the week, possibly not before Monday. I do not count on finding you there, or it would be an additional stimulus to my exertions. Much, indeed, as I should be gratified in seeing you, it would be unreasonable to desire such a protraction of your detention. I recollect that you spoke of the 11th of October, or thereabouts, as an epoch in your private business to which a transfer of your attention is now so fully due, and I hope will without scruple be decided on.

I mentioned to you that Mr. Clay had declined the executive station offered to him. Although Mr. Lowndes has had no opportunity of disclosing particular qualifications for that department, his general talents and standing with the nation turn my thoughts strongly towards him. I shall speak more fully on the subject with Mr. Monroe, who will carry to Washington the final determination, positive, or subject to consultation on his arrival there. It appears as eligible in itself, as consonant with the opinion entertained of Mr. Lowndes by the public, that he should have a place in the cabinet.

A letter from Mr. Ewing, of the last of July, describes the situation of Spain as utterly incompatible with offensive hostilities against us. Precautionary measures, as far at least as they will avoid expense and public excitement, are, notwithstanding, suggested by the possible freaks of the cabinet of Madrid and the sort of responsibility which Colonel Jessup has thrown upon us.

Be assured of my great esteem and my cordial regards,

JAMES MADISON.

Mr. DALLAS.

WASHINGTON, November 11, 1816.

DEAR SIR.—The approaching meeting of Congress requires that I should be making preparation for the event. The paragraph relating to the finances will be a very important, and, happily, a very pleasing one. Persuaded that your peculiar familiarity with the subject is as yet little impaired, I am tempted by your experienced kindness to intrude so far on moments belonging to other objects as to request from your pen a prospectus of the receipts and expenditures of the fiscal year, with the balance in the treasury, and a notice of the public debt at its latest liquidation.

The statement may be the more brief, as I wish to refer to your "Sketches" as an accompanying document; which cannot fail to be acceptable to Congress, useful to the public, and honorable under every aspect. It occurs, however, that if thus used, one or two of the topics at its close may be criticised as not exactly within the scope of a report from the particular department of the treasury, if not construable in a latitude not covered by the constitution. The remarks of either kind can be easily guarded against.

Although I presume you possess a copy of the Sketches, I inclose the original draft, that there may be no danger of needless delay, or trouble to you, in the task I am imposing.

Be pleased to accept, with my particular respects to Mrs. Dallas, my esteem and best regards,

JAMES MADISON.

Mr. DALLAS.

DEAR SIR,—An oppressive attention to the business of the court has prevented my making the inclosed draft earlier; and I send it now in a very rough state, rather than lose a mail for the purpose of copying it.

I could not venture to fill the blank in the second page; but the figures will be supplied in a moment by the Register, upon a question,—what will be the aggregate of the public *funded* debt after the dividend of the 1st of January has been paid, including the debt both before and since the late war?

My object has been to be concise and general. I feel the full responsibility of using language which is to be ascribed to you.

I am, dear sir, most affectionately and respectfully yours,

A. J. DALLAS.

The President.

20 November, 1816.

In directing the legislative attention to the state of the finances it is a subject of great gratification to find that even within the short period which has elapsed since the return of peace the revenue has far exceeded the amount of all the current demands upon the treasury; and that under any probable diminution of its future annual product which the vicissitudes of commerce may occasion, it will afford an ample fund for the effectual and early extinguishment of the whole of the public debt. It has been estimated that during the year 1816 the actual receipts of revenue at the treasury, including the balance on deposit at the commencement of the year and excluding the proceeds of loans and treasury notes, will amount to about the sum of $47,000,000; that during the same year the actual payments at the treasury, including the payment of the arrearages of the War Department as well as the payment of a considerable excess beyond the annual appropriation, will amount to about the sum of $38,000,000; and that, consequently, at the close of the year there will be a surplus in the treasury of about the sum of $9,000,000.

The operations of the treasury continue to be obstructed by difficulties arising from the condition of the national currency; but they have nevertheless been effectual to a beneficial extent in the reduction of the public debt and the establishment of the public credit. The floating debt of treasury notes and temporary loans will soon be entirely discharged. The aggregate of the funded debt, composed of the debts incurred for the wars of 1776 and 1812, has been estimated, with reference to the 1st of January next, at $109,283,485 35. The ordinary annual expenses of the government for the maintenance of all its institutions, civil, military, and naval, have been estimated at a sum less than $20,000,000. And the permanent revenue to be derived from all the existing sources has been estimated at a sum of about $25,000,000.

Upon this general view of the subject it is obvious that there is only wanting to the fiscal prosperity of the government the restoration of a uniform medium of exchange. The resources and the faith of the nation, displayed in the system which Congress has established, insure respect and confidence both at home and abroad. The local accumulations of the revenue have already enabled the treasury to meet the public engagements in the local currency of most of the States, and it is expected that the same cause will soon produce the same effect throughout the Union. But, for the interests of the community at large as well as for the purposes of the treasury, it is essential that the nation should possess a currency of equal value, credit, and use wherever it may circulate. The constitution has intrusted Congress exclusively with the power of creating and regulating a currency of that description; and the measures which were taken during the last session in execution of the power, give every promise of success. The Bank of the United States has been organized under auspices the most favorable, and cannot fail to be a valuable auxiliary to those measures; and upon a reasonable estimate of the national stock of the precious metals, there will be little difficulty in complying with the legislative demand for the payment of the public duties and taxes in coin at the period which has been prescribed.

INDEX.

(483)

THE END.